SHAUN HUTSON

Also by Shaun Hutson:

BREEDING GROUND
SHADOWS
DEATH DAY
RELICS
VICTIMS
ASSASSIN
NEMESIS
RENEGADES
CAPTIVES
HEATHEN
DEADHEAD
WHITE GHOST

SHAUN HUTSON

Three Novels in One Volume

Comprising

SLUGS
SPAWN
EREBUS

Macdonald

A Macdonald Book

First published in this omnibus edition in 1994
by Macdonald & Co

This omnibus edition was originally published in three separate volumes.
Slugs was published in hardback by W H Allen in 1982 and in paperback by Star in 1982, reprinted by Sphere Books 1990, reprinted by Warner Books 1994.

Spawn was published in hardback by W H Allen in 1983 and in paperback by Star in 1983, reprinted by Sphere Books 1990, reprinted by Warner Books 1994.

Erebus was published in paperback by Star in 1984, reprinted by Sphere Books 1990, reprinted by Warner Books 1994.

A CIP catalogue record for this book is available from the British Library

ISBN 0 316 91101 1

Printed and bound in Great Britain by
Mackays of Chatham PLC, Chatham, Kent

Macdonald & Co
Brettenham House
Lancaster Place
London WC2E 7EN

SLUGS

For Belinda

'The Devil Damn thee Black . . .

Macbeth; Act V; Scene III

Acknowledgements

I would like to thank Mr Carr and Mr Davies from the Department of Environmental Health in Letchworth and Mr Scott of the Lea Valley Water Board in Hatfield for their valuable assistance regarding some of the technical details in this book. Also, I would like to thank Bob Tanner and Nicola Davies for giving me a chance. I am grateful for their faith.

Shaun Hutson

Prologue

The slug's eye stalks waved slowly as it moved towards the crimson lump on which several of its companions were already feeding. It slithered onto the meat and buried the long central tooth in the flesh, its rows of sharp radular teeth moving back and forth like rasps as it chewed off pieces of meat, enjoying the new coppery taste of blood.

The slugs had grown accustomed to this taste over the past few months, hidden away in the cellar beneath the old house, they had discovered this new source of food. They had tired of their hunting and concentrated, instead, on the raw meat which was tossed down into the rank, fetid darkness. A dozen or so swarmed over the rotted chop, covering it with their own slime trails, chewing until there was nothing but a tiny bone left.

At one time, the slugs had been forced to compete with the other scavengers in the cellar for the precious scraps. With the cockroaches, the wood-lice and centipedes. But now, with a regular supply of meat, they were the dominant group. By sheer weight of numbers, they had made the damp cellar their own. When there were no scraps they fed on the other creatures which shared their pitch black domain. Sometimes they fed on each other.

They had begun to breed more prolifically and many had increased in size. Even though the cellar was large, its floor was covered by them, a vast seething black mass almost invisible in the impenetrable gloom. Only a single shaft of weak light broke through the darkness, forcing its way in by way of a small hole in the cellar bulkhead. But, the slugs paid it no heed. They enjoyed the blackness and the damp and they waited eagerly for the bloodied scraps.

They had heard the footsteps above them many times, felt the vibrations. It made them restless.

In that stinking cellar they slithered over one another in their impatience like an undulating black carpet.

The footsteps seemed to grow louder each day.

One

Ron Bell got through one verse of 'Mull of Kintyre' then threw up. He slumped heavily against the wooden gatepost, wondering why the world was spinning round so fast. He bent double over the fence, clutching his stomach, trying to persuade the remaining Scotch to retreat back down his gullet. He swallowed hard and blew out his cheeks. A thin film of perspiration had formed on his face and he muttered to himself as his stomach continued to somersault. He turned and gazed up at the street lamp, its sodium glare reminding him of a gigantic glow worm. Amused at his little analogy, Ron started to giggle. He pushed open the gate and stumbled down the path towards the front of the house, stumbling once over one of the chipped granite slabs. He fell forward, the bottle of Haig dropping from his grasp. It landed in the thick grass on one side of the path and remained unbroken. Ron felt something wet beneath him as he sat up and he thought it was the whisky. He put a hand to the crutch of his trousers and started to giggle again.

'Please let it be blood,' he said, laughing loudly. The sound carried far in the stillness of the night and someone walking past the gate peered at him disdainfully.

'Evening,' Ron slurred, trying to get up. He spotted the Haig bottle lying in the waist high grass and retrieved it gratefully, realising at the same time that he'd wet himself. A dark stain was fanning out from his crutch, staining one leg of his trousers too.

'Shit,' he murmured and stumbled on towards the front door. He spotted some ants hurrying away from his clumsy feet and wagged a reproachful finger at them.

'Isn't it about time you lot were in bed?' he chuckled.

'Dirty stop-outs.' With a gleeful whoop, he brought his foot down on the nearest group of insects, crushing them into the pavement. Laughing like an idiot, he made his way up the remainder of the path, rummaging through his pockets for the front door key. He stuffed the whisky bottle into his coat pocket and steadied himself for the difficult task of trying to find the key hole. At the third attempt he made it and tumbled into the hall, his nostrils immediately assailed by the familiar odour of damp. But it was a smell he'd come to live with, almost to welcome. He slapped on the hall light and, being careful to remove the Haig bottle first, slung his coat at the rack. It missed and landed in an untidy heap. Ron looked at it for a moment then blundered into the sitting room. He flicked the light switch. The bulb glowed brilliantly for a second then, with a loud pop, blew out.

'Shit,' grunted Ron. To hell with it, he'd manage without. At half past eleven at night, pissed out of his mind he didn't fancy clambering up step ladders to put a new bulb in. He staggered across the room towards the small portable TV set up on the sideboard. He yelped in pain as he banged his shin on the coffee table and he bent to rub the injured spot, cursing to himself. He finally groped his way to the TV and pressed the ON button, watching as a hazy monochrome picture gradually took shape. Ron fiddled with the aerial until the people on screen possessed the regulation number of heads then he fumbled in the cabinet beneath for a glass. All he could find was a pint pot. He shrugged and, clutching the tankard, stumbled back towards his chair. He bumped his shin again and, as he bent to massage the throbbing bruise, he caught sight of his own reflection in the glass top of the table. His eyes were sunken into their sockets and it looked as if someone had coloured his lower lids with charcoal. The accumulated growth of four days whiskers licked around his chin and cheeks and crackled as he ran a rough hand across them. He shook his head and reached his chair, slumping into the threadbare seat. A spring dug him hard in the backside and he jumped, almost dropping his tankard. Muttering to himself, he unscrewed the cap on the whisky bottle and half filled the pint pot, watching the bubbles rise to the top of the amber liquid. He swallowed the fiery fluid in deep gulps, gasping when he'd finished. He sat for long moments, gazing at the flickering TV screen, not seeing what was on. His mind was elsewhere. He rubbed his bruised shin once more and looked at the coffee table angrily.

Bloody monstrosity. Margaret had bought it not long after they moved into the house. She said it gave the house a touch of class. Ron scoffed at the recollection. What the hell had she known about class? He smiled, wondering what she would have thought seeing him the way he was now. It had been more than two years since she'd walked out on him. It was as if, all his life, he'd been living a false existence, trying to be something he really wasn't. He'd been manager at the local branch of Sainsbury's and it was his salary which had enabled them to buy the house in the first place. The last owner had left it in pretty good nick and there was no need for full scale renovation. A fact which pleased Ron no end, never having been one for painting and decorating. The house was old but without the feeling of antiquity usually felt in buildings erected at the turn of the century. In the beginning they had lived happily together, had built a nice home but Ron had just got bored. As simple as that. He started off by having an affair with one of the cashiers in the supermarket. He usually worked late hours so Margaret never suspected but his ruin had come with the arrival of Debbie. She had been seventeen the first time Ron went to bed with her and, at forty-two, he'd had trouble keeping up with her. By God, she knew what was what between the sheets, he remembered wistfully. He was smitten. He bought her gifts, he took her out, no longer seeming to care whether Margaret found out or not. The money dwindled. Bills didn't get paid.

Then, one weekend, Margaret had gone to stay with her sister and Ron had invited Debbie to stay. He'd never forgotten that weekend. They spent nearly all their time in bed and she was insatiable. So caught up in their wanton lovemaking was he, Ron didn't even notice Margaret standing in the bedroom doorway watching them. She'd come back a day early.

He didn't even try to explain.

Margaret packed her bags that night and walked out on him.

Debbie had tired of him two weeks later and finished the affair. She'd had his money and his love but she only wanted the former. So, for the past two years he'd lived alone in the old house, watching it go to seed as he did himself. His work suffered. He received endless reprimands from his superiors until, finally, after over-ordering the wrong product three weeks running, he'd been dismissed.

After that it was onto the dole. The bills piled up, the rates were overdue and, just that morning, the eviction notice had arrived. He reached for it, picking it up from the table beside him and waving the manilla envelope before him. Inside, an official notice told him that he had twenty-four hours to come up with the money or he'd be forcibly evicted. Fuck them, thought Ron, they'll have to drag me out of here bodily. He emptied the bottle of Haig into the pint pot and tossed the empty receptacle over his shoulder where it shattered against the wall. His head felt as if someone had wrapped a blanket around it. The images on the TV blurred and Ron grunted as he downed the last of the Scotch. They were playing 'God Save the Queen' on the telly and, swaying precariously, Ron stood up and saluted until the music died away. The announcer reminded him to switch his set off and the screen dissolved into a network of lines and dots, the hiss of static making it sound like an enraged snake. Ron put a hand to his head then stepped forward to turn the set off.

Once more he banged into the coffee table but, this time, he overbalanced. Arms flailing like a human windmill, he toppled over the table and crashed heavily to the ground, catching his head on the corner of the sideboard as he fell. He felt a sharp pain as his scalp seemed to split and he went down in a heap before the hissing TV. Blood began to pump freely from the ragged cut and Ron raised one hand as if in silent reproach. Then, with a final groan, he blacked out.

It was almost three a.m. when he came round. His head was thumping from the combined effect of the fall and the whisky and, above him, the TV continued to hiss and crackle. The cut on his head must have been worse than he thought because it seemed to be throbbing mightily. His hair was matted with blood and some of it had run down over his eyes, crusting on the lids and making it difficult to see.

He felt something wet on his chin and, for a second, thought he'd vomited but then he felt something fat and slimy gliding over his lips and into his open mouth. Ron snapped his teeth together, biting down on the jellied lump, cutting it in half. A foul, obscene taste filled his mouth and, as he tried to scream, half of the sticky lump rolled back into his throat. Ron coughed, feeling the hot bile clawing its way up from his stomach. He put a hand up to his cut and, as his probing fingers found the gash in his scalp, he felt a plump, mucus-covered form burrowing into the wound itself. Ron shrieked and tugged at the pulsating shape, finally pulling it free.

For long seconds he held the slug before him, his eyes bulging wide with terror, his own blood covering the head of the foul creature. Then, with a despairing moan, he hurled the monstrosity across the room. But, it was as he did so that he became aware of the pain which was gnawing at his legs and his other arm. Scarcely able to comprehend the sight before him, he saw that his limbs were covered by a seething black mass of these creatures, all slipping and sliding over one another in their efforts to get at his warm flesh. They were on his stomach too, burrowing into the skin and muscle. With a mixture of terror and disbelief, he realised that they were eating him.

He tried to crawl, dragging the monstrous parasites with him. But his hands pressed down onto a jellied carpet of slugs which seemed to be rising from the very floor itself. He fell onto his face and one of the revolting beasts slid into his mouth, fastening its razor-sharp central tooth into his tongue. He felt the bile rising once more, mingling with the taste of his own blood and the sickening mucus of the fat slug. The beast slipped down his gullet and fastened itself into the lining of his throat. Blood began to fill his mouth, spilling out onto the other slugs which were rapidly engulfing him. He felt as though his head was swelling. He couldn't breathe and even the sharp hissing of the TV seemed to have stopped. One of the slugs was burrowing into his ear, seeking out the juicy grey meat of the brain. Ron's body began to shake uncontrollably as the slugs finally swarmed over him, digging deep into his muscles, enjoying the taste of the blood which gushed so violently from his body.

One of them bored into his jugular vein and a great fountain of crimson erupted from the torn blood vessel. It splattered up the wall as if sprayed from a hose pipe.

The slugs stripped the body clean of flesh then they devoured the softer internal organs. Their eye stalks waved about as they slithered over the corpse, their mouths moving constantly, tasting the warm blood. It had formed a pool around the body, soaking into the rotted floorboards, mingling with the mucoid slime which the creatures themselves had left behind. And then, when there was nothing left worth eating, they retreated back slowly to the cellar, to the darkness.

The remains of Ron Bell lay in the centre of the room, one uneaten eyeball bulging madly in the riven socket.

Below, the slugs slithered about. There were many who had not yet eaten and they were restless, as if sensing that this was just the beginning.

Two

The alarm clock went off dead on seven, its strident ringing filling the room. Mike Brady shot out a hand to silence the clock but only succeeded in knocking it off the bedside table. Still ringing, it fell to the carpet and skidded away from his groping hand. He forced his sleep encrusted eyes open and saw that the damn thing was lying about a foot away, just out of reach.

'Oh, sod it,' he groaned, gazing at the clock as if willing it to be silent. Another few seconds ringing and he scrambled out of bed, snatched up the bloody thing and depressed the button on the top. He sat on the edge of the bed eyeing the clock malevolently. The warm shape in bed beside him didn't stir. Brady looked down at her sleeping form and smiled, then he leant over and gently bit her exposed shoulder. She awoke with a start and rolled over, looking up into Brady's smiling face. He held up the clock and tapped the perspex cover indicating the time.

'Rise and shine,' said Brady, slipping a hand under the covers. He tickled her stomach and she started to laugh, although it sounded like an effort. Kim Brady rolled onto her side and gently prodded her husband's belly.

'Fatso,' she said, tugging at a roll of fat with her thumb and forefinger.

Brady looked indignant and got to his feet, crossing to the full length mirror which covered the wardrobe door. He stood before it and drew in his stomach, holding his breath. Defiantly he turned to face her.

'Fatso my arse,' he said but then he lost control and his stomach flopped forward again. They both laughed.

'It comes with your age,' she said, smiling, watching as

Brady got down on all fours and began a series of jerky press-ups.

'Look, it's bad enough being forty without having you remind me all the time,' he wheezed, his face turning the colour of over-ripe tomatoes. He finally got to his feet. 'Oh to hell with it. You'll just have to like me fat.'

'I'm only kidding, Mike,' she said, smiling, motioning for him to come back to bed. He sat down beside her, his eyes momentarily straying to her firm breasts, rising and falling gently as she breathed. At thirty-five, Kim Brady still had a figure to be proud of. She blinked myopically at her husband and reached for her glasses, which were on the table beside her, propped up on two Erica Jong novels. But Brady stopped her, instead drawing her close, his mouth pressing urgently against hers, each tongue seeking the warmth of the other. He ran his hand gently across her face then kissed her softly on the forehead. She fumbled for her glasses and pushed them on.

'And stop going on about being forty,' she chided. 'It's not for another month yet and besides,' she started to giggle, 'life . . .'

He interrupted her. '. . . begins at forty. Yes I know, that's what everybody keeps telling me.'

'You know, I was thinking,' she said, the mischievous grin still on her face. 'Being married to a man five years older than me does have its advantages.'

He raised his eyebrows quizzically.

'It means we can both start drawing our pension at the same time.'

He nodded affably.

'It's after seven you know,' he told me. 'Isn't it time *you* got up?' He rose and crossed to the wardrobe, taking out a shirt and tie, hanging them on the handle while he took out his familiar two piece grey suit.

'I'm not going in today,' she told him. 'The nursery's closed for a couple of days.'

He looked round. 'Why?'

'Industrial action by the tea ladies or something,' she said.

Brady grunted. 'I don't blame them, the lousy bloody wages they pay them.' He sighed. 'I know one thing. I wish to Christ I didn't have to go in today.' He walked into the adjoining bathroom and Kim heard the sound of his electric razor humming.

'Why not?' she called. 'I thought you liked your job.'

'There's nothing wrong with the job,' he called back, flicking the razor off and running some hot water into the sink. 'It's just that I don't fancy what they've got lined up for me today.'

Kim sat in silence, listening as he washed his face then she heard the hiss and splutter of the shower and, a second later, a pair of pyjama trousers came flying into the bedroom. She smiled. After a moment or two, the shower was turned off and Brady re-emerged into the bedroom, a towel wrapped around his waist. He rubbed himself down and started to dress.

'They're serving an eviction notice on Ron Bell,' he told her. 'You know, the bloke who lives in that old house just outside the town centre.'

'The one near the new estate?' she asked.

He nodded. 'He's about six months behind with the rates and there's been complaints from the residents of the estate about him and the house. The garden's like a bloody jungle. I dread to think what the inside of the place looks like.'

'But I don't understand why you've got to go along,' she said, looking puzzled.

'I've got to drive the bailiff to the house,' he explained. 'They can already sling the poor sod out for non-payment of rates and because of the complaints against him but that's not enough for our council,' he said acidly. 'They want me to write a report on the state of the building, how disgusting it is and how Ron Bell isn't fit to keep it tidy. He's already hung and drawn, they've left the quartering to me'. He pulled his tie tight, smoothing it out and inspecting his image in the mirror. Brady exhaled deeply and pulled on his jacket. He gazed at his own reflection for long moments. Mike Brady, Council Health Inspector. He smiled to himself.

He'd held that exalted position for the last fourteen years, two years longer than he'd been married to Kim. Coincidentally, they'd first met at the offices. She'd been a secretary, he'd just arrived from London where he'd been doing the same job. Some of the jobs he'd had in Merton had been child's play after the revelations in London. He'd seen some things there which had made his hair curl. If he had a pound for every hamburger and hot dog seller he'd forced off the streets during those early days he wouldn't need to work, he told himself. Flies on the meat, sausages made out of boiled down pigs' heads, hamburgers with every known type of bacteria alive infesting them, fat two inches deep in the serving trays. Some of the restaurants hadn't been much better. He still remembered the time he'd nearly eaten a curry which was later found to contain mouse droppings, or the incident when he'd walked into one kitchen to see the chef removing maggots from a side of beef he was about to put into the oven.

But, things in Merton were quieter. Even so he'd had his fair share of incidents. Like the house where the ceiling had caved in because the kids had wet the bed so many times and the floorboards had rotted. Twelve of them in that family he remembered, most of the ten kids slept in one bed and they had about three pairs of shoes between them. Other than that there hadn't been too much to bother him, just the usual drizzle of complaints. Blocked drains, the occasional cockroach infestation, the odd shady snack bar but the thing which Brady liked most about his job was that he had no one breathing down his neck all the time. He could get on with things in his own way, as long as the reports were in on time he never even saw any members of the council. This fact suited him admirably, he had nothing to thank them for, there was no love lost between the Conservative council and their Public Health Officer who was fond of voicing his socialist views loudly and often. The only good thing, as far as Brady was concerned was that his job had enabled him to meet Kim. They'd been immediately attracted to one another and had married in less than a year of meeting. The only thing which hurt him, and it hurt more because he knew the heartbreak it caused Kim, was that they were childless and always would be.

Three years after they had married she had been involved in a car accident. Five months pregnant at the time she'd lost the baby and also, due to the severe internal damage she sustained, had been told that she would never be able to bear children. The shock had been overwhelming, hitting them both much harder than he could have imagined. Kim in particular went through a seemingly endless period of depression during which Brady began to fear for her sanity but she got through it in the end and the experience seemed to strengthen their marriage, intensifying their love beyond imagination. For the last six years she had worked in the local nursery, her own thwarted maternal instincts now lavished upon the children of others.

When Brady turned away from the mirror, Kim was getting out of bed. He watched her slip on a paint-stained blouse (the one which she'd worn when they had decorated the place after first moving in) and a pair of faded denims, having to pull just a bit too hard to get them up over her hips. She finally managed it and fastened the button, puffing slightly. He smiled as he watched her and she looked up to see him grinning at her.

'Looks like I'm not the only one who needs to lose some weight,' he said, nodding towards her.

She picked up one of her slippers and threw it at him.

'Cheeky bugger,' she said. 'I've a good mind to make you get your own breakfast.'

He slapped her across the backside and they both made their way downstairs.

Three

Brady wound down the window of the Vauxhall Victor and allowed some of the crisp morning air to blow into the car. It was less than ten minutes' drive from their house to the council offices where he was to pick up Archie Reece, the bailiff, and take him to Ron Bell's house to serve the eviction notice. Brady really wasn't relishing the trip. He'd only met Reece a couple of times but there was something about the man that he didn't like. He seemed to enjoy his job. Evicting people from their homes was more like a hobby for him. Brady remembered the last time it had happened. The house owner had decided that he didn't want to be moved and Reece had promptly whacked him over the head with a chair leg in full view of the poor sod's horrified family. The unfortunate man had spent two months in hospital after that particular brush with Reece. However, the Health Inspector somehow didn't see Ron Bell as the type to put up much of a fight.

He drove at a leisurely pace, taking in the long rows of trees which lined the roadside, already heavy with blossom they brought a sweet odour wafting into the car which Brady sucked in gratefully. Even though it was early, the sun had risen high in the sky and it promised to be a scorcher. The blossom seemed to catch the rays of the sun, holding it until it glowed pink and white like flimsy neon clusters.

A sixteen wheeler drove past in the opposite direction and Brady coughed as a choking cloud of diesel fumes swept into the car. He waved a hand in front of his face and glanced into the rear view mirror, watching the huge lorry swing up to the left, heading for the industrial part of town.

Despite its size, Merton had a prosperous industrial

estate, comprising a foundry, a factory which made dust-carts and, the dominant business, a huge computer complex which manufactured the machines for places all around the globe. There was also a sizeable chemical works. The town had suffered its share of closures and redundancies as had all the other towns in the area, but. on the whole, the community was thriving.

Brady swung the Vauxhall into the car park of the council offices, glancing up at the clock above the building. The metal hands had reached eight thirty and the Health Officer checked his watch. He retrieved his briefcase from the back seat, locked his door and headed towards the flight of broad stone steps which led up to the main doors of the council offices. The building itself was a large, brownstone edifice built over a hundred years ago, and a century of accumulated muck was being removed by a posse of workmen who were at this moment swarming over the lower storeys of the building like so many boiler-suited ants repairing a break in the nest wall. Brady nodded affably to the foreman as he passed. The man was sitting cross-legged on the lowest walkway of the scaffolding, drinking coffee from a thermos flask.

The Health Inspector pushed open the double doors and walked in.

Brief greetings were exchanged with the two women on the reception deck and then Brady took the stairs to the second floor where his office lay.

He found Archie Reece waiting for him outside the office door.

The bailiff tried to smile but it came out as a leer and Brady just nodded in return and walked past him into his office. The other man followed him in and stood impatiently at the door watching as Brady crossed to his desk and sat down. There were three letters lying there and Reece exhaled noisily and irritably when he saw the Health Inspector open the first of them.

The bailiff held up a brown envelope.

'The eviction order on Ron Bell,' he said.

'I know,' said Brady, opening the second letter.

'You're supposed to drive me there, Mr Brady.'

The Health Inspector looked at Reece with distaste. He was a big man, broad and very muscular even though the folds of his ill-fitting suit did their best to conceal that fact. Brady guessed his height to be around six two and his hair, although white, was thick and flowing, almost covering his collar. His hands looked huge, big enough to encircle Brady's head with little effort. He was tapping agitatedly against the door frame with his stubby fingers.

'Is there a bloody deadline on it?' asked Brady.

Reece nodded. 'I'm supposed to have him out by nine.' He looked at his watch. 'It's quarter to, now.' He turned his gaze back to the Health Inspector who rose to his feet, fumbling in his jacket pocket for his car keys.

'Come on, then,' he said, irritably.

'I'm only doing my job,' Reece protested, following the younger man out of the office towards the stairs. They descended hurriedly and Brady led him out to the waiting Vauxhall. Reece slumped heavily into the passenger seat and rummaged around in his pocket, finally producing a packet of Rothmans.

'Don't smoke in here please,' said Brady, looking at him disdainfully. 'If *you* want to die of lung cancer that's your business. I bank on being around a bit longer.' He twisted the key in the ignition, stuck the car into first and pulled out.

Reece took the cigarette from his mouth and pushed it carefully back into the packet. He found a packet of mints in his other pocket.

'Is it all right if I have one of these?' he asked, defiantly. 'Or are you frightened of catching diabetes too?'

Brady looked at the big man as he pushed the mint into his mouth.

'Do you know what they use as sweeteners in those?' he asked, a slight smile on his lips.

Reece shook his head, gazing out of the front window.

'Re-cycled pig swill,' Brady told him, laughing aloud as

the bailiff coughed and spat the mint out of the open window.

In five minutes they had reached Ron Bell's house.

Reece was out of the car with a speed implying relish and Brady could see the slight hint of a smile on the big man's lips. The Health Inspector locked the car and followed the bailiff, who, by this time, was through the gate and heading up the path to the front door of the house. Brady walked more slowly, his eyes moving slowly over the building and the garden. Jesus, he thought, talk about run-down. The grass on either side of the cracked path brushed against him as he walked and he lengthened his stride to avoid the scurrying ants which were oozing up from the crack in the granite like soil. The windows reflected the sun back at the two men, and that combined with the filth on them, made it impossible to see inside. Reece knocked three times on the front door and waited for an answer. Brady wandered across to the nearest window. It had wooden shutters on it, the wood itself rotted and yellowed in places. One was hanging off the hinges. He put his face to the pane and squinted into the gloom, trying to make out some sign of movement in what he took to be the dining room.

Reece banged the door again, harder this time.

'Perhaps he's out,' said Brady, wearily, sauntering back to the door.

Reece ignored the remark and repeated his frenzied attack on the door, as if willing it to open by itself. Brady shook his head.

'Bell,' shouted Reece, looking up at the windows of the first floor.

'For Christ's sake,' said the Health Inspector.

'I'm going to break in,' Reece told him. The bailiff strode off down the path to the window where Brady had just been. He took off his jacket, wrapped it around his elbow and, with one powerful backward stroke, broke the glass. Lumps of dirty crystal fell into the room and landed on the bare floor. Reece reached through and opened the window, hoisting himself over the sill. He landed on the broken glass which crunched beneath his heavy shoes. Brady followed him, the sound of the crushed glass reminding him of walking in heavy frost. Both men were immediately assailed by the smell of damp and Reece coughed, waving a hand in front of him. Dust particles floated lazily in the rays of sunlight which cut through the gloom.

'Bell,' Reece called again but only silence greeted his shout. He pointed to a door at the far end of the room and the two men headed towards it.

It was Brady who heard the sound first.

'Listen,' he said, lowering his voice for reasons even he didn't understand.

Reece stopped impatiently and cocked an ear in the direction of the sound. It was a high pitched, unceasing, hum which grew louder as they approached the door. The big man looked at Brady and shrugged. The handle to the door was rusty and pieces of brown metal peeled off like scabrous flesh as the bailiff turned it. It swung open with a loud creak and both men walked into the sitting room.

The stench which met them was almost palpable and even Brady recoiled at its ferocity. He just had time to register that the high pitched hum was coming from the TV which was still on, then his attention turned to the thing in the centre of the room.

Reece too saw it and Brady was vaguely aware of the big man sagging against the door frame, clutching his stomach.

'Jesus Christ,' he groaned, trying to retain his breakfast.

Brady took a step closer, the realization slowly spreading through him. The shapeless mass of torn flesh and shining bone which occupied the centre of the room was all that remained of Ron Bell. The Health Inspector moved closer, as close as the choking odour would allow him. The room was like a charnel house. Congealed blood was splattered up the walls and around the body, its rusty colour matching that of the old door handle. One sightless eye fixed Brady in a baleful stare. He pulled out his handkerchief and pressed it to his face but the foul stench even seemed to penetrate the material.

The corpse still retained some shreds of flesh, covering the shiny bones like wisps of gossamer, and clumps of hair still clung defiantly to what was left of the head. The mouth was open, revealing many rotted teeth, the lower jaw having been eaten through. It yawned soundlessly, the ligaments and tendons which had held it in place were gone. Part of the nose remained, the solitary nostril choked with clotted blood.

Reece seemed to have recovered his wits a little and he looked over at Brady, who was still kneeling beside the mutilated body.

'What the fucking hell happened to him?' gasped the bailiff, his breath coming in short gasps.

Brady didn't answer, he had finally managed to tear his gaze away from the body long enough to study the bare floorboards around it. They felt spongy because of the congealed blood which had soaked into the wood but it wasn't that which attracted the Health Inspector's eye. It was the shiny substance which seemed to cover the floor, sparkling like oil on water when the sun catches it. He noticed that it was all over the corpse too.

'How long's he been dead?' asked Reece, wiping a thin film of perspiration from his face.

Brady shrugged. 'It's hard to say. From the appearance of the body I'd say he'd been dead for months but . . .' He allowed the sentence to trail off. He stood up. 'You'd better phone the police.'

Reece nodded, happy to be able to escape the reeking confines of this slaughterhouse. Brady heard him exit then he leant back against the door frame, his eyes sweeping around the room.

There was more of the shiny substance on the far wall, only there it seemed to break apart into small trails each about an inch wide. He stroked his chin thoughtfully and looked down. There was more of the stuff at his feet. He knelt and felt tempted to touch it, much as a child does with something that arouses its curiosity but, at the last minute, he withdrew his hand, reaching instead to the inside pocket of his jacket. He took out a pencil and poked the end into the shiny stuff, seeing that it was fluid, but thick and sticky and, when he removed the pencil, the mucoid slime stuck to it. Brady wrinkled his forehead and laid the pencil down on the nearby sideboard.

He took one last look around the room and hurried out to see where Reece had got to.

The high pitched hum of the TV continued.

Four

Night brought with it a cloying humidity which made sleep, for many people, difficult. There was no moon and just the sodium glare of the street lamps penetrated the darkness.

Some of the houses on the new estate overlooked Ron Bell's house and some of those tenants had watched that afternoon as first the police and then an ambulance had arrived at the old place, but few had taken much notice. Perhaps the bloke had been taken ill, a heart attack perhaps. No one knew. No one cared. Some were pleased that he was gone, perhaps now the house would be sold to someone who would look after it and preferably to someone who would get that maze of a garden into some semblance of order. But, the subject of Ron Bell and his house was only of passing interest to the inhabitants of the new estate. Now, with night well and truly upon them, they tried to sleep in their little houses which had become like ovens due to the weather.

In dozens of red brick dwellings, they dozed, snored, made love, watched television or sat and talked. Crying children were attended to, pets dozed in the heat and, somewhere on the estate, a couple of tom-cats fought out their nightly duel. They hissed and spat at one another, scratching and biting in one of the gardens until a well aimed ash-tray, thrown from one of the bedroom windows, put an end to their squabble.

Silence descended once more.

In the cellar of Ron Bell's house it was silent too, except for the slurping, sucking sounds the slugs made as they slithered over one another. There seemed to be so many of them now. The cellar was filled practically to overflowing and, besides, their source of food had disappeared. Their hunger became uncontrollable and they began to slither up towards the hole in the bulkhead, towards the night air. Some burrowed through the ground, others slithered through the waist high grass which parted as if moved by some invisible hand. Their jet black colour helped them blend into the night.

But most crawled to the sewer cover which lay in the garden. Rusty and covered in moss, it was surrounded by broken concrete and the slugs found many holes. They crawled down into the black depths, welcoming the wetness which enabled them to move faster. Many even slipped into the filthy water, carried along by its flow.

Through the earth, over it and swept along by the fast flowing sewers, they moved towards the new estate, an invisible unstoppable black horde.

Five

Mary Forbes watched as her two children disappeared around the bend in the road, waving to them one last time before she retreated back inside the house. She smiled happily to herself as she crossed to the windows in the front room. She unfastened them and pushed them open, allowing the slight breeze to blow in. It brought with it the heady scent of lavender and Mary looked out into the garden with pride at the blossoming purple flowers. The DJ on the radio told her it was eight fifty one and then his exaggeratedly gay banter was mercilessly replaced by the strains of a Perry Como record. Mary began to sing along with it while she bustled through the house, raising her voice as she went into the kitchen. She took the breakfast dishes from the table, shaking her head when she saw how much the kids had left on their plates. It hardly seemed worth giving them anything. Such a waste, with food as expensive as it was! She shook her head as she shovelled it into the pedal bin with a fork. Perry Como meandered on and Mary joined in mightily when he got to the chorus, her voice rising above the chink of plates as she washed them. When she'd finished that particular task she cleared the table, tripping over one of Jack's slippers as she did so. She glared down at the offending article for a second, making a mental note to tell him about it when he got back home that evening. No wonder the kids are untidy when their father sets them this sort of example, she thought to herself. She and Jack had been married for twenty-four years and, not a day had gone past during that time when she hadn't had to tell him about his untidiness. He said she should stop nagging but Mary was proud of her house and how neat and tidy it was and she aimed to keep it that way. Whether the rest of the family liked it or not.

Sundays were the worst. She was always up at eight and, dead on nine, the hoover went on. The rest of the family always complained but Mary was oblivious to their protestations as she happily whizzed through the rooms with the cleaner, singing along with the radio like some demented char-lady.

Perry Como finished singing and the DJ told her it was nine o'clock. Mary dried her hands and, with the plates left on the draining rack, she scuttled upstairs to fetch the hoover.

It was the same routine every day, it never varied. Seven a.m. get up. Quarter past, get Jack and the kids up. Breakfast, get Jack off to work, make sure the kids were ready for school then, from eight fifty onwards, the house was hers. Washing up, hoovering, dusting and Mary loved every minute of it. She usually finished her housework around eleven and then she either took a trip into town (less than five minutes on the bus from the new estate) or she had coffee with one of her many friends. If there was one thing Mary enjoyed more than housework, it was a good natter.

'Did you hear about her at number 36?'

'I see so-and-so is ill.'

'Someone told me that whatsisname is having an affair with that woman, you know the one.'

But the thing which pleased her most of all was how much cleaner and tidier her house was compared to those of her friends and she felt a particular swell of pride when *they* told *her* how nice her place looked. Mary would just smile and tell them it was hard work with a family like hers but it was worth it.

Now she roared from room to room with the hoover, still singing loudly to herself despite the fact that the radio was drowned out by the din of the cleaner. She pushed it rapidly before her like some kind of jet propelled mine detector. The dusting was completed at a similarly dizzy pace and, at precisely ten fifty three, Mary tucked her duster away neatly into a drawer and wiped her hands on her apron. However, with it being Friday, there was one more thing which she had to do. Retrieving a tin of polish from the cupboard, Mary armed herself with a fresh duster and headed out to the front doorstep.

As she opened the door, Mrs Banks from next door passed by and the two women exchanged brief pleasantries before Mary knelt to begin her last job.

It was as she took the lid off the polish that she noticed the first of the slime trails.

Mary looked at it, watching as it glinted in the sunlight. Then she saw another, and another. The whole step was criss-crossed with silver threads, some hardened the others still fresh and sticky. Mary followed the course of one fresh trail, noting that it ran across the step and up the inside of the concrete porch. On either side of the porch she had baskets of flowers and, as she stood up she saw a lump of what looked like phlegm hanging from the first of the suspended baskets. She leaned closer, peering inquisitively at the almost transparent lump but, as she looked closer she could see that the stuff was like frog-spawn only instead of being round, these things were cylindrical. With a dark centre they hung in clusters of about twenty or thirty. Mary noticed that there were five or six of these clusters on each of the hanging baskets and she felt an almost unnatural disgust as she looked at them. She told herself she must show Jack when he got home, then, careful not to touch the jellied lumps, she took her duster and knocked each one from the hanging pots.

She returned to the slime trails on the doorstep and set about removing them, polishing away feverishly until all traces of them were gone, then she closed the door. But, as she put the lid back on the polish, she wondered once more what those mucoid clusters on the flower baskets had been.

Brady brought the Vauxhall to a halt and switched off the engine. He hurriedly got out of the car, anxious to be free of its stifling confines, impatient to breathe the sweet summer air once more. He locked the door behind him and strode across the deserted street to the first of the houses he was to inspect. Elm Drive was the last street on the new estate to be filled, with families due to move in at the beginning of the following week. The council had asked him to give the houses a quick look over before the new tenants took up residence, just to make sure everything was all right. But Brady's mind was not really on his present job as he walked up the short front path to the first house. Burned deep into his mind was the image of Ron Bell's mutilated body. The police had arrived within five minutes of Archie Reece's call, the ambulance another five after that. The body had been removed by two young ambulancemen, one of whom had vomited at the scene of carnage in the old house. The local police inspector had been unable to offer much in the way of explanation, insisting that they would have to wait for the results of the autopsy before pursuing any investigation. Brady had mentioned the incident only briefly to Kim, telling her that Bell had been dead when they found him, but dispensing with the worst details of the ghoulish find.

Now he stood before the front door of number one Elm Drive, fumbling in his trouser pocket for the set of pass keys which he'd been given. His jacket was draped over his shoulder and Brady could feel the perspiration sticking to his back. The concrete of the path felt hot beneath him and he could feel its searing warmth even through the soles of his shoes. The sky was cloudless, the sun hanging there defiantly. The whole town was enveloped in a blanket of blistering heat. It was like walking about inside a huge oven.

Brady found the key ring and tried one of the keys, muttering to himself when it didn't fit the lock. He tried again.

Another failure.

He sucked in an impatient breath and pushed the third key in. This time it turned and the front door swung open. He stepped into the cloying humidity which was the hall way. The place smelt of fresh wood and his shoes beat out a tattoo on the concrete floor as he walked from room to room.

He finished downstairs, did a quick tour of the upper floor and then, satisfied, moved to the next house.

He repeated the procedure in the remaining nine buildings on that side of the road, then crossed and continued his inspection of the buildings opposite.

As he entered the penultimate house, he looked up to see a couple of kids cycling past on their way to school and the Health Inspector glanced at his watch. It was almost one fifteen. After he'd finished checking these last two houses, he told himself, he'd go and get some lunch.

It was as he closed the door behind him that he saw something glinting in the rays of sunlight which fell into the hall.

Brady paused, letting go of the front door, his attention riveted to the glistening thing before him. He stepped closer, crouching slightly to get a better look.

It was a slime trail.

The front door swung back on its hinges and slammed with an almighty crash which made the Health Inspector jump. He leapt to his feet, his heart pounding.

'Shit,' he muttered, angry with himself for being so jumpy. Then he turned his attention back to the slime trail. It was dry, crumbling away when he rubbed the toe of his shoe in it. Brady followed its shiny course into the living room (or at least what would be the living room eventually), noting that there were more of the trails in the other room, one or two of them actually stretching a couple of feet up the wall. He scanned the remainder of the room then passed into the kitchen.

There were more of the trails in there.

Brady hurried out and into the last house, twisting the key almost frenziedly, pushing his way into the hall.

The slime trails were more numerous in the last house. He counted a dozen at least. For long seconds, the Health Inspector stood in the doorway, his eyes darting furtively around the humid room then he crossed to one of the trails and peered closely at it. Like the one in the house before, it was dry. Several hours, or, for all he knew, days old. All the trails were dry but Brady suddenly remembered Ron Bell and the silvery fluid which had covered his remains and he felt uneasy, suddenly anxious to be out of the house. Not really knowing why. The air seemed to be unexpectedly fetid and he hurried out into the oppressive heat once more, locking the door behind him. He crossed to his car and sat for long moments behind the wheel before leaning forward and starting the engine. He let it idle for a moment, looking at the house which he'd just left, then, with a sigh, he stuck it into first and pulled off.

Six

Bert Crossley finished his second pint of Guinness and pushed the empty pint pot back across the bar.

'Fill that up again, Tom,' he said to the barman, fumbling in his pockets for some money. 'And whatever these two silly bastards want.' He indicated the men with him both of whom shook their heads, the first of them checking his watch.

'No thanks,' Danny said. 'I'd better be getting home, the wife will wonder where I am.' He picked up a couple of full shopping bags and left to a chorus of cheers and whistles from the few remaining occupants of the public bar. As he reached the door someone shouted, 'A woman's work is never done,' and the other men laughed loudly.

'You in a hurry too, Tony?' asked Bert Crossley, watching as the second man downed what was left in his glass.

The man nodded. 'Yeah, I'd better get back to the site. I'll see you tonight though,' he assured Bert as he left.

The big man picked up his pint and swallowed two or three enormous mouthfuls, patting his swaying belly appreciatively. He belched loudly and excused himself. Bert Crossley tipped the scales at somewhere around eighteen stone and that, combined with his height, made him a formidable sight to be propping up the bar of The Swan. Bert ran a small butcher's shop in the tiny precinct of shops situated on the new estate. The precinct also comprised a newsagent's, a small supermarket and a fish and chip shop. Bert prided himself on being the only one of the shop keepers who actually owned his own business. He stood at the bar every lunchtime between one and two p.m. nattering away about football, politics and anything else anyone would care to talk about. Putting people off their ploughman's lunches by his insistence on wearing his working apron which was perpetually stained with the rusty marks of dried blood. Considering he'd been a butcher for forty-two years, Bert still didn't seem to have mastered the use of his knives and his fingers were usually swathed in blood soaked bandages, or plasters which refused to stay on and fell off to expose a jagged gash just as someone in the bar was about to tuck into their lunch. About six years back, he'd sliced off the top of his thumb while carving up a bullock carcass but, instead of calling the ambulance, Bert had calmly closed the shop and, carrying the severed end of the digit, strolled down to the doctor's surgery. That had been when he had a shop in the town centre. He'd moved into the new premises on the estate about ten months ago and had built up a good name amongst the residents. His father had always told him that there was no substitute for the family butcher's shop and Bert had been happy to find that his old man had been right. Bert had learned all he knew about the trade from his father who used to run his own shop in the days when butchers still did their own slaughtering too. Bert remembered the first time, as a child of ten, he saw his father kill a bullock. The memory was as vivid all these years later as it was at the time. In his mind's eye he could still see his father leading the animal to the centre of the yard, tethering it to an iron post there. He remembered that the animal was drooling, saliva hanging in long white streamers from its mouth. It had stood perfectly still, almost as if it realized that there was no point in running, as Bert's father had approached it with the sledgehammer. He had steadied himself, raising the heavy hammer above his head. Then, with a blow combining demonic force and years of practice, he'd brought the sledge down on the bullock's head. There was a strident snapping of bone as the skull was shattered, the beast pitching forward as its front legs buckled. It had been dead before it hit the floor. Bert had then watched as his father had hung it up, sliced open the throat to drain it and then set about cutting the animal up. He had watched it all in fascination, remembering the smells too. The overpowering smell of the blood and the pungent odour of excrement which flowed out in a trail behind the twitching beast as his father had dragged it away with a meat hook.

Bert downed the rest of his pint and sighed wistfully. There'd been an art to butchering in those days. It still needed a lot of skill, granted, but the art was gone. Now the livestock were slaughtered hundreds in a day by the pneumatic gun which shot a retractable bolt into their heads. The carcasses arrived at the butcher's in storage lorries, already prepared. The only skill that remained was in cutting the damn things up.

'Another one, Bert?' asked the barman, reaching for the empty pint pot.

The butcher shook his head. 'No thanks, Tom, I'd better get back and open up.' He glanced at the clock above the bar. It was almost two o'clock. He got to his feet and lumbered out into the sunshine, wiping his face with the back of his hand. Bert perspired a lot, even in relatively cool weather, but today he thought he must have lost a couple of pounds already. He glanced up at the blazing sun and began the short walk from the pub to the shop. It took him past some old people's flats and one or two of the old dears waved gaily to Bert as he passed. He was a popular man with all the residents and many found it a surprise that he had never married but, throughout his life, Bert had always found that his business was more important than the ties of a home life. After his father died, he'd looked after his mother, nursing her through her last few painful years until she had a stroke which proved to be fatal. By that time Bert was forty-one. He had his business and, what was more, he just thought he was too old to start chasing women around.

A fly buzzed past him, attracted by the dried blood on his apron but Bert shooed it away. He reached the back door of the shop and let himself in. It was much cooler in there and he stood beneath one of the powerful fans for a moment before walking through into the shop itself. The blinds were down so the shop was in a kind of semi-darkness. Bert was about to pull them up when something made him turn to face the display cabinets.

His mouth dropped open and, for once, he was speechless.

When he had left the shop at one o'clock, less than an hour ago, the cabinets had been full. Their trays heaped with fine cuts of beef, pork, lamb, kidneys, liver. Everything. Now, Bert ran disbelieving eyes over the remnants of his stock. The meat and offal had been devoured, only tiny scraps of it remained in the stainless steel trays. Even the blood which had run from the meat was gone, every last drop removed as if by some invisible hand. There were pieces of meat on the floor too, here and there were some dark patches of blood.

Bert put a hand to his forehead, drawing in a long, slow breath.

'My God,' he murmured softly. Then, immediately, his bewilderment turned to anger. Who the hell would do such a thing? He quickly inspected the locks on the doors and windows. If some bastard had broken in Bert promised himself he'd gut the sod personally. But a swift inspection told him that the doors and windows were still secure.

He stood silently, gazing at the empty trays before him, wondering if maybe he'd had too much to drink that lunch time and he was really imagining this.

'My God,' he muttered once more.

The shop was silent but for the bluebottle which buzzed indolently around him. Bert decided to check the back door and windows and he hurried through to the rear of the building.

In his haste he failed to notice the slime trails which led from the display cabinets to the ventilator grille on the wall. Still fresh, they glittered with a vile sparkle of their own.

Seven

Brady wiped his face with a handkerchief as he walked across the car park towards the council offices. The café where he usually had his lunch was only 200 yards from the large building and could be seen from his own office window. He looked in that direction as he crossed the car park. Christ, it was hot. The tarmac beneath his feet looked as though it was on the verge of bubbling. Brady hadn't eaten much, the experience in the two new houses had quelled his appetite but he pushed the incident to the back of his mind. The Health Inspector loosened his tie as he wearily climbed the flight of stone steps to the main doors, the sun burning fiercely on his back as he turned to enter the building.

It was cool in there and he managed to ignore the frightful rattle emitted by one defective fan. The sound reminded him of a football rattle. As he crossed reception on the way to the staircase, Julie Jenkins called him across to the desk. Brady turned, running an appraising eye over the youngest staff member in the building. She was in her early twenties and had only been working there for three months but, already, most people seemed to have taken to her. The male members of the work-force in particular. She smiled sweetly at Brady who returned the gesture, managing a quick glance at her shapely figure as he did so. Because of the hot weather she wore only a light, cheese-cloth top through which he glimpsed the dark outline of her nipples straining against the flimsy material. The blouse was undone to the third button to reveal a tiny silver crucifix hanging between her ample breasts. Brady smiled to himself, administering a swift mental rebuke for taking so much interest in a girl young enough to be his daughter. Anyway, he told himself, you're a married man. Nevertheless, just because you've bought the goods doesn't stop you window shopping, he mused.

Julie held up a piece of paper, smiling as Brady leant on the reception desk.

'A message for you, Mr Brady,' she told him. 'A lady rang up to complain about her drains and toilet.'

'Blockage?' asked the Health Inspector.

Julie nodded.

'Then it's a job for the sewage department, not me.'

'She says that there's a terrible smell coming from the drains. She wants it checked.' Julie looked at him, the deep blue of her eyes reminding Brady of the sky outside.

He sighed. 'OK. What's the name and address?'

She handed him the piece of paper and the Health Inspector pushed it into his pocket.

'It's on the new estate,' said Julie, as if she was telling him something he didn't know.

Brady exhaled deeply. 'Well, I can think of better ways of spending an afternoon than bending over drains and toilets, especially in this sort of weather.' He smiled. 'Give the sewage people a buzz anyway. I might need one of their blokes along, just in case it's anything below the surface.' He turned and headed towards the staircase.

Julie flicked a switch on the console before her, picking up the phone when a green light flickered on.

Brady reached his office and walked in to find the heat almost unbearable. He crossed to the window and heaved it up, allowing a blast of cool air to blow in. The perspiration beneath his arms and on his back suddenly felt very cold but he remained at the window, looking down on the people in the car park, as they scuttled around in the heat with their bags of shopping. All of them were probably complaining about the heat. Brady smiled to himself. When it was the depth of winter everyone longed for the summer but when *that* finally arrived they spent their time cursing the heat. He was the same. A knock on the office door broke his chain of thought.

'Come in,' he called, turning to face his visitor.

The door opened and a short stocky man in white overalls walked in. He smiled at Brady and introduced himself as Don Palmer. The Health Inspector caught the slightest hint of a cockney accent in the man's voice.

'You're from the sewage department?' he asked, although it came out more as a statement than a question.

Palmer nodded. 'That's right, guv. They call us "Effluent Operatives".' He smiled, broadly. A warm, infectious grin which caused Brady to smile too. 'Well,' he said, holding up a bag of tools. 'I've got my plunger. Shall we go?'

Brady followed the little man down to the car park where a white van with MERTON URBAN DISTRICT COUNCIL emblazoned on the sides was parked. Palmer hopped behind the steering wheel, Brady told him where to go and they set off.

Brady wound down the window of the van and allowed some cool air to blow in, and also to drive away the smoke from Palmer's cigarette which filled the van. The little man retrieved a packet of Marlboro from the parcel shelf and pointed it in the Health Inspector's direction.

'I don't smoke,' said Brady. 'Thanks all the same.'

'Wish *I* could give up,' said Palmer. 'It costs me about ten quid a week for fags.' He took a last drag and tossed the butt out of the open window. 'I've been smoking ever since I was eleven, doubt if I'll ever manage to kick it now. My old lady keeps on at me to stop but, well, you know how it is.'

'Which part of London are you from?' Brady asked, studying his companion's profile.

The little man laughed. 'Christ, is my accent *that* strong?'

The Health Inspector smiled. 'Well, let's say it's noticeable.'

'Islington,' Palmer told him.

'What did you do there?'

'Same as I do here. Effluent operative.' He laughed once more. 'Bloody stupid name isn't it? I don't know why they can't just call us shit-shovellers. They called us flushers when

I worked in the London sewers.' A wistful grin passed across his face. 'I used to do a bit of boxing before that, only amateur like. When I was a kid.'

'Why did you give up?' Brady wanted to know.

'The old lady again. She was scared I might get brain damage or something,' Palmer explained.

'Did you get very far?' the Health Inspector asked, his interest genuinely aroused by this personable little man in the white overalls.

Palmer shrugged. 'I got to the final of the ABA light weight competition one year. Albert Hall. Thousands of people there, millions watching on TV.'

'How did you get on?' Brady wanted to know.

'Well, I had the geezer worried in the third round.'

Brady was impressed. 'Yeah?'

Palmer nodded. 'Yeah.' He paused. 'He thought he'd killed me.' The little man cracked out laughing, the raucous sound filling the van and Brady chuckled too.

'What made you move to Merton?' the Health Inspector wanted to know.

'London's all right for grown-ups but I didn't want my kids living in all that smog,' Palmer explained. 'I wanted them to get up every morning and breathe fresh air instead of bloody diesel fumes.' He glanced at Brady. 'You got any kids?'

'No,' said the Health Inspector, just a little too sharply.

Palmer looked at him for a second then turned his attention back to the road ahead.

Brady changed the subject quickly. 'I used to work in London too.'

Palmer smiled. 'Yeah? Same job?'

Brady nodded.

'Why did *you* move?'

'That's something even I've never been able to work out,' he confessed. 'I think things just got on top of me. Besides, I was doing all the work in the department. I thought that if I left the other lazy bastards would have to start pulling their weight.'

The sewage man nodded.

'What the hell makes a bloke start in a business like yours?' Brady asked. 'I mean, crawling about in . . .' He hesitated.

'Crawling about in other people's shit. Was that what you were going to say?' asked Palmer.

Brady laughed, nodding.

Palmer shrugged. 'Well, look at it this way. It's a secure job. I mean, unless there's a mass outbreak of constipation, I've always got plenty to do.' He laughed his cackling laugh once more. 'There's a lot of difference between working these shite-pipes and working the ones in London,' he explained. 'I mean, the ones here are small, you have to crawl along the bloody things on all fours. At least in London you could walk through them.'

Brady frowned at the prospect.

Palmer suddenly slowed up. 'What was that address again?'

The Health Inspector found the piece of paper and scanned it.

'Twenty-two Acacia Avenue,' he said, looking out of the window to see that they had, in fact, arrived. Both men got out of the van, Brady leading the way to the front door. He saw one of the curtains parted slightly, a face peering out inquisitively from behind dirty net. He rang the doorbell and a two-tone Woolworth's chime tinkled. The two men waited, listening as several bolts were drawn back and Palmer suppressed a smile. The door opened a fraction and a woman squinted out at them, staying in the shadows, almost as if she were reluctant to feel the sun on her face.

'Mrs Fortune?' asked Brady, smiling.

The woman, who he guessed was well into her seventies, ran an appraising eye over the two newcomers.

'We're from the council. You rang about your drains,' the Health Inspector continued, still smiling. When he got no answer, he began to wonder if the woman was deaf so he raised his voice and repeated himself.

'All right,' she squawked. 'There's no need to shout. They're round the back.'

Brady nodded and was about to say something else when the front door was slammed in his face. He looked at Palmer who was laughing quietly. The two men made their way around to the rear of the house where Mrs Fortune appeared at the back door, this time emerging into the yard itself. She was a short, tubby woman, her hair done up in a bun, with horn-rimmed glasses perched precariously on the end of her nose. But the most striking thing about her was her clothes. She was wearing a huge knitted cardigan which came to well below her knees and looked as if it could have doubled as a bedspread and Brady could just detect the faint smell of mothballs.

'It's the drains,' she said, crisply.

Brady followed her pointing finger to the drain just below her kitchen window. As he stepped past her, a stench so fetid as to be obscene hit him and he recoiled. It reminded him of something between rotten vegetables and dead fish.

'Jesus Christ,' he groaned, watching as Palmer knelt beside the foul smelling drain. The sewage man pulled a pair of thick gloves from his overall pocket and slipped them on. He seemed impervious to the nauseating stench and beckoned Brady forward. The Health Inspector put a handkerchief over his nose to keep out the worst of the odour but it was so rank that it seemed to penetrate the very material itself. As he watched, Palmer took a long, hook-like implement from his canvas bag and poked it through the holes in the grate. He stirred it about, finally lifting the grille, uncovering the drain opening. There were pieces of rotten cabbage and what looked like congealed grease around the opening and Palmer scooped them away with one hand, peering closer.

'I think it's disgusting,' said Mrs Fortune, indignantly. 'Fancy letting the drains get in such a state. Why haven't the council done anything before?'

'This is the first complaint we've had from anyone on the new estate,' Brady told her, stepping back from the foul smelling opening.

She grunted indignantly.

'You say that your toilet is blocked too?' he asked her.

'Yes,' she snapped. 'It has been for more than a day now.'

'But how do . . .'

'It's only the outside one,' she snapped. 'The one upstairs is all right.' She pointed to a green door away to the right and Brady crossed to it, peering inside. The outside toilet was almost on the point of overflowing, the water already up to just below the seat. Brady closed the door and walked back into the yard.

Palmer had a torch out now and was shining it down the open drain. He finally switched it off and stood up.

'Well, I can't see anything,' he said. 'There's no external reason for the blockage or the smell.' He fumbled in his bag once more, closely watched by Brady and Mrs Fortune. The sewage man finally produced several lengths of steel tubing to which he attached what looked iike a small grappling hook. Carefully, he pushed the long probe down into the drain, hearing it clanking against the metal of the pipe as he pushed further.

'I think it's disgusting,' Mrs Fortune said once more and, with a disdainful shrug of her shoulders, she disappeared back into the house, slamming the door behind her.

'I bet she doesn't offer us a cup of tea,' said Palmer, still threading the metal probe into the drainpipe. He looked across at Brady and winked.

'How the hell can you stand that stink?' asked the Health Inspector.

'I must admit,' said Palmer, 'this one is a bit worse than usual but I'll be buggered if I can think what's causing it. It must be pretty deep down whatever it is.' He suddenly stiffened and the metal rod seemed to quiver in his hand. The little man gripped the rod tight, pressing one foot against the drain surround to steady himself. The tugging continued.

'What the fuck . . .' the sentence trailed off.

'What's wrong?' asked Brady, suddenly alarmed by the expression on Palmer's face.

The little man was straining to tug the rod free, using

every ounce of his strength to pull it from the drain.

Brady crossed to help him, fixing both hands around the probe. He felt a similar pressure being exerted from the other end.

It felt as if someone was trying to pull the rod from their hands.

'Can you feel that?' asked Palmer.

Brady nodded, anxiously. Then, finally, with a concerted burst of strength, the two men managed to heave the rod free. It came up, bringing with it a lump of brown matter. Brady looked at the lump which appeared to be a very old apple.

'Could that have been causing the blockage?' he asked.

Palmer shook his head, studying the probe closely. He sighed thoughtfully then had a quick look in the outside toilet. That done, he crossed to an iron flap which lay about ten yards down the garden. There was a disgusting smell emanating from there too. He stood on the sewer cover as if seeking inspiration.

'Whatever's causing the block is very deep,' he said. 'I can't clear it from this end.'

Brady looked apprehensive. 'Meaning?'

'Meaning, we'll have to go down.' He pointed at the rusty cover which led down into the sewer itself. 'You wait here,' he told the Health Inspector. 'I'll go and get the stuff from the van.'

Brady stood beside the flap, waving a hand before him in an effort to keep the rancid stench at bay. He heard Palmer's footsteps receding as he disappeared around the side of the house to fetch 'the stuff' – whatever the hell that might be.

He didn't have to wait long for an answer. A moment later, the little man re-appeared carrying two thick bundles of clothing and another canvas bag which he deposited on the ground.

'Put that on,' he said to Brady, pushing one of the bundles towards him. The Health Inspector picked up the bundle and opened it out, realizing that it was an overall of some kind. Made of oilskin, it looked like a shiny white boiler suit.

It fastened up the front by a zip which, in turn, was covered with a flap which both men clipped together using the large press-studs along its length. At the back, Brady found that the folds of the material could be pulled up to form a hood which was, in turn, tied at the chin with a piece of cord. As he pulled the hood up, all the sounds around him became muffled and he looked up to see a bird sitting on a nearby tree apparently whistling noiselessly. Its song could not be heard through the thick protective headgear. He pulled on the heavy gloves which Palmer handed him, watching as the little man knelt beside the other canvas bag. He finally produced a pair of large boots which Brady found he could slip over his shoes quite easily. The soles were metal and, for a moment, he found himself rooted to the spot by the weight.

The last things which Palmer took from his bag of tricks were a couple of face masks, rather like those worn by scuba divers, only curved and covering the whole of the face. Brady put his on, his breath coming in short gasps, the smell of plastic making him feel dizzy. The heat was almost unbearable. There was a small, circular, hole at the base of the mask which, Palmer informed him, was an air filter. The little man had to raise his voice to make Brady hear. The Health Inspector's breathing had slowed now, rasping loudly in the mask as he stood watching the other man.

'We've got to get this off,' shouted Palmer, his voice still sounding slightly muffled. It was as if he were talking through cotton wool. He pointed to the metal flap which covered the sewer opening and Brady looked down at the knobbed metal. Rusted with the ravages of the weather, it had two depressions in it. One at either end, both of which had a bar across them. At a signal from Palmer, both men bent, hooked their fingers under the bars and lifted.

The lid to the sewer opening came free and they deposited it on the grass nearby.

Palmer handed a torch to the Health Inspector who peered down into the darkness. It seemed to be bottomless, the iron ladder which ran down the side of the shaft disappearing into gloom so total that even the torch beams could not penetrate it for more than a couple of feet.

The sewage man looked at Brady, who was still gazing down into the darkness, and then stooped to pick up his bag of tools which he clipped to his belt.

'Last one in's a rotten egg,' he said, raising his voice once more to make himself heard. He smiled, then, watched by the Health Inspector, he clambered onto the ladder and began to make his way down into the darkness, visible, finally, only by his swaying torch beam.

Brady flicked on his own torch, took one last look around at the brightness of the day and then lowered himself onto the first rung of the ladder, his metal soled boots clanking noisily as he did so.

He steadied himself for a second, then began to descend.

Eight

Brady hadn't realized quite how narrow the shaft was until he began to climb down the ladder. Now he found that he was forced to cling tightly to the metal rungs in order to prevent his back rubbing against the other side of the tunnel. The torch wavered unsteadily in his hand and his mask had begun to cloud over, making it difficult to see. He measured his steps cautiously, careful not to miss a rung and fall. However, despite his tentative tread, he felt his left foot slide from the rung beneath him and, for a moment, his heart leapt. But he gripped the ladder tighter and continued his descent.

He heard a dull splash, signalling to him that Palmer had reached the bottom of the shaft and, a moment later, Brady himself felt his heavy boot touching something solid which he knew to be the floor of the pipe. Panting, he stood still for a moment until he felt hands tugging at his arm.

'Mind your head,' Palmer told him, shining the torch around to show him the narrowness of the pipe.

Brady guessed that it could be no more than three and a half feet from the top to bottom and both men had to get on all fours to give themselves the room to move about in it. Brady sank reluctantly to his knees, looking down to see that the trickling effluent which ran through the pipe came up as far as his forearms. He felt sick and was thankful that he had the mask on. The walls of the pipe seemed to crush in on him and the Health Inspector imagined that this was what it was like to be buried alive. Together, he and Palmer crawled through what seemed like an endless cylindrical coffin, thick with human waste and twelve instead of six feet below ground. The heat inside the suit seemed to intensify and

Brady found that he was gasping for air even though the mask was filtering it quite adequately.

'You all right?' Palmer asked him, hearing the Health Inspector's laboured, accelerated breathing. He peered over his shoulder at his companion, shining the torch at him.

Brady nodded, his breathing becoming less harsh. The perspiration was running off him and he almost slipped twice, the thought of ending up face first in a river of human excreta making him more careful.

In the darkness, neither of the men saw three or four of the slugs glide past them, carried along by the flow.

Palmer held up a hand for Brady to halt. The little man managed to scramble up onto his knees in front of a grille which was set into the tunnel roof.

'What's that?' asked Brady.

'It's the outlet from the toilet,' Palmer told him, fumbling in his bag for a screwdriver. He set to work, removing the four rusty screws which held the grille in position. As he took each one out, he handed it to Brady to hold, then, when the last one was out, he stuck the end of the screwdriver between two bars of the grille and prised it free. By torchlight he scrutinised it.

'No blockage there,' he said, puzzled.

'What now?' Brady asked, peering up the outlet.

Palmer grinned. 'We hope the old girl doesn't get taken short.'

The Health Inspector quickly withdrew his head, handing the screws, one at a time, to the sewage man who refixed the grille.

'Let's have a look at the drain outlet,' said Palmer and, pointing his torch ahead of him, crawled on. Brady followed.

'Are all the tunnels as narrow as this?' he asked.

'Most of them,' Palmer told him. 'They all work like wheels though. The pipes themselves converge in one central chamber, which is like the hub of the wheel. The tunnels are like the spokes.' He paused for a moment, steadying himself as he put his hand on something thick and soft. He grunted distastefully. He crawled on.

The large slug which Palmer had accidentally put his hand on slithered along the floor of the pipe, the stream of effluent and the impenetrable darkness hiding it.

'The manhole covers that you see in the road,' the sewage man continued. 'Each one of those goes down to one of the central chambers. They're dotted all over town. The chambers are pretty big.' The little man stopped once more, this time at a much smaller outlet which Brady realized must be the one from the drain. The same procedure was repeated, the grille removed. This time a lump of rotten potato fell out into Palmer's gloved hand. He shook his head and dropped it into the stream of effluent.

'I don't get it,' he said. 'Even down here there's nothing to show why the bloody pipes are blocked.' He pulled a curved implement from his bag and began scraping around in the drain outlet. Brady meanwhile shone his torch around the walls of the pipe. About half-way up the sides there was a scum mark of green mould which, in places, had extended to the roof of the pipe too. The concrete itself seemed to be cracked and the mould had crept into the rent like bacteria into a cut, turning it gangrenous. He remembered when he had found an old man living alone who had been infected with gangrene. Unable to move after falling and cutting his leg, Brady had found him after a next door neighbour complained about the smell coming from the man's house. He'd finally got in to discover that the old boy's leg was green and mottled with infection, black in places it was so bad. That image suddenly came to his mind as he ran the torch up the tunnel wall, following the course of the rent until it reached the roof of the tunnel. The torch beam shone on something silvery.

Brady felt the breath catch in his throat as he looked more closely. The marks were unmistakable.

The roof of the pipe was criss-crossed by dozens of slime trails.

Ron Bell's house. The two houses in Elm Drive and now here. With shaking hand he reached up and touched one of the trails with the index finger of his glove. The mucoid fluid stuck to the material, dropping away in thick globules when Brady removed his hand. Suddenly anxious, he shone the torch down the length of the tunnel but the beam faded into darkness less than three feet from him. Something bumped against his arm and he almost shouted aloud. Looking down he saw that it was a small piece of wood. His breathing once again became rapid but he tried to control it, clenching his teeth until his jaws ached. Get a bloody grip on yourself, he screamed inside his head. *Come on*. He clenched his fists, his eyes tightly closed for long seconds, then he felt Palmer touch him on the shoulder.

'Well,' said the sewage man. 'I can't find anything. We might as well go back up.'

The words were the most welcome Brady had heard in a long time. He crawled backwards (it was impossible to turn round in the narrow pipe) until his torch glinted on the bottom rung of the ladder. High above, he could see the blue of the sky and, with almost unnatural haste, he began to clamber up towards the surface.

Palmer waited at the bottom of the ladder, watching as Brady climbed up. When the Health Inspector was half way up, the little man followed him.

He didn't even see the large slug which had crawled onto his boot.

As he climbed, the slug crept higher, sensing the warmth beneath the overalls. It slithered onto his calf and prepared to sink its long central tooth into the material, eager to get at the warm flesh beneath. But, just then, Palmer brought his foot down particularly hard on the ladder, the slug lost its hold and fell back into the stream of waste below.

The sewage man heard the splash and thought he'd dropped something from his bag. He shone his torch down but could see nothing. Satisfied that he still had all his tools, he continued his ascent.

The slug had disappeared.

Nine

The heat hung heavily over Merton, like some oppressive cloud. As the afternoon wore on and the sun reached its zenith, the little town was bathed in a cloying, sticky heat which seemed to make the air itself hot, almost unbreathable.

Carol Wilton stood naked before the full length mirror studying the reflection which gazed back at her. Her eyelids felt heavy and she was tired, the heat seeming to sap her strength. Beads of perspiration had formed on her top lip and she licked them away, the salty taste remaining on her tongue momentarily. Another bead of clear liquid quivered at the hollow of her throat for a second before trickling slowly down her chest, between her taut breasts and across her flat stomach. She traced its path with the index finger of her right hand, allowing the digit to probe deeper, brushing through the soft curls of her pubic hair. She shuddered as the finger brushed against her clitoris and she felt a tingle run through her. She sighed, her nipples rising to erection at the same time. Carol moved her finger gently between her legs, feeling the first traces of moisture from her warm cleft. All the time she kept her eyes firmly on the mirror, watching the reflection before her. She parted her lips slightly and spoke one word.

'Tony.'

She stopped moving her finger, her expression changing from one of pleasure to one of anger.

'You bastard,' she said softly, withdrawing her finger.

Couldn't she forget him after four years? She shook herself out of her dream world and crossed to the bed, reaching for a pair of faded jeans which she pulled on, the tight material clinging to her slim hips and thighs. She slid further into the denims, allowing the seam to cut into her damp cleft, then she fastened the button and picked up the white t-shirt which also lay on the bed. She let it hang outside her jeans, noting how the thin material made her hardened nipples even more prominent. She slipped on a pair of backless high heels and inspected the reflection once more. You should see me now, you bastard, she thought. The image of Tony flashed into her mind once more. No, she couldn't forget him. He'd left her a permanant reminder just to make sure. She crossed to the bedroom window and looked out.

Paul was playing on the lawn, sitting contentedly beside the rabbit's pen, watching as the small white creature hopped about, stopping every now and then to munch on the pieces of lettuce which Carol had dropped in half an hour ago. Paul was four now and he'd never even seen his father. Carol watched him and felt the anger rising once more inside her. Fate had dealt her a truly cruel blow. Not only had she been left to bring up a child on her own, the child had been born slightly retarded. She bit her bottom lip, angrily. It was almost as if she blamed Tony for her son's mental deficiency. But the real anger she felt was with herself. God, she'd been a fool in those days. A sixteen-year-old girl trying to act like a woman. Tony had been twenty-four. She'd built her world around him, ignoring the warnings from her parents and friends. What did they know? He loved her and she used to show them the gifts he bought her to prove it. He loved her and she loved him. He took her virginity but she didn't care, she had given it up willingly. She had talked about getting married, though he never seemed to take much interest when it got around to that subject but then, she had told herself, not many men do talk about marriage. They made love often and he guided her, taught her things she had never even known about, introduced her to all manner of physical pleasure. And she had accepted it all. She loved him and that was all that mattered to her.

But then she became pregnant and Tony changed. They rowed constantly and, finally, he had given her his ultimatum. Get an abortion or the relationship was over. He even offered to pay for it himself.

She refused. He left her.

'Bastard,' she muttered to herself, the memory still hurting even four years later.

Of course her parents had gone through the customary procedure of disowning her. Being Catholics in a religious area didn't help matters, she supposed. Whatever would the neighbours say? How could you do such a thing, Carol? The recriminations had flown back and forth and she'd moved out. First to a flat and finally to this house she had now, on the new estate. She'd left school at sixteen with no qualifications but she'd managed to get a cleaning job at the local hospital. The meagre wages from that, together with her supplementary benefit and child allowance just about paid the rent and kept her and the child in food and clothes. With Paul being handicapped, the Government, in its infinite wisdom, saw fit to give her an extra couple of quid on top of the usual rate. And so she managed. At times she wondered how but things never got too desperate. She'd made lots of new friends on the estate, one of whom looked after Paul while Carol went out to work at nights. Back to her old job at the hospital. She sometimes wondered what it would have been like if Tony had stayed with her. Would she have been a wife by now instead of an unmarried mother, disowned by her own family? Many a night she lay awake wanting him with her. But recently, she wouldn't have cared *who* it was who shared her bed.

She pushed the thoughts to one side and made her way downstairs. Paul didn't hear her as she walked up behind him and he giggled when she tickled his ribs. He looked up at her with wide, questioning eyes for a second, almost as if he didn't recognise her. Then he gurgled something unintelligible and returned his attention to the small rabbit. Carol knelt beside him and wiped some saliva from his mouth with the tissue which she took from her jeans pocket. He didn't move, his mind still pre-occupied with the tiny white animal hopping about before him. Carol had bought it about a week ago and the man next door had helped make a pen for it. A nice bloke, Carol thought. Pity he was married. The rabbit had been an endless source of fascination for Paul and Carol could now leave him out in the garden all day, just watching the little creature.

'Paul,' she said, stroking his hair. It was blond, like her own. Soft and sleek as she touched it.

'Paul.' She gently turned his head to that he was looking at her. Once more she was faced with that vacant expression. 'Mummy's just going out for five minutes,' she told him, reaching once more for the tissue. She wiped the mucus from his nose and balled up the tissue. 'Will you be all right?'

He smiled. 'Yes,' he said, quickly. Shaking his head about. 'Yes.'

'You watch bunny, all right?' she said. 'Mummy be back in five minutes.'

'Yes,' he said again, looking back at the rabbit. He raised one chubby hand and waved in the direction of the animal. 'Bunny.'

Carol smiled. 'That's right, bunny.' She kissed him on the forehead and walked back up the garden to the house. Her purse was on the kitchen table and she opened it to reveal a pound note, some silver and an assortment of other stuff including a bus ticket, a coupon cut from a newspaper which granted her 3p off her next purchase of a certain brand of tea bag and a couple of photos. The sort taken in photo booths. The faded monochrome snaps showed her and Tony together. She snapped her purse together again and left the house. The precinct of shops was only down the road and she needed some bread and a pint of milk. Thank Christ the Giro is due in the morning, she thought.

Paul heard the clicking of his mother's heels as she walked up the path and out of the gate but he didn't turn to watch her go. He was too interested in the rabbit. He gurgled contentedly, the spittle oozing down his chin and forming a silvery pendant as it hung there.

The rabbit had stopped to eat and it crouched before him

devouring the remnants of the lettuce which it had been given. But suddenly, it jumped back, licking at its paw.

Paul laughed, throatily, watching the animal. He could see something red on its fur, on the paw it was licking but he didn't know what it was. Neither did he realize what the slimy black thing was that burrowed slowly up from the place where the rabbit had been crouching.

The slug pulled itself free of the ground and slid across the ground towards the rabbit, its antennae waving about in the air, the shorter forward tentacles flicking across the ground.

The rabbit watched the slug warily for a second and was about to leap aside when it squealed in pain. It managed to drag itself a few inches and this time, Paul saw one of the monstrous black things clinging to the animal's leg. The rabbit turned and bit into the second slug but the first and larger of the creatures had reached it by now and the terrified mammal was pulled down as the slug fastened itself onto one of the rabbit's ears. Blood ran freely from the wound as the slug used its sharp rows of radular teeth to shave off pieces of the animal's flesh.

Another slug, fully six inches long, broke the surface, dragging its vile form towards the stricken rabbit. It drove its sickle shaped tooth into the animal's side and the fur was suddenly stained crimson. The rabbit shook its head madly from side to side in an effort to dislodge the monstrous black thing but its efforts were useless and now half a dozen of the revolting gastropods were burrowing up from beneath it, each slithering across to join the attack. The rabbit tried to move but its tiny form was weighed down and all it could do was squeal as the slugs ate it alive.

Paul watched, mesmerised, his mouth open. Once he chuckled, not really knowing why but then he wrinkled his forehead as he saw the rabbit being reduced to a blood-spattered heap of fur. It had stopped moving and the slugs seethed over it, eager for the taste of its fresh, warm blood. One of its ears was eaten away, the other severed half way up. It hung uselessly, like a broken twig and, finally, the rabbit was pulled to the ground, its bloody fur almost invisible beneath the black mass of feeding slugs.

Paul gurgled as he watched, his head on one side.

Carol glanced down the garden as she walked round the house into the back garden. She looked down and saw Paul, still staring into the rabbit pen. Carol took her small bag of groceries into the house and put them on the kitchen table then she kicked off her shoes and padded down the garden towards her son, who, apparently hadn't heard her return.

'Paul,' she called but he didn't turn and it was then that Carol realized something was wrong.

She couldn't see the rabbit.

Hurrying down to the pen she stopped behind Paul, looking at the sight before her. The grass inside the pen was covered in blood and pieces of fur, here she noticed a lump of bone, beside it a piece of intestine. She turned away and closed her eyes, trying not to be sick. Gradually she regained control and looked more closely at the scene of carnage in the pen. The rabbit had disappeared completely.

Carol knelt beside Paul and held him tightly in her arms but he seemed unconcerned. He waved a hand towards the empty pen and shook his head.

'What happened?' she asked him, tears in her eyes. She glanced at the blood-stained grass once more and this time she caught sight of the mucoid fluid which also covered the pen. It sparkled in the sunlight, diffusing into a dozen different colours.

'Paul,' she repeated, holding him close to her.

He gurgled something and at first she thought he said 'cat', but when he spoke again she was able to make out the word.

'Black,' he said in his clumsy, clipped tones. He waved towards the pools of blood and slime.

'Black.'

Ten

The sun was bleeding to death in the evening sky, flooding the heavens with vivid patches of gold and crimson. Some of them eventually darkening into a cool purple as the evening drew in. Birds returning to their nests were black arrowheads against the red back-drop and the mottled sky was like a child's colouring book, layers of colour splashed brilliantly one on top of the other.

Harold Morris looked up from the begonia he was tending and marvelled at the multi-hued glory of the dusky heavens. there was nothing in the world he liked more than to be out in his greenhouse on an evening like this. Even beneath the canopy of glass and wood, the air had cooled to a pleasing temperature and Harold worked enthusiastically over his plants, tending them with a care which people usually reserve for small children.

He'd always been a keen gardener but since being made redundant from Merton's chemical works over a year ago he'd turned his hobby into something approaching an obsession. The greenhouse had been purchased with part of the sizeable pay-off he'd received. The remainder had gone into the house, new carpets and, for the first time during their thirty years marriage, a colour television. Harold's wife, Jean, was totally mesmerised by the new acquisition something which Harold himself was thankful for because it kept her out of his way while he tended to his plants. The rest of his redundancy payment had gone towards purchasing two tickets for a flight to Australia.

Their only daughter had emigrated, with her husband, six years ago and now Harold and Jean were preparing themselves to fly over for the christening of their grandson in just under a month. Harold smiled happily at the thought, dropping some Baby-Bio into a pot where he was nurturing an orchid.

As well as flowering plants he also had a sizeable choice of vegetables growing in the greenhouse and, together with those in the patch at the bottom of the garden, Jean seldom had to buy any from the shops. Apart from his cucumbers and tomatoes, Harold had also been able to grow a fair crop of aubergines. They were his particular pride and joy.

He sipped slowly from the tin of lager beside him, putting the can down beside a set of shears which lay on the work top. Then, picking up his trowel, Harold set about re-potting some geraniums.

The sun had fallen far below the horizon by now and night was seeping slowly across the sky, staining the clouds like ink on blotting paper. Harold squinted in the gloom for a few more minutes then crossed to the light switch at the end of the greenhouse and snapped it on. The bank of fluorescents flickered into life bathing the place in a cold white light. He then adjusted the thermostat control, raising the temperature just four or five degrees. He picked up the can of lager and drained the last dregs, rattling the empty receptacle in his hand before tossing it into the bin beneath the work top. He looked at his watch and decided that he had time to finish tending to the fresh crop of tomatoes before he went inside to watch the football.

It was almost ten p.m. and Harold felt like another can of lager. It was warm in the greenhouse and he had worked up a powerful thirst. He pulled off his gloves and dropped them onto the work-top, then he headed up the garden towards the house.

From beneath the bottom of the work top, the first of the three slugs slithered up, its posterior tentacles waving about. Moving slowly in their mucoid trails, the black beasts, one of them as thick as a man's index finger, crawled over the trowel leaving their mark on it. They paused at the place where Harold had left his gloves and then, after a moment's hesitation, they slithered inside.

Harold found Jean dozing in her chair, the TV still on at full blast as yet another American cop series drew mercifully to a close. He stood in the doorway of the sitting room, rolling the icy can of lager across his forehead. Jean seemed to sense his prescence and opened her eyes. She looked round and smiled.

'I thought you were busy with your plants,' she said, yawning.

'And I thought you were *watching* that,' he said, motioning towards the TV.

Jean reached for the remote control and turned down the sound.

'I nodded off,' she confessed. 'It must be this heat.'

'It'll be a lot hotter than this in Australia,' he told her, sipping at his lager.

Jean sighed wistfully. 'You know, Harry, I still can't believe we're going to see Roger and Carol again.' She smiled. 'And the little boy too. Won't it be marvellous?'

'You'll be telling me next you were pleased I got made redundant,' he said, smiling.

She held out a hand to him and he bent and kissed her on the top of the head.

'Will you be much longer?' she asked him.

Harold shook his head. 'I'll be hurrying in to you my dear,' he said, bowing exaggeratedly.

'And the football,' she said, smiling.

He winked at her and walked out. The cool evening air seemed full of the scent of flowers and Harold inhaled deeply. In next door's garden he heard a snuffling sound and, a second later, saw a hedgehog scuttle across the lawn ahead of him, trying its best to avoid the light coming from the greenhouse.

Stars stuck to the black velvet sky like pieces of tinsel which some giant hand had hurled. Harold smiled to himself and pushed open the door to the greenhouse, the temperature immediately hitting him. He hadn't realized just how hot it was in there but, after a moment or two and a hefty pull from his lager can, he re-adjusted to the heat and looked at the waiting tomatoes.

He reached for his gloves.

Yes, the tomatoes were coming along beautifully this year, he thought, pulling on the first of his gloves. Last year's crop had . . .

He stopped trying to drag the second glove on, feeling something wet and slimy blocking the fingers.

'What the hell . . .'

He never finished the sentence. Suddenly, searing pain exploded through his hand as three sets of jaws fastened themselves on his exposed fingers. The slugs inside the glove eagerly devoured the flesh offered to them, quickly tearing it away until they were nearing the very bone itself. Harold was frantic, his bulging eyes watched the material of the glove undulating rhythmically as blood began to run from his wounds and dripped from his wrist. Now he began to groan in terror, the groans gradually turning to shouts.

The pain in his hand was agonizing. Already the slugs had eaten away three of his fingers and now they slithered over the back of his hand, digging deep into muscles and sinew. Harold tugged at the glove, staggering drunkenly around the greenhouse.

He couldn't get it off.

And now his shouts became screams as he wrenched at the glove, still unable to remove it. Blood was now soaking the thick material and his arm was rapidly going numb. Harold felt the bile rising in his throat and he thought he was going to faint, but, if anything, the pain in his hand kept him concious. White hot agony lanced a path up his whole arm. Again, almost blind with pain and terror, Harold tugged at the recalcitrant glove, screaming even louder when it wouldn't come off.

He groped for the shears, the realization sweeping over him. The terrifying fact of what he must do momentarily numbing even the screaming agony in his hand. He managed to push open the twin blades of the razor sharp shears and, tears rolling down his cheeks, he put his wrist between the twin steel jaws. With his free hand he brought all his weight down on the handle, shrieking with renewed intensity as the blades sliced through the flesh of his wrist. There was a sickening grating sound as they scraped the bone and Harold was splattered with a geyser of his own blood as the veins in his arm were severed. But, despite his frenzied efforts, the shears would not cut through the bone. Skin and muscle tore like fabric, exposing ligaments and twitching sinews and he pounded on the handle like a madman, sweat pouring from his face.

It was then that Jean appeared in the doorway of the greenhouse. She had heard his screams and came running and now the sight which met her caused her stomach to somersault. She saw her husband pounding madly on the handle of the shears, the twin blades of which closed around his wrist. She saw blood spurting into the warm air, saw the shining white of bone through the pulped and torn crimson mass that had once been flesh and muscle. Blood had sprayed in all directions, onto the dusty worktop, over the glass panels of the greenhouse where it trickled down like sticky crimson rain. Harold's white shirt was covered in it. He was on his knees now, a second away from unconsciousness, the shattered wrist still firmly held in the jaws of the shears and it was at that point she ran to him. Fighting back her sickness, not even able to scream, she watched the glove, moving seemingly with a life of its own as the slugs ate further into his hand.

'The trowel,' gasped Harold, his face purple, eyes bulging like a thyroid sufferer.

Her groping hands found the implement and she stood before him, mesmerised.

'My hand,' he mumbled. 'Cut it off'.

She shook her head, her own voice now beginning to rise.

'No,' she said.

'Do it,' he shrieked and his tortured voice spurred her into action. Raising the trowel above her head, she took a last look at the torn and crushed wrist then brought the blade down with terrifying force.

Both of them screamed as the heavy implement scythed through the already shattered wrist. There was a strident snapping of bone and the hand was severed, propelled some distance from the shattered stump by the jets of blood which erupted from the arteries. Harold slumped to the ground, the remnants of his lower arm spouting red geysers into the air. Jean dropped the trowel, blood from the hewn limb splashing her feet and legs.

Harold had passed out.

Jean bolted from the greenhouse, racing back to the house and the phone. Her screams had alerted several neighbours and lights flickered on in the kitchens of the houses next door.

In the greenhouse, the three slugs finished feasting on Harold Morris's severed hand then, leaving only their thick mucoid trails as evidence of their presence, they slithered away.

Eleven

'You know, we should have lived in a bloody flat. Then we wouldn't have had all this trouble,' said Brady, driving his spade into the hard ground.

He turned a few more clods then leant on the spade, the perspiration running freely down his body. He'd removed his shirt even before he started digging and now he felt the unrelenting heat of the sun on his back.

'There's two reasons why you're so worn out,' Kim told him. She was kneeling beside him, pulling weeds from the lawn which was long overdue for a cut. 'You're either out of condition, or . . .' She looked at him, a mischievous smile on her lips.

'Or what?' he demanded.

'Or you're feeling your age.' She laughed.

Brady picked up a handful of earth and threw it at her. He returned to his digging, determined to prove to her, and to himself, that he wasn't unfit. But, Christ, his body was crying out for a rest. He ached all over and he'd only been out there for an hour. Perhaps Kim was right, perhaps he was out of condition. He slowed his pace a little and looked down at her. She was wearing a pair of dirty old jeans and just her bikini top and he looked admiringly at her deep tan. His own torso was milk white, only coloured in places by the hot sun which had reddened it. Brady didn't tan, he fried. He too wore a pair of old jeans, which hung low at the backside. Together with his big wellingtons, Kim said he looked like a farmer.

Doing the garden was something which Brady had always hated and, in blistering heat such as this, he disliked the task even more. The earth was baked hard, as ungiving as concrete and he had to drive the spade down with all his strength to even break it. But, he struggled on, turning the clods, stopping every now and then to mop his brow with a sodden handkerchief. In the end he gave it up, knotted the white linen square at each corner and pulled it onto his head. Kim looked up and immediately dissolved into fits of laughter.

'You look like Fred Gumby,' she said, referring to the resident idiot of past Monty Python shows. She got to her feet and padded back up the lawn towards the house. 'Fancy a drink?' she called.

He panted exaggeratedly and allowed his tongue to hang over his bottom lip.

'I'll take that as a yes,' said Kim, smiling.

Brady returned to his digging. Inside his thick gardening gloves, his hands felt as if they were on fire but the old spade had a shaft which had grown ragged over the years and he didn't fancy getting splinters, so he struggled on. As he threw himself into his job more, it began to seem less of a battle. Even so, Brady didn't think he could ever acquire a liking for gardening. He and Kim had lain in bed until ten that morning, as was their custom on a Saturday. They had woken at nine and made leisurely love, each seeming more responsive than usual. Brady smiled to himself at the recollection. They would probably just sit out and enjoy the sun when he finished digging. He wondered if he might try his hand at growing some vegetables and he surveyed his expanse of earth like some feudal baron looking out over his grounds.

It was as he looked down that he saw the first of the slugs slithering onto his spade.

Brady knocked it off, pushing the creature aside with the shovel but it was then that he noticed just how big the bloody thing was. He watched as it slithered away leaving its slime trail behind.

'Good God,' muttered Brady, watching the silvery trail glistening in the sunlight. His mind began to race. Ron Bell's house. The house in Elm Drive. The sewer pipe and now here, in his own garden. He knelt, watching the vile creature closely.

Then he saw another one, as black as night and, Brady guessed, a good six inches long. He swallowed hard, feeling the urge to squash the revolting creatures beneath his spade but he could do nothing but watch in fascinated distaste as the two slugs crawled over the rough ground.

He looked back at the ground he'd already dug. There were more of them. In the six or seven yards of ground which he'd overturned, the Health Inspector counted at least a dozen of the black beasts.

'Percy Thrower, your drink's here,' called Kim, seating herself in a deckchair and sipping her own glass of bacardi and coke.

Brad ignored her, his eyes still rivetted to the slugs.

'Mike,' she called again, noticing that something had caught his attention.

'Come and look at this,' he said, without taking his eyes off the slugs nearest to him. The first one had once more slithered on to his spade and, this time, Brady watched it as it crawled up the smooth metal.

Kim joined him, the glass still in her hand. She caught sight of the slug and shuddered.

'Oh God, what the hell are they?' she said, moving behind her husband as if for protection.

'They're slugs,' said Brady, still watching the crawling monstrosity.

Kim laughed nervously. 'But slugs are small.' She felt the disgust rising within her. 'These are too big.'

The Health Inspector was adamant. 'They're slugs.'

The one on the spade had almost reached the shaft now and Kim watched it with revulsion, her eyes darting over the ground in front of her which seemed to be alive with the black creatures.

'Kill it, Mike,' she urged, watching the beast slithering up the wood but Brady merely reached out and plucked the thing up, holding it between the thumb and forefinger of his thick gloves. It writhed slowly betwen the digits and reminded the Health Inspector of a fat snake. Its eye stalks swayed as if in slow motion and its mouth moved soundlessly giving the man a glimpse of its many-toothed maw.

'For God's sake, Mike,' Kim persisted. 'Kill the bloody thing.'

Suddenly the slug seemed to twist in Brady's grip, its slime making it difficult to hold, and, before the Health Inspector could react it had driven its vicious sickle shaped tooth into the tough material of his glove.

'Jesus Christ,' he yelped, the sudden attack startling him. Kim put a hand to her mouth to stifle a scream as she watched her husband pull the glove free and throw it to the floor. The slug remained anchored by the tooth, not loosing its grip even when Brady hurled it to the ground. Almost with relish he stamped on the hideous black thing, its body making a loud squish as it was crushed. The noise made Kim want to cover her ears, reminding her, as it did, of diarhoettic excretion. Brady ground the thing into shapeless pulp beneath his boot, using the end of the spade to scrape it off his glove. He pulled the glove back on, examining the hole which the tooth had made.

'The bastard tried to bite me,' he said, incredulously. Another eighth of an inch and it would have tasted flesh and that was enough to make Brady shudder.

'What kind of slug bites a man?' asked Kim, looking at the squashed remains.

'That's what I intend to find out,' said Brady, straightening up. He looked at Kim, seeing the uncertainty in her eyes and his tone softened. 'Go and get me a jar, love,' he told her. 'Anything with a screw top lid.'

She nodded and hurried back up the garden. Inside the house she picked up the money jar. They collected all their copper in it, counting it out when the huge jar was full. But, fortunately, it had only recently been emptied and there was less than thirty pence in there. Kim hurriedly emptied it, allowing it to spill out onto the kitchen table, ignoring the coins which fell to the floor. Then, she ran back to where her husband stood watching the other slugs. She put the jar down on the grass and Brady unscrewed the top. He studied the seething black shapes for long seconds then, quick as lightning, he picked one up and dropped it into the jar. He repeated the procedure with one of the larger ones, careful that the vile thing didn't take a chunk out of his finger. Kim shuddered as she saw the things slithering about on the glass, their bodies gliding on the trail of mucus they secreted. Brady snatched up a third slug and dropped it in with the others then he screwed the lid of the jar on as tightly as he could. For long seconds he watched the obnoxious animals slithering around in their efforts to escape then he crossed to the deckchair where his shirt lay discarded. As he buttoned it up, Kim looked into the jar.

'What are you going to do?' she asked.

'Find out what's happening around here,' he said. 'Come on.'

A little bewildered, Kim slipped her shoes on and followed him out to the car.

Brady fumbled in his pocket for the keys, hastily unlocking the driver and passenger doors. They both slid in, Kim yelping in pain when her exposed back came into contact with the blistering hot plastic of the seat. Brady handed her the jar of slugs which she held rather uncertainly, then he stuck the key in the ignition and started the engine. Neither of them spoke and, even as he drove, the Health Inspector couldn't resist the odd anxious look at the three slugs. Almost as if he feared they would escape their glass prison.

He put his foot down, wondering whether the perspiration on his face was entirely the product of the scorching day.

Twelve

The car park of Merton Museum was empty but for a battered old Volkswagen which lay baking in the sun.

Brady brought the Vauxhall to a halt beside it and both he and Kim got out. She handed him the jar with its monstrous black contents and wiped her hands on her jeans. Together, they approached the small flight of steps which led up to the main entrance of the museum. It was a grey stone building, three storeys high, which had been erected about ten years ago and, from the outside it looked like a block of flats but with fewer windows. The windows that were visible reflected the sun back at the two visitors as they advanced, making it difficult to see inside. A feat made all the more impossible because the venetian blinds were down. There was a small notice board outside telling of forthcoming lectures to be given there, or of special attractions to be found in the building itself but Brady was not interested in those.

Followed by Kim, he strode up the stairs, clutching the jar to him as if it were some priceless artefact he'd just dug up. The doors to the museum were open so the two of them walked straight in.

The ground floor was a natural history gallery and they found themselves faced by hundreds of stuffed birds and small animals. A thousand dead eyes followed their progress. Kim glanced into the glass cabinets. She had been here twice before with classes from the nursery and the place always gave her an odd feeling. It was almost like being in a glass fronted zoo, where all the inhabitants were in a state of permanent suspended animation. The baleful eyes of a Tawny Owl fixed her in a glassy stare and she walked on as if mesmerised by the dead orbs. The silence in the building was almost oppressive but at least it was cooler in here and both of them were glad of the respite from the blistering heat outside. Despite the apparent absence of visitors (something which seemed to be a feature of the place), the museum was freshly dusted and spotlessly clean, the wooden floor in particular so heavily polished Kim could see a distorted reflection of herself in it.

They moved through the ground floor gallery, eventually arriving at a staircase. A sign at the bottom proclaimed:

ART GALLERY
LIVE EXHIBITS
ENQUIRIES

A large white arrow showed the way and the two of them followed its course eventually emerging on a landing. To the right lay a desk on which were piled various postcards and brochures depicting exhibits in the museum. There were also pencils bearing the legend Merton Museum. A black sign told them it was an enquiry desk and another pointing arrow indicated a bell and invited them to ring for attention. Brady promptly pressed the button, looking around impatiently when no one appeared. He pressed it again, keeping his finger on it this time, the high pitched ringing echoing through the silence.

A door behind the desk opened and a young man in his early twenties emerged. He held the remains of a sandwich in his hand and was chewing the rest with difficulty, as if he'd taken too large a bite. He raised a hand in greeting, still unable to speak because of the welter of bread and salad in his mouth. Kim smiled, Brady ran an appraising eye over the youth. He wore a pair of faded jeans, crisply pressed all the same, and a T-shirt with 'Iron Maiden' emblazoned across the front. He finally managed to dispose of his mouthful of sandwich and smiled happily at the waiting couple.

'Good afternoon,' he said. 'Can I help you?'

'I want to speak to whoever's in charge, please,' Brady told him.

'Fire away,' said the youth, smiling.

The Health Inspector looked surprised and the young man saw the hint of disbelief on his face. He smiled.

'I know I don't look like a museum curator,' he said. 'That is what you were going to say, isn't it?'

Brady too smiled. 'As a matter of fact it was.'

'John Foley,' he announced, offering his right hand which Brady shook, introducing himself in his official capacity and Kim who smiled at the young man.

'And you're in charge?' Brady asked, as if anxious for re-affirmation of Foley's words.

'Monarch of all I survey,' he said, smiling. 'What can I do for you?'

Brady indicated the jar. 'Ever seen anything like that?'

Foley bent lower, peering through the glass. He frowned and shook his head as he watched the slugs sliding around in their own slime. 'Where the hell did you find these?' he asked.

Brady told him. 'One of them tried to bite me,' he added, producing the holed garden glove as evidence.

'Christ,' said Foley, picking a piece of ham from his tooth. He opened a flap in the desk and walked through, leading the couple up a short flight of stairs to a room marked: 'Staff Only'.

'Come in here,' he said, holding the door open for his two visitors.

The place was like a small laboratory and Kim wrinkled her nose as the unmistakable odour of formaldehyde assaulted her nostrils. The room was small and very hot until Foley flicked on the twin rotar fans above them. Soon, a cooling breeze began to waft around the room. It contained a table with a stainless steel top, a couple of sinks and, on the work bench which took up three sides of the laboratory, there stood some empty fish tanks.

Brady set the jar down and looked around. Foley pulled up a stool and peered once more at the large slugs in the glass container.

'Do you run this place on your own?' the Health Inspector wanted to know.

Foley shook his head, taking a pair of plastic gloves and a set of stout tweezers from a drawer beside him. 'No. During the week I have an assistant and a woman comes in to clean up but apart from that, I do the lot. Including the exhibits.' He motioned to a newly finished badger which stood on the work top on the other side of the room. 'And no jokes about mounting and stuffing please,' he said, smiling.

Brady grinned but it faded as he saw Foley slowly unscrew the top of the jar. The young man was watching the slugs intently, still not able to believe their size. One was near the top of the jar and it was this one that he aimed his tweezers at, a little disturbed when he saw that they would not reach across its girth. He discarded them in favour of a longer and larger pair, then, cautiously, he removed the lid and inched the tweezers towards the black monstrosity.

'Be careful,' said Brady, feeling Kim take hold of his arm. They both watched as Foley made sure he had a good grip on the implement, then, with a swift movement, he gripped the slug in the tweezers. It wriggled, contracting its body, immediately exuding more slime which dripped onto the work top. Foley held it firmly in the tweezers and pulled a plastic tray towards him. He carefully deposited the slug onto it and then, noticing that the other two were slithering up to the lip of the jar, he promptly knocked them back in and screwed the lid on once more. He picked up a second pair of tweezers and pulled the slug out to its full length. For the first time, Brady saw that the tray in which he'd put it had a scale on it, like a ruler.

Foley exhaled deeply. 'Five and a half inches,' he said. 'Where did you say you found this?'

Brady repeated his story.

'Is it a slug?' Kim asked.

'Oh yes,' Foley told her. 'It's a slug all right but I'll be damned if I've ever seen one this size before.'

'What kind is it?' Brady asked. 'I mean what species?'

Foley shrugged. 'I haven't a clue.'

'I thought you were supposed to be the expert,' the Health Inspector said.

The young naturalist looked at him. 'Mr Brady, you probably know as much about slugs as I do. In fact no one seems to know very much specific about them and I certainly don't know anything about this kind.' He nodded in the direction of the captive slug which was writhing and contracting its body beneath the grip of the tweezers. The mucoid coating seemed to be filling the tray around it.

'What's it doing?' asked Kim, shuddering.

'Well, with ordinary slugs, the secretion of bodily mucus is used as a defence mechanism as well as a means of locomotion,' Foley explained. 'If a bird tried to eat it, for instance, the slug would secrete more slime which would cause the bird to drop it. The mucus contains an irritant.' He paused. 'That's what happens with ordinary slugs, I'm just assuming that the same rules apply to these things.' He peered closer, still keeping a firm grip on the black creature. 'You see, when a slug moves it isn't actually in contact with the surface it's on. I know that sounds illogical but what I mean is, it lays down the mucus as a kind of "carpet" if you like, between *it* and whatever it's travelling on. It's the same with snails. Someone did an experiment with one once, they let it crawl across the edge of a razor blade but it wasn't harmed because the slime acted as a cushion.'

'How do they feed?' asked Brady.

'The mouth is on the bottom,' Foley told him. 'There's three or four rows of teeth which it uses to grind up its food.'

'Which is?' the Health Inspector asked, apprehensively.

Foley shrugged. 'Green-stuff mainly. Lettuces, cabbages. Anything they can find in a garden. They're pests, any gardener will tell you that.'

There was a long pause, the silence finally broken by Brady.

'Do any of them eat meat?' he said, quietly.

Foley laughed, softly. 'Not that I know of. There are one or two species that eat earthworms and other insects but . . .' He let the sentence trail off, his tone darkening. 'Why do you ask?'

Brady swallowed hard. 'Look, I know this is going to

sound crazy but could these slugs,' he motioned to the large creatures in the jar, 'kill a man?'

Both Foley and Kim looked at him, aghast.

The young curator smiled. 'That's hardly likely, Mr Brady'.

The Health Inspector's tone hardened. 'One of them nearly took a chunk out of my bloody finger. Now that's pretty unusual wouldn't you say?'

Foley nodded.

Brady continued.

'So there might be other unusual characteristics about them too.'

'Like being able to kill a man?' There was the tiniest trace of cynicism in the curator's voice.

'Is it possible?' the Health Inspector persisted.

'Even if it were, there would have to be hundreds of them.' The young curator quickly qualified his words. 'All the same I'd say it was,' he paused, struggling to find the word, 'unthinkable.'

Kim looked at her husband as if he were a stranger. 'Why do you need to know that, Mike?' she asked.

The Health Inspector was looking at the slug in the tray, still pinned beneath Foley's tweezers.

'A man was found dead two days ago,' he said, softly. 'Ron Bell. He lived in that big house near the new estate.'

Foley nodded.

Brady continued. 'His body looked as though it had decomposed it was . . . well it looked as though it had rotted. There was no flesh left on him but there was lots of blood in the room where we found him. Now, for a corpse to be in the state he was in, it would have taken months before that amount of tissue deterioration took place and besides that, there wouldn't have been so much blood.'

Kim paled. Foley wrinkled his brow as he listened.

'But, the thing is, all over the remains and all over the room was that slime.' He pointed to the thick, transparent mucus which the slug was exuding. 'And I've seen it again since then. When I was inspecting some new houses I found slime trails on the floor and walls.' He told them about Mrs Fortune's drains. 'I saw slime trails in the sewer too.'

Foley nodded. 'That makes sense. Slugs prefer a damp environment.'

Brady nodded, distractedly and the curator looked at him, not quite sure how he should react to what he'd just heard.

'What are you trying to say, Mr Brady?' he asked.

'I don't know what I'm trying to say, I'm just telling you what I've seen.' He sucked in a worried breath. 'And now, on top of that, I find dozens of slugs, bigger than anyone has ever seen before, in my garden. When I pick one up, it tries to bite me.'

Foley stroked his chin thoughtfully and watched the slug in the tray, slithering about in its own slime.

'So you think that old man was eaten by these slugs?' he said.

'I think it's a distinct possibility. I want to know what you think,' Brady insisted.

The younger man didn't speak.

'Could these slugs kill a man?' asked the Health Inspector again.

Foley inhaled slowly. 'Like I said, there would have to be hundreds of them.'

Brady pressed him, the vision of Ron Bell's remains burning brightly in his mind's eye. 'I'm asking you for the last time.' His voice had taken on a sharp edge. 'Could they have killed Ron Bell?'

'Yes,' said Foley, flatly, his attention now rivetted to the slug. He finally turned to face the couple. 'Look, I'll take a look at these slugs, examine them, run some tests on them, do a bit of research. I'll find out all I can about them.' His tone had darkened. 'Give me a day or two.'

Brady nodded.

'Where can I reach you?' the curator wanted to know.

The Health Inspector pulled a nearby pad towards him and scribbled down their address and phone number, then beneath that he wrote down his office number. Foley scanned it once and nodded.

'I'll be in touch,' he said.

Brady extended his right hand and the young curator shook it.

'Thanks,' said Brady and they turned to leave. Foley watched them, listening as their footsteps receded away down the stairs. He sat there for long moments then turned his attention back to the slug in the tray. It was still slithering about in its own slime and had crawled as far as the lip. The curator knocked it back into the tray but, instead of withdrawing its eye stalks like any other slug or snail, it immediately began its journey to the side of the tray again. Foley glanced across at the jar beside him and saw that the other two slugs were clinging stubbornly to the top of it. It was as if the trio of black creatures were anxious to be together again. He pushed the jar closer to the plastic tray and watched, mesmerised, as the freed slug slithered over the lip and onto the glass of the jar. It crawled up the smooth side until it was level with its companions. The curator shook his head, then, taking his tweezers, he plucked the beast from the side of the jar and dropped it into a beaker. Over this he placed a piece of asbestos, normally used in conjunction with a bunsen burner. Then, he got to his feet and passed through a door on his right.

It led into a part of the museum which boasted 'live exhibits'. He flicked the light switches and the powerful banks of fluorescents burst into life. The naturalist walked swiftly towards the thing he wanted, passing half a dozen fish tanks and a Vivarium which contained a grass snake. There was also a large tank housing three or four frogs. But it was the tank at the end of the gallery to which Foley was heading. He paused before it, running a swift eye over the inhabitants.

Pond snails.

A number were feeding on the many plants in the aquarium but a large number were clinging to the glass. Foley looked at them, selecting the largest specimens, one of which was the size of a child's fist. Then carefully, he reached into the murky water and plucked the largest animal from its position on the side of the tank. The creature immediately retracted into its shell as Foley tugged it free but, ignoring the water which ran over his hand, dripping on the polished floor, he turned and made his way back to the laboratory. For some reason, as he deposited the pond snail in the tray vacated by the slug, he felt a thin film of perspiration cover his forehead and he was surprised to find that his hand was shaking when he lifted the lid from the beaker.

He seized the slug in his tweezers and held it for a moment, gripping it at the head end just in case it decided to have a go at him as it had at Brady.

The pond snail had emerged from its shell by now and was slithering slowly about in the bottom of the tray.

Foley gently lowered the slug in beside it. He pulled up a stool and seated himself beside the work top, a pencil gripped in one hand, poised over the pad before him. Quite what he expected to happen he wasn't sure but what *did* happen both shocked and revolted him.

With almost unnatural speed, the large slug slid across to the pond snail and fastened its jaws firmly into the gastropod's head. The slug held firm, its large central tooth anchoring it to its unfortunate victim. The snail tried to withdraw into its shell but was pinned down by the weight and grip of the slug which set to work on it with the numerous rows of radular teeth. Then with one powerful movement, it tore the snail in half, wrenching its soft body from the confines of the shell.

'My God,' gasped Foley, softly, hastily scribbling notes. He watched in awed revulsion as the slug proceeded to devour the remains of the pond snail.

In fact, so intent was he on watching the scene of slaughter before him, he forgot all about the other two slugs in the jar, one of which had succeeded in slithering over the lip and was in the process of heaving its form over the glass of the exterior.

Foley had forgotten to screw the lid on.

He watched the slug in the tray finish off the snail, shaking his head as he scribbled more notes.

The second black creature was half way down the jar by now, its posterior tentacles waving silently.

The slug in the tray now turned towards the curator and he reached for his tweezers once more, ready to drop it back into the beaker.

The second slug was actually on the implement when he picked it up.

With a shout of fear and surprise, Foley dropped the tweezers, the slug falling to the floor with them. He stepped away from the creature as if it were going to leap at him. A quick glance at the one in the tray told him he was going to be forced to act fast. The first slug was slithering over the lip of the tray, leaving its thick trail behind as it gained a grip on the work top. The second was moving towards him. Foley couldn't believe what was happening.

The slug was actually coming after him.

He knelt, retrieved the tweezers and seized the second slug in a powerful grip. With disgust, he hurled it back into the jar with its companion then he turned to deal with the first of the black monstrosities. This time his lunge with the tweezers was clumsy and he snipped off one of the eye stalks.

The creature immediately contracted, slime oozing from its thick body, dark blood running from the severed tentacle. It remained still for a second then, to Foley's horror, it turned towards the metal implement which hovered over its head. The second eye stalk waved around accusingly until Foley, in a fit of anger, snipped that off too. This time the slug did stop, trying to curl up into a ball to protect itself. The naturalist picked it up in the tweezers and dropped it into the beaker, replacing the asbestos mat in position on top of it. Then, he reached into a nearby drawer and took out some adhesive tape which he used to fasten the mat in place. Satisfied that it was secure he sat back on his stool.

The beaker was small, the air supply limited and Foley estimated that it would take less than an hour before the creature suffocated. He screwed the top securely onto the jar which held the two other slugs then he pulled off his rubber gloves and tossed them onto the work top. He crossed to one of the sinks and washed his hands. He was still shaking slightly and, as he dried his hands, he watched the black creatures sliding about inside their glass prisons. He would wait until the one in the beaker was dead and then run some tests on it, perhaps open it up and see exactly what he was dealing with. He decided to go and check the library, to see what he could find out about slugs in general. He folded the towel and draped it over the rail then he headed for the door but, as he reached it he paused and Brady's words came drifting back to him through a haze of uncertainty.

'Could these slugs kill a man?'

Foley closed the lab door and, after a moment's hesitation, he locked it behind him.

Brady and Kim drove from the museum in silence, Kim in particular was disturbed by what she'd heard. She studied her husband's profile for a moment longer then said, tentatively:

'Mike.'

He glanced at her.

'What you said about Ron Bell being killed by slugs. Do you really believe that's what happened?'

He shrugged. 'I don't know what to believe.'

'What did the police report say?' she wanted to know.

'There's been no police report. They're still waiting for the coroner's verdict.'

She shook her head, almost imperceptibly. 'But slugs don't attack people.'

'That one had a pretty good go at my finger,' he snapped.

He swung the car off the side-road, guiding it towards the town centre and Kim asked him what he was doing.

'There's something I've got to get,' he told her, his tone softening slightly as he felt her hand on his thigh. He looked across and managed a thin smile and she realized just how worried he really was. He guided the Vauxhall through the heavy traffic in the centre of town and was lucky to find a parking space in the main street. He switched off the engine and took out the keys.

'Fancy a walk?' he asked her and she nodded, clambering out.

The inside of Haworth's Garden Suppliers was hot and sticky and Kim found it difficult to breathe. It was a small shop but its shelves were crammed with every kind of gardening aid and the floor was littered with lawn-mowers, rakes, hoes and all manner of other equipment. Their shoes beat out a hollow tattoo on the wooden floor as they walked in and a high pitched buzzing broke the silence as Brady opened the door. Immediately a little man with greying hair and a thin moustache appeared from behind the counter. He was wearing a grey overall and had a pipe protruding from one corner of his mouth. It had long since gone out but he either hadn't noticed or just hadn't bothered to relight it. He spoke without removing it, the bowl bouncing up and down like a rampant metronome.

'Ted Haworth,' he announced, grinning broadly. 'Welcome to my little emporium, what can I do for you?'

'Slugs,' said Brady. 'I want something to kill them.'

'Well, I didn't think you wanted something to feed them with,' said Haworth, grinning at his own quip. He looked at his two customers waiting for them to smile which they did out of politeness. Kim raised an eyebrow and Brady nodded almost imperceptibly.

Haworth scuttled round to their side of the counter, crossing to the shelves which held all manner of bottles and jars.

'Having trouble with the little buggers are you?' he said, gaily.

'You could say that,' said Brady. 'What's the strongest repellent you've got?'

'Now,' said the little man, pausing momentarily. 'Do you want something to kill them or something to just shift them to some other poor devil's garden?' He laughed again.

'I want something to kill them,' Brady told him.

Haworth nodded and reached for a bottle of brown liquid. He plonked it on the counter. Brady read the label. 'Slug-it'. He nodded. 'Anything else?'

The shop owner produced a green can which had 'Slug Pellets' written on it. He crossed back to his own side of the counter.

'I'll take them both,' said Brady, fumbling in his pocket for some money.

'You really have got problems with them, haven't you?' said Haworth, smiling. He dropped the two items into a bag and handed them to Brady along with his change.

'There's full instructions on each container,' he added. 'I had trouble with the little devils one year. They ate me out of house and home. Ruined my crop of vegetables.' He smiled at Kim who tried to look interested.

Brady turned and headed for the door. 'Thanks for your help,' he said, opening it for Kim to pass through.

'They'll get rid of the little sods,' said Haworth, grinning.

Brady nodded. 'I hope so,' he said, cryptically.

It was late afternoon when they finally got home and clouds of tiny flies hovered around Brady as he scattered slug pellets and poison over the ground. Even as he did so he could see a number of the larger slugs slithering about on the dark earth, apparently oblivious to his efforts but he felt a strange kind of pleasure knowing he was sewing the seeds of death for these black monsters. The slug pellets, according to the instructions on the tin, were consumed by the animals and worked almost immediately. There was something in them which attracted the slugs to them. The poison was intended to kill on contact.

Kim watched him from the back door, the clouds of midges swirling around in the afternoon air like flies round a rotted carcass.

When his task was completed, Brady stood back.

'Right you bastards,' he said. 'Come and get it'. He turned and headed back to the house, telling Kim that he'd check on the results next morning.

As the Health Inspector trudged back up the garden a huge black slug, fully eight inches long, slithered up onto a piece of rock. Its eye stalks moved slowly back and forth, almost mockingly.

As if it were watching Brady.

Thirteen

Kath Green picked up the small watering can and poured some of the clear liquid into the pot where the spider plant was growing. The plant was increasing at a tremendous rate and its leaves draped over the side of the pot like some kind of frozen green overflow. Kath smiled to herself and passed to the next pot where she was nurturing a bizzie-lizzie. It had just started to flower, as had a number of the other plants and a heady aroma filled the air of the outhouse.

Playing contentedly on the tiled floor of the conservatory was Kath's two year old daughter, Amanda, who was having difficulty dressing one of her dolls. Finally, when she couldn't get its coat on by conventional means, she pulled the arm off in order to ensure an adequate fit. Satisfied with her efforts, she smiled happily to herself and sat the doll down beside a couple of teddy bears and a bendy model of Kermit the frog. Amanda wiped her hands on her dungarees and clambered to her feet, wandering across towards her mother who was busy watering another of her plants. She tugged on Kath's skirt and the woman looked down.

'What is it, darling?' she asked, running her free hand through the little girl's hair.

'Ice cream,' said Amanda. looking up at her with huge brown eyes.

Kath smiled. Obviously the little girl had heard the distant chimes of the van. It usually came past the house at about three every afternoon and, when she herself heard it, she guessed that it must only be in the next street.

'The man's not here yet,' said Kath and Amanda nodded, dejectedly. 'Mummy go and get you one when the man comes round.' That suggestion seemed to brighten her up and she smiled broadly, her little face beaming. She returned to her waiting toys. Kermit and the others greeted her arrival with silence. Amanda picked up the torn off arm of her doll and set about fastening it back in position, chewing it angrily when it wouldn't fit back into the joint. Kath saw her and turned, wagging a reproachful finger at the child.

'Don't put things in your mouth, darling,' she said, taking the doll and its disjointed arm from her irate daughter. Kath fiddled about with the recalcitrant plastic limb for a moment and then she too gave it up as a bad job. 'We'll see if Daddy can fix it when he comes home,' she said, putting the doll on the shelf where she kept her plant food.

'When Daddy gets home,' Kath repeated her own words to herself, sighing wistfully. Ray Green had been working in Stowfield, about twenty miles away, for the past three days and he was due back that night. It couldn't be too soon for Kath. She missed him terribly, even on such short trips. She had never been very good at making friends and, despite the fact that they had lived on the new estate for the past five years, she still only knew most of its occupants on nodding terms. When Ray was on a job she only had Amanda for company and it was at times like that she was thankful they'd had a child. She'd been through a pretty bad bout of post-natal depression but Ray had helped her through it, showing a tolerance and understanding which she had never dreamed he possessed. They were happy in every respect now. Ray's business was flourishing and Kath was slowly learning to overcome her shyness. She had found interests of her own, the plants being her consuming passion. Ray had built the conservatory himself, an extension linked to the kitchen, afraid that the house was becoming like 'Bloody Kew Gardens'.

She smiled at the recollection and carried on watering. As if sensing something, Amanda got to her feet and wandered across to her once more and, just as Kath was going to ask what was wrong, she heard the familiar tones of the ice cream van outside.

'Mummy,' said the little girl, tugging at Kath's skirt. 'Lolly.'

'All right,' said Kath and put down her watering can. She walked through into the kitchen, retrieved her purse and headed out towards the waiting van.

The sun was still blazing away and Kath decided that she would have one herself. Why not? At twenty-six and with a figure that would make any woman envious, one ice cream wasn't going to hurt was it? She smiled to herself and got in the queue behind a couple of kids, one of whom was busily inspecting the contents of his left nostril on an index finger. Kath shook her head and smiled.

Amanda jumped up and down delightedly on the tiled floor for a moment before returning to her assembled toys. She sat cross-legged amongst them, telling them that she was going to have an ice cream. She put her hand back to steady herself and it was then that she felt something wet on her fingers. Amanda looked down and saw something glistening in the sunlight. At first she thought it was water but, as she ran her fingers through it, she noticed how thick and sticky it was. Puzzled she raised her hand, the clear liquid clinging to her fingers. Amanada brought her hand closer to her face, sniffing at the fluid, puzzled when it had no smell. She looked down and saw that it led right across the conservatory, like a trail.

Tentatively, she licked some of it from her fingers.

It was tasteless too. She swallowed quickly, wiping the rest on her dungarees. Mummy told her all the time not to put her fingers in her mouth and, if she saw her licking the sticky stuff she would be angry. Amanda ran her tongue round the inside of her mouth. The sticky stuff seemed to put her teeth on edge and she tried to wipe it away on her sleeve but, in a moment or two, she had swallowed the one or two globules and it was gone.

She heard her mother's footsteps as she returned with the ice creams and she jumped up to take hers, forgetting the sticky stuff now.

The single slug which had left the trail slithered, unseen, from the conservatory.

Kath cut Amanda's food for her and watched her as she ate. The little girl finished all her tea within about ten minutes and sat back proudly, displaying an empty plate. Kath ate her own meal, smiling as she saw Amanda rubbing her stomach the way Ray did when he had eaten. She glanced up at the wall clock and saw that the hands had crawled round to six p.m. Another three or four hours and Ray would be home. She felt a warm shudder of anticipation run through her.

She finished her own meal while Amanda scuttled off into the sitting room to watch TV. She'd brought all her toys in from the conservatory and they sat with her before the flickering picture. The multi-coloured hues reflected in their dead, glass eyes. Kath did the washing up, watching the sun slowly wane, spilling its redness into the golden heavens, tinting the clouds crimson. She left the plates to drain and padded into the sitting room. Another hour and she'd have to put Amanda to bed. The child was yawning already. Unusual for her, thought Kath. She was usually full of life and bedtimes were sometimes an impossible struggle. Getting her upstairs was bad enough but keeping her in bed was more often than not impossible. Both Kath and Ray often went through three or four story books before the little imp went off to sleep. But tonight, Amanda was dozing in front of the TV and, when seven o'clock came (traditionally a time of joyful but tiring pandemonium) she was positively insistent on going to bed. In fact, even before Kath had finished slipping on her pyjamas, the little girl had fallen asleep. Kath looked down at her as she lay on the sofa but, she reasoned, the child had been out playing all day. There was good cause for her to be tired. She lifted the sleeping form of her daughter easily and carried her up the stairs to the bedroom which had dancing rabbits on the door.

Kath laid her in bed, pulling the sheets up around her neck. She knelt beside Amanda listening to the low guttural breathing for a second then she leant over and kissed her on the cheek. The child moved slightly but did not wake.

'Goodnight, darling,' whispered Kath and crossed to the door. She stood there for a moment, watching the slow rise and fall of Amanda's chest, then she quietly pulled the door shut and made her way downstairs.

Kath heard the dog barking and looked up from her book. She muttered something to herself and got up, crossing to the big bay window in the sitting room. Outside, just passing the house, Mr Steel from next door was being dragged along the road by his Alsatian. The huge dog was yanking him all over the place and Kath couldn't resist a smile. However, he smile faded as the dog stood still before the house and began barking with renewed ferocity. The blasted thing would wake Amanda, she thought and she turned back to her seat, one ear cocked expectantly, waiting for her daughter to call or to come scampering down the stairs.

But, there was no such movement and Kath settled back into her chair, reaching for the discarded paperback. She flipped it open and tried to read but she couldn't concentrate. The barking of the dog had receded into the distance but the ticking of the sitting room clock seemed to be thunderous. Kath looked across at it and saw that it was nearly eight o'clock. She checked her watch too, as if it were going to hasten Ray on his journey home. She discarded the paperback once more and got up to switch on the TV. Kath punched buttons, trying to find something to hold her attention.

A documentary about nuclear war on one channel. She hurriedly switched over. A black and white film. She sighed and pressed the last button. It was another documentary, this time about rising street crime. Kath hovered before the set where a youth with a mohican style hair-cut was being interviewed:

'Well, the fucking law ain't no bother. Me mate, he done this fucking shop and no coppers showed up so, well, I mean they're bastards ain't they? I . . .'

Kath winced and switched the set off. She exhaled deeply and returned to her chair where she sat for long moments before deciding to make a cup of tea. At least that would keep her occupied.

It was as she rose that she heard the commotion coming from upstairs. Kath stood still for long seconds, listening to the shouts and screams coming from above then, the breath catching in her throat, she raced towards the stairs, hurrying towards the landing. It was as she reached it she realized the noises were coming from Amanda's room.

Kath pushed open the door, her hand reached frantically for the light switch.

Amanda lay across the bed, her body thrashing frenziedly about, contorting like an eel on a hot skillet. Her head was rolling back and forth at a terrifying rate and, Kath noted with horror, that there was a dark, evil smelling mucus spilling over her lips. As her head shook madly, the foul sputum flew in all directions.

Kath took a step towards the bed, the sightless eyes of a teddy bear pinning her in a glassy stare. Its sewn-on smile almost mocking her.

Amanda was rasping asthmatically, her tongue lolling wolfishly from the side of her mouth, the whites of her eyes gleaming like half moons as they rolled in their sockets.

'Oh God,' gasped Kath, and reached for her daughter, struggling to hold the squirming child still in her arms. She lifted her daughter to her shoulders, the little body twisting forcefully in her arms. Tears welled up in Kath's eyes as she struggled towards the bedroom door. Her vision blurred as the salty droplets cascaded down her cheeks but she staggered on, the wriggling form of her child clasped tightly to her as the convulsions seemed to grow in intensity. Then, suddenly, with lightning speed, Amanda snaked her head forward and bit deeply into Kaths's neck, hanging on like a ferret until her mother pushed her away. Kath was screaming now. She stood motionless for a second, gazing down at the inert body of her daughter, then she staggered as she felt the warm blood jetting from the ragged wound in her neck. She clapped a hand to it and felt the torn flap of skin. The crimson liquid was running down her chest, between the valley of her breasts, staining her blouse and she felt her right arm going numb as the pain seemed to spread through her body. The landing swam before her and she gripped the bannister to stop herself falling. She felt her knees buckle but she put out a hand and steadied herself, leaving a bloodied hand-print on the white wallpaper. The mark looked black in the twilight.

'Help me,' she gurgled, the blood flowing freely from the bite. It poured down her outstretched arm and dripped onto the carpet and she felt the sickness sweeping over her. Tears coursed down her cheeks as she turned towards the top of the stairs, the phone at the bottom beckoning her.

In her haste, she missed the first step.

For a second Kath clutched at empty air, then, with a despairing moan, she fell forward. Cartwheeling as she crashed down the stairs. She hurtled to the bottom, leaving a trail of blood behind her, some of which splattered up the walls. She smashed into the phone table at the bottom and the phone itself fell to the ground. Twisted like a broken doll, Kath lay at the foot of the stairs, her tortured mind still clinging to the last shreds of consiousness. The pain which racked her body kept her awake. Even through the agony she felt the blood running from her torn neck and, somewhere in the distance, she heard a car door slam.

Ray Green made his way up the short path to the front door and paused on the step, fumbling for his key. He cursed when he couldn't find it, eventually dropping his tool bag and rummaging in the pocket of his jeans. He finally found it and inserted it in the lock smiling wearily. The job in Stowfield had been a sod. He and his partner had worked their nuts off to get it finished on time and it had been bloody hard work, but the size of the pay cheque eased the weariness somewhat and Ray knew how glad Kath would be to see him.

He pushed open the door and walked in.

Kath practically fell into his arms.

For a second, everything seemed frozen, like a stop-frame in a cine film. Ray opened his mouth to say something as he gazed into the tortured face of his wife. She was as white as milk, the blood matted thickly in her hair and stained into her blouse. He saw the vicious bite, the crimson liquid still pumping from it. The blood spattered walls, the wrecked table, the overturned phone.

And then the film was running again.

'Kath,' he gasped, looking into her reddened eyes. She tried to hold him but her fingers slipped and she slid to the floor at his feet. He dropped to one knee, his mind trying to comprehend the sight before him. She raised one bloodied hand, as if soliciting help and he tore off his jacket, laying it over her.

'Amanda,' Kath, rasped, a sudden spasm of coughing racking her body. The movement caused more of the bright red fluid to spill over her lips but she repeated the word, motioning towards the top of the stairs. He hesitated a second then bounded up to the landing taking the steps two at a time. Passing the blood flecked walls until he was looking down at the body of his daughter, now looking so tiny and helpless. Her eyes and mouth were open, a crimson smudge across her chin and lips. He knelt beside the body, shaking his head. Then, with one quivering hand, he reached out and touched her oustretched limb and the tiny hand seemed lost in his own rough one but he clasped it tightly, tears brimming in his eyes. The child's cheeks were sunken pits, her eyes ringed black. The whites seemed to glow even more brilliantly in the darkness but Ray finally tore his gaze from them and scrambled to his feet. He hurried down the stairs, groping for the phone, dialling three nines. He gripped the receiver tightly in his impatience finally managing to blurt out the word 'Ambulance', almost screaming it down the phone. He gave the address and then dropped the receiver, crawling across to Kath who still lay motionless in the hall.

Ray reached for her hand, large salt tears now spilling down his cheeks.

'Oh God,' he breathed, quietly.

Both mother and child were dead before the ambulance arrived.

Fourteen

Brady was up early that Sunday morning. He slid noiselessly out of bed, checking to make sure that he hadn't woken Kim. She rolled onto her back, one hand flailing across the warm area he had just vacated, but she did not wake.

The Health Inspector hurriedly pulled on a pair of jeans. He looked across at Kim once more and then at the clock which told him it was six fifteen. He pushed his feet into his slippers, pulled on his bath robe and padded out of the bedroom. Quickly but quietly he made his way down the stairs, through the house until he finally reached the back door. He unlocked it and slid the bolts back, shivering slightly as an early morning breeze whistled in through the open door.

Brady peered to his right and left, checking that no one else was around. Although at six fifteen on a Sunday morning that was unlikely. Satisfied that he was alone, he padded out into the back garden, cursing as the early morning dew soaked through his slippers and wet his feet.

'Shit,' he grunted, trying to walk on tip-toe to minimise the effect of the wet grass on his fraying foot wear. He moved across to the freshly dug area of ground, some of the slug pellets still in view, scattered on the top soil where he'd left them the day before. He swallowed hard and ran a hopeful eye over the dark earth. Many of the pellets had gone, consumed by the slugs he hoped but there were no dead animals in sight either. He stepped closer, running a hand over his bristly cheeks.

A black slug, the size of his fist, moved slowly towards him and Brady recoiled in shock and disgust. He backed off, seeing that more of the obscene creatures were slithering about on the earth. Brady watched them for a second, the breath catching in his throat, then he turned and headed for the house. He opened the back door and then hurried inside, quickly locking and bolting it again.

He leant against the closed door and exhaled deeply. On the work top opposite stood the can of slug pellets and the bottle of poison.

Brady shook his head.

For all the effect they'd had, he might as well have put down sugar.

Fifteen

By noon that morning the sun had risen high in the sky and it hung in the cloudless heavens covering everything below it with a blanket of searing heat.

David Watson heard the familiar Glaswegian tones of his neighbour, Wally Mackay, and straightened up. The tall Scot had a spade over his shoulder and he sauntered over towards the wire fence which separated the two gardens.

'Hell of a bloody way to spend a Sunday morning,' said the Scot, leaning on the fence. He jumped back hastily rubbing his forearm and looking daggers at the wire which was scorching hot due to the sun. Watson suppressed a grin and tried to look enthusiastic as Mackay leant on the handle of the spade and started chattering away about the weather, his wife and any other thing which passed through his mind. David Watson loved gardening but he invariably got collared by the Scot and ended up doing nothing. It looked like today was going to be one of those days.

'My bloody old lady sent me out here to dig this lot over,' muttered Mackay, indicating the patch of miniature jungle which constituted his garden. The weeds were knee high in places and were beginning to encroach into Watson's carefully tended plot of ground.

'It is getting a bit overgrown, Wally,' he said, trying to sound tactful, but making a melodramatic effort to pull up one of the unwelcome weeds which had found its way in from the Scotsman's garden.

'Fuck it,' said the Scot, peering over his shoulder in the direction of his house. He could see no sign of his wife so he retained his position and fumbled in his trouser pocket for his tobacco tin. He swifty rolled one and then offered it to

Watson who, equally swiftly, declined. He returned to his own task of spreading some compost on his latest crop of potatoes. He'd begun growing vegetables as a joke to begin with and because his wife, Maureen, had bet him a fiver he couldn't do it. The joke turned out to be useful though and he had a fine crop of spuds, onions, carrots and lettuce to show for his efforts. He still didn't know the first thing about the technicalities of cultivating vegetables but he had been lucky. He'd planted the seeds and the things had grown.

Watson enjoyed the peace and solitude which the garden offered him (when he managed to avoid Mackay that was) and it came as a welcome relief from the hustle and bustle of his every day job. He worked for the computer firm in Merton as a rep and had done for the last seven years. The pay was good, he was proficient at the job and he enjoyed it. His wife was manageress of a small but profitable boutique in the centre of town and they were hoping to move from the new estate soon to buy their own place.

They were childless by choice, both of them preferring to pursue their careers rather than sink into a welter of wet nappies and midnight feeds. Maureen in particular, had never shown a desire or even a liking for children. It was something which Watson found unusual but nevertheless welcome. She, unlike others of her kind, never felt the urge to pick up a young child and hold it or to gurgle unintelligible words to new born babies. At twenty-eight, she was every inch the business woman and the emotion which most women possessed had been replaced, in Maureen, by a ruthless efficiency which Watson himself respected. They were a perfect match, for he too bore that unerringly ambitious streak which at times bordered on obsession and had, occasionally, been known to veer into vindictiveness. He was thirty-two and happy and, right now, he'd be a lot happier if Wally Mackay stopped nattering and let him get on with his jobs.

'I heard your place was making more redundant,' said the Scot, spitting out a piece of tobacco.

Watson shook his head. 'Just rumours.'

Mackay shrugged. 'I got the fucking push two weeks ago.'

'You told me,' said Watson. About fifteen bloody times, he thought to himself. 'Have you found anything else yet?'

'Nothing about. You haven't any vacancies at your place have you?' he asked hopefully.

Watson smiled thinly and shook his head. 'Afraid not.' He knelt again and pulled a lettuce from the row before him, holding it up to admire his handiwork.

'Got any of those to spare?' said the Scot, admiring the greenery.

Watson looked at him and smiled again. Good old Wally, always on the earhole. The younger man was about to turn when Mackay began talking about football. Reluctantly, Watson halted and listened politely, nodding every so often as the Scot rambled on, his harsh accent grating like fingernails on a blackboard. He chanced a look at his watch and saw that it was twelve-fifteen.

'Dave.'

The shout made them both turn.

Standing in the doorway was Maureen.

'Telephone for you,' she called.

Watson stifled a sigh of relief and made his way up the garden, clutching the lettuce.

Mackay watched the younger man disappear inside his house then he sucked hard on his fag and drove his spade into the iron hard earth. If only my bloody old lady looked like her, he thought.

Watson hurried into the kitchen and inhaled deeply, the delightful aroma of roast beef meeting his nostrils. He dumped the lettuce on the draining board and headed through to the lounge.

'Who is it on the phone?' he asked.

'No one,' said Maureen, laughing. 'I saw that old Rob Roy next door had got you cornered so I thought I'd rescue you.'

Watson laughed and came back into the kitchen. He took Maureen in his arms and kissed her gently on the forehead.

'You cunning bitch,' he grinned, flicking at her blonde hair with one dirty hand. He pulled her close to him feeling the warmth of her body against his. He cradled her head in his hands and kissed her, his tongue seeking hers eagerly. They remained locked together, her right hand reaching for the growing bulge in his trousers, her own nipples stiffening and pressing against the material of her shirt. He finally broke away, shaking his head.

'Lunch,' he said, smiling.

'To hell with lunch,' she said, prodding him hard with her long nail. She drew a line from the hollow of his throat, through the thick hair on his chest, to his navel. As her hand toyed with the button of his jeans he held it and smiled.

'Can't you wait?' he said, trying to sound stern but, when she shook her head he laughed. They finally pulled away from each other and Watson crossed to the sink to wash his hands. He looked at Maureen as he did. She was dressed only in a yellow shirt and a pair of tight-fitting canvas trousers, worn thin at the knees. Beneath them he knew she wore no briefs. She never wore underwear in the summer. The blonde colour was beginning to grow out of her thick hair and the darker roots were showing. Every time she said that she would let her hair return to its natural chestnut colour but, each time, she weakened and resorted to the dye. He watched her as she ran the lettuce briefly under the tap before returning it to the chopping board where she set about its crisp green leaves with a razor sharp knife. She cut it up hastily, dropping the pieces into the nearby salad bowl with the peppers and other vegetables.

'I had trouble finding a decent lettuce,' he said, indicating the vegetable as she tossed it in the bowl. 'Bloody slugs have been at them.'

'Slugs?' She shuddered.

He nodded. 'There's about a dozen out in the vegetable patch now. Damn things. I'll have to see about putting something down to kill them.'

Maureen set the bowl on the table and crossed to the oven, retrieving the meat. She set it on the table and handed the carving knife to Watson. Quickly and expertly he sliced the succulent joint and, within minutes, they were eating.

'No salad?' said Watson, offering Maureen the bowl after he'd taken his share.

She shook her head, reaching instead for the glass of red wine at her elbow. She raised it in salute and smiled.

'Here's to your success,' she said. 'I hope you get that contract signed tomorrow.'

'You're not the only one,' said Watson and joined her in the toast. He put down his glass once more and continued eating. She saw him wince as he pushed a lump of lettuce into his mouth. He chewed slowly for a second, grimaced and reached hurriedly for his wine.

'Something wrong?' she asked.

He motioned to the salad. 'I think I swallowed something,' he said. 'You did wash that lettuce properly didn't you?'

She raised an eyebrow, questioningly and Watson smiled. He continued eating, still aware of the strange flavour but, another glass of wine soon washed away the peculiar taste.

'Where are you taking them to eat tomorrow?' asked Maureen, running the index finger of one hand around the rim of her glass.

'The City Hotel,' he told her.

'That'll cost you.'

He winked. 'It's on the expense account.' He took a sip of his own wine, his voice turning reflective. 'Besides, this is an important contract. It'll be worth millions in the long run if I can secure it.'

'You're worried about it aren't you?' she said.

He nodded. The contract was a big one and, not only would it mean work for the firm for the next three years it would also bring Watson a sizeable slice of commission and almost certain promotion. Perhaps then, they could actually move out and buy their own house. He had two guests to entertain the following morning, one of them an American, and he didn't want anything to go wrong. Selling was his business and he would need all his powers of persuasion at the forthcoming business lunch. For the first time in his working life, he actually felt nervous. Four Mark-1

Computers and it would take him all his abilities to sell them and secure the contract. He sipped at his wine, pouring some more into Maureen's half empty glass with his free hand.

They ate lunch at a leisurely pace, although Watson left the rest of his salad. The strange taste seemed to have returned almost as if it were sticking to his tongue. He drank more wine in an effort to get rid of it and, even if he'd known about eating half the black slug, there was little he could have done about it.

He patted his stomach appreciatively and smiled at Maureen.

'Beautiful,' he said. 'So was the meal.'

She grinned, stood up and crossed to his chair, seating herself on his lap. She ran her carefully manicured fingers through his hair, squirming pleasurably as his left hand found its way up inside her shirt. He cupped one taut breast, rubbing his thumb across the nipple until it hardened to a firm bud. Then, with the other hand, he expertly undid the buttons until both her breasts were exposed. He bent forward and kissed each nipple in turn.

'What about the washing up?' she said, her face flushed.

He smiled. 'To hell with the washing up.'

They both laughed.

Watson checked his watch as the ten o'clock news came on. It was right to the second. He sat in the semi-darkness of the lounge with only the light from his desk lamp and the multi-coloured flickerings of the TV illuminating the room. They had only just drawn the curtains, shutting out the night but he had been sitting at his desk for more than two hours, going over blue-prints and fact-sheets. He had to be sure that he could answer any question that either of his two customers might put to him the following day. Also, he had to know every minute detail about the workings of the machines so that he could extol their worth to the best of his abilities but, as he sat, gazing at the blue-prints, his mind was not on the job at hand. His stomach felt bloated and he had already loosened his belt but, more disturbingly, he was suffering from what felt like severe flatulence. It had come on suddenly about six that evening and despite the repeated doses of Magnesia, the discomfort had not been relieved. He shifted uncomfortably in his seat, rubbing one hand across his protruding belly.

He had eaten nothing since lunch-time, but, surprisingly enough he didn't feel hungry. All he was aware of was the unrelenting pain in his stomach which sometimes felt like contractions. If he'd been a woman he might have thought he was pregnant. He smiled at his own quip but the smile dissolved into a wince as another spasm of pain hit him.

'Jesus,' he rasped, surprised at its intensity.

Maureen, crouching on the floor before the television looked round.

'What's wrong, Dave?' she asked.

He sat back in his chair. 'My bloody stomach,' he said, irritably.

She looked concerned. 'Hasn't that pain gone yet?'

He shook his head.

She got up and crossed to his desk which occupied one corner of the room. 'Do you think I should call a doctor?' she asked.

Watson grabbed hold of her and pulled her onto his knee, trying to disguise the violent stab of pain which accompanied the movement. It felt as if someone was pulling his intestines out through his navel.

'I don't need a doctor,' he said, trying to catch his breath. 'It's probably just nerves from thinking about tomorrow.'

Maureen smiled thinly, not reassured by his home-grown diagnosis. 'If you're sure.'

He nodded. 'I'm sure.' He kissed her. 'Perhaps an early night would help.'

She touched his cheek which felt hot, the perspiration beaded on it in a thin film. Maureen nodded. 'I think that's a good idea,' she said.

In fifteen minutes they were upstairs.

Watson lay in bed, the sheets pulled back. He looked down

at his naked body, studying each outline and contour. Lying flat, his stomach didn't seem to be so distended, indeed, when he stood up to examine it in the wardrobe mirror the bloated appearance it had shown earlier seemed to have gone.

The pain, however, persisted.

He crossed back to the bed and lay down again, glancing across at the bedroom curtains which billowed in the gentle breeze. Both bedside lamps were on but the corners of the room were in shadow. He lay still, his arms behind his head, supporting him. The pain seemed to have moved further up his body and, as he swallowed, a wave of agony seemed to sweep over his entire stomach and lower chest. He cursed silently. Perhaps it *was* just nerves. Maybe something he'd eaten? He nodded, yes, that was the answer. In the morning it would be fine, he'd . . .

He sat up as an excruciating pain tore through him from sternum to groin. He clutched the bed, the muscles in his arms standing out like cords of thick hemp but, after a few unbearable seconds, the spasm passed, even settling a little. He took a deep but tentative breath and lay back again. He heard the toilet flush and, a second later, Maureen's light footsteps padding across the landing.

She entered the bedroom and closed the door behind her, the long black, diaphanous, night-dress swirling around her like nylon fog. Through it, Watson could see the smooth outline of her body and she stood before him for long seconds gazing down at his own naked form. He shifted his position slightly, gritting his teeth against the onslaught of pain he expected. It came only briefly and he exhaled gratefully, watching as Maureen climbed into bed beside him.

Her left hand stroked soothingly across his belly.

'Does it feel any better?' she asked.

He nodded and leaned forward to kiss her, feeling that soft hand sliding further down his body until it enveloped his penis, stroking and caressing it until it reached full erection. Watson thrust his hips forward, forcing his shaft further up into Maureen's eager hand. He reached for the bow at her throat and pulled it, allowing the night-dress to fall away, exposing her body. He cupped one breast in his hand, bending his head to flick the rough edge of his tongue over her swollen nipple. She held his free hand, pushing it towards her mound where his fingers brushed the soft down of her pubic hair before plunging deeper to find her slippery cleft. She writhed beneath his probing digits and he pushed deeper, smiling at the look of pleasure on her face.

Her hand gripped his organ more tightly, the speed of her movements increasing and Watson felt the unmistakable waves of early pleasure sweeping over him. He kissed Maureen gently on the lips, whispering to her to slow down but her passion knew no bounds and she pulled him onto her, guiding his hardness into her moist vagina. He thrust into her, both of them gasping at this new ecstasy.

Watson almost cried out in pain as a wave of agony tore through his stomach and chest. He gritted his teeth, sucking in a tortured breath, suddenly finding that his arms would not support him. He collapsed onto Maureen, the pain driving red hot knives into him.

He withdrew from her and rolled to one side, his penis immediately losing its stiffness.

'Dave,' gasped Maureen, breathlessly. 'What is it?'

He winced. 'Jesus.' The word sounded as if it came from miles away. Watson was clutching at his stomach, lying still on his back.

'I'm going to get a doctor,' said Maureen, hauling herself out of bed.

'No,' he said, forcefully. 'It's OK now.' He nodded, noting that the pain was, indeed, diminishing.

Maureen paused, her hand still on the knob of the door but, when she saw him stand up, she crossed back to the bed. Watson stood before the mirror once more. There was no distention, just the pain. He took three or four deep breaths, relaxing more with each one. Finally he returned to bed. Maureen lay beside him, stroking his hot cheek with one index finger. He twisted his head to one side and kissed her finger, smiling at her.

'Are you going to be all right?' she said, anxiously.

Watson nodded. 'The pain's almost gone now.' He smiled. 'I'll be as right as rain in the morning.'

They switched off the bedside lamps and Maureen drew herself closer to him. It wasn't long before he heard the soft, rhythmic sound of her breathing as she drifted off to sleep. Watson watched the curtains, still billowing in the gentle breeze. Beyond them the night was black, sticky with heat.

The pain gradually lessened in David Watson's stomach but, the hands of the clock had crawled round to one twenty a.m. before he finally found the welcome oblivion of sleep.

It was Maureen who heard the alarm the following morning. She reached up and turned it off, simultaneously touching Watson gently on the shoulder.

'Dave,' she murmured, her voice thick with sleep.

He didn't move.

She called his name again, rubbing her eyes and blinking myopically at the ceiling.

Still no response.

Maureen propped herself up on one elbow and leant across her husband. He was lying on his side with his back to her and, when he made no movement on her third call, she shook him gently.

Watson remained still.

Maureen swallowed hard and swung herself out of bed, crossing to her husband's side where she knelt. She pressed a hand to his cheek which was cool and suddenly she felt afraid.

'Dave,' she repeated, more urgently, this time shaking him hard.

She gave an audible sigh of relief when he opened his eyes a fraction. Crusted and heavy-lidded, they opened slowly and he looked at her almost as if she wasn't there. He seemed to be looking through her.

Maureen called his name again and, this time, he rolled onto his back. His mouth opened slightly and he made a deep rasping noise in the back of his throat.

'God Almighty,' he moaned, covering both eyes with his hands.

'I thought you were dead,' she said, her breath coming in short gasps.

'I think I am,' croaked Watson, massaging the bridge of his nose between his thumb and forefinger. 'It feels like there's a brass band marching around inside my head.'

'What about your stomach?' she wanted to know.

He sat up slowly, the headache intensifying to a point where he felt as though someone were hitting him repeatedly across the skull with a dozen red hot hammers. He slumped against the headboard and looked down at his stomach. No distention. No pain even. With cautious hands, he pressed the firm flesh in several places.

'No pain at all,' he said, trying to smile but the blinding white agony in his head restrained him. 'It's my bloody head now.'

'I'll go and get breakfast ready. I'll get you a couple of Paracetamols,' Maureen said and pulled on her house-coat. She padded out of the bedroom leaving Watson alone. As slowly as he could he swung himself out of bed and crossed to the bedroom door. The headache seemed to intensify as he walked across the landing to the bathroom and, when he looked at his reflection in the mirror, a haggard, white-faced ghost stared back at him. His face was the colour of rancid butter, the dark circles beneath his eyes looking all the more prominent because of that. He ran some cold water and splashed it over his face, leaning over the sink for what seemed like an eternity. When he did finally straighten up, he put both hands to his temples as if he were afraid his head was going to explode. With the red hot hammers pounding away at his brain, he began to remove his shaving equipment from the glass-fronted cabinet on the wall. He filled the sink with hot water and, carefully, lathered his face.

The prospect of a day's business and hard selling seemed to make his pain all the worse.

Sixteen

The dining room of the City Hotel was already crowded with its daily quota of businessmen as Watson and his two customers entered. He'd booked a table for one fifteen and a quick glance at his watch told him that it was over thirty minutes before they were due to eat.

'How about a drink before lunch?' he said, smiling, trying to ignore the headache which still raged, threatening to split his skull in two.

'Sounds good to me,' said Edward Canning, the first of his prospective customers. Canning's thick American drawl drifted through the air, mingling with the smell of cigarettes, liquor and the tempting aroma of freshly cooked food. Canning was in his late thirties, heavily built but without a hint of fat on his powerful body. He lit up one of his huge cigars and followed Watson and the other man, Kenneth Riggs, into the smaller of the City's three bars.

Riggs was younger by a couple of years but his grey hair gave him the appearance of someone twice his age. His face was lined and his cheeks seemed to hang down like those of a bloodhound. When he laughed, which he often did, a row of double chins wobbled fluidly, spilling over onto his shirt collar which looked so tight it threatened to strangle him. Canning had removed his tie because of the heat and, as he found a table near the window, he rolled up his sleeves. Riggs joined him while Watson stood at the crowded bar brandishing a five pound note in front of him.

He looked angrily at a man who bumped into him and the unfortunate chap apologised hurriedly when he saw the expression on Watson's face. His nerves were not so much frayed as shredded. He'd picked his two customers up at nine and driven them to the factory to show them the computers in action. They had asked surprisingly few questions, only those relating to reliability, performance, output and, most importantly, cost. A fact for which Watson was grateful because he was finding it difficult to even think straight, so intense was the throbbing inside his skull. Nevertheless, he'd established a good rapport with the two men, particularly Canning. Both seemed interested and satisfied with his approach and also the computers. Watson felt almost certain that the contract would be signed but he would feel a hell of a lot happier when he could actually see their names on that dotted line. He exhaled deeply, closing his eyes momentarily. The noise in the bar seemed to swirl around him like a bank of mist yet it seemed distant, as if he were alone in a sealed compartment and everyone else was outside. He opened his eyes again, craning forward to see where the barman had got to. The little man in the red jacket was serving a couple of customers at the far end of the bar so Watson continued to stand in his place holding up the fiver as if hoping it would attract the barman. He ran one hand across his forehead, wondering if his headache was ever going to go. The two tablets he'd taken at breakfast had done nothing to help, neither had the four others he'd taken since. He just hoped that the deal could be concluded quickly. He promised himself he'd go straight home to bed afterwards.

The barman finally arrived and Watson ordered, leaning against the counter while the little man fetched the drinks. He returned with surprising speed and Watson collected both drinks and change and made his way carefully across the room to the table where his customers sat.

He almost fell into the seat, reaching for his vodka.

'Cheers,' he said, his false smile returning with effort.

The other two men echoed his toast and there was a moment's silence as they drank.

'What do you think of the place?' asked Watson, finally.

Canning scanned the bar and the dining room beyond. The walls were festooned with a mixture of rusty farming implements and old weapons. In the next, larger, bar, there was a huge open fireplace stacked high with logs over which hung a full size man-trap.

'Big mice around here, huh?' said the American, smiling.

Riggs laughed loudly, spilling some of his drink.

'They used to use them for catching poachers,' Watson told his customer.

The man-trap was about the only authentic piece of apparatus in the entire hotel. It was what some people might call a 'plastic restaurant'. The wooden beams which criss-crossed the ceiling were imitation and even the massive log fire was lit by a gas flame hidden beneath the wood. The weapons and prints were antique shop acquisitions designed to give the place a feeling of age and character which was palpably second hand. Two suits of rusty armour stood guard at either side of the fireplace, as if guarding the secret of its falseness.

The dining room itself was festooned with flags bearing the emblems of dukes and lords who had probably never existed and a stag's head hung from the central wall. Canning saw it and touched Watson on the arm.

'I was just thinking,' said the American, a wry smile on his lips. 'That goddam deer must have been doing about ninety when it hit the other side of that wall.'

Watson laughed his polite laugh and Riggs once more went into a fit of giggles, spilling more of his drink.

'Is your boss expecting us to sign a contract today?' asked Canning, sipping at his drink.

Watson shrugged. 'Well, he's not banking on it, but it'd be a nice surprise for him.'

The American smiled.

'And a nice bonus for you.'

Watson nodded, the movement sending fresh jabs of pain through his head. He gritted his teeth and smiled, downing what was left in his glass.

'You are prepared to guarantee us full maintenance, free of charge for the next five years if we accept the deal?' said Riggs, studying the salesman over the rim of his glass.

'Yes,' said Watson.

Riggs nodded. 'So, the only thing that still is to be worked out is the price.'

'The price was agreed, Mr Riggs,' said Watson. 'There's no machine comparable to the Mark-1. You'll find nothing better for your particular needs, not at the prices we're offering anyway.' He paused, seeing that he had both men's eyes on him. 'In the long run it will be an investment. You *could* buy cheaper elsewhere, I wouldn't attempt to delude you about that. But nowhere will you find a machine with the capabilities which ours can offer.'

'How long have you been doing this job?' asked Canning, a slight grin on his face.

'Seven years,' Watson told him, slightly puzzled.

The two customers exchanged an enigmatic smile which unsettled the rep slightly.

'You're very good at it,' Riggs told him.

Watson thanked the man, wishing that he'd just put his bloody name on the contract instead of lavishing compliments on him. Riggs asked a few more questions about the computers which Watson answered with his usual thoroughness. The grey haired man nodded but didn't speak. There was an awkward silence between the trio which was finally broken when a nasal sound came over the small speaker in the bar. The garbled tones chattered on for a moment and Watson finally made out the sound.

'Mr Watson,' said the voice. 'Your table for three is now ready. Mr Watson.'

The three men got to their feet, a wave of pain so powerful it staggered him, causing the rep to support himself against the wall for a second. His head felt as if it were going to split in half and he had a mental picture of his brain swelling, trying to burst free of the confines of his skull. He stood still for a moment, his fixed smile finally fading.

Canning saw him swaying slightly and put out a hand, as if fearing that the younger man were going to fall.

'You OK?' asked the American.

Watson sucked in a laboured breath. 'Yes, just a bit of a headache.' He found the smile once more and looked at the two men. 'You carry on into the dining room. I'm just going to the toilet.'

Canning hesitated but the salesman raised a hand to signal that he was all right. He watched the men walk into the dining room then he made his way to the lavatories.

The cold white light which flooded from the banks of fluorescents made him wince and his feet echoed on the white tiled floor. He found that he was alone and crossed to the nearest sink, fumbling in his jacket pocket for the jar of Paracetamol. He unscrewed the cap and scooped a handful of running water to swallow the pills with. They remained on his tongue for brief seconds, the bitter taste making him feel sick but then he swallowed them, clutching the side of the wash basin. He groaned aloud as the pain in his head pounded away. It seemed as if the red hot hammers had been replaced by hundreds of blazing chisels and someone was driving them relentlessly into his tortured brain. He bent and splashed his face with cold water, straightening up slowly to gaze at his pain racked features in the mirror.

A single drop of blood trickled from his left nostril. It ran slowly down and over his lip, falling to the sink beneath where it made a tiny crimson explosion on the white enamel.

Watson shuddered and wiped it away with the back of his hand. He washed his hands hurriedly and dried them on the nearby towel-roll then he returned to the mirror.

There was no more blood and he dabbed at the nostril with his handerchief, relieved to find that it showed no hint of red when he inspected it. He swallowed hard, steadied himself against the basin edge then walked out.

He saw Canning and Riggs seated at a table in the centre of the dining room, talking animatedly, only slowing their machinations when they saw him approaching. He smiled and sat down, draping the napkin across his knees.

'Feel any better?' the American asked.

'Yes, thank you,' Watson lied, reaching for the menu which lay before him. The waitress was approaching, order pad at the ready and Watson had only seconds to skim the menu before ordering. The waitress took the order, (steak for Watson and Canning, Spaghetti Bolognese for Riggs) and was about to walk away when the rep added a postscript.

'And a bottle of the Beaujolais please.'

The waitress nodded and disappeared.

'Well Mr Watson,' said Canning, stroking his chin thoughtfully. 'While you were elsewhere, my partner and myself made a decision.'

Watson swallowed hard, trying to forget the blinding headache for a moment.

'We'll accept the terms of your contract,' the American told him, flashing him a mouthful of capped teeth. He extended a hand which Watson shook thankfully. Riggs too repeated the gesture.

'I thought we might finalise things and sign over a drink after lunch,' said Riggs, smiling.

'Thank you,' said Watson, one hand almost unconsciously touching his nostril. He looked at the hand, relieved when he saw that it bore no crimson mark. His head was still thumping and the noise created by the many other diners made him dizzy but, the realization that he'd secured the contract was at least one worry less.

The waitress returned with the wine, uncorked it and poured some into Watson's glass. He sipped and nodded. She put it down and left them. The rep filled the other men's glasses and they raised them in salute.

'I suppose this ought to have been done with champagne really,' he said, smiling.

'What the hell,' Canning said, grinning. 'A drink's a drink. Here's to our agreement.'

They drank. The waitress returned a moment later with the food which she put down before the three men. They began eating, their conversation now veering away from business. Canning started talking about his family but the words didn't seem to register with Watson who had put down his knife and fork and was sitting motionless in his seat, his fists clenched so tightly the knuckles were white. He found it difficult to breathe and, when he tried to swallow it was almost impossible.

Canning looked up and saw him.

'Hey,' he said, a sense of urgency in his voice. 'What in the hell is wrong, David?'

Watson reached for his wine and raised it to his lips.

'I told you,' he said, his voice a dry rasp. 'It's this bloody headache.'

He managed to get a couple of mouthfuls of wine down, almost slamming the glass back onto the table. He reached for his knife and fork again and cut his steak, the pain, unbelievably, intensifying.

Riggs, peering up from his plate of spaghetti bolognese, was the first to see it.

A thin, almost watery, trickle of blood ran from Watson's nostril and dripped onto the table cloth. It left little stain but then, suddenly, it began to thicken and grow darker and within seconds, viscous clots were gushing from the nostril. They splattered onto the tablecloth and even onto Watson's plate with a force and sound which made Riggs feel sick. The rep put a hand to his face and groaned, the blood spilling through his fingers and running down the back of his hand. He remained upright in his seat, clutching at the nostril which was pouring forth blood like a tap with no washer.

'Jesus H Christ!' murmured Canning, pushing himself back and away from the table.

And now other diners had seen or heard the commotion and all eyes turned towards the horrendous scene.

Watson rocked back and forth in his seat, hands clapped to his head as the pain reached intensities beyond endurance. Blood continued to gush from his nostril and then, to the horror of all those watching, something white appeared amidst the welter of crimson. Something long and tapering which seemed to grow from the very nostril itself.

'Oh my God,' gasped Riggs.

The worm wriggled free of the nostril, its white body covered with blood. Then, as it tore its obscene form from the bursting orifice, Watson shrieked and pitched forward. He crashed into the table, plates, glasses and food cascading down after him as he grabbed at the tablecloth, which fell across him like a blood-spattered sheet. He rolled onto his back, the worm slipping down his cheek. It lay in the pool of crimson beside him.

A waitress nearby screamed and dropped an armful of plates, people began to bump into each other in their efforts to get away from the abominations before them. Only Canning remained nearby, transfixed by the sight. Watson's body was twitching madly, the muscles going into spasm so quickly he looked as if someone were tugging him about with invisible wires. Then, as the American watched, the flesh of Watson's eyelid seemed to split, as if someone had pulled it too hard. There was a small jet of clear liquid, some of which spurted onto Canning's leg and then, the eye began to bleed. The white turned crimson, the blood vessels appearing to swell and then burst.

A second white shape came writhing up from the rent in the eyeball.

The second worm was bigger and, when it finally succeeded in tearing its vile form free, Watson's eye collapsed in on itself. Blood pumped thickly from the ruined socket.

The worm slid across his face, touching the fluttering lips briefly and, with a newly awakened disgust, Canning thought that the monstrous thing was going inside his mouth but it lay there for a second then seemed to stiffen and it rolled off into the puddle of blood along with the first creature.

Watson raised one blood spattered hand as if soliciting help and his remaining eye fixed Canning in a baleful stare, then, the hand fell away and the American could see that the younger man was dead. His face a bloodied ruin, he lay amidst the spilled food and the gouts of his own blood.

Riggs had passed out.

A waiter appeared at the American's side and looked down at the body. He swiftly turned his head, fighting back the hot bile which was clawing its way up from his stomach.

'Fucking hell,' he groaned.

'Get an ambulance,' said Canning, kneeling to help Riggs up.

The dining room was filled with noise. Somewhere a woman was crying, somebody was shouting something about it being an accident. The waiter was phoning for an ambulance.

That done, he hurriedly dialled the Council Offices and asked for the local Health Inspector.

Canning took one last look at the body of David Watson, his own stomach doing somersaults but it wasn't the appearance of the body which drew his attention. It was the two white shapes which lay beside it and, finally, he lost control and retched until there was nothing left in his stomach.

Seventeen

Brady pulled up outside the City Hotel and was surprised to see up to a dozen people standing on the steps which led up to the main doorway. He locked the Vauxhall and strode across, pushing through the group into the lobby. There was no sign of any ambulance or the police and the Health Inspector wondered just what the hell was going on. He'd received the call about ten minutes ago and come straight out. Some garbled message about an accident at the Hotel, could be hygiene problems and then the caller had hung up.

The Health Inspector made his way through the group of people on the steps and walked through the lobby, his feet sinking into the deep pile of the crimson carpet. He frowned. There were more people huddled about outside the entrance to the dining room. A woman was sitting in a chair nearby and, as far as Brady could ascertain, someone was waving smelling salts under her nose.

He pushed open the door of the dining room and found several red shirted waiters standing around, all looking into the area where the tables were. There were two or three men in suits there as well and it was one of these who approached the Health Inspector. He held up his hands, as if to bar Brady's way.

'Sorry, sir,' he said. 'No one is allowed into the dining room. If you'd just like to wait . . .'

Brady cut him short. 'I'm the Health Inspector,' he said, producing a small plastic ID card which bore a very old and poorly taken photo of him.

The man looked at the card then at Brady, as if the likeness didn't fit but he handed it back, regarding the official suspiciously.

'What are you doing here?' the man wanted to know.

Brady snatched the card back, irritably.

'It's why I'm here, you should be worrying about,' he rasped. 'Now, what happened?'

'There was an accident in the dining room,' said the man. 'We're not really sure what it was.'

Brady regarded the man indifferently. 'Are you the manager?'

He shook his head. 'He's away for the day. I'm the assistant manager, anything you . . .'

The Health Inspector cut him short again. 'Can I see your . . .' he paused, '. . . accident?'

The man in the suit snapped his fingers towards a young waiter who Brady guessed must be in his early twenties. The lad looked round.

'Show this gentleman to the . . . er . . . the body,' he said.

'Why can't you show me?' asked Brady.

The man blenched and swallowed hard. 'Robinson will show you.'

The Health Inspector smiled to himself and followed the young waiter. As he walked past tables he noticed that most of them bore plates of food; some still steaming. The aroma reminded him that he hadn't had lunch.

'There,' said Robinson, pointing to a blood-stained cloth. Beneath it lay the body of David Watson.

Brady knelt and lifted one corner of the tablecloth.

'My God,' he whispered, pulling the cloth back further to reveal the upper torso as well as the face. He looked at the corpse, the blood now thickly congealed on it, the ruptured eye socket looking as if someone had filled it with rancid crimson syrup. Watson's other eye was open. It reminded Brady of Ron Bell's head with *its* single staring eye.

'Who called the ambulance?' Brady said, swallowing hard.

'I did,' the waiter told him.

Brady looked up at the youth. 'Was it you who called my office?'

Robinson nodded.

It was then that Brady noticed the worms.

He took an involuntary step back and nearly overbalanced, the tablecloth falling from his grasp and uncovering the body. For long seconds he remained crouching, looking at the motionless forms of the worms both lying in the congealed gore, then he moved closer. He estimated that the worms must be around seven or eight inches long, but, unlike ring-worm they were not segmented. Just long white threads about as thick as two spaghetti strands.

'Was that why you called my office?' asked the Health Inspector, glancing over his shoulder. The group of waiters and the three men in suits were out of earshot but, nevertheless, the older man kept his voice low.

Robinson nodded. 'I thought those . . . worms might have come from the food.' He paled. 'I mean, the fucking things came out of his eye.'

Brady reached for a knife which lay on the floor nearby. With it, he carefully lifted one of the worms into the air, making sure he kept it at arm's length. The limp body hung there without moving.

'It seems dead enough,' he said, quietly.

'What is it?' Robinson asked, revolted by the sight of the foul thing. A jellied blob of coagulated gore dripped from one end of it and narrowly missed splashing Brady's trousers.

'Give me a glass or something,' he said. 'Anything I can put them in.'

The young waiter turned and saw an empty pint glass, he snatched it up and handed it to the Health Inspector who hurriedly dropped the first worm into the bottom. Then, he scooped the second creature up out of the puddle of congealed blood and deposited that in the glass as well. The task completed, he dropped the knife, draped a serviette over the top of the glass and hurriedly fastened it to the lip with an elastic band from his pocket.

He held the glass up, studying the blood-flecked white forms inside.

It was as he was straightening up that he caught sight of two ambulance men pushing through the dining room doors. One was carrying a furled stretcher, the second a red blanket. The latter of the two recognised Brady and nodded affably, then he looked down at the body of Watson.

'What happened to him?' said the ambulance man, holding the blanket while his companion unrolled the canvas stretcher beside the corpse.

Brady shook his head slowly, holding the glass and its vile contents down by his side. He watched as the two men lifted Watson onto the stretcher. The red blanket was draped over him and they lifted the body. The Health Inspector walked behind them, keeping the glass by his side but the people outside were more interested in the shape on the stretcher and he pushed through the crowd unnoticed. A couple of police cars, their blue lights turning silently, had just pulled up across the street and Brady saw three or four uniformed men crossing towards the ambulance. He, himself, reached his car and propped the glass up on the passenger seat. He sat still for long moments, his eyes fixed on the monstrous creatures inside and he was thankful that they were dead. Now he had to find out just what they were.

He twisted the key in the ignition and the Vauxhall engine burst into life. He drove off, for some reason, feeling the need to look at the worms every so often. The glass rocked on the seat and, once, toppled over. Brady hastily stood it up again.

He drove quickly and, this time, he knew that the perspiration which stained his forehead wasn't caused by the heat.

He brought the Vauxhall to a halt in the museum car park next to Foley's battered Volkswagen. There were a couple of other cars parked there as well and a bus with 'MERTON JUNIOR SCHOOL' emblazoned on the side.

The Health Inspector snatched up the glass, locked his door and sprinted up the short flight of steps to the main door. He entered the lower gallery and was immediately surrounded by a group of kids about ten or eleven years old. They swarmed round the gallery, note-pads in hand, scrawling down the names of the exhibits while a bespectacled woman in her forties called out to them to make sure they wrote down every name. The kids babbled excitedly, one or two banging into the Health Inspector who finally fought his way through the throng and reached the stairs. He hurried up them to the enquiries desk and rang the bell, looking around impatiently when no one came. Once more he rang the ball and still no one appeared so he turned and took the three or four steps which led to the laboratory. He knocked and a familiar voice told him to wait.

A moment later, the door opened and Foley stood there. The young curator smiled broadly and ushered Brady inside.

'How's it going?' he said, wiping his wet hands on his jeans.

Brady held up the glass. 'You tell me.'

The younger man took it from him and set it down on the work top, carefully removing the makeshift cover. He reached for a specimen tray and tipped the worms into it, prodding them with the tip of a scalpel.

'Where did you get these?' he asked, his voice heavy with foreboding.

Brady caught the note of concern in the curator's voice and stepped closer.

'A man just died in the City Hotel,' he said. 'One of the waiters called me, he thought these worms might have come from the food.' Brady paused, sucking in a laboured breath. 'He said he saw one of them come out of the bloke's eye. Now what the hell do you make of that?'

Foley didn't speak, he just leant closer to the dead worms, noticing, as Brady had, that they were unsegmented.

'Well,' the Health Inspector persisted. 'That's impossible isn't it?' The question hung heavily in the air. 'I've seen ring worm, other parasites, dozens of times but never anything like this. Foley, for Christ's sake. It's not possible is it?'

The naturalist turned round to face Brady.

'Those slugs you brought in the other day,' he said. 'I ran some tests on them.'

Brady interrupted, irritably. 'All right, we'll talk about the slugs in a minute. I need to know about these bloody things.' He pointed at the worms.

'That's the whole point,' said Foley, raising his voice slightly. 'The slugs and these worms are linked.'

'How for God's sake?' asked the Health Inspector, sitting down on a stool nearby.

'After you left that day, I dissected one. I found out everything I could about it. I read as many books as I could find about the bloody things.'

'And?'

Foley exhaled deeply. 'Well, for one thing, they're not a new species. As far as I can tell they must be a kind of hybrid.'

'What makes you so sure?' Brady wanted to know.

'Because they're ordinary garden slugs,' said Foley, flatly.

Brady almost laughed. 'Foley, the damn things are eight inches long. That one you measured was five and a half inches and that was a small one. Now, anybody will tell you that a common black slug is about three-quarters of an inch long and what's more, they don't usually bite.'

'That's what I meant about them being hybrids,' the curator explained. 'They must have inter-bred with another species. There are three species of carnivorous slug in this country. Testacella maugei. Testacella haliotidea and Testacella scutulum. Now those three hunt and kill earthworms and other insects, sometimes other slugs.'

Brady interrupted him. 'Then they wouldn't mate with garden slugs, they'd eat them.' He paused. 'Besides, you said that these large slugs were the ordinary garden variety.'

'They certainly share all the same physical characteristics apart from the fact that they seem to eat meat,' said the curator.

The Health Inspector exhaled deeply.

'I just haven't got a clue why or how ordinary garden slugs could grow to sizes like we've seen, or why they should have become carnivorous,' said Foley, wearily. 'My theory about inter-breeding is all we've got.'

'But slugs are hermaphrodite aren't they?'

Foley nodded. 'But they rely mainly on ordinary mating to reproduce. That just compounds our problems. They can cross-fertilize and fertilize their own eggs.'

There was a long pause the silence finally broken by Foley.

'It might interest you to know that each female can lay up to one and a half million eggs a year.' He reached for his coffee and took a sip, wincing when he found that it was stone cold.

Brady didn't speak.

Foley tried to qualify his statement. 'There's a tremendously high mortality rate. These slugs seem to be cannibals too, the younger ones are eaten by the larger animals in the clutch. Out of a hundred eggs laid, only three or four slugs will actually reach full maturity. Even so, when each female can lay one and a half million eggs a year, that's still a hell of a lot of slugs. The only thing is, they *must* have damp conditions to lay them.'

The Health Inspector nodded. 'Like the sewers,' he whispered to himself.

'I also found out that the irritant in the slime trails of these particular slugs is lethal,' said the curator.

'How?'

'I gave some to a laboratory rat. The damn thing was dead in three hours. Now, working on that example I'd say that the slime would be fatal if consumed by, say a child for instance. What it would do to an adult I couldn't say.'

'How would it affect a child?' Brady wanted to know.

'Well, judging by the symptoms which the rat manifested,' he paused, momentarily. 'I'd say the victim would appear almost rabid. They'd probably undergo convulsions, mental disturbance. The rat turned savage, it killed the female that was in the cage with it.'

Brady wiped a hand across his forehead. 'I can't believe this,' he said, incredulously.

Foley nodded. 'I wish it wasn't true.'

'How do they move around?'

'Crawl. Burrow. Swim. Lots of ways.'

'So they could be using the sewers to move around in?' said Brady, although it sounded more like a statement than a question.

'Without a doubt,' said the curator. 'Anywhere there's plenty of moisture, and it would suit their egg laying habits.'

'But if they need moisture, how come there's so many of them about now? It's hotter out there than it has been for years.'

'These particular slugs have a very large mucus gland. They secrete huge amounts of slime so there's no danger of them "drying up" even in the hottest weather. That's what makes them so much more dangerous, they're not reliant on a damp environment. Although we're more likely to find them in one, they don't *need* it like ordinary slugs do.'

'My God,' groaned Brady.

'I don't know how long these slugs have been breeding,' said Foley, anxiously. 'But either way, there must be thousands of them by now. Maybe even tens of thousands.'

'You've certainly done your homework,' said Brady, trying to smile.

'It's best to know as much as possible about your enemy.'

'You make it sound like a war.'

Foley grinned cryptically. 'Perhaps it is and the way I figure it, they outnumber us about five hundred to one.'

Brady ran a shaking hand through his hair. 'I'll tell you something else. They're immune to ordinary repellents. I put some down in my garden and it didn't have the slightest effect.'

The curator frowned.

Neither man spoke for long moments then Brady suddenly turned his attention to the worms.

'And those?' he said, pointing to the tray. 'You said they were linked with the slugs. How?'

'Come here,' said Foley, getting up. He led the Health Inspector to a nearby microscope. There was already a slide set up beneath the powerful lens and Brady squinted down the eye-piece, adjusting the focus until everything merged into crystal clarity. Floating around before him were dozens of minute, hair-like organisms which, on closer inspection, he saw resembled tiny versions of the two worms which lay in the tray.

'What are they?' he asked.

'Schistosomes,' said Foley. 'Blood flukes. They're a type of parasite found in the blood stream of slugs. I took that sample from one of our slugs but they're found in every species.'

Brady stepped back from the microscope.

'I still don't see the tie-up,' he said.

'The schistosomes live inside the slugs, right? Now, if a slug is accidentally eaten, even if it's only the tiniest fraction of it, those parasites somehow transmit themselves to the human blood stream. They travel to the brain and form cysts. The worms grow inside these cysts.'

Brady swallowed hard as the curator continued.

'The disease is called Schistosomiasis. Once the worms encyst in the brain it causes nausea, headaches and, more often than not, death.' He paused. 'And there are at least three documented cases in Britain every year.'

'Then that was what happened to the bloke in the restaurant.'

Foley nodded. 'He must have, somehow, eaten part of one of the slugs. Everything about these bloody things is bigger or more lethal, it stands to reason the strain of disease carried by them is going to be more virulent.'

Brady sat down heavily. 'And the more of them there are, the more people they're likely to infect.' He sighed. 'The slime trails I kept seeing, Ron Bell's body and now this. It's been slugs all along.'

Foley nodded. 'Should we tell the police?'

'What the hell can they do? Arrest the damn things? Besides, if we went to them and said that there was a plague of killer slugs in the town they'd probably lock us up.'

'I wouldn't blame them,' said Foley, sardonically.

Brady drummed on the desk top with his fingers. 'So what the hell do we do?' He glanced across at the dead worms.

'I can try and perfect a poison of some kind,' Foley offered. 'Something we can use on them but, like I said, there must be thousands by now. And,' he paused, 'if they are using the sewers to move around in, they must be everywhere.'

The words hung ominously in the air and Brady felt cold fingers of fear plucking at the back of his neck.

Eighteen

Clive Talbot fiddled with the controls of the Ferguson hi-fi, trying to find the button which activated the record player. Perplexed by the profusion of dials and buttons which faced him he turned to face Donna Moss, who sat on the sofa.

'How does this fucking thing work?' grunted Clive, still holding the record in one hand.

Donna smiled inanely at him, put down her glass of bacardi and crossed to the set. She flicked a switch and the turntable buzzed into life.

'Smart arse,' said Clive, dropping the record into position. He watched Donna make her stumbling way back to the sofa then flop down. There was a half empty bottle of bacardi at her feet which she had drunk since eight o'clock. He noted that the solid silver carriage clock on the mantelpiece said nine fifteen p.m. Clive adjusted the volume as a thunderous bass line roared out of the twin speakers and the singer's voice rose over the strident wail of guitars.

'. . . what did I see? Could I believe, that what I saw
that night was real and not just fantasy'.

Satisfied with the volume, he got to his feet and slouched across to the sofa where he flopped down beside Donna. She looked round and moved towards him, her mouth seeking his, the taste of liquor strong on her tongue as it sought the warm moistness of his own. Clive responded fiercely, simultaneously sliding one hand up the inside of her skirt until he felt it brush the cool material of her panties. Donna pulled away, giggling.

'Stop it,' she said, her face flushed.

'What would your old man say if he could see us now?' said Clive, a triumphant grin on his face.

Donna shrugged and downed what was left in her glass.

'He'd probably be more annoyed to think we were using his hi-fi,' she giggled.

'Yeah, I bet he fucking would.' There was a sharp vehemence in the youth's words and his hard eyes scanned the sitting room as he spoke. He could just imagine the look on old man Moss's face if he could see his daughter now, lying across the lap of a boy he hated. Clive had never got on with either of Donna's parents. Toffee-nosed bastards they were, thought themselves a cut above the rest of the neighbourhood. Just because James Moss was on the town council and Clive's dad worked on a building site, Moss looked down on his daughter's boyfriend with ill-disguised contempt. Many times he'd tried to break up their relationship but each time they'd found a way to continue seeing each other. He'd been going out with her for over a year and she had become something of a habit. Maybe he was in love, he didn't know. Even if he was he'd certainly never let Donna know and if any of his mates should find out he wouldn't dare show his face. At eighteen, Clive Talbot was at that age when overt concern for the opposite sex was something to be frowned on. As far as his little circle of friends were concerned, girls were good for only one thing.

That was certainly true of Donna. She was a year younger than Clive but her sexual precocity bordered on nymphomania and that fact further amused the young man when he thought what her father would say if he found out his 'darling' daughter had lost her virginity at the age of thirteen. To one of Clive's mates as a matter of fact.

Clive himself was an only child and lived with his parents less than half an hour's walk from where Donna lived. It used to be a ten minute ride on his Yamaha 250 but some bastard had nicked the fucking thing about a month ago. Clive still fumed inwardly as he thought about it but he'd find out who took it and, when he did, he'd make them sorry. He wouldn't go to the police. They were bloody useless and, besides, he'd been in trouble with them a couple of times himself. Only minor offences like breaking windows or fighting but, even so, he had no desire to seek *their* assistance in retrieving his stolen bike.

It had been an eighteenth birthday present from his parents. All his mates had bikes but most of them had farting little Puch Maxis or puny 150s. Nothing like Clive's. One or two of them even had jobs. Clive himself hadn't worked since he left school two years earlier. He'd looked for work sure enough, he never stopped looking, but his father's often voiced opinions about a Government *for* the rich *by* the rich were rapidly beginning to dawn on him. He'd never listened much to what either of his parents said but his father was shop steward for his branch of the Building Workers Union and, during the past two years, Clive had come to realize that his old man's hatred of the Government was well-founded. Clive now looked across at the photo of James Moss which stood on the TV and felt the anger rising within him.

'When are your parents due back?' he asked.

'Late,' Donna said, vaguely.

'Well how late is late?' he said, irritably.

'About two in the morning,' she informed him, reaching once more for the bacardi bottle. But Clive got to it first and lifted it from her clutching grasp.

'I think you've had enough,' he said, putting the bottle out of reach.

She pouted for a second then reached up and pulled him towards her. 'Perhaps I can persuade you to give it back.'

She pressed her mouth to his, her tongue forcing its way past his teeth and he responded with equal enthusiasm. He felt a tingle run through him as one of her hands fell to the rapidly growing bulge in his jeans. Donna ran her hand over his groin, squeezing his erection through the worn material of his denims. Their mouths still locked together, he reached for the buttons on her blouse and skilfully undid them, his fingers brushing against the lace of her bra. With practised movements, he reached round and undid the clasp, pulling the garment free to expose her small, taut breasts.

She tugged at his belt irritably when it wouldn't come free and Clive finally had to help her, loosening his own button.

Donna giggled softly and plunged her hand down inside his underpants, gripping his swollen shaft. Clive squirmed and thrust it forward into her eager, pumping, hand.

He reached across and cupped one small breast in his hand, rubbing his thumb back and forth across the nipple until he felt it stiffen. Donna sighed and, taking hold of his free hand, she thrust it beneath her skirt as if guiding him. But Clive needed no prompting and soon his eager hand was flicking against the flimsy material of her panties. He stroked the silky fabric, feeling the first hint of moisture seeping through it as he pressed harder. Donna gasped and manoeuvred herself so that he could reach her pulsing desire more easily, she felt his probing digits glide through her soft pubic hair to the hardened bud of her clitoris and she felt a comforting warmth envelop her. For her own part, she lowered her head to Clive's lap, her mouth closing over his swollen penis. He sucked in a shaking breath as he felt the hot wetness gliding up and down his shaft. He continued to move his fingers, plunging deeper until he infiltrated her sleek cleft.

Donna flicked her tongue over his bulging penis and she felt the unmistakable twitchings as he neared his climax. He stiffened and grunted and it was at that point she withdrew her head and sat up.

'What the fuck are you doing?' gasped Clive, his face flushed.

Donna smiled impishly. 'Upstairs eh?' she said.

'You are a right cow at times,' he said, panting.

'But lovely with it,' she giggled. 'Do I get my drink now?'

He gave her the bottle, doing up his trousers with difficulty. Clive looked at her once more his anger and frustration quickly disappearing. He chuckled to himself.

'What's so funny?' Donna wanted to know.

'You,' he said. 'If your fucking old man knew what you were like he'd have a stroke.'

'I think mum would like to lock me up in a convent,' Donna said, giggling.

Clive shook his head and watched her as she drank. Her

blouse was still off, revealing her breasts and her long, brown hair was unkempt and ruffled. It dangled over her shoulders as she shook her head and she ran one hand through it. The perm was starting to grow out and, only at the top and sides did it still retain curls. She wore no make-up, except a little on her eyes and, when she looked at him, those twin blue orbs held him in a hypnotic stare.

Maybe he really *was* in love, after all.

Donna sipped her drink and exhaled deeply. She glanced at the clock on the mantel and it said ten p.m. She knew her parents wouldn't be back for a good four or five hours. She and Clive had plenty of time. She watched him as he got to his feet to turn the record over then, a second later, the room was shaken once more by a series of drum and guitar blasts which threatened to reach seismic proportions. She motioned to him to turn the volume down a little which he did.

Donna, unlike Clive, had stayed on at school to study for 'A' levels. She knew that her future was already mapped out for her and there seemed little she could do to alter it. After school it would be university then, hopefully, into a job in designing. She was studying Graphic Design at school and intended gaining a degree once she reached university. But, although Donna wanted the career of her own choosing she still felt a kind of unseen manipulation. The university bit was as much for her parents' sake as her own. She could just hear them at the Rotary club luncheons:

'Oh yes, our daughter is at university.'

Both were fulfilling their own failings through her and she resented it. Of course she would never do anything to hurt their feelings or to damage her own chances of success but, sometimes, she felt the mad urge to say stuff it and walk out of school right there and then. To hell with everything.

Clive was the only thing she really cared about and that was another thing which rankled with her parents. She knew how they felt about him but she would not give him up. No matter how many times her father told her she wasn't to see the young lout (his favourite description of Clive) she always found some way of being with him. In a different kind of way, she was as trapped in her lifestyle as Clive was in his. Both knew how their futures were going to turn out, he because he was unable to get a job and she because she was fulfilling the aspirations of her parents. There seemed no way out.

'. . . Not a prisoner, I'm a free man, live my life how
I want to. Don't care, where the past was, I know where
I'm going . . .'

roared the singer on the record and the words sounded all the more pertinent to Donna. She swallowed what was left in her glass and got to her feet.

'Come on,' she said, smiling, motioning towards the stairs and, in a second, Clive was behind her.

Laughing, they made their way up to Donna's bedroom.

The first half a dozen of the slugs slithered across the glass top of the large cold frame, their posterior tentacles moving silently in the night air. On the ground nearby were many more of them, a shapeless black blot on the dark earth. They slithered over James Moss's carefully tended garden all seemingly heading for one spot.

Moving as quickly as their bloated forms would allow them, the slugs slipped into the drain, crawling up the pipe itself towards the first floor of the house where they eventually emerged in the guttering which ran alongside the windows.

They filled the pipe, overflowed like thick black rain into the guttering and then, slowly, they slid across the brickwork until they were actually on the window sill of the bedroom which faced the back garden. There were many of them and they slid over the sill, dropping to the floor of the bedroom. The darkness in there was total and it was quiet, only the slight murmur of the night breeze breaking the solitude as it set the curtains gently billowing.

The slugs continued to flood into the room.

As Donna and Clive reached the landing they paused,

kissing fiercely again, his eager hands searching for her breasts once more but she knocked them away and wagged a reproachful finger at him.

'Wait,' she giggled.

Clive crossed the landing towards a door which was firmly closed.

'Wrong room, idiot,' said Donna, her hand pausing on the knob of her own door.

'I know,' Clive said. 'Is this your parents' bedroom?'

Donna nodded and crossed to the door, pushing it open. She flicked on the light and walked in. Clive followed her, his heavy shoes making deep indentations on the thick white carpet. The whole room seemed to be white. The walls, the ceiling, the wardrobe unit, the dressing table. Even the bedspread was white. It was liking walking into a blizzard. It smelt of lavender and Clive wrinkled his nose.

'Fucking hell,' he said, crossing to the bed where he saw some clothes laying. He laughed and picked up a pair of large knickers.

'Who wears these?' he said, grinning. 'Your mum or your bloody old man?'

Donna laughed, too, and walked across to the wardrobe unit which dominated one side of the large room. It was covered in mirrors and she studied her reflection for long seconds. Clive noticed.

'Mirrors, eh?' he said. 'Kinky bastards aren't they? It's a wonder they haven't got them on the ceiling too.' He made a loud whooping noise and leapt onto the bed, stretching out on it with his arms folded behind his head. 'This is comfortable. Shall we do it here?' he asked, grinning.

Donna giggled. 'Come on, or they'll know someone's been in here.'

She stepped closer and Clive shot out a hand in an attempt to grab her but Donna stepped back and he missed, overbalanced and fell off the bed. Both of them began laughing and Donna hurried to the door and flicked off the light leaving him in darkness.

'You bitch,' he chuckled and chased after her.

He grabbed her just as she reached her own bedroom door and both of them crashed against it laughing like idiots. The door flew open and Donna stepped inside. She flicked at the light switch but nothing happened.

'The bloody bulb must have gone,' she said, snapping the switch up and down.

The room was in complete darkness, only the light which flooded in from the landing lighting their way. Clive closed the door behind him and turned the key, locking it.

'Who needs lights?' he said, and tossed the key away.

Donna giggled and held him close, relaxing as he lowered her onto the bed. In the blackness, they undressed one another until their naked forms lay side by side on the bed.

The curtains billowed in the breeze and neither noticed the gobs of slime on the window sill.

They sought the pleasurable touch of the other's hands, content in the pitch black to give way to almost invisible caresses. Donna felt Clive's hands running over her breasts before sliding down to part her legs which she moved willingly. With her own hand she guided his throbbing erection towards her slipperly cleft, gasping when he drove it into her. She locked her legs around his back, increasing the depth of penetration. He began to move rhythmically inside her and she thrust her hips up to meet his every movement, raking his back with her nails. Their grunts and cries became louder as the passion within them grew in intensity.

Neither of them heard the low sucking sounds as the sea of slugs, invisible in the darkness, flowed towards the bed moving almost soundlessly over the carpet.

The eyes of numerous pop stars watched impassively from posters on the walls as the black hordes swept nearer, the warmth and scent of human flesh attracting them.

Donna rotated her hips frenziedly as she felt her orgasm approach and she was mildly disappointed when she felt Clive withdraw from her but that disappointment rapidly disappeared when she felt him sliding further down the bed until his head was resting between her thighs. She moaned with pleasure as his tongue began to flick at her clitoris.

Clive was a tall lad and, in order to position himself correctly, he was forced to allow his feet to drop off the end of the bed. He stretched his legs out behind him, attempting to get a grip on the carpet with his toes.

He almost shouted aloud when he felt his feet touch something wet and slimy.

He raised his head, feeling a jellied movement beneath his toes, then, suddenly, he felt pain lancing through his foot as two of the slugs bit into it.

'Jesus Christ,' he shouted, pulling his feet back onto the bed.

Donna looked down. 'What is it?' she asked, dreamily.

'Something's biting me,' he shrieked.

Donna sat up, her hand reaching for the bedside lamp. She switched it on and, in that same instant she let loose a scream of terror which seemed to fill the entire house. Clive was struggling to remove the monstrous black things from his foot, blood staining the sheets as the foul creatures bored into the flesh.

Donna sat transfixed, watching the black mass of slugs seething towards the bed. A number had already begun to climb up the dangling sheets and Donna screamed again when she saw two near her hand.

With a roar of pain, Clive managed to tear one of the stubborn beasts from his foot. It came away, ripping skin and muscle as it did and he groaned, trying to remove the second. However, the effort made him overbalance and he fell off the bed onto the slippery carpet of slugs. For brief, nauseating seconds he writhed in the slime then the creatures attacked, sinking their sickle shaped teeth into his twisting body. Clive screamed in pain and tried to scramble to his feet.

'Get the fucking door open,' he yelled at Donna who was crying as she watched him struggling with the black horrors, one of which was eating its way into his back.

She sat huddled on the bed, rocking back and forth like a child, her eyes wide and filled with tears.

'The door,' he bellowed, trying to claw the slugs from his back.

But Donna couldn't move and, as more of the vile beasts reached the bed, she felt one crawl onto her hand. It bit into her and she shrieked in pain, feeling the blood running freely from the wound. Another struck at her buttocks, boring deep into the flesh and now Donna struggled to her feet but, a third slug slid up the inside of her thigh and, to her horror, Donna felt it boring into her crutch. She screamed with renewed ferocity as the thick black thing forced its way into her, like some obscene bloated penis. Blood began to flood down the inside of her legs, spraying the carpet and, in a second, the slug had disappeared inside her.

Donna collapsed. Laying across the bed, she was helpless as more of the slugs slid over her body, feeding on the warm flesh and enjoying the distinctive taste of the flowing blood.

Clive saw her body, covered by the beasts and he opened his mouth in a silent scream not sure whether to yell or be sick. His own back felt as if it was on fire as a dozen black creatures ate their way into his muscles. Others were gnawing at his feet and calves but he remained upright, throwing himself against the wall in an effort to dislodge the slugs. A mixture of his own blood and the pulped slugs left a reeking imprint on the nearest poster which regarded the scene of carnage with blank eyes. Clive staggered towards the door, one of the slugs eating into his ear lobe.

He crashed into the bedside lamp and it fell to the floor, plunging the room, once again into impenetrable blackness.

Gritting his teeth, he struggled on, over the slimy sea of blood lusting slugs. The pain in his back and legs was now almost unbearable and he wanted to scream and scream as they tore into him.

He reached the door and crashed against it, one bloodied hand grabbing for the knob.

It was then, through a pain racked brain, he realized he'd locked it. He fumbled for the key, remembering that it lay somewhere in the room.

He shrieked in agonized panic and knew that he must find the key. Must get out . . .

Must . . .

The slugs ate through the flesh of his calves and slithered up towards his thighs. He felt the sickness rising inside him and he thought he was going to faint but he punched the door hard, splitting his knuckles. White hot agony lanced up his arm, keeping him conscious. Through eyes filled with tears he saw three or four of the slugs burrowing hungrily into one of Donna's breasts. Her body was still, offering no resistance as the black monstrosities devoured her.

Clive fell to his knees, crushing a number of slugs beneath him as he groped blindly for the lost key. But the black mass covered the floor and his hands only brushed over many thick bodies. One bit into his thumb and he shouted once more in pain. Others were on his thighs now, digging deep into the muscle with their razor sharp teeth. Clive began to weaken, the loss of blood finally slowing him down but still he sought the key, struggling in the darkness.

Some of the other slugs were busily devouring the remnants of their crushed companions, seemingly oblivious to the struggle before them.

Clive groaned despairingly and hauled himself upright, swaying drunkenly for a second. He knew he would never find the key and now, as the black horrors continued to feed on his living flesh, he saw his only hope.

The bedroom window beckoned.

It was a slim hope but his only one and he blundered towards it, arms outstretched. As he reached the window he looked behind him, at the remains of Donna's body. One of the slugs was in the process of eating through her tongue, its obscene form filling her mouth as it feasted.

Clive hoisted himself up onto the sill and, still with a dozen or more of the slugs clinging to him, he jumped.

For seemingly endless seconds he hung in the air as if suspended on invisible wires then, his body plummeted earthward.

He hadn't even had time to think about the cold frame.

Directly beneath Donna's window it glinted as the watery moon shone on the thick glass panels in the top of it and

Clive's last sight was of the expanse of glass rushing up to meet him.

He smashed into the cold frame, the panels shattering with an ear-splitting crash. Lumps of jagged glass flew up as if blasted by some kind of explosion, the wood snapped like matchwood and the entire frame collapsed around him.

A shard of glass fully two feet long punctured Clive's body just below the sternum, tearing its way through his chest and erupting from his back. A fountain of blood rose with it. A smaller but no less lethal sliver sliced through his throat and a torrent of crimson gushed from the wound. His body twitched spasmodically, the blood still spurting from the wound in his back, the wind rasping in his torn lung.

Lights flashed on in houses on both sides, faces appeared at windows. Someone dashed for a telephone.

The slugs finished eating and slithered back across the bedroom floor towards the window. Then, as quickly as possible, they made their way back down the drainpipe and down into the drain itself, the familiar blackness and dampness of the sewer beckoning them.

The moon caught the point of the glass shard and it sparkled for a second then faded as Clive Talbot's blood began to congeal on it.

Nineteen

Brady had got home late that evening and Kim was surprised to find that his breath smelt of whisky when he walked in. He had come in at about seven thirty, dropped his briefcase in the hall and then slumped into a chair in the sitting room. The Health Inspector kissed Kim gently on the cheek when she bent over him.

'And where have you been?' she asked, smelling the whisky on his breath. 'There I am slaving over a hot cooker while you're out boozing.' She smiled.

Brady tried to return the gesture but it dissolved away into a sneer. Kim perched on his lap and draped one arm around his neck.

'What's the matter, Mike?' she asked, realizing that there was something wrong. He rarely drank, not unless something was really worrying him.

He shook his head and pulled her closer, loosening his tie with his free hand. 'I just stopped off at the Crown on the way home. I felt as if I needed one.'

She leant closer, sniffing his breath. 'Or two,' she said.

He smiled thinly.

'The dinner's nearly spoiled,' she told him.

'I'm sorry, love,' he said. 'But I'm not very hungry anyway.'

Kim kissed the top of his head, feeling his arm squeezing her more tightly, with an urgency he didn't usually show.

'Are you going to tell me or do I have to drag it out of you?' she said.

'What do you mean?' he asked, looking into her face.

'Come on, Mike. I'm not stupid. What's bothering you?'

Brady exhaled deeply. Should he tell her? The

conversation he'd had with Foley that afternoon had unsettled him. No, that wasn't really the word. To hell with it. He was scared. For the first time in his life, and he didn't mind admitting it, Mike Brady was frightened. Not just for himself, but for the rest of the town. And, most of all for Kim. He pulled her closer to him now, wondering whether he should burden her with his newly acquired knowledge. The words whirled around inside his head and he tried to dismiss them as ridiculous. Indeed, the idea of common garden slugs turning on human beings was ludicrous. As was the thought of some of them reaching lengths of six, seven and even eight inches. But, he had seen it. He had seen these creatures at first hand and, he had seen what they could do and for fleeting seconds the image of Ron Bell's remains flashed into his mind. The vision of David Watson and those monstrous worms replaced it. But, more than the problem, the solution worried him. How the hell were they going to wipe out the menace? Dare he go to the police with such information?

Brady gently moved Kim from his lap, got to his feet and crossed to the drinks' cabinet. He took out a bottle of Teachers and poured himself a large measure, dropping a couple of ice cubes in as perfunctory afterthoughts. Just to give it the appearance of respectability he thought, taking a hefty swallow. He closed his eyes, feeling the amber liquid burn its way to his stomach. He turned and looked at Kim, holding the bottle before him.

'Join me?' he asked.

She was beginning to get annoyed. 'Mike, please.'

Brady exhaled deeply. 'All right. But what I say now is just between you and me.'

She shook her head, disconsolately. 'Mike, if you can't trust me after all these years . . .'

'It's not a matter of trust,' he snapped, angrily and she was startled by the vehemence of his outburst. They regarded one another silently for long moments then Brady's tone softened. 'I spoke to Foley this afternoon.' He sighed, sipping at his drink.

'About the slugs?' she said.

He nodded. 'They're ordinary garden slugs.'

'But garden slugs don't attack human beings,' she said.

'That's exactly what I said,' echoed Brady going on to repeat his conversation with the curator. Kim listened intently, the hairs on the back of her neck rising slightly.

'Can you be sure about it, Mike?' she asked when he'd finally finished, her voice shaky.

'All the evidence supports my ideas. Foley's investigations just confirmed them,' he said worriedly. He downed the rest of the whisky and poured himself another.

'So you think that Ron Bell was killed by slugs?' asked Kim.

'Yes,' he told her, flatly.

'Then what's to stop them killing someone else?'

His answer sent an icy ripple of fear up her spine.

'Nothing.'

Kim sat back in her chair, the colour drained from her face. She took off her glasses and wiped both eyes and, for a second, Brady thought that she was crying but, as he looked he could see that she wasn't.

'What can you do?' she wanted to know.

He shrugged. 'Foley's working on a new poison. If only, somehow, there were a way of trapping all of the bloody things together in one place perhaps we'd have a chance of destroying them.' He took a hefty swallow from his glass.

'It's hard to believe,' said Kim, softly. She looked at him, her eyes beckoning.

Brady crossed to the chair and sat on the arm, Kim clung to him, her head resting in his lap. He stroked a hand through her hair, conscious that he was shaking slightly.

'There's something else,' he said. 'A man died today at the City Hotel. He died of a disease transmitted by slugs.' The Health Inspector decided to spare her the details.

Kim sat up. 'So the trouble is worse than you first thought?'

He nodded. 'Not only are the slugs themselves attacking human beings, the slime trails they leave contain a lethal fluid and, the man who died ate part of one of them.'

Kim put a hand to her throat. 'Oh God.'

'Foley agrees that they could be using the sewers to move around in. I saw slime trails when I was down there with one of the sewage men.'

'Then they could come up anywhere?'

'Yes.'

She clutched his hand.

'There's nothing we can do at the moment,' he said. 'If I go to the police they'll laugh in my face. We can't put a warning in the papers, people will panic. We'll just have to hope that Foley can perfect a poison in time.'

'In time?' Her words echoed in the room.

'He thinks there must be thousands of them already. We've got to destroy them before they can reproduce in even greater numbers.' He swallowed the rest of his drink.

'Do you think you can?'

Brady walked back towards the drink's cabinet. 'I don't know.' Somewhere, a voice in his head was telling him that they didn't have a hope in hell. The Health Inspector closed his eyes for a moment until the voice went away then he reached for the bottle once more.

Kim got to her feet and walked slowly towards the kitchen.

'You don't want any dinner?' she said, dreamily, the knowledge she had just acquired seeming to have numbed her senses.

Brady smiled and shook his head. He walked back to the chair and flopped into it, the drink held firmly in his hand.

'Kim,' he called and she paused at the kitchen door. 'It'll be all right,' he said but the words sounded empty and reassured neither of them.

She pushed open the kitchen door.

The single scream which she unleashed seemed to shake the house. Brady leapt to his feet, the glass of whisky falling to the floor. He dashed across to her and, together they stood in the doorway, eyes riveted to the sight before them.

Slithering silently over the edge of the stainless steel sink were half a dozen of the slugs. The leading one, a huge monstrosity about six and a half inches in length, had already reached the floor and was sliding across the lino towards the two terrified onlookers. The others were close behind it and, as Brady stepped into the kitchen, he saw more crawling over the edge of the sink, the slime from their bodies making them glisten.

'Get back in there,' he shouted at Kim, pushing her into the sitting room, slamming the door behind him. The Health Inspector snatched up the broom which lay propped against the wall nearby and, using it as a club, he brought it smashing down onto the leading slug. The aim was good and the broom hit its mark. The black creature's body seemed to explode, half of it flying across the kitchen, the eye stalks still waving about silently. Brady stepped past the pulped thing and drove the bristles of the broom against two of the other slugs, watching as they dropped to the floor. He stamped on them, hearing the foul squash as they were scrambled beneath his shoes. Using the broom as a weapon he literally swept the others back over the lip and into the sink itself where, to his horror, he saw dozens more of the creatures slipping and sliding over each other.

One was on the draining board.

The Health Inspector snatched up a carving knife which lay on the drying rack nearby and sliced the foul thing in half. A gout of thick, foul smelling pus-coloured liquid spurted onto his sleeve and he tore his jacket off in disgust. He pushed the severed slug back into the sink with the blade of the knife suddenly realizing how he could destroy them.

He reached for the button which activated the waste disposal unit but his hand wavered as he looked once more into the sink, the horrific realization of how they had got there finally hitting him.

As he watched, one of the slugs eased its obscene black form from the tap.

It hung there for a second then, trailing mucus behind it, the vile beast dropped into the sink. Almost immediately, a pair of eye stalks emerged from the tap, behind it, signalling the arrival of another of the animals.

Disgusted, Brady punched the waste disposal button and the vicious blades roared into action slicing and crushing anything which came their way. Brady used the end of the broom to push the last of the slugs down into the murderous revolving blades, watching with something akin to satisfaction as their bodies were torn and pulped by the machine. He turned on both taps, flushing the last of the black creatures from its hiding place. Propelled by the powerful jet of water, the slug was hurled from the outlet and straight into the grinding jaws of the waste disposal. The water also helped to wash away the evil mixture of pus-like blood and slime which coated the bottom of the sink. Brady left the taps and the disposal unit running then bolted through the living room and up the stairs, heading for the bathroom.

As he hurtled up the stairs, visions of what he might find whirled through his brain. A bath full of the foul black animals? The whole room seething with them?

He flung open the door.

Nothing.

Breathing a sigh of relief, the Health Inspector crossed to the bath and turned both taps on full blast, the water splashing up violently when it hit the enamel. He watched for long seconds then crossed to the sink, repeating the procedure there.

Once more, there was no sign of the slugs.

Gasping for breath, Brady watched the gushing conduits finally turning them off. He reached for a towel and wrapped it around the sink taps, blocking the outlets. Then he repeated the procedure with those on the bath. Satisfied that they were secure, he hurried back downstairs. Kim looked up at him as he passed, her eyes red and puffy. Brady, breathless from his exertions and also from fear, walked back into the kitchen and switched off first the taps and then the waste disposal unit. A sudden silence descended. Only the Health Inspector's low, guttural breathing interrupting the solitude. As he fastened dishcloths around both taps, he could hear Kim in the sitting room, sobbing softly.

His task completed, he stepped back, nearly treading in the pulped mess behind him. All that remained of the slug he'd killed with the broom. He stepped back until he was leaning against the kitchen wall, his breath now slowly returning to normal.

'Mike.'

He heard Kim's subdued plea and hurried into the sitting room. She was crouching on the floor beside one of the chairs. He knelt beside her, enfolding her in his arms, rocking backward and forward as if he were comforting a child. She held him tightly, her tears staining his shirt.

'Mike,' she repeated.

'It's all right,' he said, reassuringly but couldn't resist a sly glimpse over his shoulder at the kitchen taps.

If the bastards were using the water pipes to move about in too, there was no telling where the horror would end.

Or even *if* it would.

The entire water supply of Merton could be contaminated. The thought hit Brady like a sledgehammer and he swallowed hard.

Kim looked up at him, her eyes red and bloodshot. Her glasses were steamed up and Brady removed them, wiping the big salt tears away with one finger. He held her tightly.

Brady could feel her shaking but he gripped her firmly, wondering if she could feel the powerful shudders which racked *his* body.

Twenty

Charlie Barnes struck the match, his face momentarily illuminated by the yellow light. He tossed it away, hearing it hiss on the damp grass. He sucked hard on the roll-up, leaning against the tree impatiently. The hands on the church clock had crawled on to one fifteen a.m., bathed in the cold white light of the moon, they stood out starkly against the stone face of the clock. The weather vane at the top of the spire rocked gently back and forth in the cool breeze, its squeaking carrying a long distance in the stillness of the night.

Charlie watched the metal clock hands for a few more minutes and then decided that it was now or never. He walked slowly from his hiding place behind the trees, heading towards the open grave which lay about twenty yards from him. He kept to the grassy verges, conscious of the noise his boots would make on the gravel of the path. But, he reasoned to himself, who the hell would be up and about at twenty past one in the morning? And especially in a bloody graveyard. He forgot his caution and chose the path instead, his heavy tread rattling the pieces of shale. It sounded like someone walking over a hundred bags of crisps.

His spade propped over his shoulder like some kind of mock rifle, Charlie marched up to the open grave and peered in. The moonlight glinted on the polished wooden surface of the coffin and, for a second, he could see himself reflected in it. He stood beside the grave, finishing his fag. One large lump of ash fell from the end and dropped onto the coffin lid. What the hell, Charlie thought, it wasn't going to bother the poor sod inside was it? He smiled and dropped the roll-up, grinding it out beneath his boot. Then, he rubbed his hands and drove the spade into the mound of earth at the graveside.

Charlie had been grave digger in Merton's cemetery for the last six years. Ever since he got out of the Scrubs. He'd been in and out of nick all his life, ever since he was a kid and all the people in the town knew him for what he was. But there was nothing malicious about Charlie. No GBH or mugging for him. He hadn't graduated to that, probably never would. His life of crime had consisted of things like nicking bikes or stumbling on things which had fallen from the backs of lorries. At fifty-two, Charlie was treated with something bordering on affection by the older members of Merton. 'A likeable rogue' one of the old ladies used to call him and he smiled at the recollection. The last judge had called him 'an incurable villain'. Charlie grunted indignantly to himself. Silly old sod he thought, remembering how the bastard had sat there, looking at him over the top of his hornrims like some red robed God with a plaited wig. Charlie had been caught in possession of fifty cases of Johnny Walker which had disappeared from a warehouse in Milchester, about twenty miles away. It hadn't been a case of a quick trip to the magistrate's court and a hundred quid fine (his sentence for having stolen three lawn mowers from the local garden shop). No, this time, he was hauled up to a Crown Court. The case had only taken two days and the end result had been that he'd got eighteen months in the Scrubs. A bit harsh Charlie had thought at the time but, at least, while he was in there he had had time to catch up with a couple of old friends. He smiled to himself.

When he'd come out of jail he'd returned to Merton and, much to his surprise, the local vicar had offered him the job as grave digger. Naturally he had jumped at the chance, although wondering why the old boy was so forthcoming with his offer. Charlie guessed that the vicar saw it as some kind of spiritual exercise – forgive sinners and all that. Charlie smiled to himself. Maybe it had worked because, since becoming town grave digger, he hadn't been in trouble with the law.

But, then again, dead bodies didn't make very good witnesses.

The idea had first come to Charlie after he'd seen a body laid out in the Chapel of Rest, just prior to a funeral some four years ago. The body had been of a man in his seventies and, before any mourners arrived, Charlie had wandered into the Chapel and looked into the open coffin. The body was to be buried with all its jewellery, including a gold and diamond ring which Charlie reckoned must be worth at least £500. He'd stood in awe, gazing at the glittering prize, wondering how much he could get for it if he ever managed to flog it. The point was, how could he get it? Then, that night, lying on his bed smoking, he'd had a brainwave. Along with the job of grave digger came a small wooden building which was little more than a three roomed hut. It stood just inside the main gate of the cemetery and Charlie had made it his home for the last six years. He was also entrusted with locking up the gates at night, a job which had to be done from the inside. So, from ten p.m. onwards, he was effectively sealed inside the cemetery. It became *his* domain. He was king and, as monarch he intended claiming any treasure which might lie in his mouldering kingdom.

That night, four years ago, he'd dug up the coffin, removed the lid and taken the ring from the finger of the corpse. Unfortunately, it had been a tigher fit that he'd anticipated and Charlie had winced a little when he had to sever the finger with his pocket knife. Still, what the hell, he'd collected a couple of solid gold cuff links and a diamond tie-pin too from his generous benefactor. On his next day off, Charlie had taken his little hoard up to an old friend in London. One 'Spider' Wyatt, a fence. Spider had given Charlie 900 quid for the little package, a sum which the fence knew he could recoup three times over. Unbeknownst to Charlie, the ring had been antique. But, it had been the beginning of a blossoming little business venture. Ever since that first night, Charlie had been pillaging the dead of Merton for anything he thought valuable. Just a perk of the job he thought happily as he jumped down into the open grave, screwdriver in hand.

He usually had to wait until this time to do his little job and, if the body had already been buried, it sometimes took him until four a.m. to complete his task of exhuming and then re-burial. Sometimes of course he was unlucky but, on most occasions he found something worth taking and, just lately, he'd taken to inspecting the mouths of the corpses for gold teeth. The yield had been unexpectedly fruitful, although he had to confess, prizing the teeth from dead mouths was something he hadn't quite come to terms with yet. But, he put up with the smells and the clammy touch of the bodies. He collected his prizes, hiding them carefully in a locked box beneath his bed. Then, once a month, he'd take a trip up to London and see what he could get for his latest haul. Spider had asked him once where he acquired the stuff and, giggling like an idiot, Charlie had told him. The fence had paled on hearing the news but, goods were goods in his game and the source of these particular valuables made them untraceable.

Charlie grinned to himself as he inserted the screwdriver in the slit of the first screw. Things had definitely begun to look up during the last four years. Or look down as the case may be. He chuckled to himself and removed the first screw, dropping it into the pocket of his trousers. He'd removed his jacket, despite the slight chill in the air but he knew that filling the hole in would be hard work once he got around to it.

He removed the second of the six screws and wondered what prize he would find tonight. He'd seen a particularly valuable wristwatch on the corpse when it was lying in the Chapel of Rest and there was no telling what else he would find.

Smiling happily, Charlie set to work on the third screw.

Something moved behind him and the sound startled him. His hand slipped and the screwdriver scored a deep furrow across the lid of the coffin.

'Shit,' grunted Charlie and straightened up, peering over the rim of the hole to see what was happening. He strained his ears for the slightest sound, the moon shining coldly down over the cemetery like an enormous flare.

He could see nothing and the only sound he heard was the low wailing of the wind as it sighed in the trees. It sounded like someone whistling tunelessly. Charlie remained upright for a second longer then bent once more and set about the third screw. That finally came free and he pulled it out of the hole and dropped it into his pocket.

The fourth one was a real bastard and seemed to have been wedged in with a power designed to thwart Charlie in his task. He put all his weight behind the screwdriver, trying to move the recalcitrant screw. Muttering to himself, Charlie strained with all his might to remove it, splitting the wood in one place where he bore down too hard. But, eventually, it began to give. He smiled, a thin film of perspiration forming across his forehead. He wiped it away with the back of his hand and set to work on the fifth screw.

That one came away much more easily and he moved towards the last one. The final obstacle between him and his goal.

Again something moved, closer to him this time, and he swallowed hard, his hand shaking for some reason. He wasn't sure whether to straighten up or not.

He remained still, the screwdriver firmly planted in the groove of the screw head.

The sound came again. It was much closer this time – less than ten feet away he guessed.

A thought swept through his mind. Had he remembered to lock the cemetery gates? Had the vicar walked in on him? Charlie strained his ears, trying to catch even the slightest sound. He slowed his breathing, the air stuck in his throat.

Very slowly he rose to his feet, the sound drawing closer. It sounded like a low snuffling, followed, a second later by a high-pitched scratching. Holding the screwdriver like a weapon, Charlie stood up.

He scanned the area around him.

Nothing moved.

Then he saw it, crouched on the marble plinth in the centre of one grave.

A mouse.

Charlie breathed an audible sigh of relief, angry with himself for being so jumpy. He watched the little mouse as it nibbled at some freshly laid flowers. Charlie was about to return to the coffin at his feet when he heard a screech which froze his blood.

Like a winged torpedo, an owl hurtled out of the night sky and, in one practised movement, snatched up the mouse in a powerful talon. Clutching its prize, it flew off towards one of the nearby trees to eat. Charlie watched it, the moon reflecting in its baleful eyes. It seemed to be watching him, looking up every so often, fixing him in that glassy stare. He turned his back on it and ducked down into the grave, removing the last screw. That done, he dug his fingers under the lid and lifted it free, pushing it up onto the side of the hole.

He looked down.

Had he been able to, Charlie would have probably screamed, as it was, he could only stand transfixed gazing down into the coffin, his mind reeling. He gagged and fell back against the grave wall.

The corpse was completely hidden beneath a slimy, seething black mass of slugs.

The stench which emanated from this vast horde was almost palpable in its intensity and Charlie tried to turn away but, with the same sort of deadly fascination with which a mongoose watches a cobra, he kept his gaze locked on the hideous sight before him. His hesitation proved to be his undoing.

A number of the slugs had already slithered over the edge of the coffin and two or three were sliding up Charlie's boots, up inside his trouser legs, heading for the warm flesh of his calves. He felt the sticky slime on his legs and, a second later, he screamed as the slugs bit into him. Blood began to course down his legs as the beasts burrowed deep into his muscles and Charlie groped at the side of the grave, trying to pull himself up but, as he turned, he stepped on one of the monstrous slugs. Its body was crushed under his boot and Charlie slipped in the pulped mess.

With horror, he realized he was falling.

He pitched forward, falling right into the middle of the slithering mass, into the coffin itself. He lay on top of the devoured corpse and, for nauseating seconds found himself staring into the skeletal face which seemed to grin up at him from its silk-lined box.

Charlie screamed again and tried to rise, dozens of the slugs clinging to his body, boring into his flesh. Eating him alive. He pulled a couple from him, horrified when they turned in his grip and drove their razor sharp central teeth into his fingers. He shook his hands in an effort to dislodge the creatures but they remained firmly anchored. Charlie felt something ripping at the muscles of his back, eating through to his kidneys. His back was covered in the vile things, the weight of their thick bodies holding him down. With a monumental effort, he rose, tears of pain and terror mingling with the blood on his cheeks as one of the slugs ate its way into his face. He grabbed a tuft of grass at the grave side and tried to haul himself up but his arms were weak. Blood gushed from his many wounds and he could feel nothing from the knees downward.

The slugs had already eaten his legs to the bone.

He managed to haul himself up, his upper torso actually leaving the hole but then the sheer weight of the creatures defeated him and, as a particularly large one began to burrow into the hollow at the base of his skull, he slipped back. He crashed heavily into the grave, falling once more onto the devoured corpse, his body twitching now as the slugs swarmed over him, one of them eating through the fluid filled cavity of his eye. Blood burst from the socket and Charlie found himself in darkness.

The last thing he saw was the gold wristwatch, dangling on the end of a half-eaten arm, just before his face. Then, with a final wail of despair he succumbed. The slugs slithered over him, seemingly galvanised by the flow of warm blood which pumped from his body.

The owl looked up from its meal as it heard Charlie scream. It sat on the branch of the tree, watching as the man died. Its huge eyes blinked, then it hooted twice, the sound flowing out on the wind like some kind of death knell.

Twenty-one

Mike Brady sat gazing at the phone, a pencil stuck in his mouth like a cigarette. He finally pulled the pencil out and began drawing circles on his blotter. The air conditioner in the office had packed up and the heat was oppressive even so early in the morning. His wall clock showed ten fifteen a.m. He exhaled deeply and reached for the phone, using the end of the pencil to dial. As he did so he thought back to what had happened the previous night. The idea of slugs in the water pipes both revolted and horrified him and, once again, he wondered just how far the contamination had spread. Before he and Kim had left for work that morning he'd secured all the taps with rags. Just in case. Kim, still slightly shaken by the previous night's occurrence, had promised that she would insist all water used at the nursery would be boiled before use. He had given her some story about mould in the pipes in case any of the other staff asked why.

The line was engaged and Brady tapped the pencil irritably on his desk. He let the insistent tone continue for another moment or two then pressed the cradle down and dialled again.

It was still engaged.

'Come on,' he muttered, trying his luck a third time.

At last he heard the familiar purring and he put down his pencil, waiting for the receiver to be picked up. A moment later an officious sounding woman told him that he'd reached the local doctor's surgery.

'My name's Brady,' he told her. 'I'm the Health Inspector. I'd like to speak to Dr Warwick please.'

He was told that the doctor was in surgery.

'It's important, please put me through if you can,' Brady

insisted, picking up his pencil once more. He began turning it over and over in his hand.

The receptionist told him again that the doctor was in the middle of his surgery, adding that he had a patient with him at that minute.

'Well can you put me through when that patient leaves, I'll hand on.'

Brady was told that it would have to wait until surgery was finished.

'Listen, you put me through when that next bloody patient has left or I'll be down there myself,' he rasped, finally losing his temper. 'This is important.'

The receptionist reluctantly agreed, swayed by his angry tone and Brady heard her put the receiver down on her desk top. He held his own phone, the far off noises of the surgery drifting through to him. Finally he heard a high pitched bleep and the receptionist picked up the phone and grudgingly told him that he was being connected. There was a moment's silence, a hiss of static then Brady heard another voice.

'Dr Warwick speaking.'

Brady introduced himself. He'd known the doctor for five or six years but the men were still to reach the familiarity of first name terms.

'What can I do for you, Mr Brady? I am rather busy this morning,' Warwick told him.

'I'd like to know if there's been anything unusual this morning,' said Brady.

Warwick was puzzled. 'Like what?'

'Any patients complaining of sickness, headaches anything like that?'

The doctor was mildly irritated. 'Mr Brady, I don't discuss my patients' problems over the phone. In fact, I don't discuss them at all.'

'I realize that,' said the Health Inspector. 'All I want to know is, have there been any peculiarities? Any people suffering from the same symptoms?'

I cannot divulge personal information, Mr Brady I'm sorry,' said Warwick, condescendingly.

'I'm not asking for names and addresses for Christ's sake,' snapped the Health Inspector. 'I just want to know if you've had any patients exhibiting the same sort of symptoms, similar symptoms to each other.'

Warwick sighed. 'Mr Brady I . . .'

'Doctor, this is important. I have reason to believe that the entire water system of Merton could be contaminated. Now, all I'm asking for is a little help. If you don't want to help me, fine, but I'm warning you your bloody surgery is going to be knee-deep in people if you don't.'

There was a long silence at the other end of the line and, for a moment, Brady thought that the doctor had put the phone down but then he spoke again, his tone much more subdued this time.

'What makes you think the water supply is contaminated?' he asked.

'That's information *I* can't divulge,' said Brady.

Warwick chuckled mirthlessly. 'Touché.'

'So, doctor. About your patients, have there been any similarities in their symptoms?'

The doctor exhaled deeply. 'Well, now you come to mention it, there have. I've seen twelve patients since eight thirty and nine of those have been complaining of more or less the same problems.'

Brady reached for his pencil once more, pulling a pad towards him. 'Such as?'

'Nausea, headaches, sensitivity to light, diarrhoea. Fever in one or two cases and some vomiting. Is that enough for you?'

Brady finished writing.

'What do *you* think it is?' he asked.

'It's difficult to say without the benefit of more extended diagnoses such as blood and urine tests but at first sight I'd say it was probably a virus of some kind,' Warwick told him.

'Did you prescribe anything for it?' asked Brady.'

'Only a Kaolin solution to stop the diarrhoea and vomiting. As I said, without further tests it's difficult to say what's really causing the trouble.'

'If it was a virus,' said the Health Inspector, 'wouldn't you prescribe antibiotics?'

'That depends on the severity of the symptoms. But, as I've already said, I'm not absolutely sure it is a virus. However, I will admit that if it is, your theory about it being carried by water is probably correct.'

Brady felt icy fingers tugging once more at the back of his neck. 'Why do you say that?'

'Because all water transmitted viral diseases exhibit symptoms like those I've just described to you. But to be honest, Mr Brady, the likelihood of it being a virus is small. Most diseases of that kind are transmitted by animals. Yellow fever by mosquitoes, Bilharzia by snails. Those types of disease are confined to areas where sanitation is bad, you wouldn't find anything like that . . .'

Brady cut him short. 'You said something about snails.'

'Yes. There is a species of snail which spreads a disease called Bilharzia,' Warwick explained, his voice breaking up into a soft chuckle. 'But it's not that, Mr Brady. The snail which carried the disease is confined to Africa and Asia.'

The Health Inspector wrote it on his pad all the same.

'If there's nothing else, Mr Brady' said the doctor 'I do have other patients waiting.'

'Yes. I'm sorry,' said the Health Inspector. 'Thank you very much for youı help.' He put the phone down and sat silently at his desk, reading the notes he'd scrawled:

1. Virus?
2. Water carried, contamination?
3. Nine cases so far.
4. Slugs in water pipes?

He underlined the last several times then got to his feet and headed out of his office towards the stairs which would take him up to the second floor and the offices of the Water Board.

Frank Phillips was trying to light a fag. He had dropped his lighter the day before and now the bloody thing wasn't working. Grunting to himself he put it back into his jacket and started hunting through his pockets for some matches. He found none and plucked the cigarette from his mouth angrily. It lay on the desk before him, defiantly. Phillips was in his late fifties and had been Merton's Water Board Inspector for the last nineteen years. He was a hard, uncompromising man, disliked by nearly everyone in the building but he was good at his job and when he snapped his fingers everyone in the department jumped. He ran a hand through his grey hair and picked up the first of a pile of complaints, glancing over it. He looked at the cigarette lying beside him then continued reading the sheet of yellow paper before him, simultaneously cursing the heat. His shirt was sticking to his back, dark rings of perspiration fanning out from beneath his arm pits. He got up and crossed to the water dispenser which stood in one corner of his office. Phillips took a plastic beaker from the pile beside it and filled it, drinking the clear liquid down in two enormous gulps. He filled the cup again and returned to his desk, reaching for the second sheet of paper in the tray to his left.

There was a knock on the door and Brady walked in.

'You're supposed to wait until you're bloody asked,' snapped Phillips. 'Not just walk in.'

Brady closed the door behind him. 'Yeah, never mind that, Frank, I've got to talk to you.'

'I'm busy, Mike,' he said, indicating the pile of papers.

'It's important,' Brady insisted and Phillips sat back in his chair.

'All right, but make it snappy will you?' he said, then he suddenly remembered the cigarette. 'You haven't got a light have you?' he said, hopefully.

'I don't smoke,' Brady told him.

'I should have guessed,' grunted Phillips.

'Look, Frank, just shut up and listen will you,' Brady said, his voice taking on a hard edge. Satisfied that he had the other man's attention he continued. 'I don't quite know how to say this so I won't beat about the bush.' He inhaled. 'How long would it take to cut off Merton's water supply?'

Phillips raised one eyebrow. 'How long would it what?' he said, incredulously.

Brady repeated himself.

'You are joking of course?' said Phillips, sipping at the cup of water on his desk. 'What the bloody hell should I want to cut off the water supply for?'

'Because there's something in the water,' Brady told him.

'Like what?'

'A virus of some kind.'

'How do you know?'

'I phoned the local doctor's surgery this morning,' Brady told him and went on to describe his conversation with Warwick.

'So,' said Phillips. 'Nine people have got the shits, what does that prove?'

'Even the doctor thinks that there could be something in the water,' said Brady.

Phillips sat forward in his chair. 'Yes, there is.' His voice took on a mocking tone. 'There's chlorine which is added as a gas, dissolves and forms a disinfectant. There's sulphur dioxide which is also added as a gas to neutralize any excess chlorine. There's fluoride to keep everybody's teeth in such terrific shape and occasionally, in rotten water, we use aluminium sulphate. Satisfied?'

Brady was white with rage. 'All right you smart arse bastard,' he rasped. 'Nine people are suffering from a virus which they've picked up through drinking water. That's nine people, Frank. From one surgery. There's three others in the town. Christ knows how many more poor sods have got this bloody infection.'

'So, let's get this straight, you want me to turn off the town's water?'

The Health Inspector nodded.

Phillips shrugged. 'Just how did you come to this expert diagnosis in the first place?' asked the Water Board Official, his voice heavy with sarcasm. 'I mean, what made you ring the bloody doctor anyway?'

'Something strange happened at my house last night,'

Brady began, aware that the words he was about to speak would sound ludicrous. 'I saw slugs dropping from my taps.'

'Slugs,' said Phillips, nodding.

'Yes.'

Phillips exhaled deeply. 'You want me to believe that there's slugs crawling around in our water pipes is that it? And these unfortunate buggers with the runs have got that way because of these things being in *their* water pipes. Right?'

'I know it sounds incredible,' said Brady.

Phillips laughed humourlessly. 'Incredible? It sounds bloody ridiculous.'

'I saw it,' snapped Brady. 'So did my wife.'

'I couldn't give a damn if the Band of the Coldstream Guards saw it,' snarled Phillips. 'Just assuming I shut off the water. Just assuming. What the hell am I supposed to say to the council when they ask me why I did it? I can just hear it now, "Mr Brady, our wonderful Health Inspector, says we've got slugs in our pipes". You know what this bloody lot think of you already. How the hell is that going to sound?'

'Do you need Council permission to switch it off?' Brady wanted to know.

'I don't *need* it,' Phillips told him. 'But I think they're going to want a better excuse than that. And what do I tell the public when they start ringing in and complaining because they can't make a cup of tea because they've got no bloody water?'

'So you won't do it?'

'No I won't. Not until I see some proof.' He picked up the plastic cup and pushed it towards Brady. 'I can't see anything floating about in there can you?'

'What about those nine people, aren't they proof enough?' snapped the Health Inspector.

'Coincidence,' said Phillips, dismissing it.

'Bullshit,' sharled Brady. 'That's not all, haven't you noticed the amount of slugs in the gardens lately? And another thing, I've seen their trails in three or four different places but on top of that, I told you, I saw them dropping from my taps. Slugs. Big bastards too.' He had lost his temper. 'A man died yesterday from a disease transmitted by slugs.' Brady's voice had risen in volume. 'How much more fucking proof do you want?'

The two men stared at each other in silence for long moments then Phillips smiled. 'Look, I tell you what, if *I* get a case of the runs then I'll know you were right. How's that?'

Brady got to his feet, almost knocking the chair over in his anger. He turned and made for the door, pausing before he reached it.

'You know, Frank,' he said. 'You shouldn't be working for the Council. You should be on it. You're stupid enough.'

He slammed the door behind him.

'Sod off,' grunted Phillips. He sat for a moment then crossed to the water dispenser again and poured himself another cup full of the clear liquid. He looked into it for a second.

'Slugs in the water pipes,' he said, shaking his head.

He drank the water.

Brady glanced at his watch and saw that the hands had crawled round to one fifty-five p.m. He finished his half of lager and got to his feet, leaving the half-eaten remains of a ploughman's lunch on the table before him. The lounge bar of The Ruskin Arms, the only pub in Merton's town centre, was almost empty but for those last half dozen who lingered over their drinks. Brady left the pub, walking from its subdued and dimly lit interior into the blazing sunshine of the afternoon.

It was less than ten minutes' walk from the pub to the council offices and the Health Inspector took it slowly. A barmaid was outside the pub collecting empty glasses and she smiled at Brady as he passed but it was an effort for him to return the gesture. He wiped the perspiration from his face and glanced up at the cloudless sky. The heat was unrelenting and Brady stopped at a small newsagent's nearby to purchase an ice-cream. He felt mildly ridiculous standing amidst dozens of kids, waiting for his chance to be served and he had to smile at the thought of what he must look like. The woman serving smiled broadly at him when he asked for a lolly. He handed over his money and eagerly tore off the wrapping. The ice-cream was pleasantly cool on his tongue.

It was as he was walking out, Brady noticed the newspaper rack which hung by the door. He scanned the dailies but his eye settled on the local paper. With one hand, Brady pulled it from the rack and ran his eyes over the headline:

POLICE BAFFLED BY MYSTERY DEATHS

He swallowed hard, folded the paper under his arm and tossed ten pence onto the counter. Then he walked out. On the way out, he dropped the ice-cream into a dustbin, as if he had suddenly decided he didn't want it. Brady paused outside the shop and scanned the article which accompanied the headline.

'Merton Police were baffled today after finding three mutilated bodies. The first two were discovered in a house on the town's new estate, the third in the cemetery. All three were badly mutilated and identification is still unsubstantiated regarding the third body. The other two have not yet been named. Policemen in the area are still looking for clues to the grisly trio of deaths . . .'

Brady folded the paper again and stood for a moment beneath the blazing sun, the thoughts whirling round and round in his mind. The cemetery. The new estate. They were nearly four miles apart. The slugs must be far more numerous than even *he'd* first thought. He shivered, despite the heat, then turned and headed back towards the council offices.

Brady walked with ill-disguised haste, almost as if he were anxious to be off the streets and back in the security of his office. He felt almost unaccountably nervous, wondering just where the slugs were going to strike next.

There was something black about two feet away from him and Brady froze. It was lying motionless on the pavement, and for long seconds the Health Inspector was unable to move. Then, he realized that it was nothing more than a burnt out dog-end. He breathed an audible sigh of relief and continued walking, reaching the steps that led up to the main doors of the council offices at exactly five past two. As he walked into reception he heard the familiar clacking of the defective fan but it still offered some welcome respite from the blistering sun outside.

Brady was heading for the stairs when Julie appeared from behind the desk and called him over.

'What is it?' he asked, wearily.

'There was a phone call for you, Mr Brady,' she told him. 'A man. He said it was important. He left a phone number.'

'Did he leave his name?'

She consulted a piece of paper in front of her, finally discovering it amongst numerous other jottings and scribbles.

'Foley. John Foley.'

Brady was already gone before she could finish speaking.

Twenty-two

Brady looked down into the tray where Foley had placed the slug. The animal was slithering about in a puddle of its own slime and the Health Inspector regarded it with a mixture of disgust and foreboding. Beside the tray was a small beaker filled with a thin, orange coloured fluid and it was into this that Foley now pushed a dropper. He sucked up about half an inch of the stuff into the dropper and Brady watched as he moved it over until it was poised above the slug.

'Watch,' said Foley then, gently, he squeezed the rubber bulb at the end of the dropper.

One single droplet of moisture fell from the nozzle and onto the slug.

There was a tiny flash of brilliant white light and Brady heard a loud hiss as the fluid hit the slug. The black body seemed to explode and a small shower of pus-like blood and entrails sprayed into the air. It writhed spasmodically for a second then was still.

'Good God,' gasped the Health Inspector.

Foley looked up at him and smiled.

'Is it dead?' asked Brady, peering closer to the body.

'Too right it's dead,' Foley reassured him.

'What is that stuff?' He pointed to the beaker full of fluid.

'It hasn't got a name. I invented it,' the naturalist beamed. 'Perhaps I ought to call it Foleycide.' He laughed.

'Well, whatever you call it, it certainly works. But what made it explode like that?'

'The liquid itself is arsenic based but it's got a strong lithium content. Lithium is combustible if it touches any kind of moisture. If you emptied ten or twelve gallons of it into a lake you'd have an explosion big enough to flatten this town.' He grinned triumphantly.

'Where the hell did you get the chemicals?' Brady wanted to know, his eyes still riveted to the ruptured body of the slug.

'The factory on the industrial estate,' Foley told him. 'I told them it was for use in the museum, they let me have as much as I wanted for trade price.'

'How much have you got?'

'Enough,' said the curator.

'I hope to Christ you're right,' Brady said and handed the paper to Foley. He read the article about the three deaths, his brow wrinkling as he did so.

'They got into my house last night,' said the Health Inspector. 'Dozens of them.'

'The slugs? How?'

'Through the taps. They're using the water pipes as well as the sewers to move around in.'

Foley dropped the paper. 'Then how the hell do we kill them all? We can pump this stuff into the sewers without any problem, that'll take care of the ones in there but not into the water system.'

'If what you say about this stuff being combustible when it makes contact with water is true, I'm not even sure that we can use it in the sewers.'

The curator stroked his chin thoughtfully for a second.

'The flash that you saw when the poison hit the slug,' he began. 'It looked worse than it actually was. Maybe, just maybe, we can use it in the sewers and not do too much harm.'

'By too much harm I suppose you mean demolishing the whole of Merton,' said Brady, cryptically.

'There's got to be a way,' said Foley. 'But who the hell would know?'

Brady snapped his fingers. 'Palmer.'

Foley looked vague. 'Who?'

'Don Palmer. He's one of the sewage men here. I was with him when I saw the slime trails down the sewers on the new estate. He'd know whether we could use the stuff down there or not.' The Health Inspector smiled as he thought about the little cockney. 'Have you got a phone in here?'

'At the enquiries desk,' the naturalist told him.

Brady turned and headed for the door, pausing when he got there. 'You said it contained arsenic too.'

Foley nodded. 'It works two ways. Initial contact causes the reaction you and I just saw, the arsenic penetrates their skin. It works instantly. There's no way they can survive this.' He brandished the beaker full of orange liquid before him.

Brady left the room and made for the enquiries desk where he found the phone and hurriedly dialled.

The phone was picked up at the other end and he recognised Julie's voice.

'Is Don Palmer there?' he asked.

She told him she'd check.

Brady drummed on the desk top as he waited. A second later, Julie picked up the receiver again.

No. Palmer was out on a job.

'Well, as soon as he gets back, tell him to come to the museum,' said the Health Inspector. He put the phone down and hurried back up to the lab.

'No luck,' he said, plonking himself down on a stool. 'We'll have to wait for him.' He looked down at the torn body of the large slug in the tray and shuddered.

'I've been thinking,' said Foley, 'what if these slugs have some kind of social order?'

Brady looked vague. 'What do you mean?'

'Well, maybe, and it's a long shot, the larger slugs are acting as . . .' he struggled for the word, '. . . guides, leaders for the smaller ones. Maybe it's some kind of,' he paused again, 'sonar.'

'Where's your evidence?' asked Brady.

'It's supposition at the moment but it's all we've got. Now, assuming that I'm right about the larger slugs being "controllers" of the smaller ones. If we can destroy the large creatures, the others might return to their normal behaviour patterns.'

'You mean they'd stop eating meat?' said Brady.

Foley nodded.

'But how do we destroy them?'

'The large ones are too big to move through the water pipes, right? That means they must be using the sewers to breed and move about in.'

'What's this business about a "social order" got to do with it?' asked Brady.

'Ants and other social insects have a hierarchy within the nest,' Foley explained. 'From the queen down to the soldiers and then to the workers. The queen and the soldiers "control" the smaller workers. Kill the queen, the nest dies.'

The Health Inspector shook his head. 'But slugs aren't social insects. Christ Almighty, they're not even bloody insects.'

Foley waved a hand before him. 'I know that. But the principle is the same. There's no nest and there's no queen but I'm pretty sure that the large slugs are acting as "controllers" for the small ones and I'm willing to bet that they're using the sewers as breeding grounds. The conditions down there are perfect.'

'I can't believe this,' said the Health Inspector. 'I've seen it, I've read about what they can do but I still find it hard to believe.'

'And so will everyone else,' intoned Foley. 'Have you mentioned it to anyone?'

Brady told him about the incident with Phillips and then went on to discuss the cases of illness which the doctor had told him about.

'We can't involve the police,' he said, finally.

'They are involved,' snapped Foley, holding up the paper.

'They don't know about the slugs,' said Brady. 'And they mustn't know about the poison or our attempts to destroy these things.'

Foley nodded then laughed bitterly. 'You know, for the first time in my life I thought about dying. Stupid isn't it?' He looked up and found Brady regarding him with impassive eyes. The curator continued.

'After reading what happened to those three people . . .' The sentence trailed off momentarily. 'Whatever must it be like to die like that?' He swallowed hard.

'Let's just hope none of us have to find out,' said Brady.

The curator reached into a cupboard beside him and produced a bottle of vodka. He held it up, smiling.

'Well, the water's off isn't it?'

Brady grinned, watching as the young man poured some of the clear liquor into two beakers. He handed one to the Health Inspector who drank deeply. The fiery liquid burnt a path to his stomach and he blew out his cheeks.

'How much of that poison have you got?' he asked.

'Enough to make up five gallons,' Foley told him. 'Our only other problem is how to get it into the sewer. We can't just pour it into the first outlet we find.'

'Palmer should be able to help us there.' Brady looked at his watch. 'Where the hell is he?'

'Someone is going to have to go into the sewer tunnels,' said Foley, softly.

Brady didn't answer, he just took another swallow of vodka. That particular thought had already occurred to him.

It was nearly seven thirty p.m. when Don Palmer finally arrived. He parked the white van outside the museum between Foley's Volkswagen and Brady's Vauxhall then walked up the steps to the main entrance.

In his years of living in the town, Palmer had never visited the museum and now he walked slowly through the lower gallery, admiring the handsomely mounted exhibits and making a mental note to bring the kids along some time. They'd enjoy this, he thought. The little cockney made his way up the stairs to the enquiries desk, his footsteps echoing through the silent building.

As he reached the landing Brady appeared in the doorway of the lab and beckoned Palmer up.

'What's wrong?' he asked, grinning. 'Have they got a badger stuck down the toilet?'

Brady ushered him into the lab where he was hastily

introduced to Foley. The men all sat down again and Palmer gratefully accepted the beaker of vodka which the young curator offered him.

'My old lady will think I've been out boozing,' he said, smiling, taking another sip of the liquor. It was as he put the beaker down that he noticed the dead slug.

'What the fuck is that?' he said in awe, his mouth dropping open. He looked first at Foley and then at the Health Inspector.

'It's a slug,' Foley told him.

'Leave it out,' Palmer said, his smile gradually dissolving. 'Slugs are little things about that size.' He held open his thumb and index finger to indicate the length he spoke of.

'Have you seen the paper?' Brady asked him, pushing it towards him.

Palmer nodded. 'Terrible business.'

'They were killed by slugs,' said the Health Inspector flatly. 'All three of them and Ron Bell, he was killed by them too.'

'I knew old Ron,' said the cockney, softly. Then his voice took on a harder edge. 'Killed by slugs? Is that some sort of bloody joke?'

They told him. Step by step, every incident, every sighting, every death. Brady told him about the slime trails, about the creatures in his garden, of how one tried to bite him. About the taps.

Foley explained how they fed, moved and bred. Palmer listened to every word, his face set in an attitude of horrified resignation as if that was the way it was and he would just have to get used to it. He paled visibly as the catalogue of horrors continued.

They told him about the poison and about how they intended destroying the slugs. Foley even gave him a demonstration on the last remaining creature. And the little man listened to it all, waiting until there was no more to be said. Silence descended once more on the small lab and, outside, the sky began to darken for it had taken them well over seventy minutes to tell him everything. Every mind-bending, horrifying, nauseating detail.

'Dear God,' he said, softly. He drank what was left in his beaker and gripped it until the glass threatened to break.

'Dear God.'

'We need your help, Palmer,' said Brady, putting one hand on the sewage man's shoulder.

Palmer shrugged and turned almost robotically to look at the Health Inspector.

'It could have been my kids, my wife,' he said, quietly. Visibly shaken, the sewage man put down the beaker and shook his head.

'How can I help?' he asked.

'We need a map of the sewer system,' Brady told him. 'And we need some information.'

At last, the little cockney seemed to come out of his bewildered state. He shook his head, as if trying to dispel the horror of what he'd heard. 'I've got maps in the van,' he said, getting to his feet.

Foley, too, stood up.

'I'd better make up the rest of that poison,' he said and disappeared into a small room just off from the laboratory itself.

Brady was left alone in the lab. He looked at the body of the dead slug and felt an involuntary shudder run through him. He suddenly felt as if he needed Kim. He would have to phone her soon and try to explain what was happening. She would wonder where he was. He exhaled deeply and leant on the work top.

Moments later, Palmer returned carrying a couple of rolled up pieces of paper. He took off the elastic bands and spread them out on the work top. Brady anchored them at the corners with bottles, beakers and anything else he could lay his hands on and then the two of them began to scrutinise the maps. The plans reminded Brady of the London Underground; lines criss-crossed and intercepted each other, some drawn in red, some in black. There were large red circles on many places on the maps and each was marked with a number.

'What are those?' asked the Health Inspector, pointing to one of the numbered circles.

'Manholes,' said Palmer. 'Each number designates the street it's in.'

'How the hell do you remember which is which?' Brady wanted to know but Palmer merely smiled.

'It's all part of the job.'

A moment or two later, Foley walked back into the lab. He removed a pair of rubber gloves and dumped them on the bench nearby.

'Poison's ready,' he said.

'You reckon you're going to dump that stuff into the sewers?' said Palmer.

'It's the only way,' said Foley.

'There's already a high concentration of methane down there now. That's highly combustible too,' said the sewage man. 'If you set off an explosion down there, it'll ignite the methane as well.'

'What are you saying?' asked Brady.

Palmer exhaled. 'I'm saying that the combined effect of that poison and the methane could cause a class one explosion.'

Brady swallowed hard. 'Oh Christ.'

'Is that for certain?' Foley wanted to know.

'There'll be an explosion,' Palmer told him. 'No doubt about it, all we don't know is what the effects could be.'

'What's the worst that could happen?' asked the Health Inspector.

Palmer shrugged. 'You could blow every manhole cover in town off. If the explosion was big enough you'd blast every water appliance from its housing. You might even bring the street down.'

'Maybe?' said Foley, hopefully.

Palmer nodded. 'That's the worst that could happen. But, every house has a vent outside it. Those vents would take up a lot of the blast. They might just be able to cope with the increased pressure. It all depends on how big the explosion is.'

'Then we'll have to take that chance,' said Brady, flatly.

'So now we have to find them,' Foley said and, for long minutes, the room was plunged into silence.

'The first body was found near the new estate,' said Brady, finally. 'And most of the incidents have happened in that vicinity.' He scanned the map. 'Where would that be on here?'

'Ron Bell's house you mean?' Palmer said and jabbed a finger at the map. 'There. It's got a vent in the back garden and it's also got a manhole just outside in the street.'

'We could get into the sewers there,' said the Health Inspector. 'How do these damn networks connect?' he said to Palmer.

The cockney ran his index finger over three or four of the sewer pipes which were shown in black on the map. 'All the pipes converge into one central chamber. The manholes are the routes into those vaults. That's what the numbered circles are. Each one of those has got a big chamber underneath it. There's one every two or three streets.'

Brady stroked his chin thoughtfully for a second.

'Could we crawl through those pipes? Like we did under that old woman's house?' he asked.

'We could, but we'd need special breathing apparatus. Those sewers are deeper than the rest. The pressure is far greater,' Palmer explained.

'What sort of apparatus is it?' Foley wanted to know.

'Just a face mask connected to an oxygen tank,' Palmer told him. 'But there's one snag. The tanks only hold enough air for thirty minutes.'

Another heavy silence descended finally broken by Brady.

'It's the only way. We have to go into the sewers.'

'What exactly do you think you can do?' Palmer demanded. 'If there's as many of those bloody things down there as you reckon, how the hell are you going to kill them all?'

'I'll crawl along the pipes,' said Brady, quietly.

Palmer shook his head. 'You'd never make it on your

own. It's like a bloody maze down there.' He swallowed hard. 'I'll have to go down with you.'

The two men looked at each other for long moments then Brady continued.

'There's only one way of doing it,' he said. 'We'll have to crawl through the pipes and lure the slugs towards one of these central chambers. Once we've done that, you,' he looked at Foley, 'release the poison into the sewer.'

'You're acting as human bait,' said the curator, flatly.

'There's no other way,' Brady said.

'How the hell do I know where you are? Once you're down there, I won't be able to tell whereabouts in the pipes you are. If I release the poison while you're still down there, you'll be blown to pieces along with the slugs,' Foley said.

'We can keep in contact with two-way radios,' said Palmer. 'We use them all the time when we're working down there.'

Foley nodded.

'If we keep in constant contact, you can track us on the maps,' Palmer said.

'That's it then,' said Brady, flatly. 'Palmer and I will go into the sewers near Ron Bell's house. Foley, you track us on the two-way. We'll try and lead the slugs to one of the central chambers. Once we're there, give us five minutes to get out and then let the poison go.'

'And what if you're not out in time?' said the curator.

Brady hesitated a second. 'Let it go anyway.' He turned to Palmer. 'You don't have to do this you know.'

The little cockney looked at him. 'Like I said, you'd have no chance down there on your own. I can't stand by and let you kill yourself.'

'Brady. Don't you think it might be an idea to search that old house first, before you two go into the sewers?' said Foley. 'I mean, some of the slugs could still be in there.'

The Health Inspector nodded. 'You might be right. We'll do that first.' He turned to Palmer. 'You go and get the gear from the van, you and I will travel in that. Foley you take the poison in your own car.'

'What are you going to do?' asked the curator, watching as Brady made for the door.

He turned. 'I've got to make a phone call.'

Foley went to fetch the poison, Palmer scuttled off to fetch the equipment they would need and Brady wandered down to the enquiries desk. He perched on the edge of the desk and pulled the phone towards him, trying to steady his shaking hand as he dialled. Outside, the sky was like a blanket of mottled black velvet, just the pinpricks of stars glinting on it. The trees outside the museum swayed gently in the cool breeze, the wind blowing through their leaves like some disembodied voice. Brady drummed impatiently on the desk as he waited for the received to be picked up and, when it finally was, he recognised a familiar voice.

'Hello.'

'Kim,' he said.

'Mike, where the hell are you?' She sounded distraught. 'I called your office twice but there was no answer. I was getting ready tc call the police, I wondered if you'd had an accident or . . .'

He cut her short. 'Listen to me, love. I'm at the museum.'

'What are you doing there?'

'Foley's found a way to kill the slugs,' he told her.

'Mike,' her voice had taken on a note of pleading.

'We've got a good idea where they are. I'm going down into the sewers with one of the men from the department.'

He heard the first unmistakable beginnings of a sob.

'Mike, please don't. You'll . . .' Her voice was cracking.

'Kim. Listen to me. They've got to be destroyed.'

There was silence at the other end of the line, only the low crackle of static breaking the solitude.

'Kim,' he repeated.

'Yes.' Her voice was strained.

'I want you to keep all the taps covered and lock the doors and windows.'

Silence.

'Kim. Did you hear me?'

'Yes.'

He sucked in a tortured breath, wanting so much to be close to her, to hold her. 'I love you, Kim,' he said, swallowing hard.

She was quiet for a moment then he heard her thin, worried tones once more. 'You know, I was just thinking,' she said, laughing hollowly. 'How ridiculous it is for a man of forty to be crawling about in sewer pipes.' She was crying again, sobs jerking her body as she tried to retain her composure.

Brady gritted his teeth. 'I'm still thirty-nine,' he said, trying to laugh but it wouldn't come and he could only close his eyes as he listened to her crying.

'I love you,' she said, softly.

'Keep the supper warm eh?' he said, his voice sounding empty. He slowly replaced the receiver, sitting for a moment or two on the edge of the desk. He massaged the bridge of his nose between his thumb and forefinger and exhaled deeply.

A moment later, Palmer appeared at the bottom of the stairs carrying an armful of things. He walked past Brady and up into the lab where he deposited the gear on a bench. The Health Inspector joined him.

'Put it on now, it'll save time,' said Palmer, thrusting a protective suit into the other man's hand. Both of them hurriedly pulled on the thick overalls, the little cockney completing the task first. He reached for one of the two-way radios which lay on the bench and handed it to Brady. 'Ever used one before?' he asked.

The Health Inspector shook his head and Palmer hastily demonstrated how the set worked, repeating the procedure when Foley joined them. The curator was pushing a metal drum before him and the other two men could hear fluid slapping about inside it.

'I'll need a hand to get it downstairs,' he said.

Brady helped the younger man with the bulky drum but, they eventually got it down the stairs and out into the waiting Volkswagen. The drum had a nozzle attachment to which Foley fitted a pipe. At the far end it sported what looked like the bowl of a watering can. He propped the large drum up on the passenger seat. Brady handed him the maps of the sewer and, after one final re-cap on the workings of the radio, he started the engine.

Palmer and Brady climbed into the white van and, with the breathing apparatus cradled on their laps, they drove off. Foley followed close behind.

Brady looked at his watch.

It was nearly ten fifteen p.m.

Less than fifteen minutes later, both vehicles pulled up outside Ron Bell's house.

Twenty-three

'There's the manhole cover,' said Palmer, pointing towards the large metal disc which lay in the road nearby.

Brady nodded. 'We'll look inside first.'

They clambered out of the van, leaving their masks and oxygen tanks on the seats. Foley was strolling across to join them. He'd pulled on a leather jacket just before they left but, despite the protection it offered, he was still shivering slightly.

'Cold?' said Brady.

Foley smiled, thinly. 'I'm not sure.'

'Come on,' said the Health Inspector and, led by him, they made their way up the path towards the front door of the house where Ron Bell had died. It looked evern more forbidding in the darkness and Brady's mind was suddenly wrenched back to that hot morning weeks before when he and Archie Reece had discovered the mutilated remains. Weeks. It seemed like years since all this trouble began. Brady flicked on his torch and the powerful beam lanced through the darkness, lighting their way. He shone it over the front of the building and it reflected back off the dust covered windows. The waist high grass waved silently in the breeze and Foley cursed as he stepped into a patch of stinging nettles. The other two men looked round at him and he shrugged.

'We can get in along here,' said Brady, leading them towards the window which he and Reece had climbed through, what seemed like an eternity ago. Brady clambered through first, his nostrils immediately assailed by the stench of damp and decay. Next came Foley and, finally, Palmer who, as he was clambering in, accidentally brushed against a sliver of glass which opened a minute slit in his overalls at the top of the thigh.

The three men stood in what had once been the dining room and shone their torches around. The walls were peeling and the paint had come away to reveal layers of different colour, now faded and mildewed. The floorboards felt spongy as the men walked across them and Foley put a hand across his mouth, finding it difficult to breathe in the fetid atmosphere.

Something came hurtling at them from the shadows and Brady cursed.

It was a moth. It fluttered around for a second before disappearing through the broken window.

The trio moved on, into the sitting room where the corpse of Ron Bell had first been discovered. Brady showed them where the body had been lying. The room was completely empty. All the furniture had been removed, dust several inches thick showing where the sideboard had once stood. There were marks scored in the muck, tracing the path where the heavier objects had been dragged from the house. Their footsteps were strangely muffled as they moved about in the sitting room and the silence seemed to wrap itself around them like a cloak. Torch beams cut through the blackness, the tiny spots of light seeking clues, wondering if they were going to see the first slithering dark shape dragging itself along.

There were two doors leading out of the sitting room. One into the kitchen, the other into the hall.

'You two look upstairs,' said Brady. 'I'll check in there.' He moved towards the kitchen door while the other two men made their way out into the hall.

'If you find anything, shout,' Brady called after them.

'Don't worry,' Palmer said. 'If I see one of those bloody things, you'll be the first to know.'

Brady wandered into the kitchen, stopping for a second to listen to the heavy footfalls of his companions as they moved around upstairs. He could hear them going from room to room, the low murmur of their voices occasionally drifting through to him. Eventually, he turned his attention back to the kitchen, shining his torch across the filth-encrusted lino on the floor and across to the cupboards which had been ripped out long ago.

A spider had caught a crane-fly in its web and was busily devouring it. Brady held his torch on it for a second, watching the grisly tableau, then he moved the beam across towards another door to his right. As he walked towards it, Brady glanced out of the grime-encrusted windows of the kitchen and spied the sodium glare of the lamps which marked the first street on the new estate. He returned his attention to the other door, shining the torch onto the lock. There was no key and, optimistically, he turned the handle. Needless to say it didn't budge. The door was locked. He murmured something to himself and stepped back, the torch beam still directed at the peeling door. It was as he took that pace backward he noticed the small gap in the bottom of the door. He knelt to examine it, guessing it to be about two inches high. In one corner of the door something else caught his eye.

It was a slime trail.

It glistened in the torch light and Brady extended a gloved hand, touching the mucoid path with his index finger.

It was fresh.

He swallowed hard and stood up, trying the door once again, pushing his shoulder against it when it wouldn't open. But, the hinges were old and rusted and the Health Inspector heard them shriek in protest as he threw his weight against the door once again. This time the very wood itself seemed to crack. He stepped back and aimed a kick at the stubborn lock. The handle fell away, landing with a hollow thump on the lino.

'Nothing up there.'

The voice startled him and he spun round to see Foley and Palmer standing in the doorway.

'What have you found?' asked Foley.

Brady motioned to the door. 'It's a cellar or something.' He shone his torch down at the floor and both men saw the slime trail.

Palmer crossed to the door and both of them threw their weight against it, hearing the wood groan under the pressure. Finally, under their combined assault, it gave. It flew back on its hinges and slammed into the wall behind with a loud crash. The two men paused at the opening, gazing down into the blackness below. Brady swung his torch round but the beam would only penetrate the darkness a short distance. The stone steps of the cellar stretched away beneath them, the bottom invisible in the pitch black. A rancid stench rose from the cellar, an odour so rank it caused Brady to cough. He covered his nose with one hand and took a tentative step down. The torch beam wavered in his grasp and he had difficulty keeping his feet on the slippery steps. Step by step, he descended.

Palmer followed at an arm's length behind, using his own powerful torch to sweep the walls which crowded in on both sides of the staircase.

There were slime trails on them.

'Be careful,' he said, softly.

Brady could feel his heart thumping against his ribs as he neared the bottom of the steps. A thin film of perspiration had formed on his forehead. He directed the torch beam downwards, careful not to slip on the treacherous surface.

Two steps from the bottom he saw the first slug.

He stepped back, almost knocking Palmer over. The sewage man followed Brady's pointing finger and caught sight of the glistening black horror on the step, its posterior tentacles waving about soundlessly.

'What is it?' Foley called from the doorway.

'They're down here,' said Palmer, shining his torch over the floor of the cellar. The entire surface, every square inch of earth seemed to be covered by the slithering creatures. Like a glistening, undulating black carpet.

'I'll get the poison,' said Foley.

'No, wait,' Brady called and took a step down. He crushed the first slug beneath his heavy boot and walked on. He shone the torch over the slimy sea once more, noting that there were perhaps just two or three hundred of the creatures down there. Those closest were moving towards him but the Health Inspector merely backed off.

'What are you waiting for?' asked Palmer.

'We can't afford to waste any of that poison,' Brady told him. 'There aren't many of them here. That means that most must be in the sewer itself.'

'So, what do we do?' the sewer man wanted to know.

Brady put out a hand and felt the damp walls. 'You've got a can of petrol in the back of your van haven't you?'

Palmer nodded.

'Go and get it.'

The little cockney hesitated for a moment then hurried back up the stairs, past a bewildered Foley who was descending the steps.

'What the hell are you playing at, Brady?' he demanded, seeing the slugs slithering towards them. 'We've got to destroy them.'

'This isn't the nest,' said Brady. 'Look.' He shone the torch over the hundreds of slugs. 'The rest of them, the big ones, they *must* be down in the sewers.'

Palmer returned a moment later, the petrol can in his hand. Brady took it from him and unscrewed the cap then, watched by the other two men, he walked into the cellar dousing the carpet of writhing slugs in the reeking liquid. They tried to crawl up his legs but there weren't enough of them and Brady crushed many beneath his heavy boots. He made sure every last drop of the golden fluid was drained from the can then he threw it into the cellar and retreated back up the stairs to join his companions.

Foley handed him a box of matches and the Health Inspector struck one, its yellow glow illuminating his face briefly before he tossed it down into the black mass.

There was a high pitched 'whump' as the petrol went up, followed, a moment later by a series of pops and dull bangs as the flames destroyed the bodies of the slugs. Yellow flames danced in the blackness, devouring the hideous creatures and filling the cellar with choking black smoke.

'What about the house?' asked Palmer, watching the fire.

'It's so bloody damp in there the fire will burn itself out,' said Brady with some authority.

The three men watched for a moment longer then closed the cellar door behind them. They made their way hurriedly through the house, clambering back through the broken window.

As they passed the cellar bulkhead, a thin stream of smoke rose into the night air and they could still hear the pop and crackle as the slugs were incinerated.

Palmer looked back.

'Two hundred down, 20,000 to go,' he said, cryptically.

Brady shot him an acid glance and the trio made their way out into the street. By the time they reached their parked vehicles, the smoke from the bulkhead was just a tiny plume of grey against the blackness of the night. Brady looked at it with something akin to satisfaction.

Palmer handed him his set of breathing apparatus and helped him to put it on, ensuring that he could breathe properly then the little man put on his own mask and tank. Their voices sounded muffled through the perspex and their breathing was heavy and laboured. Each of them picked up a two-way radio and Foley retrieved the third. Then, the three of them walked over to the curator's car where he quickly pulled the maps from the glove compartment.

'We're here,' Palmer told him, jabbing a gloved finger at the circle on the map marked sixteen.

Foley nodded. He got into his car and started the engine.

'We'd better synchronise watches,' said Brady.

They checked their time pieces.

'Keep in contact all the time,' said Foley and both men waved an acknowledgement.

'Remember,' said Brady. 'Five minutes after we give you the signal, let the poison go.'

The naturalist nodded and watched them as they strode over towards the manhole cover a few yards away.

It took both of them to move the huge metal disc, weighing, as it did, over a hundredweight. It fell to the road with a loud clang, spinning round and round like a dropped coin. Brady looked across at Palmer who tapped the cylinder of oxygen.

'Thirty minutes,' he said.

Brady nodded, noticing that the sewage man had a screwdriver stuck in his belt.

'What's that for?' he asked, pointing at it.

'Some of the pipes have grilles across them. I don't fancy getting caught in a dead end.'

Brady could feel his heartbeat quicken and he tried to control his breathing but it was difficult.

Led by Palmer, they began to descend.

It was eleven thirty p.m.

Twenty-four

Brady eased himself gently down from the metal ladder and stood beside Palmer, the effluent dribbling past them at about calf height. The Health Inspector swept the tunnel with his torch, noting that the beam was unable to penetrate the blackness for more than a few feet. Once again he felt that terrible claustrophobic feeling come over him as the walls of the pipe seemed to close in on him.

'We'd better check these out,' said Palmer, tapping the two-way. He switched his on and spoke into it.

Up above, the sudden crackle of static made Foley jump but the young curator picked up the set and held it to his ear.

'Foley, can you hear this?' asked Palmer, his voice buried beneath a crackling blanket of interference.

'Your voice is breaking up,' Foley told him, fiddling with the controls of the radio.

'Adjust the squelch button,' Palmer told him and, through the hissing static, Foley heard; 'Mary had a little lamb its fleece was brown not white . . .'

'Better,' said the naturalist.

Palmer continued. '. . . because the silly animal had rolled in its own shite.'

Foley laughed. 'OK, I've got it now.'

'Where the hell did you learn that?' asked Brady, smiling thinly.

Palmer shrugged and indicated that Brady should test his own equipment. A similar procedure was completed, then both men clipped the two-ways to their belts and bent low, ready to begin the tortuous crawl along the stretch of pipe which would lead to the first of the large central chambers. It was hot inside the suit and Brady felt even more uncomfortable with the breathing apparatus on. Although it was light, the tank of oxygen on his back seemed to weigh him down as he crawled and he could only hear the loud, guttural sound of his breathing as he struggled along behind Palmer. Every now and then the Health Inspector would stop, almost sitting in the flowing effluent, and shine his torch behind them, just to check that there were no slugs near them. He scanned the walls and roof of the pipe for slime trails but, as yet, saw none.

The meagre shaft of light which poured down the open manhole opening began to fade into darkness as they crawled deeper into the pipes. Brady scrambled on, anxious not to lose sight of Palmer who was about two feet ahead of him.

They passed a side outlet which was less than a foot in diameter and both men concentrated their torches into the black hole.

'Drain outlet,' Palmer told him.

Satisfied that nothing was moving in there, the two men crawled on, now totally surrounded by the cloying darkness. It seemed to swathe itself around them like a shroud and the Health Inspector felt the first drops of perspiration forming on his face. His breathing was heavy and, for a second, he wondered if he might use up his oxygen supply too quickly. The vision of Kim swam into his mind and he tried to push it to one side. Her joke about a forty-year-old man crawling around sewers was beginning to take on extra significance. He closed his eyes tight, until white stars danced before him and the vision of her finally left him. He continued crawling, the progress surprisingly fast, his torch constantly sweeping the pipe in its search for the first tell-tale signs of the slugs.

Palmer stopped.

Brady shone his torch past the little cockney and saw that a grille barred their way. The sewage man pulled the screwdriver from his belt and began working on the first of the rusty rivets which held the grille in place. Brady crouched beside him and pulled the two-way from his own belt

'Foley,' he said. 'We've reached a grille. We should be through it in a couple of minutes.'

Foley acknowledged and traced their progress on the map before him.

'Another thirty feet and you'll be at the first chamber,' the younger man told him. 'Any sign of the slugs yet?'

'Nothing moving down here except us,' Brady told him.

He clipped the radio back into place and watched as Palmer prized the last rusty screw loose. He stuck the heavy screwdriver into the jaws of the grille and put all his weight on it. The grid came free and the little man tossed it away. It landed with a clang behind them. Some rotted faeces slopped onto Brady's overalls and he paled, fighting back the nausea. He shone the torch behind them once more then waited as Palmer crawled through to take the lead again.

Up above, Foley started the engine of the Volkswagen and drove slowly to the next red circle on the map, the site of the next manhole and the central chamber. He parked the car on one side of the road and guessed that it would take them about five minutes to crawl as far as the next vault. The young man exhaled deeply. He hoped that the chamber wouldn't become their crypt. A quick glance at his watch told him that they had less than twenty-five minutes.

It was eleven forty p.m.

Brady and Palmer continued on their journey, passing two more outlets as they did so. They were much larger than the first one they'd encountered and the men found that their torch beams could not penetrate the darkness in those particular pipes.

'It's a connecting pipe from one of the other main flow pipes,' said Palmer, peering into the first of the outlets.

He could see nothing in the darkness and he swallowed hard, even shining his torch into the river of effluent which occasionally washed up as high as his elbows. He, too, was beginning to perspire and he knew that it wasn't because of the suit. All he could think of was that he hadn't got the chance to kiss his kids goodnight. The little devils were probably still up, waiting for him to get home. His wife would wonder what he was up to as well. He could imagine her moaning about how his dinner would be spoiled but, at that precise moment in time, Palmer would have given his right arm to have heard her nagging. To be up on the surface, at home. Instead of fifty feet below the ground acting as live bait for thousands of man-eating slugs.

The river of effluent did not flow high enough to alert him to the rip in his overalls.

He turned back from the outlet and looked at Brady who had been checking the other hole.

'Can't see a bloody thing,' he said.

'Me neither,' Brady told him.

They moved on.

It was a moment or two before the first of the slugs emerged from the larger of the outlets. Moving effortlessly in the slimy environment, it slithered over the damp wall of the pipe, the scent of man reaching it despite the assortment of smells down there.

In a matter of seconds, the entire pipe was filling with the obscene black monstrosities and, across from the first group, more were spilling from the second outlet. They slid into the water, others crawled along the roof and walls of the pipe, keeping just out of range of the probing torch beams. It was almost as if they knew.

Brady and Palmer crawled on unaware that, less than ten feet behind, the seething black mass of slugs pursued them.

The two men reached the first of the central chambers and Brady was glad to find that he could stand up for a minute. He shone his torch around, noting that the vault was about twelve feet in diameter. A rough circle with half a dozen outlets flowing into it. The effluent river was flowing swiftly here and it gushed past their feet with a low hiss. He shone his torch up and saw the iron ladder which led up to the manhole. Both of them knew that Foley was up there. Waiting.

'Which pipe do we go into next?' asked the Health Inspector, shining his torch over the numerous black holes.

They seemed to yawn open like huge mouths, screaming a silent warning to the men.

Palmer took the radio from his belt and raised it to his masked face.

'Foley,' he said. 'We're in the first chamber. On that map, there should be one outlet pipe marked in red, which one is it?'

Up in the car, the curator scanned the black and red lines, his finger quivering slightly as he finally found what he was looking for.

'There's about half a dozen outlets,' he said, vaguely.

'I know that,' snapped Palmer. 'Which one is marked in red?'

Foley found it. 'If you're standing with your backs to the main pipe then it's the one second from the left.'

Palmer clipped the radio back onto his belt and led Brady towards the designated outlet. They were forced to crawl once more as they entered it and the Health Inspector felt the muscles in his arms and back beginning to ache as he dragged himself along. They made their way slowly through the next pipe which seemed to narrow the deeper they got into it, but Brady told himself that his imagination was beginning to get the better of him and he struggled on behind Palmer.

He stopped suddenly as he heard a splashing from behind them.

He stuck out a hand to halt Palmer's progress.

'Listen,' said Brady and both men held their breath, torches directed down the pipe along which they had just crept. The powerful beams showed nothing.

'What was it?' asked Palmer.

Brady waved a hand to silence the sewage man and then the cockney himself heard it – the loud splashing which seemed to be growing nearer.

'It's probably just the water flowing into the chamber,' he said, reassuring no one, including himself. 'We'd better move on.'

He started to crawl again but Brady remained still, his

ears and eyes alert for the slightest sound or movement. He kept the torch beam directed behind him for long moments before finally crawling along behind Palmer. Perhaps the sewage man had been right. Perhaps it had just been the water gushing into the chamber.

Behind them, the vault was filled to overflowing with the black creatures, all slipping and sliding over one another in their haste to reach the two humans just three or four yards ahead.

'We should be reaching another of the chambers soon,' said Palmer, his own breath coming in gasps. His knees ached from crawling so much and he paused for a second beside a connecting pipe to get his breath.

Brady crouched beside him and rolled up the sleeve of his overall. He shone the torch onto his watch.

'Eleven forty-five,' he said. 'Fifteen minutes of air left.'

Palmer nodded. The Health Inspector patted him on the shoulder and they prepared to move on but, before they did, he swept the tunnel once more with his torch light.

There, glistening on the roof of the pipe, were a dozen slime trails.

'Palmer, look,' said Brady, pointing to the mucoid paths.

The sewage man turned his attention to the slime, watching as the Health Inspector touched it with a gloved finger. As he pulled it away, gobs of transparent fluid dripped from the material.

The trails were fresh.

The two men followed their course to a small outlet which Palmer said fed in from a drain. Brady bent close and shone his torch inside.

'My God,' he murmured and Palmer directed the beam of his own light inside.

Half a dozen of the slugs were in there, most of them larger than six inches. For long seconds they seemed to recoil from the bright lights but then, slowly, they began slithering towards the two men.

'Let's move,' said Brady and they suddenly found renewed strength, scrambling quickly down the pipe towards what they knew to be the second chamber.

Brady shone the torch behind him, puzzled when he saw no sign of the slugs.

There was a sibilant hiss which made both men gasp and it was a second or two before they realized that it was the static on the radio.

Foley was trying to contact them.

Brady snatched his two-way angrily from his belt.

'What is it?' he snapped. 'You scared the shit out of us.'

Palmer looked across at him. 'No pun intended I hope,' he grinned.

'Have you seen anything?' the curator wanted to know.

'We've seen half a dozen of them,' Brady told him. 'They're down here all right, it's just a matter of where.'

'Is it working?'

'If you mean are they following us, I don't know.'

Palmer tapped him on the shoulder.

'We'd better move on,' he said.

Brady nodded and switched off the set again, clipping it to his belt.

The two men found that the pipe curved slightly, eventually branching out into a kind of fork, presenting them with a choice of which one to enter. Palmer was about to radio through for directions when he saw the first of the slugs spilling from the left hand pipe ahead of them.

'Oh Jesus,' he said and tugged at Brady's arm.

The Health Inspector snatched for his radio.

'Foley,' he shouted into the set. 'We've found them.'

'Where are you?' the curator wanted to know.

It was Palmer who spoke next. 'They've got in front of us. They must have come from the second chamber. We'll have to go back the way we came.'

With the slugs less than a yard behind, the two men twisted awkwardly in the narrow pipe and scrambled back towards the first huge chamber. Brady now leading, held his torch before him and he was the first to see the other group of slugs. Those that had been pursuing them now blocked their way to the first chamber.

The two men were pinned between different groups of the black monstrosities, their route to the first and second chambers blocked off.

The seething mass approached slowly from both sides.

'In there,' shouted Palmer, pushing Brady towards a narrow outlet. 'It's a connecting pipe, it should take us through to another flow pipe.'

Brady squeezed through the narrow tunnel, finding it so confined that he had to crawl on his stomach to get through. His oxygen tank scraped against the stonework and the effluent splashed up against the perspex of his face mask but he crawled on, using his knees and elbows as means of propulsion. He slithered along like the monstrosities which pursued him.

Palmer threw himself into the narrow opening behind the Health Inspector, pushing the older man along in an effort to escape the hungry black hordes.

'Foley,' shouted the sewage man into his radio. 'They've got us trapped. We're in a connecting pipe mid-way between the first and second chambers. Where will we end up if we keep crawling?'

The curator's voice sounded a million miles away as he spoke.

'You should come into another flow pipe, if you crawl down that it'll bring you back out into the first chamber again,' he told them, tracing their progress on the map. His own heart was now thumping madly against his ribs. He started the engine of the Volkswagen again and drove to the centre of the road. There, he pushed open the passenger door and struggled to lift the heavy drum of poison onto the tarmac. With perspiration running from his face, he managed to push it over towards the manhole cover. Then, he bent and took a hold of the metal bar across the top of the heavy iron disc.

It wouldn't budge an inch.

The sewer remained sealed.

Brady was crawling as fast as he could through the rancid effluent, his breath coming in gasps. Behind him, Palmer was able to see the slugs as the first of them slithered into the pipe and made for his heavy boots. He crushed the first half a dozen beneath the weighty footwear but, in the beam of his torch, he could see more and more of the black things swarming into the tunnel. Fear gripped him tightly, and he found it difficult to swallow.

'Move,' he shouted to Brady.

The Health Inspector was scrambling along as fast as his aching limbs would allow but, suddenly, he let out a mournful groan.

The other end of the pipe was blocked by a grille.

'Give me the screwdriver, quick,' he bellowed, looking back to see the tunnel filling with the obscene fat slugs, all eager to reach their prey.

Palmer tore the implement from his belt and handed it to Brady who didn't even bother trying to loosen the screws, he merely jammed the blade between the slats and tried to tear the grid free. The screws were rusty, the stonework decaying, but still the recalcitrant grille kept its place, barring their escape.

'Hurry,' screamed Palmer, the leading slugs now seething over his legs, trying to bite through the thick material of his protective suit.

Brady beat at the grille with his hands in an effort to loosen it and, finally, the metal started to give. One screw came away and the Health Inspector used all his strength on the screwdriver, using the implement like a lever to tear off the grid.

'For fuck's sake,' shrieked Palmer and then he screamed in agony as the first slug found the rent in his suit and began eating its way into his thigh.

'Brady,' Palmer screamed but the Health Inspector could do nothing to help him. He just continued to wrench at the stubborn grille, hearing his companion's shrieks of pain. In that confined space they seemed to be deafening and Brady wanted to scream himself.

Blood spurted up from the gash in Palmer's leg and he tore at the first slug, managing to rip its vile form from his leg. But its head remained embedded in the flesh and it was just the bloated body which he tossed away. And now more of the creatures were swarming over him, tasting the fast-flowing blood, burrowing deep into his meaty thigh, sliding up inside the suit until they reached his genitals. The sewer man shrieked again as two of the slugs began boring their way into his scrotum. He felt waves of unbelievable pain lance through him as more of the creatures found the rip in the suit. They slithered inside to feast on his shaking body. He tried to swat at them with his hands, feeling one huge fat body burst under his fist. It squashed against his torn thigh, its own pus-like bodily fluid mingling with his spurting blood.

Brady began to shout in rage and terrified frustration when the grille wouldn't come away and, behind him, Palmer's screams became fainter as the slugs ate their way into him, a number burrowing up through his torn genitals, using his anus as a means of access in their search for the softer, more succulent parts of his body. Blood filled his mouth and gushed out into his face mask, bubbling up behind the perspex, running back down the tube to the oxygen cylinder until he was breathing the coppery fumes of his own life fluid.

With an angry yell, Brady finally tore the grid free.

He slithered through and found himself, as Foley had said, in another flow-pipe.

He shot out a hand and began to haul Palmer free of the connecting tunnel but it was too late, the little man was already dead. The only movements his body made were spasmodic contractions of the muscles and now many of the slugs were sliding over his torn body in their efforts to reach Brady.

Panting for air, the Health Inspector began to crawl back towards the first chamber.

He had just five minutes of oxygen left.

Foley tried one last time to remove the manhole cover but could make no impression on the heavy disc. Looking around in panic he saw a piece of wood lying by the roadside – the branch of a tree torn down by some kids a day before. He hurried across to it, relieved to find that it was reasonably stout. The curator stuck it into the indentation in the lid and put all his weight on it.

The lid still refused to move and Foley put more pressure on it.

There was a loud groan and the wood snapped.

He threw one half to the ground, his mind desperately searching for a means to lift the heavy lid.

The radio crackled and he snatched it up.

'Yes,' he said.

'Foley.' The curator recognised Brady's voice. 'The slugs are right behind me,' he gasped. 'I'm coming up. Get ready to let the poison in.'

Foley hesitated a second. 'I can't get the lid up,' he said, flatly.

'Oh God. Have you tried prizing it open?' gasped the Health Inspector.

Foley said that he had.

'For Christ's sake, hurry,' Brady implored him. 'I'm at the main chamber now, the bloody things are right behind me.' His voice rose to a shout. 'Hurry, Foley.'

'Rope,' the naturalist said aloud and hurried to the boot of his car. He flung it open and rummaged through the other debris in search of the thick hemp which he knew to be in there.

He found it and scurried back to the manhole cover where he slipped the rope under the metal bar in the lid. He tied a hasty knot, tugged on the rope then secured the other end to his front bumper. Then he leapt behind the wheel and reversed slowly.

Inch by agonising inch, the lid began to lift.

Foley smiled, triumphantly.

It was almost halfway up when the rope began to fray.

Brady stood in the central chamber looking up, watching as the lid was lifted. He shot a glance towards the pipes which opened into the vault and shuddered.

From every outlet, hundreds of black shapes were spilling. Like an unstoppable tide of death, they poured out of the pipes into the central chamber and Brady could only guess at how many thousand there were. Led by the huge seven and eight inch monsters, they piled on top of one another, gliding effortlessly towards their helpless prey.

He stood transfixed for long seconds, watching as the seething black mass drew towards him, then, he grabbed at the metal ladder and began to climb towards the rapidly opening gap above him.

The slugs reached the spot where he had been standing and he saw a number trying to slither up the ladder after him but they could gain no adequate hold and fell back amongst the rest of their companions.

Brady was halfway up the ladder now and his oxygen was running out rapidly. His head felt swollen, as if someone were filling it with air. The ladder swam before him and, once, he nearly lost his footing but he continued up, gripping each rung tighter than the next until he was mere feet from the opening.

It was at that point that the rope snapped.

All Foley heard was the dull clang as the manhole cover fell back into place. He looked round in alarm and saw what had happened, leaping from behind the steering wheel to re-affix the rope. He could hear Brady's weak banging on the bottom of the lid as he fastened the hemp once more. Then the Health Inspector's voice drifted wearily over the two-way.

'Running out of oxygen,' he groaned. 'I can't breathe. I . . .'

Brady found himself nearing unconsciousness, he looked down into the darkness and saw the slugs seething about below him almost as if they were waiting for him to drop into their midst. He lost his footing and thought he was going to faint but he gritted his teeth, trying to hold his breath to prevent himself inhaling his own carbon dioxide. He heard the roar of the Volkswagen's engine and then suddenly, the manhole cover was torn free. In a daze, Brady felt strong arms grabbing him, pulling him from that hell hole. He felt hands struggling to remove his mask and then he was breathing fresh air again. Fresh clean air.

His head was throbbing but he scrambled to his feet when he saw Foley struggling with the large drum of poison, attempting to tip it over.

Brady joined him and both men put their weight to it, feeling the drum teeter then finally fall.

Five gallons of the deadly substance spilled from it and rained down into the sewer, onto the writhing slugs.

There was a flash of light so brilliant that both men thought they must be blinded, then a blistering geyser of white flame rose almost silently from the manhole. It rocketed up into the heavens a full fifty feet before disappearing in a billowing mushroom cloud of grey smoke. The ground shook as, beneath them, the poison set off a chain reaction which swept through the entire sewer system of Merton. As Palmer had warned them, the fire-flash set off the clouds of methane and the earth rocked. Both Foley and Brady were thrown to the floor and, below a lightning tongue of flame tore along the pipes in all directions, fanning out like some kind of fiery amoebic creature. Tentacles of screaming flame ripped through pipes and tunnels. The taps in the houses nearby were blasted from their housings and in many places, the water boiled in lavatory bowls. In the street nearby, a manhole cover was blasted a full thirty feet into the air by the explosion and, all over town, sewer vents lit up momentarily as the flames roared beneath them.

Then, as suddenly as it had come, the fire died and just a mournful plume of grey smoke wafted up from the open hole.

Brady rose slowly to his feet, the smell of burning strong in his nostrils. A moment later Foley joined him and both of them peered down into the smoke-filled maw below. They could see nothing.

'I'm sorry about Palmer,' said Foley, softly.

The Health Inspector nodded. 'The slugs killed him. The poor bastard was dead before the explosion.'

Brady was suddenly aware of a foul smell and he realized that it was his overalls. Pieces of dried excrement still stuck to them in places and he hurriedly pulled them off, dropping the stinking garments in an untidy heap on the road beside the manhole.

'What now?' asked Foley.

The Health Inspector exhaled deeply. 'The sewers will have to be checked. We can't take any chances. I'll go down again in the morning with some more men, just to be sure.'

It was as they turned to head back to Foley's car that they saw it.

Crawling in the road was a single solitary slug.

'Oh my God,' whispered Brady.

Before he could react, Foley had snatched up one of the discarded gloves and was moving towards the slug which looked to be about two or three inches long. He knelt and, watched by Brady, picked the black creature up. It tried to contract itself, anxious to be free of the grip and, when Brady stepped closer he saw that the animal had retracted its posterior tentacles.

Foley put it down on the pavement and it crawled away towards the safety of the bushes nearby.

Brady breathed an audible sigh of relief.

'Looks like my theory was right,' said Foley but there was no joy in his words, just a thankful affirmation of his beliefs.

'Let's wait and see shall we,' said Brady, patting the younger man on the back.

Lights were going on in houses all over the street, people were peering out of doors and windows and, far away, the two men heard the wail of police and ambulance sirens.

'I think you and I are going to have some questions to answer,' said Foley, pulling a packet of cigarettes from his pocket.

Brady nodded. 'Don Palmer's wife will have to be told,' he said, softly.

'The police will do it,' said Foley.

'No. It was my fault he died. It's my job to tell her.'

'He knew the risks involved,' said Foley.

'Yeah. But I'm still going to be the one to tell her.'
Foley offered him a cigarette.
'I don't smoke,' Brady said.
'Perhaps it's time you started,' said the curator and both men smiled.

Epilogue

George Thomas watched as the crates of lettuce were unloaded from the back of the lorry. He chewed the end of his pipe which, as always, remained unlit.

All around him the place was alive with the sound of crashing boxes, raised voices, laughing. The usual cacophony of noise which went to make up Covent Garden.

He'd arrived later than usual that morning due to the traffic on the roads leading into London. The drive from his farm in Merton usually took him less than an hour but he'd left at five a.m. that morning, when the mist still lay heavy on the ground, and now at seven o'clock he had finally managed to struggle through. The sun was already high in the sky above the city, pouring its unrelenting heat down over the people scurrying for buses and tubes.

George always hated coming to London. He'd lived in the country all his life and the hustle and bustle of the city unsettled him. Everybody was always in such a bloody hurry and George liked to take things easy. However, at sixty-two he was as sprightly as a teenager and ran his little farm in Merton only with the help of his two sons. It was a small piece of land but it yielded a good crop of vegetables and George had found a regular buyer for his produce. He watched now as the man picked quickly but expertly through the crates laid out before him, occasionally taking out one of the lettuces and tossing it onto a nearby pile of rotting vegetables. He went along all the crates with similar expertise, muttering to himself as he did.

'Good crop again,' said George.

'Yeah, only a few bad ones,' said the buyer, picking up another lettuce. He ran an expert eye over it, noticing something inside the inner leaves. He threw it onto the pile with the other rejects.

After about fifteen minutes he finished. The deal was concluded and George climbed thankfully back into his lorry. He waved a hurried farewell to his buyer, who was already having the crates removed, and then set off to battle his way through the traffic on his way home to Merton.

He couldn't wait to be out of the bloody city.

The pile of discarded vegetables grew higher as the day progressed, until it seemed to tower as tall as a man. Under the heat of the sun the green stuff began to wilt and smell, but no one paid it any attention. People came and went and the noise grew louder, with stall-holders shouting out their prices, bickering with their neighbours. It was a normal day really.

No one paid the slightest attention to the lettuce which lay near the bottom of the pile, one of George's crop, rejected because of the strange cylindrical objects in its inner leaves. The transparent mucoid tubes with the black centres.

Who cared about a few slugs' eggs anyway?

SPAWN

For Mike Brett
with thanks and admiration

Acknowledgements

Some of the research which went into this book was difficult, to put it mildly and I would like to thank everyone who answered my questions, however bizarre they may have seemed. Particular thanks to Nurse Anne Bozia for her help. I would also like to thank Niki, whose criticism was as hard but as helpful as always. Also thanks to everyone concerned with the production of the book, particularly Mike Bailey, my editor, who put up with my numerous phone calls and lousy spelling. And, as ever, to Bob Tanner. Indirect thanks to John Carpenter, Iron Maiden, Black Sabbath, Tobe Hooper. All worshipped from afar. And lastly and most important, to my family. My parents, who thought I was mad to write a book like this and to Belinda, who *knows* I'm mad. For suffering my obsessions these past few years I am indebted to her. One day soon . . .

Shaun Hutson

Part One

". . . some of us are born posthumously. . ."
– *Nietzsche*

". . . the foetus is conscious or aware. It can sense and react not only to emotions such as love and hate, but to more complex and ambiguous feelings."
– *Dr Thomas Verny*

One

The flickering wings of the crane-flies inside the jar sounded like whispers in the darkness and Harold Pierce held it to his ear, listening. He smiled and looked at the three insects struggling helplessly inside their glass prison. It was the light that attracted them, he had reasoned, as it did the moths. But Harold wasn't interested in moths, they moved too quickly. They were too hard to catch but the daddy-long-legs were easy prey. He smiled as he repeated the name. Daddy-long-legs. He stifled a giggle. His mother called them Tommies and that amused him even more. She was sleeping across the narrow hallway now, alone for once. Harold didn't remember the succession of men who she brought home, he wasn't really interested either. All he knew was that his father would not be coming back.

Jack Pierce had been killed at Dunkirk six years earlier and, since then, Harold's mother had entertained a never-ending series of men. Sometimes Harold had seen them give her money as they left but, it not being in the nature of fourteen-year-olds to question strangers, he had never asked any of them why. One night he had crept across the narrow landing and squinted through the key hole of his mother's room. She'd had two men in there with her. All of them were laughing and Harold had smelt liquor. They had been naked, all three of them, and for long moments he had watched, puzzled by the strange goings-on before him.

It was shortly after that night that his mother announced he was to have a brother or sister. The baby had duly arrived and Harold had been dragged off to church for the Christening, puzzled when there was only him and his mother present to witness the ceremony. In fact, his mother was shunned by most of the women in the neighbourhood. They spoke to her in the street but it was never anything more than a cursory 'hello'.

Harold held the jar of crane-flies up before him once more, wondering if their whispers would tell him the answers he needed to know.

He lowered the jar and looked across at the cot which held his baby brother, Gordon. The child was sleeping, lying on its back with the thick flannelette sheet pulled up around its face. Harold hated having to share a room with his brother. In the beginning, it had been all right. Gordon had slept in his cot in his mother's room but, since his first birthday, he had been put in with Harold. That meant that Harold was forced to come to bed when Gordon was tucked up for the night and that could be as early as seven in the evening. Most of the time, Harold would sit in the bedroom window watching the other kids kicking a big old leather football about in the street below. He had watched them doing that tonight, perched in his customary position until nine o'clock came around and the other kids were called indoors. Then, Harold had switched on his bedside lamp and watched as the crane-flies and moths flittered in through the open window.

Gordon was sound asleep, little gurgling noises came from his cot as he shifted position occasionally. The nylon eiderdown was crumpled at his feet where he'd kicked it off. It was covered with stitched-on rabbits. Beside the heavy wooden cot stood a pile of yellowing newspapers. Harold didn't read very well but he knew that the papers were called *The News Chronicle*. Just why his mother kept them he didn't know. There was another stack downstairs beside the coal fire, those she used to get the fire started in the mornings. Perhaps the pile in his bedroom were destined for the same purpose.

He crouched on the end of the bed for long moments, propping the jar of crane-flies on the window sill. The night was still and windless and, from somewhere nearby the strains of "String of Pearls" came drifting in with the night. Harold listened to the distant music for a moment then he swung himself off the bed and padded across to the door. The lino was cold beneath his feet and he hissed softly as he tip-toed from the bedroom, across the hall to the door of his mother's room. A framed painting of George VI watched him impassively as he gently turned the handle and popped his head round. His mother was asleep, her black hair smeared across her face in untidy patterns. Harold stood there for long seconds, watching the steady rise and fall of her chest, almost coughing as the strong odour of lavender assaulted his nostrils. Finally, satisfied that she wasn't likely to disturb him, he gently pushed the door closed and tip-toed back to his own room.

"String of Pearls" had been replaced by "Moonlight Serenade" when he got back but he ignored the music, more intent on the task at hand. He reached beneath his pillow and took out a box of Swan Vestas matches. Harold held them in his sweaty hand for a moment then he took hold of the glass jar. The crane-flies began flapping about even more frenziedly as Harold began to unscrew the top, as if sensing freedom. When it was fully loosened he held the jar before him, eyeing the insect closest to the neck of the jar. With lightning movements, he reached in and grabbed it by one membranous wing, simultaneously pushing the lid back in place.

The insect tried to escape his grasp and, quickly,

Harold pulled both its wings off. He did the same with three of its legs. The unfortunate creature was then dropped onto a sheet of newspaper where it tried, in vain, to scuttle away. Harold watched its helpless writhings for a moment then he picked up the box of Swan Vestas and slid the tray out, taking a match. It flared orange and the smell of sulphur filled his nostrils momentarily. He bent lower, bringing the burning match to within an inch of the crane-fly which immediately began to wriggle more frantically. Harold pressed the tiny flame to one of its legs, watching as the spindly limb seemed to retract, much like hair does when it is burned. The insect rolled onto its back, its two remaining legs thrashing wildly, its tiny head moving frenziedly. Harold burnt off another of its limbs then pressed the spent match-head against its slender abdomen. There was a slight hiss and the creature's head and remaining leg began moving even more rapidly.

Harold hurriedly lit another match.

This one he held right over the crane-fly, giggling when the stumps of its legs moved spasmodically as the flame drew closer. He dropped the match onto the insect, smiling as it was incinerated, its body rapidly consumed by the flame, charred black by the tiny plume of yellow. A whisp of grey smoke rose into the air. When the match had finished burning, Harold took another and prodded the blackened remains of the insect. It merely disintegrated.

Totally enthralled, Harold stuck his hand inside the jar and took out another of the crane-flies. This one he held by its wings, waving the match beneath it until all its legs had been burnt off. He twisted the wings so it couldn't fly away then he dropped it onto the newspaper and finished the cremation job with another match.

For the last insect, Harold had reserved something

special. His *pièce de résistance.* He took a handful of matches from the box and, with infinite care and patience, built them up until they were stacked cross-ways, on top of one another in a kind of well. Into the centre of this well, after removing its wings, he dropped the last insect. Then, quickly, he covered the top with three more matches. There must have been about twenty-five in all comprising that miniature funeral pyre and Harold sat back for a second admiring his handy-work. He could see the crane-fly inside the little stack of matches, its long legs protruding through the slits here and there as it tried to escape.

There were half a dozen matches left in the box and Harold struck one, gazing into the flame for a second before carefully applying it to the head of the match at the bottom of the pile.

It ignited with a hiss, burning for a second then setting off a chain reaction. The little structure went up in a flash of yellow and white flame and Harold grinned broadly.

He grinned until he saw that his blazing creation had set light to the paper it rested on.

The newspaper was dry and the flames devoured it hungrily. Harold felt a sudden surge of panic and he snatched up the blazing paper, scattering the burning remains of the tiny pyre as he did so. Matches which still hissed, alive with wisps of yellow, were scattered all over the room. One fell beside the pile of *News Chronicle*s and licked at the edge of the dry papers. Flames began to rise. The room was filled with the smell of charred paper and smoke wafted in the still air.

Another of the blazing matches fell into Gordon's cot. It hit the nylon eiderdown and seemed to explode, the quilt suddenly flaring as bright tongues of fire sprang from it.

Gordon woke up and began to scream as the fire touched his skin.

For long seconds, Harold was frozen, not knowing what to do. He took a step towards the cot, then backed off, his eyes bulging wide. Gordon's night-shirt was on fire. The baby was screaming, trying to drag itself away from the all-consuming inferno. Already, the skin on its arms and legs was a vivid scarlet.

Harold opened his mouth to scream but no sound would come out. The pile of newspapers beside the cot had ignited with a frightening vehemence and the tongues of flame rose a full three feet into the air. The whole room was ablaze. His own bed was seething, a mass of writhing fire. Smoke, thick and noxious, filled his nostrils and finally, as a piece of burning wallpaper fell and stuck to his arm, Harold found the breath for a scream. For interminable seconds, the paper clung to his arm, searing the flesh. He tore it away to see that the skin was red and blistered. His head swam and for a second he thought he was going to faint but, as he saw the cot disappear beneath a flickering haze of fire, he spun round and dashed for the door.

His mother had heard the screams and they crashed into one another on the landing. She saw the smoke billowing from the children's room, saw the leaping flames and she shook her head in disbelief. Pushing Harold aside, she ran into the room – into the furnace and flames which seared her flesh and set her clothes ablaze. Harold followed her back in, watching as she fought her way to the cot, reaching in to lift something which had once been her baby son. The body of Gordon was little more than a blackened shell. One arm had been completely burned off from the elbow down, the stump was still flaming. His mouth was open to reveal a blackened, tumefied tongue. The flesh looked as if it had been peeled away with red hot pincers. Through the charred flesh, white bone showed in places.

Harold's mother screamed and clutched the baby to her. Her own hair was now ablaze, the stench filling the room. She turned, a look of agony etched on her face and she screamed something at him but he couldn't hear through the roaring flames. As he turned to open the door a particularly violent eruption of flame exploded before him. Harold shrieked and felt one side of his face sizzling. The skin rose swiftly into blisters which immediately burst, the welts hardening as the fire stripped his flesh away as surely as if someone had thrust a blow torch at him. He felt something wet dripping from his burning cheek. Things went black as his right eye swelled under the intense heat then, in a moment of mind blowing agony, the sensitive orb seemed to bulge and burst. Blood gushed freely from the ruptured eye, turning immediately to charcoal under the ferocity of the flames. Harold clapped a hand to his face and felt the oblivion of unconciousness creeping over him but the pain kept him awake and he managed to yank open the bedroom door. The hair on his arms was singed and his veins seemed to bulge as his skin contracted. He turned to see his mother, on her hands and knees, crawling towards him, the flesh of her body apparently bubbling, lumps of it falling from calcified bones. She raised an accusing finger at him and screamed:

"You're to blame!"

The empty box of matches lay close beside her. Her hair was burnt off and the stench of charred skin was overpowering. Smoke poured from the open window and those living nearby hurried out into the street to see what was happening. The fire-engine was called.

Harold reeled amongst the flames, screaming in agony as what remained of his face was stripped clean by the flames. But, shielding himself as best he could, he stumbled out onto the landing, throwing himself against the wall in an effort to put out the fire which still devoured his clothes. He stumbled and fell, crashing heavily to the floor.

Downstairs, someone was trying to batter down the front door.

Harold looked round.

Through the haze of pain he saw his mother, a blackened vision which seemed to have risen from the fires of hell, standing in the bedroom doorway. She had her arms outstretched, the skin like crumbling parchment. When she opened her mouth, smoke billowed forth. Her eyes were gone, they were now just black pits in a bleeding, ruined face. Bone shone through the charred skin as blisters formed then burst with rapidity. She no longer had hair just the dancing snakes of flame which topped her skull, like some kind of fiery Gorgon.

She swayed for long seconds then, as the front door was broken down, she toppled backwards into the flames.

Harold began to scream.

"Mr Pierce."

Everything was darkness, he could feel his body shaking.

"Mr Pierce." The tone was more forceful this time.

He could hear screams, close by, drumming in his ears.

"Harold. Wake up."

He realized that the screams were his and, suddenly, he opened his eye and sat up, panting for breath, his body bathed in sweat. He looked round, fixing the woman in a glassy stare.

"Harold, are you all right?" she asked him.

He exhaled deeply and rubbed his eye. His hands were shaking madly, like a junkie who needs a fix. But, finally, his breathing slowed and he felt his heart returning to its usual rhythm. He looked at the woman, at her blue and white uniform, the small triangular hat which perched precariously on her head. Gradually the realization spread over him and he smiled thinly.

"I was dreaming," he said apologetically.

The woman smiled and nodded.

"I know," she said. "But you frightened the life out of all of us."

He apologized once more and wiped his forehead with the back of his hand. He looked up to see two maroon-coated interns standing on the other side of his bed. He recognized one as Pat Leary, a big Irishman who bore a bottle scar just above his right eye.

"You all right, Harold?" he asked.

The older man nodded and swung himself onto the edge of the bed. His pyjama jacket was soaked with sweat, a dark stain running from the nape of his neck to the small of his back. He pulled it off and began searching in his locker for his clothes.

His audience left, the interns moving off towards the exit at the far end of the ward, Nurse Beaton ambling across to the bed next to Harold to wake its occupant. He was a man older than Harold, completely bald and with skin like the folds of a badly fitting jacket. In fact that was what his face reminded Harold of. Harold watched as Nurse Beaton woke the man and then took two red pills from a plastic container she held. She supported the bald man while he took the pills, wiping away the water from his chin when it spilled over his rubbery lips. He heard her ask the man if he'd swallowed them and he nodded slowly. The nurse gently lowered him back into bed and moved on.

Harold was dressed by this time. He picked up a small imitation leather shaving-bag from his locker and headed towards the toilets at the far end of the corridor. The place smelt of disinfectant, as usual, but it was a smell with which he was well acquainted after so long.

Harold Pierce had been a patient in Exham Mental Hospital since 1946. Apart from the first fourteen years of his life, the institution had been his only home. It had been his world. And, in all that time things hadn't changed much. He'd seen scores of people, both staff and patients, come and go and now he was as much a part of the hospital as the yellow-painted walls.

He reached the toilets and selected his usual wash basin. He filled it with water and splashed his face, reaching beneath to find a towel. Slowly he straightened up, regarding the image which stared back at him from the mirror.

Harold sucked in a shaking breath. Even after all these years the sight of his own hideously scarred face repulsed him. It was a patchwork of welts and indentations, the whole thing a vivid red. The hair over his left eye was gone, as was the eye itself. A glass one now sparkled blindly in its place. His left ear was bent, minus the lobe it was in fact little more than a hole in the side of his head. One corner of his mouth was swollen, the lip turned up in a kind of obscene grin. A dark growth of flesh, what had once been a large mole, protruded from just below his left cheek bone, jutting out like the gnarled end of an incinerated tree branch. His left nostril was flared wide. What little hair remained on the left side of his head was thin and grey, a marked contrast to the thick black strands on the other side.

In fact, the right side of his face was relatively unmarked except for a slight scar on his forehead, most of the damage had been done to the left side of his body.

Harold took out his electric razor and ran it swiftly over the right cheek and beneath his chin. No stubble would grow on the left side.

He turned to see two interns carrying another patient from a wheel chair into one of the toilet cubicles. The old man was paralysed from the neck downwards, leaving one intern with the unsavoury task of cleaning him up when he'd finished. The old man was well into his eighties and suffered from Senile Dementia too. A common complaint amongst most of the patients at the institution.

One of the other patients, a man in his thirties who Harold knew as John, was cleaning the floor of the toilet with a mop, slopping the water everywhere in his haste.

"Careful, John," said Phil Coot, trying to slow him down. "You'll drown us all."

John laughed throatily and plunged the mop back into the bucket making a monumental splash. Coot, who was senior male nurse on the ward shook his head and smiled, watching the patient merrily slopping his way across the tiled floor.

"How are you this morning, Harold?" he said as he passed.

"Very well, Mr Coot, thank you."

Coot paused.

"You had some trouble last night?" he said.

Harold looked puzzled.

"The dream," Coot reminded him.

"Oh yes, that." Harold smiled thinly and raised one hand to cover the scarred side of his face but Coot reached up and gently pulled the hand away.

"The usual thing?" he asked.

Harold nodded.

"You're not on medication any more are you?" asked the male nurse.

"No, Mr Coot."

"This is the first time you've had this dream for a long time isn't it?"

"Yes, I don't know why. I'm sorry."

Coot smiled.

"No need to be sorry, Harold," he said. "Some of it is probably just tension at the thought of leaving here after so long." He patted Harold on the shoulder. "Once you get out of here you'll be OK. You'll settle into your new job and forget you've ever seen this place." He gestured around him, his tone turning reflective. "To tell you the truth, I shan't be sorry when we all leave here. The place is falling down around our ears it's so old."

"Where are you going then?" Harold wanted to know.

"The staff and patients are being moved to a new hospital on the other side of Exham in a couple of weeks time."

Harold nodded absently, lowering his gaze. He felt Coot touch him once more on the shoulder and then the male nurse was gone.

Harold took one last look in the mirror then pulled the plug in the sink, watching as the water swirled around the hole before disappearing. It was something which never failed to fascinate him.

Back by his bed, Harold put away his razor and smoothed out the creases in his trousers with the palms of his hands. He glanced out of the nearest window and scanned the grounds. The wind of the previous night had dropped and the leaves which had fallen from the trees now lay still on the lawns below. There were already a number of patients at work with large rakes, gathering the leaves up. Two interns stood close by, smoking.

Three nurses were walking past and they paused to speak with a doctor. Harold could see that they were laughing together and he saw the doctor kiss one of them on the cheek. They all laughed again. Laughter was something which Harold didn't hear too much of these days. He watched the little group almost enviously for long moments then turned away from the window and set about making his bed.

Finally satisfied that all was in order, he wandered off towards the staircase which would take him down a floor to the Therapy rooms.

There were already two other patients at work in the

large room when Harold walked in. He inhaled deeply, enjoying the odour of the oil paint. His own easel was set up close to one of the meshed windows and he crossed to it, inspecting the canvas which he had lovingly decorated these past three weeks. The picture was a series of bright colour flashes, mainly reds and yellows. What it was no one was quite sure, not even Harold, but he swiftly hunted out a brush and some paint from the wooden cupboard nearby and set to work.

Harold looked carefully at his canvas before applying the first vivid brush stroke. It was as if he saw something in those reds and yellows, something which stirred a memory inside him. His brush hovered over the place on his palette where he squeezed a blob of orange.

Flames.

He swallowed hard. Yes, they looked like flames. The memories of his nightmare came flooding back to him and he took a step back from the canvas as if he had discovered something vile and obscene about it. Perhaps, unconsciously, he was painting that nightmare scene as it had appeared to him all those years ago. Was this his punishment? To commit his crime to canvas for eternity? He bowed his head and, with his free hand, touched the scarred side of his face. A single tear blossomed in his eye corner and rolled down his unmarked cheek. Harold wiped it away angrily. He looked up and gazed at the painting once again. The bright colours *did* look like flames.

He dabbed the brush into the puddle of orange paint and tentatively applied a few strokes. For some reason, he found that his hand was shaking but he persevered. Why, in the last few weeks, had the canvas never appeared to be a canopy of dancing flames, he wondered? Was it because of the nightmare? The re-kindling of memories which he thought he had at last succeeded in pushing to the back of his tortured mind? Harold could not, would not, forget that horrific night in 1946 and he had more than his scar to remind him of it.

Along the length of his arms, from elbow to wrist, long white marks showed. They were all that now remained of the near-fatal attempt he'd made to kill himself. The scars were barely visible now but he would sit and look at them sometimes remembering the day when he'd inflicted the cuts which he had hoped would bring him the welcome oblivion of death – the ultimate darkness which would rid him of the guilt that gnawed away at his mind like a hungry rat. He had locked himself in the toilet and slashed his forearms open with a piece of broken glass. He'd smashed the window in the toilet with one powerful fist and then drawn his arms back and forth across the jagged shards on the frame until his thin forearms were crimson tatters. The blood had pooled at his feet and Harold could still remember the strange feeling of serenity which had fallen over him as he'd watched his arteries and veins spewing forth their vivid red fluid. The pain had been excruciating but not as bad as the fire. The fire. That was all he could think of as he stood there that day, his arms reduced to dripping rags as he tugged them back and forth across the glass.

But two interns had battered the door down and found him. They dragged him away, one of them applying make-shift tourniquets to his arms while Harold burbled:

"I'm sorry, I'm sorry."

They tried to comfort him as he slid into unconsciousness, not understanding that his words were for his dead brother and mother.

Now Harold stood in the Therapy room, brush in hand, his eyes lowered. The thoughts tumbling over in his mind.

He had learned to live with the guilt. He knew it

was something he would always have to bear and he accepted that. He *had* been responsible for the death of his brother. He knew that and it was something that would haunt him forever. There was no atonement for him, no way of releasing that guilt. It grew and festered in his mind like some kind of poisonous growth, the dreams which it brought like the discharge from a rank boil.

"Good morning, Harold."

The voice startled him and he turned quickly, almost dropping his palette. The Occupational Therapist, Jenny Clark, stood beside him looking at his canvas. "What are you going to call your painting, Harold?" she asked.

"It looks like a fire to me," he told her. "Can't you see the flames?" He looked directly at her and she tried to fix her gaze on his one good eye, deliberately avoiding his burned skin. She held the questioning stare for long moments then looked back at the canvas.

Jenny smiled thinly,

"Yes, they do look like flames don't they?" she said, softly.

They stood in silence for long moments, both inhaling the cloying odour of the oil paint, then Harold spoke again.

"Have you ever done anything you're ashamed of, Miss Clark?"

The question came completely out of the blue and took her by surprise. She swallowed hard, her brow furrowing slightly.

"I suppose so, Harold. Why do you ask?"

"This painting," he told her. "I think it's like a punishment. A reminder to me never to forget what I did to my brother. I was ashamed of that. I still am. I killed my brother, Miss Clark. I think that's what I'm painting."

Jenny exhaled deeply.

She was about to say something when he spoke again.

"I think it's my way of saying sorry. Sorry for what I did."

She was silent for a moment, her eyes searching his, straying from that wretched glass orb to the real one and then back again.

His tone suddenly lightened.

"I'll call it 'Fire'," he announced. "Just 'Fire'."

More patients were arriving now and Jenny left Harold alone with his masterpiece in order to help the others. Soon the room was alive with activity and noise. Someone knocked over an easel but Harold ignored the clatter and continued with his painting. Finally, satisfied that it was complete, he picked up a tube of red paint and squeezed some of the sticky liquid onto his palette. He dipped his brush into it and, in thick letters at the top of the canvas, painted one word:

FIRE

Two

The road which led from Exham itself, to the larger town of Cornford twelve miles away, was flanked on both sides by wide expanses of fields. Some belonged to the handful of small farms which dotted the countryside round about, but others just sprouted weeds, they stood unwanted and untended.

The road was usually busy but, as the early morning mist cleared slowly, it was strangely devoid of the customary bustle of commuters who clogged it. The

Panda car passed just three other vehicles, one of which was a large lorry carrying vegetables.

Constable Bill Higgins stepped on the brake, simultaneously easing the Panda to one side of the road, its nearside wheels actually mounting the footpath at the side of the tarmac. The lorry swept past, its tail flap rattling loudly and Higgins watched it in the rear view mirror, half expecting to see it spill its load behind it. He swung the car back in lane and drove on.

Beside him, in the passenger seat, his superior gazed out of the side window, watching as the trees sped past. The window was open to allow some cool air into the stifling confines of the car. Despite the slight chill, the refreshing breeze was welcomed by both men. The Panda's heater was on the blink, jammed at maximum output it transformed the vehicle into some kind of mobile sauna.

Inspector Lou Randall fumbled in the pocket of his jacket for a packet of Rothmans and lit one, the wind blowing smoke back into his face. He coughed and waved a hand in front of him. A stronger smell reached his nostrils through the bluish haze of fumes and he winced as he realized that it was manure.

"Why does the countryside always smell like a shithouse?" he said, blowing out a disapproving breath.

"What is it about fresh air that you hate so much, guv?" asked the driver, grinning.

"I wouldn't call *that* fresh air."

Randall had been born and brought up in London, always used to its cramped confines. To the steady crush of buildings and people around him. He felt strangely exposed in the countryside, as if light and space were somehow alien to him. Apart from holidays when he was a kid, he'd never been out of London longer than two weeks at a time. He remembered how his parents always took him to the Lake District when he was a nipper, and how much he hated water too. Large expanses of it always put the fear of Christ into him even though he was a good swimmer. The strange brooding silence which seemed to hang over the lakes always disturbed him just as now the perpetual solitude of endless fields brought back that youthful unease. Randall was thirty-six, stocky and heavily muscled. He usually put himself through a routine of exercises three or four times a week to keep in shape. Not that much happened in Exham to compel sudden strenuous physical activity though. In his sixteen months as head of the small force, he'd dealt with nothing more serious than a couple of rape cases.

He slumped in the seat, the plastic hot against his back, puffing on his fag, his blue eyes scanning the endless tracts of arable land. He ran a hand through his brown hair and exhaled deeply. The clock on the dashboard showed 8.09 a.m. and Randall yawned. He hadn't slept too well the previous night and his eyes felt as if someone had sewed the lids together. He took a last drag on his cigarette and tossed the butt out of the window. Grunting, he straightened up in the passenger seat. He reached over onto the back seat and picked up a manila file, which he flipped open. Inside was a report and, clipped to that, another sheet of paper which bore the signature of the county coroner. Randall yawned again and ran his eyes over the typewritten report which he'd already looked at half a dozen times that morning.

"Paul Harvey," he read aloud. "Age twenty-nine. Detained Cornford Maximum Security Prison, June 1979. No previous prison record." He closed the file, drumming on it agitatedly. "Convicted of two murders, sentenced to life."

"I can still remember when he was arrested," said Higgins, some of the colour draining from his normally ruddy complexion. "It took four of us to hold the bastard down long enough to cuff him. He was a bloody maniac."

Randall raised an eyebrow.

"The reports seem to agree with you," he said. "It must have been quite a shaker for a little place like Exham."

"It was," Higgins confirmed.

"The killings were random. There was never any motive established," said the Inspector, reflectively.

"What exactly *did* he do to them?" Higgins wanted to know. "We never did find out for sure."

Randall opened the file again.

"Both victims were dismembered," he read. "Apparently there was so little of them left that identification was almost impossible. Fond of the old carving knife our Harvey," he added, sardonically.

"Most of the bits were never even found."

"Oh Jesus," murmured Higgins.

"And now he's out again," said Randall, flatly. "He escaped at five o'clock this morning."

The two men continued their journey in silence. Higgins swung the Panda off the main road and down a narrower off-shoot flanked on both sides by trees. Through the windscreen both men could make out the gaunt edifice of Cornford prison. It was built of red brick, discoloured with the ravages of time and the elements. The high wall which surrounded it was similarly scarred, a row of iron spikes and barbed wire running along the top. Two huge black-painted doors barred their way as the constable brought the Panda to a halt.

Randall straightened his tie, cursing when one of the buttons popped off. Higgins grinned.

"Get your wife to sew it. . ."

The smile and the sentence trailed off and the constable coloured as he felt Randall's eyes on him.

"Sorry, guv," he said, softly.

Randall found the button and dropped it into his pocket. Then, clambering out of the car he said:

"I don't know how long I'll be."

Higgins nodded and watched as his superior walked across the tarmac towards the towering black gates. On his way he passed a blue sign which proclaimed in large white letters:

HER MAJESTY'S PRISON: CORNFORD

There was an old mini parked outside the gates, its side panels rotting, the white paint peeling away to reveal the rust beneath. The decaying metal was the colour of dried blood and the peeling paint reminded the Inspector of a picked scab.

He reached the huge gates and banged on a small door set into the right hand one. After a few seconds a panel slid open and a face appeared.

Randall showed his ID and the panel closed. A moment later the door opened and the policeman stepped through to find himself in the courtyard of the prison. A uniformed warder showed him the main entrance of the building and Randall set off across the vast expanse of wet tarmac.

To his left a group of prisoners, dressed in their familiar dark blue overalls, were standing or shuffling idly about while two warders stood chatting. One or two heads turned as he made his way towards the huge main building which was still wreathed in the early morning mist, the grey fog drifting round it like some kind of ethereal shroud.

The Governor's office was enormous, fully thirty feet long and perhaps twenty wide. A huge oak table stood in the centre, an oval shaped antique which sparkled brightly. The legacy of many years polishing. It had nine chairs around it and, suppressing a smile, Randall wondered where King Arthur and his knights had got to. The thought quickly vanished however.

The walls were a sky blue colour dull with the dust

of the years, as with most of the paintwork in the prison it seemed. The ceiling rose high above him, three large banks of fluorescents set into it – the only concession to progress. The rest of the room seemed forty years out of date. Large windows looked out onto the West Wing of the prison, the office itself separated from the prisoners' quarters by a high stone wall and a large expanse of well-kept lawn. The carpet on the floor was so threadbare that Randall's footsteps echoed as he walked towards the desk at the far end of the office. As he approached, Governor George Stokes rose to greet him.

The two men introduced themselves, a sign on Stokes's desk adding a silently corroborative affirmation that he was indeed Governor. He was well into his sixties, his hair almost white, even the wisps that curled from his wide nostrils. But his handshake was strong, belying his years. He was tall, ungainly. Dressed in a two piece brown suit, the trousers of which were an inch too short, he looked like some kind of be-spectacled stick insect.

Stokes introduced the other man in the room as Doctor Kevin Hayes. He was, or had been up until his escape, Harvey's psychiatrist. A short, nervous looking man in his fifties, he was prodding one ear with the blunt end of a pin.

"You're probably wondering why I called you, Randall?" said Stokes, clasping his hands before him and leaning on his blotter.

"It had crossed my mind," said the Inspector.

"We have reason to believe that Harvey will return to Exham," Stokes told him. "We thought you should be forewarned." The older man plucked at the end of his nose. "If there's anything we can do to help you, ask."

"Well, for one thing, I'd like to know why he was having psychiatric treatment," the Inspector said.

"From what I've read about the case there was never any hint of mental disturbance."

"During the last six months," said Hayes, "Harvey had become very introverted. He brooded. He'd always been a loner but he seemed to become more hostile towards the other prisoners. He got into fights frequently."

"We had him in solitary most of the time," Stokes interjected. "As much for the safety of the other men as anything else."

"How dangerous is he?" Randall wanted to know.

Hayes stroked his chin thoughtfully.

"It's difficult to say," he said, evasively.

"Could he kill again?" Randall demanded. "*Would* he kill again?"

The psychiatrist exchanged a brief glance with Stokes then looked at Randall.

"It's possible," he said, almost reluctantly.

"How the hell did he manage to get out of here in the first place?" Randall snapped, just a little too forcefully.

"That, Randall, is not your concern," rasped Stokes. "Catching him again is all that matters. *That's* your job I suggest you set about doing it." The two men locked stares for long seconds and the Inspector could see the anger in the older man's eyes. The escape had hurt his pride, it might, Randall reasoned, cost him his job. He probably had every right to be angry. But there was fear there too.

Randall got to his feet.

Randall didn't speak much on the way back to Exham, his mind was too full of thoughts and questions, one in particular nagging at him.

Where and when would Paul Harvey turn up?

Three

Paul Harvey stumbled and fell, crashing heavily against a nearby tree. He lay still on the damp moss for long seconds, sucking in painful breaths, each of which seemed to sear his lungs. His calves and thighs were stiff, as if someone had clamped a vice on each leg and was slowly turning the screw. He dragged himself upright, using a low branch for support. Panting like a bloodhound, he leant against the tree and massaged the top of his legs. He licked a furred, tumefied tongue over his cracked lips. It felt as if someone had stuffed his mouth with cotton wool. He stood still for a moment longer then blundered on through the small wood.

He walked awkwardly, like a drunkard and was forced to use the trees and bushes to hold him up. He couldn't remember how long he'd been running. Four, five hours. Perhaps more. He wasn't sure of anything except the gnawing pain in his legs and the burning in his belly. He must have food, that much he *did* know. The prison was a good six miles behind him now and he afforded himself a smile as he continued his haphazard course through the woods.

A bird twittered overhead and he spun round, taken aback by this sudden sound. He raised a hand as if trying to pluck it from its perch. When that failed he attempted to shout at it but no sound would come. His throat was like parchment. He slumped against another tree, head bowed, ears alert for the slightest movement. *They* would be after him by now but they would not catch him. Not this time.

He cocked an ear expectantly but heard nothing, just the ever-present sound of the birds and. . .

A twig snapped close by and he froze, pressing himself closer to the trunk of the elm, trying to become a part of it.

As he watched, a small boy, no more than twelve years old, pushed his way through the bushes and picked up a football. With the object safely retrieved, he scrambled back towards the clearing beyond where two of his companions waited. Harvey could see the other children now. He relaxed slightly and moved forward with surprising agility for a man of his size. He was well over six feet two, weighing around fourteen stone. His hair was black, closely cropped and shining. Pupils like chips of emerald glittered amidst whites criss-crossed by bulging red veins.

He moved closer to the edge of the woods, keeping low, well away from the children playing beyond. There were three of them he could see, all engrossed in their game. Harvey parted a bush to peer out at them. His large fingers twitched spasmodically but a look of bewilderment crossed his face when he saw them stop kicking the orange ball around and cross to a large plastic bag which lay behind one of the make-shift goal posts.

They took out some sandwiches and began eating.

Harvey put a hand to his stomach as it rumbled loudly.

He watched the three of them eating.

The time would come.

He watched and waited.

Graham Phelps stuffed the remains of the ham sandwich into his mouth and chewed noisily.

"Let's have a drink," he said, motioning towards one of the two thermos flasks.

Colin Fulton dutifully poured him a cup of steaming hot chocolate which he swigged, burning his tongue.

"Fucking hell," he gasped. "That's hot."

Colin and his younger brother, Miles, both chuckled.

Graham, on the other hand, didn't see the joke.

"What's so fucking funny?" he demanded, angrily.

He swore a lot. His father and his elder brothers did it too. His eldest brother had been in Borstal for six months and Graham hero-worshipped him, as he did his father. Both of them would think nothing of smacking a woman in the teeth too, if the need arose. They were really hard. Graham's mind contained a simple equation because he was somewhat simple minded:

Swearing and hitting women = manliness.

As easy as that.

Now he rounded on Miles again. The twelve-year-old, three years younger than Graham and Colin, was an ideal target.

"I said, what's so fucking funny?" he persisted.

"You, burning your mouth," Miles told him. "You shouldn't be such a pig."

"Fuck off," rasped Graham and got to his feet, kicking the ball about, dribbling it close to the brothers, bouncing it off Miles's legs every so often. They finally took the hint and got wearily to their feet, dropping the remnants of half-eaten sandwiches back into the plastic Tesco bag.

Paul Harvey kept perfectly still amongst the trees and bushes, his breath now slowed to a rasping hiss. He watched the three boys kicking the ball about and a twisted grin spread across his face.

Graham decided to show off his shooting ability and lashed a shot in the direction of the makeshift goal but a gust of wind caught the ball and it went flying wide, hurtling into the trees beyond. Graham planted his hands on his hips and looked at his companion.

"Well, go and get the fucking thing," he shouted, watching as Miles sloped off in the direction of the trees.

Paul Harvey saw him coming.

Miles pushed his way into the bushes and onward until he was surrounded by trees. For the first time that morning he noticed just how quiet it was inside the copse. His feet hardly made a sound as he walked over the carpet of moss, glancing around in his search for the ball. It obviously must have gone further than usual. Even its bright orange colour seemed invisible in the maze of greens and browns which made up the small wood. He stepped up onto a fallen, rotting tree stump, hoping to get a better view. At his feet a large spider had succeeded in trapping a fly in its web and, for a moment, Miles watched the hairy horror devouring its prey. He shuddered and moved away, his eyes still scanning the copse for the lost ball. He stepped into some stinging nettles and yelped in pain as one of them found its way to the exposed area between his sock top and the turn-up of his jeans. He rubbed the painful spot and wandered further into the wood. Where the hell was that ball?

He stood still, hands on his hips, squinting in the dull light. Mist still hung low on the floor of the copse, like a blanket of dry ice, it covered his feet as he walked. Droplets of moisture hung like shimmering crystal from the few leaves which remained on the trees. They reminded Miles of cold tears.

Something caught his eye.

He smiled. It was the ball, about ten yards away, stuck in the top of a stunted bush. He hurried towards it, suddenly aware of the unearthly silence which seemed to have closed around him like some kind of invisible velvet glove. He shivered and scurried forward to retrieve the ball, tugging it loose from the grasping branches of the bush.

Something moved close behind him, a soft footfall on the carpet of moss. He spun round, his heart thumping hard against his ribs.

A sudden light breeze sprang up, whipping the mist into thin spirals.

Miles started back towards the openness of the rec, away from the stifling confines of the copse. He clutched the ball to his chest, ignoring the mud which was staining his jumper. The odour of damp wood and moss was almost asphyxiating, as palpable as the gossamer wisps of fog which swirled around him.

Something cold touched his arm and he gasped, dropping the ball, spinning round, ready to run.

It was a low branch.

As he bent to pick up the ball, Miles could see that his hands were shaking. He straightened up, a thin film of perspiration on his forehead. And it was at that moment he felt the hand grip his shoulder.

This time he screamed, trying to pull away but the hand held him back and he heard raucous laughter ringing in his ears.

"All right, don't shit yourself," said a familiar voice and Miles finally found the courage to turn. He saw Graham Phelps standing there, his hand gripping Miles's shoulder. "Just thought I'd give you a bit of a fright." He laughed again, pushing Miles towards the clearing ahead of them.

"How would you like it if someone had done that to you?" Miles bleated.

"Oh shut up and give me the ball," said Graham, snatching it from him.

The huge frame of Paul Harvey loomed ahead of them, rising from behind a fallen tree stump as if he had sprung from the very ground itself. He towered over them, huge hands bunched into fists which looked like ham hocks. Wreathed in mist, he looked like something from a nightmare and, when he took a step towards them, both boys screamed and ran. They darted in opposite directions, the football falling to the ground where it bounced three or four times. Forgotten. They ran and Harvey ran after them.

They crashed through bushes, ignoring the low branches of trees which clawed at their faces, oblivious to the thorns which scraped their flesh. They both burst into the open, running like frightened rabbits. Colin saw them, saw the terror in their eyes and he too, without knowing why, joined them in their crazed flight.

Harvey watched the children as they dashed across the clearing. He waited until they were out of sight, then, scanning the open ground ahead, anxiously emerged from the trees. He crossed to the Tesco bag and rummaged inside, finding several sandwiches, some of which he stuffed into his mouth immediately. The others he jammed into his pockets. He picked up the first thermos flask, flinging it to one side when he discovered it was empty. The second one, however, was full and he could hear the contents slopping about as he shook it. Pieces of half-eaten sandwich fell from his mouth as he tried to swallow as much as he could.

Beyond the clearing lay the rolling fields which marked the outskirts of Exham. Careful not to drop any of his food, he loped off.

In twenty minutes he had disappeared.

It was 10.05 a.m.

Four

The Exham police station was a two storey red brick building set on the perimeter of the town centre. A small construction, barely large enough to house the force of nine men and three women, Randall himself excluded.

At 2.56 p.m., the entire force was crowded into what normally passed as the rest room. There wasn't enough seats for everyone to sit down so one or two of the constables leant against the white-washed walls, their attention focused on the Inspector who stood beside a board at the far end of the room. There were several monochrome photos stuck to it and, resting precariously on the chair in front of him, Randall had a dozen or so more of them.

"Paul Harvey," he said, motioning towards the photos. "Get to know that face because we've got to find him and quick."

The Inspector lit up a cigarette and sucked hard on it.

"Exham's quite a big town," he said. "So there's plenty of places for the bastard to hide. That's if he's even got here yet." He paused. "Or even coming that is."

A murmur of sardonic laughter rippled around the room.

"I want a thorough search of the whole town. Any disused houses, places like that and ask people too. Take one of these with you." He held up the photo and waved it before him. "But just be careful with your questioning. If word gets around that Harvey is on his way back to Exham then we could have a panic on our hands. It's going to be difficult enough finding him without having people ringing up every five minutes wanting to know if we've caught him." He blew out a stream of smoke. "And if the local press ask any questions, tell them to sod off. This lot around here can't write about jumble sales without getting the facts wrong so we don't want stories about Harvey splashed all over the front page of the local rags." A lump of ash dropped from the end of his fag and Randall ground it into the carpet.

"Any questions?" he asked.

"Did Harvey have any family, guv?" The question came from P C Charlton,

"Yes he did. If you can call it a family. The information's a bit vague but it seems he lived with his father up until three years ago when the old boy died. Nobody could find any trace of his mother though. The murders were committed after his father's death."

"How do you know he's coming back here?" It was Constable Reed this time.

Randall repeated his conversation with Stokes and the psychiatrist, expressing his own doubts about the killer returning to Exham. Reed seemed satisfied with the explanation.

There was an uneasy silence and Randall scanned the collection of faces before him

"Any more questions?" he asked.

There were none.

"Right," he glanced at his watch. "There's a couple of hours of daylight left. We may as well make a start."

The uniformed men and women got to their feet, filing past Randall and the board, each one picking up a couple of the black and white photos. The inspector himself waited until they had all departed and then made his way up to his office on the first floor. He lit up another cigarette and sat down at his desk, flicking on the desk lamp. Already the sky outside was overcast, heavy with rain, it hastened the onset of dusk and the watery sun which had tried to shine for most of the day had finally been swallowed up by the banks of thick cloud.

Randall held one of the photos before him, studying Harvey's chiselled features. There was a piercing intensity in those eyes which seemed to bore into the policeman even from the dull monochrome of the picture. Harvey carried two distinctive scars on his right cheek which Randall guessed were bottle scars. They were deep and the Inspector wondered how and when the escaped prisoner had sustained them. He sat back in his seat, tossing the photo onto his desk. The smoke from the cigarette drifted lazily in the air, curling into spirals around him. He closed his eyes.

The wind moaned despairingly at his window.

Five

He couldn't remember how long he'd been running, only that it had been daylight when he'd begun but now the countryside was wrapped in an almost impenetrable cloak of darkness. He wondered if he had been running in circles, chasing his own tracks round and round as he sought some vague escape route. The hills and fields all looked alike in the blackness. His legs felt like ton weights, burdened as they were by clods of mud. His heart thumped hard against his ribs and the breath rasped in his lungs as if it were being pumped by defective bellows.

He paused for a moment, atop a hill, and looked around. Below and behind him lights were shining. In some places the sodium glare of street lamps, in others the brighter glow which spilled from the windows of houses. If he had been able to calculate distance, Paul Harvey might well have guessed that he was about two miles from the centre of Exham. The town was little more than a collection of dim lights in the distance. Like a scattering of fire-flies. He panted loudly, his mouth filled with a bitter taste. He was cold, the first particles of frost now sparkling on the grass around him as the moon fumbled its way from behind a bank of thick cloud. Harvey looked up at the wreathed white orb and blinked. He put up a hand, as if trying to sweep it from the sky and, when this ploy didn't work he decided to keep on running.

The hill dipped away sharply before him and he slipped on the slick grass as he descended the slope. He lay still for what seemed like an eternity, ignoring the dampness which he felt seeping through his clothes. He merely lay on his back, gazing up at the moon, sucking in huge lungfuls of air. Every muscle in his body ached but he knew he couldn't stop. Not yet. Grunting painfully, he hauled himself upright and stumbled on. As he ran he could feel the sandwiches bumping in his coat pockets. He'd eaten one or two since taking them from the children earlier in the day and the flask was now half empty, its contents only luke-warm. He realized that he would have to eat as soon as he found shelter. Eat and drink. But what would he do when that source of food was exhausted? The question tumbled over in his mind as he ran. Yes, the food was important but so was shelter. The night was already digging icy fingers into him, he needed somewhere to hide. And not just from the elements. From *them*. *They* would be looking for him. He knew they would come soon but perhaps not for a few days. Even *they* would have difficulty finding him out here.

The moon escaped a bank of cloud once more and, in its cold white light, Harvey saw a group of buildings ahead of him.

He stopped dead in his tracks, even his breathing slowed for a moment.

Shelter.

He was sure it was a farm. There were. . .

He clenched his fists. Why was it so difficult to think?

One, two, three. There were perhaps more buildings,

arranged in a quadrangle, with a large open area at their centre – a farm house, a barn, a pig pen, another barn. He moved closer, his wide eyes ever watchful. There were no lights on in the house, perhaps whoever lived there was out, gone to bed maybe. Or perhaps *they* were in there, watching him. Just waiting for him to walk into their trap. He stood still, panting. No, there was no possible way they would find him here, they couldn't know he would find this place. Harvey smiled crookedly and licked his lips, advancing a few more yards. It was certainly quiet, there didn't appear to be anyone around.

He reached the broken fence which surrounded the entrance to the farmyard. It was rotten with damp, the wood black where at one time it had been regularly creosoted. The gate hung from one hinge, an invitation to enter which Harvey took. The yard itself was covered with weeds, some as high as his knees. He walked across to the overgrown hedge which surrounded the garden. There was no gate here, just a weather-beaten arch covered with the spidery remains of a rose plant. Harvey moved tentatively up the path towards the front door of the house, his eyes moving back and forth, waiting for the slightest sign of movement.

When nothing had happened by the time he'd reached the front door, he began to relax slightly. He went from window to window, trying to peer through the grime-encrusted panes in an effort to see what lay inside the house but he could make out no shapes in the gloom. He thought about breaking in. He could smash a window. With his tremendous strength he could even break down one of the doors.

But, what if someone came by? They would see that the farmhouse had been damaged. They would know something was wrong. He would be found. *They* would come for him again. He smiled crookedly again, pleased with his own cunning. He turned and scuttled back down the path, crossing the yard in the direction of the barn. This time, two huge wooden doors stood open and Harvey walked cautiously into the black maw which lay beyond.

The barn smelt of dampness and rotting straw. Bales of it were stacked in one corner and also up in the loft. A rickety looking ladder offered a route up to the loft and the big man put one huge foot on the first rung, testing it. It groaned under his weight but held and he began to climb.

There were about a dozen bales of damp straw in the loft, the wooden floor itself covered with a thin carpet of the fibrous stuff. The stench was almost overpowering but Harvey seemed not to notice it. The darkness inside the barn was broken only by the weak light provided by the moon, the beams creeping in through the numerous cracks in the roof. Here and there, large chunks of the slate roof were gone and Harvey shied away from these as if anxious to remain in the enveloping darkness. He settled down against a straw bale and rummaged through his coat pockets for the remaining sandwiches he'd taken from the three boys that morning. He ate ravenously, stuffing the food into his cavernous mouth until it was gone then he reached for the thermos flask. He took a large mouthful but the contents were cold and Harvey spat the liquid out angrily, hurling the empty receptacle away.

He felt tired, needed to sleep and something told him that this was the safest place to spend the night. Even *they* would not find him in this place, he was certain of that. He stretched out his arms and yawned.

Something cold touched his right hand and he almost shouted in surprise.

He spun round, crawling away but simultaneously trying to see what his hand had brushed against. He listened for sounds of movement but there was nothing, just the hammering of his heart against his ribs and, gradually, he regained his composure. The moon, spilling through one of the many cracks in the roof, fell onto the cold object and, eyes fixed on it, Harvey got slowly to his feet.

It was a sickle.

Stuck into a straw bale, it protruded from the rotted bundle, its rusty blade still wickedly sharp. Harvey reached out and grasped the handle, pulling the sickle clear. He hefted it before him, tracing the curve of the blade with his forefinger. He grinned and swung it through the air, the swish disturbing the solitude of the silent barn. Harvey chuckled throatily, excited by his discovery as a child would be with a new toy. He wiped the wooden handle on his trousers in an effort to remove the dampness which seemed to have penetrated the wood. His stomach rumbled noisily and, once more, he was reminded of the craving gnawing deep inside him. He gritted his teeth and swung the blade at a nearby bale of straw, watching as his powerful blow hacked off a large chunk of it. He rubbed his belly with his other hand and grunted irritably.

The big man turned the sickle over in his hand, his eyes drawn to the cutting edge. He rubbed it with his thumb, pressing just a little too hard and a small globule of blood welled from the cut. He cursed and sucked the wounded digit. He grunted. So sharp. His father used to have an open razor and occasionally, as a child, Harvey had watched the man shaving with it. It always remained in its wooden case at other times, on a small ledge in the bathroom. The strop hung next to it. Harvey remembered the strop well, its smell. That cloying odour of oiled leather which he had come to hate.

And he remembered how it felt.

A vision swam into his mind and it brought almost physical pain with it. The vision of a small child being beaten by a raging drunken man who laughed as he brought the strop down across the boy's pale body.

Across Harvey's pale body.

He swung the sickle through the air, slicing off more of the straw bale. The memories of his childhood were burned indelibly in his mind like a brand. A festering sore which would always be there to torment him.

He was an only child. There had never been brothers or sisters for him to share his miserable world with. His mother, Elizabeth, had seen to that. Harvey had been a breech birth. The labour had been long and agonising and, after it, his mother had vowed never to go through that hell again. Eventually she came to deny Harvey's father intercourse so great was her fear of another pregnancy. But Richard Harvey was not a man to be refused. In the beginning he had sought solace in drink, turning in three years from a large muscular man to a dark, haunted, shadow. When he drank, it seemed a part of himself was sucked into the bottle.

Harvey could still remember the night he had come home, drunk as usual, but this time raving, demanding that Elizabeth allow him what he said was rightfully his. Young Harvey, then just four years old, had heard them rowing in the room next door. He had heard the words turn to shouts and finally to screams and at that point he had climbed out of bed and padded along the landing towards the sounds of the screams and curses. He had pushed the door open and stood watching as his father tried to hold Elizabeth down, forcing her legs apart with one rough hand. Attempting to guide his own puny erection towards her with the other and, when she screamed, he would butt her with his wrinkled forehead until finally, he broke her nose and they were writhing on the bed like bloodstained puppets. Their movements jerky and uncoordinated.

Young Harvey had turned to leave but his father had roared at him to stay. And he had obeyed. Quivering helplessly, watching in bewilderment as his mother moved painfully beneath his father who finally achieved his climax and rolled off the bed, leaving Elizabeth almost unconscious. Richard Harvey had grabbed his son by the shoulders and rasped some whisky soaked words into his face, then he had dragged him to the bathroom and beaten him with the strop until the skin had risen in welts all the time screaming at him that *he* was to blame for what had gone wrong between his parents. If *he* had not been so difficult to bring into the world then things might have been different.

His mother had left the next day.

But for Paul Harvey, the nightmare had just begun. His father's drinking had grown worse. He would drag Paul out of bed at nights and shout and curse at him. Telling him that it was *his* fault Elizabeth had left.

And there was always the strop.

But, even as he grew older, Harvey was forced to put up with it because it became his accepted way of life. Abuse, both physical and verbal became commonplace for him and he stayed with his father in that tiny house in Exham where he had lived his life because he knew nothing else. He had no friends, no relatives he could go to and, somewhere, beneath that hatred which he felt, there was something akin to pity for this shrivelled-up piece of humanity which was his father. For perhaps Harvey had come to believe that he *was* responsible for the break-up of his parents' marriage. Maybe the punishment *was* deserved.

His father had died three years earlier and Harvey's world had collapsed around him. What remained of his self-control and esteem had died too.

Freed from the living hell in which he'd grown up, alone in a harsh world where there was no one he could turn to for solace, he had snapped.

He didn't know how to make friends. He was spurned by the people of Exham, and treated with ill-disguised scorn, for everyone had known what Richard Harvey had been like. Why should his son be any different?

Paul Harvey had taken a fearful revenge. He had killed two of them those three years ago. They had not spoken to him but he had sensed, behind their eyes, the disgust which they felt for him. And he had killed them. For that he had been locked away but now things were different. He was free once more and the people of Exham would be made to pay. *They* would not find him. Not until it was too late.

He smiled crookedly and hefted the sickle before him.

There was movement below him.

He froze, listening to the sound. A steady but cautious sound which wafted up from below on the reeking air. Harvey dropped to his knees and peered through the gaps in the beams, trying to see what was making the sound. Could *they* have found him already? He gripped the sickle tighter.

There was more movement.

He spun round, his heart pounding.

This time it was in the loft.

Harvey struggled to his feet, squinting in the gloom. He gripped the sickle tightly, ready to defend himself.

The moon was suddenly enveloped by clouds and the barn plunged into deep, impenetrable darkness. Harvey felt a strange mixture of fear and anger. He sucked in an anxious breath.

Something brushed against his leg and he shrieked.

He heard a rustling sound from behind him and turned, blind in the darkness, striking out helplessly with the sickle. Something else touched his leg and he jumped back, twisting his ankle in the gap between two beams. He fell forward and a foul smell filled his nostrils. Something rubbed against his face. Something wet.

At that precise moment, the moon broke free of the

enveloping cloud and cold light flooded the barn once more.

Harvey found himself staring into the cold black eyes of a rat. There was another one behind him. It had been their scratchings and scurryings which he'd heard. He got to his knees, grinning, watching the rat as it sat on its haunches nibbling at something it held between its forepaws. Harvey kept his eyes fixed on it, then, with a devastatingly quick movement, he brought the sickle down. Before the rat had a chance to move, the lethal point of the blade had pierced its back, the steel itself ripping through its tiny body until it thudded into the beam beneath. The rat squealed and Harvey grabbed it by the head, ignoring its feeble attempts to bite him. He pulled it free of the sickle, ignoring the blood which dripped onto his trousers. The big man held it in one huge hand, thick streamers of saliva dripping from his mouth. The rat felt so warm. So warm. The gnawing in his belly seemed to become a raging fire.

So warm. . .

He bit the creature's small head off with one powerful bite, chewed twice, feeling bones splinter and then swallowed. With his bare hands he tore the rat open, chewing on the raw flesh, tugging the matted fur away with his teeth, swallowing the jellied pulp of intestines. He even chewed on the tail before tossing the remains away. His stomach glowed, despite the fact that he thought, for a second, he was going to be sick. But, nevertheless, he wiped the rat's blood from his chin and, sickle in hand, went looking for another of the furry creatures. As he grabbed a second one he decided not to eat the head and lopped it off with the sickle. Blood spurted from the tiny arteries and Harvey giggled childishly for a second, watching the headless animal bucking spasmodically in his huge hand.

He ate that one too.

By the time the gnawing in his belly had been quelled,

he felt drowsy, ready for sleep. He was even more satisfied now that this place was safe. *They* would not find him here. Not yet anyway and even if they did, it didn't matter. He touched the blade of the sickle and smiled.

Besides, he had other things on his mind.

He went to sleep with the vicious blade held in one hand.

Six

Harold Pierce brushed away an imaginary speck of dust from the sleeve of his white overall and swallowed hard. He was staring at the floor of the lift as it descended, listening to the steady drone as it headed for the next floor. On the other side of the cramped enclosure stood Winston Greaves. He glanced across at Harold, his eyes straying to the disfiguring scar which covered half of his companion's face. He looked at the burn with the same hypnotic fascination as a child stares at something unusual and he felt all the more self-conscious because of this. He tried to look away but couldn't. Only when Harold raised his head to smile sheepishly did Greaves suddenly find the ability to avert his eyes.

Harold knew that the other porter was looking at him. Just as he had felt the stares and sometimes heard the jibes of others, so many times before. He could understand their fascination, even revulsion, with his own disfigurement but their prolonged stares nevertheless still made him feel awkward.

For his own part, Greaves had only succeeded by a

monumental effort of will from openly expressing his horror at the sight of Harold's face. He told himself that, in time, he would come to accept it but, at the moment, he still found his attention drawn to the red and black mess. His eyes fastened like magnets to the vision of tissue destruction. And yet, he had been a hospital porter for over fifteen years, he had seen many appalling sights during his working life. The road crash victims (one of whom, he remembered, had been brought in DOA after taking a dive through his windscreen – when Greaves and another man had lifted the body from the gurney on which it lay, the head had dropped off, so bad were the lacerations to the man's neck), the injured children, other burn victims, casualties of modern day living such as the victims of muggings. The youth who had staggered into casualty trying to push his intestines back through a knife wound which he'd sustained in a gang fight. The woman who had been so badly beaten by her husband that, not only had her skull been fractured, part of her brain had been exposed. The child with the severed hand, a legacy of playing near farm machinery. The old lady with a cut on her hip which had been left unattended for so long there were actually maggots writhing in the wound.

The list was endless.

Small wonder then that Greaves's black, wiry hair was shot through with streaks of grey. They looked all the more incongruous against his black skin. He was a small man with large forearms and huge hands which seemed quite disproportionate to the size of his body. He was a hard worker and good at his job which was probably the reason, he thought, why he'd been saddled with the task of showing Harold the ropes.

For the first week, until he became accustomed to hospital procedure and proficient in his duties, Harold was to be under almost constant supervision by

Greaves. Now he looked across at his black companion and smiled again, conscious of his scar but trying not to hide it. Greaves smiled back at him and it reminded Harold of a piano keyboard. The black man's teeth were dazzling. It looked as if someone had stuck several lumps of porcelain into his mouth. His eyes however, were rheumy and bloodshot but nevertheless there was a warmth in that smile and in those sad eyes which Harold responded to.

He had arrived at Fairvale Hospital just the day before. Phil Coot had driven him there from the asylum and helped him unpack his meagre belongings, moving them into the small hut-like dwelling which was to be his new home. The small building stood close by the perimeter fence which surrounded the hospital grounds, about 400 yards from the central block, sheltered by clumps of beech and elder.

Fairvale itself consisted of three main buildings. The central block contained most of the twelve wards and rose more than eighty feet into the air, each storey bore an A and B ward, both able to maintain over sixty patients. The children's wing was attached to the ground floor part of the hospital and connected to it by a long corridor, thus it was effectively classified as a thirteenth ward. Also separate from the main building was an occupational therapy unit where a small but dedicated staff helped the older patients, and those recovering from debilitating illnesses, to regain some of the basic skills which they had possessed before being admitted. It was here that the previously simple task of making a cup of tea now seemed like the twelfth labour of Hercules. Also attached to this wing was a small gymnasium where patients with heart complaints were encouraged to undergo mild exercise and those with broken legs or arms underwent rigorous tests to regain the proper use of their damaged limbs. Also separate from the main building, accessible only by a brief walk across the car park, were the red brick buildings of the nurses' quarters.

Fairvale, standing as it did about a mile from the centre of Exham, served an area of about thirty square miles. It was the only hospital within that radius to offer emergency care and its turnover of patients was large. It also boasted a dazzling array of medical paraphernalia, including a cancer scanner and many other modern devices. Its X-Ray, EEG, ECG, and Pathology departments ensured that the turnover of out-patients matched, if not exceeded, the number of those confined. But the Pathology department which the out-patients saw was the one which took blood samples and urine samples. The real work of Fairvale's team of pathologists took place in the basement of the main building. Here, in four separate labs, each containing three stainless steel slabs and a work-top, bodies were examined and dissected. Pieces of tissue were pored over. Moles, growths, even skin-tags were examined and put through the same rigorous tests. There were no secrets to be kept in the pathology labs, detailed notes were made on each specimen be it a full scale post-mortem or the examination of a lump of benign cells. The filing cabinets which held this information stretched the full length of two of the large rooms. Each one was more than twenty feet wide, double that in length. Inside the labs, cold white light poured down from the banks of fluorescents set into the ceilings but, outside, in the wide corridor which led from the lift to the labs, it seemed to be forbiddingly dark. A perpetual twilight of dim lights which reflected a dull yellow glow off the polished floor and walls.

Harold looked up as the lift came to a halt and saw that the line of numbers and letters above the lift entrance were now dark. Just the "B" flared in the gloom. Winston Greaves ushered him out into the corridor which led towards the pathology labs and

Harold felt a curious chill run through him. He shivered.

"It's always cold down here," Greaves told him. "The labs are kept at fifty-five degrees. Otherwise, things start to smell." He smiled, his teeth looking yellow in the dim light.

Harold nodded and walked along beside him, his skin rising into goose-pimples as they neared the door of the nearest lab. A sign greeted them defiantly:

NO ENTRY BY UNAUTHORISED STAFF

"That includes you at the moment," said Greaves, smiling at Harold. He told him to wait then he himself knocked and, after a moment or two, heard a voice telling him to enter which he duly did, closing the door behind him. Harold was left alone. He stood still for long moments, wrinkling his nose at the odour which came from inside the lab. It wasn't the familiar antiseptic smell to which he'd become accustomed, it was something more pungent, more unpleasant. It was in fact, formaldehyde. He dug his hands into the pockets of his overall and began pacing up and down before the door, looking around him. The labs seemed to be silent, if anyone was working inside there, they certainly weren't making any noise. Harold walked past the door of first one then two. He came to a bend in the corridor.

Straight ahead of him, another twenty feet further down a shorter corridor, was a plain wooden door. Harold advanced towards it and stood silently before the entry way. There were no signs on this door telling him to keep out and, as he stood there, he could hear no sound coming from inside. Except. . .

He took a step closer.

There was a low rumbling sound coming from inside the room, punctuated every now and then by what sounded like extremely loud asthmatic breathing.

He put his hand on the knob and turned it.

The door was unlocked and Harold walked inside.

The heat hit him in a palpable wave and he recoiled. For long seconds he struggled to adjust to his new surroundings; then, as he looked around he saw just how large the room really was. It must have been a good forty feet square, the ceiling rising high above him. The paintwork which had once been white, was dirty and blackened in places and, directly ahead of him, over a bare floor, lay a huge metal boiler. A chimney thrust up from it, disappearing through the ceiling. It was the boiler that was rumbling but now Harold noticed another sound. A loud humming and, turning to his left he saw what he took to be a generator. It was covered by a profusion of dials, switches and gauges but Harold's attention was quickly diverted away from the generator back to the boiler and its adjacent furnace. The heavy iron door was firmly closed and the metal looked rusty. The wall above it was blackened and scorched and there was a faint odour of burning material in the air. Harold shuddered, felt his hands beginning to shake, his body trembling slightly. He sucked in a slow breath which rattled in his throat and when he tried to swallow he found it difficult.

There were half a dozen trolleys in one corner of the room, each piled high with linen and as Harold took a step closer towards the strange bundles he coughed at the vile stench which emanated from them. He recognized them as sheets; some soiled with excrement, some stained dark with dried blood or vomit.

A bead of perspiration formed on his forehead and he wiped it away with a shaking hand as he moved closer towards the door of the furnace, the heat growing more powerful as he did so. He saw a pair of thick gloves lying on a ledge close to the tightly sealed door, beside them a set of long tongs and a wrench. Coal was piled in countless buckets nearby, some of it having spilled over onto the floor, its black dust swirling in the hot air.

Harold was trembling uncontrollably now and, as he strained his ears, he could actually hear the sound of the roaring flames from within.

A nightmare vision of his mother flashed into his mind. She was on fire, the skin peeling from her face and arms as the flames devoured her and she was holding something in those blazing arms. It was Harold's baby brother. The child was little more than a ball of flame, one stubby, blackened arm reaching out from the searing fire-ball which consumed it.

Harold closed his eyes tight, trying to force the image from his mind. He took a step back, away from the furnace.

"Harold."

He almost shouted aloud when he heard the voice behind him. He spun round, his face flushed, his breath coming in short gasps.

Winston Greaves stood in the doorway looking at him.

"Are you all right?" he asked, seeing his companion's obvious distress.

Harold nodded.

"I'm sorry," he said. "I wandered off. I found this room."

Greaves nodded.

"The furnace," he said. "The boiler heats some parts of the hospital and that," he motioned to the generator, "that's for auxiliary power, in case we get any power failures or anything, the system is wired so that the emergency generator switches on straight away."

"What about those?" said Harold, motioning to the piles of reeking laundry.

"Some of it is kept here until the laundry department can take it away," Greaves told him. "Some of it is so bad, we just have to burn it." The black man turned and motioned Harold out of the room, closing the door behind him. They made their way back down the corridor, back to the lift. "I would have showed you that room anyway," said Greaves. "That was what I came down here for in the first place. You and I have got some work to do in there this afternoon."

Harold swallowed hard but didn't speak. He gently, almost unconciously, touched the scarred side of his face and remembered the awful cloying heat inside the furnace room, the terrifying vision of his mother and brother flashing briefly into his mind once more. Greaves had told him they had work to do in there. What sort of work? His mind was spinning.

As they waited for the lift to descend, Harold felt the perspiration clinging to his back.

For some unfathomable reason he felt terribly afraid.

For the remainder of that first morning, Greaves took Harold on a conducted tour of the hospital, telling him what his duties would be, showing him where things were kept, introducing him to other members of staff all but a couple of whom managed to disguise their revulsion at the sight of Harold's scarred face. Greaves chattered good-naturedly about all sorts of things, the weather, hospital work, football, politics, and Harold listened to him. Or at least he gave the impression that he was listening. His mind was elsewhere, more specifically on just what he and Greaves had to do in the furnace room that coming afternoon.

The two of them went along to the hospital canteen at about one fifteen and ate lunch. Harold managed a couple of sausages but merely prodded the rest of his dinner with his knife and fork. Greaves, on the other hand, between mouthfuls of fish and chips continued to babble happily to his new companion. But, gradually, the extent of Harold's worry filtered through to the other porter.

"What's wrong, Harold?" he asked, sipping at a large mug of tea.

Harold shrugged and looked around him. The canteen was full of people, nurses, porters, doctors, all sitting around tables eating and chatting. The steady drone of conversation reminded him of the hum of the generator.

"Is it about the furnace?" Greaves asked, cautiously.

"I'm frightened of fire," said Harold, flatly.

Greaves studied his companion over the lip of his mug.

"I'm sorry to ask but. . ." He struggled to find the words. "Your face. Was that . . . is it a burn?"

Harold nodded.

"I've had it since I was fourteen," he said but didn't continue. The rest was knowledge for him alone. He tried to smile and, indeed, his tone lightened somewhat. "I suppose I'll get over my fear sooner or later."

Greaves nodded, benignly and took another hefty swallow of tea. The two men sat and talked and, this time Harold found himself contributing to the conversation instead of merely acting as listener. The images of the morning began to recede somewhat. He relaxed, telling himself that he was tense. After all, it was his first day at work. His first *ever* day at work. Greaves asked him, coyly, about the asylum but Harold answered his questions candidly not wishing to hide anything. He felt no shame about having spent over thirty-five years in a mental home. No, his shame was reserved for that particular subject which Greaves had touched on briefly just moments before. Fortunately the coloured porter didn't ask how Harold had come to be in a mental home since he was fourteen and he himself certainly didn't volunteer the information.

Greaves finally finished his meal and pushed the plate away from him, downing what was left in his mug as well. He patted his stomach appreciatively and smiled at Harold who returned the gesture with more assurance. He looked around him and saw a group of nurses sitting nearby. They were all in their early twenties, pretty girls tending towards plumpness as is the habit of their profession. Harold found himself captivated. One of them, the youngest of the group, her brown hair tucked up beneath her white cap, noticed his obvious interest and smiled at him. Harold smiled, lowering his gaze, one hand reaching up to cover the scarred side of his face in a gesture which had become all too familiar for him. He coloured and turn back to face Greaves who was smiling.

"Are you married?" Harold asked him.

"Yes," his colleague told him.

"What's your wife's name?"

"Linda. We've been married for twenty years."

Harold nodded. He wondered what it was like to be married. What was it like to have someone who cared for you, who needed you? To be wanted, loved – it must be a wonderful feeling. He had loved his mother but it had been so long ago he'd forgotten what the emotion felt like. All that was left inside him now was a hole. A kind of emotional dustbin filled only with guilt and want. He needed someone but was equally resigned to the fact that he would end his life alone, dying with only his memories and his shame for company. He swallowed hard.

Greaves got to his feet and tapped the table top.

"Well, we'd better get on," he said. "I think it's about time you and I did some work."

Harold nodded and followed his companion out of the canteen, leaving the sounds of joyful chatter behind, moving out once more into the hushed corridors of the hospital.

He worked hard that afternoon. On the third floor landing between Wards 3A and 3B, Harold swept and polished the lino until it shone. He muttered to himself when visitors walked over his handiwork in their muddy shoes, for it was raining outside, but no sooner had they passed than he was scrubbing away again.

It was approaching 3.15 p.m. when Winston Greaves arrived. Harold stopped what he was doing, put the cleaning materials away neatly in the cupboard indicated by Greaves then followed his coloured companion into the lift. The senior porter punched a button and the car began its descent towards the basement.

Harold felt a chill filling him, an unexplainable foreboding which seemed to intensify as they drew nearer the basement.

The lift bumped to a halt and the doors slid open. Both men walked out, immediately assailed by the cold. They walked to the end of the corridor to one of the labs, outside which stood a gurney. Whatever was on the trolley was hidden beneath a white plastic sheet. Hanging from one corner were two aprons. Greaves handed one to Harold and told him to put it on which he did, repeating the procedure with a pair of thin rubber gloves that the porter handed him. Suitably decked out for their task, the two men headed left, pushing the gurney towards the room which housed the furnace.

As he opened the door, Harold once again felt the heat, smelled the cloying stench of the coal dust. He saw the black particles swirling in the warm air. The piles of filthy linen had been disturbed, one or two of them removed.

"We'll have to burn what's left as well," said Greaves, indicating the reeking material. He pushed the trolley close to the furnace and, as Harold watched, he slipped on the pair of thick gloves which lay on the ledge before the rumbling boiler, pulling them over his rubber ones. That done, he reached for the wrench and used it to knock the latch on the furnace door up. Immediately the rusty iron door swung open. A blast of searing air swept out, causing the men to gasp for breath. Harold stood transfixed, gazing into the blazing maw. White and yellow flames danced frenziedly inside the furnace which yawned open like the mouth of a dragon. Like the entrance to hell, thought Harold.

"Fetch those sheets," said Greaves. "We'll do those first."

Harold paused before the roaring flames, seemingly hypnotized by the patterns they weaved as they fluttered before him. A low roar issued forth from the blazing hole. Even standing six feet away, the heat stung him and he took a step back.

"Harold," said Greaves, more forcefully. "The sheets."

He seemed to come out of his trance, nodded and crossed to the corner of the room, gathering up as many of the soiled sheets as he could carry. The stench was appalling and his head swam. A piece of rotted excrement squashed against his apron and he winced, trying to hold his breath as he struggled back to the waiting furnace. Greaves took them from him and began pushing them into the flames on the end of a large poker. The ferocity of the fire hardly diminished and even sheets damp with urine and blood were quickly engulfed by the furious fire. Dark smoke billowed momentarily from the gaping mouth of the furnace, bringing with it acrid fumes which made both men cough.

"I hate this job," gasped Greaves, pushing more of the filthy material into the fire.

Harold returned with the last of the faecal linen and together they shoved it into the furnace, watching as it was consumed.

"We'll clean those trolleys up later," said Greaves, motioning to the reeking gurneys in the corner of the room.

Harold nodded blankly, his eyes now turning to the trolley before them and its blanketed offerings. He watched as Greaves took hold of the blanket and pulled it free, exposing what lay beneath.

Harold moaned aloud and stepped back, eyes rivetted to the trolley. His one good eye bulged in its socket, the glass one regarded all proceedings impassively. He clenched his teeth together, felt the hot bile gushing up from his stomach, fought to control the spasms which racked his insides. The veins at either temple throbbed wildly and his body shook.

The foetus was in a receiver, dark liquid puddled around it. It was a little over six inches long, its head bulbous, its eyes black and sightless. It had been cleaned up a little after coming from pathology but not enough to disguise the damage done to it. The umbilicus was little more than a purple knot, gouts of thick yellowish fluid mingling with the blood that oozed from it. Its tiny mouth was open. There was more blood around the head which looked soft, the fontanelles not having sealed yet. The entire organism looked jellied, shrunken, threatening to dissolve when touched.

Harold backed off another step watched by Greaves.

"Not a pretty sight is it?" he said, apparently unperturbed. But then why should he be? He'd done this sort of thing often enough before. Harold gagged, put both hands on the trolley to steady himself and stared down at the foetus, his heart thudding madly against his ribs. He watched as Greaves picked up a pair of forceps, large stainless steel ones, from the trolley beside the receiver. Then, he picked the occupant of the tray up by the head, having to readjust his grip when the body nearly fell out. A foul-smelling mixture of blood, pus and chemicals dripped from the tiny body and Greaves wrinkled his nose slightly. Then, almost with disgust, he cast the foetus into the furnace. Immediately the body was consumed and there were a series of loud pops and hisses as the tiny shape was devoured by the flames.

Harold watched, mesmerized.

"Gordon," he whispered, watching the tiny foetus disappear, reduced in seconds to ashes.

He thought of his brother.

"Gordon," he whimpered again.

But, this time there was no screaming. His mother didn't dash in and try to drag the small creature from the roaring inferno. There was nothing this time. Just the terrible feeling inside himself. A cold shiver, as if someone had gently run a carving knife into his genitals and torn it upward to his breastbone. He felt as if he'd been gutted.

Greaves pushed the furnace door shut and hammered the latch back into place with the wrench then he turned to look at Harold who was still swaying uncertainly. For a moment, the senior porter thought his companion was going to faint.

"Are you all right?" he said.

Harold gripped the edge of the gurney and nodded almost imperceptibly.

"You'll get used to it," Greaves told him, trying to inject some compassion into his voice.

Harold was confused. He looked imploringly at Greaves as if wanting him to elaborate on the statement.

"That's how all the abortions are disposed of," the coloured porter told him. "We get through above five a month."

"Will I have to do this?" said Harold.

"Eventually."

The two of them stood there for long moments, neither one speaking, only the roaring of the flames from inside the furnace and the persistent hum of the generator interrupting the silence.

Harold drew a shaking hand through his hair. His face was bathed in perspiration and he was finding it difficult to swallow, as if the furnace had sucked in all the air from the room. He was suddenly anxious to be out of this place, back into the chill of the corridors. Away from the furnace. Away from the dragon's mouth that devoured children. Away from the memories. But he knew that they were one thing that would always pursue him. No matter where he ran or hid they would always find him because they were always inside him and now, as he thought about that tiny body being incinerated, his mind flashed back to another body burning, to another time. To 1946. To Gordon.

He turned and blundered out of the room, leaning against the wall, panting as he waited for Greaves to join him. The black man closed the door behind them, sealing off the sounds of the generator and the furnace.

He touched Harold gently on the shoulder, urging him to follow.

"Come on," he said, softly and Harold walked beside him, brushing one solitary tear from the corner of his eye.

And Greaves's words echoed in his mind:

"You'll get used to it."

Seven

One of the barn doors creaked loudly in the wind and the high pitched whine made Paul Harvey sit up. He gripped the sickle tightly in his hand, trying to control his breathing. The creak came once more and he realized that it was the door. Exhaling wearily, he lay down on the bed of straw again, gazing up through the hole in the roof immediately above him. Clouds skudded past, buffeted by the wind, passing swiftly before the moon until it resembled some kind of celestial stroboscope. The unrelenting glare reminded Harvey of an unshaded light bulb.

There are many things which stick in the memory, some of them inconsequential, and one of the things which now came to the big man's mind was the fact that, in the house where he grew up, not one single light possessed a shade. The rooms downstairs were bright but those upstairs were lit by dim sixty watt bulbs. His own bedroom included. He could still see it in his mind's eye. The unshaded bulb, the large bed with its rusty legs, the dusty floorboards. After his mother had left, the house had become steadily filthy. His father was never there to clean it and, even when he was, the dirt and grime didn't seem to bother him. During summer, the kitchen became a playground for all kinds of insects. Flies would feast on the congealed grease and rotting food which coated plates and saucepans. They were tossed, unwashed, into the chipped sink. Perhaps once a week, Harvey's father would force him to wash them and Harvey would obey because he feared his father. Fear was a stronger emotion even than hatred, over the years Harvey had come to learn that much. He had, even as a teenager, been a big lad, powerfully built. It would have been relatively easy to snap his father's frail neck with one strong hand. But, the spectre of fear, ingrained within him for so long, always seemed to be there, preventing him from harming his father who was, after all, the only person he had to share his worthless existence with. He cooked for him, he cleaned as best he could. Sometimes forced to launder sheets which his drunken father had fouled the night before. Harvey had done it all because, along with the fear was a perverted sense of duty. He owed this shrunken, sadistic little bastard his existence and that was what hurt most of all.

He wondered what it would have been like if he had left home with his mother. Would it have been different? Perhaps there wouldn't have been the beatings and the abuse but words sometimes hurt more than actions and his mother did not easily let him forget the pain she had gone through to give him life.

Harvey pressed both his hands to his temples as if the thoughts hurt him. He screwed his eyes up until white stars danced behind the lids. The knot of muscles at the side of his jaw throbbed angrily and he kept his teeth clenched until his head began to ache. Only then did the images begin to recede somewhat. He sat up rubbing his face with both huge hands, head bowed. And he remained in that position for some time.

The wind howled around the barn.

Eight

Harold watched the milk bubbling in the battered pan and listened to the powerful wind outside. At times, the gusts grew to such awesome proportions it seemed they would demolish the little hut. Built only of wood, it shook with each fresh onslaught of the gale.

The solitary dwelling was about 300 yards from the main building, which was itself visible through the window in the other room. There were no windows in the kitchen and Harold now stood in the yellowish light provided by an unshaded fifty watt bulb which dangled from the ceiling by a worn flex. The kitchen contained a hotplate, an old enamel sink and some cupboards which had been hastily nailed to the wooden wall at some time. The rusted heads of the nails were still visible in places. The tiny room was less than twelve feet square and it smelt of damp. There was mould on the west wall but at least, thought Harold, the place didn't leak. It had been cleaned up somewhat before his arrival but still showed the signs that it had been uninhabited for more than six years. There was a deep layer of dust and grime on nearly everything and Harold decided that he must clean the place up on his day off. It was, after all, to be his home from this point onwards.

He switched off the gas and removed the saucepan of milk, carefully pouring the contents into a mug which stood nearby. He then dropped the pan into the sink where it landed with a clang. Harold shuffled into the other room. It was slightly larger than the kitchen, boasting a single bed, a table and two battered chairs and more cupboards which looked as if they'd been assembled by a group of unenthusiastic woodwork students. The room was heated by a parafin stove which stood close to the bed and Harold warmed himself beside it before crossing to the window and peering out. He scraped away some of the accumulated muck from the window pane and squinted through the darkness. The lights of the hospital blazed in the night.

Harold lowered his head, the memory of what he'd seen that afternoon suddenly filling his mind. He turned his back on the hospital as if, by doing so, he would be able to blot out the visions of what he'd witnessed there earlier. He crossed to the bed and sat on the edge of it, sipping at the milk. It was hot. It burned.

He exhaled deeply, the thought of that tiny foetus consumed by the hungry furnace causing him to shudder. My God, that sight brought so many unwanted memories with it. He had thought that when he took this job it might help him to forget or at least come to terms with what had happened all those years ago. But now he had learned that it was to be his duty to burn things. Things. Were they human? he asked himself. The one in the tray had looked like something from Outer Space but it was still human. It was still a child. They were asking him to burn children. Asking him to relive his nightmare day in, day out.

Asking him to burn Gordon, to burn his brother, over and over again.

Harold walked slowly towards the door of the furnace room. Even ten feet away he could hear the steady hum of the generator. His footsteps echoed in the dimly lit corridor and his breath formed small vapour clouds in the heavy air. For some reason it seemed colder in the basement than usual. Behind him, the pathology lab doors were closed, retaining their secrets. Harold put his hand on the furnace room door and pushed it open. He stepped inside, immediately recoiling from the all too familiar smell of soiled linen. He walked across to the furnace itself, the generator humming noisily nearby. He could hear the muffled roar of the flames as he picked up the thick gloves which lay on the ledge before the furnace door. He pulled them on then reached for the wrench, giving the lock a hefty whack.

It sprang open.

Flames, white and orange, danced madly before him and Harold felt their searing heat on his face. The air seemed to be sucked into the blazing hole and he struggled to get his breath. He took a step back, wincing at the intensity of the heat.

The door behind him swung shut with a loud bang and Harold spun round, heart thumping hard against his ribs. For long seconds he watched the door, expecting someone to walk in – Winston Greaves or maybe one of the other porters. The door remained firmly closed. Harold turned slowly back to look into the roaring furnace. As he stared into the raging inferno his one good eye began to pick out shapes in the blazing hell which was the furnace. Much as children watch the dancing flames of a coal fire. A vision slowly formed before Harold.

He wanted to move away but it was as if his feet were nailed to the ground and, all he could do was stare into the fire.

A single tear blossomed in the corner of his eye and rolled down his cheek. They were in there, the charred remnants of countless children like the one he had seen Greaves burn.

He had felt so powerless as he had watched the tiny body consumed. Just as he had felt powerless that night in 1946 when he had seen his mother and Gordon burned to death in the fire.

The fire which *he* had started.

The leaping flames seemed to alter shape, reform until Harold found himself looking into the face of his dead brother and, all at once, he realized that he must pluck Gordon from the flames.

He plunged both hands into the firebox.

Mind shattering pain enveloped his arms, the gloves which he wore disintegrating in seconds as the flames devoured them. Harold found that he could not move and, as the agonizing pain began to spread through his entire body he actually saw the flesh of his arms turning black, huge blisters growing and bursting like flowering plants which spilled their fluid in thick gouts. Bone showed white through the charred stumps and finally Harold found the breath to scream.

He was still screaming when he woke up, propelled from the dream with a force he could almost feel. For long seconds he continued to scream but then, as he realized where he was, he quietened down and his screams turned first to whimpers and then to tears.

Curling up beneath the covers he sobbed uncontrollably.

Nine

Judith Myers stood before the bedroom mirror and studied her reflection in the glass. She ran a hand over the small, almost imperceptible bulge below her sternum then turned sideways for a better view. She touched the shape gently, allowing her eyes to stray momentarily from it, studying the rest of her naked body. Her hair was still wet from the shower she'd just taken and it hung in dark dripping strands, the droplets of water making brief circlets on the beige carpet. Her make-up had been washed off but her face was all the more striking for that. It seemed to glow in the half-light cast by the bedside lamp, her cheeks seeming sunken and hollow in the twilight. She ran an apprai-sing eye over the rest of her body – the taut breasts, the unwanted bulge of her belly, the dark nest of pubic hair at its base. She'd put on some weight around her bottom and that fact made her even more irritable. Finally, after taking one last look at her slightly distended stomach, she turned away from the mirror and reached for the large fluffy towel which lay on the bottom of the large double bed. She began to dry her hair.

"You still intend to go through with it then?" said Andy Parker. He was stretched out beneath the sheets, watching her. He took a last drag on his cigarette and ground it out in the ash-tray on the bedside table.

"I thought I asked you not to smoke up here," said Judith, still rubbing frenziedly at her hair.

"Don't evade the question," he said.

She paused for a second and looked at him.

"Yes, I am still going through with it."

Parker held her gaze for a moment then he shook his head resignedly.

"Look, Andy," she said, irritably. "We've been over

this time and time again. Now I don't want to keep talking about it."

"I wonder sometimes if you've given it enough thought," he said.

"Christ," she threw the towel down. "I've done nothing *but* think about it ever since I found out I was pregnant." There was a long silence then Judith retrieved the towel and set about drying her hair once more. Her tone was more subdued when she spoke again. "Look, I can understand the way *you* feel, but try and understand how *I* feel. A baby at this time just wouldn't be. . ." She struggled to find the word.

"Convenient?" said Parker.

She nodded.

"I don't know why you're so worried, Judith. I mean, if it's the money that's bothering you, my wage is plenty for the two of us. We don't *need* the money you bring in."

"The money's got nothing to do with it and you know that," she told him, folding the towel. She shook her head, her shoulder-length hair flowing tantalizingly as she got up and crossed to the linen basket in the corner of the bedroom. He watched her, still naked, as she tossed the towel in amongst the other dirty washing. She stooped to pick up one of his handkerchiefs which was lying nearby. She glanced at it, saw that it was clean so proceeded to fold it neatly and push it into the drawer with the others. She was a stickler for neatness, everything must be in its place. It was one of the many little things which Parker had noticed about her during their six years together. She was twenty-five, eight years younger than him and they had shared each other's lives for the past six years, four of which they had spent living together in a house on the edge of Exham town centre. There had never been any mention of marriage, in truth it was an unspoken fact that they would probably live out their days together without the intrusion of matrimony. It was something which suited them both. But the subject of children was another matter. At thirty-three, Parker was keen, almost anxious, to be a father. He had everything else he wanted. He owned a highly successful restaurant in Exham, he had gone through his hell-raising days and enjoyed every minute of it but now he was ready to set the seal on his success, their relationship and his own newly-found passivity by drawing the cosy cocoon of a family around himself.

Judith, apparently, had other ideas. She worked for one of Exham's biggest firms as a graphic designer and she took her job very seriously. She was in with the chance of promotion, the opportunity to take charge of her own department and she certainly didn't want to jeopardize the impending promotion by the unwelcome intrusion of a child.

She crossed to the dressing table and picked up a brush, sitting before the mirror to sweep the bristles through her hair. She glanced at Parker's reflection as she removed the knots and tangles from her hair, brushing away enthusiastically until it sprang up to its usual lustrous fullness. She dug fingers into it then crossed to the bed and slid in beside him.

"Is this bloody promotion *so* important?" Parker demanded, scarcely concealing his annoyance.

"To me it is," she told him. "I want that department."

"You could go back after you'd had the baby," he suggested.

She snorted.

"And start at the bottom again? No thanks."

She put one hand on his chest, curling the thick hair with her index finger, tracing the outline of his muscles with her long nail, allowing it to glide down towards his navel. The muscles of his stomach tightened slightly as she drew patterns across his belly, working lower until she was at the forest of his pubic hair. The head of his erection nudged against the probing digit and she enveloped it with her whole hand, feeling its hardness. With her free hand, she reached up and touched his face, curious at his apparent lack of response.

"You realize the moral implications of what you intend to do?" he asked, unexpectedly.

She looked puzzled.

"You're over four months pregnant."

She released his penis immediately, rolling onto her back. Judith let out a long, angry breath then propped herself up on one elbow, glaring at him. "You never give up do you?" she said. Her voice took on a hard edge. "Just drop it, Andy. Once and for all. Drop it."

"Judith, it's a human life," he insisted.

"For God's sake, shut up about the bloody child." She sat up, looking down at him. "For the last time, I'm having the abortion. Don't start this philosophical crap about taking a human life because, apart from being about the lowest trick you've pulled so far to try and stop me, it doesn't make the slightest bit of difference to the way I feel. Nothing you can say or do will make me change my mind." Her face was flushed with anger and it was reflected in her voice. "I don't *need* this baby. I don't *want* this baby."

She suddenly sucked in a tortured breath as a violent stab of pain lanced through her.

"Oh God," she gasped and rolled onto her back again.

Parker threw back the sheets, seeing that her hands had gone to her belly, were pressing the slight distension. She winced again. It felt as if someone were jabbing her stomach wall with a red hot knife, just below the navel. She inhaled deeply and the movement brought a renewed wave of pain. As a child she had been bitten by the family cat once, and the pain which she now felt inside her abdomen reminded her of that pain.

She allowed her hands to slide away from her belly and both she and Parker watched as the flesh rose slightly, first above the navel and then to one side of it. Her stomach undulated slowly for long seconds then was still. The pain ceased as abruptly as it had come.

She lay still for what seemed like an eternity, afraid to move in case the agonizing torment returned. Her forehead was greasy with perspiration and her breath came in shallow gasps. Eventually she touched her stomach. There was no discomfort.

"What the hell happened?" Parker asked, anxiously.

Judith smiled thinly, her face pale.

"I don't know. I think it must have been a muscle spasm," she said. But, even as she spoke, she looked down at her stomach, remembering the undulations.

She turned, trembling, to face Parker, who took her in his arms.

It was a long time before either of them slept.

Ten

Randall got out of the car and walked across the pavement towards the front of the cinema. A few red letters still hung from the track which ran around its canopy, others had been displaced long ago by the wind. He looked up and read:

TH P LA E

"I can remember when the Palace used to be the best cinema in Exham," P C Higgins told him, scanning the front of the building.

"Well, it's been empty for two years," said Randall. "It's as good a place as any to hide."

"You don't really think he'd pick somewhere in the middle of town do you, guv?" asked the constable.

"I doubt it," Randall confessed, "but we'd better check it anyway." He pulled a large key from his jacket pocket, one which they'd picked up from the owner of the building earlier that morning. He owned both The Palace and The Gaumont further up the road and had asked why the police should be showing so much interest in the deserted cinema. Randall had told him there'd been a spate of arson recently and they wanted to check the building out in case the fire-raiser should strike there next. The owner had not asked any more questions.

"You stop in the car," Randall told his driver. "Just in case anything comes over on the two-way."

Higgins hesitated for a moment.

"I'll be OK," the Inspector reassured him. He waited until the constable had retreated to the car then inserted the key in one of the padlocks which hung from the four sets of double doors. The Inspector threw his weight against the doors and they swung open reluctantly. He coughed at the smell of damp and decay inside.

A door to his left led into the stalls, to his right, a staircase which would take him up to the circle. He checked the stalls, the beam of his torch scarcely able to penetrate the gloom. Dust, at least a couple of inches thick, swirled up and around him, the particles drifting lazily in the glow of the torch.

The circle was worse.

Seats had been torn up and piled at both sides of the balcony and Randall had to put a handkerchief across his face so foul was the odour of decay. He checked everywhere, including the projection box, but all he found up there were a couple of yellowed copies of *Men*

Only. He glanced through one, smiling thinly to himself then dropped it back into the dustbin. Rusted spool cans lay discarded on the stone floor.

Satisfied that the cinema was, indeed, deserted, Randall made his way back outside and across to the waiting Panda car.

"Not a bloody trace," he said, dropping the torch on the parcel shelf.

It had been the same story all day, not just in the places where Randall had searched but from the other members of the force. The Inspector had ordered hourly reports from each car but, as yet, with the time now approaching noon, no sign had been found of Harvey. There was no hint that he was anywhere near, let alone in, Exham. As Higgins moved the Panda gently out into traffic, Randall looked at the people who thronged the streets of the town. Some were shopping, some stood talking. There were children with their mothers, youngsters standing in groups smoking. The Inspector exhaled deeply wondering what any of them would think or say if they knew that there was a psychopath heading for their quiet little town. If that fact was correct of course. Randall hated trusting other people and he felt especially reluctant to trust the opinions of a prison psychiatrist and a jumped-up bastard like George Stokes.

As yet another report came in, again drawing a blank, Randall began to think that he and all of his force were on one big wild goose chase.

Paul Harvey slept until almost one o'clock in the afternoon, a fitful, dreamless sleep which he awoke from abruptly. He tasted something bitter in his mouth and he spat as he clambered to his feet. He stretched, the joints in his arms cracking loudly. He bent and picked up the sickle, gripping it tight in one huge hand. From his perch inside the barn, he could see the farmhouse.

His stomach rumbled noisily and he belched loudly. Perhaps there was food in the house.

Either way, he decided to find out.

Eleven

Harold Pierce worked unsupervised now and, freed from the watchful but helpful eyes of Greaves, he became more confident. Now, as he mopped the floor, he hummed a tune merrily to himself.

Harold was still humming his tuneless ditty when the lift nearby opened and Brian Cayton stepped out. He too was dressed in a porter's overall, a small blue name badge attached to his lapel. Cayton was a young man, yet to reach his thirties, with a shock of red hair and a smattering of freckles, Harold had seen him about the hospital many times.

"Harold, do me a favour will you?" he said.

Harold put down his mop.

"What is it?" he asked, smiling, noticing that Cayton made a point of not looking at him. He was one of the few members of staff who had not yet become accustomed to the sight of the vile scar.

"There's some work to be done down in bloody pathology," said Cayton. "I would help you only there's an emergency op. about to go ahead on nine and I'm supposed to be there. So, if you wouldn't mind helping them out down in pathology."

Harold's smile faded quickly and he swallowed hard.

"What do they want?" he asked, warily.

"I'm not sure," said Cayton, stepping back into the lift and punching the button marked nine.

The doors slid shut and there was a loud burring as the lift rose.

Harold stood still for long moments, gazing at the floor, staring at his own distorted image on the wet surface. Then, leaving the mop and bucket in the middle of the floor, he headed for the steps which would take him down to the basement.

Harold found that, by the time he reached the door of Pathology One, his body was sheathed in a fine film of perspiration. He knocked tentatively and stood waiting, listening to the sound of footsteps approaching from inside. The door opened and a middle-aged man in a white plastic apron peered out. He looked at Harold over the rims of his thick spectacles, brushing a loose strand of hair from his forehead. He glanced briefly at the scar then ran an appraising eye over the nervous porter.

"Wait there," said the man, attempting a smile but not quite managing it.

Harold peered through the half-open door, at the stainless steel slab nearest the door which, he noted, bore an occupant. The other men in white overalls were poring over it. There was a type of scale suspended over the slab and, as Harold watched, one of the men lifted a crimson lump from the slab and laid it in the bowl which registered a weight on the metric scale it bore. The man ran a blood-soaked finger along the scale, recording the weight to the last gramme. He then said something about the liver and Harold saw his companion jot the weight down on a clipboard which he held. The crimson lump was removed and placed on a trolley nearby, some congealed blood spilling in blackened gouts from the organ. Harold blenched and turned away, his stomach somersaulting.

"Here you are."

The voice startled him and he turned to see the

bespectacled man standing in the doorway, leaning on a trolley covered with a white sheet.

"Just some specimens to dispose of," he said and pushed the trolley out.

Harold took a firm grip on the gurney and began to push it in the direction of the furnace room, hearing the door close behind him as the pathologist retreated back inside the lab. One of the wheels squeaked and it offered a discordant accompaniment to the rhythmic tattoo beaten out by Harold's shoes which echoed through the chill, silent corridor. He looked down at the trolley as he walked, running a suspicious eye over the sheeted exhibits hidden from view. He could detect that familiar smell, the cloying, pungent odour of chemicals which made his eyes water. Harold tried to swallow but found that his throat was parchment dry, his tongue felt like a piece of sun-baked meat. He paused at the door of the furnace room and opened it, feeling the familiar blast of warm air as it greeted him. The generator hummed unceasingly as he dragged the gurney in beside him and closed the door. Unable to contain his curiosity any longer he pulled back the sheet, uncovering the objects which lay on the trolley.

He moaned as if in pain. His one good eye riveted to the foetus which lay in the tray. For long seconds, Harold stared at it, tears brimming in his eye. He didn't know at what stage the thing had been aborted but it was slightly larger than the one he'd seen Greaves incinerate on the first day. Its eyes were sealed shut by membranous skin. The head once more looked swollen and liquescent but this time it had a thin, almost invisible covering of fine hair. The whole body was covered by the langou and Harold reached out a shaking hand to touch the silken fibres. But the body was cold and dripping with chemicals and it felt so obscenely soft that he hastily withdrew his hand. The forceps lay beside the receiver and they glinted in the cold white light cast by the overhead banks of fluorescents.

Harold pushed the trolley closer to the furnace, using the wrench and gloves to open it as he had seen Greaves do. The door swung open and a blistering wave of heat gushed forth, sweeping over Harold like a burning tide. He took a step back, recoiling from the sudden intense temperature. He pulled on a pair of thin rubber gloves and looked down at the foetus, then at the forceps. The furnace yawned invitingly. Harold picked up the metallic clamp and prepared to pick up the tiny body. His breath was coming in gasps, a single tear now rolling down his unscarred cheek.

He reached for the foetus.

"No."

He threw the forceps down and gripped the side of the trolley to steady himself.

"No," he said again, his voice cracking. "No."

He looked at the body, lying in its pool of rancid fluid, the arms and legs drawn up stiffly in a pose which reminded him of some kind of vile, hairless cat waiting to have its belly stroked. He sucked in huge lungfuls of stagnant air, his head bowed. When he finally managed to straighten up he looked into the furnace until the roaring flames burned yellow and white patterns on his retina. He could not, *would* not, put the foetus into that hungry mouth. His anxious gaze strayed back to the liquid-covered body and he shook convulsively.

"Gordon," he whispered, softly.

His head was beginning to throb, his nostrils and eye stinging from the odorous substances which lay in the tray with the abortion. He looked around him, at the generator, at the filthy trolleys which stood in one corner of the room, at the piles of fouled linen. There was something else too, something which he hadn't noticed the first time. It was like a large plastic dustbin standing near to the piles of filthy laundry. Harold crossed hastily to it and lifted the lid, immediately gagging at the disgusting stench which rose from it. He looked down and saw that it was full of old dressings. Some were stiff with dried blood, others still crimson and fresh. There were gauze pads soaked with yellowish fluid, bandages that had pieces of skin sticking to them. Harold backed away, his mind churning with ideas. He crossed to the gurney and, with infinite care, as if he were lifting a sleeping child, picked up the foetus with both gloved hands. A drop of fluid burst from the umbilicus and splashed Harold's overall but he ignored it, carrying the tiny creature towards the bandage filled dustbin. There, he gently layed it on the ground and dug deep into the mass of bloodied dressings, making room at the bottom. This done, he once more lifted the foetus and placed it in the dustbin, covering it with the used bandages and pads, hiding it from view. He wiped some pus from his glove and then hastily put back the lid of the dustbin.

The furnace room door opened and Winston Greaves walked in.

Harold spun round, heart hammering against his ribs. Greaves looked at him for a moment, at the dustbin, at Harold's bloodstained hands. Then he smiled thinly.

"I thought I'd see how you were getting on," said the senior porter.

Harold walked back to the furnace, satisfied that Greaves suspected nothing. After all, he reasoned, what *could* he suspect? Together they disposed of the remaining things on the gurney, consigning them to the blazing fire then returning the trolley to pathology.

As they left the furnace room, Greaves leading the way, Harold took one last look across at the dustbin. The foetus would remain hidden in there, free from prying eyes. As far as anyone else was concerned, it had been incinerated along with everything else. He had told Greaves that he'd burned the contents of the dustbin along with the pathology specimens and the coloured porter nodded his approval. Harold smiled to himself and pulled the furnace room door closed.

The foetus would be safe in its hiding place until he could return.

Night came without bringing the rain which had threatened earlier. Instead, the air was filled with a numbing frost which glittered on the grass and trees, reflecting the light from the hospital like millions of tiny diamonds. Harold stood at his window, watching as more and more lights were extinguished in the huge building as the hour grew late. He watched with almost inhuman patience, his mind a blank; the only thing scratching the surface of his consciousness being the persistent ticking of his alarm clock. He stood in the hut in darkness, not having bothered to turn on the light and, when he glanced behind him, the phosphorescent arms of the clock radiated their greenish glow revealing that it was almost 12.36 a.m.

Harold didn't feel tired, despite the fact that he'd been up since six that morning. His mind was too full of ideas for him to notice any fatigue. In another twenty-five minutes or so he would slip out of the hut, cross the few hundred yards of open ground which separated his own dwelling from the main building and go through the entrance which faced him.

It led past the mortuary to a flight of steps and a lift which would take him down to the basement and, eventually, to the furnace room.

The hands of the clock crawled slowly to one o'clock and Harold decided that it was time to leave. He slipped silently out of the door and locked it behind him, hurriedly making his way across the large expanse of grass between his hut and the nearest entrance. The frost crunched beneath his feet but, despite its severity, it had done little to harden up the ground and Harold twice nearly slipped in the mud. His breath came in short gasps, each of which was signalled by a small cloud of misty condensation. As he drew closer he realized just how dark the hospital was. There seemed to be only a couple of lights burning on each floor and that was not enough to illuminate his dark shape in the blackness.

He paused, ducking behind a nearby bush when he heard a clicking sound. Looking up he saw that it was two of the nurses returning to their quarters. They were laughing happily, the sounds of merriment drifting through the chill, silent night. Harold watched them until they disappeared out of sight then he continued forward, almost running the last few yards to the entrance.

A blue sign to his right proclaimed:

MORTUARY

He pushed open one of the swing doors and moved as quietly as he could into a short corridor which led to a staircase. He blinked hard in the darkness, for no light had been left on. Indeed, as he reached the top of the stairs, he grabbed the handrail to guide himself, so impenetrable was the darkness.

It seemed even colder inside the building than out and Harold shuddered as he made his way tentatively down the stairs. How he wished he had a torch. He was completely and utterly blind, unable to see a hand in front of him and this sensation made him feel all the more uneasy. He could feel his body trembling and, as he put his foot down to find the next step, he stumbled. Harold gasped in shocked surprise and fell hard on the base of his spine. The impact sent a pain right through his body and, for long seconds, he sat where he was, moaning softly, one hand still gripping the handrail, the other massaging his back. He slowed his breathing, afraid that someone might hear him, worried that his little venture would be halted because some conscientious pathology assistant had decided to stay late and finish some work in the labs. His trepidation grew stronger when he noticed that there was a light burning at the bottom of the staircase. He had to round a corner to reach the base and that was still a dozen or more steps down. As yet the light was indistinct but, hauling himself up, Harold moved on, drawn towards the light like a moth to a flame.

He reached the bottom of the stairs, emerging in the area before the lift. The doors to all the labs were closed. Perhaps, he reasoned, someone had left and forgotten to turn out the light. But another part of his mind told him that the men who worked down here were too thorough to let such a minor thing as a light escape their notice. Heart pounding against his ribs, he walked to the door of the first lab and pressed his ear to it.

There was no sound coming from inside.

He twisted the handle and found that the door was locked. The same procedure was repeated with the other three labs and Harold was finally satisfied that the light had simply been overlooked. For that, to some degree, he was grateful. Although it lit only the area near the lift, it did provide at least some light for him as he made his way up the corridor.

In the furnace room the heat was as powerful as ever, but this time he welcomed it for it drove some of the chill from his bones. The generator kept up its ceaseless humming. Harold crossed quickly to the plastic dustbin and lifted the lid, pulling the used dressings aside, ignoring the blood and other discharge which sometimes stuck to his flesh. He finally felt something soft and jellied beneath his hands.

Very carefully, he lifted the foetus out, holding the tiny body before him for long seconds. Even in the half-light, he could see that the skin was already turning blue. He turned and laid it on one of the soiled sheets which were stacked on the gurneys behind him, then, as if he were wrapping a fragile Christmas present, he carefully pulled the dirty linen around the foetus. A rank odour filled his nostrils but he tried to ignore it and, with his "prize" secured, he made his way back towards the door, holding the small thing as a mother would hold her baby.

Harold ran across the open ground towards his hut finally slowing down when he reached the flimsy dwelling. He leant against the wall, trying to catch his breath, his one good eye squinting through the gloom to the doors he'd come through. No one had heard or seen him. There was no one following. Harold smiled thinly and closed his eyes. He took great gulps of cold air, trying to ignore the rancid stench which rose from the sheet and its dead occupant but that didn't seem to matter any longer. He had completed the first and most hazardous part of his venture, the second step was merely a formality.

The hut in which Harold lived stood about ten yards from a low barbed wire fence which marked the perimeter of the hospital beyond it lay large expanses of open fields, some of the ground was owned by the hospital but it was fenced off nevertheless. In the far distance, Harold could see the lights of Exham and, occasionally, the headlamps of a vehicle travelling along the dual-carriageway which led into the town. He headed towards the fence and cautiously stepped over it, catching his trousers on one of the vicious barbs. The material ripped slightly and Harold pulled himself free.

The ground sloped away before him slightly, leading down towards a deep cleft in the field which looked like an open black mouth in the darkness of the night. Harold steadied himself and made his way towards the depression. Above him tall electricity pylons rose high into the sky, their metal legs straddling the field, the high voltage cables they carried invisible in the gloom. There was a smell of ozone in the air, rather like the aftermath of a thunderstorm and Harold could hear a distant crackling sound from overhead.

He reached the foot of the small hill and stood close by the foot of a pylon. He was exhausted, both mentally and physically drained. His eye felt gritty and his throat was dry but he walked on, finally finding what he thought looked like a suitable spot. There was enough natural light for him to see what he was doing. He paused and laid the bundle of dirty sheet on the frosty grass, then he knelt and began scraping at the earth with his bare hands. He found that it was soft enough for him to achieve the necessary depth. Like a dog who's found a good spot to hide a bone, Harold pawed the earth away until it began to form a sizeable mound behind him. By the time he'd finished he estimated that the hole must be about two feet deep and twice that in length. He was panting loudly, his hands caked in mud, his clothes already reeking from the foul smell of the soiled linen. With the hole prepared, he unrolled the sheet, exposing the foetus inside. He lifted it gently from the cover and laid it in the hole.

For long seconds he stared down at it, tears brimming in his eye. He lowered his head, his body shaking.

"Gordon," he whispered. "Forgive me."

He felt a strange contradiction inside himself, a great sadness but also something akin to relief. Had he at last found a means of atonement? He began pushing the wet earth back into place, covering the tiny body.

"Mother," he said, as he continued to pile earth back into the grave. "It's different this time. This time I won't let it happen again. There'll be no more burnings."

He looked up, as if expecting to see someone standing

over him. Expecting to hear voices. There was only the far-off whistle of the wind in the pylons.

Harold finished piling in the earth and stood up, flattening it down with his shoe. He wiped his hands on the piece of soiled sheet then balled it up and hid it beneath a nearby bush. That done, he returned to the small grave. At first, when he tried to speak, no sound would come and his lips fluttered noiselessly but he swallowed hard and clasped his dirty hands before him.

He didn't know anything religious. No prayers. No hymns. He lowered his head, his eyes closed.

"Now I lay me down to sleep," he began, falteringly. "I pray the Lord. . ." He struggled to remember. "I pray the Lord my soul to keep." A long silence. "If . . . If I would . . . should," he corrected himself. "If I should die before I wake. I pray the Lord my soul to take." Tears were coursing freely down his cheek by now.

"Amen."

He turned and headed back to his hut.

It was not to be the last time he performed the cathartic ritual.

Twelve

Lynn Tyler prodded the bacon with a fork, turning it over in the hot fat. She hated fried food and the small kitchen already smelt strongly of it, the odour making her feel queasy. How the hell anyone could ever eat a cooked breakfast she didn't know but, in about five minutes, Chris would come downstairs and devour his usual four rashes of bacon, two eggs and a couple of slices of fried bread. He was sleeping upstairs at the moment, undisturbed by the sounds coming from the room below him. The radio competed with the frying bacon for supremacy in the cramped area.

Lynn jumped back as the fat spat at her, some of it catching the arm of the sweatshirt which she wore. At least three sizes too big for her and with "Judas Priest" printed across it, the garment came to just below her bottom. She wore nothing else and the lino in the kitchen felt cold beneath her bare feet. She ran a hand through her uncombed black hair and exhaled deeply, looking down at the pan but also at herself. She was almost shapeless beneath the thick folds of the sweatshirt but even that wasn't enough to disguise some painfully obvious facts about her body. Her breasts, for so long unfettered by a bra, were beginning to droop – legacy of all those years she had spent enticing men. Ever since she'd reached her fourteenth birthday, just over five years ago, she had flaunted herself in every flimsy blouse and T-shirt she could find. There had been dozens of men in the intervening years, too many for her to count, attracted not just by her sizeable bust but by her easy manner – and easy was the operative word. She knew that some called her a tart, a slag, someone had even called her a whore once, but to Lynn Tyler the moral double-standard which governed the sex lives of men and women was ludicrous. And unfair. If a man slept around he was patted on the back and admired, earning the name of stud with each new conquest. If a woman chose to take different men to bed for her own private pleasure, she was sneered at, insulted and, in Lynn's case, thrown out of the house. Her parents had kicked her out when she was seventeen after coming home to find her locked in a torrid embrace on the floor of their sitting room with her boyfriend of the time. Since then she had shared a three-bedroomed house near the centre of Exham with her best friend, Jill Wallace. Jill worked in nearby Camford and her job often took her away from the house for days at a time. It was during these respites that Lynn invited Chris to stay. She herself was unemployed and had been for over a year. Chris worked in Exham's largest engineering firm. They had been together for over nine months. It was something of a record for Lynn and, during that span of time, something had happened to her which she had always consciously avoided before. She had fallen in love. All the countless other men, they had been for *her* private gratification although more often than not it had not turned out that way. But it was different with Chris. She had never had any intention of falling in love, in fact the emotion had proved so alien to her that at first she hadn't been sure what she was feeling, but she knew it was ten times stronger than anything she'd felt in her life before. And she knew she wanted Chris on a more permanent basis than meetings three times a week and the odd weekend together. She wanted to marry him.

That was why she had stopped taking her pill. For the last three months she had left it untouched in its green packet. And, finally, she was sure. She was pregnant. She'd missed two periods, and a trip to the doctor last week had confirmed her suspicions. Surely with a baby on the way Chris would marry her? But she had yet to tell him her news.

She finished cooking his breakfast and while the kettle boiled for coffee she lit a cigarette, went to the bottom of the stairs and called him. She waited until she heard the creak of the bedsprings, signalling that he was up then she padded back into the kitchen and sat down to her own breakfast – a cup of Nescafé and a Marlboro.

He was down in a matter of moments, chest bare to expose his hard lean body with its tangled growth of light hair on the chest and stomach. He wore a faded pair of jeans, held up by a studded leather belt. Around one wrist was a leather band, similarly dotted with studs. He rubbed his stomach and sat down in front of the plateful of food.

"Don't you ever wash in the mornings?" she asked him, smiling. She watched as he started hacking away at the bacon.

"Well, I didn't have time this morning," he told her, chewing furiously. "I felt hungry."

She shuddered.

"I don't know how the hell you can eat *that* first thing in the morning." She took a drag on her cigarette, blowing out a long stream of smoke. She crossed her legs beneath the table, tapping her feet together agitatedly. Should she tell him now? Excuse me Chris but you're going to be a father? She took a sip of her coffee instead.

The DJ on the radio was babbling some hip bullshit which neither of them seemed to hear. Chris because he was too engrossed in his breakfast and Lynn because she was too wrapped up in her own thoughts. She watched him as he set about the first egg, slicing it in two, dipping his fried bread in the runny yolk. He looked up at her and smiled that warm, welcoming smile she had come to know so well these past nine months. She wondered if there was room for love in that smile.

"What's on your mind?" he said.

She looked surprised.

"Not a lot," she lied. "Why do you ask?"

"You're not usually this quiet," he told her.

Lynn smiled weakly, taking mock offence.

"Thanks a lot."

He smiled again, pushing half the egg into his mouth.

She sucked hard on her cigarette, held the smoke in

her mouth for long seconds then blew it out in a long blue stream.

"Chris, I'm pregnant."

The words came out as easily as that but, once she'd said them, it felt as if a hole had opened up inside her. Well, there it was. She'd told him, flat out. She sipped at her coffee and eyed him warily over the rim of the mug.

He slowed the pace of his chewing, looking down at his plate, not, as she'd expected, at her. He didn't speak.

"I said. . ."

He cut her short.

"Yeah, I heard you." There was an edge to his voice, almost imperceptible but nevertheless present. Like a knife blade in the darkness, invisible but razor sharp.

She ground out the fag in a nearby saucer, the plume of smoke rising mournfully, disappearing above her like a forgotten dream.

"Haven't you got anything to say?" she wanted to know.

"Are you sure?" he asked, still looking at his plate.

She told him about the visit to the doctors, the missed periods. He nodded.

They sat in silence for an eternity then he dropped his knife and fork onto the plate where they clattered noisily. Finally, he looked her in the eye.

"I thought you were on the bloody pill," he said, exasperatedly.

"I was," she told him. "I just didn't take it for a few weeks."

With the deception now revealed, it was she who dropped her gaze, unable to meet the unrelenting stare from his green eyes.

"Jesus Christ," he murmured, then his voice gradually grew in volume. "You bloody tricked me didn't you?"

"I didn't," she countered although the accusation bore weight and she was crumbling beneath that weight.

"You had me thinking it was safe and all the time you weren't taking your pill. You made a fucking mug out of me for all that time?" He was struggling to keep his anger in check and he wasn't making much of a job of it.

"It was just two months, Chris," she said.

"Two months. Two *years*. What's the difference? It's still me who ends up looking the twat, isn't it?"

She could feel the tears building but she fought them back, angry with herself now. They sat in silence for a long time. A silence finally broken by Chris.

"So what are you going to do?" he demanded.

"What do you mean?"

"About the kid."

"I'm going to have it."

He shook his head.

"Well, it's your business I suppose but I think you're stupid," he told her.

Her brow furrowed.

"It's not just *my* business," she said, defiantly. "It's yours too. You are the father after all."

"Are you sure?"

The remark was barbed and it cut deeply.

"You bastard," she growled. "Yes, I'm sure it's yours. If anyone else had been fucking me in the last nine months I think you might have found out about it."

"So, what are you going to do about it?" he asked again.

"I've told you once. I'm going to have it. I wanted the child. It's *our* child."

The realization gradually swept over him and a bitter smile creased his face.

"You know, Lynn, you've got more brains than I gave you credit for," he said.

"What's that supposed to mean?" she said.

"The baby. Not taking the pill. You planned it all didn't you?"

She reached for his hand, almost surprised when he didn't pull away. When she spoke again her tone was low, almost pleading.

"Chris, it was the only way I knew of keeping you," she said. "I love you. I've never loved anyone else in my life before. I didn't want to lose you."

"So you thought you'd trick me into becoming a daddy?" His voice was heavy with sarcasm.

She pulled her hand away.

"I hoped you'd marry me when you heard about the kid," she confessed. "You are its father after all."

"Only because you didn't take your fucking pill," he rasped. She watched as he got to his feet. "I'm sorry, Lynn but I'm not ready for this." He swallowed hard, not sure whether to pity her or punch her in the teeth. She too got to her feet.

"I love you, I want your baby. I want *you*," she said, the first salty tear sliding down her cheek.

"I'm sorry," he said. "Look, I think a lot of you, you're a good kid, fun to be with. . ."

She cut him short, her own anger now overriding his.

"And an easy fuck," she growled.

"I just don't love you," he told her, almost reluctantly.

She stood quivering for a moment, trying to hold back the flood of tears which she knew would come any minute. Her voice was cracking.

"So what's *your* answer then?" she demanded.

He stepped away from the table.

"I think it'd be simpler if we just didn't see each other again," he said.

"As easy as that? Forget the relationship. Nine months down the drain. Is that all it meant to you? Is it?" She was shouting now, the tears flooding down her cheeks. "A good screw when you wanted it? What was I, just a convenient piece of equipment when you got fed up with wanking?"

"I think I'd better go," he said, quietly.

"Yes, go on. Go. Fuck off." She started to tug the sweatshirt off, despite his pleas for her to stop. Eventually she pulled it free and threw it at him, standing there naked in that smoke filled kitchen, the odour of fried food heavy in the air.

"I'm sorry, Lynn," he said.

"Get out," she screamed at him, hurling the sauce bottle in his direction. It hit the wall close by him and exploded, splattering the sticky red liquid all over the place. Lumps of glass skittered across the lino.

She sat down at the table, sobbing, her head resting on her arms and she heard the front door close behind him as he left.

Naked, she sat alone in the kitchen her tears falling onto the paper table cloth and spreading out like transparent ink on blotting paper.

She remained like that for at least thirty minutes before wiping her face and shuffling upstairs to dress. She pulled on a pair of drain-pipe jeans and hauled a khaki coloured T-shirt over her head. She went back downstairs and cleaned up the mess in the kitchen.

At 10.03 a.m. she phoned her doctor and made an appointment to see about getting an abortion.

Thirteen

"Well, this is better than standing under a fucking tree isn't it?" said Keith Todd, adjusting the volume control on the Dolomite's cassette.

Penny Walsh giggled and moved closer to him, gazing out through the windscreen at the rain clouds which were gathering ominously. It was already dark but the impending storm seemed to bring a heaviness to the air, gripping the small car in a black velvet fist. The headlamps were off and the only light came from the sodium lamp about ten yards behind then down the lane. Flanked on both sides by trees and high bushes, it had wide grass verges on either side and it was on one of these that Keith had parked the car.

"And you're really going to buy this off your dad?" Penny said, patting the passenger seat.

"Once I get a job, yeah," Keith reassured her. "He doesn't mind me borrowing it until then."

Neither of them had jobs, both Keith and Penny had left school at sixteen, just two years earlier. The ritual of signing on had become, as it had to hundreds of thousands more of their generation, a way of life. But Keith was an eternal optimist and, tonight, in particular, he felt lucky. That feeling proved to have foundation as he felt Penny slide one hand onto his thigh. He responded by pulling her towards him, their mouths locking, tongues darting feverishly back and forth, each anxious to taste the other.

Keith felt her hand clawing its way up to the growing bulge in his jeans. He responded by squeezing her left breast feeling the nipple stiffen through the thin material of her blouse.

She turned in her seat, one leg now drawn up beneath her. His rough hand found the buttons on her blouse and undid them, moving more urgently now as he massaged her plump breasts. For her own part she managed to undo the zip of his jeans, coaxing his stiffness free, running one finger along the shaft from tip to base before enveloping it with her warm hand.

Keith grunted and reached beneath her short skirt. As her hand began to move rhythmically up and down, he felt her part her legs slightly and his probing digits pulled the slinky material of her panties aside in an effort to reach the moist warmth beyond. He slid two fingers into her eager cleft and she stiffened in response.

Paul Harvey was less than ten yards from the car.

He crouched in the bushes, the sickle held firmly in his hand, watching the young couple inside the vehicle, his expression a mixture of disgust and bewilderment. The first spots of rain began to fall but Harvey ignored them, his attention riveted to the car. The windows were steaming up and it was becoming difficult to see inside from his present vantage point. The two youngsters inside were merely indistinct blurs before him. He gripped the sickle tighter.

During his own teenage years he had never known the pleasure of a companion, male or female. He had tried to make friends, when his father had allowed it but Harvey's self-consciousness and naivety had let him down until at last, he resigned himself to being a loner. Not that the people of Exham did anything to help him overcome those shortcomings. Fate, and the townspeople, seemed to be conspiring against him, trying to ensure that he would never know what it was like to be a part of society. And, in truth, perhaps Harvey didn't want to be a part of it.

He moved slowly towards the car.

Penny bent her head and closed her mouth over the bulging purple head of Keith's penis, flicking some drops of clear liquid from its tip. He gasped as he felt her warm tongue curling around his erection, the sensations which he felt becoming stronger by the second. He, himself, continued to move his fingers within her, using his thumb to tease the hardened bud of her clitoris. Keith allowed his head to loll back onto the head-rest, closing his eyes as he felt her pushing more urgently against his hand. He could hear her rasping breath, feel its hotness on his slippery shaft.

There was a thunderous roar as the first rumble of thunder broke like a wave on a rock and the sound make Keith open his eyes.

He almost screamed.

Glaring in at him through the side window, his face distorted by the swiftly flowing rain, was Harvey.

Keith, pulling Penny upright, withdrew his fingers and reached frantically for the ignition key. The girl sat back, dazed and confused.

"Keith, what. . ."

The engine roared into life and the young lad looked once more out of the side window.

The face had gone. Of Harvey there was no sign.

Keith slumped back, shaking uncontrollably and, high above them, a powerful fork of lightning tore open the clouds.

Fourteen

The eighth foetus had been buried, its tiny body now lying beneath the slippery mud with the others. Harold dried his hair with a towel and checked on the milk bubbling in the pan on the hot-plate.

Eight of them in that shallow grave. He yawned and glanced across at the alarm clock. It was 1.45 a.m. It hadn't taken him so long to bury the last one. The constant rain had transformed the earth into a quagmire. Indeed, it had been raining for the past two days on and off and that, at least, made his task easier. The clods came away easily.

He lifted the saucepan just in time to prevent it boiling over, poured the milk into a mug and tossed the pan into the sink.

Outside, there was a particularly loud growl of thunder which seemed to roll across the land like an unfurling blanket. The little hut shook and Harold stood still for a moment, wondering if the entire flimsy structure was going to collapse around his head. The rumbling died away to be replaced by a whiplash crack of lightning which seared across the bloated, mottled sky and, for brief seconds, left a brilliant white afterburn on Harold's retina as he watched it. Mesmerized by the sight of nature's fury at its most potent, he crossed to the tiny window and stood looking out as the storm gathered for its furious onslaught on Exham and the countryside round about. Black cloud, buffeted by the wind, came rolling in to empty its load while lightning split the heavens with blazing white forks of pure energy. The thunder grew to a crescendo, like a thousand cannons being fired at once. The little hut shook once more as the storm intensified. Harold watched in awe, recoiling every now and then from the particularly violent flashes of lightning or the seemingly endless volleys of thunder. And, through it all, came the persistent pounding of the rain as it hammered against buildings and turned the ground into sticky slime. On the tarmac around the hospital entrance, the water puddled in pools ankle deep, each droplet exploding on the black, saturated surface. Even inside the hut, Harold could detect the strong smell of ozone as the sky was torn open by the powerful fingers of light which rent the thick black clouds like hands through wet tissue paper. Thunder roared menacingly and, in one or two places in the hospital, windows rattled in their frames. For those patients still awake, the world outside became a blur as they squinted through the rain-drenched windows. There was no steady trickle of tear-like droplets this time but a massive deluge which seemed to strike the windows and cascade down in one liquid flow, as if there were many men standing out there throwing buckets of the stuff at the panes. The few lights that burned outside were diffused into mere blurs through the rain-battered windows.

Harold sipped at his milk and watched the celestial fireworks, drawing back slightly as each blinding burst of forked or sheet lightning exploded across the sky, to be followed by a deafening blast of thunder. It sounded like some gigantic animal roaring in pain, the lowing of a massive steer lashed by a whip of ferociously undiluted force.

In the field behind Harold's hut, the pylons swayed ominously in the high wind, their normally stable structures looking suddenly vulnerable. They crackled loudly and the thick power lines hummed as they were rocked back and forth by the onslaught. The metal groaned as it was bent and blasted by the wind and, beneath one of the pylons, less than fifty feet from its base, the shallow grave which Harold had dug was saturated to the extent that some of the top soil began to wash away.

There was a crack of lightning which screamed across the black heavens for a full five seconds, a blast of energy so powerful that for long moments even the thunder seemed to cease. The crackling fork hit the pylon nearest to the hospital fence, striking it at the very point where the huge power lines were attached. There was a blinding flash of blue and white sparks and an angry sputtering as the thick cable, twice as thick as a man's torso was wrenched free of its housing by the fury of the impact. Then, it simply fell to earth, the other end of it still attached to the preceding pylon. But the severed end twisted and writhed on the wet earth like some kind of gigantic snake, showering the sodden mud with sparks and pumping hundreds of thousands of volts into the sticky ooze. The pylon itself shook violently as the cable twisted at its base, contorting madly like an eel on a hot skillet as it poured its immense reservoir of energy into the earth. The grass nearby was immediately blackened by the furious discharge, the mud even bubbling in places as the endless supply of electricity continued to gush into the ground. The cable twisted and whiplashed for what seemed like an eternity as it unleashed its pent-up power in a display which even overshadowed the mighty forks of lightning still flashing across the sky. The power line poured seemingly endless stores of crackling volts into the wet earth which, itself, acted as a conductor, further aiding the explosive exhibition.

Fifteen

The picture on the TV broke up into a maze of static and Judith Myers looked up as she heard Andy Parker curse.

"I knew we should have got a different set," he grunted, thumping the TV with the flat of his hand.

"It's the storm," said Judith, gazing out of the bedroom window at the forks of lightning that rattled across the sky. She lowered her book and ran an appraising eye over Parker who stood naked before the television as if daring it to start playing up again. The picture gradually gained clarity and he nodded appreciatively, but still waited defiantly. Judith giggled.

"What's so funny?" he asked, without turning to look at her.

"You," she said. "Get back into bed or at least draw the curtains. Someone will be calling the police. They'll lock you up for indecent exposure." She chuckled again. Parker remained where he was.

Slowly, almost reluctantly, she slid the sheets down a little way to uncover her stomach, stroking a hand over its firm flatness. Gone was the bulge she had hated so much. The abortion had been successful and she had been out of Fairvale for more than a week now and had even been into work for a couple of hours.

A particularly thunderous crack of lightning tore across the sky as the storm reached ever greater heights and Judith winced as she felt sudden, unexpected pain just below her navel. She pressed the area gingerly, as Parker shouted and cursed at the TV which was again hissing at the onslaught of so much static in the air.

Judith sucked in a painful breath, eyes fixed on her abdomen. The flesh seemed to stretch across her pelvic bone, becoming shiny, then, as she watched, a single drop of blood welled inside her navel. It spread outwards until it overflowed and trickled down her side like a solitary crimson tear.

"Oh my God," she gasped, her eyes bulging.

"What's wrong?" asked Parker, still more concerned with the recalcitrant TV. He had his back to Judith.

She opened her mouth to speak but no words would come. The single drop of blood dripped onto the sheet beside her, blossoming on the material. The pain below her navel grew stronger and it felt as if someone had punched her. The flesh suddenly contracted then rose an inch or two, rising and falling almost rhythmically.

She threw back the covers and finally, Parker *did* turn round.

He saw the blood, saw the skin on Judith's abdomen stretching and contracting, saw her naked body trembling.

She tensed for immeasurable seconds, her entire body stiff then, with a gasp, she crumpled. He dashed for the phone but she stopped him.

"Judith, for Christ's sake. . ." he said, fear in his voice.

"The pain's stopped," she told him, her voice quivering.

She reached for a tissue and wiped away the blood from her belly. "I'm all right."

He slammed the receiver down.

"All right," he shouted. "It's that fucking abortion. I told you not to have it. I'm getting a doctor, now." He reached for the receiver once more and dialled.

She pressed her abdomen once more but there was no pain. Parker was speaking to someone now, telling them that it was urgent but his words didn't seem to register with her. The blood in her navel had congealed into a sticky red syrup which she wiped away. Parker slammed the phone down and told her that the doctor was on his way.

Outside, another shaft of lightning ripped across the sky, followed a second later by a clap of thunder which threatened to bring the house down around their heads.

They both sat in stunned silence, waiting.

Sixteen

Even in the deep gloom inside the hut, Harold could make out his mother's features. Her skin was peeling away, mottled green in places where it had turned gangrenous. Her hair hung in loose, flame-seared strands, blackened wisps against the pale pink of her scalp. When she opened her mouth no sound came forth, just a swollen blackened tongue which dripped dark fluid over her scorched lips. She moved towards him, her own putrefying odour almost palpable, wrapping itself around his throat like obscene tentacles.

As her stench filled his nostrils, Harold screamed and screamed. . .

He awoke beating at his pillow, the covers thrown off. His body was soaked in sweat and his throat felt raw from screaming. Gradually he realized that it had been yet another dream.

Someone was pounding on the door of his hut.

Harold uttered a small moan of fear then, as he saw the murky daylight flooding through the window, he found the courage to get to his feet. He padded across to the door.

"Who is it?" he called.

"Harold are you all right?" the voice from the other side asked and, after a moment or two, he recognised it. Harold unlocked the door and pulled it open to find Winston Greaves standing there. The senior porter was spattered with rain which was still falling from the banks of grey cloud overhead. He looked Harold up and down, noticing how pale the unscarred side of his face looked. There were deep pits beneath both his eyes and his hair was plastered to his head with sweat.

"Are you OK?" asked Greaves, stepping inside.

Harold nodded.

"Do you know what the time is?" Greaves asked him.

He shook his head, sitting down on the edge of the bed.

"It's after nine o'clock," the coloured porter told him. "You should have been on duty over an hour ago. I thought you were ill or something."

"I'm sorry," said Harold, apologetically. "I didn't sleep very well last night." He got to his feet. "If you give me a minute, I'll get ready."

"If you don't feel well, I can get one of the doctors to come over and have a look at you. You. . ."

Harold cut him short.

"No. I'll be all right. I'm just tired," he explained.

Greaves nodded and sat down on one of the rickety old wooden chairs while Harold padded into the small room which housed the chemical toilet. He emerged a moment later and, after splashing his face with water from the cold tap in the kitchen, he began dressing. The muddy clothes which he'd worn the previous night to bury the foetus were pushed out of sight beneath the bed. Finally, he pulled on his overall and together he and Greaves began the walk across the open ground towards the main building. Harold looked up at the sky which still promised rain but now was falling in small droplets, quite different from the downpour of the previous night.

"I hear there was a blackout last night," said Greaves.

Harold nodded.

"It's the worst storm I can remember," Greaves confessed. "Still, the electricity company should have everything fixed by this afternoon. I heard that one of the cables was brought down." He stopped and looked behind him towards the field where the damaged pylon was. "They're trying to fix it up now."

Harold spun round and his eye bulged. There were indeed men moving about in the field near to the pylon, some climbing on it, others using ladders to reach inaccessible areas. There was even a small crane crawling through the mud.

"Oh my God," he murmured, softly.

The men were all around the pylon. They were working in *that* field.

Near to the grave.

Harold swallowed hard. If they should find it. . .

Greaves walked on but Harold remained where he was, his gaze fixed worriedly on the men in dark blue overalls who swarmed over the pylon in their efforts to repair it. He saw the crane, the large white and blue van parked nearby and he began to tremble. They would find it. They must do. But, it was at least fifty yards from the base of the pylon he told himself. It should be relatively safe. His ready-made assurances did not have the desired effect and he wondered if the rain might have washed the shallow covering of soil right off exposing the bodies beneath. He hurried on to join Greaves, his mind in a turmoil.

He spent most of the day thinking about the men in that field, expecting at any time one of them to walk into the hospital and tell of the grave that they'd discovered. Then his secret would be there for all to see. His crime would be exposed. For that was what they would call it. A crime. Not understanding, they would punish him, they would not want to listen to his reasons. They would not be able to comprehend the thought behind his actions.

Every chance he got, he stole a look at them, to see how far their work was progressing. To see if they had stumbled on the grave. He could eat no lunch, so knotted with fear was his stomach. He spent his entire break standing in the rain outside watching the blue-clad men repairing the damage to the pylon.

When, at three fifteen that afternoon, they finally left, Harold breathed an audible sigh of relief.

Seventeen

Harold pulled on his shirt, wincing when he felt the damp material touch his skin. He hadn't had time to wash the garment since the previous night and it was still stiff with dried mud. So were the trousers which he put on but, after a moment or two, he grew to accept the cloying feel of the odorous cloth against his skin. He pulled on his coat and tucked the torch into one pocket – he'd taken it from a store-room in the hospital earlier in the day. The fifty watt bulb hung above him. He hadn't put it on since returning to the hut over four hours ago and the hands on his alarm clock had crawled around to 12.26 a.m. Harold knew that he was taking a small risk leaving the hut earlier than usual but, he reasoned, his business in the muddy quagmire was more important than usual and, besides, if someone did see him it would be easy enough to explain away the fact that he was out that late. Also, he was carrying nothing with him tonight. Nothing, that was, except his fear. He realized that the men from the electricity company who had repaired the downed power line could not have discovered the grave of foetuses, he would have known about it by now. However, he was worried that the driving rain might have disturbed the top soil which covered the grave.

He folded the blanket up as small as he could and tucked it inside his coat. It was to be used as an extra covering on the grave. He would drape it over the eight bodies interred there and then build more layers of earth over the blanket, ensuring once and for all that they were hidden from prying eyes. It was cold but, despite that, Harold could feel the beads of perspiration on his forehead and between his shoulder blades. He swallowed hard, checked everything one final time and then headed for the door of the hut.

Harold peered out, making sure that there was no one about, then he slipped around the side of the small building and was swallowed up in the shadows which formed so thickly at its rear. He walked to the low barbed wire fence and clambered over it, nearly slipping on some damp grass at the top of the ridge. It had stopped raining and the night air smelt crisp, filled with the aroma of wet grass. His hot breath formed small white clouds every time he exhaled and Harold was pleased when he finally reached the bottom of the ridge, almost slipping half way down. He walked across to the pylon and felt his feet sinking into the mud at its base – a testament to the comings and goings of men and machinery earlier in the day. He flicked on the torch and shone it over the ground, seeing the outline of heavy footprints in the soft soil.

There was not enough natural light for him to find his way so he kept the torch on.

Above him, the sky was a patchwork of clouds and stars. It looked like a canopy of soggy black velvet that someone had thrown a handful of sequins onto. There was a slight breeze, cold and just strong enough to send the clouds rolling across the dark backdrop.

Harold shone the torch down once more and saw where the fallen power cable had scorched the earth over a wide area. He didn't know how many volts each of those massive overhead wires carried but it certainly had done some damage. The blackened grass and mud seemed to extend as far as thirty yards, perhaps more. He could pick out the tracks of the crane in the mud too and, close by, someone had dropped an empty cigarette packet. He kicked it aimlessly with the toe of his shoe and walked on, the breath now rasping in his throat. He was very close to the grave.

The boot marks and crane tracks ended abruptly and Harold realized that the men had not gone anywhere near to the hole. He moved on, slowing his pace somewhat. He sucked in a shaking breath, the frosty air making his mouth and the back of his throat even drier. He tried to swallow but couldn't. It felt as if his heart was trying to smash its way through his ribcage. He played the powerful torch beam over the area ahead of him, his boots creaking on the soft mud as he advanced.

Something pale gleamed in the shaft of light and Harold held the torch on it, moving forward with even more deliberate steps until he was at the spot which he knew so well.

"Oh God," he croaked.

The bulbous head of one of the foetuses had been exposed when the constant rain had washed away the covering of earth. As Harold had feared, the top soil had been almost completely eroded and, as he shone the torch over the length of the grave, he saw that more of the tiny creatures lay virtually in the open, only the tiniest covering of mud hid them from view. He scratched his head in puzzlement. Even if the men from the electricity company hadn't actually come as far as this, surely, he reasoned, they could not have avoided seeing the exposed bodies? The grass round about, what remained of it, was blackened so the cable had discharged its power into this part of the field too. How could they have missed the small grave? However, the important thing was that he was still undiscovered. He knelt, and scooped up a handful of wet earth, ready to cover the corpses once again.

But, looking down at the vile array of abortions which lay before him, something nagged at the back of his mind. He dropped the handful of soggy muck and frowned. It was something about the position of the creatures. Harold had buried them in a straight line and yet, three, perhaps more, were lying sideways now. One even lay spread-eagled across one of its unfortunate companions. The driving rain would have been enough to wash away the top soil but not to move the position of the foetuses. Had the men from the electricity board found them? Had he been reported? His mind suddenly began to race, his heart beat even faster. It would take maybe a day or two for the people at the hospital to discover that *he* was responsible. He would not know immediately that he had been found out. He began to shudder with cold and fear. What would they do to him? He clenched his fists, his confused mind searching for some other answer. *Any* other answer. Perhaps animals had disturbed the grave. A fox? A badger perhaps? He picked up his torch and shone it over the nearest foetus, inspecting the small body for damage. The arms, the legs, the body were all untouched. Harold leaned closer, casting furtive eyes over the head. It looked swollen, mottled red and black in places, it appeared like a huge festering sore. The tiny mouth was open, pieces of mud clogging it. Harold reached forward with one shaking finger and brushed the muck away. The body looked so limp, not rigored as would be expected, but soft and malleable. Harold shone the torch close to it, prodding the skin with his fingers, mildly disgusted by its slimy softness. He was breathing hard now but his fear had been replaced, to some degree, by an appalling kind of curiosity. He prodded the tiny body with his fingers, even touching the torn, putrescent umbilicus for a second before returning his attention to its face. The stench which rose from the grave was almost overpowering, a cloying odour of decay which couldn't even be driven away by the fresh breeze which sprang up but Harold didn't seem to notice it. He shone the torch over the other bodies, some of which were in an advanced state of decomposition. Harold looked on them with a feeling akin to pity and, for long moments, he crouched in the mud gazing at the bodies, then, he took the blanket from his coat and laid it beside him. He decided to lay the foetuses back in their original position before completing the burial so he lifted the one nearest to him and placed it gently between two smaller specimens, one of which had already had its sightless eyes devoured by worms. Harold shuddered and hurried to complete his task. The smell, which he had not noticed before, suddenly seemed to be unbearable to him, filling his nostrils and making his head ache.

Each foetus he touched felt similarly cold and soft, the touch of their flesh on his fingers making him quiver violently. But, nevertheless, he completed his task, finally reaching for the body which he had first inspected. Puzzled once more by its position in the grave, Harold lifted it gently in order to replace it in the original space he had made for it. It seemed heavier than the rest and he guessed that it must have been aborted at a much later stage than the others. He lowered it gently into place and shone his torch over it one last time.

The foetus opened its eyes.

Harold's body stiffened, his hand almost crushing the torch. It was as if thousands of volts of electricity were being pumped through him, the shock making him rigid. His single good eye bulged madly in the socket, he shook his head gently from side to side.

The foetus moved one arm, raising it slowly, as if soliciting help and Harold heard a low sucking sound as its mouth opened. A blob of black fluid appeared on its lip and trickled down its chin. The tiny chest heaved once then settled into a more rhythmic motion.

He kept the torch aimed at the thing, his entire body shaking uncontrollably.

To his left there was another low, liquid, noise which reminded him of asthmatic breathing only it was thicker, more mucoid and Harold swung the torch beam around. He began to mouth silent words as he saw a second foetus slithering awkwardly in the sticky ooze.

It was smaller than the first one, its umbilicus moving tentacle-like, as it struggled in the slime.

Harold felt his heart beginning to pound. He felt as though his head were swelling. The execrable stench filled his nostrils, hanging in the air like an almost palpable cloud of corruption. He dropped the torch but it fell to the ground with its light pointing into the grave and, in that light, Harold saw a third creature begin to move. It rolled onto its side, yellowish fluid so viscous it was almost jellied, oozing from the hole in its belly where the umbilicus should have been. Part of its body was blackened and rotted, one arm mottled, two of the tiny stubby fingers missing. It clambered up and fixed Harold in a hypnotic gaze, the twin black orbs which were its eyes holding him immobile.

He pressed both hands to his head and screamed but no sound would come. His mouth was stretched open as far as it would go, the shriek of terror and revulsion waiting to be released but he could not summon it. That ultimate exclamation of disgust remained deep within him. He tried to stand, to get away but his knees buckled and he fell face down in the mud, close to the edge of the grave, watching helplessly as the three living foetuses crawled towards him. He felt as if someone had laid a huge weight on his body, for when he tried to rise again he felt an intolerable pressure pinning him down as surely as if he'd been skewered to the mud with a long knife. He could only watch, mesmerized, as the trio of abominations drew closer to him. He was babbling incoherently now, his words unintelligible even to himself. His mind struggled to accept what his eye saw but could not, *would* not. He fought against the pressure above him and managed to rise, dragging himself to his knees, eyes still locked on the monstrosities before him.

"No," he murmured, his entire body trembling.

The leading foetus had reached the edge of the grave and was trying to crawl up the side.

Harold shook his head violently. He heard voices.

Was there someone else with him?

He spun round, searching for the source of the voice.

Had someone discovered him?

"Who's there?" he gasped, his gaze still riveted to the trio of creatures beneath him.

Again the voice came only this time it was joined by another, and another. Soft, hissing words which he could barely understand seemed to flicker inside his head like a dying candle flame. He stopped trying to back away and watched the three foetuses writhing in the grave. He tried to tell himself that he would awake in a moment, safe, in his hut. He would leave this nightmare behind him, wake up to find that it had all been a figment of his imagination.

He bowed his head and tears began to flood down his cheek. Kneeling like some kind of penitent, he remained where he was, his body racked by sobs, his vision blurring as he cried like a child. Gradually, the spasms subsided and he stared down at the three creatures which lay in the sticky mud, pinned in their collective gaze. Then, very slowly, he unrolled the blanket and lifted the first of them out, putting it gently onto the soft material. He repeated the procedure with the other two. They lay before him, grotesque parodies of human babies – living nightmares. The third moved slightly and Harold reached forward and wiped some of the thick yellow discharge from its belly, rubbing his hand clean on the wet earth.

"Yes, the grave," he said, nodding blankly, as if speaking to some invisible companion. He began scraping huge clods of reeking soil onto the other five bodies in the grave, sweating with the exertion. It took him nearly half an hour to fill it in then he turned back to the three creatures who lay on the blanket.

"I will find you shelter," he said. He smiled crookedly. "Gordon." He looked down at them.

"Gordon."

The word echoed inside his head, swirling around in a fog of confusion that seemed to be thickening by the second. A mist made of nightmares from which there was to be no escape.

Harold sat on the edge of his bed, looking down at the three foetuses on the blanket before him. He had left the light off in the hut and, in the darkness, the hands of his clock glowed dully. Harold noted that it was approaching 2.23 a.m. His head was throbbing and his body felt stiff, every muscle crying out for rest but he could only sit. Sit and stare at these. . .

He didn't even know what they were. He realized that they were abortions but, more than that. . . The thought trailed off once more.

Words. Soft, sibilant, came hissing inside his head once more and Harold wondered if he was imagining them. Were they really his own thoughts? He swallowed hard. The voices seemed more distinct now, as if they were speaking directly to him.

He nodded in response to the silent question.

"Yes," he said, softly. "I am afraid of you."

A pause.

"Because I don't know what you are." If not for the fact that he was constantly pulling at the flesh on the back of his right hand, he might still have thought that this was some horrendous nightmare from which he would be hurled screaming at any second, to wake up sweating and trembling in his bed with the daylight streaming in through his window. As it was, all he heard were the voices again, echoing, resonating like whispers in a cave.

He gave answers to unspoken questions.

"Food? What can *I* do?"

Hissing inside his head.

Harold shook his head and stood up.

"I can't."

The whispers became louder.

"No." He backed off until suddenly he felt a searing pain explode inside his head. White light danced before his eyes and he felt something warm and wet trickle from his nostril. He put a finger to the orifice, withdrawing it to see dark fluid on the tip. The blood looked black in the darkness. Harold swayed drunkenly. It felt as if someone had clamped a vice on his skull and were twisting the screw as tightly as possible.

"All right," he yelled and the pain receded. He leant against the nearest wall, panting. "Tell me how," he sobbed.

The words came slowly and, at first he recoiled again but remembrance of the awful pain when he disobeyed forced him to listen. Tears streaming down his face, he sat motionless, hands clasped together, head bowed until finally he got to his feet and walked into the tiny kitchen. He pulled open one of the rotting wooden drawers and rummaged through until he found a butcher's knife. It was a heavy bladed implement, rusty in places, its black handle missing a screw but, as Harold pressed his thumb to the cutting edge he found that it was still wickedly sharp. He shambled back into the other room and sat down on the bed, the knife held in one unsteady hand. The ghostly voices spoke to him once more and he put down the vicious blade in order to undo his shirt. As each successive button was unfastened, he could hear the soft sucking sounds which the foetuses made echoing around the room. They moved only occasionally on the blanket but, all the while, their black glistening eyes were fixed upon him. One of them, the smallest of the trio was gurgling thickly, a stream of fluid spilling from its mouth which it kept opening and closing rather like a goldfish. Harold looked at it and then across at the knife.

Perhaps he should kill them now, destroy these foul things. Cut. . .

He groaned once more as a white hot burst of agony seared his brain. He imagined his head swelling then exploding into a thousand sticky pieces. He undid the final button and pulled his shirt off then, with shaking hands, he reached for the long bladed knife. His own body looked pale in the gloom and his skin was puckered into goose-pimples. He held the knife before him, looking at the wicked weapon then, with infinite care, almost without looking, he pressed the sharp edge to his chest. It felt cold and he held it there for what seemed like an eternity then, with one swift movement, he drew it across his pectoral muscle, opening the flesh, slicing through veins. He moaned in pain, felt the hot bile bubbling up in his throat but he fought it back, hacking at himself once more until a bright stream of blood gushed from the torn breast. His second cut was more random and he was fortunate not to carve his left nipple off. His chest felt as if it were on fire and he swayed for a second, some of his blood splashing the bedclothes and, all the time, the voices inside his head urged him on.

He bent forward and lifted the first of the foetuses, cradling it in his arms for long seconds, allowing some of his blood to drip onto the tiny body, then he raised it to his torn chest. He felt its jellied, putrescent flesh in his hands, he smelt the stench which it gave off and he allowed it to press its bulbous head against his wounds. Harold was shaking uncontrollably as he felt the thing's lips on his chest, probing the ragged edges of the twin gashes, burying its small mouth inside the bleeding maw as it swallowed his life fluid. It bucked violently in his hands and he felt that familiar wave of sickness sweeping over him again but the pain in his chest kept him conscious. Tears streamed down his face, dripping from his chin to mingle with his blood and the odorous fluid which the foetus itself seemed to exude.

He heard the voice deep within the darkest recesses of his mind and he laid the creature back on the cover where it lay still, its face slick with blood, its body bloated and immobile.

He repeated the procedure with the second monstrosity, opening a third wound on the other breast to satiate it. He moaned once more, feeling the thing grip his flesh with stubby fingers as it pressed itself tightly to the weeping wound. It too signalled its satisfaction and Harold completed the vile ritual by lifting the third foetus to his torn pectoral.

When the task was over, Harold got to his feet, unhindered, and staggered into the kitchen. He hung over the sink and vomited violently, remaining there for a long time afterwards, finally spinning both taps and washing the foul mess down the plug-hole. Then he sponged down his chest wounds with a wet towel, pressing it hard against the wounds in an effort to seal them. When he withdrew it, the material was stained orange and red. He was bruised black in some places where the creatures had fed. Harold held the towel in place until he was satisfied that the bleeding had stopped then he dried himself and sought out some adhesive strip which he had in the bedside cabinet. He carefully cut some lengths of it and placed it delicately over the wounds. It still felt as if someone were using a blow torch on his chest but the pain was diminishing somewhat.

Bleary eyed, he looked down at the three abortions.

Where the hell was he going to hide them?

He inhaled deeply, wincing as his torso began to throb once more, looking around for a suitable place. There seemed to be just one.

There was a large cupboard beneath the sink which appeared to be ideal. He carried them, one by one into the kitchen and knelt before the cupboard door, a sliding effort with a metal handle.

"I have to hide you," he said. "Someone might come here."

Silent questions.

He nodded, pulling open the door. A strong odour of mildew wafted out, taking Harold's breath away momentarily. He looked inside and saw that, but for a couple of old saucepans and a plastic bucket, the cupboard was empty. He hastily removed the offending articles, pushing them to one side. A silver-fish scurried from the dark confines of the enclosure and Harold crushed it beneath his foot, gazing down at the shapeless mess for a second before lifting the blanket into the cupboard. This done, he carefully laid the foetus' onto it, finally pulling it over them. He gazed into the darkness, heard the vile mewling sounds which they made, the soft mucoid snortings and gurglings and he closed his eyes. Then, the voices came to him again, soft but full of menace. Full of power. He slid the cupboard door shut and stumbled back into the other room where he collapsed on the bed. Immediately, he was overcome with the welcome oblivion of unconsciousness but whether it was sleep or a blackout he was never to know. Either way, he sprawled on the blood-speckled bed, the odour of the creatures still strong in the air.

Outside, the rain had begun to fall again, pattering against the window, thrown by the wind which rattled the glass in its frame. Inside, the steady ticking of the clock was the only sound.

It was 3.17 a.m.

Part Two

". . . death could drop from the dark
As easily as song."
– Isaac Rosenberg

Eighteen

Inspector Lou Randall pushed two coins into the vending machine at the end of the corridor and pressed one of the buttons. A plastic cup dropped down but no tea followed it. Randall muttered something to himself and pressed the reject button but the machine had swallowed his money and obviously didn't intend parting with it. The Inspector swore and kicked the recalcitrant contraption, smiling when he saw a stream of tea suddenly gush forth into the waiting cup. Grinning, he retrieved the tea and retreated back to his office, closing the door behind him.

He crossed to his desk and sat down, lighting up a cigarette before flipping open the first of half a dozen files spread on the work-top.

They were statements from four residents of Exham, all of whom claimed to have seen Paul Harvey in the past two days. Randall read each one slowly, shaking his head every now and then. Every one gave a different description and at least two of the sightings had happened at exactly the same time but on different sides of town. He closed the file and dropped it amongst the others. He sat back in his chair, the plastic beaker in one hand, the cigarette in the other. His office was already full of smoke and an empty packet of Rothmans lay at his elbow. He put down his tea and massaged the bridge of his nose between thumb and forefinger, trying to assess what little he knew of the investigation so far.

He ticked the items off mentally, as if striking them from some kind of psychological shopping list.

1. Harvey escaped six weeks ago.
2. Four sightings so far, all unsubstantiated.
3. All possible hiding places searched.

Randall sat forward in his chair. If the escaped prisoner *was* in or around Exham then where the hell was he hiding? He reached for a green file and opened it. It was a psychiatric report on Harvey, something which the Inspector had read before but now scanned yet again in an effort to glean some insight into the man he was hunting.

Harvey was dangerous – there was no doubt about that – but, as far as he could tell, the man was no idiot. A number of tests had been carried out on him by the prison psychiatrist. The results showed that he was prone to bouts of manic depression. His IQ was below average, his faculties not quite spot on but he wasn't crazy. That was what made him more dangerous, thought Randall. Harvey was unpredictable.

Randall shut the file and closed his eyes for a moment. So far no one had been harmed and the Inspector was becoming more and more convinced that the prisoner was nowhere near the town. Nevertheless, somewhere, nagging at the back of his mind was the conviction that eventually he would meet Paul Harvey face to face and it was a prospect he did not relish.

Lynn Tyler hauled herself out of bed, wincing slightly at the pain from her abdomen. She straightened up and the pain receded. The doctors had told her to expect a little discomfort after the abortion and, after all, she had only been home for a week. She stood up and looked down at her pale body, noticing how her stomach had begun to fill out. She was surprised at this, expecting that it would flatten after the operation. She drew in a breath and held it, pulling in her belly for a moment. It didn't flop forward when she exhaled, the skin remained taut across her pelvis and stomach and she ran both hands over it. It felt hot, as if she had been standing next to a radiator and Lynn pressed the tight skin cautiously, puzzled by its feel. There was no pain, just the peculiar sensation of heat. She sat down on the edge of the bed once more, one leg hooked beneath her, both hands still pressed to her belly. She lay back, letting her hands slip to her sides and, gradually, the burning seemed to disappear. When she replaced her hands she felt only the familiar coolness of her skin. She gazed at the ceiling, tracing the many cracks, her thoughts rerunning the events of the last couple of weeks, as if she were rewinding a piece of cine-film – with each frame a memory.

She thought of how happy she'd been when she first discovered she was pregnant but of her fear at telling Chris. And how well that fear had been founded. She could still remember that morning he walked out on her, the morning she had decided to have the abortion.

As she lay there, a feeling of bitterness swept through her. Not only had she lost Chris, the one man she had ever loved, she had also lost the child she wanted. She had been forced out of necessity to have the abortion, knowing she would never be able to bring up a child alone.

The tears came suddenly and unexpectedly and she rolled onto her stomach in an effort to stifle them in the pillow. She wanted to forget him, tell him to fuck off, that she didn't need him. She wanted to yell it in his face. Tell him that there were plenty more men around. Her mind was in a turmoil and, as she rolled back onto her side, the tears dripped onto the sheets and soaked into the material. She wiped them away, smearing her mascara, wincing slightly when she felt the peculiar burning sensation return, the skin stretching across her stomach and pelvis until it seemed it would tear.

She gasped at the stab of pain below her navel.

But, as quickly as it had come, it vanished and, tentatively, Lynn Tyler got to her feet, her hands gently stroking her belly.

There was no more discomfort.

She crossed to the wardrobe and began to dress.

Nineteen

Harold leant on the edge of the sink and gazed at the pale, ghost-like image which stared back at him from the mirror. There were deep, dark pits beneath both his eyes, his eyelids looked crusted and heavy and, when he exhaled, it came out as a deep sigh. There was no one else in the hospital toilet to see him and, for that, Harold was thankful.

God, how the day had dragged. It seemed more like eight years not eight hours since he'd started work. He'd been in on time and had done his best to disguise the fact that he felt so wretched. The three vicious cuts on his chest ached beneath the plaster and his joints seemed to groan in protest every time he moved.

His efforts to disguise how he *felt* might have been successful but there was no hiding his appearance. He looked, in the tradition of that time-honoured phrase, like death warmed up. He'd only eaten a small lunch and a couple of chocolate biscuits and even they had made him feel sick. His stomach rebelled at each new intrusion and, at one point, he had thought he was going to vomit.

He pulled the plug in the sink and shuffled over to the towel-roll, tugging hard on it to find a clean piece. Then he dried his face and hands, took one last look at his drawn visage and walked out into the corridor.

The wall clock opposite him showed 7.30 p.m. He still had another two hours before he was finished for the day. Harold sighed, thankful, at least, that it was time for a break. He made his way to the lifts and found an empty one. He punched the five button and leant back against the rear wall as the car rose swiftly. He would have preferred to have spent his break alone but Winston Greaves had insisted that he come to the office so that the two of them could talk. As the lift reached five and the doors slid open, Harold decided that talk was the last thing he needed but, nevertheless, he had to keep up appearances as best he could. As he walked towards the door of Greaves's office he felt his legs go weak and, for long seconds, he thought he was going to faint. Thankful that no one was around, he stood still for a moment, supporting himself against a wall. His head was spinning, the floor swimming before him. That ever-present pulse of pain at the back of his neck had now developed into a series of hammer blows to his skull and, once again, he fought back the urge to be sick. Sucking in deep breaths of stale, antiseptic air, he walked on.

Greaves had the kettle on when Harold entered the small office. The coloured porter looked up and smiled and Harold managed a thin grin in return. He sat down heavily, leaning back in the plastic chair. Greaves eyed him appraisingly. He too noticed the pallor, the milkiness of Harold's unscarred skin. The dark rings beneath his eyes looked as if they had been made by soot. The one good eye was bloodshot, the glass one sparkled with its customary unsettling brilliance. It looked all the more incongruous set against the drawn quality of the rest of his face.

Greaves waited for the kettle to boil then made the tea, handing Harold a mug. He watched as his companion struggled to remove the tea bag, scalding his fingers in the hot liquid. Greaves handed him a spoon and Harold finally succeeded in lifting the tiny bag out. He dropped it into a nearby ashtray and sat gazing down into his mug.

"Are you all right, Harold?" asked Greaves, sitting down opposite him.

"Yes."

The answer came a little too quickly, full of mock assurance.

"You look a bit under the weather," Greaves told him. Actually, Harold, he thought, you look half-dead.

"I'm OK," Harold told him, sipping at his tea.

"The job isn't getting you down is it?" Greaves asked. "I mean, I know it can be depressing sometimes."

Harold ran a hand through his hair again.

"I didn't sleep well last night," he confessed.

"That's not the first time is it? Why don't you ask one of the doctors for some sleeping pills?"

Harold shook his head.

"I'll be all right. I've just got a bit of a headache."

"There's nothing worrying you is there?"

Harold looked up.

"Why?" His voice was heavy with suspicion, perhaps a little over-cautious.

Greaves caught the inflection.

"I just asked," he said, smiling, trying to sound calm.

When Harold raised his mug to drink again, his hands were shaking, something which did not go unnoticed by his companion. Greaves regarded him warily over the rim of his own mug. Harold certainly looked rough, he thought, and he was unusually jumpy. Still, if he hadn't had any sleep. . .

He sat up as Harold swayed uncertainly in the chair.

The coloured porter was on his feet in an instant,

moving around the desk towards his companion. Harold put one hand to his head and leant forward, taking the weight on his other elbow.

"Harold," said Greaves.

The older man waved him back.

"I'll be all right," he said. "I just felt faint."

Harold was shaking all over and a fine film of perspiration had greased his skin. He sucked in deep lungfuls of air and gradually straightened up but Greaves remained where he was.

"I think it might be best if you went back to your hut for half an hour or so, just for a lay down," the coloured porter said. "And while you're there, get something to eat. That's half of your trouble, you don't eat enough." He put out a hand which Harold grasped, allowing himself to be helped up.

"Come on," said Greaves. "I'll help you."

Together, the two of them made their way to the lift, descending to the ground floor. They headed for the main entrance without Harold speaking a solitary word. He stopped twice, worried that he was going to pass out but Greaves supported him. The senior porter suggested they see a doctor but Harold resisted the offer with a determination bordering on panic. So, slowly, they made their way out of the main building and towards the stretch of grass which led to Harold's hut. As they drew closer, perhaps a hundred yards from the flimsy structure, the older man pulled away and stood, swaying uncertainly, his good eye looking as glazed as the false one.

"I'm all right now," he said.

Greaves looked puzzled.

"I'll just see you inside," he said. "Make sure –"

Harold cut him short.

"No."

There was a note of near pleading in the word and Greaves wrinkled his brow.

"Don't come inside," said Harold, then he managed a weak smile. "I'm OK. Really."

Greaves did not move but he remained unconvinced.

"I'll be back on the ward at quarter past eight," Harold promised, nodding vigorously. "Quarter past eight."

He turned and headed for the hut, tottering drunkenly until he finally reached the hut. Greaves watched him through the darkness his eyes fixed to the small dwelling, waiting for the light to be put on inside. The hut remained in darkness. The coloured porter stroked his chin thoughtfully. Perhaps he should go and check on Harold anyway.

He began walking towards the hut.

Less than ten yards further on, he slowed his pace then finally stopped. No, he told himself, Harold must be allowed some privacy and, after all, he had promised to be back at work in less than forty-five minutes. Greaves stood a moment longer, his eyes riveted to the hut. Still no light came on. The senior porter sucked in a deep breath then turned and headed back towards the main entrance. His mind was full of unanswered questions the main one being, why would Harold not let him inside the hut? What was he hiding? Greaves administered a mental rebuke for himself. Harold probably had nothing to hide. He was probably just ashamed of the fact that the hut was a bit of a shambles. Nevertheless, as he reached the main entrance to the hospital, Greaves looked round once more, expecting to see a light coming from the hut and he was mildly disturbed when he saw nothing.

His curiosity was aroused and, as he made his way back up to his office, he became more and more convinced that Harold was hiding something. Perhaps he'd been stealing? Greaves swiftly dismissed that particular notion. For one thing there was nothing worth nicking in the hospital and, secondly, Harold probably wouldn't have the intelligence to pass for a thief. It was probably a quite innocent reason, Greaves told himself as he reached his office. He sat down and sipped his tea which was now stone cold. He put the kettle on to make a fresh cup, glancing at his watch.

It was 7.46. Harold would be back in half an hour.

Greaves waited for the kettle to boil.

Harold stood in the darkness, his back to the door of the hut, his eyes closed. He finally crept across to the window and, squinting out, he could see Greaves as he stood and watched and then finally turned and left. Harold had breathed an audible sigh of relief at that point. He didn't reach for the light switch but moved furtively in the gloom, making his way into the kitchen. He stood staring at the cupboard door for long seconds, the cupboard beneath the sink with its sliding door. With a shaking hand he reached out to open it then swiftly withdrew, the breath catching in his throat. The cuts on his chest began to throb and he took a step backward.

The hissing began.

He placed both hands to his temples as his headache seemed to intensify, the voices fluttering inside his mind like dialogue from a half remembered dream.

He moved towards the door.

Harold knelt and opened it, sliding the cupboard opening back an inch at a time, recoiling from the rancid odour of mildew and something stronger. Something more pungent and cloying. The stench of decay. It wafted out of the cupboard in an almost visible cloud making Harold cough.

He had covered the three foetuses with the blanket and now he could see their dark shapes moving slowly beneath the material.

Words came into his head, words which he had heard before. Mutterings and commands which he knew he must obey and which, now, he found himself wanting to obey.

The kitchen knife was still lying beside the sink, its blade dull with rust and dried blood and Harold's groping hands closed around the handle. He swallowed hard, listening to the words which whirled around inside his head, making him dizzy. His ears were buzzing and he was finding it difficult to focus on the three writhing shapes beneath the blanket but, finally, the feeling diminished somewhat and he reached for the loose corner of the material, pulling it back to expose the trio of creatures beneath.

Harold gaped at them, the breath rasping louding in his throat as he inhaled the rank air. At first he thought he was mistaken but, on closer inspection he realized that his first reaction had been correct. There was *no* mistake.

All three of the foetuses were growing.

Twenty

Winston Greaves glanced at his watch, drumming on his desk top with his free hand. It was almost 8.35 p.m. Where the hell was Harold? He had promised to be back on the ward by quarter past eight. Greaves chewed his bottom lip contemplatively. Perhaps the other porter had just returned and gone back to work without letting him know. Greaves pushed the thought to one side. No. Harold would have come up to the office first, to let him know that everything was all right. Greaves stared at the bottom of his own empty mug. Perhaps everything *wasn't* all right. Harold had looked ill, maybe he'd been unable to return to work. He might even need medical attention of some kind.

Greaves sat for five more anxious minutes then he got to his feet and headed out of his office towards the lifts. He reached the ground floor asking a number of other staff members if any of them had seen Harold. None had. Greaves exhaled deeply. Obviously he had not returned to the main building. Not sure whether to be angry or anxious, Greaves headed for the main doors, intent on finding Harold. He must still be in his hut after all. Perhaps he'd just fallen asleep. Was he really ill? These and other thoughts passed through the coloured porter's mind as he crossed the expanse of grass which led to the small dwelling where his companion lived.

There was still no light on in there.

Greaves wondered how Harold would react to his appearing at the hut this way. Would he refuse him entry as he had done earlier? Maybe he *did* have something to hide. If that was the case, Greaves told himself, he would find out what it was.

As he drew nearer the hut he became aware of how quiet it was. The darkness seemed to envelope the tiny hut like a black velvet glove, shutting out all sounds too. Greaves slowed his pace as he approached the door, straining his ears to pick up the slightest hint of movement from inside. It remained as quiet and forbidding as a tomb. For the first time, Greaves became aware of the cold, not just the ever-present chill in the air but a deeper more numbing cold which seemed to seep into his bones. He shuddered and glanced around him. Trees nearby swayed gently in the breeze, the beginnings of a mist swirled in the hollows of the field beyond the hospital grounds.

Greaves knocked hard on the door of the hut.

No response.

He knocked again, tapping his thigh with the flat of his other hand.

Nothing. Just silence. And the cold.

"Harold," he called, knocking again.

This time he knelt and tried to see through the keyhole but it was too dark inside the hut. He clambered to his feet and moved across to the window, cupping both hands over his eyes as he pressed his face to the soiled pane. He narrowed his eyes and could just make out a dark form on the bed. He banged the window but the shape on the bed remained immobile. He returned to the door and twisted the handle.

It was locked.

Perhaps he should go back and get help. For a moment he considered the idea but then decided that he should deal with it himself if possible. He didn't want to get Harold into trouble unnecessarily. Greaves put his hand on the door knob and twisted it again, this time throwing his weight against it. The lock was old and rusted and it came away with relative ease. The subsequent momentum sent Greaves stumbling into the hut itself. He almost fell, only retaining his balance by hanging onto the door. Then he gently pushed it shut behind him, immediately aware of the appalling stench which filled the hut – a pungent, nauseating odour which made him gag. It seemed to have no source but to be permeating the entire hut, oozing from the woodwork like sweat from pores.

He flicked the light switch. The bulb flickered, buzzed irritably then blew out. Greaves fumbled in his overall pocket for his lighter. He flicked it on and held the small flame above his head. It cast a pool of weak orange light and, in that sparse illumination, the porter saw the shape on the bed was Harold.

Greaves crossed to the prone body, his mouth dropping open.

Harold lay on his back, one leg drawn up foot resting

on the bed, the other stretched out so that the heel of his shoe was touching the floor. One arm lay across his stomach whilst the other hung limply at his side. Greaves stepped closer, seeing the dark stains on the floor, on the bedclothes. He realized that it was blood and, as he leant over the older man his foot brushed against Harold's outstretched arm. The knife fell with a dull clatter and Greaves almost shouted aloud. The blade was slick with blood too. There were pieces of plaster lying on the bedside cabinet and some soaking cotton wool. The crimson gore on it looked black in the darkness. But it was Harold himself who gave Greaves the biggest shock. The coloured porter leant as close as he could, staring at the vicious cuts on his companion's chest, one of them still weeping blood. The others were in the process of sealing, their ragged edges held together by congealing gore.

"Oh God," murmured the porter and he reached out to touch Harold's shoulder. He could see the man's torn chest rising and falling but he could solicit no reaction from him. Greaves prised open the unconscious man's eyelids and held the lighter close. Its flame sparkled in the glass orb. The pupil of the good eye contracted. Greaves pressed a tentative index finger to the older man's jugular vein and felt it pumping.

I've got to get help, he thought. He flicked off the lighter and headed towards the door.

Something fell with a crash in the kitchen and Greaves spun round.

"Who's there?" he said.

Silence.

He moved towards the other room, once more flicking the lighter on, using its meagre light as a guide. His own footsteps sounded heavy and conspicuous on the wooden floor as he advanced.

He heard breathing. Faint, mucoid breathing which seemed to grow louder as he paused in the doorway of the kitchen. He held the lighter higher. It was beginning to get hot and he changed hands as his eyes scanned the tiny room. A plate lay shattered close by. There were drops of dark fluid on the enamel of the sink. Greaves crossed to it, his nostrils once more filled with an unbearable carrion stench. He dipped a finger in the dark fluid and sniffed it.

It was blood.

There was more of it on the door of the sliding cupboard opening beneath and Greaves knelt, pulling the door back as far as it would go. A blast of almost palpably rancid air gushed out and he had to fight hard to prevent himself from vomiting. He saw the blanket inside the cupboard, the dried blood caked on it. He reached out to touch it.

The first foetus seemed to roll into view from a darkened corner of the cupboard.

Greaves opened his mouth to scream, his eyes bulging as he saw the monstrosity. It pinned him in a hypnotic stare, its own black eyes glinting with a vile lustre. There was blood around its mouth and on its chest – even on the minute, shrunken genitals.

Greaves tried to back away, the lighter falling from his grasp, but he was unable to tear his horrified gaze away from the foetus's twin black orbs. He saw the second one drag itself into view, its own eyes focusing on him too. He reached back to grip the door jamb in an effort to pull himself away but his hand closed over something soft and jellied. He shrieked and looked down to see the third of the creatures. Greaves had grabbed its arm. He hurriedly pulled his hand away, noticing the trail of blood which the thing had left behind when it had dragged itself from beneath Harold's bed.

He was trapped. Pinned by their gaze, he was a prisoner of his own crippling terror. Now he felt the pain begin to build behind his eyes and at the base of his skull as the three abominations concentrated their fearful powers on him. It felt as if their eyes were burning into his head, like black laser beams they bored through his skull to his brain. He moaned and put both hands to his head in an effort to stop the pain which was growing more intense by the second. He tried to shut his eyes and blot out the insane vision before him but he couldn't and now he felt blood running from his nostrils. Filling his ears. Even his tear ducts seemed to swell and burst until he was weeping crimson. The pain in his head reached unbearable heights. He felt his legs go numb. He opened his mouth to scream but his tongue felt thick and useless, as if it had been injected with novocaine. Blood gurgled in his throat. His hands dropped from his head as he lost the use of them and finally he could only sit and watch, through a haze of red as the three creatures made one more concerted effort against him. Both his temporal arteries seemed to swell, pulsing madly for agonising seconds. His eyes seemed to swell and protrude as if pushed from the inside. But, somehow, Greaves managed to roll onto his belly and, using his legs as a means of propulsion, he pushed himself away from these nameless monstrosities. Into the other room he crawled, past the still motionless form of Harold, until he reached the door, the pain now reaching heights beyond endurance. Greaves managed to haul himself upright and, with a despairing moan, he flung the door open and staggered out, tottering drunkenly towards the beckoning lights of the main building.

He was almost there when, in a blinding moment of incredible agony, the veins and arteries inside his brain ruptured with so much force that most of the frontal and temporal lobes were destroyed. Winston Greaves collapsed but his body continued to jerk spasmodically for a few moments even after his death.

His body was found the next morning by an ambulance driver and the autopsy revealed that Greaves had died as the result of a massive cerebral haemorrhage.

Harold took the news of his friend's death badly. So badly that he spent his day off lying in bed but he did not sleep because, all the time, inside his head, the voices whispered.

It was to be a long time before he recovered from the news of Winston's death and the loneliness which he had thought banished now returned with numbing intensity.

Twenty-one

The onset of night brought about contradictory feelings within Paul Harvey. He welcomed it because it hid him and cloaked his furtive excursions from the farm. But he feared it too because it brought memories. Night had, in the past, always been a time of fear for him. The time when his father and mother would fight or when, in later years, he would be dragged from his bed and beaten, forced to bear that reeking stench of stale whisky and tobacco in his face as his father shouted at him.

Harvey hated to be shut in. It was another legacy of his childhood. His bedroom door was always locked from the outside, and this practice continued right up until his father died. There was no chamber pot in his room and, more often than not, he would be forced to urinate out of the window if he awoke during the night. Before he understood that trick he would simply wet the bed or do it into one of the drawers. Consequently, the clothes inside stank most of the time. However, whichever course of action Harvey had taken it had brought savage retribution from his father. During his troubled years at school, Harvey had been quizzed by teachers and taunted by his fellow pupils about the cuts and bruises which he bore almost all the time but, of course, he never dared to divulge the truth of how he sustained them.

His hatred of enclosed places had intensified during his stay in Cornford prison. The fact that he was kept in solitary, for the sake of the other prisoners, made things worse. But now, to a certain extent, he was free to wander the open fields and hillsides of Exham for the first time in his life and, with night now draped across the countryside like a shroud, he did just that.

As he stood at the top of a hill, the lights of the town glittered invitingly below him and Harvey gripped the sickle tightly as he made his way down the incline. An owl hooted close by but Harvey ignored its cry.

The town beckoned and Harvey did not refuse its call. He felt no fear, just a peculiar feeling that was something like exhilaration.

The woods on the outskirts of town swallowed him up.

Twenty-two

Ian Logan pulled up the zip on his leather jacket and shivered. He stood beneath the swaying sign of "The Black Swan", fumbling in his pocket for the packet of Marlboro and a box of matches. Thanks to the gusting wind, it took him three attempts to light the fag but finally he succeeded and, hands dug deep into his pockets, he started walking.

Other staff members, another barman included, were also leaving and Logan muttered cursory farewells to them. They all seemed to have cars except him and nearly all of them were going in the opposite direction. Even the one vehicle that was going his way sped past without offering him a lift. Logan exhaled deeply, his breath clouding in the night air.

He glanced at his watch and saw that it was approaching 12.15 a.m. He was usually home by half past eleven at the latest. He could imagine Sally's reaction now, almost hear her whinings as he walked in the front door. Moaning that his supper was spoiled, asking him where he'd been. He worked six nights a week, the only other day he spent at home listening to Sally moaning about how he should get a better job so that they could move into a *decent* house.

He decided to take a short-cut. There was bound to be an argument when he got in anyway so he might as well get it over and done with.

He cut down the lane to his left, knowing that he could be home in ten minutes. He quickened his step, the cigarette bouncing up and down between his lips as he walked.

The lane was dimly lit at the best of times but now, with the witching hour twenty minutes old, all but three of the lamps had been extinguished. There was the odd porch light on outside one or two of the cottages but, apart from that, the lane was wreathed in a heavy gloom. Visibility was made all the worse by a writhing mist which seemed to have settled over the fields. Blown by the wind, it seemed to ooze over the hedges like some kind of ethereal sea whose waves moved in slow motion.

Logan glanced at the white-washed cottages as he walked. Each one had its own drive and there was hardly one which did not boast two cars. These private dwellings stood out in marked contrast to the estate on which he lived. It lay a mere few hundred yards down the lane and the staid uniformity of the council houses offered a marked contrast to the gleaming individuality of these expensive properties. Perhaps Sally was right, he thought, it would be nice to live in a place like that. He was contemplating that thought when something moved away to his right.

He glanced round, slowing down only slightly, squinting into the blackness in an attempt to see what had made the sound. He heard a shuffling, scratching noise and, a moment later, a hedgehog scuttled out from beneath one of the hedges and trundled across the lane. Logan smiled to himself as he watched it disappear into one of the gardens opposite. A few yards further on another of the tiny creatures was splattered across the road. Cars sometimes drove down the lane and, obviously, this one had squashed the unfortunate hedgehog. It had been there a long time for, even in the gloom, Logan could see that its flattened remains were stiff, giving it the appearance of a spiky frisbee. He smiled at his analogy and walked on.

There was a farmhouse on the right. Painted black, it was almost invisible in the darkness but, from inside, he could hear the barking of a dog. The bloody thing had gone for him a couple of times in the past and he passed by hurriedly despite the fact that the animal was safely penned in the building. He walked another few yards and came to a rotting wooden stile. Beside it a bent and battered sign declared:

FOOTPATH

The so-called footpath led across a field and came out right opposite his own house. He decided to risk the many cow-pats which littered the field and cross it in an effort to get home quicker. He put his foot on the bottom plank of the stile and hoisted himself up. It creaked ominously under his weight and for a second he thought it was going to collapse but, as nimbly as possible, he swung himself over and landed with a loud plop in the mud on the other side.

"Sod it," he said, aloud, scraping some of the glutinous muck off on the bottom plank. That done, he set off across the field.

The light from the lane diminished to a point where his only guide was the odd light burning in the houses which backed on to the field. It was virtually impossible to see more than fifteen or twenty feet ahead. The crispness of the night air made the smells around him seem all the more prominent and he winced at the strong odour of cow dung. The ground was soft despite the frost and he almost slipped over twice, the second time shooting out a hand to grasp the fence which ran alongside him. He yelped in pain as his groping fingers closed over some barbed wire. Logan stopped dead, fumbling in his trouser pocket for a handkerchief, dabbing at the small cuts and muttering irritably to himself. He reached into his coat pocket for his fags and lit one up, puffing at it for a second before moving on.

The field was separated from the nearest house by a double row of trees, the ground in between each one thick with underbrush. Gorse and blackberry bushes grew in rampant abundance, in many places reaching shoulder height. There was a powerful smell of rotted vegetation in the air and Logan muttered to himself as he walked.

A twig snapped close by and, instinctively, he stepped back, the noise sounding thunderous in the stillness of the night.

His foot sank into something soft and he realized that it wasn't mud.

"Bloody cows," he groaned, shaking his foot.

However, his complaints were cut short when he heard another sound – the low rustling of bushes being parted. Logan squinted into the thick underbrush but he could see nothing. There was a moment's silence then the sound came again, closer this time.

A fox perhaps? Probably another hedgehog.

He swallowed hard and walked on, quickening his step for reasons he himself was not sure of. The other stile which marked the far end of the footpath was less than a hundred yards away and Logan could see the light from a nearby house beckoning him. His feet made squelching sounds in the mud and, as he walked, he glanced towards the trees nearby.

There was a loud scratching sound in the bushes less than two feet from him and he opened his mouth, allowing a small gasp to escape his lips. A sibilant rasping sounded so loud in the stillness and, at last, Logan broke into a run. He kept his eyes firmly fixed on the light ahead of him but it seemed to be a million miles away.

Beside him, the snapping of twigs seemed to grow to deafening proportions and he realized with horror that whatever was in the bushes was keeping pace with him.

His mind sought an explanation. It wanted to find a logical answer but all he could think of was getting to that bloody stile and clambering out of the field.

It was fifty yards away and he was still running, the bushes actually moving beside him now, some pushed over by his invisible companion. He could not bring himself to look for fear of what he might see.

Thirty yards.

The light ahead gleamed brighter and Logan found renewed strength in his legs as, beside him, he heard a low whining sound.

His breath was rasping in his lungs, his mouth dry.

Ten yards and he could see that stile. It was broken

in two places and for that he was grateful, because it meant he wouldn't have to waste time clambering over it.

Five yards.

He almost fell, slipping in another cow-pat. His arms pinwheeled wildly for a moment but he retained his balance. The perspiration was now heavy on his face, his breath harsh and almost painful. His legs ached from running and he could feel his heart hammering against his ribs.

There was a loud screech and a snapping of wood to his right, so close it seemed that it was coming from inside his own head. Something burst from the underbush and flew at him. He tried to scream but couldn't find the breath. He went down, face first into the mud, rolling over quickly, his eyes bulging and terror winding icy tendrils around his throat.

The cat which had leapt out of the bushes at him was already scampering off into the darkness, a mouse held firmly in its jaws.

"Jesus Christ," he gasped, wiping his face and dragging himself to his feet. For long seconds he stood there, trying to regain his composure. He closed his eyes and sucked in a deep breath, holding it for a second before exhaling in an audible sigh of relief. His clothes were splattered with mud and cow dung and he tried to brush it off with his hands. What the hell would Sally say about this? He suddenly found that he could smile and, as he watched the cat loping off across the field, he began to laugh.

"Bloody idiot," he said to himself and, still chuckling, he clambered over the stile.

The dark shape which loomed behind him seemed to grow from the blackness itself. Where gloom and night air had swirled around, there was suddenly something tangible.

Ian Logan thought he had heard a gust of wind but

what he did hear, *all* he heard, was the arc of metal as the weapon descended. The scream was locked in his throat. His eyes bulged wildly as he saw something metallic glinting above him. The dark outline of. . .

Before he had time to discern the shape, his throat was slashed open.

Darkness became eternal night.

Twenty-three

Despite the fact that the sun was shining, there was a harsh chill in the air and Randall shivered involuntarily as he stepped out of the Panda car. He yawned and rubbed a hand across his face. Behind him, the radio crackled and Constable Higgins reached for it; Randall didn't hear what he said because he was already making his way up the small incline that led to the footpath. A piece of rope had been tied across the entrance to the footpath and another uniformed constable stood there. The Inspector recognized him as Chris Fowler, the youngest man on the force. Yet to reach his twenty-sixth birthday, the constable looked fresh-faced and alert and seemed to remind Randall of his own weariness.

"Morning, sir," said Fowler.

Randall smiled thinly. The youngster was still nervous, only having been on the force for six months and he was still somewhat in awe of his superior. The Inspector patted the younger man on the shoulder as he passed. He swung his leg over the piece of rope and started up the narrow path. There were houses on either side of it, both separated from it by high hedges and a welter of rampant wild plants which seemed still to be flourishing despite the onset of the cold weather. Clumps of stinging nettles grew thickly on either side, spilling over onto and into the cracks in the broken concrete in places. Long fingers of blackberry bush clutched at the policeman's jacket as he passed. Muttering irritably to himself, Randall tugged the jacket free and walked on. The heady aroma of wet grass and damp wood filled his nostrils and he reached for a cigarette, lighting it hurriedly as if trying to dispel the fresh natural odour of the countryside. He sucked hard on the filter and walked on.

Ahead of him, tall trees were dotted with black clumps which signalled the presence of crows' nests. Most of them were abandoned by the look of it. Just one solitary bird hovered in the crisp blue sky, as if casting an eye over the proceedings beneath it. Randall glanced at the houses on either side of the path. They were all simple red-brick buildings, with neatly kept gardens and suitably gleaming windows. Nothing seemed out of place on the estate, for every building appeared similarly immaculate.

Opposite him at the moment, in the house across the street, Sally Logan was being comforted by her mother while a perplexed police-woman tried to make some sense out of her hysterical blubberings.

Yes, everything was in its place on the estate. Even the corpse in the field just ahead.

Randall clambered over the wooden stile at the end of the footpath and eased himself down, trying to avoid the glutinous pools of mud. There was a powerful smell of rancid muck and, Randall suspected, cow shit. His suspicions were well founded when he nearly stepped in a pat. He glanced around, at the trees and undergrowth which ran alongside the barbed wire fence marking the boundaries of the field to his right. To his left ran another fence which separated the back gardens of nearby houses from the expanse of field and, straight ahead, he saw a group of three men standing around a blanketed shape. All three turned to face him as he drew nearer.

Two were on his force, Constable Roy Charlton and Sergeant Norman Willis. The third man looked like a midget placed beside the two burly policemen. He nodded a greeting to Randall and the Inspector returned the gesture. Dr Richard Higham stepped back from the shape at his feet and took off his glasses, polishing them enthusiastically with the monogrammed handkerchief he took from his trouser pocket. Randall exhaled deeply, looking down at the grey blanket. All around it, the mud was stained a deep rust colour, the dried blood mingling with the thick, oozing slime. The Inspector sucked hard on his cigarette and blew the smoke out in a long thin stream.

"What have we got?" he asked, his question addressed to no one in particular, his gaze riveted to the shapeless form at his feet. A hand protruded from beneath the blanket, the fingers curled and rigored.

Sergeant Willis handed the inspector a wallet and watched as his superior flipped it open. It contained about twenty pounds, mostly in pound notes, an Access card which bore the embossed name Ian J Logan and a couple of small photos. The photos showed a young woman, the man's wife Randall reasoned, and the other had her smiling out at the camera, a dark-haired man beside her. Randall held the photo before him and then looked down at the shape beneath the blanket.

"We haven't been able to make positive identification yet, guv," said Willis. "But we're pretty sure it's him."

Randall looked puzzled and handed the wallet back to his sergeant.

"What's the problem with identification then?" Randall wanted to know. He looked at Higham who knelt down and took hold of one corner of the blanket.

"The bloke under there is the one in the picture, isn't it?" He took a final drag on his fag.

"You tell me," said the doctor and pulled the material away to expose the corpse.

"Jesus Christ Almighty," murmured Randall, quickly clenching his teeth together, fighting to control the somersaults which his stomach was performing.

Willis lowered his head, Charlton looked away. Only Higham glanced first at Randall and then at the corpse.

The head was missing.

Randall wiped a hand across his face and sucked in several lungfuls of air. His stomach was still churning and he could almost feel the colour drain from his cheeks. Yet, somehow, he managed to keep his gaze fixed on the decapitated body. Blood was caked thickly all down the front of Logan's coat and for many yards around the body. The dark stains were everywhere. Randall felt a bead of perspiration burst onto his forehead as he studied the hacked and torn stump of the neck, a portion of spinal cord visible through the pulped mess. The head had been severed very close to the shoulders and apparently with some difficulty because there were a dozen or more other equally savage gashes at the base of the neck and even on the shoulders themselves. At first sight however, the damage seemed to be confined to that particular area, the blood which covered the body having come from the severed veins and arteries of the neck rather than from any wounds in the torso.

"Put it back," said Randall, motioning to the blanket and Higham duly obliged. The Inspector reached for his cigarettes and hurriedly lit another.

"The ambulance is on its way," Willis told him. "They'll take the body to the hospital."

"How long has he been dead?" asked Randall, looking at the doctor.

"It's difficult to say without the benefit of a thorough

post-mortem," Higham told him. "The pathologist at Fairvale will be able to tell you that more precisely than I can."

"Try guessing," said Randall, taking a puff on his cigarette.

Higham shrugged.

"There's very little surface lividity," he pulled back the blanket once more and indicated the pale hand with its clawed fingers. "Although the massive loss of blood may well be a cause of that." He sighed. "I'd say he'd been dead about eight or nine hours."

Randall looked at his watch. The hands showed 9.06 a.m. He nodded.

"Who found him?" he asked.

"A couple of kids," Willis said. "On their way to school."

"Christ," muttered Randall. "Where are they now?"

Willis explained that both children were being treated for shock at their homes close by.

The Inspector walked around the corpse and ambled over towards the thick bushes close by. A portion of the fence had been broken down and some of the underbrush crushed flat.

"Have you checked this out?" he asked, indicating the overgrown area.

Willis joined him.

"We found footprints in there and in the field over here," he motioned for Randall to follow him. He motioned to the single set of deep indentations in the mud. The Inspector knelt and examined the imprints more closely.

"Looks as if he was running," he said, blowing out another stream of smoke. "But why the hell are there only one set of tracks? It doesn't look as if anyone was chasing him."

"Whoever did it must be a right fucking maniac,"

said Willis. "I mean, who the hell cuts off a bloke's head and. . ."

Randall cut him short.

"By the way, where is the head?" he asked.

"It was taken, guv." The words came out slowly. "We can't find it anywhere."

Randall raised one eyebrow questioningly, his mind suddenly preoccupied with another thought.

"Paul Harvey," he said. "How long is it since he escaped?"

Willis shrugged.

"It must be going on for eight weeks, maybe longer," the sergeant said. "We haven't been able to find hide nor hair of him. He's probably in another part of the country by now, guv." The two men looked at each other for long seconds, the gravity and drift of Randall's suspicions gradually dawning on the older man.

"Get all the cars out. I want this bloody town searched again," Randall said.

"But guvnor, we hunted high and low for him for over a month," Willis protested. "There's no way he can still be in or around Exham."

"I want that search initiated, sergeant." The Inspector paused. "Look, there's been two murders in the history of this town, both committed by Paul Harvey. In the last two days, four people reckon to have seen him. Now we've got this," he pointed to the covered remains of Ian Logan. "Doesn't it seem just a little *too* coincidental?"

Willis shrugged.

"So you reckon Harvey killed Logan?"

"I'd lay money on it and, once the pathologist's report is in, then I'll have an ever clearer picture." The Inspector walked over to the fence. "The footprints you found in the bushes, can you get casts from them?"

Willis shook his head.

"There's too many and, what with the rain last night. . ." He allowed the sentence to trail off.

"Shit," muttered Randall. He turned to see a couple of uniformed men clambering over the stile, one of them carrying a furled stretcher. They made their way across to the body and, under the careful supervision of Higham, lifted the corpse onto the stretcher. Randall watched them as they carried the headless body away, struggling to get back over the stile with their recumbent load.

"I want that coroner's report as soon as it's completed," he said to Willis. "Send one of the men over to the hospital to pick it up as soon as it's ready."

The sergeant nodded. The two men walked back towards the waiting figure of Higham and Charlton, then the four of them made their way back down the footpath behind the two stretcher bearers. The ambulance itself was parked behind one of the Pandas, two of its wheels up on the grass verge to allow cars easy passage in the narrow street. Randall watched as the body was loaded into the back of the vehicle and he could see people peering from their front windows to see what was happening. Some had even opened their front doors and were standing there quite unconcerned in their efforts to get a better view of the proceedings. A handful of people already knew that something sinister had happened in the field. By lunch-time probably the entire street and half the estate would know what was going on, such was people's fascination with the macabre, Randall had found. Anything even slightly out of the ordinary was a source of endless curiosity to them and, in a way, he felt a curious kind of pity for these people whose hum-drum existences were only brightened up by the occasional death or break-in on the estate. A murder would no doubt fuel their coffee time chats for months to come as they speculated and fabricated, each teller adding his or her own particular brand of exaggeration until the tale would eventually become local folk-lore. It was something to be mulled over in years to come – and perhaps even laughed about.

As he climbed wearily into the waiting Panda, the last thing Lou Randall felt like doing was laughing.

The afternoon grew dark early and, at four o'clock, Randall found that he had to switch on the lights in his office at Exham's police station. The building itself was a two storey, red brick edifice about five minutes walk from the centre of the town. Its ground floor comprised an entrance hall, the complaints desk (where Willis now stood doing a crossword) and, beyond that, a type of rest room which doubled as a briefing base for the small force. A flight of steps led down to the basement and its six cells whilst the upper floor was made up of offices and store-rooms. There was a vending machine at the head of the stairs and Randall had managed to coax a cup of luke-warm coffee from it by the simple expedient of kicking it. The bloody machine was playing up and force seemed to be the only thing it responded to. Usually, one of the men popped in his twenty pence and the machine swallowed it gratefully without offering a drink in return. There'd been numerous complaints about it and Randall had decided it was time to get in touch with the manufacturers to see about getting it replaced. However, his thoughts lay on matters other than vending machines as he sat at his desk tapping his blotter with the end of a pencil.

Thoughts raced through his mind at break-neck speed, not allowing him to focus on them.

The murder of Ian Logan. The hunt for Paul Harvey. Even now, men were out searching for him, retracing ground which *he* knew they had already covered in the first early days when the maniac escaped. Randall sipped his coffee but found that it was cold. He winced and put the cup down. Harvey. Harvey. Harvey. The name rolled around in his mind like a loose marble. He thumped his desk irritably and got to his feet. There *had* to be a link between Logan's murder and the escaped maniac. He walked to the window of his office and gazed out. From his vantage point he could see the small railway station which served Exham. A train was just pulling out, heading for London. The people of Exham were lucky in so far as they were able to reach the capital direct. Just a few stops up the line, in Conninford, lay Regional HQ and Randall's superiors. They had already been on to him about his failure to find Harvey, once they discovered that the wanted man had committed a murder they would probably try and nail Randall to their office wall.

He sighed and ran a hand through his hair. He felt so helpless, so frustrated. He looked out over the town.

"Where are you, Harvey?" he muttered, aloud.

He knew he would return home that night, the problem still on his mind. It was always like that now. He had many sleepless nights sifting through problems, unable to divorce work from home any longer. Home. He smiled bitterly at the irony of the word. It wasn't a home any longer, not without Fiona and Lisa to welcome him. The house was still and lifeless without them and had been for the past five years. There was no warmth any more, just the harsh white greeting of the walls and their glass smiles beaming out at him from behind carefully framed photos. When it had happened, Randall had wondered whether or not he would ever recover. It had felt as if something had been torn from inside him, as if a part of his being had ceased to exist, robbed of their love and companionship. He had seen the change in himself over the past few years. He had his work and that was something but it was precious little substitute for a wife and daughter. He had become, against his own will, a cynical and embittered man. To a certain extent the cynicism had always been present – it went with the job someone had once told him. The bitterness, however, and the feeling of desolation which sometimes bordered on anger, was something which he had only recently learned to live with and even, in his worst moments, to nurture. He had allowed the seeds of resentment to blossom into blooms of hatred and fury. He closed his eyes, feeling as lost and lonely as he had ever done in his life.

The knock on the office door brought him back into the real world so fast that the thoughts vanished from his mind.

It was Constable Stuart Reed, a tall, gangling individual with a heavily pitted complexion. He was in his mid-thirties, perhaps two or three years younger than Randall himself. The constable was carrying a thin file.

"Coroner's report on Ian Logan, guv," he announced, waving the file in the air.

"Thanks," said Randall, taking it from him.

The PC turned to leave but the Inspector called to him.

"See if Norman's got any coffee or tea on the go will you?" he asked. "The stuff out of that bloody machine tastes like cat's piss."

Stuart nodded and, smiling, left his superior alone. Randall flipped open the file and found that it contained just three pieces of paper. The coroner's report, another report on the possible murder weapon and a carbon headed:

FAIRVALE HOSPITAL/NOTICE OF DECEASE

All three were signed with the same sweeping signature – *Ronald Potter*.

Potter was chief pathologist at Fairvale, a fact born out by the legend below his name stating that in block letters.

Randall ran a close eye over each of the three documents in turn, pausing here and there to reread certain sections. He fumbled in his jacket pocket for his cigarettes and took out the packet muttering irritably to himself when he found it was empty. He picked up his biro and chewed on the end of that instead. The initial report ran for four pages much of which was comprised of medical jargon but, by the time he put it down, Randall understood how, if not why, Ian Logan had died.

"Eight lateral wounds on the shoulders and neck," he read aloud. "The head was severed by a single edged weapon. Depth of wounds ranges from a quarter of an inch to two and a half inches. No other external damage."

Randall dropped the report onto his desk and leant forward in his seat, glancing at the second sheet. It was a short piece on the possible nature of the murder weapon. Once more he read aloud.

"Traces of rust found in all but one of the wounds." The Inspector drummed softly on the desk top with his fingers.

"Rust," he murmured. He pulled a notepad towards him and scribbled on it:

1. Rusty knife?
2. Strong man (depth of cuts)?
3. No motive?

He pulled at one eyebrow as he considered his own scribblings. It would take someone of extraordinary strength and savagery to sever a man's head without the aid of a serrated tool. The implement appeared to be straight-edged. He checked back over the first report. No, there was no mention of any straight blade. A single edge, yes. He ringed the word knife and drew three question marks beside it. An axe maybe. He quickly dismissed the thought. The wounds would be much deeper if an axe had been used. Even so, the deepest had penetrated two and a half inches. To Randall, that implied the weapon had been used in a swatting not stabbing action. Ian Logan's head had been hacked off, not sliced off. He glanced back over the report and noted that portions of chipped spinal cord had been found, something which further indicated that the head had been cut off by repeated powerful blows. Where the severed appendage was now remained to be seen.

Randall exhaled deeply and sank back in his chair. He tapped on the arm agitatedly, wondering if any of his men had found Paul Harvey yet. It had to be Harvey, he reasoned. Everything pointed to that. The bastard was still in or around Exham somewhere. The Inspector gritted his teeth. He had to be found, even if it meant tearing every house and building down brick by brick. He glanced at the pathologist's report a last time and felt the hairs prickle on the back of his neck. He had the unshakeable feeling that it would not be the last such report he read.

Twenty-four

The staff canteen at Fairvale seemed more than usually crowded and Harold Pierce found that he had to move carefully with his tray of lunch. The mug of tea lurched violently and threatened to spill and, twice, the plate which bore his beans on toast slid dangerously near to the edge of the laminated board. Harold eventually found a seat alone and set his lunch down, almost grateful to have reached the haven of a chair. He sat, exhaling heavily. His stomach was rumbling and he felt hungry but the sight of the food made him feel nauseous. He picked up the knife and fork and held them before him, gazing down at his steaming food but, after a moment or two, he put the cutlery down and contented himself with sipping at his tea.

His head ached, something not helped by the constant hum of conversation which filled the canteen.

All around him, groups of nurses, doctors, porters and other hospital staff chatted and laughed, complained and swore. Harold sat alone, the sea of sound washing over him like an unstoppable current. It had seemed like a loud buzzing at first but, as the day wore on, the buzzing had diminished until it became words. Admittedly they were fuzzy and indistinct, but they were words nevertheless. Harold could not make out what the voices said but they persisted. He closed his eyes and put one hand to his ear as if he thought it possible to pluck these ever-present sounds from inside his head with his finger-tips. But the noises continued, mingling with the cacophony of sound in the canteen.

Harold sipped his tea, wincing as he picked up the mug. He raised it to his lips with effort, almost as if it were made of lead instead of porcelain. The brown liquid tasted bland on his furred tongue.

Someone asked him to move his chair and Harold turned to see a very attractive woman standing behind him. She was dressed in a white coat, open to reveal the full swell of her breasts beneath the blouse she wore. The skirt hugged her slender waist and hips and as Harold looked into her face he found himself captivated by a pair of the brightest blue eyes he'd ever seen. Her thin face was framed by short, brown hair. She was smiling.

For long seconds, Harold gazed at her, realizing from her attire that she was a lady doctor. He woke up to the fact that he was blocking her way and hurriedly pulled his chair in, allowing her through. She smiled again and thanked him, and he watched her as she made her way up to the food counter and began picking things out, talking happily to the women there. Harold touched the scarred side of his face with a shaking hand, his one good eye still riveted to the woman in the white coat. All the other sounds in the canteen seemed to fade as his attention focused exclusively on the doctor. She had carried her tray of food to a table where a number of other doctors sat and he could see her laughing and joking with them. He lowered his head again, once more aware of the pain which gnawed at the back of his neck and head. The voices in his mind continued to mutter and mumble their incomprehensible dialogue and Harold gritted his teeth until his jaw ached.

Finally, he got to his feet but as he did so he felt his knees buckle and he shot out a hand to steady himself. His flailing hand caught the edge of the plate and, before he realized what was happening, it had fallen from the table and smashed on the floor. Those nearby turned to see what had happened and Harold coloured beneath their curious gaze. He looked down at the mess of broken porcelain and baked beans and shrugged apologetically as a large woman in a green overall waddled across the canteen carrying a mop and bucket.

"I'm sorry," mumbled Harold.

"That's all right, love," said the woman. "It happens all the time. But if you didn't like our cooking you could have told us. You didn't have to chuck it all over the floor." She looked up at him, laughing loudly.

Harold swallowed hard, his body trembling.

"I'm sorry," he repeated, not seeing the joke. He hesitated for a moment then turned briskly and made for the exit door, imagining all eyes were on him.

"Who is that man?" asked Dr Maggie Ford, running a hand through her short brown hair. She watched

Harold's rushed departure with a feeling akin to pity. "I don't remember seeing him around the hospital before."

Frederick Parkin drained what was left in his coffee cup and dabbed at the corner of his mouth with a handkerchief, paying particular attention to the thick white moustache that overhung his top lip.

"His name is Pierce as far as I know," he told Maggie. "He was a patient at the old mental hospital until recently."

Maggie nodded slowly.

"I wonder how he got that terrible scar? Poor devil."

"No one seems to know too much about him," Parkin told her. "A fire I would think, looking at it." His tone brightened and he smiled broadly at Maggie. "Why the sudden interest?"

"You know me, Fred," she said. She pointed to her nose and winked. Both of them laughed. "I just feel sorry for him," she added finally. "It must be an awful burden going through life like that. He's got guts to walk about in that state."

"Your compassion is overwhelming, Maggie," said Parkin, good-naturedly. "Sometimes I think you're in the wrong job. You should have been a social worker."

"There's nothing wrong with taking an interest in people," she said, defensively. "After all that's what we're all paid for isn't it?"

Parkin smiled.

"I bow to your superior logic," he said. He got to his feet, said a few words to another man at the end of the table and then made his way out. Maggie sipped her coffee, her mind still unaccountably fixed on Pierce.

She was thirty-two and had been a consultant gynaecologist at Fairvale for the last four years during which time she'd built up an enviable reputation for herself. She had not, as might have been expected, encountered any resentment from her male colleagues – rather the opposite in fact. They had welcomed her eagerly into their midst, impressed by her abilities and also, she thought with a smile, by her female assets. She was the sort of woman who exuded that peculiarly ambiguous demeanour that combined sensuality with innocence; although, with a handful of lovers behind her, Maggie could scarcely claim the word innocent in its literal sense. She was a dedicated woman, single-minded to the point of obsession about her work, something which had caused conflict in many of her relationships but it was not a matter on which she was prepared to compromise. Her mother was always telling her that she should be married but, for Maggie, a career was the only thing which mattered. Men, when she found the time for them, were little more than a brief interlude. At the moment, she lived alone in a small flat about twenty minutes drive from the hospital and she went back to an empty home every night. She said this did not bother her and, on the surface, it appeared that she was telling the truth. However, somewhere inside her was a need which had to be fulfilled and fulfilled by far more than the occasional brief relationship or one night stand. Maggie harboured a brooding fear of loneliness. Some nights, lying alone in her bed she would contemplate the idea of sharing the rest of her years with a partner who cared for *her* above all else. But that thought was always tempered by the fear that she would not be able to reciprocate that bond no matter how hard she wanted to. If many people struggled with the problem of wanting to *be* loved, Maggie Ford was trying to come to terms with the fact that she wanted *to* love. It seemed as if that pleasure were to be denied.

She sat in the canteen and finished her coffee then, finally, she got to her feet. Glancing at her watch she remembered she had a patient to see in ten minutes.

It was almost 1.55 p.m.

Harold pushed the trolley out of the lift into the eerie twilight of the basement. He guided it over the polished floor, past the pathology labs, towards the furnace room. His head felt as if it were swelling and then contracting like some bulbous extension of his pulse. The voices inside his head continued to hiss but they were gaining a startling clarity now. Harold listened to his own footsteps echoing in the corridor as he approached the furnace room, surprised to see that the door was open.

He hesitated, his hands suddenly trembling and he gripped the handrail of the trolley until his knuckles turned white. The noise inside his head grew to a fresh crescendo and it sounded as if someone were holding two gigantic sea-shells against his head such was the roaring in his ears.

He could see the furnace through the open door, its great metal door yawning open to reveal the blistering flames within, competing with the ever-present hum of the generator. Harold's world had become one of noises and he closed his eyes momentarily before walking on towards the room. He could already feel the heat from inside. He bumped the door open with one end of the trolley.

Brian Cayton turned as the door opened. He recognized Harold and smiled.

"Hello, Harold," he said, reaching for a pair of forceps which lay on the trolley which he himself stood next to.

As Harold watched, he saw Cayton grip the forceps and clamp them around the limp and dripping form of a foetus which he took from a receiver. Its head lolled back as if the neck had been snapped and Harold saw blood running from its tiny mouth.

"What are you doing?" he demanded, stepping towards the other porter who was still holding the tiny body before him, trying not to inhale the rank odour which it gave off.

"You know what I'm doing," said Cayton, a little impatiently. "I've just come from pathology."

He held the foetus closer to the hungry mouth of the furnace.

"You're going to burn that child," said Harold, flatly.

The smile faded from Cayton's face.

"Yes. Of course I'm going to burn it." He paused, fixing his gaze on Harold's good eye. "Besides, it isn't a child."

The words inside Harold's tortured mind finally burst through the fog of indecision like diamond bullets.

"Stop it," he said, moving closer.

Cayton raised a hand to ward him off.

"Look, Harold, I know it's not very pleasant but it's got to be done," he said, forcefully. "Christ, you've done it yourself, what's the big deal?"

Harold felt searing pain inside his head and he blundered towards the other porter who stepped back, bewildered. Then, suddenly, he turned and tossed the foetus into the flames.

Harold screamed. A high keening wail torn raw from his throat, the wild ululation of a creature in pain. He crashed to the ground heavily, pulling the trolley over with him. His last conscious thought and sight, one of the foetuses being devoured by the ravenous fire. He rolled onto his back, vaguely aware that Cayton was heading for the door.

"I tried to stop him."

Words pounded in his ears, low guttural raspings, thick with power.

"I tried, I. . ."

Pain. Agonizing, white hot pain, filled his head for interminable seconds. Mercifully, Harold Pierce blacked out.

Maggie Ford yawned and reached up to massage her neck, allowing her head to rest against the rear wall of the lift. There was no one else in it and Maggie slipped one foot out of her shoe, flexing her toes. Her feet were killing her. Come to think of it, she ached all over.

"A good hot bath when you get home," she said aloud, suddenly embarrassed with herself when the lift doors slid open, the car having bumped to a stop without her even noticing.

She saw Brian Cayton standing there, his face flushed, a thin film of perspiration on his face.

"Doctor," he gasped, jumping into the lift. "Can you come down to the basement straight away? One of the other porters has collapsed."

She was going to protest but the concern on the young porter's face was such that she decided to remain silent. He jabbed the basement button and the lift dropped the remaining floors. When it came to a halt at its appointed place, Maggie found herself running behind Cayton, so infectious was his anxiety. She followed him to the furnace room, immediately struck by the foul odour of soiled linen and the blistering heat which poured forth from the still open metal door. She saw Harold lying prone beside the overturned trolley, arms outstretched.

"Go and get help," she told Cayton. "Get someone to help you, we've got to get him up." Even as she spoke, she slid back the lid of one eye and shone her penlight on it mildly repelled by the feel of the cracked skin beneath her fingers but she administered a swift mental rebuke to herself at her reactions, now more concerned when she realized that Harold's pupil didn't react to the light. She tried again, feeling mildly foolish when she realized that it was the glass eye she was gazing into. She repeated the procedure with the good eye, relieved to see that this time there was pupilary contraction. Even as she pocketed the penlight, he began to stir. He tried to sit up but Maggie restrained him.

"Just take it easy," she said, softly and the initial look of fear on Harold's face was replaced by one of pained bewilderment.

He found himself looking into the face which he'd seen earlier. That beautiful thin face framed with the brown hair. *Her* soft hands were touching his wrist, feeling for his pulse.

"Why do they do it?" he croaked.

"Do what?" she wanted to know, checking his pulse against the second hand of her watch.

"Burn the children."

She looked puzzled.

"They burn babies in there," Harold said, tearfully, motioning towards the furnace.

Maggie understood and was thankful that, at that precise moment, Cayton arrived with another porter. On her instructions, they helped Harold to his feet and supported him to the lift.

"Shall we take him to casualty?" asked Cayton.

Maggie shook her head.

"No. Take him to my room on the fourth floor. I think it's time someone examined him."

All four of them climbed into the lift and, in seconds, it was rising.

Twenty-five

Harold sat on the edge of the couch, fidgeting uncomfortably. He watched Maggie as she crossed to her desk and selected a number of implements with which she obviously intended to perform the examination. He didn't know what the things were although he had seen one or two of them many times during his spell in the hospital.

It was warm in the office, the gentle hum of the radiator reminding him of the furnace room. The walls were a brilliant white, the snowy expanse broken only by one large picture window to his right which looked out over much of the hospital below. The room itself was sparsely decked out, containing three hard chairs, a large desk and the couch upon which he now sat. There were filing cabinets against the far wall, each drawer marked with red labels bearing letters. On the desk itself there was a small pile of books, a pencil holder and a clock. The ticking seemed unnaturally loud in the silence.

"When was the last time you had an examination, Mr Pierce?" Maggie asked him, turning back to the couch.

Harold smiled weakly.

"I don't remember," he said. "You can call me Harold if you want to," he added, falteringly.

Maggie smiled and asked him to take off his overall which he did. Beneath it he wore a slightly off-white shirt, the cuffs fraying and worn. She asked him to undo his sleeve which he also did, being careful not to pull the material any further than an inch or two from his wrist, ensuring that his forearm was still covered. Maggie took his pulse once again and scribbled something down on a piece of paper.

"How long have you been working here, Harold?" she asked him, reaching for the opthalmoscope, flicking it on and testing the tiny beam of light against the palm of her hand. Satisfied, she peered into his one good eye, adjusting the implement until she found the correct magnification.

"About eight or nine weeks," he told her.

As she leant close to him he could smell her perfume. Just a vague hint but nevertheless detectable. She smelt so clean and fresh and, as she peered through the opthalmoscope, her silky hair brushed the unscarred side of his face. He felt a peculiar tingle run through him and his breathing quickened slightly.

"Have you ever had blackouts before?" she wanted to know.

Harold shrugged.

"I don't think so."

She asked him to take off his shirt.

A look of panic flashed across his face, as if she had just asked him to jump from the fourth storey window. He quivered, the breath catching in his throat.

"Why?" he asked, agitatedly.

She smiled, surprised by his reaction.

"I want to check your heart and lungs." She was already reaching for the stethoscope.

Still he hesitated, dropping his gaze momentarily then looking up at her with something akin to pleading sparkling in his eye.

"I'm all right," he told her, his voice cracking.

"Please, Harold," she persisted.

His mind was racing. What would she say when he took it off? Should he leave now, run out of the room? But then, he knew that they would come for him and when that happened. . . He pushed the thought to one side.

"Harold, please take off your shirt."

With shaking hands, he began to undo the buttons, pulling the bottom free of his trousers. Maggie took the sphygmomanometer from its metal case, preparing to test his blood pressure when she'd finished the chest examination. She tugged the cuff open, the velcro rasping noisily in the silence of the room.

Harold pulled his shirt free, balled it up and held it on his lap, his body trembling.

Maggie turned to look at him.

She swallowed hard, trying hard to disguise her horror at what she saw. Harold sat impassively, his eyes closed as if ashamed of the sight of his body.

His chest and arms were covered by numerous raw, angry cuts. Some had scabbed over, others were purple knots where the scar tissue had formed, only to be picked or cut away later. Dark, vicious welts covered his arms from the wrist to the elbow and the parts of his torso and limbs not disfigured by the multitude of sores and wounds were milk white. He had obviously lost a lot of blood from the cuts. One or two were festering, a large one just below his left elbow was a suppurating cleft in the mottled flesh. The most striking thing about the wounds, however, was their positioning. Each seemed to be a measured distance from the next, almost like carefully carved tribal scars. His chest was a patchwork of crusted flesh and dried blood, one nipple having been sliced in two. It was so badly bruised it was black. And that was the curious thing about all the cuts. Around each one was a dark area which, if anything reminded Maggie of a love-bite. It was as if the skin on Harold's body had been drawn between someone's lips, the suction causing the resultant discoloration of the flesh.

"Where did you get these cuts?" she asked him, her voice low and full of muted fear. Fear? Yes, Maggie told herself. Spidery fingers were playing a symphony along the nape of her neck and she felt the hairs rise in response.

Harold didn't answer, he just continued gazing down at the floor.

She moved closer, taking hold of his left wrist, anxious to get a closer look at the numerous gashes. He pulled away from her, his breath coming in gasps.

"Did you cut yourself like this for a reason?" she wanted to know.

He opened his mouth to speak, thoughts still whirling around inside his head and now, he began to hear the familiar voices growing in volume as he fought to find some kind of explanation for the shocking appearance of his upper body.

"I think I should call Dr Parkin, let him. . ."

"No." He practically shouted at her. "No."

"Something has got to be done about these cuts, Harold," she said. "Now, will you please tell me how you got them?"

"I . . . I dream," he mumbled.

"About what?" she asked him, taking his left arm in her hand and, this time, she encountered no opposition. She probed the edges of the nearest gash with a wooden spatula, withdrawing it when Harold winced.

"I dream about different things," he said, vaguely, gazing ahead as if he were addressing someone on the other side of the room.

"What do you see in these dreams, Harold?" she asked him. She was using the conversation as a means of distraction while she got a better look at the cuts on his body. The one below his elbow was undoubtedly fresh. She wiped some sticky liquid from it with a piece of gauze and prodded the torn flesh but, this time, Harold didn't react.

"Fire," he said, flatly. "I see fire."

"Can you tell me more about the dreams?" she asked.

"I killed my brother and my mother," he said, almost as if it were a confession. "That was why they put me away." The smile that he flashed at her caused her flesh to rise into goose-pimples. Maggie wondered just how deeply Harold's apparent obsession with the disposal of abortions, and his insistence on calling them "children", went. It made her wonder just how much more he could cope with. The wounds on his body were obviously self-inflicted, perhaps, she thought, as some kind of bizarre revenge against himself for the crime which he felt he'd committed.

"How did your mother and brother die?" she asked.

He told her, and the significance of the fire, the destruction of the embryonic creatures, immediately fell into place.

"I dream about them sometimes," he said. "I dreamt about the furnace room once, I. . ."

He felt a stab of pain inside his head and the voices were there, loud and commanding.

"Tell me about the dream," Maggie said. He swallowed hard, his tone lightening somewhat.

"I don't think I remember now," he told her. "It's best if I don't talk about it. I don't like to think about it."

Maggie nodded, pressing the stethoscope to his chest. His heartbeat was slow. When she took his blood pressure she found it was a fraction lower than normal. Harold may have appeared to be anxious and disturbed but none of his bodily signs showed anything to back that up. She told him to put his shirt back on, dressing the worst of the cuts first.

"Can I go now?" he asked.

"If you're sure you're all right," she said. "But I'd still feel better if you'd let me call Dr Parkin in to have a look at you."

He refused, tucking his shirt back into his trousers and pulling on his overall.

"I'd like you to come back and see me in a couple of days, Harold," Maggie told him.

He nodded, still eager to leave.

"Why don't you go and lie down for a while."

"I feel much better, thank you."

Maggie shrugged. They said brief goodbyes and Harold left, closing the door behind him. He walked slowly down the corridor, the voices inside his head buzzing agitatedly.

"I didn't say anything. I kept the secret," Harold whispered to empty air.

"Will you hurt her?" he wanted to know.

The voices continued to speak and Harold listened intently.

Maggie sat down at her desk and ran a hand through her hair. Outside, grey rain clouds were gathering and the first fine particles of drizzle were beginning to coat the window like early morning dew on a spider's web. It was gloomy in the office but she did not switch the lights on, merely sat in the deepening shadows, lost in her own thoughts, the vision of Harold's savaged body still vivid in her mind. What could drive a man to inflict such damage on himself, she wondered? She looked at the phone on her desk for a long time, pondering on whether or not to ring Harold's old psychiatrist. Perhaps if she knew more about his background she would better understand why he had done what he'd done. She drummed restlessly on the desk top, her eyes still fixed on the phone then, finally, she got to her feet and crossed to the window, gazing out at the approaching banks of grey cloud.

If he had dreams, nightmares, she reasoned, then maybe the cuts had been inflicted whilst he was in the dream-state. She had heard of people lifting objects in their sleep which they would never be able to move while awake. Perhaps the same principle applied in Harold's case. What he could not bring himself to do in his waking state, he found the subconscious strength to do during his dreams. Namely the self-mutilation. She exhaled deeply. It was too simple an explanation. The cuts seemed *too* carefully spaced, there was nothing random about them. Unlike other psychotics who, given a sharp instrument, would carve themselves up just for the hell of it, Harold seemed to have chosen the spots where he inflicted the damage. It was almost as if he had been guided.

Maggie shook her head, trying to dismiss the thought. For one thing, Harold, as far as she knew, lived alone. He had few friends and certainly no enemies. And, as for the theory of him inflicting the wounds in a psychotic orgy of masochism – well, that didn't tie up because, although he may be mildly disturbed, Harold was certainly not psychotic.

She crossed back to her desk and glanced at the clock.

4.11 p.m.

What really puzzled her was the dark, bruised area around each cut. If Harold was a haematophile and thereby obsessed with the drinking of his own blood then the bruises on his arms could be easily explained but, she thought, that seemed unlikely.

Besides, it still wouldn't explain how his chest came to be in the same state.

Maggie chewed her bottom lip thoughtfully, already determined that if she had not heard from Harold in two days' time, she would personally go to his home and find out just what was happening to him.

Twenty-six

Judith Myers got up from her desk, smiling happily at the other people in the room, anxious to disguise the pain which was gnawing at her stomach and groin. She tried to tell herself that it was muscle strain. She'd been away from work for too long and now bending over a drawing board all day. . .

The idea quickly vanished as she felt a searing jab of

agony in her side. She stood still in the corridor for a moment, leaning against the wall, feeling as if someone had kicked her in the side. She put one hand to the throbbing area and felt it gently, the pain seemed to recede somewhat and she hurried down the short flight of steps which would take her to the toilets.

Once inside, she was relieved to discover that she was alone. She locked herself in one of the cubicles and sat down on the toilet seat, rubbing both sides now, taking short breaths. The pain seemed to be moving deeper into her groin so she stood up and slipped her tights and panties down to her knees, probing gently at the lips of her vagina with her index finger. She withdrew the digit after a couple of minutes, her hand shaking, her eyes half expecting to see it stained with blood. The incident the other night had frightened her but the doctor had told her that slight bleeding was not uncommon so soon after an abortion. Bleeding from the navel however, *was* uncommon but a trip to her own GP had revealed no complications and, despite Andy Parker's protestations, she had returned to work as soon as possible.

Now she pulled up her underclothes and unlocked the cubicle aware still of the pain which seemed to be spreading throughout her abdomen. She felt a sudden wave of nausea sweep over her and just made it to one of the sinks. Bent double over it, she retched until there was nothing left in her stomach. The pain, curiously, seemed to vanish. Judith spun both taps to wash away the mess, cupping some water in one palm and swilling it around her mouth. She looked up, studying her reflection in the mirror. Her face was the colour of rancid butter, the dark brown of her eye-shadow giving her the appearance of a skull. She pulled some paper towels from the dispenser and wiped her mouth, tossing the used articles into a nearby bin. Then, once again, she pressed both hands to her stomach.

"Judith, are you all right?"

The voice startled her and she turned to see Theresa Holmes standing just inside the door.

"It's OK, Terri," she said.

"You look awful," Theresa told her. "Do you want me to fetch the first aid bloke?"

"No, I'll be all right. I just felt sick."

Terri crossed to the sink and stood beside her, the ruddiness of her own complexion a marked contrast to the palour of Judith's. She was two years older and the women had been friends ever since Judith joined the firm.

"A friend of mine, she had an abortion," Terri said. "She had stomach trouble for months afterwards."

Judith smiled sardonically.

"Thanks, Terri, you're a great comfort."

"Sorry, I didn't mean it like that. All I'm saying is, I think it's common to feel bad soon after one."

Judith shrugged.

"It's been over three weeks now," she said.

She went on to describe the incident the other night.

Terri frowned but could offer no helpful information or advice. She asked Judith once more if she felt fit enough to come back to work and the younger woman nodded.

At two o'clock that afternoon, Judith Myers collapsed and was taken home, a slight swelling in her stomach noticed by no one.

Twenty-seven

The doors of the cellar bulkhead rattled in the powerful wind and Paul Harvey grunted irritably, awoken by the sound. He sat, screwing his eyes up in an effort to re-orientate himself with his surroundings. It was dark in the cellar, the only light coming through the slight gap where the two bulkhead doors met. Outside, the moon hung high in the sky, a solitary cold white beam finding its way down into the subterranean gloom. The cellar was large, stretching far away from him on three sides. It ran all the way beneath the farmhouse but he had not ventured far from his present hiding place for some time now. Not during daylight at least.

They had come, as he had expected. Two of them in one of their cars but, he had seen them and he had hidden. Pleased with his own cunning, he had gained entry to the house by breaking one of the small glass panels in the front door and simply wrenching the lock off with one huge hand. He had blundered around inside the empty, dust-choked dwelling until he finally found the cellar door. The rusty key still in the lock. He had unlocked the door and taken the key in with him. *They* had searched the house, he had heard them moving about inside, one of them had even mentioned something about a break-in but, when they had tried the door to the cellar and found it locked, they had gone away. Harvey had remained silent all the time they searched, the sickle held tightly in his grasp just in case. When one of them had tugged at the rusty iron chain on the bulkhead doors, Harvey had thought that they would discover him but his luck had persisted. Through the gap in the doors he had been able to see one of them in his blue uniform, speaking into the box which he carried and which seemed to answer him back. But, after what seemed like an eternity, Harvey had heard them return to their car and drive off. However, determined not to fall into one of *their* traps, he had remained in his hiding place. They would not catch him out again.

The cellar had proved to be far more than somewhere to hole up. Harvey had found that it was full of wooden shelves, each stocked with dusty jars of home-made preserves, pickles and even some bottles of amateur wine. The previous owners of the farm had obviously gone in for that kind of thing and Harvey had been glad to find a seemingly endless supply of food. He'd scooped jam from jars with his bare hands, drunk dandelion wine until his head ached, devoured entire jars full of pickled onions, upturning the receptacle to swallow the vinegar when all the other contents were gone. But his ravenous appetite had proved his undoing. He didn't know how long it was since he'd eaten – three, maybe four days. He'd lost track of time down there in that dank hole. The cellar smelt like an open sewer, splattered as it was with excrement and rat droppings. In the beginning the rodents had competed for the pieces of food which Harvey had dropped but now, as his hunger reached new heights, the rats themselves, as in the barn, had become the prey.

Broken jars littered the floor, their contents now rotting and moulding. Lumps of glass lay everywhere, two of the wooden shelves had been torn down during one of Harvey's frenzied moments. He had tried to eat some rotting marmalade which he scraped up off the floor but it had made him vomit and he sat in one corner now, his trousers damp and reeking of urine. Surrounded by his own excrement, the gnawing in his stomach seemed to fuel the anger which was growing within him. He had left the cellar just once, two nights ago, breathing clean fresh air instead of the fetid cloying odour of putrescence he had come to know so well. He had wandered over the fields, the lights of Exham acting like beacons, attracting him as surely as a candle would attract a moth. He had carried the sickle with him, its rusty blade tucked into his belt.

Now he hefted it before him, running one finger over the cutting edge, pieces of dried blood flaking off along with some minute fragments of rust. He stood up, reaching for the key in his pocket, realizing that he would have to leave this place again. But, the night was his friend, it hid him. Allowed him to move freely. He began climbing the cellar steps towards the door, the gnawing in his belly growing stronger by the second.

Liz Maynard held the book close to her face, peering through her glasses at the print before her. She was holding the paperback in one hand, the other she had balled into a fist beneath the sheet. As she read she would murmur aloud at each fresh development in the chapter, turning the pages with trepidation as the huge flesh-eating creature drew nearer to the hero and heroine who were trapped in a deserted house. She shuddered, lowering the book for a moment when a particularly powerful gust of wind rattled the bedroom window in its frame. After a moment she returned to the book, reading more quickly than usual now. The creature was stalking the young couple and Liz began to tug on the sheet in the anxiousness. The dull glow of the bedside lamp added even more atmosphere to the proceedings and she was completely caught up in her horrifying read. So caught up that she didn't notice she was pulling all of the sheets and covers to her side of the bed.

The creature in the book had found the young couple and was now chasing them.

A hand reached up and grabbed her wrist.

Liz yelped and dropped the book, looking down to

see her husband glaring up at her, trying to claw back some of the covers which she had pulled off him.

She let out a sigh of relief and glared down at Jack.

"You frightened me to death," she said.

"You were pulling all the bloody clothes off," he protested. Then he smiled, picking up the book which she'd dropped. He glanced at the cover. It showed a creature with glowing red eyes and huge teeth, dripping blood. "How the hell can you read this sort of rubbish?" he asked, grinning.

She snatched back the book indignantly and placed it on the bedside table with half a dozen others like it.

"It's very good actually," she said, defensively. "Besides, reading this sort of book is good for you. It's a medical fact, and so is watching horror films. It does you good to have a fright every now and then."

Jack nodded.

"Well, the bloody tax man frightens me, without having to read about monsters from hell and things with two heads." He exhaled deeply. "You know I don't know what's more disturbing, the fact that people part with good money to buy the damn things or that there's someone somewhere who dreams them up. I mean, what sort of mentality must a bloke have to write a book like that?"

"You've got no imagination, Jack, that's your trouble," she told him. "You should let yourself go every once in a while. Try reading one of these."

He snorted indignantly.

"I should think so. There's enough horrors in the real world without having to make them up."

She blew a raspberry at him and they both laughed. Married for twenty-eight years, they ran a small shop on the outskirts of Exham selling everything from fresh vegetables to newspapers. They were a rare and welcome commodity in the age of the supermarket and had a large and loyal clientele to prove it.

Liz leant over flicked off the bedside lamp, pulling the covers up around her neck as she settled down.

She was in the process of adjusting her pillows when she heard a distant crash. It sounded distinctly like breaking glass. She sat up, ears straining to pick up any other noise. The window rattled frenziedly in the frame for a second then the powerful gust seemed to ease and silence descended once more. Liz lay down again, ears pricked, heart thumping just that bit faster. She closed her eyes. Jack was already snoring softly beside her, he took a short course in death when he went to bed.

The noise came again and this time she was sure it was breaking glass. Liz sat up, simultaneously shaking her husband. He grunted and opened his eyes.

"What's wrong?" he said, thickly.

"Listen," she said. "I heard something."

Jack Maynard hauled himself up the bed and propped his head against the board at the top.

"I know I heard something," she repeated.

"What was it?"

She told him.

"Probably the wind, love." He smiled. "Or your imagination running away with you after reading that bloody book."

She was just about to agree with him when they both heard a much louder crash. This time it was Jack who reacted. He swung himself out of bed and walked to the bedroom door, opening it as quietly as he could. There was no light on in the landing and it was like looking out into a wall of blackness. A couple of yards ahead lay the staircase which led down into their sitting room. Beyond that, lay the shop itself. As he stood there, he heard unmistakable sounds of movement from below him. Hurriedly, he closed the door and padded back towards the bed.

"I think there's someone in the shop," he said, quietly.

"Oh God," Liz murmured. "We'll have to call the police."

Jack nodded.

"I know," he said, cryptically. "But just in case you'd forgotten, the bloody phone is in the living room. I'll have to go downstairs anyway." Even as he spoke he knelt, reaching beneath the bed and pulling out a long leather case. He lifted it up onto the bed and unzipped it, pulling back the cover to reveal a gleaming double-barrelled shotgun which he hurriedly loaded.

Liz reached across and flicked the lamp switch.

Nothing happened.

She got out of bed and crossed to the main point, flicking it on. The room, however, remained in darkness.

"Oh Christ," muttered Jack. "The wind must have brought a power line down."

"Or someone's been at the fuse box," Liz said, ominously.

He nodded, touching her cheek with his free hand, noticing how cold it was.

"Jack, please be careful," she whispered.

"It's probably just somebody larking about," he said, reassuring neither Liz or himself. "I'll give them a bit of a fright." He hefted the shotgun in front of him. "You close this door behind me."

She nodded, watching as he moved cautiously out onto the landing, immediately enveloped by the inky blackness. He motioned to her to close the door which she did, resting her forehead against it for long moments, her heart hammering against her ribs.

The wind swept around the shop, growling at the windows like some beast of prey.

Jack Maynard could hear it too as he padded stealthily across the landing, moving with surprising agility for a man of his size. He paused at the top step and peered down into the gloom. The darkness was like a thick, clinging blanket wrapping itself around him as he stood there, breathing softly. He gripped the shotgun tighter but, he reasoned, with it being so dark he wouldn't even be able to see the intruder if he decided to come at him. The bloody gun was useless in such impenetrable gloom. It was like trying to teach a blind man to shoot bottles.

Cursing the power failure, Jack began to descend the stairs.

The third one creaked beneath him and he stood still, a thin film of perspiration greasing his face. He could still hear some distant scrabblings from beyond, now certain that the intruder was in the shop. He moved more quickly down the stairs, the shotgun held across his chest, ready to swing up to his shoulder at the slightest hint of movement. As he reached the bottom of the stairs he flicked the light switch there.

The room remained in darkness.

Jack swallowed hard and moved cautiously through the living room, narrowing his eyes in an effort to make out the dark shapes before him. Some light was coming in through a window but most of that was masked by the large tree which towered outside. To his left lay the door to the kitchen. Straight ahead the door which would take him through into the shop.

He banged his shin against the coffee table and almost overbalanced, stifling a yelp of surprise as he struggled to remain upright. He cursed silently and rubbed his injured leg, ears still alert for any sounds. Other than the howling of the wind, he could hear nothing. His heart jumped a beat and he strained his ears for the noises which he'd heard just moments earlier.

Something cracked against the window pane and Jack swung round, bringing the shotgun up, his thumb instinctively jerking one of the twin hammers back. He saw that it was a tree branch which had struck the glass, the bony fingers of low branches clawing at the window as if seeking entry. He breathed an audible sigh of relief then, turning, decided to check the kitchen before progessing into the shop itself.

It too was empty.

As Jack stepped back into the sitting room the lights flashed on momentarily but the welcome illumination was all too brief and, seconds later, the house was plunged back into darkness.

He reached the door which would take him through into the shop, his hand quivering as he reached for the key. He glimpsed the phone out of the corner of his eye. Should he call the police now? He inhaled deeply. Sod it, he'd have a look for himself.

The lights flickered once more as he reached for the key and turned it.

Paul Harvey heard the door open slightly as Jack Maynard entered the shop. He had heard the other man moving about in the sitting room moments earlier and so he had ducked down behind one of the three counters inside the main room. The one behind which he sought shelter was topped by tin cans and through those Harvey could see the man edge his way cautiously forwards, towards the front door. A small pane in the door had been broken and, as Jack touched it, the wooden partition was blown open by a particularly violent gust of wind.

The shopkeeper jumped back, the gun at hip height.

Harvey saw the weapon and touched his chin thoughtfully. He looked up and saw the door through which the other man had come. Moving as swiftly and silently as he could, he scuttled towards it and disappeared inside the sitting room.

Liz Maynard paced back and forth beside the bed listening for any sounds of movement from beneath her. She looked at the clock on the bedside table, then checked it against her own watch. Jack seemed to have been gone an eternity. The lights flickered on briefly yet again and she gasped aloud at the suddenness of it. What the hell was he doing down there? She hadn't heard his voice. Why wasn't he phoning the police? Perhaps whoever it was that had broken in had attacked him down there in the dark, he could be lying there now with his throat cut. Thoughts tumbled wildly through her mind. She sat on the edge of the bed but her entire body was trembling so she took to her pacings once more. Another glance at the clock. She would give him one more minute then, warning or not, she would go down after him. Her own anxiety about Jack had to a certain extent overcome her fear. She watched as the second hand swept round, marking off the minute.

"Bastards," muttered Jack Maynard.

He was standing before one of the shelves in the shop. The jars had been taken down, the tops wrenched off and some of the contents spread over the floor of the shop. Remnants of half eaten fruit also littered the dusty floor. A can of soup had been gashed open with something sharp, the cold contents now gone. Jack frowned, whoever had broken in must have been *really* hungry if they were prepared to drink cold soup. He hefted the riven can before him, the shotgun cradled over his other arm. Other cans and jars had been taken, one of the shelves all but empty. Sweets, kept on the counter to his right with the newspapers, had also been taken by the handful. Kids? He shook his head. Kids wouldn't do this. He put the can down wondering just who the hell would?

Liz Maynard could wait no longer. She opened the bedroom door and peered out onto the landing, her heart pounding. It was still pitch black out there and she moved somewhat nervously towards the hand-rail.

There was no sound from the sitting room below or the shop itself, only the ever-present roaring of the wind. She placed one hand against the wall and took the stairs tentatively, one at a time. As she reached the third one, the lights flashed on and continued to fill the house with their glow for a full minute and a half.

Liz Maynard screamed.

Harvey was already half way up the stairs, the sickle gripped in his fist.

She turned and ran back to the bedroom, hearing the heavy footsteps thudding up the stairs behind her. She screamed again as she threw the door shut and pressed her pitiful weight against it, expecting at any second for him to launch his huge bulk against it. Instead, she heard the loud thud and the splintering of wood as he buried the sickle's vicious curved blade in the door. The point protruded a few inches through it and, as Harvey tore it free, a panel was ripped loose.

She screamed again.

Jack heard her and dashed into the sitting room, looking up to see the large figure of Harvey poised before the bedroom door, the sickle swinging back and forth as it made matchwood of the partition. Jack raised the shotgun to his shoulder simultaneously yelling something at the madman who turned to face him. Harvey moved with lightning speed and, slobbering like a rabid animal, threw himself to the ground.

There was a thunderous roar as the shotgun barrel exploded in an orgasm of fire and lead, the sound amplified by the enclosed space. The deadly load struck the wall just above Harvey's head. Paint and lumps of plaster were blasted away by the impact and Jack cursed aloud when he saw Harvey scramble to his feet, running across the landing towards the solitary window there.

He hit it with the force of a steam train, crashing through the glass and wood, heedless of what lay below. Shards of crystal sprayed out in all directions as Harvey hurtled through. He clutched at empty air for a second before plummeting to earth. He crashed into a privet hedge, the wind knocked from him, but, other than that, he was unharmed. He rolled clear and got to his feet.

Jack Maynard ran to the window and looked out in time to see Harvey loping off into the darkness. Then, the shotgun still gripped tight in his hand, he dashed into the bedroom where he found Liz on her knees beside the bed sobbing uncontrollably. It took him fully fifteen minutes to calm her down then, that done, he made his way downstairs and dialled three nines.

Twenty-eight

Inspector Lou Randall skimmed the file once more then threw it down onto his desk.

"Jesus Christ," he growled. "Doesn't anybody ever see this bastard? What is he a man or a fucking ghost?" He leant back in his chair and rubbed his face with both hands, feeling the stubble on his cheeks and chin as he did so. He'd been called out at six that morning and had driven to the police station without shaving or eating. His stomach rumbled disapprovingly and his mouth felt like the bottom of a birdcage.

"Who found this one?" he asked, wearily.

"A milkman," Norman Willis told him. "He said the body was lying in the road. No attempt to hide it." The sergeant studied his superior's worried face. "He wasn't making much sense when Charlton took the statement from him." He paused. "He's still badly shaken up."

Randall grunted.

"I'm not surprised," he said. "Finding a headless body at half past five in the morning lying in the middle of the street is enough to give anyone the bloody shakes." He glanced at the report again. "Same murder weapon?" It came out more as a confirmation than a question.

Willis nodded.

"Everything about it is the same as Ian Logan's murder. Rust in the wounds, a single-bladed weapon and the head was taken."

Randall fumbled in his pocket for his cigarettes, finding them with some difficulty. There was only one in the packet and he tossed the empty receptacle away, not really bothering whether it reached the waste-bin or not. He lit the fag and drew hard on it.

"What about this other incident?" he said, picking up Jack Maynard's statement regarding Harvey's attack and break-in. Willis told his superior about it while Randall quickly read the statement himself.

"The break-in happened at half past one," said Randall. He flipped open the file in front of him. "The pathologist's report puts the time of death at around two." He tapped on the desk top with his index finger as if seeking some kind of magical inspiration, a clue to what the hell he was going to do next. "He didn't kill anyone at the shop where he broke in, maybe he lost his rag and decided he owed himself one anyway. This poor sod just happened to be the first one he came across." He took another drag on his cigarette. "Where was the body found? Which side of town?"

"Going out towards the main road into Mayford. There's lots of fields out that way," Willis explained.

"Is it being checked?" Randall wanted to know.

"Not yet, we're spread a bit thin at the moment trying to find him but as soon as a car calls in I'll send them out that way."

The Inspector nodded.

"I just don't get it," he said, wearily. "How the hell can Harvey just keep disappearing like he does? He must be hiding somewhere around Exham and yet we've already checked it over once." The Inspector smiled sardonically. "Perhaps he's not as mad as everyone seems to think he is."

"They always say that it's the brains who are locked up and the lunatics who are free," added Willis, shrugging.

"I'm beginning to agree," said Randall. He ground out his cigarette, watching the plume of grey smoke rise mournfully into the air.

"We'll get him, guv," said Willis.

Randall raised an eyebrow, questioningly.

"Can I have that in writing?" he said, humourlessly. The phone rang and, as he picked it up, Willis turned to leave. Randall picked up the receiver, quickly cupping his hand over the mouthpiece. "Hey, Norman, a cup of tea would go down a treat."

Willis smiled and left.

Randall pressed the phone to his ear.

"Inspector Randall speaking."

"I'm not going to beat about the bush, Randall," said the voice at the other end, one which the Inspector immediately recognized as belonging to Chief Inspector Frank Allen. There was a harsh, cold quality to the CI's voice which made it unmistakable. The younger man stiffened in his chair.

"Yes, sir," he said, wondering what his superior wanted. He glanced across at the wall clock opposite him and saw that it was almost 9.05 a.m. Whatever the miserable old sod wanted must be important, Randall mused.

"I understand you're having some problems down there," said Allen. "This escaped maniac, Harvey isn't it? How long has he been free now?"

Randall swallowed hard.

"Just over nine weeks, sir. Everything possible is being done to apprehend him. My men. . ."

"And how many has he killed. One or two?"

Randall paled.

"Two, sir." It came out almost as a confession.

Allen exhaled deeply, his voice taking on an even harder edge.

"I see," he said. "Well, look Randall, you don't need me to tell you how serious this whole business is. Your inability to find the man in the beginning was bad enough but now this. For Christ's sake put the lid on it and find Harvey quickly." There was a pause, during which time the CI's mood seemed to lighten a little. "Do you need any help?"

"A couple of bloodhounds I think, sir," he japed.

"Don't be facetious, Randall," Allen snapped. "This series of events is not going to look very good on your record. Now, I asked if you needed any help."

The Inspector clenched his fists until the knuckles were bloodless, trying hard to control his anger.

"Some extra men wouldn't go amiss, sir," he said, brusquely.

"Very well. But catch this bastard. Quick."

"Yes, sir."

Allen hung up.

Randall held the receiver in his hand for a second, listening to the persistent drone then, angrily, he slammed it down onto the cradle. He had the uncomfortable suspicion that someone was keeping tabs on him. Christ, he wanted a cigarette but, as he peered at the empty packet nearby he could only mutter irritably to himself. "Catch Harvey". He shook his head. Any ideas where we should start, big head? He thought, glaring at the phone, the anger still boiling inside him. He got to his feet and looked at the map of the town on his office wall. It bore two red crosses, each marking the scene of the murders. Both were in different parts of Exham. At least two miles separated the scene of each crime. Randall stood gazing helplessly at the map.

"Come out, come out wherever you are, you bastard," murmured the Inspector.

Twenty-nine

The windscreen wipers of the Audi swept slowly back and forth across the glass, brushing away the rain which had been falling steadily for the past three hours.

"I need a new set of blades," muttered Mick Calvin, jabbing a finger at the area on the windscreen which was still rainsoaked.

"You always need something, Mick," said his wife, Diane, firmly belted into the passenger seat beside him. "I think it's about time we had a new car."

Calvin snorted.

"Well, my darling," he said, sarcastically. "As soon as we get home you write me a cheque for six thousand and I'll nip out and get us one."

"You know what I mean," she said, irritably. "*You've* been saying the same yourself for months."

"I just wish your bloody mother didn't live so far away," he added.

Diane studied his profile for a second.

"I suppose it's her fault that the car's falling to bits?" she said, acidly.

"Did I say that? I just said that it's a long drive to where she lives."

Diane smiled impishly.

"She could always come and live with us, that would save the journey."

She laughed aloud at the expression which crossed her husband's face.

"I could get to like long journeys," he said, smiling.

"She wouldn't be any trouble."

"That's what they said about Hitler."

Diane punched him playfully on the arm.

"Dad, can we stop?"

The voice came from the back seat where Richie, their eldest son at eleven, was dressed in a pair of freshly pressed jeans and a Spiderman sweatshirt. He was on his knees, pulling at his crutch agitatedly. Beside him sat his brother, Wayne, two years younger, his face round and red as if he'd been holding his breath for a long time.

"Dad."

"What?" said Calvin.

"Can't we stop? Wayne and me both want to go for a wee," he protested.

"Can't you hold it? We're nearly home now," said Calvin. "And it's Wayne and *I*," he added as an afterthought.

The oldest lad was bouncing up and down now.

"Dad," he persisted, clutching his groin with both hands, as if letting go would release a flood tide.

"Oh, pull over, Mick," Diane said. "They can nip behind a hedge."

"It's wet out there you know," said Calvin, as if trying to deter his two sons.

Diane looked at Wayne who was going ever redder in a monumental effort of self-control which he was obviously going to lose at any minute.

"It's going to be wet in here if you don't pull over," she said.

Calvin nodded and glanced ahead for a suitable place to stop. There were fields all around them but few seemed to be blessed with bushes. He saw the massive edifice of Fairvale hospital towering above a row of trees and remembered that there was a lay-by just beyond. The fields that backed onto the hospital itself would offer plenty of cover for the two kids. He could see the electricity pylons towering over the field, their cables swaying in the breeze. Checking his rear-view mirror, he swung the Audi across the road and into the lay-by. Immediately, the two kids were fumbling for the door locks in their efforts to get out and Calvin couldn't resist a smile as he watched them both scramble out of the car.

"Go behind those bushes over there," he said, pointing towards some bare gorse bushes which masked a sizeable hollow in the field. The hollow ran from the base of one of the towering pylons.

He and Diane watched as the kids clambered over the low fence which separated the lay-by from the field, then both of the boys were racing towards the bushes. They disappeared behind the bushes and Calvin grinned broadly.

"Do you want to go as well?" he asked Diane. "There's plenty more bushes in the field." He laughed.

"No," she whispered, leaning closer. "But I'll tell you what I do want." She pulled him to her and their mouths met eagerly. She spoke something into his ear, kissing the lobe as she did so, one hand straying to his thigh.

"Now that *will* have to wait until we get home," he said.

They both laughed.

The screams which they heard made them both sit bolt upright, but it was a matter of seconds before Calvin was unhooking his seat belt, pushing open the car door. He slipped as he leapt out onto the wet tarmac but regained his balance and hurried towards the fence. Diane was close behind him, her high heels sinking into the mud as she reached the low wooden fence. She struggled over it, seeing that her husband was already racing towards the bushes where the screams were coming from.

He was panting madly, the high pitched screams of his sons ringing in his ears as he ran. The rain plastered hair to his face but he ignored it and ran on, his only concern to reach his children. As he drew closer, he saw Richie staggering from behind the bushes, his face colourless, his mouth open. Behind him came Wayne, his jeans wet around the crutch, his flies still open. By now, Diane could see them. She called their names but no sound seemed to come, she was mouthing the words but only silence escaped her.

Calvin reached his eldest son and held him by the shoulders, gazing into his eyes that were bulging wide and red-rimmed. He was motioning behind him, his breath coming out in deep, racking sobs. Wayne merely stood where he was, apparently oblivious to the rain. Calvin hurried across and lifted the boy into his arms. He seemed limp, like a puppet with its wires cut and, but for the fact that his eyes were open and blinking, he had the appearance of a waxwork model.

"What's wrong?"

It was Diane's voice, trembling and full of fear.

"Wayne, Richie, what is it?" she repeated.

Calvin himself held the eldest boy close to his chest while Diane took over the responsibility for Wayne.

"There," gasped Richie, once more motioning behind him.

"Take them both back to the car," said Calvin but Diane hesitated, watching as he walked behind the bushes and along the depression in the field, stopping at one point. He turned to face Diane, her hair now hanging in dripping coils.

"Take them back," said Calvin, waving Diane away.

"What is it, Mick?" she demanded.

"Take them back to the car," he shouted and the vehemence in his voice startled her. She turned and led the two children back across the field towards the shelter of the Audi.

Calvin watched them, waiting until he saw them reach the vehicle before returning his attention to what he had found. He bent, squatting on his haunches, peering at the rain-sodden earth. The grass had been dug over in an area he guessed measuring about twelve feet by six. The mud was sticky and oozing, like reeking gravy and, through this thin film of muck, he could see a face. It was the face of a baby although the definition was questionable. The head, uncovered by the torrential rain, was bulbous with two large growths over the holes where the eyes should have been. In the black pits of sockets worms writhed, one of them disappearing into the open mouth of the putrescing body and it was all Calvin could do to stop himself from vomiting. One rotted, mottled arm protruded from the earth nearby, the fingers stubby, two of them missing. Close to that an entire tiny corpse had been uncovered by the elements. What remained of it had been gnawed in places, maybe by rats or a badger. The stomach had been torn open to reveal a seething mess of mouldering viscera. The stench rising from the grave was overpowering and Calvin took a handkerchief from his pocket to cover his nose, his head swimming. He counted at least half a dozen pieces of human debris and one complete corpse. What lay deeper he could only guess at. He stood up, swaying slightly, the realization that he was indeed standing beside some kind of grave, sweeping over him as surely as the choking stench which wafted from it on invisible clouds. He stood there for long seconds, his eyes fixed on the worm-eaten, ravaged body of one of the foetuses then, as he saw one of the slimy creatures wriggle from a hole in the corpse's stomach like some kind of animated umbilical cord, he finally lost control and vomited violently.

Diane, watching from the back seat of the car, where she was doing her best to comfort the two boys, saw her husband tottering drunkenly back across the field. He finally reached the wooden fence and swung himself over it, supporting himself against the Audi before pulling the driver's side door open. He flopped heavily into the seat and sat motionless, gazing ahead. Diane could hear his laboured breathing.

"We've got to report this," he said, falteringly, reaching for the ignition key and turning it.

"What did you find, Mick?" she demanded. "For God's sake tell me."

He lowered his head momentarily.

"There's . . . something buried." He coughed and, for a moment, thought he was going to be sick again. He gritted his teeth and the feeling diminished somewhat. "Something . . . embryos. There's a grave in that field." He sucked in a deep breath. "We've got to report it, now."

He started the car, swung it round and headed back towards Fairvale's main entrance.

Within an hour he had made a full report to a senior doctor and, thirty minutes later, Mick Calvin led that same doctor and three porters, Harold Pierce amongst them, to the spot where he'd found the grave. And there, under the watchful eyes of both men, five aborted foetuses were uncovered. The bodies were put into a sack and carried back to the hospital where they were disposed of in the usual way. Cast into the mouth of the furnace as they should have been weeks before.

Harold watched as the tiny bodies were born away for disposal his body shaking.

The voices inside his head had begun to chatter once more.

Thirty

Harold sat nervously in the outer office, his hands clasped on his knees. The room was large, a white-walled enclosure which he shared with just three leather chairs and a secretary who sat across from him hammering away at the keys of an old Imperial type-writer. The constant clacking sounded like dozens of tiny explosions. The secretary herself was a woman in her forties, a plump lady with greying hair swept back from a face coated with far too much make-up. It seemed to shine beneath the banks of fluorescents set into the ceiling. There was a mug on her desk with a slogan written on it in large red letters. Harold wond-ered if it was her name as he saw the word June on it. She glanced up at him every now and then and, when she did, he would self-consciously touch the scarred side of his face as if trying to shield it from her gaze. She smiled at him warmly and he returned the gesture sheepishly. He shifted uncomfortably in his seat which made a sound like someone breaking wind, as is the wont of leather chairs. Harold tried to sit still but it was a difficult task. He glanced up at the wall clock above the secretary's head. It showed 4.26 p.m. Below it was a painting which Harold could not make out. It was just squares, all painted different colours, forming no pattern or shape. Not unlike the paintings Harold himself had done in occupational therapy.

The memory of those days seemed so distant now. Then he had felt as if he belonged at the hospital. He had friends and, more importantly, he was not burd-ened with responsibility as he was now. It seemed like a million years ago. Now he sat in the outer office, waiting, remembering back to just a few hours ago when he had helped to disinter the foetuses which he had spent so much care saving in the first place. Saving was the word to describe his actions but now he feared that they would punish him for it. He closed his eyes and allowed his head to rest against the wall. Immediately, the buzzing in his ears became the rasping voices which he had come to know so well.

Harold sat up, his eyelids jerking open. He looked around, as if expecting to see someone sitting next to him but then he realized that the voices were inside his head.

He swallowed hard.

There was a loud bleep and a green light flared on the console beside the secretary. She flipped a switch and Harold heard her say something into the inter-com. When she'd finished speaking she looked up at Harold, smiled and told him to go in. He nodded, got to his feet and made for the varnished door to his right. It bore a nameplate:

Dr Kenneth McManus, R.C.S.

Harold knocked and received the instruction to enter. He walked in to find Brian Cayton in there as well as McManus who was shielded behind a huge mahogany desk. He motioned for Harold to sit down and brief pleasantries were exchanged. McManus was a big man, tall but muscular with sunken cheeks and lustrous black hair which was brushed back, accentuating the widow's peak he had. His eyes were set close together, rather like fog lamps on the front of a car, only these particular lights glowed with a pale grey hue as Harold found himself pinned beneath their gaze.

"Pierce, isn't it," said McManus, smiling thinly.

Harold nodded.

"How long have you been with us?"

"Two months, sir," said Harold, lowering his head, slightly. "Perhaps a bit longer."

"And you were entrusted with the disposal of aborted foetuses on a number of occasions during this time.

Correct?" The words had a harsh, almost accusatory ring to them.

Harold nodded.

"Did you in fact complete the disposal procedure?" McManus wanted to know.

"I did as I was told, sir," Harold insisted, a slight pain gnawing at the back of his neck.

McManus nodded in the direction of Cayton who was sitting to Harold's left.

"Mr Cayton tells me that you tried to prevent him from disposing of a dead foetus," said the doctor. "Is this true?"

"I didn't feel well that day," Harold said, blankly, his one good eye staring right through McManus. He appeared to be in a dazed condition, his mouth forming words which his mind had not formulated.

"How many other times have you tried to interfere with the disposal procedure?"

"I haven't done . . . I didn't try to stop anyone else." The words were coming slowly, monosyllabically. As if each one were an effort. Something not unnoticed by either the doctor or Cayton.

"Are you all right, Pierce?" asked McManus.

"Yes, sir," Harold insisted.

Doctor and porter exchanged puzzled looks.

"Did *you* bury those bodies in the field, Pierce?" McManus wanted to know.

Harold hesitated, closing his eyes for a moment.

He shook his head.

"Why do the children have to be burned?" he asked, looking straight at the doctor with a stare which made the other man recoil.

McManus sucked in a troubled breath.

"Could you wait outside for a while please, Pierce?" he said, watching as the porter got unsteadily to his feet and walked to the door, closing it gently behind him.

"Pierce was the only one who could have prevented the disposal of the five foetuses we found in the field. Correct?" said McManus.

Cayton nodded.

"Yes, sir, but God knows how he did it," the porter confessed.

"I think it's more to the point, *why* he did it? Although his past would go some way to explaining that I suppose." The doctor exhaled deeply. "I don't see that we have any alternative other than to dismiss him. It's unfortunate but I'm just grateful the papers didn't find out about it."

"Wasn't there a similar case in Germany a few years ago?" said Cayton. "Only there, they'd been making soap out of the remains."

McManus raised one eyebrow.

"He lives on the grounds doesn't he?"

"Yes," Cayton told him. "In that old hut."

"Well, I'm afraid he'll have to leave there too."

"What if he's got nowhere to go, sir?"

"That's not our problem, Cayton. The man is obviously unbalanced in some way. He'll probably end up back in an institution. Probably the best place for him. I just don't want him in *my* hospital." The doctor was already reaching for a switch on the console before him. He flipped it up.

"Send Pierce back in will you, please," he said, settling back in his chair, hands clasped across his lap.

Harold re-entered and sat down, listening unconcernedly as McManus explained that he was to lose his job. It wasn't until the doctor mentioned leaving the hut that the older porter showed any trace of reaction. His one good eye seemed to bulge momentarily but the moment passed and he sat in silence as the reasons for his dismissal were reeled off. But Harold wasn't listening to McManus, his attention was focused on the voices which spoke to him from within. The doctor finally finished and leant forward in his chair, glancing first at Cayton and then at Harold.

"I'm sorry things turned out like this, Pierce," he said. "I realize your problems. Perhaps you would be better off. . ." he was struggling to find the words, rummaging amidst the welter of bluntness for a few morsels of tact. "It might be best if you returned to the institution. I can contact doctor Vincent, I'm sure, if you have nowhere else to go, he would understand."

"Thank you," said Harold, blankly, absently touching the scarred side of his face. It felt dry beneath his fingers.

"Do you have somewhere to go, Harold?" asked Cayton.

"Yes." The word came out almost angrily. "I have somewhere to go." He got to his feet, a new found strength filling him. "I have somewhere to go."

A hissing, sibilant command sounded so loud inside his head that he almost winced but he turned and walked towards the door, moving as if each step were an effort.

"Goodbye," he said and left them.

It was a long time before either McManus or Cayton spoke.

As Harold stepped into the lift he looked straight through Maggie Ford. She smiled at him but the gesture provoked no response. His one good eye looked as glassy as the false one, his skin was the colour of rancid butter.

"Harold." Maggie put out her hand to touch his shoulder.

He looked at her again, some of the mistiness vanishing from that blank stare. He touched his face and swallowed hard.

"Harold, are you all right?" she asked him, as the lift doors slid shut.

He opened his mouth to speak, his lips fluttering noiselessly.

The words inside his head became warnings.

Harold looked squarely at Maggie, his brow furrowing slightly. She released her grip on his shoulder, much as someone would let go of a dog when they'd just discovered it was liable to bite them at any minute. The doctor regarded Harold warily, somewhat relieved when his expression changed to its customary calm blankness.

"I'm leaving here," he said, softly.

Maggie looked puzzled.

"Leaving? Why?"

"They told me to leave. Because of the children."

"What children, Harold?" she demanded. "And who asked you to leave?"

"Doctor McManus told me to leave." He gazed at her with that seething vehemence once more, his face darkening.

"They kill the children," he hissed.

Maggie was almost relieved when the lift reached its appointed floor and she could step out and away from Harold. She glanced back at him, watching as the doors slid shut on his disfigured visage. She waited a moment then took the stairs up to the fourth floor and Doctor McManus's office.

Maggie didn't time how long she was in the senior consultant's office but she guessed later that it couldn't have been more than five minutes. She tried to persuade her superior that Harold was in a bad way both physically and mentally.

"He's ill," she insisted. "He should be taken into care, not thrown out onto the streets."

McManus was unimpressed.

"He committed a breach of hospital regulations," the

older man said. "He's lucky he's not being prosecuted never mind dismissed."

When she asked what he meant, he explained about the foetuses, the grave in the field, how Harold had hidden the bodies and then interred them in secret rather than incinerating them.

"Oh God," murmured Maggie.

"*Now* do you understand why he has to go?" said McManus, irritably. "The man's disturbed. I should never have taken him on in the first place."

"Well then that's all the more reason to take him into care," Maggie insisted.

"He needs psychiatric help, not medical help."

She told him about the cuts on Harold's body but McManus was obviously tiring of the conversation and it showed in the sharp edge which his words acquired.

"As far as I'm concerned, Miss Ford, the matter is closed. Pierce will be out of the grounds by tomorrow morning." He looked at his watch, tapping the glass. "Now I suggest you return to *your* duties. I presume you have patients to attend to?"

"Yes, doctor," she said, her face flushed.

She left the office, closing the door just a little too firmly behind her. There was something badly wrong with Harold and she was determined to find out what it was. She glanced at her watch. It was 5.30 p.m., in another two hours she would be off duty. When that time came, she decided she would go to Harold's hut and speak to him.

Thirty-one

Harold moved slowly about the hut collecting what few possessions he had, bundling them into the battered old suitcase he'd been lent. Every now and then he would stop still and glance towards the kitchen, as if trying to catch sight of something. The voices whispered insistently inside his head, like the wind rustling paper.

He heard scuffling sounds coming from the cupboard in the kitchen. There was hessian laid out before it and, when the last item was dropped into the suitcase, Harold passed into the other room and knelt before the door, his hand quivering slightly as he slid it open.

A vile, cloying stench billowed from the hiding place and Harold recoiled at the ferocity of the odour. He gazed into the cupboard, mesmerized.

All three of the foetuses had doubled in size.

Maggie Ford glanced at the clock on the wall of her office and noted that it was approaching 7.40 p.m. She sat back in her seat, slipping the cap back onto her pen. Her neck and shoulders ached and she reached up with both hands to perform some swift massage. Outside, the sky was mottled with rain clouds and a thin film of drizzle covered the office window like a gossamer shroud. Maggie yawned and got to her feet, remembering that she'd promised herself a visit to Harold's hut before she went home that night. She took off her white coat and hung it up on the hook, pulling on a lightweight mac in its place. She glanced at a chart on the office wall and noticed that she was due in surgery at eight-thirty the following morning. Maggie took one final look around the office then flicked off the light and left.

She took the lift down to the ground floor, mumbling

a few hasty "goodnights" on her way to the main entrance. When she reached it she paused, pulling up her collar to protect herself from the worst ravages of the icy wind. The chill in the air was turning the drizzle into particles of sleet and Maggie shivered, turning to her left, heading towards the open stretch of ground which would take her to Harold's hut. Almost invisible in the gloom, she could see that no lights burned inside and she wondered if perhaps he'd gone to bed. As far as she knew he didn't go out at nights so it was more than likely that he was in the small dwelling. She muttered to herself as her heels sank into the soft earth but she struggled on towards the still and black shrouded hut.

She found herself shivering but the movements were not merely a product of the cold weather. She felt an unaccountable fear rising within her as she drew nearer to the building. Perhaps it had been Harold's reactions in the lift which had unsettled her, she thought, angry with herself for feeling the trepidation she now experienced. It was pity she should be feeling for Harold, not fear.

Maggie found that the door of the hut was slightly ajar. She knocked all the same, simultaneously calling the older man's name. When she received no answer, she cautiously pushed the wooden door which swung back on its hinges with a high pitched shriek. Maggie called Harold's name once more then stepped inside.

The smell of damp was almost overpowering but mingled with it was a more pungent odour which she had difficulty identifying. She looked around the interior of the place. The bed had been stripped, the sheets and blankets gone but, on the mattress she noticed a dark stain. Now dried and powdery, the substance seemed to crumble beneath her probing fingers. She wet the tip of her index finger and on withdrawing it from the mysterious patch she found that it was congealed blood. Maggie swallowed hard and looked around. The door to her right, the one which led through to the kitchen, was closed.

"Harold," she called, moving towards the door.

The hut greeted her with silence.

She pushed the door but found that it was stuck.

Maggie tried again and, this time, it budged a few inches. She put her weight against it, realizing that the door was a fraction of an inch too large and was sticking. Eventually, she succeeded in opening it and found herself standing in the tiny kitchen.

The door of the cupboard beneath the sink was open, the handle splashed with blood.

Maggie squatted before it and squinted through the gloom at the crimson liquid. It glistened in the half-light and she could see that it was fresh. There was a fetid stench coming from the cupboard and Maggie paused for long seconds before deciding to look inside. She gripped the handle, trying to avoid the blood, and pulled it open.

There was something inside the cupboard, something which she couldn't see in the blackness. Something moving.

She could hear a faint scratching too, an agitated skittering which stopped abruptly. The cupboard was large, large enough for a fully grown man to climb into but Maggie certainly had no intentions of crawling inside to see what was making the noise. She coughed, her eye suddenly caught by something which lay on the wooden floor beside her. She picked up the matted strands, turning them over in her fingers.

There was a sudden movement from within the cupboard and Maggie screamed as something soft and furry brushed against her leg. She dropped the stiff fur, almost overbalancing.

The mouse scampered away, past her and disappeared through a hole in the wall.

Maggie sucked in a deep breath, held it for a second then exhaled.

"God," she murmured and got to her feet.

She ran both hands through her hair and blew out a troubled breath. Harold Pierce was gone, no doubt about that. But exactly where, she had no idea.

The old Exham Mental Hospital now stood deserted and already dust had begun to accumulate in thick layers on the floors and window-ledges. Some of the windows had been broken, the dirty glass lying in the wards which were now empty of beds. It was as black as pitch in the empty building and Harold blinked his one good eye repeatedly, as if the action would somehow give him the power to see through the darkness. But he had lived at the hospital for so long he knew every inch of it and he moved with assurance through the long corridors, his tired footsteps echoing loudly in the silence. He was aware of nothing but the musty smell of the place and the aching in his legs where he had walked for so long. He had no idea what the time was but, outside, a large watery moon gave him some light and illuminated his stumbling progess somewhat.

He had left the three foetuses in a room on the first floor while he himself explored the remains of the deserted asylum. For the first time in months he actually felt happy. It was like a homecoming for him. He belonged here in this place, in this empty Victorian shell which smelt of damp and was thick with dust. It had been his home for so many years before and now it would be his home again.

He paused at the foot of the staircase which would take him up to the first floor, the voices hissing in his ears again. They were calling him and Harold made his way almost eagerly to his room where they waited.

Thirty-two

Lynn Tyler grunted as she felt the weight of the man's body on top of her. She sucked in a deep breath but it slowly subsided into a groan of pleasure as she felt his swollen penis slide into her. He bent his head forward, his unshaven cheek scraping her.

"Don't you ever shave?" she murmured, her complaint dissolving away into another exclamation of pleasure as he began thrusting into her with firm strokes.

She couldn't remember his name. Barry or Gary. Something like that. It didn't matter much to her either way. She'd picked him up at a disco about two hours earlier and was now enjoying the consummation of what, for her, was to be yet another notch on the bed-stead.

She ran a hand through his thick black hair, wincing slightly as she felt the slick greasiness of it. His breath smelt of beer and, when he kissed her, it was a clumsy slobbering action, rather like being accosted by a Saint Bernard. However, she weathered his attentions, enjoying the sensations he was creating within her. One of his rough hands went to her breast and squeezed hard. So hard that she yelped in pain but all he did was grin and squeeze the other one with equal force. Her nipples rose to meet his strong advances, her hips now beginning to rotate in time to his thrusts.

She felt a glow around her groin which spread slowly to her belly but it was not the pleasant warmth that signals the approach of orgasm. It was an uncomfortably familiar burning sensation which she had experienced two or three times since returning from hospital. Lynn sucked in a sharp breath as a stab of pain jolted her. Her lover took it to be a sign of her excitement and grunted something but she didn't hear him, her mind was now occupied with the growing pain in her lower region which seemed to be intensifying. The weight on top of her seemed almost unbearable but she gritted her teeth, whispering words of encouragement in his ear, trying by any means she could to drive the thoughts of the searing pain from her mind.

Barry or Gary or whatever his name was, suddenly withdrew his organ, leaving her panting in frustration but that feeling of frustration did not remain long as, a moment later, she felt his hot breath on her left breast then the right. His tongue flicked against her swollen nipples and he drew them between his teeth making them even harder and more erect.

The pain in her abdomen grew more acute. The skin across her belly seemed first to contract and then to stretch, rising in two places in the form of almost imperceptible bumps. Lynn swallowed hard, the burning sensation now even stronger. It felt as if someone had poured a kettle full of boiling water all over her abdomen.

A particularly prominent bulge rose just to the right of her navel, strained against the flesh defiantly for long seconds then vanished.

The man was up on his knees now, looking down at her vagina and she almost screamed aloud as she saw the blood.

Lynn Tyler thrust a shaking hand between her legs and withdrew it slowly to see crimson staining her fingertips. She felt the burning inside her, stared at the blood as it trickled down her quivering digits and, finally, she did scream.

Thirty-three

It was cold inside the pathology lab and Randall dug both hands deep inside his trouser pockets. The smell of chemicals was strong and the inspector wrinkled his nose, peering around the large room with its green painted, white tiled walls. There were three stainless steel slabs set side by side, the last of which bore a sheet covered occupant. There was a small tag attached to the big toe of the left foot. It bore a name and a three digit number. The number coincided with one of the many lockers that ran the full length of the far wall. A storecase for sightless eyes.

Above the slab dangled a scale, beside it there was a tray littered with surgical instruments, one of which, Randall noticed with revulsion, was a saw. He glanced across at PC Fowler who looked even paler than usual beneath the glare of the fluorescents. The young constable was gazing at the covered body on the far slab. He was shivering and, he told himself, it was not solely the product of the chill air.

In one corner of the lab there was a sink and it was there that the hospital's chief pathologist stood. He washed his hands then pulled on a pair of rubber gloves, pressing his fingers together to ensure that they fitted like a second skin. Ronald Potter turned and headed for the slab. He was in his forties, his bald dome hidden by the toupée which he wore. It was a bad fit because flecks of what little hair he retained showed beneath it at the rear but Randall was concerned with more important things than ill-fitting hair pieces at the moment. Both he and Fowler moved forward as Potter reached the slab and pulled back the sheet.

The pathologist eyed the corpse indifferently, leaning over it, inspecting the preliminary damage. He stroked his chin thoughtfully, considering the object before him with the same concentration which a child would apply to selecting a sweet from a chocolate box.

Randall looked at the body for a moment then diverted his gaze towards the pathologist.

Fowler gritted his teeth and looked away, trying to retain his breakfast.

The body was badly mutilated about the shoulders and was, once again, headless. Blood had trickled into the gutter which ran around the rim of the slab, most of it from the torn stump of the neck. The head had been severed much higher up this time, just below the bottom jaw as far as Randall could see. Indeed, fragments of bone and even a tooth also lay on the slab where the head should have been.

Potter reached for a metal probe and began poking about in one of the many gashes that criss-crossed the remains of the neck.

"This is becoming something of a habit isn't it, Inspector?" he asked, plucking a pair of tweezers from the trolley.

"What?" asked Randall, puzzled, his attention riveted to the stomach-turning sight before him.

"Finding headless corpses." The pathologist looked up and smiled, humorlessly. "How many is this now? Three isn't it?"

Randall clenched his fists at his side and glared at the older man.

"Someone somewhere must have quite a collection. I didn't know we had head-hunters in Exham."

"What are you a pathologist or a fucking comedian?" snapped the Inspector, irritably. "I want to know what he was killed with. I don't want Sunday Night at the London Palladium."

It was Potter's turn to glare. The two men locked stares for a moment then the pathologist returned to his work. He laboured in silence for a good ten minutes then straightened up, wiping some blood off on his apron.

"As far as I can see, the head was severed with the same weapon as the one used on the two previous victims." He paused. "A single-edged blade of some kind. There's rust in two or three of the wounds as well." The older man pulled the sheet further back and regarded the remains of the body. "No other external damage. The pattern's the same."

"With the other two you said that there was a lot of blood in the lungs," Randall reminded him. "What about this one?"

Potter smiled thinly and reached for a new tool. He held it before him and Randall saw that it was a tiny buzz-saw, its steel blade glinting beneath the lights.

"Let's have a look, shall we?" said Potter and checked to see if the instrument was plugged in. It was. He stepped on a pedal near his left foot and the buzz-saw whirred into action with a sound that reminded Randall of a dentist's drill. As he watched, the pathologist lowered the spinning blade to a point just below the sternum of the corpse, then, with one expert movement, he buried it in the flesh, allowing the screaming blade to carve a path through dead flesh and bone, opening the rib cage until the lungs were exposed. A foul stench rose from the open chest cavity and both Randall and Fowler backed away.

The high-pitched whine ceased abruptly, to be replaced by a sickening crack as the older man prized open the sawn-through rib cage exposing the vital organs beneath. He picked up a pair of scissors and carefully snipped away at the lining of the chest, finally cutting into the left lung just below the trachea. As the expertly-wielded scissors sliced through the pleura, a clear fluid spilled out to be followed, a second later, by the first dark, almost black, clots of congealed blood. Seemingly oblivious to the thick red cascade, Potter opened the lung from top to bottom finally pulling open the organ with his gloved hands. Randall swallowed hard.

"Exactly the same as the other two," said Potter.

"What exactly does that mean?" the Inspector asked, trying to look anywhere but at the ruined torso of the corpse before him. He wanted a smoke and his fingers anxiously toyed with the packet of Rothmans in his pocket but he kept his composure as best he could and waited for an answer.

Potter shrugged.

"The killer attacked from behind. That's easy enough to see from these wounds here," he pointed to three particularly large gashes on the lower part of the neck. "The blade was used in a type of swatting action. These are cuts, not punctures. The fact that there are no defence cuts on the hands or arms would seem to indicate that the victim was dead after the first or second blow."

"Could the head have been severed with one stroke?" Randall wanted to know. "By a very strong man for instance."

Potter shook his head.

"No,"

"You sound very sure."

"Well, Inspector, for one thing, strength has nothing to do with it." He smiled thinly. "It's technique. When beheading was the accepted form of execution during the Middle Ages, right up to the sixteenth century, there was a certain art to it. The headsmen were trained for their job and even then it was common for them to take two or three blows to sever the head completely. And they used axes or large swords. These wounds were inflicted with a small weapon."

Randall nodded.

"Thanks for the history lesson," he said.

"Besides, in this case," he motioned towards the

corpse, "As with the previous two, the head was removed by a series of blows. Chopped not sliced off."

Fowler blenched and decided he needed some fresh air. Randall told him to wait in the car outside. The young constable left, gratefully, his footsteps echoing around the large cold room. The other two men waited until the PC had departed then they spoke briskly, Randall watching as the pathologist completed the autopsy. His mind was brimming over with ideas and thoughts. Harvey. The murder weapon. But, something which Potter had said troubled him, something about strength having nothing to do with it. He turned the thought over in his mind finally dismissing it. The incident at the grocer's shop the other night had confirmed his suspicions once and for all. Paul Harvey was responsible for these killings. It was just a matter of finding him. Randall chewed his bottom lip contemplatively. Find Harvey. That was what he'd been trying to do for nearly three months now and he was still no closer. As he stood in this cold room his men were out searching Exham and the surrounding countryside, covering ground which they'd already searched months before in a vain effort to find the maniac. Randall exhaled deeply and looked at his watch. It was 10.34 a.m. He'd been at the hospital for over three hours, ever since the corpse had been discovered in the front garden of a house on the south side of town. The Inspector had driven to the scene of the crime and then ridden the ambulance to the hospital to await the autopsy report. He had not intended to stay for the actual event but, he had reasoned, there was nothing for him to do back at his office except twiddle his thumbs and lose his temper trying to figure out just where the hell Harvey was. So he had stayed.

Potter completed his work and pulled the sheet back over the body, calling in one of the lab technicians to complete the task of sewing the corpse up again.

Randall watched as the older man washed his hands at the sink, humming happily to himself as he did so. When he'd finished he turned to face the policeman.

"Is there anything else I can do for you, Inspector?" he said, sardonically.

Randall shook his head.

"I do have other work to do," the pathologist reminded him, motioning towards the door.

The policeman shot him an acid glance and headed towards the exit, glad to leave this foul place. He slammed the door behind him and headed for the lift, jabbing the button which would take him up to the ground floor. He closed his eyes as the car rose the short distance to the upper level. It smelt of plastic and perspiration in there and Randall was pleased when he could step out. He fumbled in his jacket pocket and retrieved his cigarettes, hurriedly lighting one up. He'd taken two drags on it when a voice called to him and he turned to see an attractive woman walking towards him. She wore a long white coat, open to reveal a green blouse and grey skirt. But, as she drew closer, Randall found himself captivated by a pair of piercing blue eyes. They gleamed like chips of sapphire but there was a warmth to them.

She pointed to a sign on the wall to his left which said "NO SMOKING" in large red letters. He took the cigarette from his mouth and dropped it, grinding it out beneath his foot.

She had seen him emerge from the lift and, immediately, her curiosity had been aroused.

"You're not a member of staff are you?" It was a statement, not a question.

"No." He smiled, still gazing into those gleaming blue eyes. "You could say I was here on business."

She looked puzzled but Randall fumbled in his pocket for his ID. He flipped the slim wallet open and showed it to her.

"Police," she said.

He nodded.

"It's not a very good photo," she said, indicating the small snap in the wallet. Their eyes locked for brief seconds and Randall detected the hint of a smile on her lips.

"Is it about the murders?"

He snapped the wallet shut, his expression hardening.

"What makes you think that?" he asked, sharply.

"Because we don't have too many policemen calling here at this time in the morning." She studied his face, hard and lined, puffy beneath the eyes from lack of sleep. He still had some stubble on his chin from his hasty shave. "Don't look so alarmed," she told him. "Word does travel you know. Three murders in less than a week is bound to be news."

Randall nodded.

"So who are you?" he wanted to know.

She introduced herself and, as he held her hand he found his gaze drawn once more to those blue orbs. She was, indeed, a very attractive woman. He looked for the wedding ring on her left hand but didn't see one, something which surprised him. They exchanged brief pleasantries then Randall announced that he should be going.

She called him back.

"Have you got any idea who you're looking for?" she asked.

Randall eyed her suspiciously.

"That's police information, Miss Ford," he said. "Why do you ask?"

"Well, it's probably nothing. . ." She allowed the sentence to trail off but Randall's curiosity was suddenly and unexpectedly aroused.

"What is it? If you've heard anything, tell me." There was a note of urgency in his voice now.

She explained about Harold. Falteringly, not sure whether she was making a fool of herself or not, she told Randall about the ex-porter's background, about the examination she had carried out, and about Harold's apparent regression. Randall listened but was unimpressed. She mentioned her search of the hut, the discovery of the blood and finally, almost reluctantly, the incident with the foetuses' grave.

"Jesus Christ," muttered Randall. "Where is he now?"

"No one knows," said Maggie.

The Inspector ran a hand through his hair.

"Everybody seems to be disappearing," he said, wearily.

"Maybe it's just my imagination but, well, he was disturbed," she said.

Randall nodded.

"I don't think this. . ." He asked the porter's name again and she told him. "I don't think Pierce is tied up with these killings. The severed heads, they're like Harvey's trade-mark. I can't see that it's anyone but him." He hesitated. "But I'll check out this Pierce anyway." He turned to leave but paused. "Thanks, Miss Ford."

"Maggie," she said.

"Thanks, Maggie," he said, smiling. "You know, if every doctor looked like you the Health Service would have an even longer waiting list." He winked and headed for the exit.

She watched him go, wondering if she had done the right thing. She doubted that Harold was connected in any way with the killings but if Randall could find out where he was she would feel a little easier. She took the lift to her office, the vision of Randall's hard but appealing face still strong in her mind. It was a vision that would not fade easily.

Randall slid into the passenger seat beside Fowler and nodded for the constable to start the car. He told the young PC to drive out to the new psychiatric hospital on the outskirts of Exham and the journey was completed in less than twenty minutes. Neither of the men spoke, each wrapped up in his own thoughts. Fowler still felt queasy at the thought of the autopsy and Randall's mind was trying to digest the information which Maggie had given him. However, there was something else on the Inspector's mind, something not directly linked with police business. It was the doctor herself and, as he allowed his head to loll back against the head-rest he thought about those sparkling blue eyes and that soft brown hair. He even afforded himself a smile.

Messages came through over the two-way as they travelled as other cars reported in. The news was the same every time – not a trace of Harvey. Randall hooked the receiver back into place and looked up as Fowler swung the Panda into the driveway which led up to the new psychiatric hospital. What a contrast to the old place, thought Randall as he got out. Where there had been granite there was now glass. Where there'd been barred windows there was now double glazing. The entire structure looked light and airy, a marked contrast to the forbidding monolithic bearing of the old asylum.

Randall got out of the car, telling Fowler he wasn't sure how long he'd be. The Inspector discovered that Doctor Vincent was with a patient so Randall paced up and down a spacious outer office until the head of the hospital found time to see him. He smoked six cigarettes in the thirty minutes he was forced to wait, gleefully ignoring the sign which asked visitors to refrain from the habit. He ground out the final butt just as the doctor's door opened to admit him.

Randall declined the offer of a cup of coffee, more interested to know what Vincent could tell him about

Harold Pierce. The psychiatrist seemed puzzled at first but then produced a file which included a photo. Randall looked at it, struck immediately by the appalling disfiguring scar which covered half of Harold's face. He asked how the man came to bear it and Vincent told him the whole story.

"Have you seen anything of Pierce since he left the old asylum?" Randall wanted to know.

Vincent shook his head.

"He hasn't been readmitted?"

The psychiatrist looked puzzled.

"Is Harold in some sort of trouble, Inspector?" he asked.

Randall shook his head and asked, "Have you any idea where he might go? Did he have any relatives around here?"

"Look, Inspector Randall, is there something I should know? What exactly *is* going on?"

"Nothing as far as I know," said the policeman. "It's just that Pierce has gone missing. I wondered if you might know of his whereabouts. That's all."

Vincent stroked his chin thoughtfully, looking hurt, as if Harold's aberrations were some kind of personal slight against *him*.

"I haven't a clue where he might be," said Vincent.

The two men sat in silence for long moments then Randall coughed preemptively.

"While Pierce was under your care did he ever display any violent tendencies towards other patients?" he asked.

"Absolutely not," said Vincent, emphatically.

"What about against himself? Self-mutiliation, that type of thing?"

Vincent looked shocked.

"No."

Randall nodded, took one last look at the photo of Harold Pierce then got to his feet. He thanked the psychiatrist for his time and walked back out to the waiting Panda.

Fowler was dozing behind the wheel, the unrepaired heater still blasting out its full fury. The PC jerked upright when Randall knocked on the window. The Inspector climbed in and, after rubbing his face with both hands, Fowler started the engine, swinging the car round in the direction of Exham. They were back at the police station in less than thirty minutes.

Randall pulled off his coat and stuck it on the hanger on the back of his office door. He took the cigarettes from the pocket and crossed to his desk, lighting one up as he did so. He slumped into his chair and blew out a mouthful of smoke in a long blue stream. It swirled before him, writhing gently in the still air, forming patterns then dissipating. He sat forward and pulled a pencil and notepad towards him then, with rough strokes, he sketched a passing likeness of Harold Pierce's face somewhat over-emphasising the scarred side. Tiring of his attempts at art he wrote down two names beneath the sketch.

Paul Harvey

Harold Pierce

He considered them both for a moment then crossed out the bottom one, tapping on the pad with the end of the pencil.

Both men had disappeared, apparently without trace. Was there some bizarre link which he hadn't yet thought of? Randall scribbled across the rough sketch, tore the leaf from the pad and tossed it into the waste-bin. He pushed the thought from his mind. There was no link between the two men, he was searching for answers where there were none. Clutching at straws had become something of a hobby for him just lately.

The phone rang.

"Randall speaking."

"Inspector, it's me," the voice was immediately recognizable. "Maggie Ford."

Randall smiled to himself.

"What can I do for you, Miss. . ." He corrected himself. "Maggie?" He heard her laugh at the other end.

"It's about what I said earlier, about Harold Pierce. I didn't think at the time but I remember now, when he was dismissed, apparently he said that he *did* have somewhere to go."

"You wouldn't happen to know where that was?" Randall enquired.

She didn't.

"Well, not to worry. I've got some news for you too. After I left the hospital this morning, I went out to the new psychiatric place and did some checking up on your friend Harold. I think you can stop worrying. I spoke to the Chief Consultant psychiatrist there and he assured me that Pierce had never shown any signs of violence. If I had a list of suspects I'd cross him off it right now." He laughed, humourlessly.

"So you're convinced it's Harvey?" she said.

"No doubt about it."

There was silence at the other end for a moment. Randall frowned.

"Maggie."

"Yes," she said. "I'm still here." The pause was a nervous one, both anxious to prolong the conversation but not sure how to progress. Randall felt like a schoolkid and noticed, with amusement, that his hand was trembling slightly.

"What time do you finish work tonight?" he asked.

"I'm off at ten," she said, almost apologetically.

"I know a nice little restaurant that stays open until late. I can pick you up outside the hospital."

Maggie laughed.

"If you're asking me to dinner the answer is no."

Randall felt suddenly deflated, almost shocked at her refusal but his mood rapidly lightened as she continued speaking.

"I know the restaurant you're talking about," she said. "It's too expensive. Besides, I'm a better cook anyway and, my flat's nearer. You wouldn't have so far to drive."

It was Randall's turn to laugh.

She gave him her address.

"Be there at about quarter to eleven."

They exchanged farewells and Randall put the phone down, feeling happier than he'd felt for a long time.

There was a knock on the office door and Randall shouted for the visitor to enter. It was Sergeant Willis.

"Thought you might have brought me a cuppa, Norman," said the Inspector.

"Sorry, guv," said Willis. "Just the pathologist's full report and this." He handed another piece of paper to his superior. It bore the numbers of all the Panda cars belonging to the Exham force. Each number had the driver's name next to it.

"They've all just checked in," said Willis. "The East side of the town is clear. There's still no sign of Harvey."

The smile faded rapidly from Randall's face and the familiar feeling of angry frustration swiftly drove away the fleeting twinge of elation he'd experienced moments before.

"I suppose we just keep looking then?" said Willis.

Randall nodded.

"Yes," he muttered, his voice low. "We just keep looking."

Outside, it was beginning to get dark.

Thirty-four

"Well, I don't think the bus is coming," said Debbie Snell pushing another stick of Juicy Fruit into her mouth.

"If we hadn't been mucking about in maths we wouldn't have got detention and we wouldn't have missed the bloody bus would we?" Colette Hill told her irritably.

"Well we *were* mucking about and we *did* get detention," Debbie said, leaning against the bus stop.

"Why don't you ring your precious Tony up," Belinda Vernon told her. "If you hadn't been going on about him we wouldn't have got told off in the beginning."

"Oh piss off," Debbie said, defiantly. "Anyway, if the bus isn't here soon I might just do that."

All three girls were from Exham Comprehensive School, the largest of the town's three schools and they wore its distinctive maroon blazer. Which, in Debbie's case refused to do up because of her mountainous breasts. All three girls were fifteen but Debbie was a taller, more mature-looking youngster than her two companions. They stood forlornly at the stop glancing agitatedly at their watches or periodically glancing up the road in the hope that a bus would appear from around the corner. The bus stop itself, complete with its glass shelter, backed onto a thick outcrop of trees which, in turn, masked some of the rolling fields that formed Exham's boundaries.

It was from these trees that Paul Harvey watched the three girls.

As a teenager he had always found girls impossible to cope with. Their jokes, their jibes, their little tricks. He had not known how to react and, on one occasion, when one of them had made exaggerated advances towards him, he had been left humiliated – standing alone amidst the jeers and laughter trying to hide an uncontrollable erection. The memory, as did so many of the others, still hurt.

Now he watched the girls from the shelter of the trees, close enough to hear what they were saying. The sickle was gripped tightly in his hand.

Debbie took one more look at her watch.

"Well, I'm not waiting around any longer," she proclaimed. "I'm going to phone Tony."

She rummaged through her pocket for a coin and, with a haughty "Goodbye" set off down the hill towards the phone box. The other girls watched her go until finally she turned a corner and disappeared from view.

Harvey moved swiftly but stealthily through the trees, tracing a parallel path with the lone girl. The dusk was deepening into darkness now, further adding to his concealment and he was content to remain within the confines of the woods, his eyes constantly on Debbie.

She reached the phone box and pulled open the door.

Harvey watched as she dialled. He could see her speaking into the mouthpiece and, a few minutes later, she put the receiver down and stepped back outside.

He watched her for a full five minutes as she paced back and forth then, slowly, he rose to his full height and moved through the trees towards her.

Debbie had her back to him and the growing wind masked the sound of breaking twigs and the big man emerged from the woods.

He was within ten yards of her now, almost clear of the trees.

She looked at her watch, oblivious to his approach.

The black Capri came speeding round the corner, headlamps blazing. Debbie ran across the road to meet it, jumping in happily. The driver a young man in his early twenties, spun the wheel and the vehicle turned full circle, heading back to Exham.

Harvey melted back into the woods, merging with the darkness as if he were a shadow.

Thirty-five

Harold sat up, the nightmare fading rapidly as consciousness swept over him. He blinked in the darkness, rubbed his eyes and, as he did so, he felt the perspiration on his face.

It was almost pitch black in the deserted asylum. He had a hurricane lamp in the room but he dare not light it. He sat shivering in the darkness, listening to the high mournful wailing of the wind as it whistled through the countless broken windows on the lower floor, stirring the dust which coated the floors so thickly.

The foetuses were in one corner of the room, covered by a blanket to protect them from the cold. Harold squinted through the gloom, his ears picking up the sounds of their low guttural raspings. He could see the blanket rising and falling intermittently. For what seemed like an eternity he sat cross-legged on the dirty floor then, slowly, he reached for the hurricane lamp and the box of matches nearby. He struck a match, lifted the housing on the lamp and watched as the wick began to glow yellow then he dropped the housing back into place, the dull light gradually filling the room, spreading out like an ink blot around him, driving back the darkness. Holding the lamp in one hand, Harold crawled towards the dormant foetuses.

His hand hovered over the blanket for what seemed like an eternity, then he slowly pulled it back.

The creatures appeared to be sleeping, their eyes closed, sealed only by the thin membrane of skin through which the gleaming blackness of those magnetic orbs still showed. Harold ran an appraising eye over them, swallowing hard.

One of them moved and its arm flopped limply against his knee. Harold let out a low moan and held the hurricane lamp closer to the outstretched limb. The breath caught in his throat and his one good eye bulged in its socket.

As if pulled by invisible wires, the stubby fingers of the nearest foetus slowly elongated, lengthened into spidery tendrils. The flesh looked soft but leathery. Harold pulled the cover back a little more and watched in fascination as the same thing happened with the creature's other hand.

He backed off, heart pounding hard against his ribs.

They were developing at a faster rate than even *he* had first imagined.

Harold sat gazing at them, his mind in a turmoil. Torn between fear and fascination. There was no revulsion any longer, just foreboding.

He wondered how long it would be before the foetuses completed their growth.

Thirty-six

Randall parked his car and walked across to the small group of flats on the other side of the street. Beneath the sodium glare of the street-lamp he checked his watch.

10.43 p.m.

"Spot on," he said to himself, pushing open the double doors which led into the hallway. There was a staircase ahead of him and a lift to his right. He chose the stairs, walking up slowly, feeling somewhat self-conscious carrying the spray of red carnations. Two kids, about fifteen, bundled their way past him laughing raucously and, minutes later, Randall heard the roar of motor-bike engines as the two of them sped off. They'll probably be wrapped round a tree by midnight, he thought. He'd always wanted a motor-bike when he was a kid but his parents had resolutely forbidden it. Death traps, his father had called them. Over the years, with the number of accidents he'd seen, Randall had come to agree.

He reached the landing and found that it was bright and clean-looking with paintings hung on two of the walls. There was an enormous rubber plant outside one of the flat doors which looked like something out of "The Day of the Triffids". The building consisted of just three storeys, six flats on each floor and it bore a marked contrast to the flats on the larger estates on the other side of Exham. No grafitti here, he thought. No dog shit in the hallway or cat's piss on the landings. Sweetness and light he mused, somewhat sardonically. The small block was quiet, everyone either went to bed early or Maggie was the only one on this floor he thought as he found her number. He pressed the bell and a two tone chime answered him. He held the carnations beside him, finally producing them when Maggie herself opened the door.

She smiled broadly, her face lighting up and, once more, Randall was struck by her extraordinarily sparkling eyes. It was like looking at a June sky – two pieces of heaven captured within those glittering orbs. She was dressed in a crisply laundered grey dress and a pair of high-heeled gold shoes which seemed to accentuate the smooth curve of her calves. Maggie was a small woman, about five-three Randall guessed, but the graceful suppleness of her legs made her appear taller. He ran a quick, appreciative eye over her, thinking how different she looked from when he'd first seen her that morning.

She ushered him in, taking the flowers gratefully.

"I didn't know what sort of chocolates you liked," he said, somewhat self-consciously. "So I thought I'd play safe."

"They're beautiful," she said and went off to find a vase. "Sit down."

He sank into the welcoming luxuriance of the sofa and looked around him. The room was quite large but sparsely furnished with just the three piece suite, a sideboard and a coffee table. A gas fire blazed before him, one of those with mock flames. There was a portable TV perched on a high table in the far corner of the room, a small music centre to his left. Two doors led out of the room, the one which Maggie had disappeared through led into the kitchen, the other one, closed at the moment, led to the bedroom and bathroom.

Behind the sofa on which he sat there was a small dining table set for two and the policeman could smell food cooking. The lights were dimmed and the whole room had a cosy feel to it. Immediately Randall felt relaxed.

Maggie returned a moment later carrying the flowers in a white vase. She set it down on the coffee table. He smelt her perfume as she leant over, a subtle aroma which lingered after her.

She poured him a drink and they talked gaily for a while until Maggie got up, announcing that the supper was ready. Randall got to his feet and wandered across to the table, watching her as she carried the meal in.

Randall savoured the meal. It was indeed a treat to eat something prepared by a woman's hands, especially when she was as attractive as Maggie. He looked up at her and for long seconds he imagined he was sitting opposite his dead wife but the vision hastily vanished.

"I'm not used to cooking for two," she said.

He reached for the wine bottle and poured them both a glass.

"That surprises me," he said.

"Why?"

"You're an attractive woman. It's not usual to find women like you on their own."

"Men don't seem interested in women who can compete with them on the same level," she said. "I mean, as far as a career goes. It seems to frighten them off. A woman anywhere else but the kitchen sink is a threat to their egos."

Randall raised his glass in salute.

"Come back Germaine Greer, all is forgiven," he said, smiling. "Where did you dig that speech up from?"

"I'm sorry," she said.

"It's ok, but, like I said, I'm still surprised you're single."

"I could say the same about you," she said, smiling.

Randall grinned.

"I think there's a compliment in there somewhere but I can't quite find it."

"You do live alone though?" she asked.

His smile faded somewhat. He nodded and sipped at his wine.

"Yeah, I have done for the last five years," he told her.

He returned to his food, aware that her eyes were upon him.

"I *was* married. I had a little girl: Lisa. She was two when it happened." He chewed his food slowly, finally sitting back in his chair, running the tip of his index finger around the rim of his glass. Maggie watched him silently.

"My wife, Fiona," he began, "she asked me to drive her and Lisa to her mother's. Well, I was just about to set off when I got a call through, could I come down to the station? They'd hauled a suspect in, wanted me to talk to him. I forget what it was about. Anyway, I told her that she'd have to drive herself, that the case was important." He sipped his wine, the voice which he heard sounded alien, distant, as if it didn't belong to him and he realized that he was speaking about the event for the first time since it had happened all those years ago. It seemed like an eternity.

"She'd only passed her test a few weeks earlier." He smiled thinly. "I remember how pleased she was when she *did* pass. But she didn't fancy driving at night, that was why she asked me to take her and Lisa." He paused again. "A lorry hit the car. Big bastard it was, sixteen wheeler. It took the fire brigade four hours to cut them loose from the wreckage. Of course they were both dead by that time anyway." He took a long swallow from his glass.

"Oh God, I'm sorry, Lou," she said.

He nodded.

"If *I'd* have been driving, it probably wouldn't have happened."

"You can't know that," she said.

"Sometimes I wish I'd have died with them," he confessed.

"You shouldn't blame yourself," she said.

He smiled, humourlessly.

"People used to say that to me all the time after it happened. All except Fiona's mother who seemed to agree that it *was* my fault. She hasn't spoken to me since the day it happened."

There was a long silence finally broken by Randall.

"Well, things are getting a bit morbid, aren't they? Shall we change the subject?"

He suggested they clear the table, offering to help

with the washing up. They carried the plates into the kitchen where she washed and he dried. They talked unceasingly, as if each had finally found some kind of confessor. Someone to whom their life's secrets could be revealed without the risk of scorn or judgement. And, in their openness they discovered just how desolate and empty their lives really were, but the discovery of that fact seemed only to pull them closer until, by midnight when they moved back into the sitting room with a cup of coffee each, they felt as if they'd known one another all their lives.

Randall sat down on the sofa, Maggie kicked off her shoes and sat beside him on the floor, legs tucked beneath her. She rested her coffee cup on the cushion next to him and ran a hand through her hair.

Randall watched her, realizing that he wanted her badly. Maggie felt a similar yearning but there was something nagging at the back of her mind. Something which she had not experienced with the other men she'd known. She wanted him, that much she knew but, for some unknown reason, she was afraid of rejection. She knew that he felt something for her, even if it was only physical, but she could not shake the feeling that she would be betraying the memory of his wife and child if she gave herself up to her feelings. But those feelings were powerful and, even as she sat talking to him, she felt compelled to take his heavy hand in hers, gently stroking the back, tracing the outline of his thick veins, stirring the hair which grew thickly on his hand and wrist.

Randall too was thinking about Fiona, wondering if he should be sitting here with this very attractive young woman wanting so badly to feel his body pressing against hers, to feel her hands on him and his on her. He had lost more than his family when Fiona and Lisa had been killed, he had lost a part of himself. The part that once knew happiness, compassion and optimism, but, in Maggie, maybe he had found someone who might help him to rediscover what he had lost. He gazed down at her as she bent forward to kiss the back of his hand and he could not resist the urge to lay one hand on the back of her neck, kneading the flesh there with his strong fingers. She felt so soft, so pliant and a tingle ran through him. You only met her this morning, he told himself, but that didn't seem to matter anymore. They were together and it seemed so right. As if they belonged with one another. He felt a single tear burst from his eye corner. There was fear there too. It had been so long. So long since he'd allowed himself to share any feelings he wondered if, when the time came, he would be able to.

Maggie climbed up onto the sofa beside him. She brushed the tear from his cheek with her index finger but she did not speak.

She thought of all those men before. Was this one going to be different? Could she actually find someone to love? She felt his arms pull her closer and she rested her head on his shoulder. For long seconds they remained still then she twisted around to face him and, tenderly at first, leant forward and kissed him on the lips. Randall responded and suddenly their kisses were deep and probing, making them both shudder. Almost reluctantly, Maggie broke away, her eyes wide, searching his.

"Does it bother you that I've been to bed with men in the past just because *I* wanted to?" she asked.

"Why should it?" he said. "It's your business, Maggie and, besides, the past doesn't matter."

"I think I've been very naive," she confessed. "I was confusing want with need. I wanted physical relationships but I needed something more."

Randall slid his arm around her, shuddering as he felt her hand touch his thigh.

"Do you always get philosophical at this time of night?" he asked, smiling.

"It depends on who I'm with," she said, grinning. "You're a good listener."

They lay down together on the floor and made love in the heat from the fire.

For long seconds afterwards, both of them gasped and shuddered with the intensity of their passion. Coupled together and breathless, they held each other tightly.

She bit his shoulder, drawing the skin between her teeth for brief moments until, when she withdrew her head, there was a small red mark there.

"Ouch," he said and nipped her ear lobe.

Maggie laughed, one hand stroking his hair, her finger finally tracing the outline of his eyebrows and, above those, the deep furrows which creased his forehead. She propped herself up on one elbow, looking down at him. She seemed fascinated by his hard face with its many lines and creases, each of which she seemed to follow with her nail.

"You must worry a lot," she said.

He looked vague.

"Wrinkles," she said, kissing him gently on the end of his nose. He frowned and she giggled.

"Do you know it takes forty-five facial muscles to frown but only fifteen to smile?" she asked.

"Thank you, doctor," he said, gripping her soft hand in his. "I don't usually have much to smile about."

She nodded, her expression softening.

"Will I still be smiling tomorrow, Maggie?" he asked.

"What do you mean?"

"This," he said. "Was this just another one night stand?"

She kissed him softly on the lips.

"I hope not," she whispered.

"The lonely doctor and the cynical, embittered copper

eh?" he said and, for a moment, she thought she heard a note of sarcasm in his voice. "Sounds like a perfect match."

She smiled as his tone lightened somewhat. He reached up and pulled her to him, holding her tightly. They gazed into each other's eyes, he, once more captivated by those glittering blue jewels with which she stared back at him.

"Would it surprise you to know that you are the first woman I've had since Fiona died?" he said.

Maggie looked a little shocked.

"Lou, I'm sorry if I've made you feel guilty. I. . ."

He put a finger to her lips to silence her.

"I suppose I can't live in the past forever," he said softly. "Nothing is going to bring her or Lisa back. I've got my memories and I'm grateful for them. I loved Fiona more than I thought it was possible to love anyone, and even more so when Lisa was born. When they were killed, something inside me died with them." He paused, swallowed hard and she could see his eyes misting over.

"Don't talk about it," she said, stroking his face.

"No, it's all right," he reassured her. "For the first time since it happened, I *want* to talk about it. For five years it's been bottled up. Because, until now there's been no one who I wanted to tell."

Maggie felt something stirring deep inside her. A feeling almost of pity for Randall.

Her voice took on a reflective tone.

"You know, all these years I've been calling myself liberated," she said, bitterly, "when all I've really been is a slag."

"Don't say that," he said.

She shook her head.

"It's true. I can't remember how many men I've had or maybe I've been fooling myself there too. Perhaps they've been having me." She kissed him on the cheek.

"And do you know what I've missed more than anything?"

He shook his head.

"Kids," she told him. "I've always loved kids but my bloody career came first where they were concerned too. Maybe that's why I work with kids. I'm a frustrated mother. Parent by proxy." She smiled humourlessly. "What I wouldn't give for my own child. . ." She allowed the sentence to trail off.

"I think that's enough soul-searching for one night, don't you?" said Randall, touching her face. He pulled her close to him once again and kissed her. She responded fiercely for a moment then broke away and got to her feet. For precious seconds, she stood, naked, before him and Randall gazed almost wonderingly at the smooth outlines of her glowing body.

"Let's go to bed," she said, flicking off the light.

Once in bed they found their passions roused once again and this time they were joined with an abandoned intensity.

Finally, exhausted, they fell asleep, clutching one another feeling that a shared demon was in the process of being exorcised.

PART THREE

". . . Evil, what is evil? There is only one evil, to deny life."

– D. H. Lawrence

". . . And after the fire a still small voice. . ."

– Kings 19:12

Thirty-seven

Harold was shaking, his entire body racked by uncontrollable shudders. He knelt over the three foetuses and tentatively reached out a hand to touch the one closest to him. Its skin felt soft and puffy, like the swollen flesh on a blister. It moved only slightly as his probing fingers pressed against its chest. The creature made a low gurgling sound and Harold recoiled slightly as some yellowish fluid oozed slowly from one corner of its mouth. The foetus had its eyes closed, the thin membranes of skin scarcely concealing the dark pits beneath.

Close by, the other two creatures dragged themselves towards it, black eyes shining malevolently. Harold looked round, heard the sounds as they approached, shook his head as if to dispel the sibilant hissing within. The voices gradually took on a sharp clarity. It was like the static clearing from a radio transmitter. First there would be just rasping sounds then the words would come through.

"What's wrong with him?" asked Harold, gazing down at the barely moving foetus before him. The thing lay completely motionless by this time, just its thin lips fluttering, the thick pus-like liquid dripping from its mouth.

"Please tell me," Harold said, almost pleadingly.

Hissing, more loudly now.

Harold shook his head.

"No."

They were more insistent.

"What should I do?"

Commands, which he knew must be obeyed.

Harold looked at the ailing foetus and then at its stronger companions. He hesitated for a moment realizing what must be done. But, his reluctance was momentary. He got to his feet and crossed the room to the blanket where he himself slept. Beneath the rolled up coat which passed as a pillow lay the kitchen knife. Harold picked it up, glancing at the dull blade for a second before hurrying back to the trio of creatures. He could feel a slight gnawing pain at the back of his neck and, when he knelt beside the first foetus again, he found that the other two were glaring at him. They fixed him in that formidable stare, watching as he rolled up one sleeve exposing a forearm already criss-crossed with purple scabs and welts. Taking the knife in his right hand, he extended his left arm, flexing his fingers until the veins stood out. He swallowed hard, the razor sharp blade hovering over his own flesh.

Harold drew the knife swiftly across his arm, wincing in pain as the cold metal cut easily through his skin, opening the bulging veins. Blood spurted from the wound and Harold gripped the top of his left arm, dropping the blade beside him. The gash seemed to burn for long seconds and his arm felt as if it were going numb but he fought back the nausea and slowly lowered the slashed appendage, allowing the crimson liquid to run down. It oozed over his hand and dripped from his fingers and Harold carefully dangled the limb above the mouth of the dying foetus, watching as the blood formed red droplets on his fingertips before falling into the open mouth of the creature. Its lips moved slightly but some of the blood splashed onto its face and chest. It made a low mewling sound as it tried to swallow the blood which was mingling with the yellowish secretion already pumping from its mouth. Harold was shaking, the pain now consuming his entire arm. He held the limb steady, watching as the crimson fluid dripped onto the foetus. A swollen tongue lapped at it hungrily. Harold reached out to touch it with his free hand.

"I did as you said," he croaked, looking at the other two creatures. God, they were much larger now, he thought, and he recoiled slightly, whimpering. He gripped the rent in his arm, his fingers brushing against the hardened skin of the freshly healed scabs elsewhere on his forearm. Blood from the most recent cut was seeping through his fingers.

The voices were chattering once more, accusatory this time.

"I didn't kill Gordon," Harold gasped. "I didn't kill my brother."

The voices grew louder until finally, Harold shrieked. It was a cry which came from deep within him. As he looked down at the foetus, it seemed to metamorphosise, its shape changing, its features altering until it was his baby brother lying beside him. After all those years, Gordon was here in this dank, dark place. Harold began to sob uncontrollably as he reached out to pick up the small body. It felt so soft and jellied, as if his rough fingers would go right through the skin, but he lifted it nonetheless, holding the body to his chest, gazing into its face.

"Gordon," he whispered, tears rolling down his cheeks.

The accusations were there once again, whispered words of contempt from inside his head.

"I didn't kill him," he screamed. "It was an accident." Harold lifted its head, feeling how slack the neck was. Its chest was moving but only slightly and he could no longer hear the rasping, guttural breathing. Harold bent forward to kiss the thin lips and, as he did so, the face seemed, in his mind's eye, to alter shape again until it was no longer his baby brother he held but the familiar form of the bloated foetus. He found his lips pressed to cold, wet flesh. He felt and tasted the blood, his blood. The pus stuck to his lips in oozing gobs and Harold shrieked once more, trying to wipe the vile substance from his mouth. He fell backwards, the body of the creature falling from his arms. Harold gagged as the obscene mixture of blood and pus clogged on his tongue. He rolled onto his side and retched until there was nothing left in his stomach.

When the spasms had finally passed, he hauled himself up on one elbow, his head spinning. He wiped the tears from his cheeks and gazed down at the dying foetus, the bitter aftertaste of his vomit still strong in his mouth.

"Oh God," he murmured.

He felt weak, barely able to support himself as he tried to stand. He managed it with effort, reaching for a filthy handkerchief which he pulled from his trouser pocket. He pressed it to the wound on his arm and held it firmly until the worst of the bleeding had stopped.

"I'll always do my best," he gasped, looking down at the foetal monstrosities. "I promise."

Harold took a step backwards. In the darkness of the room he almost stumbled over some of the other debris. The floor was smeared with excrement and dried blood. It smelt like an open sewer. The pungent odour of decaying, putrescent flesh was also noticeable. He dropped to his knees, exhausted by his sleepless night and also by the mental strain which he had been under for so long. He lay on the blanket but he dare not sleep. If he did, the dreams would come and he could not stand that. How he wished he had the tablets they used to give him, with those he never dreamed. There were no spectres waiting in his subconscious then, nothing to crawl out during sleeping hours to torment his mind.

But the dreams *had* returned now. So vividly at times that it was almost impossible to separate imagination from reality. He glanced across at the foetuses and shivered, pulling the blanket tighter around him.

The voices, now that little bit quieter, still hissed inside his head.

Thirty-eight

Maggie Ford washed her hands quickly and dried them on the sterilized towel before pulling on the surgical gloves. With her hair pinned up beneath her white cap she made her way hurriedly into the operating room where the unconscious body of a young woman lay on the table. Around her stood nurses and the anaesthetist who was checking his equipment. He already had his mask on and Maggie followed suit a moment later, crossing to her patient.

"What have we got?" said Maggie, looking down at the young woman whose smock had been opened to reveal her body. Her pubic hair had been hurriedly shaved and the area looked raw and angry but it was the blood seeping from the woman's vagina which disturbed Maggie most of all. There was a prominent bulge around the left hand side of the patient's abdomen, the skin shining beneath the lights of the operating theatre. It looked as if it were being stretched from inside.

"Suspected ectopic pregnancy," Maggie was told by a nurse standing close by. "The woman's name is Judith Myers, they rushed her in about ten minutes ago. She collapsed at work."

Maggie frowned. She inhaled and took a closer look at the bulge in Judith Myer's abdomen. It seemed to be pulsating.

The doctor wasted no time, realizing that the woman's life could be lost or saved in a matter of minutes. She set to work, something nagging at the back of her mind. She had heard the name Myers before, recently too.

The initial incision was made and Maggie worked as fast as she was able until she finally exposed the bulging Fallopian tube. There were audible gasps about the theatre.

"My God," she muttered. "It's a long way advanced isn't it?" She took the instruments that were handed to her, a bead of perspiration popping onto her forehead. The bulge was very large and, impossibly seemed to be moving even as she watched it. The blip on the nearby oscilloscope dipped violently, the rhythmic high-pitched sound fluctuating alarmingly once or twice. A nurse checked Judith Myers's blood pressure.

"Her blood pressure is falling," she said, anxiously.

Maggie held the scalpel in one hand, realizing what she must do but her hands suddenly seemed leaden, her gaze riveted to that pulsing protruberance which was stretching her patient's Fallopian tube practically to bursting point.

Harold huddled in one corner of the room watching the foetuses. They lay still, only the almost imperceptible rise and fall of their chests signalling that they were still alive. But, as he watched, he saw the veins on their bulbous heads swell and throb and their eyes gradually darken until they seemed to be glowing with some mysterious black light that filled the room, drifting like smoke all around them. Their bodies began to shake.

The blip on the oscilloscope was still diving wildly, the

sound occasionally shutting down for brief seconds. Maggie swallowed hard, noting that the membranous covering of the bulging Fallopian tube was actually beginning to tear. She heard muttered words around her as she worked to cut the tube free. She called for a swab, alarmed at the amount of blood which seemed to be forming in the abdominal cavity. It was lifted, dripping crimson, from the danger area to be replaced a second later by another. Then another.

A second split appeared in the thin wall of the Fallopian tube, the membrane tearing like overstretched fabric.

"We're losing her, doctor," someone called and Maggie looked up to see that the oscilloscope pattern had almost levelled out.

Harold opened his mouth in a silent scream as the entire room seemed to fill with a deafening roar. He clapped both hands to his ears but the sound continued. It was inside his head, it was all around him, filling the room until it seemed the walls must explode outwards. The foetuses continued to shudder violently, the veins on their bodies now turning purple, their eyes glowing red like pools of boiling blood.

Maggie recoiled as the large bulge in Judith Myers's Fallopian tube seemed first to contract and then erupt. There was a fountain of blood, pus and pieces of human tissue as the internal organ literally exploded showering those nearby with viscera. A young nurse fainted. The anaesthetist leapt from his seat and dashed across to Maggie's side. Both of them turned to see that the oscilloscope blip had stopped bobbing and bouncing, it just ran in an uninterrupted straight line now, its mournful note filling the operating room. Maggie worked to remove the ruptured tube, trying in vain to save her patient's life. There was blood everywhere, even on the large light above the operating table. Maggie herself wiped some from her face, gazing down almost in disbelief at the damage before her. The young nurse was being helped to her feet and supported out of the theatre.

While another nurse checked the patient's blood pressure for one last time, Maggie herself listened for any sign of heartbeat. There was none. She pulled a penlight from her smock pocket and shone it into the woman's eyes. There was no pupillary reaction.

Judith Myers was dead.

Maggie untied her mask and turned to the nearest nurse.

"Fetch a porter," she said. "I want an autopsy done immediately."

Maggie, her smock and face spattered with blood, made her way back to the wash-room, her movements almost mechanical. She knew what she had just seen but she did not believe it. The ectopic pregnancy had been too far advanced. If her guess was corrent, Judith Myers would have had to have been at least five months pregnant for her Fallopian tube to be in that condition. Myers. Judith Myers. Again she felt that nagging at the back of her mind. She knew that name from somewhere.

She pulled off her blood-stained gloves and tossed them into the bin, washing her hands beneath the swiftly flowing water from the tap.

The realization hit her with the force of a steam-hammer and, for long seconds she stood still. Thoughts tumbled through her mind and she exhaled deeply. She finished washing and pulled her white coat back on, heading out into the corridor. Before she took a trip down to the pathology lab, she intended visiting the records department. She had just remembered where she'd heard the name Judith Myers.

It took the clerk in the records office less than five minutes to find the file on Judith Myers. Maggie took the file gratefully and walked across to the desk on the other side of the room. There she sat down and flipped the folder open.

NAME: Judith Myers. DATE OF BIRTH: 14/3/57.
REASON FOR ADMISSION: Clinical Abortion

Maggie scanned the rest of the sheet, her eyes straying to the date of admission. She looked at it again. Could there have been some mistake? She doubted it. She herself had performed the abortion. She looked yet again at the admission date. Finally, clutching the file to her chest she got to her feet. She asked the clerk if she could take the file with her, promising to return it in an hour or so. Maggie left the records office and headed towards the pathology labs.

It took Ronald Potter less than an hour to complete the autopsy on Judith Myers. Maggie sat in his office drinking coffee until the chief pathologist finally joined her. He sat down heavily in his chair and ran a hand through his false hair, careful not to dislodge the toupée.

"Well?" Maggie said.

Potter sniffed.

"Well, Doctor Ford, I'm sure you don't need me to tell you that it was an ectopic pregnancy. She died of massive internal bleeding."

"Did you examine the Fallopian tube itself?" Maggie wanted to know.

Potter stroked his chin thoughtfully.

"Yes I did." His tone was heavy, troubled even.

"What caused the rupture to be so. . ." she struggled for the word, "so violent?"

"Well, the curious thing is, I don't know," said the pathologist, colouring slightly. "The size and nature of the Fallopian rupture would indicate that she was carrying a foetus of over six months which as we both know is clinically impossible. But there's something else puzzling." He paused. "My examination showed no sign of a foetus, any embryonic life or even an egg. There was nothing in her Fallopian tube to cause a rupture of that size. In fact there was nothing in there, full stop."

"So you're saying that she died of a condition that was not pathological," said Maggie.

"That's correct. There was no evidence of any fertilized life-form in the Fallopian tube. It's almost as if the swelling and the subsequent rupture were. . ." He grinned humourlessly.

"Were what?" Maggie demanded.

"It's as if they were psychosomatically induced. There is *no* trace of foetus, embryo or egg in that woman's Fallopian tube." The pathologist exhaled deeply and traced a line across his forehead with one index finger.

"Well, I found something too," said Maggie, holding up the file. "How old did you say the foetus would have to be to cause a Fallopian rupture of that size?"

"Six months, at least," said Potter.

"Judith Myers underwent a clinical abortion in this hospital less than six weeks ago."

"That's impossible," said the pathologist, reaching for the file as if he doubted the truth of Maggie's words. He scanned the admission sheet, his brow wrinkling. "There must be some mistake."

"That's what I thought," she confessed. "But, as you can see from the notes, I did the operation myself."

Potter sat back in his chair and shook his head almost imperceptibly.

"A woman has an abortion six weeks ago," said Maggie. "Then dies of a Fallopian rupture that could only have been caused by the lodging of a foetus at least six months old in her tube and yet you find no trace of any foetus. Not even an egg."

Both of them stared at each other not knowing what to say. The silence in the office was heavy, like a weight pressing down on them and Maggie was not the only one to feel spidery fingers of fear plucking at the back of her neck.

Thirty-nine

PC Stuart Reed brought the Panda car to a halt outside the gate which led into the farmyard. The gate, like the fence it was attached to, was rotting. Pieces of broken, splintered wood jutting out like a series of compound fractures from the untended surround.

The farm buildings themselves looked dark and dirty in the mid-morning sunshine and the slight breeze moved the weather vane atop the barn, causing it to squeak loudly like a trapped mouse.

"Why the bloody hell do we have to check this place again?" groaned Constable Charlton. "I mean we've already been out here twice and there was no sign of Harvey."

Reed shrugged.

"Sergeant Willis said we had to go over everything with a fine toothcomb," said the younger man, glancing out at the collection of buildings. "I'd better check in." He reached for the two-way and relayed their position to the station. Willis's voice acknowledged the call.

"Do you want to toss for it?" said Ray Charlton.

Reed looked blank.

"For the privilege of looking around," Charlton clarified.

"Perhaps we should both go," said the younger man.

"And leave the car? Sod off, if the Sergeant calls through and finds out we've both gone for a walk he'll string us up by the bollocks." Charlton studied his companion's face for a moment then he reached for a walkie-talkie, taking it from the parcel shelf. "I'll go," he muttered, pushing open the door. He stepped out into a pool of muddy water and it was all Reed could do to suppress a grin.

"Shit," grunted Charlton and slammed the door behind him. The younger man watched as his companion trudged across the muddy ground, having to lift the farmyard gate out of the sticky muck before he could open it enough to squeeze through. Reed picked up his own walkie-talkie and flicked it on.

"Why didn't you jump it?" he asked, chuckling.

Charlton turned and raised two fingers in a familiar gesture. He walked on, finding, thankfully, that the ground was becoming firmer. The sun wasn't strong enough to dry it out but the chill wind probably helped to toughen up the top soil. He stood still in the centre of the yard and looked around. It was as quiet as a grave. To his right lay two barns, to his left the farmhouse itself. All the buildings had been searched before. When Harvey first escaped he and Reed had been ordered to scout the deserted farm and, as Charlton had expected, they had found nothing. That had been nearly three months ago and now they expected the bloody maniac to be still holed up here when, in reality, he was probably long gone and had been since the first day of his escape. However, Charlton's cynicism did not take into account the three murders and he, as well as everyone on the Exham force, realized that the decapitations were Harvey's trade mark. The bastard was still in or around Exham somewhere but he doubted if it was here.

He decided to check the barns initially and made his way across the yard to the first of the large buildings. The door was open so the constable walked straight in, coughing as the smell of damp and rotting straw hit him. He peered up towards the loft and, glancing across at the ladder which led to the higher level, decided to check it. He reached for the walkie-talkie and switched it on.

"Stuart, come in."

Reed's voice sounded metallic as he replied.

"Have you found something?" the younger man wanted to know.

"No," Charlton snapped. "And not likely to. I'm just checking the first barn."

He switched off the two-way and clipped it to his belt as he began to climb the ladder which would take him up into the loft. The floorboards creaked menacingly beneath his weight and the policeman stood still for long seconds wondering if the entire floor were going to collapse beneath him but then, cautiously, he made a quick inspection of the upper level. A couple of dead rats and some small bones were all he found. He knelt and picked up one of the bones. It looked like a tiny femur and he surmised that one of the rodents that inhabited the barn had served as a midnight meal for an owl. He tossed the tiny bone away and headed back towards the ladder, pausing long enough to tell Reed that the first barn was clear.

It was the same story in the second of the buildings. It held just a couple of pieces of rusty farm machinery, otherwise the place was empty.

"I'm going to check the house now," Charlton said and started across the yard towards the last building.

Reed, still watching from the Panda, saw his companion approach the farmhouse and was puzzled when he hesitated before it. The walkie-talkie crackled into life.

"The door's open," said Charlton, a vague note of surprise in his voice. "Probably the wind."

"Do you want any help?" Reed asked.

Charlton didn't. He slowed his pace as he drew closer to the house, nudging the door back the last few inches with the toe of his boot. The hinges screeched protestingly and, as the constable advanced, he was enveloped by the overpowering odour of damp once again. The house smelt musty, closing around him like an invisible hand. He coughed and moved further into the room. It was a hallway. Straight ahead was a flight of stairs, now devoid of carpet, some of the steps were already eaten through by woodworm or rising damp. To his right lay a door, to his left another, this one slightly ajar. He hesitated, not sure which way to go first. He decided to look upstairs so, negotiating the rickety steps, he climbed to the higher level. The curtains had been left drawn up there and it was difficult to see in the almost impenetrable gloom.

Three closed doors confronted him.

Pulling the torch from his belt with one hand, Charlton reached for the handle of the first door and rammed it down, pushing the door open simultaneously. It swung back against the wall and he immediately brought the torch beam to bear on the contents of the room. There was an old chest of drawers, obviously too big to be moved when the owners' left but, apart from that, there was nothing. The floor was thick with dust and a quick inspection told the PC that it was undisturbed.

He moved to the second door.

Once more the door opened with no trouble, this time into a cramped toilet cum bathroom. The taps were mottled and rusty, the bath itself crusted with mould.

He closed that door behind him and moved across to the last.

The door knob twisted in his grasp but would not turn. Charlton tried again, this time throwing his weight against it but still the door wouldn't budge. He flicked off the torch and slipped it back into his belt then, taking a step back, he aimed a powerful kick at the handle which promptly dropped off.

The door opened a few inches.

Charlton, feeling unaccountably nervous, pushed the door open and stood motionless in the frame, eyes alert for any movement. As with the other two rooms, things were untouched and, almost gratefully, he reached for the two-way.

"The upstairs is clear," he said. "I'm just going to check the lower floor."

"Any sign of life?" Reed wanted to know.

"There's more life in a bloody graveyard," said the older man and flicked off the set. Feeling somewhat more relaxed, he made his way back down the stairs, his heavy boots clumping on the damp wood.

He looked into the sitting room and found it to be empty then he passed into the last room in the house, the kitchen.

He paused at the cellar door, his hand hovering over the knob. Last time he and Reed had been out here, they had left without checking the cellar but, this time, Charlton knew the job must be done. The lock was old and rusty but nevertheless strong and, at first, resisted even his most powerful kicks as he attempted to break it off. Finally, the recalcitrant lump of rusted metal dropped to the floor with a clang and the door opened outwards a fraction. The constable reached for his torch once more and edged inside the doorway until he was standing on the top step of the flight of stone stairs that led down into the all-enveloping gloom of the cellar.

The smell which met him was almost palpable in its

intensity and he raised one hand to his face in an effort to keep the fetid stench away. He shone his torch down, the beam scarcely penetrating the blackness. Cautiously, careful not to slip in any of the puddles of moisture on the steps, he descended, breathing through his mouth in an effort to counteract the appalling stench.

He reached the bottom and shone the torch around, playing its beam over the floor, picking out the broken bottles, the shattered lumps of wood where some of the shelves had been overturned. His heart was beating just that little bit faster as he moved further into the dark recesses of the subterranean hole, the torch lancing through the blackness like some kind of laser beam.

He stepped in something soft and cursed, looking down to see what it was.

"Oh Christ," he murmured.

It was excrement.

He winced and tried to wipe the worst of it off, realizing that it was of human origin. A sudden cold chill nipped at the back of his neck and he stood still, sure that he'd heard something. A low rasping sound came from close by. He spun round, his torch beam searching the darkness.

There was nothing.

A loud crackle ripped through the silence and Charlton almost shouted aloud in fear, his mind taking precious seconds to adjust to the fact that it was the two-way. He snatched it from his belt angrily.

"Found anything?" Reed wanted to know

"For fuck's sake don't do that again," rasped Charlton, his hand shaking.

"What's wrong?" his companion wanted to know.

The other constable recovered his breath, angry with himself too for letting the situation get a hold of him.

"I'm down in the cellar of the house," he said. "We didn't check it out last time we were here."

"And?"

"Someone's been here. Whether it's Harvey or not I can't say but, by the look of the place whoever it was was holed up here for quite a time. The cellar's been wrecked." He described the scene of devastation and filth before him. "Call the station," he added as a postscript. "You'd better get them to send another car out here." He flicked off the two-way. Charlton shone the torch beam around the reeking confines of the cellar one last time then he turned back towards the stairs.

The massive bulk of Paul Harvey loomed before him, silhouetted in the dim light which filtered in from the kitchen and, in that half-light, Charlton caught sight of the sickle as it swept down.

Paralysed, momentarily, by the sight of the figure before him, Charlton was unable to move as quickly as he would usually have done. He tried to avoid the vicious blade but it caught him on the left arm, tearing through the fabric of his uniform and slicing open skin and muscle from the shoulder to the elbow. Blood burst from the ragged wound and, with a shriek, Charlton fell backwards, the two-way skidding from his grasp. He tried to scramble to his feet, blood pumping thickly from the hideous rent in his arm.

Harvey advanced quickly, swinging the curved blade down once more. This time the policeman managed to roll clear and the wicked point embedded itself in a broken shelf. Harvey grunted and tore it free, noticing that Charlton was making for the stairs.

"Ray, are you all right?"

Reed's disembodied voice floated up from the discarded walkie-talkie.

Charlton reached the bottom step and, clutching his torn arm, raced up the slippery steps but Harvey moved with surprising agility for a man of his size. He swiped wildly at the fleeing policeman, the sickle blade slicing through the man's thigh, hamstringing him. Charlton crashed down onto the stone steps, white hot pain gnawing at his leg.

"Ray. Come in. What's happening?"

Dazed by his fall and weak from loss of blood, Charlton rolled onto his back to see Harvey towering over him. The sickle swept down once again, this time to its appointed mark. It pierced the policeman's chest just below the sternum, then, using his enormous stength, Harvey ripped it downwards, gutting Charlton with one stroke. A tangled mess of intestines spilled from the riven torso and the policeman's scream was lost as his mouth filled with blood. His head sagged forward as he plunged both hands into the steaming maze of his own entrails, trying to push them back in.

"Ray, for Christ's sake."

Harvey looked around for the source of the voice but realized that it was the two-way. He headed up the stairs towards the kitchen, stepping over the eviscerated body of the dead policeman.

Reed actually heard the sirens in the distance as he looked up towards the farmhouse and, as he opened the door to clamber out, he heard a familiar voice rasping over the two way in the car.

"Alpha one come in," said Randall.

"Reed here," he answered. "I think we've found Harvey."

"Stop the bastard," Randall ordered. "I don't care if you have to kill him. Just stop him."

The sirens were growing louder as the other two Pandas drew closer but, when Reed looked up he saw Harvey emerge into the daylight, his clothes splashed with blood. The young PC shouted to him to stop but the desperate convict merely slowed his pace, as if waiting for Reed to come closer and, as he drew nearer, the policeman saw the sickle. Blood was dripping from its curved blade.

Reed ran across the muddy yard, tripping on something as he did so. He scrambled to his feet to see that it was a rake. He picked it up, hefting the rusty metal head before him like some kind of ancient quarter-staff.

Harvey remained motionless, even when the first of the Pandas skidded to a halt in the yard. Randall leapt out and moved towards the big man.

It was at that moment Harvey chose to strike.

He lunged towards Reed who managed to bring the rake up to shield himself. The sickle struck the wooden shaft and cut through it easily. Reed fell backwards, trying to crawl away through the mud as the big man came for him.

Randall, who had moved closer by this time, picked up a handful of mud and hurled it into the man's face, momentarily blinding him. Harvey raised a hand to wipe the oozing muck away and Randall took his chance. He launched himself at his opponent, smashing into him just above the pelvis. Both of them went sprawling, the sickle flying from Harvey's grasp. Randall reacted first and, with a vicious grunt, drove two fingers into the big man's left eye. Harvey shrieked in pain and rage and scrambled to his feet as Randall backed off, looking for something to defend himself with. Harvey roared and charged at him, catching the Inspector by the shoulder, pulling him down. Randall gasped as he felt strong hands encircle his throat. White light flashed before his eyes. His face began to turn the colour of dark grapes and it was as if his head were going to burst. Then, through a haze of pain, he saw Reed retrieve the metal topped end of the rake.

With a blow combining demonic force and terrified desperation, the young PC brought the rusty metal down on the back of Harvey's head. There was a dull clang, combined with the strident snapping of bone and Randall suddenly felt the pressure on his throat ease.

The big man tottered, then tumbled forward into the mud, groaning. Randall rolled clear, helped to his feet by PC Higgins. Both of them watched, almost in awe, as Harvey raised himself up on one elbow and tried to get up. Randall stepped forward and, with all the power he could muster, drove his foot into the big man's face. The impact shattered his nose, blood and small fragments of bone flying into the air.

"Bastard," muttered Randall, massaging his throat. He prodded the prone body with his foot then turned to Higgins.

"Get an ambulance for him," snapped the Inspector. "But put the cuffs on the bastard first."

Higgins scuttled off to call an emergency vehicle while Fowler cuffed the unconscious convict.

"He killed PC Charlton," said Reed, motioning towards the house. Randall walked slowly towards the deserted dwelling. He did, indeed, find Charlton in the house, his stomach somersaulting as he gazed at the mutilated corpse. He lingered in the reeking cellar for a moment then walked back out into the yard sucking in huge lungfuls of clean air.

An ambulance was approaching, its blue light spinning frenziedly and Randall watched as Harvey was lifted into the back of it by the dark uniformed men. The vehicle turned full circle and sped off in the direction of Fairvale, its siren gradually dying on the wind as it got further away.

"Thank Christ we found him, guv," said Higgins.

Randall nodded.

"Yeah," he said acidly. "But we were three months too late, weren't we?"

Forty

Randall lit up another cigarette and blew out a stream of smoke which diffused in the warm air. It drifted lazily in the lounge bar of "The Gamekeeper". The pub was quieter than usual but, nevertheless, Ralph the landlord busied himself behind the bar, serving and chatting, dispensing booze and gossip in equal proportions. He was a big man, about four years older than Randall and he carried a bad limp (beneath his trousers he wore callipers). He'd been landlord of the pub for the past eight years, prior to which he'd been in the Scots Guards. The limp was a legacy from one of his spells in Northern Ireland.

Every so often he would look across and nod agreeably at the Inspector who was sitting on the other side of the room beside the blazing log fire which roared in the grate. The hiss and pop of burning wood seemed unnaturally loud in the relative calm of the lounge. From the public bar, the far off sound of a juke-box cut through the subdued nattering. The pub was old but the juke-box was its concession to a livelier, more hectic age, one which was lived out in the public bar, frequented mostly by youngsters. The older regulars were content to down their pints and to play dominoes in the snug. Cocooned within that cosy environment, they were oblivious to all around them.

"Penny for them," said Maggie, studying Randall's expression.

He looked up and smiled.

"Sorry, Maggie," he said. "I was miles away."

"I noticed. What's wrong, Lou? You've been quiet ever since we got here."

"Be thankful for small mercies," he grinned.

"*Is* there something on your mind?" she persisted.

He reached for his pint and took a hefty swallow.

"I was thinking about Harvey," he confessed. "I rang my superior, Frank Allen, to tell him we'd got Harvey. Do you know what he said? 'About time'." He paused. "Bastard."

"What happens to him now?" Maggie wanted to know.

"They'll stick him in Rampton or Broadmoor I suppose. He'll be taken back to Cornford prison in the meantime. Though to be honest, I couldn't give a toss where they put him as long as he's out of the way. I just wish I could have got hold of him sooner than I did. Four people are dead now who might still be alive if I had."

"Come on, Lou, you can't carry the blame for those deaths too." There was a note of irritation in her voice. "Stop shouldering the responsibilities for everything that goes wrong. You did your job. What more could you do?"

He raised his glass to her and smiled.

"Point taken." He wiped some froth from his top lip. "What sort of day have *you* had?"

She considered telling him about Judith Myers but decided against it.

"Routine," she lied. "You wouldn't want to hear about it." She sipped her drink, changing the subject swiftly. "It's my day off tomorrow, can you get away a little earlier?"

Randall smiled.

"Well, with Harvey out of the way, there's just the paperwork to be written up." He reached out and touched her hand. "I should think I can sneak out around five."

Maggie smiled.

"What do you usually do on your day off?" he asked.

"Lie in bed," she began.

He cut her short.

"Now that sounds like a perfect way of spending a day."

They both laughed.

"I clean the flat, watch TV, read. Go shopping." She raised an eyebrow. "Really exciting isn't it?"

He smiled thinly, gazing into the bottom of his glass for a moment.

"Maggie, I hope you don't mind me asking but, well, these other men that you had relationships with –"

It was her turn to interrupt.

"I'd hardly call them relationships."

"Well, you know what I mean. Haven't you ever felt anything for any of them?"

"Why does it matter, Lou?" she wanted to know.

He shrugged.

"I'm a copper aren't I? Asking questions is second nature. I'm curious that's all."

She took another sip of her drink.

"No, there hasn't been anyone serious before. As I said to you the other night, I envy you your memories. All I've got is notches on the headboard." She smiled, bitterly. "And I'm sure that to most of the men I've slept with that's all I've been. Just another name in the little black book." She paused. "There was one man who wanted to marry me."

"What happened?" he asked.

She smiled.

"He worked for an oil company. They wanted him to move out to Bahrain for six months, he asked me to go with him. I said no. It was as simple as that. I'd just got the job at Fairvale and I didn't intend letting it go. He said that I wouldn't need to work, that we'd have plenty of money anyway but that wasn't the point. He didn't understand how important it was for me to feel needed. I enjoy the responsibilities I've got at the hospital. It makes me feel. . ." She struggled to find the word. "Accepted." She looked at him. "Anyway, I didn't love him." She drained what was left in her glass and put it down.

Ralph appeared at the table, collecting empty glasses.

"Hello, Lou," he said. "You'd better make sure one of your boys doesn't catch you boozing, you might get breathalized." The Scotsman laughed. He looked at Maggie and smiled.

"Mrs Randall," he said. "How are you?"

Maggie swallowed hard and looked at the policeman, then at the landlord. She smiled thinly in response, colouring slightly as the Scotsman made his way back to the bar.

"I'm sorry, Lou," she said, softly.

"For what?" he asked, smiling.

"The barman . . . he thought I was your wife."

"Nothing to worry about. It's not your fault and Ralph doesn't know about Fiona anyway." He took a hefty swallow from his glass. "Perhaps we look married," he said.

"Who *does* know about your wife?" asked Maggie. "About what happened to her?"

"I think most of the men on the Exham force know," he said. "Word travels fast. Coppers like to rabbit as much as anyone else. But, other than them and you," he glanced up at her, "no one here knows I was ever married or that I had a child." He lit up a cigarette. "That was one of the reasons I came to Exham. After it happened, I put in for a transfer. I thought if I got away from London and the places that reminded me of the accident, then it might help me to forget it. So, they shunted me around for a couple of years until I ended up here."

She touched his hand.

"You still miss them?" she asked.

"Naturally." He touched her hand with his own. "But not as much as I used to."

He squeezed her hand, as if afraid that she was going

to somehow disappear and she felt the urgency in his touch.

Forty-one

Sergeant Norman Willis checked that Paul Harvey was securely strapped down in the back of the ambulance before making his way back to the waiting Panda close by. He slid into the passenger seat, watching as the rear doors of the emergency vehicle were pulled shut. The blue light was spinning but the siren was turned off. Willis looked at his watch and saw that it was approaching 10.08 p.m. The ambulance pulled away, behind it PC Fowler started the engine of the police car and both vehicles pulled out into traffic.

Willis and Fowler had both been ordered by Randall to remain at Fairvale while Harvey was treated for his injuries (a hair-line fracture of the skull and a broken nose) and then to ensure that the captured prisoner reached Cornford prison.

Willis yawned and rubbed his eyes, blowing out his cheeks.

"It's bloody hot in here, isn't it?" he said.

"The heater's up the creek, Sarge," Fowler told him, without taking his eyes off the ambulance which was travelling at a steady thirty about forty yards ahead of them.

"I think you'd better wake me up when we get to Cornford," said the sergeant, smiling.

Inside the ambulance itself a uniformed attendant sat on the seat opposite the stretcher where Harvey lay. He was reading an old copy of "Reader's Digest", alternately looking up to see if Harvey was OK. The big man moved occasionally, once even moaning softly and the attendant got to his feet and looked down at the patient. Harvey's head was heavily bandaged and a large dressing covered his nose and most of his cheeks. His mouth, however, was open and there was a dribble of thick saliva coming from one corner. The attendant, identified as Peter Smart by the small blue badge on his jacket, looked at the restraining straps and stroked his chin thoughtfully. Harvey was making even louder gurgling sounds now and Smart was worried in case the big man should choke on his own spittle. He hesitated a second longer then began to undo the first of the straps, intending to roll Harvey over onto his side.

The first strap came loose and Smart set to work on the second, the one which secured Harvey's feet.

With his back to the prisoner, Smart didn't see Harvey's eyes flicker open.

For long moments he tried to reorientate himself with his surroundings, with what was going on. There was a dull ache in his head and it felt as if someone were standing on his face but, as he saw the uniformed man undoing the strap on his legs, Harvey realized what was happening.

As the strap came free, he lashed out with his large foot, catching Smart in the solar plexus. The impact of the blow sent the ambulanceman flying backward and he thumped his head hard against the far wall of the vehicle.

Harvey, meantime, was sitting up, tugging wildly at the third and final strap which was across his midsection.

Smart reached for the small box close by, trying to get to the syringe, desperate to inject the prisoner with the 25mg of Promazine before it was too late. He scrambled towards Harvey who, by this time, had managed to free himself and was in the process of getting to his feet.

Smart brought the needle down in a stabbing action, aiming for the big man's chest but Harvey was too fast for him and he clamped one huge hand around Smart's wrist, squeezing it like a vice until the appendage went white. With a despairing groan, Smart dropped the syringe. Harvey drove a powerful fist into the uniformed man's face, feeling bone splinter under the impact. He held his victim by the wrist for a second longer then, using both hands, hurled him against the other wall of the ambulance.

The driver felt the thump and slowed down.

Fowler, following close behind, saw the ambulance brake lights flare and nudged Willis.

"Sarge," he said, anxiously. "They're stopping."

Willis yawned.

"One of them probably wants to have a piss," he said.

By this time the emergency vehicle had indeed stopped. Fowler brought the Panda to a halt about twenty yards behind, watching as the driver got out and walked to the back of the vehicle. He fumbled with the doors, finally turning the handle.

Harvey came crashing out of the ambulance like a tank through a wall. The door slammed into the driver, knocking him flat and, before anyone could react, he was dashing off into the darkened woods to the left, disappearing like a fading nightmare.

Both Willis and Fowler leapt out of the car, the sergeant dashing after Harvey but it was useless. He saw the big man crashing through the undergrowth in his wild flight but the sergeant knew that he could never catch him. He ran back across the road to check on the injured ambulancemen. The driver was bleeding from a cut on the forehead, his companion inside lay unconscious.

"Get on the two-way, quick," Willis told Fowler. "Alert all cars. Tell them what's happened."

Fowler ran back to the car and snatched up the radio.

Within minutes, every man on the Exham force was picking up his frantic message.

Outside the pub, Maggie pulled up the collar of her coat and waited as Randall fumbled in his pocket for the car keys. A slight fog had come down during the evening and Maggie noticed how halos seemed to have formed around the sodium street lamps. Objects looked blurred and indistinct through the thin film of mist.

Randall finally found the keys and unlocked the car. Both of them climbed in. He was about to start the engine when the two-way hissed into life. Randall picked it up.

"Randall here, what is it?" he asked.

"It's Harvey," the voice at the other end said.

Maggie saw Randall's expression darken.

"Harvey's loose," the voice said.

Forty-two

Harold paced the corridors of the deserted asylum agitatedly. The wind was whispering through the many broken windows and it seemed to add an accompaniment to his apparently aimless wanderings. He moved with assurance through the dark avenues, through rooms which he had come to know only too well in the past and with which he was now becoming reacquainted. He could not sleep. It wasn't that he dare not but, for the first time in many years, the welcome oblivion of unconsciousness eluded him.

He pushed open a door and walked into what had once been a dormitory. One or two beds, considered too old to be moved to the new psychiatric hospital, still stood in their familiar places. The iron work was rusted, the old mattresses damp and torn. Harold walked across to one and looked down at it. In his mind's eye he could see himself lying there, sleeping peacefully.

Crossing to one of the windows, he stared out into the night. It seemed a million years since he had been here, the memories now like fading photographs, the images becoming more and more indistinct.

He remained at the window for a long time then finally turned and walked back towards the door of the dormitory, pushing it shut behind him. He made his way slowly along the corridor, one hand absent-mindedly touching the scarred side of his face. Harold reached the foot of the staircase which would take him up to the first floor and the room where the foetuses lay. He paused for a moment, gazing up, as if expecting to see someone standing at the top, then, wearily, he began to climb. His legs and head ached and, as he drew nearer to the room, the stench which he had come to know so well wrapped itself around him like invisible tentacles.

He stumbled into the room and froze, both hands gripping the door frame until his knuckles turned white.

The first, and largest, of the three creatures was standing up.

It wavered uncertainly at first, those black pits of eyes pinning Harold in a hypnotic stare. Then, as if moving in slow motion, it began to walk.

Forty-three

Paul Harvey tore the last of the dressing from his nose and cheeks and tossed it aside. He had already removed the bandages around his head. Now he moved slowly down the lane, sucking in lungfuls of early morning air. He still found it difficult to breathe through his nose and his breathing was harsh and guttural. A persistent pain gnawed at the back of his head where he'd sustained the fracture and, periodically, he would press tentative fingers to it.

Exham had yet to come to life. The town seemed to be sleeping as dawn broke but Harvey knew that, soon, there would be people on the streets, in their gardens, walking their dogs. He had to find shelter. He'd spent the night in a shed at the bottom of a large garden. It was from there he'd picked up the shears which he now held in one huge hand but, as the daylight began to creep inexorably across the heavens, he knew he must find somewhere to hide.

The church stood on a hill, on the very edge of one of Exham's many estates. It was old, its stone-work worn and chipped, the colours in its stained-glass windows now faded somewhat. A weather vane squeaked mournfully in the light breeze and Harvey ran appraising eyes over the building as he approached it. Many of the gravestones were coloured with moss and a good number of the plots were overgrown. Here and there, dead flowers lay like discarded confetti, their petals now brown and wrinkled.

He reached the main door but found it locked. He

slammed a powerful fist against it twice, angry that he could not gain entry. Muttering to himself, he made his way around the building until he found another door. This one was old too, the woodwork the colour of dried blood. It was splintered in many places and the chain which held it shut looked brittle. Harvey tugged hard on it, gritting his teeth as he felt the rusty links give. It snapped with a dull clang and he tossed the pieces away, wedging his fingers in the gap between door and frame in an effort to get it open.

The hinges screamed alarmingly but Harvey persevered, finally opening it far enough to give himself access. He slipped inside. The stench and the impenetrable darkness nearly made him change his mind but, fortunately, due to his broken nose he could not detect too much of the fetid odour and he soon found that there was some light coming into the subterranean room. He descended the stone steps cautiously only realizing when he reached the bottom that he was in a crypt.

Nevertheless, it was shelter. He sat down, the shears across his lap.

He waited for the darkness.

Forty-four

Maggie stood still at the top of the stairs, trying to catch her breath. She considered herself a fit woman but climbing up a long flight of stairs with two armfuls of shopping had all but exhausted her. She walked across towards the door of her flat, wishing that she'd put some lower shoes on. Her feet were throbbing and she decided to run a bath as soon as she got inside. She put down her bags and fumbled in the pocket of her jeans for the key.

The phone was ringing inside and Maggie muttered irritably to herself as she struggled to unlock the door; she pushed it open, snatched up the bag and hurried in, one eye on the phone, convinced that it would stop ringing the moment she picked it up. She made a dash for it and lifted the receiver.

"Hello," she said.

"Doctor Ford?"

She recognized the voice at the other end of the line but could not identify it immediately.

"It's Ronald Potter here."

Maggie wrinkled her brow.

"What can I do for you?" she wanted to know.

Potter sounded anxious, distraught even.

"I've been trying to get hold of you for the last three hours," he said, speaking quickly, not giving her time to ask why. She glanced across at the clock on the mantlepiece which showed 4.35 p.m. "There's been another death. The symptoms are identical to those of that woman the other day." Maggie heard rustling of paper on the other end of the line. "The ectopic pregnancy, Judith Myers."

"I remember," she said.

"There was another one this afternoon and the results of the autopsy are exactly the same. No foetus, no embryo, not even an egg and yet she died of a Fallopian rupture."

Maggie let out a long, slow breath, gripping the receiver until her knuckles turned white.

"Doctor Ford."

Potter's voice seemed to shake her out of her trance.

"Yes, I'm still here," she told him. "Look, I'm coming over to the hospital now. I'll be there in about ten minutes." She put the phone down and, without changing, she rushed out once more. The shopping was left discarded on the sitting room floor.

Maggie sipped at the cup of luke-warm coffee and winced. On the desk before her lay half a dozen different files, including those on Judith Myers but the thing which was holding her attention was the neatly typed sheet headed:

FAIRVALE HOSPITAL: NOTICE OF DECEASE.

The name entered in the appropriate box was one which she recognized:

Lynn Tyler.

Maggie exhaled deeply and ran her eyes over the sheet for the fourth time. She had read the autopsy report countless times too, glancing at that of Judith Myers as well. From the wording, it might have been a duplicate of the same woman's autopsy. *Everything* was the same about the two cases. Both young women, apparently healthy, had died from internal haemorrhage due to the rupturing of a Fallopian tube. But it was not just a rupture, it was the complete destruction of that particular internal organ. There were no warning signs, just the rapid onset of symptoms so virulent they had caused death in a matter of hours.

"No evidence of any embryonic or foetal development," Maggie read aloud. The words were the same on both reports. It wasn't a virus of any kind, that she was sure of. Could it be coincidence? The chances must be astronomical. Lynn Tyler had suffered a Fallopian rupture which would have corresponded to her carrying a foetus of over six months. Even the size of the bursts was the same, thought Maggie, and there was one more thing which made her uneasy.

Lynn Tyler, like Judith Myers, had undergone a clinical abortion just seven weeks earlier.

She swept her hair back and tried to find some kind

of explanation for the two deaths in the facts and figures laid out before her. There seemed to be no answers, just the unnervingly exact similarities between the two deaths.

There was another file on her desk, one which she now picked up and glanced through. It was a report by the senior porter on the discovery of the foetuses which Harold Pierce had buried in the field beyond the hospital grounds. She read it once, then twice, this time more slowly. It told of how the grave had been discovered, the remains disinterred and disposed of and ended with a note about Harold's dismissal because of his part in the action. Five foetuses had been dug up and incinerated. Maggie frowned and glanced across at another piece of paper to her left. It was a record of all clinical abortions carried out between the beginning of August and the end of September. There had been eight. The porter assigned to dispose of each one had been Harold Pierce.

Eight abortions but only five foetuses found in the grave.

Perhaps he just missed three Maggie reasoned. She chewed her bottom lip, contemplatively. Harold's obsession with the "burning of children", as he put it, was something which had surprised her but now, as she sat alone in her office, she began to wonder just how deep that obsession went.

"Eight abortions carried out," she muttered. "Five bodies exhumed." She drummed on the desk top with her fingers.

There was a knock on the door.

"Come in," Maggie called and was surprised to see Randall standing there.

"I went to your flat," he said. "There was no answer so I thought I'd try here."

"I'm sorry," she said, "something came up." Then, remembering he had problems of his own she added:

"Any sign of Harvey yet?"

He shook his head, producing a newspaper from behind his back. He held it before him.

"I could have done without this too," he muttered, handing her the paper.

She opened it and read the headline:

MANIAC HARVEY ELUDES POLICE AGAIN

"Oh Christ," said Maggie, quickly scanning the story that accompanied the headline. " 'Mass murderer, Paul Harvey, already thought to be responsible for four deaths in Exham recently, escaped from the police for the second time in as many days. . .' " She allowed the sentence to trail off. "What are you going to do?" she asked him.

Randall was gazing out of the window into the darkening evening sky. The first droplets of rain were coursing down the pane like silent tears.

"About what?" he demanded. "Harvey, or that fucking article?"

"Both."

"Bloody local papers," rasped Randall. "They're all the same. A bunch of two-bit scribblers. They might as well write on toilet paper because the stuff they write is only fit for wiping your arse on." He banged the window frame angrily.

"And Harvey?" she said.

Randall sucked in a troubled breath.

"My men are out there now looking for him, they've got orders to call me the minute they find anything." He turned, scanning the piles of paper and files on her desk. "What's *your* problem?" He sat down opposite her and Maggie began speaking. She explained everything. About the two deaths, about the autopsy reports, the abortions, even the discovery of the foetuses' grave.

"Christ," murmured Randall when she'd finally finished. "How do you explain it?"

"I can't," she told him.

"And the pathologist has no answer either?"

She shook her head.

He asked if it could be a virus.

"Any infection would have shown up in the examination," she told him.

He reached forward and picked up one of the files, flipping through it.

"In both cases," she said, "there was no *physical* cause for the Fallopian ruptures, that's the most puzzling thing. It's as if they were, well. . ." she struggled to find the words, "induced."

Randall looked up.

"I don't get you," he said.

"Every woman reacts differently to an abortion," Maggie explained. "For some it's a great relief but even the ones who want abortions and realize how necessary they are still feel guilty. It might only be in their subconcious but the guilt is still there."

"So you're trying to say that these two women induced the symptoms of ectopic pregnancy in themselves to compensate for the kids they'd had aborted?" he said.

Maggie raised an eyebrow.

"Does it sound crazy?"

Randall dropped the file back onto the desk.

"It sounds bloody ridiculous, Maggie," he said.

"Well then what the hell do you think happened?" she asked.

"Look, you're the doctor not me but you must admit that theory is stretching things a bit."

"Do you know anything about the power of the mind, Lou?"

"About as much as the average man in the street. What kind of power?"

"Thought projection, auto-suggestion, self-hypnosis. That kind of thing."

He sighed.

"Come on, Lou," she muttered, "I know it's clutching at straws but it's all I've got. Both women aborted for non-medical reasons."

"Meaning what?" he demanded.

"Usually abortions are carried out if the baby is found to be malformed, retarded or sometimes even dead. Both Judith Myers and Lynn Tyler would have given birth to perfectly healthy children. There was nothing clinically wrong with the babies they were carrying. They had abortions for convenience not necessity."

"You said there were three bodies missing from the grave," he said. "What about the mother of the third aborted child?"

Maggie flicked through one of the files.

"That abortion was a medical necessity," she told him. "The scan showed that the child would have been malformed."

Randall nodded.

"If your theory about the ectopic pregnancies is right," the Inspector said, "then you realize you're trying to tell me they committed suicide."

Maggie sighed.

"I know it sounds ridiculous, you're right." There was a long pause. "Lou, it's almost as if they'd both still had the foetuses gestating inside their Fallopian tubes despite the fact that they'd undergone abortions just weeks before. I don't know what to think."

"What about this business with the grave?" he asked. "Were the three missing bodies ever found?"

"Not to my knowledge."

Randall frowned, aware that what he was about to say was going to sound idiotic. He coughed.

"Is there any way a foetus could continue to grow once it had been removed from the womb?" he asked.

"No. Even in laboratory conditions it would be difficult. Not impossible but extremely unlikely."

He exhaled deeply.

"Now I'm not sure what *I'm* trying to say," he confessed. "But I know one thing, I'd like to talk to Harold Pierce."

"How could he be linked with this?" she wanted to know.

"Maybe he knows what happened to those other three bodies."

Maggie closed the files and stacked them on one corner of the desk. She got to her feet, switching off the lamp. The room was momentarily plunged into darkness.

"Perhaps we'll both think straighter on a full stomach," said Randall, opening the office door for her.

They walked out into the corridor, heading for the lift. Maggie looked worried and, as they reached the ground floor, she took his hand and held it tightly. The two of them walked out to the car park where Randall's Chevette waited. As he opened the passenger door to let her in, Maggie seemed reluctant to let go of his hand. He touched her cheek gently and kissed her softly on the lips.

Inside the car, despite the warmth from the heater, both of them shivered.

They were back at Randall's place in less than twenty minutes.

Neither of them ate much. They spoke quietly, as if afraid that their conversation would be overheard by someone. Again and again they discussed what had transpired at the hospital, as if repeated examination of the bizarre events would somehow lead to a solution. There was no need for either of them to suspect anything out of the ordinary but nevertheless an atmosphere of foreboding seemed to descend over them as they spoke. In the sitting room, Maggie sat close to

Randall, glad to feel his arm around her shoulder. Still they talked and still they could find no answers.

"We could go on like this all night," said Maggie, "and it still wouldn't get us anywhere." She smiled humourlessly. "Now I know what you feel like trying to find Paul Harvey."

"There seems to be more than one needle in *this* haystack, though," he said, taking a drag on the cigarette he'd just lit up. He got to his feet and crossed to a drinks cabinet where he poured them both a large measure of brandy.

Maggie glanced around the room. It was small and tidy. Randall obviously took care of the place. There was a pleasing smell of lemon in the room (from a carpet cleaner, she guessed) which further attested to its cleanliness. On the mantlepiece above the glowing gas fire there were three photos. The first was of Randall and his wife and daughter, the second and third of Fiona and Lisa alone. Maggie was struck by how attractive the dead woman had been. The little girl too, smiling out from behind the glass in the frame, sported two dimples which only added to the cheeky playfulness mirrored in her eyes.

"Your wife was very pretty," said Maggie.

Randall smiled.

"I know," he said, handing her a drink. "Lisa looked a lot like her." He crossed to the mantlepiece and lifted the photo of his daughter. "My little lady," he said, smiling. He replaced the photo almost reluctantly and turned back to face Maggie.

"She would have thought the same about you." He smiled and raised his glass.

He took a long swallow, allowing the amber fluid to burn its way down to his stomach. Maggie sipped at hers.

"So," said Randall. "What else can you do about

these deaths? Is there anything more the pathologist can tell you?"

Maggie shook her head.

"I don't know, Lou," she confessed. She gazed into the bottom of her glass and then up at him. "The only thing that bothers me is, if there's no explanation for these two deaths, what's to stop it happening to other women? Maybe even women who aren't pregnant?"

"Why should it affect them?"

"If there was no foetus or embryo in the Fallopian tubes then, theoretically, it could happen to any woman of child-bearing age."

"You can't say that until you know the cause," he protested.

"That's the whole problem isn't it? We don't know the cause."

They both lapsed into silence, a solitude broken by the strident ringing of the phone. Randall crossed to it and lifted the receiver to his ear.

"Randall."

Maggie looked at him and could only guess at what the caller was saying but, from the expression on Randall's face, it obviously wasn't good news. She got to her feet and walked across to him.

"Yeah. When? Whereabouts?" He pulled a pad towards him and wrote something on it. As he listened, the policeman was drawing small circles on the pad with his pencil.

"What's wrong?" Maggie whispered.

"A murder," he told her, handing her the note which bore the location. "But we've got a witness."

She swallowed hard, watching him as he listened, the pencil still performing its spyrographic rotations on the pad.

"Willis," said Randall. "Did the victim have any ID on him?"

"No, guv." The sergeant's voice sounded strained.

"We did some finger-print tests just to be sure. We double-checked. Triple-checked."

"Checked what for Christ's sake?" Randall demanded.

Willis sighed.

"The victim was decapitated."

Randall's pencil snapped with a loud crunch.

"What's that got to do with bloody fingerprints?" he demanded.

"The victim was Paul Harvey."

Forty-five

Randall brought the Chevette to a screeching halt, the tyres spinning for a second on the wet tarmac. Across the street he could see an ambulance, its blue light spinning noiselessly, and two Panda cars. Uniformed men moved around in the darkness and, as he pushed open the door, the Inspector saw that much of the far side of the road was lined with trees. Beyond them was a narrow pathway which led between two houses. The pathway was masked by high hedges on both sides. There were lights on in both of the houses and also in some further down the street. Indeed, some people had even braved the rain to stand at their gates in an effort to see what was going on.

Maggie got out too, slamming her door behind her. Together they crossed to the scene of feverish activity. Randall caught sight of PC Higgins and called him over.

"Where's the body?" he said.

"This way, guv," he said. "We didn't move anything until you arrived." He led them a little way down the narrow path to a sheet shrouded object. Randall knelt and pulled back one corner of the covering, wincing as he did so.

"Shit," he muttered.

Maggie too looked at the headless body, letting out a long, slow breath.

"Where's the witness?" the inspector wanted to know.

"He's in the ambulance. Some old girl from the house next door gave him a cup of tea. The poor sod's in quite a state. He's only a kid."

Randall and Maggie followed Higgins to the ambulance, the Inspector hauling himself up into the back of the vehicle. The youth, no more than fifteen, was milk white and shaking like a leaf. He held a mug of tea in both hands as if not quite sure what to do with it.

He looked up anxiously as Randall joined him in the back of the ambulance. Maggie climbed in behind him.

"What's your name, son?" Randall asked him.

The lad picked nervously at one of the spots on his chin and swallowed hard.

"M-Mark Rawlings," he stammered.

"I just want to know what you saw," said Randall, softly.

The youth tried to stop himself shaking but found it an impossible task. Some of the tea slopped over the lip of the mug and burned his hand. Maggie took it from him.

"Well," he began. "I was coming home from the pictures, I'd just left my girlfriend. She only lives round the corner see. So I thought I'd take a short-cut up the lane. I saw this bloke with a knife."

"In the alley?" Randall asked.

"Yeah. He was bending over something. I just saw him lifting the knife. Then I saw that there was a body there. He cut the fucking head off." The youth turned even paler and clenched his teeth together. "I saw him pick it up. He put it in a sack or bag or something. He didn't see me."

"But you got a look at *his* face? The man with the knife?" Randall said.

"Yeah. I know it was dark but, well he had this great big scar or something all down one side of his face."

Randall shot Maggie an anxious glance, the same thought registering in their minds.

"He looked like something out of a fucking horror film," Rawlings continued. "Like he'd been burned or something."

Randall got to his feet, patted the youth on the shoulder and jumped down from the ambulance, helping Maggie down after him. Neither of them spoke. They didn't have to. Randall had a quick word with Sergeant Willis then led Maggie back to the Chevette. They both climbed in, sitting there for a moment, the Inspector breathing heavily.

"When Pierce left the hospital," he said. "Where did he go?"

"I told you before, Lou, nobody knew," Maggie told him.

Randall banged the steering wheel angrily but then, his initial anger subsided. He looked at her.

"He was locked up in that asylum for more than thirty years, wasn't he?"

She nodded.

"I don't get you."

"It's the only home he's ever known." Randall started the engine.

She suddenly understood.

He put the car in gear and swung it round in the wide road. In a few minutes, they were heading out towards the road which would take them to the deserted asylum.

Forty-six

"How can you be sure he's here?" said Maggie as Randall stepped on the brake and brought the Chevette to a halt.

"I can't," he said, opening his door. "Let's just hope this is one hunch that's right." The policeman clambered out from behind the wheel and walked across to the metal gates which barred the way to the asylum. In the darkness he could just discern three words on the stone archway above him.

EXHAM MENTAL HOSPITAL

There was a padlock on the gates and Randall tugged on it. The rusty gates creaked protestingly but didn't budge. The Inspector looked round. The driveway was the only means of getting a car into the grounds but a man could slip through one of the many gaps in the hedge. Randall scanned the ground around him and finally spotted a large stone. He retrieved it and set about the padlock, striking it with all his strength. It eventually came free with a dull clang and dropped to the ground. The Inspector put his shoulder to one of the gates and pushed. It was heavier than it looked and the exertion made him sweat but he finally succeeded in opening it as far as it would go. He repeated the procedure with the other one then hurried back to the car. Starting the engine he guided the Chevette through the archway and along the drive towards the asylum itself.

Flanked on both sides by leafless trees, he estimated

that the driveway must be at least half a mile long. He drove slowly, eyes alert for the slightest movement in the darkness.

"What are you going to do if Harold is here?" Maggie wanted to know.

"I'll tell you that when I find him," Randall told her, cryptically.

He brought the vehicle to a halt before the main entrance and both of them peered out at the building itself. It was an awesome sight, a Victorian edifice which, in the darkness, looked not as if it had been built with separate bricks but hewn from one enormous lump of granite. Five storeys high, it was built in the shape of an "E", the apex of which rose like a church spire. The figure of the weather vane on the top surveyed the bleak and ghostly scene with indifference.

The policeman climbed out of the car. Maggie also pushed open her door but Randall held up a hand to stop her.

"You stay here," he told her.

"But Lou, you don't know for certain that he's here," she protested. "And, even if he is, at least *I* know him. I could talk to him."

"The man's a bloody maniac," he rasped. "Now get back in the car, lock both doors and don't move until I get back. If I'm not here in an hour use this." He grabbed the two-way and held it up. "Contact the station and tell them where we are. Right?"

She didn't speak.

"Right?" he said, more forcefully.

"All right. Lou, be careful."

He nodded, slammed the door behind him and waited until he heard both locks drop then he made his way slowly towards what had once been the main entrance. As he'd suspected, the doors were locked so he moved along, peering at all the windows, eyes alert for any sign of a break-in, any tell-tale evidence of

Pierce's whereabouts. He rounded a corner and disappeared from Maggie's view. She sat impatiently, hands clenched on her thighs.

Randall moved cautiously, noticing how many of the asylum windows had been broken but he could tell which had been smashed by kids. Just round holes in the panes showed where stones had been hurled. As yet, there was no sign of forced entry. He sucked in an impatient breath wondering if his hunch had been wrong. He rested his hand on one of the sills and felt something wet beneath his fingers. The Inspector turned and looked down. There was a dark stain on the peeling paint. Tentatively he raised his fingers to his nose, sniffing the substance. There was no mistaking the distinctive coppery odour of blood.

He looked up and saw that the dark liquid was puddled beneath a set of double windows, one of which had been broken about half-way up, near the handle. The policeman gripped both sides of the frame and hauled himself up onto the sill, perching there for a second before pushing the two windows. They swung open invitingly and he jumped down into the building itself.

The smell of damp was almost overpowering and the Inspector blinked hard in an effort to combat the cloying darkness. There was some natural light spilling through the windows, enough to reveal to him that he was in what had once been an office. Dust swirled around him, the particles irritating his nose and throat but he fought back the urge to cough, anxious not to alert anyone who might be hiding inside.

There was more blood on the floor just ahead of him – a large splash and then droplets of the thick crimson fluid which was in the process of congealing. The trail led to the door and Randall paused before it a moment, listening. The asylum greeted him with silence and a kind of conspiratorial solitude which made him feel uneasy.

He slowly opened the door.

Corridors faced him and, after a moment's hesitation, he chose the one straight ahead.

Harold heard the noise from downstairs.

He snatched up the long kitchen knife, its blade still wet with blood, and scuttled out into the corridor his own ears now attuned to the sounds within the asylum. There was a crooked grin on his face. Someone was inside *his* home. They would not escape. His mind suddenly seemed clearer than it had done for months and he hurried through the darkened corridors as if drawn by some huge magnet, bearing down on the intruder.

It would only be a matter of time before he found the unwanted guest.

Maggie looked at her watch. The hands had crawled round to 11.49 p.m. Randall had been gone for nearly fifteen minutes. She sighed, shifting impatiently in her seat. There was a torch on the parcel shelf before her and she eyed it with a look akin to temptation. She closed her eyes for a second, trying to think about what had happened. The thought of Harold Pierce as a killer was still one she found hard to accept but it seemed clear enough. Nevertheless, if only she could speak to him, reason with him. . .

From where she sat she could see that many of the windows had been broken. It should be relatively easy to slip the catch on one and get in. She looked at the torch once again, this time picking it up. She unlocked her door and closed it behind her then she scuttled across to the nearest window, slipped her hand through a break in the pane and undid the latch. It opened and Maggie dragged herself up onto the sill. She steadied herself for a moment then jumped down into the room beyond. As she switched on the torch she saw that the door ahead of her was already open. The powerful beam shone through the darkness, lighting her way. She swallowed hard and moved quietly out into the corridor.

Randall pushed open the door of a room, surprised that so many of the asylum's places had been left unlocked but then, he reasoned, no one could have foreseen anyone returning here. Why bother? He edged cautiously into what he guessed had once been the dining room. There were a number of long tables stacked at one side and, at the far end of the vast room, a long counter. It was fronted by a corrugated metal sheet which had been pulled down and padlocked. The Inspector walked across to it, his footsteps clacking on the stone floor. Large picture windows, meshed, gave him some added light but already his eyes were beginning to ache from the effort of squinting in the gloom. He stood still for long moments, listening, trying to catch even the slightest hint of movement.

Silence.

He exhaled deeply and turned towards a door nearby which was also unlocked. It was as he passed through it that the Inspector realized he had nothing to defend himself with should he come upon Pierce. He swallowed hard and moved on, finding himself in another corridor. There were rooms every fifteen yards and each one would have to be checked.

He pushed open the first door.

Harold paused at the bottom of the stairs, looking round. He could see no sign of the intruder but he knew that his quarry was here somewhere. A surge of adrenalin swept through him and he gripped the knife tighter, his breath now coming in short, excited gasps.

He touched the scarred side of his face, feeling the crusted flesh beneath his fingertips. He moved slowly along the corridor to his right, stopping dead when he heard movement ahead of him. His knife gripped firmly in his fist, he ducked into a nearby room.

Maggie put her hand on the bannister of the staircase and hurriedly withdrew it as she felt something sticky on her fingers.

It was blood.

There was more on the bannister, even some on the steps themselves. She shone the torch on the crimson liquid and, slowly began to climb. She wiped the blood off on her jeans her heart now beating just that little bit faster. The staircase rose precipitously until, at last, it levelled out onto a landing. Faced by two corridors, Maggie took the one on her left, tip-toeing in an effort to diminish the clicking of her heels on the stone floor.

She recoiled from a sudden, nauseating stench which seemed to drift around her like an invisible cloud. She put a hand to her mouth and stifled a cough. As she moved further down the corridor the smell became almost unbearable. Her head began to swim and she was forced to lean momentarily against the wall for support. She played the torch beam before her in an effort to discover the source of the rank odour and, as she moved on, she found that the end door in the corridor was open. Maggie pressed herself against the wall once again, listening. From inside the room she could hear soft, liquid sounds – a series of rasping gurgles. She closed her eyes for a second, at once revolted by the sounds and desperate to discover their source. A part of her was wishing she had stayed in the car.

She held the torch beam up and peered round the door.

For brief seconds, Maggie had to use all her self-control to prevent herself from vomiting. She swayed slightly, supporting herself against the door frame, then, almost drawn to the sight before her, she walked slowly into the room.

Maggie shook her head, unable to believe what she saw, convinced that, any second she was going to wake up to discover that this was a nightmare. But no nightmare could be as vile as what she now saw before her.

She shone the torch on the first foetus and the creature recoiled slightly from the piercing beam, its dark eyes glinting menacingly. It was standing, something wet and sticky gripped in its fingers. The other two were on the floor, the second one pawing at something before it.

It was a few more seconds before Maggie realized that the object was a human head.

And now, as she stepped back, her foot brushed something else. Something which rolled when she made contact. She swung the torch beam round, the gruesome discovery pinned in the beam.

The second head was partially decomposed, the skin around the neck and eyes mottled green in places. The skull had been split open with a heavy object, exposing the brain and, as Maggie turned the torch back onto the abominations before her, she realized just what the sticky grey substance was which the larger creature held. As she watched, it raised the jellied matter to its mouth and clumsily pushed some in.

Maggie closed her eyes momentarily.

The foetuses seemed unconcerned at her presence. They were more interested in the severed head they were toying with. There was blood everywhere, mingling on the floor with slicks of excrement and pieces of hair. Greyish brain matter seemed to sparkle in the light.

Suddenly, everything seemed to take on a horrendous clarity: the headless murder victims that the police had found, Harold's obsession with the incineration of foetuses and, worst of all, she now understood why only five babies instead of eight had been disinterred from the grave near Fairvale.

She stood still, frozen by the sight before her, trying to find either the will to move or the power to scream but she could do neither. She felt faint, her stomach finally beginning to churn uncontrollably and she felt the vomit begin its journey up her throat. She turned away, retching violently, the foul stench of her vomit mingling with the choking odours already filling the room. But, the action seemed to shake her out of her trance and she moved for the door.

(*STOP*)

Maggie clapped both hands to her head, the torch dropping to the ground.

(*You will not leave*)

It's my imagination, she told herself.

(*No, it is not your imagination*)

She turned back to face the creatures.

Could it be telepathy? she wondered, hurriedly dismissing the thought. Her mind was over-reacting to the situation.

(*Your thoughts are open to us*)

She gazed at them, her face twisted into an expression which combined revulsion and fascination.

"What are you?" she said.

(*Nothing. We are nothing*)

"How do you know what I'm thinking?"

A soft chuckling and Maggie felt the hairs on the back of her neck prickle.

(*There can be no secrets. We know your thoughts and your fears*)

She thought about Randall. If only she could alert him to the danger.

In the blinking of an eye he was standing before her, smiling.

"Lou," she said and stepped forward to touch him but, even as she did so, the vision faded and she was alone once more.

The soft chuckling filled her ears.

(*Thoughts. Fears. There are no secrets*)

Thought projection, Maggie wondered? Auto-suggestion? The very things which she had mentioned to Randall and now she began to realize how Judith Myers and Lynn Tyler had come to die. The foetuses were the exact size which they would needed to have been to cause the Fallopian ruptures.

"You killed two women," she said.

(*They had to die*)

"Why?"

(*THEY WOULD HAVE KILLED US*)

Despite herself, Maggie moved closer to the largest of the creatures, kneeling before it, running expert eyes over its body. It was perfectly formed, as if it had grown within the mother's womb, reaching maturity as originally intended. The most frightening thing about it was its eyes. Black pits devoid of emotion, they pinned her in an hypnotic stare.

Randall heard the sounds of movement from upstairs and he ran towards the foot of the staircase, pausing momentarily when he reached it.

Harold came hurtling out of the room behind him, the knife held high above his head.

Randall heard the vicious arc of the steel and tried to turn but Harold was too quick for him. The blade powered down, catching the policeman in the shoulder. It tore through the flesh and actually scraped the clavical as it finally burst through his pectoral muscle, the point dripping blood. Harold pressed his advantage, wrenched the knife free and drove it down again but this time Randall managed to get his hand up in time. He deflected the blow, the knife striking concrete as the two men fell to the ground. The Inspector was surprised at his assailant's strength; despite Harold's age he seemed to possess an energy which belied his years. Randall struck out with his right fist, his left arm already numb from the knife wound. The blow caught Harold squarely in the side of the head but the impact only staggered him for a minute. However, that minute was enough to allow Randall the chance to wriggle free. He hauled himself upright and, as Harold tried to follow him, he drove a foot hard into the older man's side. There was a strident snapping of bone as one brittle rib splintered under the impact.

Harold went down in a heap, the knife held in one outstretched hand. Randall dropped to his knees, grabbing for it but Harold struck out again, the wild blow slicing open the policeman's palm. He yelped in pain but closed his injured hand around Harold's wrist, banging the hand on the ground repeatedly in an effort to make him drop the knife.

The older man clawed at Randall's face, gripping him by the hair, yanking his head to one side and both of them went sprawling again. This time Harold was first on his feet and Randall saw the scarred attacker advancing on him. The Inspector waited until his opponent was mere inches away then lashed out, catching Harold in the crutch with a powerful kick. He doubled up and Randall hastily scrambled to his feet. He grabbed Harold's hair and, in one skilful movement, brought his knee up to meet Harold's down-rushing head. The older man's nose seemed to explode, splattering the policeman's trousers with blood. Randall wrenched his attacker upright, hitting him hard in the stomach, his hand still gripping Harold's hair. The knife finally fell to the ground and Randall drove another powerful kick into the other man's stomach, watching as he crashed heavily to the ground.

"Lou!" – the scream came from upstairs. It was Maggie's voice.

Randall snatched up the knife and started up the stairs.

"No," Harold shouted and staggered after him.

He caught the Inspector half way up but, the older man was weak and, as Randall spun round he drove the knife forward. It caught Harold just above the right hip, deflected off the pelvis and ripped into his intestines. The policeman tore it free, watching as Harold tottered drunkenly on the stairs, blood pouring through his fingers as he tried to hold the ragged edges of the wound together. Then, with a final despairing moan he toppled backwards, crashing head-over-heels until he lay still at the foot of the stairs.

Randall's breath was coming in gasps. His left shoulder and most of his left arm felt numb and the slashed palm of his right hand felt as if it were on fire. He turned wearily and climbed the last few steps to the landing casting a perfunctory look back at Harold when he reached the top. The older man lay still, face down in the dust which covered the floor, a dark pool spreading out around him.

The Inspector turned and walked on towards the junction of the two corridors before him, not sure which one to check out first. Then he noticed the vile stench and moved cautiously along the left hand one, the knife gripped tightly in his throbbing hand.

He reached the last door and slumped against the frame, his mind reeling from the pain of his wounds and the sight before him.

"Oh my God," he croaked, his eyes scanning the scene of horror which confronted him. The heads, the blood, the excrement and. . .

He stared at the foetuses, shaking his head slowly from side to side. Then he took a step into the room, noticing Maggie for the first time.

"Get out," he told her, gripping the knife tighter.

The foetuses turned their black eyes on him and Randall felt the first gnawings of pain at the back of his neck. He advanced slowly on them, taking in each monstrous detail.

"Lou, don't touch them," said Maggie, her voice low.

Randall seemed not to hear, he just kept moving closer. So slowly, so feebly, as if someone had attached lead weights to his limbs.

"Don't touch them," Maggie implored.

"What are they?" he croaked.

"The grave of abortions that Pierce dug up, these are the three that were missing. They've grown."

"Oh Jesus," murmured the policeman.

(*GET BACK*)

He felt as if he'd been struck with an iron bar. He reeled, almost fell and a thin trickle of blood dribbled from one nostril.

"Lou," Maggie shouted. "Stay away, they'll kill you."

Randall gritted his teeth, raised the knife in his bloodied hand. It seemed as if someone were inflating his head with a high-pressure pump. His eyes bulged in their sockets, a small crimson orb burst from one tear duct and ran down his cheek. Still he advanced on them, the pain in his head growing.

He was less than ten yards away from them.

"Lou."

His legs gave out and he dropped to his knees but still he crawled onward. The veins in his arms and neck bulged menacingly, the wounds in his hand and shoulder bleeding freely. It was like pushing open a thousand ton door, pressing against it, moving a fraction of an inch at a time. He clenched his teeth until his jaws ached, the knife clanking on the concrete as he dropped to all fours.

He almost screamed aloud as he found himself staring into the sightless eyes of Paul Harvey.

The dead man's head lay in a pool of congealing blood, inches from the policeman's face. Thick crimson streamers still dripped from the nostrils and ears. The tongue protruded over white lips. The skull had been smashed in just above the right ear and Randall could still see fragments of brain matter sticking to the hair. The cavity had been emptied, the soft tissue devoured by the monstrosities before him, torn out with their eager hands.

As Randall crawled on, he bumped the head and it rolled over to reveal the severed stump of the neck, the slashed veins and arteries hanging like dripping bloodied tendrils.

The foetuses concentrated their mind power with greater accuracy, focusing it on Randall like some kind of invisible laser beam.

Blood burst from his ears and he went deaf for precious seconds.

"Lou," Maggie shrieked. "Stop."

He was just feet away from them now, their rancid stench filling his nostrils, mingling with the coppery smell of his own blood which was flowing from his nose and dripping onto the floor. He groaned more loudly now as his efforts to reach the creatures became greater.

He raised the knife to strike.

Randall almost screamed aloud as he found himself gazing into the eyes of his daughter.

(*No*)

"Lisa," he croaked, the knife hovering above her head.

(*Don't kill me*)

He swayed, thought he was going to pass out then, slowly, he lowered the knife, eyes fixed on the vision of his daughter.

(*Put the knife down*)

He dropped it in front of him, staring at her. God,

she was beautiful. She lay before him, her body unblemished. He reached out his arms to touch her smooth skin but, as he felt her body, he gagged. The flesh was soft and jellied. As cold as ice. The vision faded instantly and he found himself staring once more at the foetuses.

"No," he screamed and snatched up the knife, plunging it into the one closest to him.

A huge gout of blood erupted from the wound splattering Randall who was sobbing now as he brought the knife down again, the second blow hacking off the foetus's right arm. The tiny limb fell to one side twitching spasmodically, blood gushing from the severed arteries. He struck again and again until the knife was slippery with his blood and that of the creature. The other one tried to crawl away but Randall was upon it in a flash, driving the blade down between its shoulder blades, tearing downwards to rip through its kidneys and liver. He held it by the back of the head and drove the knife into the hollow at the nape of its neck, ignoring the blood which spurted up into his face. He hacked off an ear, part of its nose, buried the blade in one of those dark pits of eyes.

The third creature didn't even move as he gutted it, ripping the small tangle of intestines free with his bare hands.

Finally, he toppled over onto his back, eyes staring blankly at the ceiling. Maggie rushed across to him, wiping some of the blood from his face with her handkerchief. There was so much of the sticky crimson gore on him it was difficult to tell which was from his wounds and which was from the creatures. She helped him to his feet, supporting him out of the room and out into the corridor.

"Got to get back to the car," he whispered, almost collapsing.

She held him, ignoring the blood which dripped from his hands and arms and stained her own clothes.

They reached the landing and began, cautiously, to descend the stairs.

"Harold?" asked Maggie.

"I killed him," said Randall.

But, as they reached the bottom of the stairs, the policeman saw only the pool of blood there. Of Harold there was no sign.

"Come on, hurry," the Inspector said, leading her back through the maze of corridors. "He can't have got far, we've got to get help."

Harold emerged from the door opposite like a vision from hell. Mouth agape, blood spread darkly around his stomach and crutch, he was on them in a second, hurling Maggie to one side. Randall tried to strike out with the knife but Harold was too fast. The older man, wounded though he was, had the element of surprise in his favour. He swung a lump of wood which looked like a chair leg and the blow caught Randall in the side of the face, felling him like a tree-trunk.

Maggie screamed and ran, looking back in time to see Harold snatch up the knife and set off in pursuit of her.

She barged through a door and found herself in the old canteen. Maggie slammed the door behind her and ran for the window, reaching it just as Harold sent the door crashing inwards. He came after her, the bloodied knife raised above his head. Maggie turned to see him gaining and, gritting her teeth, she broke the window with her hand. Crystal shards sliced open her flesh and she screamed, but she managed to push the window open and scramble out, falling heavily onto the grass below. Harold clambered after her, seeing that she was running for the car parked nearby.

Maggie reached it and tore open the door, locking it quickly behind her as Harold advanced. He struck at the windscreen with the knife and, as Maggie recoiled from the expected explosion of glass she saw that the passenger side door was still unlocked. She flung herself across in an effort to reach the lock but Harold saw her and slid off the bonnet, grabbing for the door which he managed to pull open a fraction. Maggie screamed as she tugged with all her strength on the handle but he was slowly forcing it open an inch at a time.

He snaked one hand inside, the knife driving down, missing her by inches as it buried itself in the seat.

Maggie tugged hard on the handle and smashed his arm between door and frame, almost smiling when she heard his yelp of pain. Harold withdrew his hand and she was able to lock the door. He rushed round to the front of the car again and leapt up onto the bonnet, pounding on the glass with his hands.

Maggie snatched up the two-way radio and flicked it on, babbling into the set, not waiting for an answer.

The first hair-line splinters appeared in the windscreen as Harold continued his relentless pounding.

"Help me," Maggie screamed into the two-way. "The old asylum. Inspector Randall is here too. Help."

There was a garbled answer then the set went dead.

The cracks in the glass were spreading, spider-webbing until the driver's side resembled nothing more than crushed ice. Maggie turned the key in the ignition and the engine roared into life. She stuck it in gear but her foot slipped off the clutch and the vehicle stalled.

Almost in tears, she twisted the key again.

Glass sprayed inwards as Harold's fist crashed through the windscreen, groping around blindly as he searched for her, the jagged edges cutting his wrist, trapping him. Maggie stepped on the accelerator and the car shot forward. She heard Harold's shouts of alarm for he could see the wall which Maggie couldn't.

The Chevette hit it doing about twenty-five. The impact sent Harold hurtling into the brickwork with a sickening thud. He staggered, watching helplessly as Maggie reversed. As the car ploughed into Harold, Maggie threw herself clear.

There was a blood-chilling scream of pain followed a second later by a high pitched thump as the car exploded. Pinned between car and wall, Harold could only scream in anguish as the flames licked around him eagerly devouring his flesh. He clapped both hands to his face as he burned, his false eye falling from its socket to reveal the dark mess beneath. His hair went up in wisps of smoke and the flesh peeled from his body like a snake shedding its skin. He let out one final caterwaul of agony then the roaring flames drowned everything out. The heat rolled over Maggie, bringing with it the sickly sweet stench of charred flesh.

She dragged herself upright, the pain in her hand from the cuts keeping her conscious. Mesmerized, she gazed at the burning car and, before her eyes, Harold Pierce seemed to melt away beneath the roaring inferno.

Maggie sucked in huge lungfuls of air, suddenly remembering Randall.

It was as she was heading back towards the asylum that the first of the police cars arrived.

Forty-seven

Randall had regained consciousness by the time they lifted him into the ambulance. He even managed a smile before they closed the doors on him. Maggie had kissed him softly on the lips and then watched as the ambulance sped away.

The firemen, called to the scene by Sergeant Willis, put out the blazing Chevette and then cut the remains of Harold Pierce loose. What was left of him was put into another ambulance and taken away, then Maggie led the police up into the room where the dead foetuses were. PC Fowler threw up at the sight of so much carnage and even Willis found it difficult to retain his dinner. But, nevertheless, the room was eventually cleared, each mutilated body and severed head wrapped in a separate blanket and taken away. Maggie asked for the foetuses to be taken to Fairvale for examination.

All that had happened fifteen minutes ago; now she stood alone in the corridor looking into the room, the vile stench still strong in the air. The room, for what it was worth, was to be inspected by forensic men and then hosed down. Willis himself was coming back to take Maggie home as soon as he'd dropped the specimens off at Fairvale.

She had plenty of time.

She went to the door of another room across the corridor and pushed it open.

The surviving foetus lay in the centre of the room.

No one had thought to check any of the other rooms in the building – why should they? The power of the foetuses' thought projection had been stronger than even she had imagined. So powerful in fact that Randall could not have realized that the third foetus he had killed was merely a projection of his own subconscious.

She herself had hidden the creature in this other room before the Inspector had even reached the first floor. While he had been struggling with Harold Pierce she had lifted the foetus and carried it across the corridor to its new hiding place.

Maggie crossed to it and knelt beside the body.

It *was* rather beautiful she had decided. A perfectly formed child. *Her* child. She lifted it, surprised at its weight and it looked at her, those twin black eyes glinting malevolently.

She pulled it close to her, kissing its bulbous head, allowing it to nuzzle against her. Its lips moved slowly.

The words echoed loudly, not inside her head this time but booming off the walls, all the more incongruous because of the tiny body they came from. The words filled the small room. Deep bass, thick and full of power.

"Hold me."

EREBUS

To Peter Williams
Make mine de-caffeinated with honey

Acknowledgements

To everyone who helped with this book, thank you. On the research side, I would like to thank Mr Peter Milton. Regarding the actual writing, many thanks to Niki, who helped me even more than usual. Thanks also to Bob Tanner who, at the beginning, gave me the kick up the backside I so richly deserved. And I am grateful to everyone at W. H. Allen concerned with the production and distribution of this book.

Shaun Hutson

Erebus (er-u-bus):

1. A region beyond Hades; the abode of the Dead.
2. The Greek God of darkness, born of chaos.

PART ONE

'The motions of his spirit are dull as night,
And his affections dark as Erebus . . .'
– *The Merchant of Venice*; Act V; scene 1

'Shame on the night.
For places I've been
And what I've seen . . .'
– Ronnie James Dio

One

The gravel of the driveway crunched loudly beneath the wheels of the Rolls Royce as Terence Bristow brought the vehicle to a halt.

He switched off the engine and glanced across to the passenger seat where his wife, Laura, sat. They exchanged smiles and clambered out of the car. The drive from their home some eight miles from Wakely, to the stables, had taken less than fifteen minutes and they had passed just two vehicles on the way.

It was still early and Laura pulled her white mink jacket tighter around her in an effort to ward off the slight chill in the air. Fingers of mist drew patterns across the grass which surrounded the complex of white-washed buildings. She wasn't normally up so early in the morning, and, glancing down, she saw that the hands of her solid gold Cartier watch had barely reached 7.06 a.m.

Bristow rubbed his hands together, smiling as he saw the senior stud-groom approaching from one of the stables. They exchanged pleasantries and proceeded up a narrow path towards another building.

'How are things today?' asked Bristow.

'Fine, Mr Bristow,' said John Peters, scratching at his left ear. 'We had the foal out in the paddock yesterday. He's feeding well and he looks strong.'

Bristow nodded approvingly. The foal had been late, born just two days ago. A May foal. Something of a rarity in the world of racing but, Bristow reasoned, the animal would be worth millions. Sired, as it had been, by Regal Gent, winner of both the English and Irish Derbies the previous year. After the second win, Bristow had decided to put the animal out to stud. Now, as he leant on the gate of the box and looked in, he smiled contentedly.

The smell of fresh straw was strong in his nostrils and, inside the box, one young studman was busily turning the yellow strands over with a small pitchfork. Another lad, a rotund, red-faced youth in his teens, was brushing the tail of the mare which stood quietly before him. Bristow's eyes strayed to the foal and he was suitably satisfied by the sleek sheen of both animals' coats. The mare was a bay, a large animal perhaps eighteen or nineteen hands and she seemed to dwarf the foal which nuzzled her flanks.

'A winner if ever I saw one,' said Bristow reaching across to grip his wife's hand.

Laura was looking at the mare which had begun to move its head back and forth somewhat agitatedly.

'She's lathering up a little, isn't she?' Laura said, noticing some flecks of sweat around the animal's neck.

The studman brushing the mare's tail merely continued with his task. He stepped back, accidentally treading in some droppings. His companion held back a chuckle and continued turning the straw. But, as he looked up, he too saw that the bay was beginning to sweat. She continued to swing her head back and forth for a moment longer then she suddenly froze. But her ears were pricked, her nostrils flared wide and, as he watched, her eyes seemed to roll in the sockets. She snorted loudly.

With lightning speed, the mare lashed out with her offside hind leg, driving her hoof back savagely, catching the younger studman in the solar plexus. There was a sickening thud, accompanied by the strident cracking of bone as several ribs splintered under the impact and he was propelled backward by the blow, crashing into the far wall of the box. In the twelve foot square area all hell suddenly seemed to break loose.

'What's wrong with her?' Bristow shouted at Peters who was already slipping the catch on the door in an effort to get inside the enclosure but, as he saw the mare rear up, he slowed his pace.

The first studman dropped his fork and pressed himself against the wall, heart hammering against his ribs. He glanced at the mare and then at his companion who was slumped against the rear wall, blood dribbling over his lips. He had no means of restraining the mare for she wore no harness of any kind. The foal took a couple of nervous steps back, whinneying softly.

'For God's sake do something,' Bristow demanded as he watched the mare turn its attention to the foal.

The larger animal struck swiftly, its head snaking forward cobra-like to strike at the bewildered foal. Powerful teeth were clamped together like a vice and the mare bit hard, twisting its head for a second, tearing a large lump of flesh and muscle free. The bite was a lethal one for it severed one of the foal's carotid arteries. Blood exploded from the savage wound with the force of a high pressure hose, spraying the horrified onlookers.

Laura Bristow screamed as the crimson fluid splattered across her face and body, turning her white mink the colour of poppies. Bristow himself could only watch mesmerised as the mare reared high in the air before bringing both front hooves crashing down onto the smaller animal's back, smashing its spine. The foal crumpled beneath the onslaught, its legs collapsing under it. The little animal raised its head as if soliciting help but a piledriver blow from the mare caught it above the right eye. The sharp edge of the hoof shaved away a portion of the skull and tore the glistening orb from the socket. Still attached by the optic nerve, it dangled like some bloodied table tennis ball from the gaping hole in its head.

The first studman took his chance and ran for the unlatched door. The mare struck at him but missed and the youth vaulted the partition, rolling over in the gravel on the other side.

'Get some help! Hurry!' shouted Peters and the lad scrambled to his feet.

Laura had fainted but Bristow himself could only stand and stare, as if entranced by the horrendous tableau before him. He failed to notice that Peters had turned away and was shouting to several other men nearby, motioning for them to join him.

The foal was already dead and the mare stood over the body, her mad eyes fixing Bristow in a challenging stare. The air was thick with the stench of blood and excrement, the only sounds now the low snorting of the horse and the moans of pain from the injured studman.

Bristow heard voices drawing closer. He felt his stomach begin to churn and then, as he took one last look at the foal, he bent double and retched until there was nothing left in his stomach.

Two

The mist hung thickly around the hills and hollows which surrounded the town of Wakely. But, as a watery sun began to haul itself across the sky, those shreds of condensation began to disperse, as if a veil were being drawn back to reveal the small town.

It stood amidst a patchwork of woods and fields, some of the many farms which dotted its outskirts clung to the sides of the low hills. Others, like the town itself, seemed to be hiding away in shallow valleys.

The closest town to it, about twenty minutes drive along the main road which bisected the countryside, was Arkham. The two places could not have been more different. The latter being a thriving, bustling centre of industry and commerce whilst Wakely depended largely on its livestock and arable farming. The economy of the whole place seemed to revolve around the dozen or so farms nearby. The land rewarded the efforts of those who toiled on it. The soil was rich in minerals and, other than a disastrous failed harvest back in 1964, no one in Wakely could remember when nature had denied them full bounty.

The town itself was a curious amalgam of ancient and modern. In the high street, one or two half-timbered houses sat almost reluctantly alongside red brick shops and small offices. The town was regarded affectionately by its older inhabitants, sometimes reviled by the younger members of the community due to its lack of leisure amenities. But for a bingo hall and a twice weekly disco (held in the small youth club) Wakely offered little in the way of entertainment. Days were spent at work, nights in front of the television or at one of the six pubs. Once more the clash of chronology showed itself in the architecture of the pubs themselves. There were those which still burned real fires in their grates in winter and refused the intrusion of a juke-box, whilst others sported pool tables and drinking was done to the accompaniment of pop music and the electronic bleeping of Space Invaders.

The town seemed to represent a polarisation of styles

and opinions but its inhabitants were united by one thing. Their reliance on the land.

Butchers bought local livestock at the weekly market. The numerous grocers purchased their goods from those farmers who maintained arable lands. Even bakeries made their own flour from wheat and corn supplied locally. Outsiders came to buy, naturally, but the town seemed to guard its yields jealously and buyers from anywhere other than Wakely itself usually went home with little or nothing.

But, if the produce of the surrounding countryside was something to be horded, friendship was not. Isolated it might have been but Wakely's inhabitants were not imbued with the coldness which sometimes afflicts residents of isolated communities. Nonetheless, it remained a town in hiding. Nestled within its cocoon of hills, trees and fields Wakely and its residents survived admirably without the help or hindrance of outsiders.

In the stillness of the morning, sounds of men at work were already beginning to fill the air. Those who worked on the farms had been on the go since before the break of dawn and now, as the sun burned away the last wraith-like vestiges of mist, Wakely began to come to life.

Three

Ken Hargreaves put down his slice of cake and grunted irritably.

'Do you have to do that at the bloody table?' he

rasped, looking across at his companion who was busily inspecting the contents of one nostril on the end of his finger.

Nick Daley apologised and returned to his cup of tea instead. At just twenty-nine he was almost twenty years younger than his thick-set colleague opposite. Ken Hargreaves took one more fleeting look at the younger man then stuffed what was left of the cake into his mouth, his attention shifting to the newspaper spread out before him. All around other men chatted, smoked, drank tea or coffee and ate. Some with hearty appetites, others more perfunctorily. Hargreaves saw this same ritual every day and had done for the past thirty-two years.

In the canteen of Wakely abattoir men discovered whether they really *were* hungry or not. Of the younger men, Daley amongst them, few ate with such gusto as Hargreaves and his older workmates. He, himself, had just demolished three rashers of bacon and two eggs before his cake. Daley had prodded at a piece of apple pie, more interested in gazing round about him than eating. Or, Hargreaves reasoned, somewhat reluctant to fill his stomach, imagining the sight he would shortly be witnessing.

The only thing which Hargreaves had not been able to get used to in all his years at the place was the smell. He expected it to smell like a charnel house downstairs because that was what it was. The stench of blood and excrement was almost palpable, such was its intensity. But, even now, in the light, air-conditioned canteen, that smell still followed him – the smell of death which clung to him after work like a second skin, resistant to even the strongest soaps, unremovable by countless showers and baths. His clothes were washed every night yet still that pungent odour seemed to permeate the very fibres as an ever-present reminder of the job he did.

Wakely abattoir employed just over fifty men engaged in tasks ranging from the unloading of livestock, the inspecting of those animals for disease, preparation of the carcasses and, naturally, killing. That was the job which Hargreaves performed. As many as 500 animals a day passed through the slaughterhouse, arriving in twos and threes, brought by individual farmers. Some arrived in the huge two-tier trucks which could hold as many as eighty pigs.

Hargreaves had been given the task of showing young Daley the ropes and, as he glanced up periodically from his paper, he could see that the younger man was nervous. He had only worked at the slaughterhouse for two days and it was to be his first time in the killing room, nicknamed 'the carcass cave' by the men who worked in it. In five minutes' time, when the hands on the wall clock crawled round to 10.15 a.m., he would follow Hargreaves down to the pens where the various livestock were waiting to be despatched. Already he looked pale and the older man smiled to himself, wondering if Daley would be like the last youngster they'd assigned to him. The youth had watched fascinated as Hargreaves had loaded the humane killer then, as it was pressed to the cow's head he had keeled over, falling face down in the sea of crimson which swam ankle deep on the floor of the killing room. No one had seen him since.

'If you think you're going to throw up, go outside and do it,' said Hargreaves, glancing up at Daley.

The younger man swallowed hard.

'What?'

'If you want to puke,' Hargreaves expanded. 'Don't do it in the meat room.'

Daley nodded, a thin film of perspiration sheathing his forehead as he saw Hargreaves down the last of his tea and get to his feet. He motioned for his younger companion to follow.

They left the canteen and headed down a flight of stairs which brought them into a long corridor, sealed at the far end by a heavy steel door. Hargreaves opened it and ushered Daley through. They emerged onto a high walkway which ran around the cavernous interior of the meat room. The slatted metal cat-walk had a handrail and Daley leant against this in order to look down into the pens below. Tethered there were up to two dozen bullocks, some standing still, others pawing the blood-soaked floor in bewilderment. The stench was unbelievable. Despite six powerful extractor fans which hummed loudly inside the large room, the smell still drifted up in invisible tendrils, causing Daley to recoil slightly. A large set of double doors to his right were open and he could see two men pulling away the carcass of a dead bullock, a large hook driven through its nose. He swallowed hard as he saw that the body was still twitching. The lowing of the cattle seemed to bounce off the walls, rolling around inside Daley's head like slowly breaking waves.

'Put these on,' said Hargreaves, handing the younger man a pair of what looked like waders. They fastened by a strap at his thigh and he saw that the older man also wore a pair. When both were suitably attired, Hargreaves led the way down another flight of steps to the floor of the room. Daley saw the blood lap around his ankles and he gritted his teeth as a portion of bone floated past on the sea of gore, bound for one of the many drains which dotted the concrete floor. One or two had already become clogged with pieces of animal debris and excrement and Hargreaves decided that the place would have to be hosed down before he started on the next group of animals. However, he intended to dispose of the bullocks first.

Near to the animal pens was a wide, stainless steel-topped bench. On top of it lay an assortment of tools. Daley noticed a small sledgehammer, a couple of saws and what looked like a large air pistol. It was that particular device which Hargreaves picked up. It had a vicious looking metal bolt extending from it, protruding about an inch from the end of the barrel.

'The humane killer,' Hargreaves announced, holding up the weapon. He then crossed to the nearest of the pens and approached a bullock which was licking the metal struts of the enclosure, apparently unconcerned by the presence of the two men. Hargreaves leant forward, pressed the bolt to the animal's forehead and pulled the trigger.

There was a loud thud. The implement bucked in the older man's hand as the bolt slammed into the bullocks's skull then quickly retracted, bringing with it a sizeable lump of bone. The animal let out a low grunt then dropped as if pole-axed. Streams of blood erupted from the hole in its forehead. The sphincter muscle gave out and, as the bullock underwent its death-throes, Daley heard the rapid splattering of excrement in the sea of red fluid beneath. He blenched, gripped the pen with both hands and coughed.

Hargreaves watched him for a second, noticing that his skin had taken on a pale, yellowish tinge.

A blast of coppery-smelling fumes swept over them both and, almost immediately, the two men from the double doors to the right emerged and headed for the dead bullock. They nodded a greeting to Hargreaves who exchanged brief words with one of them. Both men were sweating profusely.

'There's eighty pigs coming in at eleven, Ken,' said the first man. 'If you can shift this lot,' he made a sweeping gesture towards the penned bullocks, 'I'd be grateful.'

Hargreaves nodded.

Daley was still gazing down at the body of the dead animal.

'First time in here, is it?' asked the man with the meat hook.

The youngster could only nod.

Hargreaves suppressed a grin as he saw the first man squat down beside the dead bullock. He pulled back the animal's lips and bared its teeth, turning the head in Daley's direction.

'Say cheese,' said the first man, grinning.

Hargreaves and the other two cracked out laughing but Daley didn't see the joke. He merely watched in silence as the carcass was dragged away.

'You all right?' Hargreaves asked him.

The younger man nodded although the gesture was a mechanical one. He could feel his stomach somersaulting.

They moved to the next pen.

The animal inside it was still but it watched the slaughterer with rheumy eyes that seemed to hide a glint of fear. Fear? Anger? Realization? He had often wondered, during his years in the abattoir, whether the animals actually knew what was going to happen to them. Did this particular bullock somehow understand what was about to take place?

He steadied the humane killer in his hand and took a step closer.

Suddenly the animal lunged forward, slamming itself into the metal pen. The impact shook the small enclosure, causing the two bullocks next to it to spring into action as well. There wasn't much room inside the pen for it to gather momentum but, nonetheless, the bullock still managed to attain sufficient impetus to bend the top two struts of the enclosure.

'Jesus,' muttered Hargreaves, stepping back for a second.

The steer let out a low rumbling bellow and launched itself at the frame once more.

Daley saw the gate buckling.

The other two bullocks by now were also slamming repeatedly against their pens and Hargreaves realized that he must act quickly. He stepped forward and lowered the bolt. However, the animal brought its head up sharply and knocked the device from the slaughterer's hand. It flew into the air, disappearing beneath the tide of crimson.

'Christ,' he growled. Then turning to Daley.

'Get the other one – it's on the workbench.'

Daley was frozen for long seconds but the sight of the pen gate bending spurred him on. He waded through the blood, nearly slipping once, and snatched up the second of the bolt-loaded killers.

'Hurry,' shouted Hargreaves.

The first bullock let out a booming roar and drove its way through the battered metal of the pen.

Rivets, screws and pieces of aluminium exploded into the air, showering the two men who raised their hands to shield their faces. The large animal skidded on the slippery floor but then regained its footing and turned on its would-be executioners. Hargreaves managed to leap aside, blood spraying up in a crimson wave as he went sprawling in the mess, but Daley was too slow.

The bullock hit him in the stomach with its left horn, driving him up against the metal work-bench, the lethal stubby protuberance gouging his skin. He screamed in agony as he felt his stomach wall give way beneath the unbearable pressure. The stench of the bullock mingled with the powerful odour of his own viscera as the crushing impact first mangled the lower part of his ribcage to a pulp, rupturing both lungs, then tore open his belly, releasing a tangle of intestines.

'Oh my God,' gasped Hargreaves, rolling over. He was lying less than two feet from the maddened bullock and its victim, his hand still firmly clamped around the humane killer. Daley's screams filled his ears like the cries of the damned, echoing off the walls.

The slaughterer dragged himself to his feet and pressed the bolt to the bullock's side.

With a roar of rage and pain it backed off, the hole in its left shoulder gradually growing bigger as the flesh seemed to rip like tearing material. A mess of entrails began to bulge from the riven hide. The beast snorted, blood spilling from its nostrils. It tried to turn but staggered and fell as its bolt-blasted shoulder gave out. Hargreaves leapt back, hearing the sound of tearing metal from behind him.

The other two bullocks had broken free.

The meat room had become a madhouse, a deafening cacophony of bellows, roars and screams, both human and animal. Hargreaves found his breath coming in gasps and he looked around desperately for a means of escape. There was an alarm bell on the far wall. Whether he could reach it or not was another matter.

The second bullock spun round and headed towards him, stumbling momentarily, giving him precious seconds. But, the waders slowed Hargreaves down. In his mind's eye he could see the bullock. Head lowered, charging towards him, ready to grind him into the ground beneath its crushing weight.

The alarm looked a hundred miles away.

'What the fuck is happening?'

He heard the shout of surprise and horror as the first of the men with meat hooks appeared and looked in upon the scene of carnage. He barely had time to shout a warning to them and they slammed the metal doors, dropping the locking bar in place as the third bullock smashed into it. Then they stood helpless, listening to the unholy commotion from inside the meat room itself.

Hargreaves reached the alarm and smashed the glass with one bloodied fist, the strident shriek of the siren immediately joining the fierce bellowing of the maddened cattle. There was no more sound from Daley.

Hargreaves turned.

The bullock slammed into him, shattering his pelvis, destroying kidneys and liver in the fearful impact. He felt as if his internal organs were being forced upwards first into his chest and then into his throat. What was, in fact, filling his throat was a mixture of blood and bile which, seconds later, gushed from his mouth like water from a broken dam. As the animal backed off, the slaughterer slumped to his knees and found himself gazing into the burning eyes. The beast fixed him in an insane stare, eyeballs bulging madly in red rimmed sockets, thick streamers of saliva hanging from its mouth.

The bullock drew back a foot or so then butted him again, pushing him down into the ocean of blood, pressing hard on his chest until the sternum collapsed and his body seemed to fold in upon itself.

A moment before he lost consciousness he heard footsteps above him on the metal cat-walk, the metallic rattle as a shotgun cartridge was chambered and, a second later, the deafening blast as the weapon was fired. The bullock was hit just behind the left eye, most of its head exploding, showering Hargreaves with a confetti of bone, blood and brain. The creature lowed and its legs buckled as a second discharge tore a hole in its side the size of a football.

The body collapsed beside the fallen man.

Hargreaves could only lie motionless as footsteps drew nearer. He heard shouts then another thunderous gunshot this time close to him.

Then he heard nothing at all.

Four

The light breeze set the curtains billowing, fluttering like the membranous wings of giant moths. The cool air was welcome because the room was stifling.

Vic Tyler lay on his back watching as the curtains danced softly at the bidding of the wind. A single bead of perspiration trickled from his forehead and he wiped it away with the back of his hand. Beneath him the sheets felt damp, a legacy of the warm night, and he shifted uncomfortably, finally swinging himself upright. Perched on the edge of the bed he sat motionless, head lowered, inhaling deeply in an effort to draw some sweet fresh air from the atmosphere of musty stale sweat and freshly laundered linen.

Outside the window birds sang in the clutch of willows which bent and sagged in the bright sunlight. Despite the fact that it was still relatively early, the burning orb in the cloudless sky blazed with savage intensity. Tyler glanced at the clock on the dressing table and saw that it was 10.30 a.m.

He muttered something to himself and ran a hand through his short brown hair. He'd overslept, or rather he'd been allowed to oversleep. If his father had still been alive . . .

The thought trailed off and Tyler swallowed hard, getting to his feet. He padded out of the bedroom across the landing to the bathroom where he switched on the shower, testing the water. He studied his reflection in the mirror, satisfied with what he saw. Tyler stood about six foot two, his body thick with muscle. At thirty-two he was in reasonably good shape for a man who had spent the last six years of his life working behind a desk. The transformation had not been easy for him. Born and brought up on a farm in Wakely, the farm to which he had now been forced to return, Tyler had always known and loved the freedom of the countryside. The city made him feel like a prisoner, an outsider. He had felt like a child, thrust into a strange environment.

At his father's suggestion he had left the farm just after his eighteenth birthday to attend agricultural college. Jack Tyler had seen the wisdom of allowing his son to learn that there was more to farming than driving a tractor and shovelling manure. Tyler himself had left with mixed feelings. Nevertheless, he settled to his new task. However, when his mother died three years later, he had been devastated.

He had returned to Wakely for the funeral and considered whether or not he should even contemplate making the trip back to college but his father persuaded him. He returned and completed the course, but the death of his mother was something which obsessed him. Guilt began to loom large in his mind. Would it have been any different if *he'd* been there? The spectre of that guilt still plagued him. From college he had moved on to work for the Ministry of Agriculture itself. He was good at his job, he earned an excellent salary and he had his own flat in Bayswater. He had friends too. Tyler was a likeable man, always quick to smile, ever ready with a warm handshake and a pleasant word. There had been a succession of girls, mostly one night stands but that was sufficient for him. It was how he wanted it. Yet still he felt a curious ambivalence towards the city. He welcomed what it gave him but he hated it for what it was. And he missed the country.

On hearing of his father's death his actions had been instantaneous. He had handed in his notice, packed his belongings into every available suitcase and carrier he could find and headed back to Wakely, leaving London and his memories behind him.

Now he stood beneath the shower, eyes closed, his mind full of thoughts and ideas yet somehow able to appraise the situation clearly and rationally. He was back where he belonged. Back in Wakely on the farm which had been his home for so many years and which, he promised himself, would remain so until his own death. There was a savage irony to the entire scenario which Tyler was not slow to consider. His father had originally sent him off to college and now, with Jack's death, he was home once more.

The last of the Tylers, he mused to himself. He smiled thinly but the gesture faded rapidly, as if washed from his face by the swiftly flowing water. He was back where he belonged but God alone knew that he would have given anything for it to be under different circumstances.

He turned off the shower and stood for long moments, watching the last of the water swirl away down the plughole. Then, he stepped out, wrapped a towel around himself and began drying his hair.

From the bathroom window he could see the red bulk of the Massey-Ferguson moving slowly across one of the fields to the North of the farm. It was driven by Russell Jenkins, one of two farmhands who Jack had employed. The other, Jim Harrison, was feeding the livestock elsewhere. Both men were in their forties and had worked for the family for as long as Tyler could remember.

Both had been present at yesterday's funeral.

Indeed, Tyler had been surprised at the number of people who had turned up. It had seemed as if the whole of Wakely had come to stand at his father's graveside. Each one of them carrying their individual memories of the man. Tyler had been both grateful and moved by their gesture. The townspeople had welcomed him back amongst them as if he had never been away. The place seemed to radiate cordiality, the homecoming only soured by the circumstances which necessitated it.

Tyler dried himself thoroughly then wandered back into the bedroom where he pulled on a pair of jeans and some old wellingtons. There was a crack in one of the toes and Tyler muttered irritably. There had been several violent thunderstorms recently and the earth of the farm was caught in a curious kind of limbo. Some parts were cracked and parched, others were like a quagmire. From the humidity in the air, Tyler had every reason to believe that they were in for another storm that night.

He went downstairs and, unable to face anything cooked, devoured six rounds of toast which he washed down with several large mugs of tea. Formica cupboards and stainless steel glinted in the rays of the sun which streamed through the open windows. The farm might be old and traditional on the outside but its amenities were strictly modern. The only concession to a bygone, less hectic and mechanised age were a couple of antiques housed in the sitting room: a full size man-trap which hung over the fire place and the rusted blade of a horse-drawn plough. Both had been put there by his father.

His father.

He exhaled deeply then got to his feet, wandering out of the house into the yard itself.

He winced momentarily, shielding his eyes from the glare, but then he relaxed, drawing in a deep breath which smelt of wet grass, hay and manure. The smell had a welcome familiarity about it and Tyler smiled as he headed towards the pig-sty which stood near to the farm's main gate. There was a barn close by which housed the sows and boars but the sty was used for weaners and it was obviously well populated judging by the noise which was coming from inside.

Tyler saw Jim Harrison standing amongst the hungry piglets, his gloved hand dispensing meal to them.

'Morning, Jim,' said Tyler, approaching the sty.

The farmhand looked up, the sun glinting on his bald head.

He nodded at Tyler, momentarily stopping his task.

'Me and Russ thought it best to let you sleep in, Mr Tyler,' said the bald man. 'With all what's happened, like.' He swallowed hard, as if embarrassed.

Tyler nodded.

'I appreciate it but I've got to get used to being up at dawn again now I'm here to stay.'

'Well, the work's underway anyhow, Mr Tyler.'

'Thanks. And you can drop the *Mr* Tyler bit too, Jim. Call me Vic.'

Harrison smiled, mischievously.

'OK,' he paused. 'Vic.'

Tyler peered into the sty and ran an appraising eye over the pigs inside.

'I thought we just used this sty for weaners,' he said, puzzled, looking at the size of the pigs rummaging around for the food which Harrison dropped.

'We do.'

'*These* are weaners?' asked Tyler, almost incredulously. 'But the bloody things are twice the size they should be. You're trying to tell me that these pigs are only ten weeks old?'

'We found it hard to believe at first,' Harrison told him. 'But it's the same with all the animals fed on that new meal.'

Tyler frowned, looking first at Harrison and then at the pigs again. One of them raised its head, nostrils flared, small eyes fixing him in a glassy stare.

'Your father,' Harrison said, dropping his gaze as he spoke, 'he bought some new multi-purpose feed a few weeks back. The fellow who sold it to him said it would increase growth in livestock.'

Tyler nodded approvingly.

'What about the milk yield from the cows, has it affected that?' he wanted to know.

The farm hand shook his head.

'Where did my father get this feed?' asked Tyler.

'There's a new company just outside town,' Harrison said, struggling to remember the name. 'But I'm buggered if I can remember what they're called.' Harrison shrugged. 'Anyway, they make and sell the stuff.'

Tyler nodded.

'Well, it obviously works. We should get a better price for the stock at market.'

'Most of the farms around here are using it,' Harrison added. He tossed what was left of the meal into a small trough then unlatched the sty and eased himself out. He lingered for a moment then wiped his head, leaving a dark smear on his bald dome.

'If it's all right with you, Mr Ty . . . sorry, Vic, I'll get on with my other jobs.'

'Right, I'll be along to help in a minute,' Tyler said, listening as Harrison picked his way across the muddy yard, his boots squelching in the thick ooze.

The younger man leant on the wall of the sty and gazed in at the weaners gathered around the trough. As he had first noticed, for their age, most of the animals inside the enclosure were twice their normal size. It looked as though he was going to make a sizeable profit at the market in two days' time.

Tyler stroked his chin thoughtfully.

He wondered how big the weaners would be when they had finished growing.

Five

The first low rumblings of thunder rolled across the bruised sky, banks of blue-black cloud giving it a mottled appearance. The first silent forks of lightning pushed their way tentatively across the darkened heavens.

The lights in the laboratory flickered once then regained their initial brilliance. The banks of fluorescents in the ceiling reflected off the work tops in the large room. The animals in the rows of cages scurried back and forth nervously as the storm drew nearer.

Geoffrey Anderson crossed to the lab door and peered through the meshed glass panel near the top then, still not fully satisfied that he was alone, he pushed the door open a fraction and peered out. The corridor on either side of him was deserted, the floor sparkling as if someone had been over it with a gigantic buffing machine. The white walls reflected the glow from the strip lights overhead making it seem brighter in the corridor and Anderson felt suddenly conspicuous. But he was satisfied that he was alone.

The clock behind him ticked noisily in the silence, the hands having crawled around to 10.15 p.m. Apart from the rhythmic sound of the timepiece the only disturbance in the solitude was the distant thunder and the agitated squeaking of the animals.

Anderson locked the door behind him, flicked off the lights and stood silently for long seconds. There was a film of perspiration clinging to his face which he hurriedly wiped off with the sleeve of his white overall. As he looked down, the red and silver V C, the logo worn by all Vanderburg employees, seemed to wink at him. He swallowed hard then moved across to the wall phone, looking over his shoulder once more towards the meshed window.

His hand was shaking slightly as he began to dial.

The staccato clatter of typewriter keys sounded like machine-gun fire in the confines of the small office and Jo Ward sighed as she read and re-read the piece she had just finished. There was something not quite right about it but she couldn't put her finger on what it was. To hell with it, she thought, at least she'd make the deadline with time to spare. The stories didn't have to go to press until eleven in order for them to reach the morning edition of the *Arkham Comet*. Elsewhere in the office things were at various stages of organized pandemonium as other reporters rushed to complete their assignments, some hampered by the fact that their typewriting dexterity had not yet extended to more than one finger.

The phone on Jo's desk rang and she picked it up.

'*Arkham Comet*,' she said, her American accent sounding as strong now as it had been when she had first come to work for the paper six months ago.

'I want to speak to Joanna Ward,' the voice at the other end said, breathlessly. It sounded as if the man had been running.

'Speaking. Who is this?' she wanted to know.

'There isn't much time. My name is Anderson. Geoffrey Anderson, I've spoken to you before.'

Jo ran a hand through her chestnut hair, brushing two or three long strands from her forehead.

'Oh, the guy who works at Vanderburg Chemicals,' she said, finally recognizing his voice. She had, indeed, spoken to him before but his voice sounded different this time. There was a strong note of urgency in it, fear even.

'I have to meet you,' he said. 'Tonight.'

Jo reached for a pencil and began drawing irregular shapes on the pad before her. She glanced briefly at her watch.

'It's getting late, Mr Anderson, surely we could discuss it tomorrow or . . .'

He cut her short.

'No.' He almost shouted the word at her. 'It must be tonight.' She could hear him breathing hard.

'Whereabouts?' she wanted to know. 'A pub maybe, there's . . .'

Again he interrupted.

'No. Nowhere where there are people. What I have to say . . .'

The sentence trailed off and, for long seconds, Jo thought that the phone had gone dead. Outside there was a loud growl of thunder.

'Mr Anderson,' she said.

Silence then a burst of static.

'Mr Anderson, are you still there?'

'Yes.' His voice was lower but still strained. 'There's a lay-by on the main road between Wakely and Arkham, it's near an old roadside café. The place is deserted now. Meet me there at eleven-thirty.'

She scribbled something on her pad.

'Hello,' he babbled. 'Did you hear me?'

'Yeah, I got it. Eleven-thirty. I'll see you then.'

'Don't tell anyone,' he gasped. 'I . . .'

The line went dead.

Jo flicked the cradle but there was just the steady hum of static. Finally she put down the receiver, replacing it slowly as if she expected it to burst into life once more. Whatever it was that Anderson wanted he was certainly in a hurry to tell her. She chewed the end of her pencil thoughtfully then glanced down at the location she had scribbled on the pad. A lay-by in the middle of nowhere – what the hell would he want to meet her there for? She wondered if the guy was some kind of creep, maybe he was going to try and jump her the minute he got her alone. She shook her head. He didn't sound like that sort of person. He *did* sound frightened however.

She got to her feet, slipped the notepad into her handbag and headed for the door.

Outside, the storm was drawing closer.

Geoffrey Anderson drew in a deep breath, held it a second then opened the door of the darkened lab. The corridor outside was still empty, all the doors leading down to the lifts tightly locked. He had removed his white coat and stood now in his two-piece suit, his tie undone. He felt as if it were strangling him and, when he swallowed, the muscles of his throat seemed to be swollen. He wiped a hand across his face, salty drops of perspiration stinging his eyes. Overhead, the strip lights buzzed like indolent bluebottles and Anderson paused momentarily as he heard the distant thunder growl menacingly.

He locked the lab door and began walking along the corridor, his shoes beating out an urgent tattoo in the preternatural silence of the deserted building.

Anderson turned a corner and found himself at the lifts. He jabbed the button which would take him to the ground floor, shuffling impatiently as the car rose. His eyes were fixed on the glowing white numbers which lit up as it passed each floor.

It stopped at 3 and his heart missed a beat, the breath frozen in his lungs, but when the lift finally arrived it was empty. He stepped in and rode down to the ground floor.

The reception area of Vanderburg Chemicals was vast, large enough to hold a football pitch. Doors and corridors led off from this carpeted central chamber like the tunnels in a termite nest. At the far end were six sets of reinforced glass double doors. Rain was already coursing down them as the deluge outside began and now bright forks of lightning tore through the blanket of clouds. There were just three lights burning in the reception area, the shadows in the corners seeming thicker, conspiratorial. As if they were hiding something.

Anderson walked quickly towards the exit, his feet now cushioned by the carpet. In the dull light its normal orange colour reminded him of congealed blood.

He reached the doors and paused for a second. His car, a blue Ford Granada, was parked on the other side of the car park. There were other vehicles out there and he counted six large Scania lorries, each one with a tanker attached. The black tankers bore the familiar red and silver logo of Vanderburg Chemicals, the two letters joined together at the curve of the C.

Rain was beating heavily against the glass doors of the main building and, every so often, Anderson would shield his eyes as the sky exploded into a patchwork of searing lightning which left an afterburn on his retina.

There were one or two lights still glowing in windows on the East side of the building and Anderson wondered who could still be working at 10.45. He just hoped they hadn't seen him.

The large sheds to his right were silent, huge black leering shapes, they seemed to grow from the night itself. These were the warehouses and manufacturing buildings where hundreds of tons of the new Vanderburg multi-purpose feed were stored and created using a formula which Anderson himself had worked on. Beyond them stood the well-lit living quarters used by all but a handful of Vanderburg's employees.

There was movement behind him.

He spun round, the breath catching in his throat. In the abyss of the large reception area he could see nothing. The shadows seemed to grow darker, the lightning momentarily abating as if even the elements were combining to conceal the source of the sound from him.

It came again.

A soft, swishing sound, close to him.

A particularly vehement crack of lightning suddenly

lit the entire area, bathing it for precious seconds in cold blue light and, in that light, Anderson saw what was making the noise.

Someone had forgotten to close a window and the broad leaves of a rubber plant were swatting the glass nearby. He smiled thinly, a whisper of relief escaping him.

He almost laughed aloud at his own foolishness. He was, he told himself, becoming paranoid. Nevertheless, his heart would not stop pounding.

There was a loud ring as the lift purred into action.

Someone was descending.

Anderson moved quickly, pushing open the exit doors, ignoring the rain which drenched him. He ran across the tarmac to his car, fumbling in his jacket pocket for his keys as the heavens exploded in a deafening symphony of power above him. He jammed the key in the lock and slid, gratefully, behind the wheel. For long moments he sat there, his breath coming in gasps, head bowed. Then, he pulled the handkerchief from his pocket and mopped his face as best he could. His breathing began to slow down somewhat. Anderson inserted the key in the ignition and gripped the wheel, glancing down at the clock on the dashboard as he did so.

It was almost 10.59.

He prepared to start the engine.

The dark shape rose from the back of the Granada as if it had materialized from the blackness itself. Something cold and thin was looped around Anderson's neck and it was a second or two before he realized what was going on. He was slammed back in his seat as the wire was pulled tight.

He tried to grip the lethal strand, to ease the mounting pressure on his oesophagus, but the more he struggled, the tighter it was pulled. A second tug nearly hauled him over the back of the seat and now the cheese wire began to cut through his flesh, through his windpipe. Jets of blood sprayed the windscreen as veins and arteries were cut. Anderson's eyes bulged in their sockets and his attempt at a scream came out as a liquid gurgle. Blood poured down the front of his shirt as his body began to go into an uncontrollable spasm.

The dark shape in the back seat made no sound but merely pulled harder on the wire, wrenching Anderson several inches up from his seat.

His bladder gave out and a dark stain spread rapidly across his crotch, mingling with the blood which was puddling on the mock leather beneath him. His eyes rolled upwards in their sockets, bulging like swollen boiled eggs, as he felt the tide of unconciousness roll over him. There was a sound in his ears like that of the sea. A great pounding, churning noise which blotted out everything else.

The sound of fluid excretion signalled his death but Anderson's executioner pulled the wire tight against the dead man's spinal cord. Only the bone prevented Anderson from being decapitated.

The car smelt like a slaughterhouse.

The dark shape in the back sat perfectly still for long seconds just gazing at the body of Anderson.

Outside the rain lashed the car unmercifully. Inside, blood trickled down the windscreen like crimson tears.

Six

Jo Ward wiped the condensation from her windscreen and peered through the lashing rain which slammed against the glass. The wiper blades seemed unable to clear the torrents and she wondered if she was going to have to stop.

The road between Wakely and Arkham was badly lit, framed as it was on both sides by trees. They bent and bowed beneath the driving rain, spidery branches reaching down towards the slowly moving Chevette. The headlamps cut a swathe through the blackness but still Jo found visibility was down to about fifty feet. The dull orange glare of the sodium lamps were like pools across the road, islands of light in a sea of darkness.

Why the hell did Anderson have to pick a place like this to meet her? she thought.

She caught sight of the disused transport cafe from her side window. Just beyond it, shrouded by trees, was the lay-by which Anderson had spoken of.

Jo eased the Chevette along the last few tortuous yards of slick tarmac then drew to a halt, the car facing Wakely. She wondered whether or not to switch off her headlamps. Surely he would find her anyway? She decided to leave just the side lights burning. A rolling crack of thunder seemed to shake the car and Jo shuddered involuntarily. She reached for her handbag and pulled out a pack of cigarettes, easing the window down slightly to let the smoke out but rain poured in too freely and she hastily wound it up again. The car began to fill with a blue haze.

Jo smiled thinly to herself. It was like breathing New York air. The smile faded rapidly. Even the thought of that dirty city sent a shudder through her. She'd been born and brought up on Manhattan's East Side, overlooking the slimy brown tongue which was the East river. Some days, she and her friends would stand on the Queensboro bridge and look down at the small boats and tugs which moved along that aquatic thoroughfare. Jo often wondered where the boats were heading, her curiosity more usually extending to the men who worked on them as well. Were they going home to loving wives? To endless rows? Had some of them even got homes to go to? All through her early years Jo's interest in other people had been something which amused and surprised those who knew her. Not least her parents. Her father worked for a cab company while her mother cleaned rooms at the Hotel Roosevelt, less than three blocks from where they lived.

Jo began her own working life at the hotel, earning enough money to support herself while she pursued a faltering career as a freelance journalist. Her interest in people and her curiosity seemed to find a pefect outlet in the articles she wrote. Forever probing and searching for something, she would work an eight hour day at the Roosevelt then begin anew when she got back to her home at night. But journalism was her real love and, as the years passed and her payment cheques totalled just 1,500 dollars, she began to despair of ever making a real breakthrough into the profession she craved so much to be a part of.

Then she met Tony.

Tony Hagen was a guest at the Roosevelt when he first met Jo. Immediately impressed by his appearance and looks she was at first taken aback by his advances. She was a very attractive girl and she was aware of that fact but they came from such vastly different ends of the social spectrum that contact seemed impossible. However, as she got to know him better she found that the fancy suits and expensive jewellery came from an unexpected source. Hagen worked for Alberto Scalise, great grandson of one of Al Capone's top trigger men and then head of the largest of New York's five families.

The temptation was too great for her. She slept with Hagen, she used him, remembering each little piece of information he let slip until she had enough material for an article which she managed to sell to *The New York Times*. They wanted more and they were willing to pay a high price. The opportunity was irresistible.

After the third article appeared she was offered a job on the paper which she took immediately. However, Hagen became more evasive, frightened even. He warned her off, telling her not to write anything else about Scalise but Jo had always been stubborn.

She continued seeing Hagen who, she realized, had fallen in love with her despite the dangers to himself. But she could prise no more information out of him. Or so it seemed.

When he asked her to marry him she agreed and Hagen once more allowed his tongue to flap.

The next story she wrote made the front page.

Within two days it was all over.

They had been sitting in a bar on Lexington Avenue when two men walked in who Hagen instantly recognized.

Now, as Jo sat in the Chevette sucking hard on her cigarette she could still see the scene, printed indelibly on her mind. The first of the men had been carrying a coat over his right arm, the second merely stood in the doorway. Hagen had turned to face them, the beer glass still mid-way between his mouth and the bar top. The first man had let the coat slide away to reveal what he held beneath. Jo had recognized it as a .45 automatic. The man had fired three times.

The first shot caught Hagen in the face, shattering the beer glass before ploughing into his chin, blasting away most of his bottom jaw. The second shot hit him in the chest and lifted him off his feet. The third blew a fist-sized hole through his left shoulder, the impact spinning him round. He dropped to his knees, the screams of the customers ringing loud in his ears.

Jo had thrown herself over the bar, pulling her legs up and shielding her head as more slugs ploughed into the thick wood, blasting long shards away. She heard the hammer slam down on an empty chamber and she took her chance. Leaping to her feet she pushed past the terrified barman and scrambled for the rear exit.

Neither of the men followed her.

Naturally, the incident itself made front page news but Jo had been shaken nonetheless, and then when someone blew the windscreen of her Lincoln away with a shotgun as she was driving home one evening, it was the last straw.

She left America and came to London where she found freelance work relatively easily, but London seemed too central. Too exposed. She moved to Arkham and had worked on the *Arkham Comet* for six months.

She ground out the cigarette in the ashtray and lit up another, glancing at her watch as she did so.

11.48 p.m.

Where in the hell was Anderson?

No other vehicles had passed by, coming from or going to Wakely. She drummed on the wheel irritably and peered out into the storm blasted night.

Away to her left stood the old transport café, now a hollow shell. The only thing moving was a rusty old sign which swayed and rocked precariously as it was buffeted by the wind. The large windows which had once formed the front of the dining area had been smashed and scores of stones lay in the forecourt. There was even the wreck of a Volkswagen rusting in what used to be the car park. The entire, decaying complex was cloaked in blackness, illuminated only occasionally by the bursts of lightning which ripped across the rain-sodden sky.

Jo ran both hands through her hair and glanced at herself in the rear-view mirror. Considering some of the things she had been through in her life she looked remarkably fresh for her twenty-eight years. There wasn't a worry line to be seen and the almost perfect curve of her skin was broken only by a small scar near her right eye – the legacy of that night in the bar on Lexington Avenue. She wore little or no make-up, except for some eye-liner. Even in the darkness of the car, those twin green orbs seemed to glow like jade beacons. She wore a pair of jeans, cut off at the bottom, the material slightly frayed, and a dark blue sweatshirt accentuated her breasts.

She was in the process of lighting another cigarette when she heard the loud drone of a car engine.

Seconds later, powerful headlights cut through the night, shining brightly in her face for fleeting moments as the car drove past.

'Goddamit,' she muttered as the vehicle disappeared in the direction of Arkham.

Jo looked at her watch again. It was almost 12.15. After another five minutes she intended leaving. She'd stop at the first phone she came across and ring Anderson's home. Maybe the stupid son of a bitch had forgotten. Jo quickly dismissed the thought. He had sounded too anxious on the phone, too distraught. He needed to see her and she believed him. Perhaps his car had broken down. She quickly ran through a list of reasons why he hadn't turned up then looked at her watch once again. Three more minutes and she was going.

She snapped her fingers. She'd noticed a phone box on the forecourt of the deserted transport cafe. If it was still working she could ring from there. She had his number at Vanderburg too in case something had prevented him leaving. Jo decided to ring there first.

She twisted the key in the ignition and started the

engine, swinging the Chevette around, heading back towards the night shrouded derelict cafe. She pulled into the kerb and pushed open her door. Leaving the engine idling she sprinted the twenty yards to the phone box.

In the Stygian gloom of the rain-soaked woods something moved.

Something large.

Across the other side of the road, hidden by the impenetrable blackness and the stifling confines of the trees, a portion of the night seemed to detach itself and find animation. The shape moved slowly through the trees, watching as Jo first stopped her car and then clambered out to scuttle to the phone box. She could be seen quite clearly because the lightning now lashed the sky with increasing rapidity, casting a cold bluish glow over the landscape.

The shape watched intently as Jo lifted the receiver, then, like a shadow, it seemed to spread as it approached the roadside.

There was a particularly vehement explosion across the heavens and the shape paused, ducking down behind some bushes.

Jo's car was just ten yards away.

The box smelt fusty and Jo wiped the dirty receiver on her jeans when she lifted it, relieved to hear the steady purring which signalled that it was still in working order. She fumbled in the pocket of her jeans for some change and pulled out a handful of ten pence pieces which she laid on the metal shelf beside her. She dialled Vanderburg Chemicals.

Behind her, the wind whistled mournfully through the smashed windows of the deserted café. A sign proclaiming

HOT MEALS SERVED HERE

hung crookedly, one end of it having come loose. It slapped against the wall of the main building beating out an intermittent rhythm.

The ringing tone sounded and Jo prepared to push one of the coins into the slot.

It continued to ring.

No one answered.

She let it ring fifteen times then put the receiver back down and pulled a piece of paper from her coat pocket which had Anderson's home number on it. She dialled once more. This time it rang just three times before it was picked up. Hearing the rapid pips, Jo pushed her money in.

'Mr Anderson?' she said.

Silence.

'Mr Anderson. Hello.'

Just a low hiss of static. Nothing more.

'Do I have the right number?' she asked.

There was a thunderous explosion of lightning which caused the receiver to crackle alarmingly. It was so loud that Jo held it away from her ear for a second. When she listened again, the line was dead. She put the receiver down angrily.

'Shit,' she muttered, scooping up what was left of the change and shoving it back into her pocket. She paused in the phone box for a moment, preparing herself for the dash through the rain to the car. Then she pushed open the door and scurried across to the waiting Chevette. Was Anderson playing some kind of game with her? she wondered. If so, why? She exhaled deeply and reached into her purse, pulling out her diary. Jo reached back to flick on the car light, puzzled to find that it didn't come on when she touched the switch. She sat in darkness for a second before turning slightly in her chair to see why it hadn't come on.

The bulb was missing.

Not just blown, the entire bracket which held the light, including screws, was gone.

She frowned. It had been fine before she got out of the car . . .

It had been removed. Torn out.

But by whom she wondered? her heart unaccountably beating that little bit quicker. She put the Chevette in gear and stepped on the accelerator, anxious to get away from this place, to get home. However, her curiosity was aroused and she was already determined to visit Anderson the following day.

The light and bracket from inside the Chevette lay on the roadside until a foot came down slowly and deliberately on them, grinding them into splinters. The dark shape watched as the tail lights of Jo's car disappeared around a bend then, as stealthily as it had come, the shape dissolved back into the trees and became as one with the night once more.

Seven

Ronald Faber barely heard the alarm. As he woke he reached out instinctively to switch it off but the clock had already run down. Instead he lay beneath the sheets his eyes crusted shut as if someone had sealed the lids during the night. He raised both hands to his face and murmured something to himself. The sheets beneath him were sodden with perspiration and, as he swung himself upright, he swept some matted strands from his forehead. His breathing was shallow, asthmatic almost, and when his body was suddenly racked by a powerful spasm of coughing he gripped his chest in alarm. It certainly wasn't smoker's cough. He hadn't touched the damned weed in any form in all of his forty-two years.

The spasm passed and he got slowly to his feet, a strange gnawing pain in the pit of his stomach. He rubbed his mountainous belly gently as he crossed to the window and looked out.

Sunlight blazed brightly through the chink in the curtains and Faber closed his eyes tight once again, recoiling from the blistering heat and brightness. Below him, the main street of Wakely was starting to come to life as early morning shoppers moved about and some of the other businesses opened their doors for the beginning of another trading day.

Faber knew that he too must have his shop open at nine o'clock, just as he had done every day for the last twenty years. As sole owner and proprietor of Faber Menswear he prided himself on not having missed a single day through illness or anything else. But, today, he would have given anything not to have to go down into the shop and work.

He was a big man, perhaps twenty stone, and the dressing gown which he pulled on barely met around his ample stomach. His black hair was plastered to his head by perspiration and, when he tried to swallow, it seemed as if his throat had seized up. His mouth was dry, his tongue felt as if it had been turned to chalk.

He passed slowly into the bathroom and gazed at himself in the mirror, a little disturbed at what he saw.

His skin was milk white, not just on his face but all over his body. And it had a uniformity to it, there didn't seem to be one part of him that had any colour. Even the dark mole which stood out so prominently on his chin appeared to have been drained. He raised one hand to his cheek and rubbed gently at the skin, his eyes narrowing as some pieces of flesh came away. He looked as though he'd been exposed to the sun for a great length of time but for the deathly pallor of his skin. The flesh around his nails was cracked and split, the nails themselves broken. His lips were swollen, puffy and thick and when he opened his mouth, a strangled cry escaped him.

As he pulled his dressing gown open he saw that the skin on his chest was coming away in great coils. Like some kind of obscene sloughing he looked like a man in transition, shedding one skin for another. And, everywhere was the bloodless colour of his flesh.

He splashed his face with water, quivering slightly when he stepped back and saw that there were fragments of skin floating on the surface of the water.

'Oh God,' he muttered, his words strained.

He turned to the toilet and began urinating.

As the first spurts of blood jetted from his penis and spattered the white porcelain of the lavatory bowl, Ronald Faber fought back a scream.

The water began to turn a dark red colour as the thick fluid continued gushing forth. It was as if his bladder were filled with red ink. His eyes bulged in horror as the bowl seemed to fill with the crimson liquid then the coppery odour reached his nostrils and he realized that his urine wasn't merely the *colour* of blood.

It was blood.

At that point he did scream.

Eight

From its exterior it could well have been a concentration camp. All it lacked were the machine-gun nests.

The complex of buildings which made up Vanderburg Chemicals stood in the middle of thirty acres of countryside about a mile or so off the main Wakely-Arkham road. The entire collection of monolithic structures was enclosed by a wire fence fully twelve feet high. A daunting enough prospect as it was, topped by several lengths of barbed wire, the fence also bore a sign. Stencilled in large red letters, it proclaimed:

DANGER ELECTRIFIED FENCE

Beneath that, as if any would-be interloper should be foolish enough to ignore the warning, another, smaller, sign read:

THESE PREMISES ARE PATROLLED
BY GUARD DOGS

Jo Ward pushed her sunglasses back onto her nose and ran an appraising eye over the array of fortifications before her. She was driving parallel to the high fence, looking alternately through her windscreen and open side window. A cool breeze wafted into the car and for that she was thankful. High above her the sun had already risen in the cloudless sky, its powerful rays bathing the countryside beneath. Jo drove slowly, the Chevette bumping over the uneven road.

So, she thought, this is where Geoffrey Anderson works. She turned the name over in her mind, wondering just what the hell he'd been playing at the previous night. Two or three things still puzzled her about the events surrounding the mystery. She had recognized the click on the other end of the phone as she'd reached Anderson's house. It had been an answering machine switching itself on. But, she reasoned, why no message? What good was a goddam answering phone without a tape in it? Secondly, the light bracket which had been taken. She glanced up at the place where it had been. Taken. That was something of an understatement. It had been ripped out, by hand too from the look of it. Jo pressed her foot down on the accelerator a little harder. The sooner she saw Anderson the better. Besides, she was anxious to find out what he had to tell her.

After another minute's drive she found herself approaching a set of gates. They were topped with barbed wire like the fence but both stood open and only a narrow yellow barrier separated her from the long driveway which led up to the Vanderburg complex. Jo took off her sunglasses, ran a hand through her hair and pulled up at the barrier. She banged her hooter twice, trying to illicit some response from the blue uniformed men seated in a yellow Porta-cabin to the left of the barrier. They were drinking tea and chatting but one finally sauntered out, brushing the sleeve of his uniform as he approached. Jo caught sight of the red and silver VC on his breast pocket as he drew closer.

'Good morning,' said Jo.

'Morning, Miss,' said the guard, eyeing first the car and then Jo, his attention drawn momentarily to the valley between her breasts, visible in the vee of her white blouse.

'I have an appointment with a Mr Anderson,' Jo told him.

'Who are you?' the guard wanted to know.

She told him her name.

'What do you want to see him for?' the man asked, his eyes now turned on Jo's face.

The lie was ready on her tongue.

'I represent a company which is interested in amalgamating with Vanderburg. Mr Anderson told me he could introduce me to the right people.'

The guard licked his lips, gazing once more at Jo's breasts. His brow furrowed. She hoped he wouldn't notice how tightly she was gripping the steering wheel. The plastic felt clammy beneath her sweaty palms.

She played her trump card.

'Call him – you must have a phone in there,' she motioned towards the yellow cabin.

The guard took a step back.

Jo felt her heart beating faster. He had called her bluff; now she had to hope it worked.

'What was the name of your company?' he asked.

'That's really between Mr Anderson and myself,' she told him. She pushed open her door and stepped out. 'Look, let me call him.'

The guard appreciated the chance to see her standing upright and he nodded approvingly as she walked towards him. He held up a hand to halt her.

'OK, we'll let you through,' he said.

Jo slid back behind the wheel, her whole body shaking in a mixture of anxiety and triumph. The barrier was raised and she drove through, smiling at the guard as she passed. She watched him in the rear-view mirror for a moment, relieved when he didn't go back into the cabin. He might just decide to alert the main building while she was on her way up the drive. The macadamized surface was wide enough to accommodate four or more cars driving abreast of each other and, a moment later, Jo saw why.

A huge Scania rolled towards her from the opposite direction, the sun glinting off its metal tanker. The juggernaut sped past and she felt the Chevette tugged momentarily into the larger vehicle's slip-stream. The large lorry rumbled away towards the main gate.

She finally reached the maze of buildings and pulled up before the main block. There were numerous other cars parked outside. She spotted a Jensen, even a Porsche, amongst the lesser vehicles. Her own car she left right outside the six sets of double doors which led into the main reception area.

It was cool inside the cavernous arena, a welcome change from the heat outside and Jo felt the perspiration chill on her skin. Two large fans, set near the doors, rotated full circle, ensuring that the whole reception was kept at a comfortable temperature. Her high heels sank into the thick carpet as she approached a desk behind which sat a girl of about her own age. She was dressed in a dark blue skirt and jacket which reminded Jo of an Air Hostess. The only difference was the familiar VC on the breast pocket. The girl wore a name tag on her lapel which identified her as Julie.

She gave her perfect practised smile as Jo approached the desk.

'Good morning,' said Jo. 'I'd like to see Geoffrey Anderson please.'

'Do you have an appointment?' asked Julie, the smile apparently bolted to her face for it didn't fade even when she spoke.

'He's expecting me.'

'Who shall I say is here?'

'My name's Joanna Ward.'

Julie flicked a switch on the console before her, reaching for a small set of earphones as she did so. There was a loud bleeping, rather like an overloud pager.

'There's a Miss Joanna Ward in reception,' said Julie, into a mouthpiece, the smile still not slipping. 'She says she wants to see Mr Anderson.'

There was a moment's silence, mutterings at the other end of the line and Julie listened. Jo took the opportunity to glance around. There were a number of people moving about in and around the reception area, coming and going through the corridors which led off, spoke-like from the central chamber. Some were in pairs, others alone. All wore the dark blue uniform of Vanderburg or white coats, some even had overalls on. Two young men, both in their early twenties, passed by and cast approving looks at Jo. Even their overalls bore the red and silver VC. The reception smelt of carpet cleaner and polish. The drone of muzak added a background to the chatter of typewriters and the almost constant purring of lift doors as people came and went.

'Someone will be down in a moment,' said Julie, flicking the switch on her console to 'Off'. 'Would you like a cup of coffee?'

Jo availed herself of the offer then went to sit down in one of the soft leather chairs near the lifts. She had hardly seated herself when a tall, white-haired man in a three piece suit emerged from the lift nearest to her. His shoes, she noticed, were in need of cleaning. He headed straight towards her, as if he'd known her for years but, she reasoned, considering she was the only person in sight not sporting a Vanderburg logo, it was safe for him to assume she was a visitor.

She got to her feet as he drew closer.

'Miss Ward,' he said, smiling. He extended a hand which was dotted with liver spots but there was a warmth in his handshake. Jo looked at him carefully. He was in his fifties, perhaps older but his blue eyes twinkled with a radiance which belied his years. His skin was wrinkled, a double chin wobbling fluidly as he shook her hand.

'What can I do for you?' he asked.

'You're not the guy I spoke to last night,' she said.

He smiled.

'No. My name is Glendenning. Martin Glendenning.'

'I wanted to see Geoffrey Anderson.'

'So I understand.' He motioned her towards a door on the left and she began walking towards it. When he opened it, she found herself in an office. It was a small room, the desk and filing cabinets making it seem overcrowded. He invited her to sit down, taking up position himself on the other side of the desk. The room was obviously sound proof because Jo could no longer hear the muzak from the reception area once Glendenning closed the door.

'As I was saying,' he began. 'I realize that it was Mr Anderson you wanted to see. Might I ask in what connection?'

'I'm a journalist,' she told him. 'He rang me last night and said he wanted to speak to me.'

'Really,' said Glendenning, his smile fading slightly. 'How did you manage to get past the security men at the gate? They have instructions not to let members of the press in.'

'Something to hide?' said Jo, grinning.

Glendenning chuckled.

'I wish it were that exciting here, Miss Ward,' he said. 'No, it's nothing like that but we're a new company and our backers are somewhat shy of publicity.'

'Who are your backers?' she asked.

He smiled.

'Do journalists always leave the office in the morning with the intention of finding a story?'

'We do our best.'

Glendenning nodded. He rested his elbows on the desk and propped his chin on his hands.

'Well, Miss Ward, I'm afraid there seems to have been some kind of misunderstanding. Mr Anderson doesn't work here any more. In fact he moved on some time ago.'

'He spoke to me from here last night,' Jo protested.

'That's impossible. Besides there is no record of a call, all phone messages are monitored you see.'

'You mean the phones are bugged?' said Jo, flatly.

'Not in the sense you mean,' Glendenning told her. 'It's just part of security procedure.'

Jo exhaled in exasperation.

'He called me about eleven last night, maybe a little earlier.'

Glendenning shook his head.

'Most of our employees leave the main building at seven,' he said. 'It's extremely unlikely that anyone would be working at such a late hour in any case. Besides, as I said, Mr Anderson has not worked at Vanderburg for some time.'

'What do you call some time?' Jo demanded.

The older man shrugged.

'Weeks.'

The American shook her head.

'If you'll excuse the expression, Mr Glendenning, someone's been shafted and I get the impression it's me. Some guy calls me last night, says his name's Anderson. I know the man's voice for God's sake. He says he has to meet me. Now you tell me he's been gone for weeks.'

'I'm sorry I can't be more helpful, Miss Ward,' Glendenning said, getting to his feet. He walked to the door and opened it, a gesture which was unmistakable. Jo rose and walked past him into the reception area.

'You never did tell me how you got past the Security men,' the older man asked her, smiling.

'I lied to them,' said Jo. 'All part of the job.'

He chuckled and they exchanged pleasant farewells. Glendenning closed the door behind her and, only then, did his smile dissolve into a frown.

'Left weeks ago, my ass,' Jo rasped, fumbling for the pack of Marlboro. She lit one and sucked hard on it. On the seat beside her was a piece of paper.

It bore the address of Geoffrey Anderson.

One way or another she was going to find out where he was.

Nine

The cow tried to rise but then dropped forward onto its spindly front legs. It raised its head and snorted in pain, its body lathered in thick white sweat. A Friesian, it was virtually all white due to the creamy coating of fluid it exuded. The barn smelt of damp straw, mingling with the fusty odour of cattle and the more pungent stench of excrement. The cow twitched its tail frenziedly as if trying to brush away some non-existent flies and, as he watched, Tyler saw blood trickling from both its anus and also from the gaping opening to its womb.

'Did you call the vet?' he asked, agitatedly, looking round at Russell Jenkins who was carrying a bucket of hot water and some cloths.

'He said he should be here in ten minutes,' Jenkins replied setting the bucket down.

Tyler looked back to the cow.

'I hope to God she lasts that long,' he murmured.

The animal had managed to lift itself up onto its forelegs once again and stood swaying uncertainly, its eyes bulging in pain. Its stomach and much of its hind quarters appeared grossly swollen and, as he watched, Tyler could see rapid undulations beneath the skin. The calf was a large one and it was due to be dropped very soon. Tyler crossed to the cow and laid his hand on its muzzle, disturbed to see that there was blood coming from its nostrils too. The animal was bleeding internally.

'Come on, Hawley, for Christ sake,' he rasped under his breath.

'Is there anything more we can do?' asked Russell Jenkins, watching as the cow's hind legs buckled as if unable to bear the immense weight they were supporting. Tyler coaxed the animal into lying down but it seemed unable to do so adequately. The huge protuberances in its hindquarters making this almost impossible. It was as if someone had inflated the creature with a high pressure pump. The undulations became more rapid, more violent and the cow tossed its head about spraying Tyler with the foam like perspiration.

From outside the barn, both men heard a car pull up. A door slammed and Jenkins ran across to see who it was.

Dan Hawley walked in carrying a large black bag which he swiftly opened, pulling out a stethoscope.

'Get her up if you can,' he said, tugging off his tie, hurriedly unfastening his shirt. He crossed to the stricken cow and pressed the stethoscope to its ribs. The heart beat was faint. He moved down and tried to locate the calf's upper-body. There was no sound but the animal was obviously still alive because Hawley could see the frantic movements inside the cow itself. He pulled off his shirt, quickly washed his hands in the bucket of hot water then approached the rear end of the cow which was now on its feet, partially supported by Tyler and Jenkins.

'What the hell is wrong with her?' asked Tyler, perspiration coursing down his face.

'The calf's stuck lengthways by the looks of it,' Hawley told him. 'I'll have to right it.' He steadied himself. 'Hold her tight,' he said. Ignoring the vile odour which was coming from the groaning beast, Hawley slid first one then two dripping hands into the bleeding orifice before him, feeling for the calf's head. He found the feet, the fore-legs he guessed.

'Give me some rope, quick,' he snapped, withdrawing his hands, both of which were dripping crimson.

Tyler scuttled across to the other side of the barn and snatched up a piece of stout hemp, almost knocking a pitchfork over in the process. He cursed and threw the rope to Hawley.

'Why didn't you call me earlier, Vic?' asked the vet.

'Because things didn't start to get bad until about twenty minutes ago,' Tyler told him.

'Here,' said Hawley. 'You'll have to help me, we're going to have to pull the calf free.' He plunged his hands back inside the cow's riven uterine passage and tried to loop the rope around the forelegs of the calf. He cursed as he attempted to complete the difficult task, sweat running off him in salty rivulets. He was a thick set man, powerfully built but he showed remarkable dexterity when dealing with animals, and now Tyler saw a slight grin spread across his face as he succeeded in fastening the rope around the calf's legs. He gripped it hard and Tyler did likewise.

'Hold her head,' the vet told Jenkins.

The cow let out a bellow of pain which sent shivers through all three men – a low rumbling ululation the like of which Tyler had never heard before. Jenkins stepped back in surprise.

'Hold her, dammit,' snarled Hawley but, a second later, he too stepped back as he saw blood begin to pour even more rapidly from her gaping median vagina.

'Oh Christ, the Müllerian duct has ruptured,' the vet rasped. 'The bloody thing could bleed to death.'

'Is there anything you can do?' Tyler demanded.

'We can at least save the calf,' Hawley told him.

The cow bellowed once more, even more loudly this time. The sound seemed to thunder from the very walls themselves then, as that roaring sound of agony subsided, another very different noise took its place.

There was a sound like tearing fabric and the cow's side began to split open. Blood burst from the gash and, a second later, what looked like a hoof tore through the rent.

Tyler stepped back in horror and, even Hawley could only stand transfixed as part of the cow's rump seemed first to be sucked in and then to rapidly bulge, the flesh straining to the point where it became shiny, as if pushed from the inside by some impossible force.

There was a rasping sound and the skin broke. Blood and excrement sprayed upwards in an obscene fountain and, from the ruins of the cow's hindquarters, a head appeared. It rose on a long, snake-like neck. It was the head of the calf, but no calf any of them had ever seen before, and it gazed defiantly at them for long seconds. Then the rear end of the cow literally exploded as the calf tore itself free.

Tyler and Hawley recoiled, splattered with blood, watching as the calf, which they could now see was huge, struggled to free itself from the torn body of its mother. Pieces of cow and calf became momentarily as one and it was as if the men were witnessing some monstrous kind of binary fission as one animal became two. Like the nuclei of two cells, the animals separated, the cow going into spasm as the calf continued to tear itself free. It burst from the torn remnants of its mother, lumps of the allanta chorium hanging from it, the membranous sack sticking to it like grotesque streamers of translucent flesh.

'What the fuck is it?' gasped Jenkins, looking at the calf which now stood upright.

The creature was at least four feet high at the shoulder. A living nightmare. A patchwork of life. Bumps and growths seemed to cover it, leaving not one square of skin unaffected. Its head was heavy, weighed down by what appeared to be a large tumescent protuberance on one side. Tyler noticed with horror that this additional growth had an eye and for fleeting seconds he thought the monstrosity had two heads. It stood perfectly still, watching them, blood and pieces of internal tissue dripping from its gore soaked hide. Then it moved towards Jenkins.

The calf opened its mouth to reveal a set of powerful

teeth and Jenkins pressed himself back against the wall of the barn.

Tyler leapt to one side, grabbing the pitchfork, lowering the two prongs at the deformed calf.

'Don't touch it,' screamed Hawley, as the abomination spun round to face him, lips drawn back in a grimace of rage. It uttered a low sound in its throat, a noise which gradually grew in volume, impossibly loud for a creature of its size.

Tyler gritted his teeth and thrust the pitchfork forward, driving it into the chest of the calf, ignoring the fresh gouts of blood which sprayed him. He wrenched the weapon free and struck again, this time piercing the calf's side, pushing deeper until he caused it to topple over. He leant on the fork with all his strength, holding the creature down as it bucked and twisted frantically, trying to escape the twin prongs which pinned it to the floor like a butterfly to a board. The calf raised its head and tried to bite him but Tyler merely stepped back a foot or two, tore the fork free then rammed it through the dying monstrosity's head. One of the prongs punctured an eye on the way and, amidst the cracking of bone, the thing writhed one last time then was still.

Panting, Tyler staggered away, looking down with digust at the calf and what was left of the cow. Blood had sprayed everywhere and the barn reeked of the coppery smelling substance.

'What is it?' Jenkins asked once more, looking down at the body.

Hawley knelt beside the dead calf.

'It's a mutation of some kind,' he said. The vet turned to look at Tyler. 'I'll have to do an autopsy.'

Tyler nodded, wiping some blood from his face.

'What the fuck would make it grow like that?' he said, his voice a hoarse whisper.

'I won't know that until I've done the autopsy,' Hawley told him.

'Call me as soon as you've got any information,' said the farmer.

'I'll need something to put it in,' the vet told him.

'Russell,' Tyler hooked a thumb towards the other barn and Jenkins scuttled out to fetch something in which to wrap the monster.

'I've never seen anything like this in my life,' Hawley confessed, prodding the calf with his index finger. 'Mutations yes, but never as advanced as this.'

'Could the growths be tumours?' said Tyler.

'I doubt it, not as large as this, especially the one on the head.' The vet looked at the bulge with its extra eye. 'What about the bull that serviced this cow. Is *it* all right?'

'I told you, Dan, there was nothing out of the ordinary until about thirty minutes ago when the cow started bleeding. I thought it was an ovarian rupture like you did but . . . not this.'

'I'll need to examine the cow as well, chances are there was some kind of genetic fault with either the bull or the cow – some kind of change in the DNA, perhaps a translocation of chromosomes.' He exhaled deeply. 'I won't be able to say until I've given them both a thorough going over.'

The two men stood in silence for long seconds, their gaze fixed on the mutation at their feet.

'Have you had any other breeding problems?' Hawley asked.

Tyler caught the note of concern in his voice.

'No, why do you ask?'

'Just curious,' said the vet.

'I *have* got weaners and lambs that are twice the size they should be for their age,' Tyler said.

'You're not the only one, Vic,' said Hawley, flatly.

'You know Stuart Nichols over in Western Orchard farm and old Ben Thurston? So have they.'

Tyler looked puzzled.

'But no mutations?' he said.

Hawley shook his head.

Both of them returned their gaze to the deformed calf, its third eye fixing them in a glassy stare.

Tyler exhaled deeply, the blood starting to congeal on his hands.

'What the hell is going on?'

Ten

The multi-coloured awnings which adorned the stalls of Wakely market flapped in the wind. The central square of the town was awash with colour. It resembled the palette of a mad artist, greens, blues, reds and all manner of stripes alongside each other in bright rows.

Jo drove slowly past, glancing over at the market. The clock on the council building across the square struck eleven, trading was in full swing. Why then, Jo wondered, were there so few people around? She had been in Wakely on market day before and had always found it practically impossible to walk around the central square let alone drive. But today was different. People moved about quietly and few voices were raised for there was no need to shout. Everything had a calmness about it and a serenity which was almost unnerving.

Anxious for some fresh air, Jo stopped the car and

got out. She had parked next to a large fruit van and two men were unloading it, one of them struggling across to a nearby stall with crates of oranges. The man seemed to be managing without too much trouble but, half-way to the stall, he sagged and dropped the crate which promptly burst open. Jaffas went rolling in all directions like huge orange marbles.

'Oh sod it,' grunted the man and began picking them up.

His companion chuckled, jumped down from the van and they set about gathering the dropped fruit.

Jo ran an appraising eye over them. Both men were in their early twenties, stripped to the waist, one of them with dark hair that reached his shoulders. Yet what struck her as most odd was the colour of their skin. Considering it had been so hot during the past few weeks and these men were obviously from one of the farms around Wakely, both were milk white. There wasn't the slightest trace of sun tan on either of them which was something Jo found surprising. She walked past, aware that the one with the long hair was gazing at her legs.

'Morning,' he said, cheerfully, looking up at her.

Jo smiled, even more aware of her own smoothly tanned skin as she looked into the pale face of the farm hand. His eyes were narrowed against the sun as he looked at her, his glance shifting furtively from her face to her breasts.

'I thought you were supposed to sell your goods,' she said, motioning towards the oranges. 'Not throw them around.'

The two men finished gathering up the fruit and succeeded in placing it amongst the other produce. The stall seemed unusually well stocked.

'Business not too good?' Jo asked.

'There aren't that many people around today,' said the one with the long hair.

Jo scanned the first aisle, flanked on both sides by stalls selling everything from wet fish to brass antiques. It stretched for at least a hundred yards ahead of her yet there were barely two dozen people in it. They seemed, some of them, to be moving in slow motion, as if every step were an effort.

'I thought it was usually busy in town on market days,' she said.

'It is,' the first man said, touching his cheek. Jo frowned, noticing how sunken his features were, the dark rings beneath both eyes which looked as though someone had smudged soot there. She put it down to a rough night.

'Can we interest you in anything, love?' said the second man brandishing a cucumber before him. Both he and his companion laughed.

Jo grinned.

'Maybe some other time,' she said and wandered off.

The town square of Wakely was cobbled and she found that she had to walk slowly for fear of overbalancing in her high heels. As she passed up the aisle, glancing at each stall, she noticed again just how quiet it was, even in the centre of the market. A few people chatted animatedly and every so often a peal of laughter would ring out but, in the main, the shoppers and traders were subdued.

Jo paused at a stall which sold miniature glass animals. All of them, she guessed, made by the proprietor. He was sitting at the rear of the stall reading a tatty paperback, his face hidden from view. The journalist looked at him, studying his hands which were large, comfortably enclosing the book. She frowned slightly.

The fingernails of his left hand were long and pointed, the skin of the cuticles cracked and raw. The nails of the other hand were the same, the index finger particularly long to the point where it had begun to curve over.

Jo picked up one of the glass animals, an elephant sitting up balancing a ball on its trunk, and inspected it.

'Need any help, lady?' said the man, his voice low.

The American looked up and, once again, found herself looking into a face the colour of sour cream. Only this time the man's lips were cracked too, as if he'd been exposed to the sun for a long time. Yet he had no colour. His cheek bones were high, the skin looking as if it had been stretched over them. She saw that it was peeling in places, just small fragments which flaked off as he rubbed his chin.

'These models are very nice,' she said, replacing the elephant.

'All my own work,' said the man, proudly.

'I was saying to some guys back there, it's not very busy for market day,' said Jo.

The man shook his head.

'It might buck up a bit later on,' he explained. 'The livestock market is held this afternoon.'

Jo nodded.

'Nice talking to you. I like your models very much,' she told him as she walked away.

The man returned to his paperback.

It must have taken Jo thirty minutes to walk up and down all six aisles of Wakely market and she found that she managed it without the customary barging and bumping which usually occurred on this, the town's busiest day of the week. She headed back to her car, passing the fruit stall where the man with the long hair winked at her and smiled. She returned the gesture, noticing that he too had long, hooked fingernails on at least four of the spindly digits. Her initial surprise and curiosity had diminished somewhat and, by the time she slid back behind the wheel of the Chevette, her mind had returned to more important things.

She glanced down at the piece of paper beside her which bore Geoffrey Anderson's address.

Jo started the engine and drove off. She wriggled uncomfortably in her seat at first. The sun, pouring through the windows, had turned the plastic seats of the car into a hot plate which seared her legs and even burned her backside through the thin material of her skirt. As she drove, she rolled her head back and forth in an effort to release some of the tension which was gnawing at her shoulders.

Anderson's house stood amidst a large expanse of garden, separated from his neighbours on both sides by a high wooden fence. The grass, Jo noticed as she got out of the car, looked short, freshly mown even. The man she sought might indeed have left Vanderburg Chemicals but he certainly hadn't left Wakely. The garden looked immaculate. She approached the front gate, inhaling a heady mixture of blossom from the trees and the numerous fragrances of flowers growing in abundance in all the gardens before her.

There was a sign on the gate which read: 'Avalon'.

She double checked her piece of paper, although it was a formality. This was definitely Anderson's house. Jo walked briskly up the path, noticing as she did so that the curtains at the front of the house were drawn – doubtless to keep out the scorching sun. She knocked on the door and waited.

There was no answer. No sounds of movement from inside.

She tried again.

Still nothing.

She pushed open the letter box and tried to peer into the gloom inside the hall. It was like looking into a pit. She could see nothing. Jo followed the path around to the back of the house where she banged on the rear door. Once again she noticed that the curtains, both upstairs and down, were drawn. The American tapped on the kitchen window with her car keys and still she received no answer. She wandered down the garden to a large shed, surprised to find it unlocked. It smelt fusty inside, an odour of damp wood and earth. The windows were dirty, the tools inside caked with dried mud.

Jo walked back to the house, around to the front and along to the house next door.

The curtains there were drawn too.

She banged the front door twice, stepping back to look up at the red brick dwelling.

She waited for five minutes but there was no answer.

She was becoming increasingly irritable by now and walked back the way she had come, to the house which stood on the other side of Anderson's.

She almost breathed a sigh of relief when she saw a woman, a little older than herself, emerge from the front door, a plastic bucket in one hand, a wash leather in the other.

'Excuse me,' Jo called.

The woman looked up as the journalist walked up the path towards her.

'Sorry to intrude,' said the American. 'I won't keep you a minute.'

'If you're a Jehovah's Witness I'm afraid I'm busy,' said the woman, taking a step back.

Jo smiled.

She held out her hands.

'No Bible, see.'

The woman smiled, running a hand through her tousled blonde hair. She was a trifle on the plump side, the jeans she wore just that little bit too tight around the thighs. Her face was aglow, her ruddy complexion making it look as though someone had scrubbed her cheeks with a wire brush.

Jo could hear the sound of a record player from inside the house.

'I'm sorry to stop you working,' said Jo. 'I won't take up a minute of your time.'

'Who are you?' the woman wanted to know.

'I'm a journalist, my name's Joanna Ward. I work for the *Arkham Comet*.'

The woman nodded.

'I'm looking for the guy who lives next door, Geoffrey Anderson. I wondered if you'd seen him.'

'You're American, aren't you?' the woman said, smiling as if she'd just made some earth-shattering discovery.

Jo nodded.

'About Mr Anderson,' she persisted, 'I wondered if you'd be able to tell me anything about him.'

'Is he in trouble?' asked the woman almost excitedly.

'No, it's nothing like that. *Have* you seen him lately?'

'Not since Sunday, he was out there cutting his grass,' the woman told her. 'A nice man. He kept himself to himself but there's nothing wrong with that is there?'

Sunday, Jo thought. 'He was here two days ago?'

'Yes.'

'But you haven't seen him since?'

'No. You could probably contact him at work. I think he's got something to do with that new chemical place.'

Jo fumbled in her pocket and produced a card.

'Look, if you see him, could you call me on that number, please.'

'I can't really tell you much about him,' said the woman, apologetically. She ran her eyes over the card which Jo had given her.

'Do you know if he finished working for Vanderburg Chemicals recently?' Jo enquired.

'He's worked for them since they started.'

'So he hasn't left or been fired in the last three or four days?'

'Not as far as I know.'

Jo nodded.

'Thanks very much, you've been a great help.' She turned and headed back to her car.

The woman looked at the card once more then pushed it into her back pocket. By the time she had done that, Jo had driven off.

Eleven

'I reckon you must be using the wrong soap, Jack. You've frightened all the bloody customers away.'

A chorus of laughter and cheers greeted Stuart Nichols' remark. He downed what was left in his cider glass and ordered another round, pushing the other empty glasses towards the barman. Nichols was a big man, a year or two older than Tyler. He ran a farm to the west of Wakely, a large holding on which he kept a herd of more than two hundred cattle. He and his wife, Bet, had lived there for the past twelve years.

'It's not me,' Jack Vernon told him. 'It's you lot, come trooping in here with your sodding great boots covered in cow shit.'

The group of men gathered around the bar of 'The Black Swan' laughed.

'That's a fine way to talk to your best customers,' said Tyler, taking a hefty swig from the fresh pint which Vernon handed to him.

'It is quiet in here though,' said Reg Gentry, looking around the bar. He chewed thoughtfully on the stem of his pipe and scratched his face, careful to avoid the nasty scar on his left cheek. He'd been kicked in the face by a pony when he was eleven. It had broken his jaw in four places and cost him five teeth as well as leaving him with the scar.

As he sat on the bar stool he glanced up at the light above him and winced slightly.

'I bet you don't know where you are, now you're back doing some real work again, Vic,' said Nichols, taking a hefty swallow from his pint pot.

'Well, it beats sitting on your arse behind a desk I'll say that,' Tyler told him.

'How are you settling in?' asked Ben Thurston.

'Fine thanks, Ben,' said the younger man warmly. 'It's great to be able to breathe clean air again.' He chuckled.

Tyler had always reserved a certain affection for Thurston. The man was in his early sixties, the oldest of the landowners around Wakely. He and his three sons ran a fifty acre farm to the North. Thurston had intended to retire when he reached his sixtieth birthday but, with the passing on of his wife, that had not transpired. He reminded Tyler of his own father in many ways; his dogged determination, sharp business mind and other, less noticeable features further endeared him to the younger man.

Nichols took another swig of his pint, wiping his mouth with the back of his hand.

'One of my sows gave birth to a litter,' he said. 'About two days ago and every one of the little buggers was dead. All seven of them. I can't understand it.'

'Dan Hawley told me you'd been having trouble with your weaners,' said Tyler, wondering whether or not to mention the incident with the calf.

'When did you see Dan?' asked Nichols.

'This morning, about three hours ago,' Tyler told him. He decided *not* to mention the deformed animal. 'I said to him that my weaners were twice the size they should be and he mentioned that you and Ben too were getting the same results.'

'I'm not complaining,' said Thurston. 'With the stock as big as it is we should all get better prices.'

'Bloody right,' echoed Nichols. 'I'll be asking more than usual I'll tell you that.'

'Bred a super-pig have you, Stuart?' asked Jack Vernon, grinning.

'You could say that,' Nichols told him, smugly, then he laughed.

'It's been the same with my lambs,' Thurston added. 'Only three weeks old but some of them are as big as collies.'

'What do you think's causing it?' said Reg Gentry.

'I couldn't give a sod what's causing it,' Stuart Nichols told him. 'All I know is my profits are going to rise.'

Tyler was the first to notice Jo when she walked into the bar. She strode past the farmers, smiled softly at them and ordered herself a drink.

'If there's any more like that come in today, profits won't be the only thing rising,' Nichols said, lecherously. He watched as Jo seated herself on a stool at the far end of the bar, hitching her skirt up until it was well above her knee, revealing her slim tanned thigh. She took a notepad from her handbag and began scribbling something down.

'I've not seen her around before,' Gentry said.

Tyler didn't speak. He had his eyes fixed firmly but discreetly on Jo, watching her over the rim of his glass.

'I believe we were talking about livestock,' said Ben Thurston, smiling.

The other men seemed to come out of their trance, their eyes turning away from Jo who could see them out of her eye corner. She smiled to herself and continued writing.

'What about you, Vic?' said Nichols. 'You're the one

with the brains, you went to college. What do you think's causing the accelerated growth?'

Tyler shrugged.

'It's difficult to say. My farmhands were telling me about some new multi-purpose feed they'd been using.'

Nichols nodded.

'That stuff from Vanderburg or whatever the hell it's called?' he asked.

'I don't know the name of it,' Tyler said.

'It's from Vanderburg Chemicals,' the other farmer continued. 'The bloke who sold it to me said it would increase growth.'

Jo sat up at the mention of the word Vanderburg. She swung round on her stool and faced the men.

'Pardon me,' she said. 'Don't think I'm eavesdropping but I did hear one of you mention Vanderburg Chemicals, didn't I?'

The men were a little taken aback by her accent but Tyler broke the sudden silence, hesitantly at first perhaps but thankful for the opportunity to converse with such an attractive young woman.

'Yes you did,' he said. 'Do you know something about them?'

'Not as much as I'd like too,' said Jo. She picked up her drink and walked over to the group of men. Thurston offered her his stool.

'You're a Yank, aren't you?' said Nichols.

'I'm an *American*, yes.'

'What are you doing here?' asked Gentry.

'I work for the *Arkham Comet*. I'm just covering a local story,' she said.

'Anything interesting?' asked Nichols.

Jo shook her head.

'Not really.' She sipped at her drink. 'Are you all in town for the cattle market?'

Tyler nodded.

'Was that an educated guess?' he asked, smiling at her.

'I've been to it before,' she told him.

Jo looked deep into his blue eyes and could almost feel the warmth there. She afforded herself a quick inspection of this tall, hard-faced man dressed in jeans, boots and a check shirt. His face was pleasantly tanned, the material of his shirt unable to conceal the powerful body beneath.

'To be accurate,' said Thurston, 'it's a livestock market.'

Jo shrugged.

'Whatever it is I was surprised there weren't more people around.'

'So were we,' Nichols told her. He eyed the newcomer up and down, noticing that her full breasts were unfettered by a bra, the twin peaks of her nipples dark beneath the fabric. 'What's a Yank doing working for the *Arkham Comet*?'

'It's a living,' she told him.

Gentry looked at his watch. The hands were approaching 1.00 p.m. He downed what was left in his glass and got to his feet.

'If we don't get a move on we'll miss the bloody market,' he said and the other men also finished their drinks. Tyler hesitated.

'Want to come along?' he asked her. 'You can see how we yokels spend the day.'

He smiled at her and Jo responded. Tyler found himself drawn to those twinkling green eyes of hers, hypnotized by them.

'I have to make a phone call first,' she told him.

He nodded.

'Jack, the lady would like to borrow your phone,' he said.

The barman smiled and ushered Jo towards the end of the bar where, from beneath the counter, he produced a phone and set it down before her. Tyler watched her as she jabbed at the numbers, drumming agitatedly on the bar top as she waited for the receiver to be lifted at the other end. When it finally was, she recognized the voice.

'It's Jo Ward,' she babbled. 'Put me through to Doug Clark, please.'

Another moment's silence at the other end then she heard the familiar voice of the editor.

He wanted to know where she was.

'I'm in Wakely,' Jo said and then, before he could ask why, 'Listen, Doug, this could be important.' She told him about the phone call of the previous night, about her visit to Vanderburg Chemicals, of Glendenning's lie about Anderson and of that particular man's disappearance. 'I think Anderson is still in Wakely. I have to find him.'

He asked how long it would take her.

'That's impossible to say but, whatever it was he wanted to talk about must have been pretty goddam important. I have to stay here until I find him.'

Clark suggested that her imagination might be getting the better of her.

'For Christ's sake,' she blurted, 'you know me better than that. Besides, when I asked Glendenning who Vanderburg's backers were he changed the subject. I'm sure Anderson knows something worth knowing and I want to hear it.'

She hung up and rejoined Tyler.

'Do you want to follow my truck in your car?' he asked her.

'What's wrong with me riding in the cab with you?' she wanted to know.

Tyler smiled.

'Fair enough, if you don't mind the twelve cattle and sixteen pigs in the back. It doesn't exactly smell like a rose garden in there.'

He led her out to the waiting truck, a large van that looked like a container lorry, its sides painted white. He opened the passenger side door and helped her up onto the running platform. From there she scrambled into the cab.

'You weren't joking, were you?' she said, wrinkling her nose.

Tyler chuckled and scuttled around to the driver's side where he hauled himself up and started the engine, the smell of diesel mingling with the odour of livestock.

'I did warn you,' he said and, this time, they both laughed.

Twelve

The livestock market was held in a maze of yards and sheds on the main road leading out of Wakely. It always attracted a sizeable gathering of people: buyers, livestock breeders and interested onlookers. It was, like the other market in the town square, something of an event for Wakely's inhabitants and also those who made the trip from outside the town be it for business purposes or just plain curiosity.

The trucks and vans which carried the animals were parked in a large tarmac area to the rear of two corrugated iron sheds. From there, the animals were herded through a series of pens and enclosures, separating them into varying sizes, breeds and species.

Some of the farmers were under contract to the various butchers, restaurants or hotels in and around the town so business was done briskly. It was just a matter of deciding on a price. The livestock would then be herded back into their respective transporters and driven straight to the abattoir for slaughtering. The whole process took less than a day from arrival at the market to delivery of the prepared carcasses to the appointed destination.

Those animals belonging to farmers not under contract were open for auction to anyone who cared to pay the right price for them. Tyler's stock came into this latter category but he felt confident about making a healthy price on all his stock. Some of the animals were occasionally bought by other farmers. Particularly dairy cattle and pigs. One or two of the small-holders specialized in one type of livestock, so bidding for what was termed 'independent stock' was also their privilege.

Jo lit up a cigarette and offered the pack to Tyler.

He declined.

'I don't smoke.'

Jo lit one and blew out a funnel of the bluish haze.

'Does this place always smell as bad as this?' she asked, waving a hand in front of her as if to drive away the odour of animal excretion and damp straw.

Tyler grinned.

'Country air is good for you. You've lived in towns too long.'

'I intend staying in towns if the country smells as bad as this.'

They were standing beside a small enclosure which housed a sow and six piglets. Tyler ran an interested eye over the smaller creatures, at once impressed and puzzled by their exaggerated size. The largest was at least twelve inches high at the shoulder. Nevertheless they had, as he'd expected, brought him an excellent price and he'd already negotiated a deal for the litter with a buyer from a restaurant in Arkham. He watched as the animals moved agitatedly around the sow, one or two trying to reach her swollen teats in order to feed. The sow herself grunted and moved around the pen as if attempting to keep away from her hungry offspring.

'Look, mum.'

The shout startled Tyler and he turned to see a small boy, about twelve, clambering onto the metal struts of the enclosure, leaning over to get a better look at the animals inside. His mother, who had two other younger children with her, trudged wearily over to her son and joined him at Tyler's side.

The farmer looked at the little group and then at Jo who smiled, as the boy began to make grunting noises like the pig.

The sow had finally stopped her agitated pacings and remained still long enough for one or two of the piglets to begin feeding. They were swiftly joined by the others, all jostling one another in an effort to reach the milk secreting glands.

'They're sucking her tits,' said the boy loudly, laughing raucously.

'Teats,' said his mother, slapping him on the back of the head, looking around to see if anyone else had heard. She looked at Tyler and coloured slightly. He smiled.

The piglets were becoming more excited and Tyler could hear a series of low grunts coming from the sow. A grunt that suddenly turned into a bellow of pain.

One of the litter had gripped a teat in its mouth and, with a powerful twist of its neck, wrung the swollen appendage off.

Blood jetted from the gash, splattering the other animals.

It was like a signal for them.

Almost as one, they began gnawing and tearing at the teats, ripping them free, swallowing them, the mixture of milk and blood cascading from their jaws. Then, as the sow toppled over they moved in frenziedly upon her, almost burrowing into the soft flesh of her underbelly, seeking out the vital organs inside.

Tyler began to clamber over the rail as he saw two of them use their trotters to gouge a cleft in the bloodied flesh. A foul-smelling flux of viscera erupted from the wound and the piglets squealed excitedly, devouring the bulging intestines which presented themselves, bursting forth from the sow's mutilated stomach. She tried to rise, to shake off the cannabalistic horde but it was no good.

The boy on the fence had turned the colour of rancid butter, his sisters screaming hysterically, his mother trying to drag all three of the children away.

Tyler grabbed one of the piglets and pulled it off. He hurled the animal to one side, horrified when it rolled over and then came at him, trying to bite his leg. He kicked it hard in the face, the blow momentarily felling it.

Jo saw two men nearby, dressed in dark green overalls, one of them carrying a small sledgehammer. She called to them, one eye still fixed on Tyler who was trying to save the dying sow.

The men in the overalls were stockmen, employees of the livestock market and both came running when they heard the commotion. The one carrying the hammer vaulted the rail, heading for the nearest piglet.

'Kill them,' shouted Tyler, driving his foot into the side of another of the litter.

The stockman needed no second bidding. He brought the hammer down on the head of the nearest piglet and killed it with that one crushing blow.

The sow was trying to crawl away, her intestines dragging in the straw like bulging bloodied party streamers. Jo gripped the rail tight, the cigarette stuck to her bottom lip. She watched as the squealing piglets were despatched, each one killed by a blow of the sledgehammer. Except for the last which Tyler himself finished off. Sliding his sheath knife across its throat he dropped the writhing body to the ground and watched as it quivered violently. Blood jetted from the slashed throat.

'What happened?' asked the stockman with the hammer.

Tyler told him.

'I've heard of sows eating piglets before,' said the man. 'But not the other way around. What the hell caused it?'

'How should I know?' snapped Tyler, irritably. He looked down at the sow. The animal was dead, sprawled amongst her dead litter. One of the stockman hurried off to get something in which to conceal the carcasses.

Jo merely stood gazing at the scene of carnage. She looked at Tyler who was shaking his head slowly, trying to wipe some blood from his hands.

The stockman returned with a number of sacks, one of which Tyler took from him. He bent and lifted the nearest dead piglet by the ears, tossing it into the hessian bag then he clambered back over the fence, clutching his grisly acquisition in one gore-soaked hand.

'Come on,' he said to Jo, walking briskly towards the car park and his waiting truck.

'Where are we going?' she asked, hurrying to keep up with him.

'To see about this,' he told her, holding up the sack.

They were back in town in less than ten minutes.

Thirteen

Dan Hawley's veterinary surgery stood in a quiet, residential area of Wakely about two minutes' drive from the centre of the town. A large, detached house with white-washed walls and a spacious garden, it looked more like a rest home than a place of work. Hawley worked alone, helped out during the day by his receptionist, Mandy Potter, a lively girl in her early thirties who, because of the enormous glasses she wore, reminded Tyler of a barn owl.

The house had a sign outside with Hawley's name and credentials engraved on it and, on either side of the front door, two large stone dogs stood sentinel. It was a garish touch which never failed to amuse Tyler but, as he pulled the truck into Hawley's driveway, the last thing he felt like doing was laughing.

Jo followed him as he got down from the cab, clutching the sack and its bloodied load. He had hardly spoken during the drive from the livestock market and his face was set in tense lines as he approached the front door of the surgery. He walked into the reception and found that there were perhaps half a dozen other people waiting inside.

Dogs began to howl and bark at him. An elderly man who was balancing a parrot in a cage on his knee coughed as the bird began squawking, sending feathers and sand in all directions.

The smell from the sack which Tyler held began to fill the waiting room.

'Hello, Mr Tyler,' said Mandy, eyeing the sack curiously.

'Is Dan in there?' Tyler asked, motioning towards a green door to his right which led into the surgery proper.

'Yes, he is but . . .'

The farmer spun round and headed for the green door, Jo right behind him.

Mandy got to her feet, pushing her glasses back on her nose.

'You can't go in there yet,' she protested, but already Tyler was pushing his way in, leaving Mandy to cope with the complaints of the other visitors.

'Knock before you come in for Christ's sake,' said Hawley, without looking up. He was hunched over his desk writing something in a large red book. The vet turned when he heard the door slam.

'Vic, what the hell do you want?' he asked, his gaze quickly shifting to Jo.

Hawley got to his feet, watching as Tyler upended the sack and dumped the dead piglet on the stainless steel work top nearest to him.

'First calves, now weaners,' said Tyler angrily. 'Six of the fucking things, from the same litter, have just torn one of my sows to shreds.'

Hawley frowned and moved over to look at the still body of the piglet.

'It was like they were crazy, rabid or something,' said Jo.

The vet momentarily transferred his gaze from the dead pig to Jo. Tyler made hurried introductions then all three of them returned their attention to the carcass before them.

'What exactly happened?' asked Hawley, pulling on a pair of rubber gloves and reaching for a probe.

Tyler told him.

The vet nodded almost imperceptibly, using the probe to open the jaws of the piglet. A thick slush of blood and bile oozed from the open mouth and puddled beneath the piglet's head.

'What about that calf?' asked Tyler. 'Have you had the chance to examine it yet?'

Hawley shook his head.

'As soon as I find anything I'll let you know. No doubt you're expecting there to be some kind of link between the calf and this weaner?'

'Yes,' said Tyler. 'Perhaps some kind of genetic defect that's peculiar to both of them.'

'It's unlikely, Vic.'

'Then what's your bloody answer, Dan?'

'I haven't get one yet. I wish to Christ I had. Deformed calves, still-born litters, weaners that tear their own mother to pieces, baby animals that are growing at four times the rate they should be. I can't come up with answers to problems like those in a couple of hours.'

'How long has this been going on?' Jo asked.

Hawley shrugged.

'Well, for one thing, we don't even know if any of the incidents are related.'

'Don't tell me that these things are coincidence,' Tyler snapped.

'I didn't say they were,' Hawley muttered. 'But you can't put your finger on a calendar and say "it started then".'

'But when *would* you say the incidents began?' Jo asked again.

'Four, five weeks ago,' Hawley told her.

Jo nodded, her eyes flicking around the large surgery as the vet returned to the animal before him. The room was large, with a table and what looked like two operating tables inside. Powerful arc lamps on adjustable arms were arranged over each one. Rows of filing cabinets filled one wall and above those hung Hawley's certificates of practice. The other three walls were covered with shelves. Medicines, tonics and pills of all descriptions were contained there and, as Jo looked more carefully she saw that there was a larger jar containing some amber coloured fluid.

Floating in it was a small dog, which, on closer

inspection, she noticed had just three legs and no eyes. The journalist shuddered involuntarily.

'Like I said, Vic, I can't tell you anything until I've done autopsies on the animals. You'll just have to wait for my call.' Hawley pulled off his rubber gloves, muttering to himself as some skin flaked off in the process. He rubbed the back of his hand gently, more flesh peeling away to reveal a raw area beneath.

Jo looked at the hand and then at the vet's face which was pale, dark rings beneath his eyes. He turned off the light over the table, massaging his temple as he did so.

'I *will* get back to you,' he said again.

They all exchanged brief farewells and Hawley showed them to the door. As he walked back inside the surgery he took a last look at the dead piglet and pulled a sheet over it.

'What do *you* think is going on?' said Jo, studying Tyler's profile.

'I wish I knew,' he said.

Tyler drove slowly through the narrow streets of Wakely, heading back towards the pub where Jo had parked her car.

'For a quiet town this place sure has its share of mysteries,' she said, smiling.

Tyler nodded.

'It seems like we both have problems,' she said. 'You need answers, so do I, I have to find Geoffrey Anderson.'

'What's so special about this bloke anyway?' asked Tyler.

'Well, between you and me, I think he knows something that someone doesn't want him to talk about.'

'Like what?'

'If I knew that I wouldn't have a problem would I?'

'Ask a silly question . . .' Tyler let the sentence trail off.

'Look, you've lived in this place for most of your life. You know the people, you know the places.'

'You're asking me to help you find Geoffrey Anderson?'

'Right.'

Tyler brought the truck to a halt alongside Jo's Chevette. He switched off his engine and looked across at her.

'Look, Jo, I don't know anything about Anderson. I don't even know much about you.'

'We can soon put that right,' she said. 'How about dinner tonight?'

Tyler grinned, finally chuckling aloud.

'What's so funny?' Jo wanted to know.

'It's the first time any woman has asked me to dinner.'

'So, is it a date?'

'How could I refuse? What time?'

She checked her watch and saw that it was almost 3.45 p.m.

'I've got to go back to Arkham and pick up some stuff, then I'll check into a hotel here. I need to be in town. If Anderson's in Wakely and I'm damn sure he is, I mean to find him.'

'And dinner?'

'How about eight-thirty?'

He nodded, watching her as she jumped down from the cab.

'Eight-thirty in the hotel, I'll meet you in the bar,' she nodded in the direction of 'The King George', one of two hotels which overlooked the main square of the town.

Tyler nodded.

He watched her as she crossed to her car, started the engine and drove off. Then he himself turned the key in his ignition and the big truck roared into life. He swung it around, squinting up at the burnished sun as he did so.

By 4.00 he was back at the farm.

Fourteen

The late afternoon sunlight crept like an intruder through the chinks in the venetian blinds. Vera Duggan stood at the sink peering at the partially hidden glowing orb which still burned brightly in the cloudless sky. As she watched it she felt her skin begin to tingle and her eyes begin to water. Vera looked away, moving across to one of the yellow painted cupboards on the wall by the fridge. She moved slowly. Arthritis had eaten deep into her joints and now, at sixty-eight, there were times when she could hardly move her hands. Ordinarily the sun eased the tightness in her joints but, for the past two or three weeks, it had been having the opposite effect. She felt stiff all over and she had been forced to retrieve the thick walking stick which she had discarded ten years before.

It had belonged to her husband, now dead for more than fifteen years. But his slippers were still in the same place in the hall, his photo still on the wall. He had looked so handsome in his uniform. Arthur Duggan of the King's Own Yorkshire Rifles. He had been wounded at Amiens in 1917. Gassed at Passchendaele. It had been that which had brought on his bronchitis. The same complaint which had taken him from her those fifteen years ago. Since then she had lived alone but for her succession of cats. Her sons rarely visited her but she didn't really miss them. One was an engineer, the other a plasterer. They took turns to look after her at Christmas but, other than that, she hardly saw them from one year to the next.

She hobbled to the pantry and retrieved a tin opener, working it with difficulty around the lip of the tin until she finally managed to open it. She scooped out the contents with a fork, pushing them into a bowl which bore the name 'Beth'. The cat finished preening itself and looked up, smelling its food.

'Come on,' said Vera, holding the bowl before her.

The cat, impatient for its food, leapt up onto the table and pawed at her hand.

'Get off,' Vera told it.

The cat continued trying to reach the food.

'Get down, now,' she snarled.

The cat hissed and tried once again to reach the dish of food, only this time it scratched Vera's hand. The claws cut easily through her thin flesh and she yelped, dropping the bowl, looking down at the four gashes on the back of her hand. The cat remained standing on the table, looking at her as if it realized that it had done wrong. It meowed and jumped down off the table, eagerly devouring the spilt food.

Vera muttered something under her breath and raised the walking stick above her head, steadying herself against the table.

With a grunt she brought it crashing down again.

There was a strength and ferocity to the blow which belied her years and condition for, so powerful was the impact, she heard the crack of bone as the walking stick connected with the cat's head. It screeched and tried to run but the blow had stunned it and, as Vera struck again, blood burst from its skull. The animal fell forward and Vera drove the end of the stout stick into its side, pressing down until she heard the breaking of ribs. The cat rasped, blood spilling from its mouth. The sight of the blood seemed to inflame Vera even more for she brought the walking stick down once more on the creature's head. This time the force was enough to rend bone and a gobbet of grey and red brain matter welled up through the smashed skull.

Still Vera continued beating at it until the kitchen floor was spattered with blood. Only when the cat was completely motionless did she sink to her knees, hands in the mess of grey and crimson. She was panting from the effort but there was a crooked smile on her face and, as she gazed at the dead animal, she began to salivate madly until streamers of sputum hung from her false teeth.

She shielded her eyes from the sun and began to laugh.

Fifteen

Despite the approach of evening, the sun still remained dominant in the sky. Now bleeding some of its colour into the heavens it retained its heat and Jo wiped a bead of perspiration from her forehead as she parked the Chevette in the car park beside 'The King George'. It had taken her just over an hour to drive back to her home in Arkham and pick up a few clothes.

Now she checked that the vehicle was securely locked up and walked around to the main entrance of the hotel.

Ivy grew thickly all over the old stonework, so thick in places it seemed that if it were cut down the entire building would collapse. The dining room was as yet in darkness, the only lights burning were those in the reception.

It was cool inside the hotel and Jo welcomed the respite for the cloying humidity in the air was making her feel uncomfortable. She smiled to herself, realizing that she must already have been away from New York too long. Out there residents learned to cope with eighty per cent humidity during the summer. But, the heat had unpleasant side-effects. Jo knew that the murder rate rose by almost double during those dog-days.

Now she carried her suitcase up to the reception desk and scanned the place for a member of staff. The hotel smelt of polish and new wood and, from somewhere nearby, there was a tempting aroma of food. Jo rubbed her stomach as she heard it rumble. There were two old pikes crossed on the wall over the open fire place behind her and on either side were metal pots which looked like witches' cauldrons. The entire place was panelled in dark oak, the beams, from the look of the tiny holes in them, being genuine.

Jo spotted a bell and shook it.

She looked around to see if anyone was going to respond. There didn't seem to be any guests or staff about.

The man rose from behind the desk, a tall fellow who towered over Jo.

'Can I help you?'

She spun round, shocked at the sudden sound.

'Damn,' she gasped, her hand going to her throat. 'Where did you come from?'

'Sorry if I startled you, Miss,' the man said, apologetically. 'I was down behind the desk, I didn't hear you come in.'

Jo nodded, regaining her breath.

'I'd like a room please. For a week.' She gave him her name and address. When she filled in the confirmation form she charged it to the *Arkham Comet*.

He turned and selected a key.

'Number 24,' he told her. 'On the second floor.' When he spoke, his voice was low and rasping, his teeth reducing the sounds he made to harsh whispers. His teeth looked huge, to the point where he had difficulty closing his mouth.

Jo nodded, looking more closely at the man. The badge on his lapel read 'Mark Bates'. He was in his late thirties, although it was virtually impossible to guess his age accurately. His skin was pale, shrivelled around the eyes and lip corners, sunken around the cheeks. It was peeling in places, particularly on the backs of his hands which, she noticed, bore the long, hooked nails she had seen earlier in the day on other Wakely residents. But his most striking features were his eyes. The irises glowed with an unnatural brilliance, quite in contrast to the yellowish, vein-infested whites.

Jo picked up her case.

'There aren't any porters,' said Bates. 'But I can help you with that.' He nodded towards the case.

'No that's fine. Thanks anyway,' Jo said.

She'd got as far as the lifts when he called her back.

'You forgot your key,' he informed her, walking out from behind the desk.

Jo smiled.

'One of these days I'll forget my name,' she said, reaching out to take it from him.

For a second she almost gasped aloud but she clenched her teeth together, the breath caught in her throat.

She could see it. There before her. The key was in his hand but she hesitated.

She looked at Bates and then down again.

There was hair growing on the palm of his hand.

Sixteen

'There's no one else for me to see is there, Mandy?' Dan Hawley asked, peering out from inside the surgery.

The receptionist was sitting at her desk glancing at *Cosmopolitan*. She put the magazine down and ran a finger through the list of names in the appointment book.

'No, Mr Hawley,' she said. 'But Stuart Nichols rang about half an hour ago and asked if you could go out to his farm tomorrow.'

'Did he say what was wrong?'

'Something about his lambs losing wool.'

Hawley nodded. He pulled off his rubber gloves and balled them up, pushing them into a pocket in his apron.

'You can drop the formalities now, Mandy,' he said.

She smiled and got to her feet.

The vet pulled her close, their mouths meeting, tongues probing urgently. She snaked her arms up around his neck, eager to prolong the sensation. When, finally, they did separate Mandy found that her glasses were misted over. She removed them, laying them on the desk behind her. Hawley brushed a speck of dust from her long lashes then kissed her softly on the end of the nose.

'If you're going to call me Mr Hawley during working hours,' he said. 'Perhaps I ought to call you Miss Potter.'

She chuckled.

'I don't know why we bother keeping up the pretence, Dan, everyone in Wakely knows what's going on between us.'

'You make it sound like something from a Barbara Cartland novel,' Hawley said, brushing a strand of hair from her forehead.

'You know what I mean.'

'People in Wakely are what you might call traditionalists. They have their standards and they expect everyone to conform to them. But they turn a blind eye when what they see starts to offend their moral sensibilities.'

'Very philosophical,' she said.

'And very true,' he added, kissing her again.

They had lived together for nearly a year in the vet's house. Prior to that, Mandy had been married to a plumber named Andy. There had been two children from the marriage, both boys. With Andy, she had endured a secure and steady way of life. He was a dependable, even predictable man. But that had not been enough for Mandy. She deplored his lack of ambition, his willingness to settle for what life gave him rather than taking it with both hands. And, over the years, she had seen her children being moulded into the same shape as their father. Neither of the boys had any desire to leave Wakely or the surroundings they had grown up in. At thirteen and eleven, she could see them as mirrors of their father and she began to resent them for it.

Hawley had been everything she had always hoped to find in a man.

She'd met him quite by chance. One day, taking the family dog along for its distemper shot, she had encountered the thick set, dark-haired man who was to become her lover.

Hawley had been in partnership with an older man for some time and, eager to have his own practice, he had often thought of leaving Wakely and setting up somewhere else. The problem had been solved for him when his partner had been killed in a car crash some eighteen months earlier. The practice had automatically come to him and since taking over he had expanded it until he alone now served Wakely and all areas for thirty miles round about.

She had found him so easy going on that first meeting. Mandy relaxed in his company until it felt as if she had known him all her life and, before she left the surgery, he asked her to have dinner with him one night.

She had agreed, thinking for days beforehand of an excuse which would not arouse her husband's insane jealousy and suspicion. She had gone to Hawley's house where he had cooked them a lavish meal and, afterwards, as if it were the most natural thing in the world, they had gone to bed together. Through him she had found her true self, discovering passions which she had thought dormant, finding others she never knew she possessed. He helped her shed her inhibitions until *she* became the teacher. Revelling in her newly awakened sexuality, overcome by Hawley's own expertise, she became insatiable. They were fused together by a ferocity of feeling which surprised them both.

She had found it easy to leave Andy and the two boys. At least, she had in the emotional sense. When he found out where she had gone he turned up at the house carrying a crow bar and he broke every window he could until, that night, Hawley had emerged to face him. The two men had exchanged blows, the vet sustaining a hairline fracture of the left tibia from a blow with the metal bar but he had left Andy with a broken nose and two fewer teeth.

It had been Hawley's suggestion that Mandy become his receptionist. At first she had been reluctant, realizing how quickly word of what had happened would spread around Wakely. However, she agreed eventually and, after the first few weeks of knowing looks and sly remarks, she had come to accept and enjoy her new way of life.

She didn't intend to contest the divorce case. She

didn't want anything from Andy and she certainly didn't wish for custody of the children. She had all she wanted with Hawley.

The cuckoo clock on the wall above the desk signalled its presence by screeching six times.

Mandy touched Hawley's cheek, tutting when some skin came off. Small flakes of it stuck under her nails.

'You look pale, Dan, are you feeling OK?' she asked, noticing also that his lips were swollen and cracked.

'I'm a bit tired, nothing more,' he told her.

'Then don't you think it's time you packed up?' She began undoing her white overall. 'I'll go and get dinner ready.' He ran an appreciative eye over the figure previously concealed by the overall. She was blessed with large but firm breasts, her figure narrowing slightly at the waist before filling out again into a well rounded bottom. Her stomach was flat, her legs long and slender.

'Are you going to eat some proper food tonight?' Hawley asked her, smiling.

Mandy feigned irritation.

'And what's that supposed to mean?'

'It means, when are you coming off that bloody stupid diet?'

'A fish and fruit diet is good for you. I've already lost three pounds in the last two weeks.'

He slapped her backside.

'From where?' he japed.

Mandy stuck her tongue out at him.

'I won't be long,' Hawley said. 'I've got something to do first.'

She hesitated.

'I promise,' he said and headed back into the surgery. Mandy disappeared into what were the living quarters of the house.

Hawley crossed to the work top nearest him and slipped on a fresh pair of rubber gloves. Then, slowly, he pulled back the sheet which covered the remains of the piglet brought in by Tyler that afternoon. The vet pulled one of the arc lamps over and flicked it on, wincing at the powerful light. He closed his eyes for a moment, a sharp pain jabbing at his temples, and when he finally opened his eyes it was as narrow slits. The light felt hot on his skin.

He reached for a scalpel and steadied his hand then, with consummate skill, be began to cut a hole in the pig's skull.

Jesus, the light was bright. His eyes were almost watering now, making it difficult to concentrate. He put down the scalpel and blinked hard. His eyes felt gritty, as if he'd gone for too long without sleep.

The lamp felt even hotter on his skin.

He took a small saw and set about opening the cranium of the piglet, finally exposing the brain. This done, he cut two thin sections, small enough to fit on a microscope slide. He carried them across to the magnifying instrument and slid one beneath the powerful lens.

'Now,' he murmured to himself, relieved to be out of the rays of the arc light. 'Let's see what we've got.'

Seventeen

The bar of 'The King George' was empty but for Tyler, the barman and a couple of other people. The barman, dressed in white shirt and jacket and a pair of black trousers which had gone shiny around the backside, was busy cleaning glasses. Hardly for the rush of business, Tyler mused.

He pulled self-conciously at the top button of his shirt, anxious to loosen his tie a little. He had got out of the habit of wearing one and it was beginning to feel a little uncomfortable. Nevertheless, he had made a special effort for this night. As soon as he'd returned to the farm he'd taken his blue suit from the wardrobe where it had hung since his father's funeral and pressed it over, careful not to burn it. Then he'd showered, shaved and dressed, discovering that he'd been too early, so he drove into Wakely anyway and had a pint or two at 'The Black Knight' enduring the warmly sarcastic comments of his friends who had only once seen him in a suit.

Now he sat glancing alternately at the clock in the corner and his own watch.

It was 8.30 p.m.

With the timing of an actress who has just received her cue, Jo emerged from one of the lifts to the right. Tyler smiled at her across the darkened bar, immediately impressed by her appearance.

Her thick hair had been recently washed and allowed to dry naturally, making it look shaggy. She wore little make-up, the near perfect bone structure of her face making her features glow in the dull light. She wore a black dress, slashed across one shoulder and also up as far as the thigh. The curve of her tanned legs was accentuated by the silver high heels which she wore.

'Hi,' she beamed, seating herself beside him.

'Hello,' he said, smiling at her. 'What will you have to drink?'

She asked for a vodka and lime and, when the barman had poured it, heaping the glass with ice first, she sipped slowly at it, regarding Tyler over the rim.

'So, you hung up your wellington boots for the night, huh?'

'Yes, ma'am,' he said, saluting. He raised his glass. 'Cheers.'

'Here's to secrets,' she said and smiled that radiant smile once more.

Tyler nodded.

'Secrets,' he muttered. 'I still don't know what it is you're looking for, apart from this bloke called Anderson.'

Jo sighed.

'Maybe I don't either. Doug said it was just my suspicious mind.'

'Who's Doug?'

'Doug Clark. My editor and . . . friend.'

'What's that supposed to mean?'

'We had a thing going for a time. Notice I use the past tense.'

'Serious?'

'It would have been if I'd let it go that far. He wanted it to. I didn't.'

'So you split up.'

She ran the tip of her index finger around the rim of her glass.

'There was never too much there to begin with,' she told him. 'It wasn't long after I came to Arkham. I was lonely I guess. If it hadn't been Doug it would've been someone else.'

'And now you're not lonely anymore is that it?' he asked.

'Hey, you ask a lot of questions. I think you're in the wrong job. You should be a private detective.'

'Just curious.'

'What about you? Any sordid truths to tell?'

'I should be so lucky.'

They both laughed.

At nine they got up and walked through into the dining room. But for one man alone in a corner the place was devoid of people. They ordered, the menu brought to them by a thin waitress whose face looked like a skull in the dim light. Jo frowned.

'I'll tell you one thing I've noticed,' she said. 'There seem to be a hell of a lot of people in this town who need some sun. Did you see that waitress? She looked anaemic.'

Tyler scratched his chin thoughtfully.

'Now you come to mention it I *have* noticed. Perhaps it's a virus of some kind.'

The first course arrived and they began eating. Both had prawn cocktail.

'So, how did you come to be a farmer?' Jo asked him.

'My father died, not long ago, left me to look after the place.'

'I'm sorry.'

'That's OK.' He smiled at her, mesmerized once more by her raw beauty, her mixture of sensuality and pure animal magnetism. She reminded Tyler of a caged beast, forever on the move, her questions probing, her manner relaxed and yet possessing a certain urgency. 'I'd been brought up on the land, it's what I know best.'

'I didn't even see anything green until I was seven and that was Central Park.' She laughed, sardonically. 'Muggers parade. Do you know that one in three families in New York have had someone amongst them mugged? That's a lot of people.'

'It's a lot of muggers.'

'They tell us to feel sorry for minority groups. You know, Negroes, Chicanos, Puerto Ricans. The underprivileged.' She shook her head. 'The underprivileged are beating our goddam brains out.'

'It's the same in some parts of Britain. I used to live in London. That's going the same way, you can't walk the streets in some areas without getting attacked. It's the political situation as much as anything, if people can't get money by working, then they'll nick it. No jobs, no money, no future.' He stuffed a spoonful of prawns into his mouth.

'Some of the city cynicism rubbed off on you,' she said.

'Perhaps. Why did you leave America?'

She told him about Tony, about the stories in the papers, about the murder, about the attempt on her own life.

'Christ,' he muttered when she'd finished. 'It must be quite boring living in Arkham after what you've seen.'

'I'd rather be bored and *alive*,' she told him and they both laughed. 'Anyhow, it's fine here for me. There's no pressure on me now like there used to be.'

The waitress returned and took away the empty dishes.

'You said your father was dead,' Jo said, softly. 'You haven't told me about your mother.'

Tyler lowered his gaze momentarily, staring into the bottom of his glass as if seeking an explanation of some kind.

'She died when I was twenty-one. A heart attack.'

Jo sensed she'd struck a wrong chord in his emotions.

'I still blame myself for her death in a way,' Tyler continued. 'She never wanted me to go away to college. It was all my father's idea. I knew that whatever I did I'd end up hurting one of them. It turned out to be my mother. She never did forgive me for going.'

'You shouldn't feel guilty about her death,' said Jo.

'I've come to terms with it now but it was difficult in the beginning.'

The main course arrived. Tyler had fish. Jo had chicken.

'Why not steak?' she asked, smiling, grateful for the opportunity to change the subject.

'I work with meat, so I don't feel like eating it too,'

he explained. 'I haven't touched meat or poultry for years.'

He re-filled Jo's wine glass. Then, he watched, amused, as she cut up her food, switched hands and began picking up the pieces, holding her fork in her right hand.

'Have you heard anything about this Anderson bloke?' he asked.

Jo sighed.

'No, but I know he had something important to tell me. I know he sounded frightened when I spoke to him on the phone.' She paused to swallow. 'And, what's more, I also know that the people he worked for lied to me about him. I'm sure he's around here somewhere, it's just a matter of finding him.'

'He could have left the country.'

'He had no reason to, besides, one of his neighbours saw him two days ago.'

'There's probably a perfectly simple explanation for it.'

'Terrific. If there is then I'm happy but I'd like to know one way or the other, you know what I mean?'

'And how do you intend doing that?'

'By breaking into his house.'

Tyler looked at her carefully across the table.

'What the hell will that solve?' he asked. 'You're a reporter not a bloody copper, you can't just go around breaking into people's houses.'

'Got any better suggestions?'

'And you want me to help you?'

She nodded.

'When do we do it?' His tone had lost some of its surprise.

'Tonight.'

'Fair enough.' He couldn't resist a smile. 'I reckon the Mafia should have tried to recruit you, not kill you.'

They both laughed.

Jo found herself gazing deep into the blue pools that were Tyler's eyes. Like twin circlets of June sky they seemed to glow with a radiance which she found both sensitive and arousing. As she ate she looked closely at him, the chiselled features, the broad shoulders, and she felt a stirring within her. She was drawn not just to his physical appearance but also by his easy manner. Christ, she was hot for him. It was as simple as that.

Tyler himself found his gaze drawn to her. She looked like something from an erotic dream, sitting opposite him with one tanned shoulder bare, the hair cascading over it. The tips of her nipples nudging the material of the dress. When she moved her foot he felt one of her legs brush against his and a feeling much akin to an electric shock ran up his spine. He watched her eating, fascinated and attracted by the way she licked her pouting lips after each mouthful. He saw the pink tip of her tongue flick forward, snake-like before disappearing back inside that moist orifice.

'You said you had some problems of your own,' said Jo over coffee.

The farmer nodded, as if reluctant to talk about them.

'It's the animals,' he said, finally. 'Well, you saw what happened at the market today with the weaners.'

The American shuddered at the recollection.

'It's not just that, it's other things and not only on *my* farm either. Those fellows you saw me with this afternoon in the pub, each one of them has been having problems with his stock.'

Jo rubbed her stomach and pulled a face, remembering the chicken she'd eaten.

'Thank God it seems confined to the bigger animals. Cattle, sheep and pigs and it's mainly affecting the young.'

'You say "it", what do you think it is?'

He shrugged.

'I don't know, I'm just hoping that Dan Hawley can come up with some answers.'

Jo sipped at her coffee and considered the farmer's troubled expression. He had his hands clasped on the table before him.

Putting her cup down, she reached forward and gently squeezed Tyler's arm.

He looked up, a little surprised then responded by pressing her slim hand between his. Their eyes locked.

'A town full of secrets,' he whispered.

She nodded almost imperceptibly, enjoying the contact with him. The strength in those hands.

'Maybe we won't like the answers we find,' she murmured.

They regarded each other a moment longer, as if disturbed by her words. Tyler finally managed to look away from those hypnotic green orbs of hers, the pupils now dilated.

He paid the bill and they left.

A cool breeze had sprung up and Jo shivered as they walked to her car. Above them, dark clouds conspired to blot out the watery moon. She shuddered as she slid behind the wheel, taking a glance at Tyler as she started the engine.

She guided the Chevette out into the road. The drive to Geoffrey Anderson's house should take about ten minutes.

It was almost 10.48 p.m.

Eighteen

The ticking of the wall clock sounded deafening in the silence of the kitchen. There was no other sound and the dull green luminosity of the clock hands was the only thing which was able to infiltrate the totality of the darkness. The room, in fact the entire house, was swamped in a gloom as impenetrable as pitch. All curtains were drawn, as they had been for the last two days. Not even the sodium glare of the street lamps outside was able to penetrate the abyss.

But, inside the home of Geoffrey Anderson, there was movement.

The darkness may have been almost palpable but there was a part of it which seemed to move independently of the rest. It was no shadow for there was no light to cast one. As if a piece of the gloom had gained form, the shape moved effortlessly through the black house. It walked slowly, noiselessly, completely at one with the cloying funereal surroundings.

It moved through the kitchen, opening the fridge door. There was a pool of water near the door, a spillage from the melted ice inside. The shape pulled out drawers and rummaged through them but all with an economy of movement which caused little sound.

It passed through into the sitting room, discovering a bureau. This it inspected more thoroughly, pulling open the cupboards and drawers but discovering nothing. Still it made no sound and even its breathing was muted and low, scarcely audible.

The shape froze in mid-stride as it heard a car drive past. It stood for long seconds then, satisfied that it would not be disturbed, it headed for the door which led to the hall.

The stairs creaked slightly as it ascended. Four closed

doors confronted it as it reached the landing and it moved towards the closest one.

It was open and the shape entered quickly.

Outside a car pulled up, the powerful headlamps cutting through the blackness.

The shape moved cautiously to the window and pulled the curtain back slightly, gazing out. It looked down upon the two people who had clambered out of the car and who, it now saw, were coming towards the house.

It watched as they approached then it let the curtain go and retreated back into the gloom.

There were sounds of movement from outside the house but, hidden within, surrounded by the cocoon of blackness, the shape waited.

Tyler closed the car door behind him and ran an appraising eye up and down the street. But for the odd light burning in sitting rooms or bedrooms, the tree-lined thoroughfare was in darkness broken only by the dull glow of the street lamps. A moth fluttered lazily around one of them, its wings skittering against the housing.

Jo pulled a torch from her coat pocket and flicked it on. Satisfied that it worked she headed towards the house which bore the sign 'Avalon'.

'It looks quiet enough,' said Tyler as he opened the gate.

'That's how it looked earlier,' Jo told him.

She moved impatiently forward but the farmer blocked her way. He shook his head.

'Let me go first,' he said, softly.

She agreed, allowing him to lead the way, furtively, up the garden path. They decided to break in via the back way in order to make themselves less conspicuous. Jo looked to her left, watching for any lights in the house of the woman she'd spoken to that morning. There were no lights to be seen anywhere.

The moon had been well and truly smothered by dark cloud so they hadn't even the advantage of natural light.

As they reached the back door Jo flicked on the torch.

'Shine it on the lock,' whispered Tyler, fumbling in his pocket. 'Shit,' he grunted. Then, turning to Jo, he asked, 'Have you got a hair clip or something like that?'

She hadn't.

Tyler pulled off his jacket, wrapped the garment around his elbow and, looking around one last time, drove it into the glass panelled door.

The pane spider-webbed but didn't break.

He hit it again, wincing as some glass smashed loudly on the kitchen floor inside. Then the farmer hurriedly slipped his hand through and unlocked the door. They both scuttled inside.

'Burglar I'm not,' he muttered, pulling his jacket back on. 'Now tell me what the hell we're looking for?'

Jo shone the torch around the kitchen, playing the beam over the beige walls. She picked out a calendar, a rack of knives, a couple of shelves and cupboards.

'I'm not even sure myself,' she told him, walking cautiously towards the door which led into the sitting room. Her high heels clicked loudly on the lino.

Tyler followed, noticing that one of the knives was missing from the rack. It was nothing extraordinary in itself but, with the rest of the room being so well ordered, this particular abberrance seemed all the more prominent.

The shape moved quietly from one bedroom to the next, listening to the muffled sounds of movement below. Finally it emerged on the landing and peered over the banister into the seething pit of Stygian blackness beneath.

The long-bladed kitchen knife, held in one black hand, seemed almost to be floating on air.

'Does this place look lived in to you?' said Jo, shining the torch around the sitting room.

'Well, someone's been here recently,' Tyler proclaimed, motioning towards an open drawer in the bureau. He hunted through it but found nothing. Jo moved to join him, picking up some pieces of paper which she discovered elsewhere on the cabinet.

'There might be notes of some kind,' she said.

'About what?' he enquired.

'I don't know. Anything, just to tell us where the hell Anderson is.'

Tyler moved into the hallway where he discovered the phone and the answering machine.

'Jo,' he called.

She joined him, shining the torch over the machine.

The cassette had been removed, the tape torn out. It hung like long streamers from the shattered cassette case. Even the plug on the machine itself had been removed.

'I told you there was something going on,' she said almost triumphantly.

'Let's not jump the gun,' said Tyler. 'There could be a logical explanation for this.'

'Like hell,' she rasped.

The American shone the torch around, bringing the beam to bear on the doormat.

There were two letters lying there, both addressed to Anderson and both bearing postmarks two days old. She looked at Tyler and an unspoken acknowledgement passed between them.

'Let's check upstairs,' said the farmer, taking the torch from her and mounting the first step.

The dark shape heard the sound of footfalls on the steps and it melted back into the darkness. It stepped into the bath and drew the shower curtain slowly around to conceal itself still further. It gripped the knife tightly and listened intently as the stairs creaked.

'We can get it done quicker if we check the rooms separately,' said Jo. 'If you find anything, shout.'

He nodded and pushed open the door of the nearest room. She, for her own part, took the one to the left.

Tyler found himself in what appeared to be a spare bedroom. A single bed was made up neatly and the room smelt of fresh linen. There was a wardrobe too and he tried the key, wincing at the squeak as he turned it. The door came open and Tyler shone the torch inside.

Apart from a set of blankets, it was empty. No clothes, no shoes. Even the coat hangers were gone.

He pushed the door to and crossed to a bedside cabinet, sliding open a top drawer.

It too was empty.

Tyler frowned, repeating the procedure with the solid oak dressing table which stood beneath the window. The entire thing had been cleared, all the drawers were empty.

He exhaled deeply.

Jo, meanwhile, found herself in what looked like an office of some kind. There was a desk, a couple of filing cabinets and piles of paper and envelopes of varying sizes. The desk itself had just two pencils and a small writing pad on it. She checked the drawers which, to her surprise, were empty. Puzzled, she ran a hand through her hair and decided to flip through the pad. Several pages had been torn out, the tops of the perforated paper still in place.

She crossed to the filing cabinets and pulled the top one open. There were about three dozen manila files inside. All unmarked. All empty.

'Christ,' muttered Jo, her voice a mixture of anger and frustration. She pushed the cabinet shut a little too hard, the sound of metal on metal ringing around the silent house.

Tyler heard it and called to her.

She answered that she was OK.

The farmer moved into a second, larger bedroom.

Once more he was confronted with a wardrobe, a bigger one, and this one was locked. He tugged at the recalcitrant fastening. Finally putting down the torch and using both hands. It wouldn't budge. He looked around for something with which to break the handle and retrieved a brass paper weight from a nearby sideboard. He struck the handle twice and, on the second impact, it dropped away.

Jo heard the clatter but paid it no heed as she moved into the bathroom. She blinked hard, her eyes having become accustomed to the gloom, but in this particular room it seemed darker still. It was small, with just a toilet, a wash basin and a bath. The shower curtain, she noticed, was drawn.

Her heels sounded loud in the stillness as she crossed to the nylon curtain and prepared to pull it back.

Behind it, the shape raised the knife.

Jo took a firm hold on the curtain.

'Come here.'

The shout startled her. She spun round, letting go of the curtain, and headed in the direction of Tyler's voice.

She found him in the larger bedroom, two suitcases lying on the floor before him. They were both open. Both filled with clothes.

'If he'd gone away,' said the farmer. 'I think he might have taken his things with him.'

Jo nodded, looking down at the cases. Someone had gone through the wardrobe, removed every item of clothing and meticulously packed them into the tan suitcases.

'The wardrobe in the other room is empty too,' Tyler told her.

'I told you there was something wrong here,' she said.

'That still doesn't explain where Anderson is.'

'No,' murmured the American.

'I think we should call the police but not from here. This is out of our hands now. We'll report him as a missing person, tell them what's happened.'

'When?'

He looked at his watch beneath the torch light.

It was approaching 11.42.

'If he's already been missing for two days another few hours won't hurt. We'll wait until morning.'

Jo agreed.

They left everything as it was and made their way back down the stairs then outside once more. Tyler flicked off the torch as they reached the back door and they scuttled across the front lawn back to the waiting Chevette.

From the window of the larger bedroom the shape watched the car pull away, the kitchen knife still cradled in its hand.

Nineteen

As the sound of the Chevette's engine receded into the night, the curtain was slowly pushed back into position and the inside of Geoffrey Anderson's house once more became as black as pitch. Nevertheless, the lone intruder moved, as he always did at night, with an assurance few others possessed. His footsteps were as noiseless as before and he crossed to the larger bedroom, retracing his own steps and also those of Tyler and Jo.

He stood, a dark shape amongst so much gloom, gazing down at the open suitcases, the long bladed kitchen knife still gripped firmly in his hand. He hefted the lethal blade before him a second then dropped it onto the bed. His breathing was shallow but more guttural now and he suppressed a cough as he reached into his jacket pocket for a pack of Rothmans. There was one in the box, crumpled. What the hell, he'd make do. He'd started smoking when he was five and now, at fifty-three, he was on over eighty a day. His fingers, long and slender, were stained almost black with nicotine. He lit the cigarette and sucked hard on it. A spasm of coughing racked his body and he banged his chest angrily.

Carlo Fanducci was dying.

He knew it, he didn't need any doctor to tell him. He was fucking dying. The mornings when he coughed until he spat blood, the pains in his chest, the bouts of wheezing. They had told him that, he didn't need any goddam medical genius to confirm it. But what the hell, everybody had to die sometime. Fanducci smiled thinly, running a hand through his lank grey hair. Despite the fact that his hairline was receding, the lustrous grey strands still grew in abundance over his ears and the back of his head. Deep creases scarred almost every inch of his face, particularly his forehead which looked as though someone had pulled a fork across it. Someone had once told him he had a face like an unkept grave and he smiled once more at the recollection.

He sat down on the edge of the bed to finish his cigarette, the glowing tip the only light in the room.

Fanducci inhaled painfully.

He'd thought he was going to have to kill the man

and the girl when they'd entered the house. He didn't recognise the man but he'd seen the girl before. He'd listened in on the phone tap the night Anderson had called her then he'd watched her from the trees as she'd used the call box. He'd ripped the car light from inside the Chevette with his bare hands. He smiled and flexed his fingers. There was enormous strength in those hands. He might be dying but he sure as hell didn't intend going down weak and enfeebled.

The vision of the girl floated into his mind once more. He thought he'd seen her before that night in the lay-by. She was American, like himself. He had detected her accent – East Side, New York. Different from his own which was a curious amalgam of Italian and Lower Manhattan. He'd been born in Mott Street, at the very centre of 'Little Italy'. His father had been a bartender, running one of the joints owned by the Molinaro family, one of New York's largest and most powerful families. Fanducci himself had graduated, over the years, from collector to soldier and, finally, to trigger man.

Cosa Nostra. He almost said the words aloud. *Our thing*. *Our* fucking *thing*. Only he was no longer a part of it. Don Vito Molinaro had seen to that. The old bastard had given him a job to do. There had been a Union boss called Bishop. He wouldn't toe the line, wouldn't pay his dues to the collectors. Had even pulled a .45 on them, told them to fuck off and stop bothering him. Fanducci had been told to warn the Union leader off, frighten him a bit. So he had paid a visit to the man's factory, spoken to him. Ended up sticking the barrel of his .357 between the motherfucker's legs.

It hadn't been warning enough.

Old man Molinaro had finally given Fanducci the go ahead to push the button on Bishop. The Union Leader had to go and Fanducci was only too happy to do the job. He'd trailed the man home one night, then sat in his car until late finally emerging around midnight.

He'd cut through one of the windows with a glass cutter and entered the building.

Bishop had woken up as the Italian had entered the room and Fanducci could still remember the look of horrified realization on the Union leader's face as he saw the .357 being drawn. The big gun had not had the benefit of a silencer and the bang when it came had been thunderous. The hollow-tipped bullet had caught Bishop in the chest, exploding as it shattered bone, ripping an exit hole the size of a fist as it punched its way out of his back spraying Mrs Bishop with gobbets of lung and smashed scapula.

She'd started screaming when Fanducci had fired the second bullet into the nape of her husband's neck.

In the darkness her screams had seemed to be coming from some disembodied ghost but, in the pale light from outside, he could see her, drenched in her husband's blood. She continued to shriek. Then the two kids appeared from another room and *they* were screaming.

All of them were fucking screaming.

The only way to shut them up was by blowing their heads off and that was precisely what he'd done.

It had been plastered all over the papers the next day. Fanducci had been summoned before the Don and told that he was outcast. The family didn't want him any longer. Fuck them, he thought, and he went.

There was no shortage of buyers for his services. During his years as a family member he had met many top industrialists. These powerful men always needed bodyguards and Fanducci had found himself another employer with ease. He'd enjoyed that way of life. There had been more women in those years than he'd ever had before. One of them had become his wife.

By that time in his fiftieth year, Fanducci had married a girl half his age. She had the face and body of a movie star and a mind like a child. However, in bed she was something else. And, she was too much for him to handle. She had, he'd later discovered, a string of lovers but it wasn't until he walked in one night and found her being well and truly shafted by some goddam nigger that he'd found out. He'd beaten them both with a chair leg. Then he'd broken the nigger's fingers for good measure and thrown the girl out. Little bitch.

At roughly the same time, he'd been approached by John Stark. A mysterious man about six years younger than Fanducci himself. He'd asked the Italian what he was earning, then offered to double it. The condition was, he would have to up roots and move to England. Stark was opening a chemical research plant of some kind and he needed someone like Fanducci working for him. The Italian had agreed and, for the past three years he'd lived in England, working for what was to become Vanderburg Chemicals. He saw little of Stark, taking most of his orders from a guy called Thorndike, an Englishman who he could not learn to trust but then, Fanducci reasoned, trust was a hard thing to come by.

It had been Thorndike who had told him to kill Anderson. He hadn't reckoned on any interference though. Now, as he sat on the edge of the bed he tried to remember where he'd seen that dark-haired girl who'd not long ago left the house. Quite a looker, not the sort you'd easily forget – nice tits. No. The memory eluded him. He took one last suck on the cigarette, nipped it out and dropped the butt into his jacket pocket.

Then he set about his task.

Twenty

It was just after midnight as Jo and Tyler stood facing each other in the car park of 'The King George'. She had locked her own vehicle and now they stood beside the farmer's landrover.

'I'll meet you in the morning,' he said. 'We'll go to the police, tell them everything. They'll find Anderson.'

Jo nodded.

'Thanks for your help,' she said. 'I appreciate it.'

He leant forward and kissed her softly on the lips, feeling that familiar tingle run the length of his spine as he did so.

Jo felt the same sensation and she pulled Tyler closer, her lips parting, brushing the hard edges of his teeth before probing deeper into his mouth. He responded fiercely and they remained locked together for long moments, each enjoying the touch of the other. He felt her soft hair brush against his hand and he shuddered. As she slipped one hand inside his jacket it was all he could do to contain the erection he felt beginning. They finally broke apart, gazing into each other's eyes.

'I'd better go,' he said, opening the door of the landrover.

She watched as he climbed in and started the engine. He smiled at her, then spun the wheel and drove off. Jo stood in the car park for a moment longer, then she headed for the side entrance to the hotel.

There wasn't a soul in the reception as she entered. The American wandered into the darkened bar and found that too was deserted. She felt a sudden pang of hunger and knew she would have to eat something before she turned in for the night. Just a sandwich would do. Jo crossed to the reception and rang the bell.

No one appeared.

There were some papers on the desk top and a half

finished glass of beer but there didn't appear to be anyone around to claim them.

'Hello,' she called, her voice sounding strangely muffled in the silent confines of the reception.

The night porter or some member of staff had to be around she reasoned. Maybe they'd gone for a leak. She waited a moment longer, walking across to the open fire place, looking up at the two large pikes crossed above it. The weapons had been polished recently and glinted in the half light. Jo wandered back to the desk and rang the bell once more.

When the second attempt failed to secure any response, Jo lifted the flap which led behind the counter and walked through. There were two doors before her, both closed, both marked 'Private'. She knocked on the first one, peering inside when she got no answer. It was a small room, one wall being lined with leather chairs. There were a couple of coffee tables in there too, some magazines lying around. Jo guessed that it must be the staff room, a suspicion confirmed when she saw a rota pinned to a notice board on her right. There was another door before her which led through into the kitchen. This door was slightly ajar and she could see light spilling through the crack. There were vague sounds of movement from inside so she headed towards the door.

Of four banks of fluorescent lights set into the ceiling of the kitchen, only one was lit and, from where she stood, Jo could see a dark figure standing near to one of the fridges at the far end of the room.

As he turned, she saw that it was Mark Bates. She watched in silence as he opened the fridge door and took out a large piece of raw steak, the blood dripping from it as he removed it from the metal tray.

Jo was hidden from him by the darkness and by a rack of cooking utensils which hung before her. She watched, mesmerized, as he lifted the steak in one hairy-palmed hand, looked at it for a moment, then tore off a chunk with his teeth. He chewed with difficulty, blood from the meat dripping from his chin. Bates grunted in satisfaction as he indulged his gluttony. Dark, rusty stains smeared his cheeks and some of the red liquid dripped from his long nails. When he opened his mouth, a gobbet fell to the floor and, quick as a flash, he scooped it up and rammed it back into his mouth.

Jo turned away, revolted, and fled from the kitchen. She felt sick and, when she finally reached her room, she drank several glasses of water before she felt the nausea pass off.

Downstairs, Bates stuffed the last of the steak into his mouth, then he fastidiously licked every last drop of blood from his fingers.

Twenty-one

The following morning, Jo ate a light breakfast of toast and jam washed down with a cup of coffee. She couldn't face the bacon and eggs which she saw one of the other guests tucking into, not after what she'd seen the previous night. She hadn't slept too well and there were dark rings beneath her eyes. Dressed in a pair of jeans and a red T-shirt she was already beginning to feel warm as, outside, the sun rose in a cloudless sky and began its merciless grilling of the land beneath.

She had looked for Bates but not seen him. There were just two waitresses and a porter, all three of whom looked lethargic and pale. Perhaps Tyler had been right? There might be a virus going around. She sipped at her coffee. A virus which caused hair to grow on the palm of a man's hand and made him eat raw meat? Jo almost chuckled aloud.

Her thoughts turned to other things. The incident at Anderson's house last night had unsettled her. Although at least now she felt secure in the knowledge that her hunch had been correct. There *was* something going on which he had known about and which someone at Vanderburg didn't want him to talk about. At least it looked that way. Obviously they wouldn't know for sure until they found him. She paused. *If* they found him. Jo hastily dismissed the idea. After all, this was England, not New York. Things like that didn't happen here. She finished her coffee, seeds of doubt already sown and growing in her mind. The American lit up a cigarette, took a few drags on it and left the dining room.

Tyler was waiting for her in reception.

'I wondered if you'd be up yet,' he said, smiling.

'With the lark,' she told him as they headed out to his waiting landrover.

As they drove to the police station she told him about Bates and the raw meat.

'Christ, what would make him do that?' Tyler wondered aloud.

She mentioned what he himself had said about a virus.

'It's possible I suppose but if it is a virus which is affecting so many people how the hell is it transmitted?'

'I'm a journalist not a doctor, Vic,' she said.

'Curiously enough, neither of my farm hands have turned up this morning but no one's rung in to say if they're sick or not. One of Stuart Nichols' blokes is taking care of things for me.'

They drove slowly through the quiet streets, noticing

just how few people there were about. Granted it was only ten o'clock but Wakely town centre was usually bustling by now. Those few people who were on the streets seemed to be moving in slow motion, heads bowed as if searching for something on the ground beneath them.

Tyler turned a corner, braking hard as a man stepped out in front of him.

'You silly sod,' Tyler shouted angrily. 'I could have killed you.'

The man merely looked round and both Jo and Tyler saw how bloodless his features were, the cheeks sunken, the eyes dark rimmed and yellowed. The man narrowed them against the glare of the sun. He gazed at the occupants of the landrover in bewilderment and, as he did so, Jo noticed that the flesh was flaking from his hands and curling back in almost transparent wisps. His nails were hooked, those that weren't broken. He stood motionless for a moment, then walked on as if nothing had happened.

Tyler looked anxiously at Jo and started the engine again.

'Maybe we should stop off at the doctor's surgery,' Jo said. 'See if he's had many cases like we've been seeing.'

'First things first, eh?' said the farmer. 'Let's find out where Geoffrey Anderson is. Besides, we don't know there *is* anything wrong with the people in Wakely yet.'

Jo opened her mouth to speak but Tyler cut her short.

'And even if there is, I don't see that there's much we can do about it.'

'But if it's affecting so many of them it must be communicable. What the hell is to stop us catching it?'

The farmer seemed not to have considered that possibility. As if troubled by the realization, he drove the rest of the way in silence.

There were two Panda cars parked outside Wakely police station, both with their windows wound down in an effort to let some air into the stifling confines of the vehicles. The police station itself was a large, white-washed building; just one storey, it was about the size of a supermarket and quite disproportionately large for the number of men on the force. Tyler knew four of them well, the other three just well enough to nod too.

He swung the landrover around and parked in front of the main doors, then he and Jo climbed out and strode down the six wide stone steps which led to the forecourt.

Inside the building it was cool, two powerful fans droning in opposite corners of the entry-way giving some respite from the blistering heat outside. Tyler crossed to a meshed glass partition and rapped sharply on it.

There were sounds of movement from behind, of a bolt being slipped and then the partition opened to reveal a red-faced man with a thick growth of beard. He had his white shirt rolled up to the elbows but there was still perspiration glistening on the thick hairs of his forearms. Rotund and quick to smile, he reminded Jo of a dark-haired, sweaty Santa Claus.

'Hello, Vic,' said Sergeant Don Mason. 'How are you?'

'Not so bad,' said Tyler, then he introduced Jo.

Mason smiled even more broadly and shook hands with the American who did her best to retain her smile as she felt her hand engulfed by the sticky puffiness of Mason's appendage.

'What's wrong? One of your pigs got lost has it?' Mason said, chuckling.

'I want to file a missing persons report,' the farmer told him.

Mason raised his eyebrows quizzically. He reached for the appropriate form and stood there, pen poised.

'What's the name?' he asked.

'Geoffrey Anderson,' Jo told him. 'He's been missing since Sunday.'

'Three days,' said Mason to himself, scribbling on the form. 'Description?'

There was an awkward silence.

Mason looked up.

Tyler exhaled deeply.

'We don't know what he looks like. Neither of us have ever seen him.'

'So how do you know he's missing?' Mason wanted to know.

'We broke into his house last night,' Jo said. 'All his clothes were packed as if he was going away but there was no sign of him. I think someone had been through the house.'

The policeman tapped on the desk top with the end of his pen.

'*You* broke into someone's house?' he said.

They both nodded.

'Perhaps I should be filling out a bloody charge sheet, not a missing persons form. What the hell were you doing breaking into somebody's house?'

'Don, for Heaven's sake listen to me,' said Tyler. 'I'm telling you, Anderson has disappeared.'

Mason wiped a bead of perspiration from his forehead.

'We'll soon sort this out,' he muttered. 'Peck.'

A constable appeared from one of the back rooms. He was tall, perhaps six five and he moved slowly as if each step were an effort. Both Jo and Tyler noticed the pallor of his skin, the way his teeth protruded from his swollen lips.

'Peck, drive out to this address,' said Mason handing the P.C. a page from his notebook. 'See what you can find.'

Peck nodded, blinked hard and rubbed his eyes.

'Come on, move yourself, lad, we haven't got all day. Radio in as soon as you've found out what's happening there.'

The constable nodded and made his way slowly out to one of the Pandas. They heard the engine being revved up, then the car pulled away.

'He needs a bloody bomb behind him that lad,' said Mason. 'He's been moping around looking like a wet weekend for the last week or so.'

'He looks ill,' said Jo.

'Well, if he is, he's not the only one on the force who is. Two of my constables called in sick five days ago and I haven't heard anything from them since and the others here, apart from myself and P.C. Dagless, look like death warmed up.'

'So do most of the people we've seen,' said Jo.

'I reckon there must be a virus or something going round,' Tyler added.

'Probably bloody flu,' Mason said, scornfully. He considered the missing persons report again. 'What makes this Anderson so important anyway?'

'He works for Vanderburg Chemicals,' Jo said. She paused. 'Or *worked*. He was a research scientist. He wanted to speak to me about something but he never got the chance.'

'So you two thought you'd break into his house and see if you could find him?' Mason said, sarcastically.

'Goddamit, we had no choice,' Jo snapped.

'Perhaps he's gone on holiday,' Mason insisted.

Tyler shook his head.

'No,' he said, emphatically.

The sergeant offered them some tea and they sat in the entry-way and drank it, waiting for Peck to radio in.

'When he gets inside he'll find the suitcases,' Jo said to Tyler. 'They'll know we're telling the truth then.'

There was a hiss of static from the microphone on

the desk close to Mason. He picked it up and flicked the transmitter switch. Tyler and Jo got up and crossed to the partition in an effort to hear the conversation.

'Tango One come in,' said Mason.

More static.

'Peck, for Christ's sake come in you idiot.'

'Sorry, sarge, I was having trouble with the handset.' The constable's voice sounded tinny.

'Have you checked the house out?' Mason asked.

'I didn't have to.'

'Why not?'

'Anderson's here.'

'What?' snapped Tyler.

Mason waved a hand for him to be quiet.

'You're sure it's him. Geoffrey Anderson. You have got the right address haven't you?'

'Sarge, it's him, I'm telling you. He said he was leaving for a few weeks' holiday. I saw his cases in the hall.'

Mason exhaled through clenched teeth, his eyes fixed on Jo and Tyler.

'OK, Peck, come back to the station. Over and out.' He flicked off the set.

Mason held up the missing persons report and very carefully tore it up.

'Next time, Vic, get your facts right before you come bothering me. Now clear out before I charge you both with breaking and entering.'

The two men glared at each other for long moments, then Tyler spun round and, followed by Jo, left.

As they clambered into the landrover Tyler banged the steering wheel angrily.

'What the bloody hell is going on?' he snarled.

'Vic, it couldn't have been Anderson,' Jo insisted.

'Well, as far as the police are concerned, it *was* and the case is closed.' He started the engine and turned the vehicle around, heading in the direction of his farm.

'I'm not letting it drop, Vic.'

'We were taken for mugs,' he snapped. 'Someone fooled both of us.'

They drove the rest of the way in silence.

Carlo Fanducci stood in the doorway and watched the Panda pull away. He couldn't resist a smile. Jesus, what a dumb bastard that cop had been. He hadn't even asked him for any I.D. A real lame fuck. Fanducci had said he was Geoffrey Anderson and the cop had believed him, even fallen for the line he'd shot him about going away for a few weeks. Dumb motherfucker. The ex-Mafia man chuckled to himself and closed the door.

He wondered if he'd get any more trouble from the two bastards he'd seen in the house last night.

If they wanted trouble, fine.

As he moved, the .357 Magnum felt heavy in its shoulder holster.

Twenty-two

The cow walked by slowly, followed by its calf. The larger of the two animals paused momentarily and looked at the two onlookers, then it found some grass and began eating. All over the field animals were doing likewise. In some places, the young were almost as big as the parents. It was difficult to distinguish them.

'See what I mean,' said Tyler, indicating one of the over-developed calves. 'Twice as big as they should be for their age.'

Jo nodded.

'But you said it wasn't just the cows.'

'It isn't,' said Tyler, heading back across the yard towards a barn. Jo followed him, trying to avoid the mud patches, muttering to herself when her heels sank into the sticky ooze. Tyler looked down at her feet and grinned.

'Not the most practical footwear for a farm,' he japed.

The American was about to say something when her left shoe was actually pulled off by the clinging mud. She hopped about on one leg, hurriedly tugged the shoe free and slipped it back on.

The farmer led her into a barn which contained a number of pigs. In small pens were about two dozen sows, most with litters. The noise in the building was almost deafening. Jo looked into the first pen and saw three large weaners feeding from their mother's teats. She shuddered involuntarily, remembering what had happened at the livestock market. In the next pen were more piglets, only here some of them were normal size. One lay motionless in the straw whilst another, larger one, sniffed at it.

'Some are affected, some are normal,' said Tyler, wearily.

'I don't know what to make of it.'

He turned and headed for the exit but Jo lingered for a moment, her attention caught by the small pig before her. It was still lying in the straw but whether or not it was dead she didn't know. Its larger companion continued to nuzzle against it until finally it gripped one of the creatures floppy ears in its mouth and tore it away.

Jo winced.

'Oh God,' she murmured, then she found the breath to call Tyler. He scuttled back to the pen and glanced in at the tableau before him. The larger piglet had taken another chunk out of the dead one and was chewing hungrily. The smell of blood had created squeals of excitement amongst the remainder of the litter and, in seconds, they were crowding around the body of the dead weaner. Tyler reached for a nearby broom and, stepping over the rail, drove the litter away. He picked up the dead pig by one of its hind legs and lifted it out of the pen. The others returned to the sow as if nothing had happened.

Jo had turned pale and she headed for the door ahead of Tyler who carried the torn carcass of the dead weaner with him. He tossed it onto the ground outside and sighed.

'Are you OK?' he asked the journalist.

She nodded.

'When is this going to stop?' she wanted to know.

'I wish I knew.'

There was a large compost heap nearby, the stench even more unbearable due to the fact that the sun had been baking it for the past few weeks. Tyler tossed the weaner onto it and pitched a few forkfuls of the muck over the carcass. Beside the heap Jo noticed some large bags, like the bags supermarkets sold potatoes in. They were of a strong plastic, silver in colour and she could also see some red letters on them. The American squatted down and pulled one of the bags free.

'What was in here, Vic?' she asked.

'A new multi-purpose feed,' he told her.

They looked at one another as Jo uncovered the label:

VANDERBURG CHEMICALS.

The same thought struck them simultaneously.

'Then it is something to do with the feed,' she said. 'I mean, what's been happening to the animals? The accelerated growth, them turning crazy?'

Tyler nodded.

'I'm pretty sure none of this started happening until the Vanderburg feed was introduced to the stock. Hawley said that other farmers around here have been having the same sort of problems as I have.' He scratched his chin thoughtfully.

'Christ,' he muttered. 'Stuart Nichols was using it, so was old Ben Thurston. They *did* both mention peculiarities in their stock.'

'Increased growth,' Jo added. 'I heard one of them say that when I was in the bar before the livestock market.'

'Still-born litters and Ben said his lambs were as big as dogs. It has to be the feed.'

'Maybe Anderson ties in to this somehow,' she said.

Tyler frowned.

'Come on, Jo, you're obsessed with this bloody bloke. How could he have anything to do with what's been happening at the farms in Wakely?'

'Look, Anderson worked for Vanderburg Chemicals. These sacks belong to Vanderburg Chemicals. The feed they produce has caused abnormalities in livestock. There . . .'

He cut her short.

'We won't know that for *sure*, not until Dan Hawley completes the autopsies.'

'Goddamit, Vic, there has to be a link,' she shouted at him. She threw the bag down angrily.

'You want there to be a link,' he countered. 'Anderson probably doesn't even know anything about this multi-purpose feed, let alone its effects.'

'He was a research scientist for Christ's sake, he was one of the guys working on the project.'

'Where's your proof?'

She was silent for a moment. Her breath was coming in short gasps, her eyes aglow with anger.

'Let's see what Hawley says first,' Tyler said. 'But I think you're wrong about the link between Anderson and what's going on here.'

'Maybe you're right,' she conceded. 'Maybe I am

paranoid about Anderson but it's one hell of a coincidence.'

Tyler nodded. They stood for a moment longer, then he walked back to the house with her. He asked if she wanted a coffee. She said yes.

'I'll make you a cup when I've tried to reach my two farmhands.' He crossed to the phone.

'I can do it. Just tell me where everything is,' said Jo.

'In the kitchen, you can't miss it, it's still out from breakfast time.'

She wandered through into the kitchen. Tyler picked up the phone and dialled Harrison's number.

No answer.

He let it ring half a dozen times.

Still there was nothing.

Tyler put the phone down. If Harrison was that ill, then surely his wife would have called in for him. Unless she too was sick. But too sick to reach the telephone? He tried Jenkins's number. The result was the same. No answer.

He replaced the receiver and wandered into the kitchen where he found Jo standing over two steaming mugs of coffee. She handed one to him.

'No luck?' she asked.

He shook his head.

'Maybe they've got that virus,' she offered.

Tyler smiled thinly.

'Now you *are* clutching at straws. You'll be telling me next that Anderson's mixed up with that as well.'

Jo smiled wryly.

'I don't discount the possibility.'

'Don't journalists ever stop speculating?'

'No.'

They carried their coffee into the sitting room and Tyler seated himself on the sofa. Jo sat next to him, lighting up a cigarette. She looked around the room, taking in every detail.

'It's a nice house,' she said. 'Not what you'd expect a farmhouse to look like.'

'You mean where are the horse brasses and carved wood furniture?'

She chuckled.

'A bit of a cliché that,' he said, smiling. 'Farmers are businessmen these days. We're more concerned with stock figures and V.A.T. than we are with weaving our own sweaters and making oak tables.'

'I *never* had you figured as a cliché, Vic,' she told him. She noticed two photos on the mantelpiece over the fire.

'Your parents?' she asked, motioning towards them.

'Yes.'

Jo got to her feet and crossed to the fireplace, looking at the photograph of the man and then at Tyler.

'There's a resemblance.'

'Same face, same temperament my mother used to say.'

'Don't you ever get lonely out here by yourself?' she asked, returning to the seat beside him.

'No. I could ask you the same question, you're thousands of miles away from home. Don't you ever miss it?'

'I don't miss New York. Though maybe one day I'll go back, just to see if things have changed.'

She looked down into her coffee as if trying to discover her next few words there.

'Who am I kidding?' she confessed. 'I wouldn't dare go back.'

'You mean because of the Mafia?'

She nodded.

'They're like the goddam Mounties, they always get their man.'

Vic squeezed her hand and she turned to look at him. As on the previous night, Tyler sensed that curious duality within her. The raw, smouldering sexuality mingling with the softness. It was a combination which aroused him deeply and he found himself gazing deep into those jade eyes. He leant forward and kissed her softly on the lips. Jo touched his stubbled cheek with one long nail, listening to it rasp across the bristles. Then she pulled him closer, her mouth eager to find his, her tongue probing deeply.

Tyler slid his right hand up her back until he felt her soft lustrous hair. Without breaking the kiss, Jo moved closer to him, her hands sliding inside his shirt to explore his muscular chest. He felt her long nails rake his flesh and the sensation sent waves of pleasure through him.

He slipped his free hand up her T-shirt, his eager fingers brushing her left nipple. It stiffened to a hard bud and he transferred his attention to the other one. Jo let out a low gasp of pleasure and lay back, allowing the farmer to reach her more easily. She pulled the T-shirt over her head and dropped it behind her, treating Tyler to the sight of her firm breasts. He bent forward and kissed each nipple in turn, drawing it between his teeth, leaving a trail of saliva as he licked his way down to her navel.

She loosened the button of her jeans, closing her eyes as he eased her zip down. She lifted her bottom so he could pull the denim free. He removed her jeans and panties in one movement. He nuzzled the area between her legs, his hands parting her thighs a little more. He kissed her mound, allowing his tongue to snake lower until he was flicking her clitoris.

Jo arched her back, pushing her pelvis hard against his questing, darting tongue, wanting him to push it into that most sensitive area. Her entire body felt as if it was on fire and, as he probed her moist cleft, she jerked spasmodically beneath the attentions of his tongue.

She opened her eyes and looked at him as he knelt

before her, freeing his own bulging erection. Jo reached for it eagerly, moving her hand gently up and down the shaft until Tyler himself began to shudder.

He entered her with ease, both of them gasping at the sensation and he began to move rhythmically inside her. Jo raised her hips to meet each of his thrusts, her hands resting on his buttocks as she drew him in deeper.

Tyler bent his head and lapped at her swollen nipples and he felt her body begin to tense.

She murmured something in his ear, her hair brushing against his shoulder as she leant forward. She licked some perspiration from his face, gritting her teeth as she felt the first sensations of impending orgasm. Tyler quickened his pace and, seconds later, Jo was moaning loudly, raking his back with her nails as the fury of her climax racked her body. Tyler tensed and, a moment later, he too joined her in ecstasy and she writhed with renewed pleasure as she felt his hot seed spurting into her.

For long moments they lay breathless, Jo running her fingers through his hair. Her body seemed to be glowing and both of them were covered by a thin film of perspiration. He withdrew gently from her, allowing his eyes to trace a pattern once more over her shapely body. Jo lay back, naked, on the sofa, her eyes closed.

Tyler ran his hand up her leg, pausing just short of her slippery cleft.

'It's more comfortable upstairs,' he said.

They both laughed.

Twenty-three

Wakely's only General Practitioner's surgery was crowded as usual. The waiting-room, which seated twenty people, was full and there were even patients standing in the corridors waiting their turn. A chorus of coughs and mutterings drifted from the room, mingling with the strident ringing of the phones on the front desk. One harrassed receptionist tried to deal with patients wanting appointments and manage those who already had them.

In a room to the right sat half-a-dozen more people, some clutching green cards, others pink ones. The pink cards signified blood tests and nurse Jan Williams peered through her appointment book to see how many more she had to do before she finished at one o'clock. She had a splitting headache, not helped by the glaring fluorescent lights above. As she swabbed the arm of a patient and steadied the syringe over the bulging vein, she blinked hard. The needle seemed to swim into separate images for a second before clarifying.

She'd had the headache for the past two days but the tablets which usually relieved it had not worked this time. She'd thought about phoning in to say she was going to have a day off but had decided against it. Besides, if she was at home she would only sit around feeling sorry for herself and the kids would drive her potty. They always did during the school holidays. They got so bored and ended up fighting. Jan had two children, both boys, both ten years old, identical twins in fact. They were the image of their father. Joe Williams had been made redundant two months ago from his job in Arkham and now spent his days sitting around the house worrying where the rent was going to come from. Jan didn't fancy a day at home in *that* atmosphere.

The patient got up and left and Jan transferred the

blood to a phial, placing it alongside the other eight which she had already collected that morning. As she gazed at the crimson liquid she felt her stomach churning and, for a moment, she thought she was going to be sick. She bowed her head and massaged her temples, a little disturbed to find flakes of skin coming away beneath her finger tips. Her hands and arms looked milk white and, when she caught sight of her face in an upturned kidney bowl, she thought she was looking at a skull. The distorted vision leered back at her, eyes sunken, the orbs bulging from the sockets. The blood vessels seemed swollen in places as if threatening to burst but the whites were sepia coloured.

Jan Williams closed her eyes, hoping that the pain in her head would go, but it showed no signs of abating.

She called her next patient.

A urine test this time. She gave the man a small bottle and directed him towards the lavatory, reminding him that the sample must be 'mid-stream'. He looked vague and she started to explain but then he smiled as if something had clicked and he marched off to the toilet.

Jan consulted her book once more, readying a fresh syringe as she saw that she had yet another blood test to do. She ushered the woman behind the curtain and sat her down, fastening the velcro pad around her bicep. Jan blinked hard under the light and stuck the needle in.

It missed the vein and the woman yelped in pain and surprise.

The nurse apologized and tried again. This time the needle punctured the pulsing vein. She let the tourniquet go and drew the required amount of blood. As before, she deposited it in a tube and reached for the seal but, as she held the bottle in her hand, she began to salivate wildly until streamers of sputum dribbled from her mouth. The pain in her head seemed to grow in intensity until it felt as if her eyes were going to burst from her skull.

The woman who had just had her blood taken sat mesmerized, watching the nurse who had clamped her hand around the bottle and was squeezing. With her free hand she reached for two more of the phials, crushing the glass inside her fist.

There was a loud crack as it broke.

Blood cascaded from her hands, pieces of glass falling also, other shards slicing open Jan's palms. She opened her hands to see that the glass had lacerated her hands badly. Broken pieces of crystal protruded from the torn flesh as thick crimson liquid pumped out.

Jan raised both hands to her mouth and lapped at the swiftly flowing blood.

The woman in the chair fainted.

The man returned from the lavatory, apologising for only having half filled the bottle but, when he saw what the nurse was doing, his bladder seemed to find hidden reserves and a dark stain appeared at the front of his trousers.

Jan Williams sank to her knees amidst the blood and glass, both hands held up, the crimson liquid running down her arms to stain her white overall. Ignoring the pieces of glass which cut her tongue, she sucked and licked frenziedly at the life fluid.

When a doctor tore back the curtain and looked down at her she merely turned and smiled, her teeth and lips dripping red, her hands in bloody tatters.

Her wild laughter began to fill the room.

Twenty-four

Dan Hawley wiped some perspiration from his forehead with the back of his hand and steadied the scalpel above the calf. The animal was lying spread-eagled on one of the dissection tables, the vet's trolley full of implements beside it. He cut carefully into it, just above the anus and opened the alimentary canal. A vile-smelling dark fluid spilled from the rent and, even though he was wearing a mask, Hawley winced slightly. He cut a piece of the slippery internal tube and placed it carefully on a microscope slide, then he turned his attention to the calf's stomach.

The accumulation of gas had caused it to swell up so that when the vet cut into it, it deflated rapidly. Bile spurted onto his gloved hand. He sliced off a section of the stomach wall and placed that on a slide too.

He coughed and supported himself against the work bench for a moment, wincing beneath the powerful overhead lights which blazed like minute suns. Then he pressed his eye to the microscope, slid the specimen beneath the powerful lens and peered at it. He adjusted the focus until things swam into crystal clarity, carefully scrutinizing what he saw before him.

Hawley exhaled deeply and reached for the second slide.

What he saw was the same.

Ordinarily, bacteria will survive in a dead body for anything up to three days before dying. The microscopic organisms which he saw before him had come from an animal that had been dead for two days and yet they were still moving amongst the other debris. But what surprised Hawley was the fact that they were multiplying.

Instead of dying, the bacteria were increasing.

He stepped back from the microscope and crossed to

a small incubator nearby. From it he took a third slide, one which held a section of the piglet's brain which Tyler had brought in the day before.

Hawley looked once more at the third slide.

The bacteria had begun to form spores.

He swallowed hard, his mouth feeling as if it were full of chalk. His tongue seemed swollen, his lips dry. He crossed to the sink and filled a plastic cup with water but, instead of slaking his thirst, it made him feel sick. The vet held his stomach for a moment, then returned to the spread-eagled calf. He took a saw from his trolley and set to work opening the skull. The tumescent growth on the side of the head had begun to shrivel like an old grape but, Hawley noticed, the eye which was attached to it still gazed glassily at him.

He prized away the portion of skull he'd cut, exposing the brain, then he retrieved his scalpel and carefully cut a sliver of the grey-red matter, dropping it onto a slide as he had done the other specimens.

There were spores in there too.

Whatever kind of bacteria it was, Hawley had never seen its like before. It was multiplying at a greatly accelerated speed, forming spores in order to hibernate. But why? He coughed again and pulled off his rubber gloves, then he walked across to a small bookshelf on the far wall. From it he took down a heavy tome and flicked agitatedly through it. There were diagrams of every known bacteria but nothing remotely like what he'd seen on his slides. He slammed the book shut and stood there for what seemed like an eternity then, pulling the gloves back on, he returned to the calf.

He'd already examined the cow which had given birth to it and found traces of exactly the same bacteria in both her bloodstream and placenta. It had also been present in the remains of the stomach.

The cow, the calf and the weaner. All three had

become breeding grounds for the new strain of bacteria, their carcasses infested with the microscopic life form.

Hawley took one last look at the writhing shapes on the slide, then he hurried to the phone and dialled Tyler's number.

Mandy Potter opened the door when Tyler and Jo arrived. She ushered them through into the surgery, then disappeared.

The hands of the wall clock had just crawled past noon.

As the farmer and the journalist entered the surgery they were immediately struck by the foul smell. The body of the calf had been covered by a rubber sheet but, nevertheless, the strong odour hung heavily in the air making Jo cough.

Hawley was sitting on a stool beside the microscope. The room was stuffy, the blinds down, the overhead lights having been turned off.

The vet looked up wearily as his two visitors entered.

'What have you found, Dan?' asked Tyler.

Hawley exhaled deeply.

'I wish I could tell you,' said the vet, enigmatically. He motioned for the farmer to look into the microscope which he did, squinting down the eye piece. He saw the bacteria moving rapidly amongst the tissue, then he stepped back to let Jo have a look.

'It's bacteria,' said Hawley, answering an unasked question. 'There are four separate specimens taken from the weaner, the calf's brain and stomach and from the cow. They're all identical.'

'What does that mean?' asked Jo.

'A virus?' asked Tyler.

'I don't think so,' the vet told him. 'The bacteria which cause viral infections in livestock aren't as. . . .' He struggled to find the word. 'They're not as powerful.

This bacteria is not only multiplying, it's creating spores.'

'Meaning what?' said Tyler.

'Meaning that it intends or intended to go into a period of dormancy, of hibernation. Now, very few bacteria are able to do that and those that do are normally confined to plants. This is a completely new strain. Not different. New. *I've* never seen anything like it before.'

'How does that explain what's been happening to the animals lately?' the farmer enquired. 'The cannibalism, the still-born litters, the increased growth?'

Hawley exhaled deeply.

'As I said, I took samples from the stomachs of all three animals. There was a greater abundance of the bacteria in the stomach of the cow. She ate something which induced the growth of this bacteria. It was passed on through her bloodstream to the calf. That was what happened with the sow and her piglets. That's what's been happening with *all* the livestock around here. The parent animal has been passing on the bacteria through the bloodstream to the unborn young which have been developing more rapidly. The bacteria have, somehow, caused a change in the DNA of the young animals.'

'What could they have eaten that would do this?' asked Jo.

'It's a toxic agent of some kind. It's impossible to say without a sample of it,' Hawley told her. 'All I do know is, whatever it is, it's inorganic.'

'You mean it's man-made?' said Tyler.

Hawley nodded.

'The feed,' said the farmer, wearily. 'The Vanderburg feed. It's the only inorganic compound that any of my animals have had lately.'

'What about the other farmers?' asked Jo.

'We'll have to find out.'

'I need to run some tests on this feed,' said Hawley. 'Break it down, find out what exactly it's comprised of.'

Tyler nodded.

'And then what?' Jo asked.

'I'm going to see how long the bacteria survive for,' Hawley told her. 'I need to know as much as possible about it if I'm going to help. Get me a sample of it.'

Tyler turned and headed for the door. Jo followed.

'I'll be in touch, Dan,' he said.

'Where are we going now?' she asked.

'Visiting,' Tyler said, enigmatically.

They sprinted across to the waiting landrover and climbed in and, in seconds, were heading out towards Stuart Nichols's farm.

Hawley stood before the bathroom mirror, reluctant to turn on the light above it. As if the sight of his own face were too abhorrent to him. But finally he did so, wincing painfully as the fluorescent sputtered into life. The vet inspected his skin, both surprised and anxious by its pale, dry appearance. He put a tentative finger to his cheek and rubbed, watching as a thin coil of skin came away. It left a red patch beneath and Hawley swallowed hard.

Perhaps Tyler was right. Perhaps there *was* some kind of virus going around.

The vet moaned and pressed both hands to his temples. The light seemed to sear his eyeballs until he could stand it no longer. He shot out a hand and switched if off.

In the silence of the bathroom he listened to his own low, guttural breathing. His body felt tight, his skin itched. With clumsy fingers he began unfastening his shirt finally pulling it free to expose the wasted flesh beneath.

Skin was coming off in great long tendrils, hanging from him like leprous rolls.

Hawley sucked in a frightened breath. He pulled at one of the coils and it came free, much like sunburnt flesh, but it felt moist. He dropped it into the sink and tried to wash it away. His throat was dry and sore and he scooped a handful of water from the swiftly flowing tap. It made him feel sick and he steadied himself against the basin, gazing through bloodshot eyes at his own ghastly visage.

He pulled another of the flesh coils from his chest, held it in his hand for a second, then pushed it into his mouth and chewed hungrily.

Twenty-five

The windows of the landrover were open but the slight breeze which they allowed in offered no respite from the scorching heat. Tyler wiped a hand across his forehead and brushed away the film of perspiration. Above them, the sun blazed with unrelenting fury.

Jo tossed the butt of her cigarette out of the window and gazed at the surrounding countryside. The road which led out of Wakely towards Stuart Nichols's farm was flanked on both sides by thick forest and gently sloping hills but, as they left the town further behind, the land flattened into rolling fields.

Ahead of them on the right, Jo spotted something.

'What's that?' she asked, pointing.

Tyler smiled and slowed down as they reached it.

'It's Wakely football club,' he told her.

'It used to be one of the best equipped non-League

clubs in the country. The old chairman was a builder. Now he's dead the whole place has gone to ruin.'

The ground was compact, surrounded on all sides by a high wooden fence which was now broken in many places. The six floodlight staunchions still rose into the air although somewhat less majestically than in the past. The steel girders were rusted, weeds and overgrown grass lapping at their bases like some kind of floral sea. The smaller stands were roofed with corrugated iron looking more like enlarged sheds and they too carried a patina of rust, so bad in some places that there were holes in them. The pitch was like a jungle, infested with weeds. Grass grew wildly in places but, in others, it had been trampled flat. The kids from the town cycled out to the old stadium in the summer and played in the disused goals but there were none to be seen on this particular day. Wakely Town F.C. had gone broke in the end after many years of struggling with low attendances – the same fate which was befalling many other league and non-league clubs. However, Tyler could still remember the days when people had come from all around to watch, filling the ground to capacity.

'I used to go there with my father when I was a kid,' said the farmer as they left the place behind. Soon, it was nothing more than a vague outline in the rear view mirror.

'How far to the farm?' asked Jo.

'It's just up ahead,' Tyler told her, pointing through some trees.

He swung the landrover off the main road onto a sun-baked track. The vehicle bounced over the hardened ruts and Jo gripped the door handle to prevent herself being shaken too badly. There was a clatter in the back as the farmer's shotgun fell from its hooks and skittered across the rear of the landrover. Tyler stuck it into a low gear and slowed down, lessening the effect of the bumps. As he drove, he scanned the fields around them. His forehead puckered into a frown.

Jo glanced to one side and caught his worried expression.

'Something wrong?' she asked.

'I don't know yet,' he murmured.

The gate which led into the farm yard itself was open. Tyler swung the landrover around and brought it to a halt beside a large shed which he knew Nichols used for milking. They both got out.

Immediately, the silence seemed to wrap itself around them like a glove.

Tyler looked around and exhaled deeply.

'Where the hell are all the animals?' he mused.

There was a sty to the left but it was empty, the gate open. Even in the fields there was nothing to be seen and yet Nichols owned a herd of over 200 cattle. Tyler wandered into the milking shed, alert for any sign or sound of movement. Jo followed him, wrinkling her nose at the cloying stench inside the shed. It seemed even hotter inside the metal construction, like walking into an oven.

Tyler was the first one to spot the dead cow.

It was lying near the far exit of the shed and he walked cautiously across to it. The buzzing of flies could clearly be heard and there were dozens of the things crawling on the carcass. Tyler got as close as he needed to and peered at the cow. Its eyes were open, its tongue lolling from one side of its open mouth. Flies crawled eagerly over the glassy orbs. There were no external signs of damage to the animal. No wounds. No blood. He and Jo stood there for long moments, gazing down at the body, then they turned and headed outside once more.

The yard was rectangular, sheds and barns forming the enclosure which led up to the farm house itself.

Lying in the open doorway of another barn were two dead pigs – big boars, saddlebacks by the look of them.

Tyler held up a hand for Jo to stay back, then he crossed to the door of the barn and looked in, careful to avoid the carcasses. The stench from them was appalling, exposed, as they were, to the sun. And, this time, as well as flies, the carcasses had drawn the attention of some ants. The insects crawled frenziedly over the bodies, some of the flies feasting on a gaping sore near one boar's ear.

Inside the barn were a number of pens, designed to hold pigs, very similar to the ones Tyler had on his own farm.

The gates to every single one were open, the animals gone.

'What is it?' asked Jo, appearing at his shoulder.

'See for yourself,' he said.

She peered into the barn, then stepped outside again, almost tripping over one of the dead boars. She looked down and noted with disgust that a large blow-fly was just disappearing into the animal's nostril.

'What could have killed them, Vic?' she asked.

'There's no sign of injury on any of them,' said the farmer. He shrugged helplessly.

'A disease?' she said, cryptically.

'Could be. But where the bloody hell are the rest of the stock?'

He turned and headed towards the farm house itself. It was a two-storey, pebble-dashed building with a grey slate roof and a genuine nineteenth-century chimney stack. In fact, the whole building looked somewhat anachronistic amongst the modern machinery which lay around in the yard.

As they approached the house, Jo noticed that the curtains, both upstairs and down, were drawn.

Tyler reached the front door and knocked hard.

It swung open.

'Stuart. Bet,' he called. 'It's Vic Tyler.'

Silence.

'We'd better take a look inside,' said Jo.

They walked into the hall, squinting in the gloom.

'Stuart,' Tyler shouted once more, passing into the sitting room. He bumped his leg on a table and cursed. It was so dark in the room. The place smelt fusty, the humidity wrapping itself around them like a sweaty glove. Jo felt her T-shirt sticking to her back and she ran both hands through her thick hair.

Tyler pushed open the door to the kitchen.

There was some food on the table. A piece of cheese and a couple of slices of bread, the edges curled up. The silence in the room was broken, yet again, by the loud buzzing of flies.

'Let's try upstairs,' said Tyler, leading the way.

As he opened the door from the hallway to the staircase he had to stop for a moment. The steps were immersed in a blackness so total it was virtually impossible to see a hand in front of him. He moved cautiously, slipping on a step half way up.

'Shit,' he grunted and continued his ascent, finally reaching the landing. There, he was grateful to find that the powerful rays of the sun had managed to find a chink in the curtains and a single powerful ray of light lit up the area. Jo joined him and they approached the first of three doors which confronted them. Tyler knocked loudly on the closest before turning the handle.

'Stuart,' he shouted.

They walked into the room.

It was empty. The bed was unmade, the sheets rumpled, one pillow lying on the floor close by. The room smelt of copper, a strange metallic smell which reminded the farmer of rotting meat.

'Let's try the next one,' he said.

He repeated the same procedure, banging loudly on the door, calling Nichols' name and then entering.

It seemed darker in the second room, a blanket having been pinned across the window as well as the drawn curtains.

Lying prone on the bed, arms by his sides, was Stuart Nichols.

Tyler and Jo moved quietly into the room, the only sound being the low, guttural breathing of the other man. His chest rose and fell almost imperceptibly, his mouth open to reveal protruding teeth. Even in the gloom, Tyler could see how pale Nichols's skin was. His hands, palms turned upward, bore the long hooked nails which both Jo and Tyler had come to recognise by now.

Tyler took a step closer, recoiling slightly from the stench which seemed to be emanating from Nichols's body. A combination of rancid sweat and an overpoweringly fetid odour which made the farmer cough.

'Stuart,' he said, reaching out a hand but not touching the motionless form of his friend.

Nichols didn't stir.

The pillow beneath his head was dirty and, as Tyler looked more closely, he saw that there were several sizeable growths of hair lying there. Not mere strands of it but thick hanks. Nichols's scalp was bared in places where the hair had come out, raw and angry as if it had been torn away.

'He looks as if he's in a coma,' said Jo. 'Maybe we ought to ring a doctor.'

There was a low rasping sound from nearby and both of them spun round, their eyes searching the gloom.

It came from behind them, from the other bed in the room.

So mesmerized had they been by the sight of Nichols, neither had noticed the hunched form of his wife lying on the other bed.

Bet Nichols was, Tyler remembered, a large woman but now, she looked as though she was suffering from anorexia. Her body, covered only by a thin nightdress, was emaciated, as if she hadn't eaten for days. For weeks. The pallor of her skin was even more alarming than that of her husband and her hair, usually done up in a bun, was hanging loose.

Tyler reached forward and shook Nichols, trying to rouse him from his deathly slumber.

'There's a phone downstairs,' said Jo, 'maybe we ought to ring a doctor.'

Tyler didn't speak, he was still gazing down at his friend. He touched Nichols's cheek, withdrawing his hand quickly as he felt how clammy the skin was but, after a moment's hesitation, he cautiously opened the other man's crusted eyelids. His eyes were dark ringed, the whites flecked with yellow, the normally steely eyes now dull and lifeless. Tyler shuddered. It was like looking at a corpse.

'Stuart,' Tyler called, shaking Nichols hard until he saw his eyelids flicker open.

He turned his head to look at Tyler, his cracked lips sliding back in a bestial sneer.

Tyler took a step backwards.

'What do you want?' Nichols croaked, trying to swing himself upright. He finally managed it and sat on the edge of the bed, head bowed.

'How long have you been like this?' Tyler asked him.

'I don't remember,' said the other farmer, sounding as if he had gravel in his throat. He put both hands to his temples and winced. Tyler crossed to the window and pulled down the blanket, then he dragged the curtains open, flooding the room with sunlight.

Nichols let out a howl. A deafening shriek torn raw from his throat, from the depths of his soul. A sound which was a mixture of rage and pain. He staggered to his feet, shielding his face from the powerful rays of the sun and Tyler looked on in horror as the flesh on his friend's arms rose swiftly into half a dozen reddening welts. The flesh was actually blistering as surely as if a red hot iron had been pressed to it.

'Shut them,' screamed Nichols.

He crashed into the bed and overbalanced, trying to slide down beside it to hide from the sunlight. He had one hand across his face, the other outstretched before him. Jo, too, saw the skin rise into a series of liquescent blisters which, all at once, burst. They left dark crimson gouges in the flesh and Nichols's fingers curled round, his nails tearing the palm of his hand.

'Shut the fucking curtains, for God's sake shut the fucking curtains,' he roared, dragging himself to his feet.

Tyler was in the process of doing what Nichols wanted when he heard the click of a shotgun hammer. The other farmer, his face now a malevolent mask of pain and anger, had snatched a twelve bore from beneath his bed and was aiming the barrels at Tyler.

'Shut them,' he bellowed once again.

Tyler complied hurriedly.

'Now get out of here,' snarled Nichols. 'Leave us.' One side of his face looked as if someone had thrust a blow torch at it. Huge suppurating sores dribbled their sticky contents down his torn cheek, one of them having formed over his left eye, nearly closing it.

Bet Nichols writhed silently on her own bed, her flesh similarly scorched. But Nichols had taken the full brunt of the intruding sunlight and he swayed uncertainly, the shotgun levelled at Tyler's stomach. He edged cautiously towards the door, ushering Jo before him.

'Get out now,' rasped Nichols, licking his swollen lips. He raised the shotgun and, for one interminable second, Tyler thought he was going to fire but, as the farmer and the American stepped out of the room, he lowered it once again.

Tyler closed the door behind him.

There were sounds of movement from inside and, a second later, Nichols burst out of the room, staggering drunkenly.

'Don't come back here,' he said. 'If you do I'll kill you.'

'Stuart, you need help,' Tyler said, his eyes never leaving the gaping mouths of the twin barrels.

'I told you, just get away from me,' Nichols growled and he stood sentinel at the top of the darkened stairs as Jo and Tyler retreated. 'And don't try sending anyone else or I'll kill them too.'

Jo was the first to reach the hallway and she pulled open the door, hurrying out into the blazing sunlight. Tyler followed a second later.

'My God,' muttered Jo. 'What the hell happened to him?'

Tyler could only shake his head vacantly.

'It must be a disease of some sort,' he said, almost incredulously.

'Rabies?'

'No. He isn't exhibiting the symptoms.'

'Hawley said that the bacteria was a new strain. Maybe he's got a new kind of rabies.'

Tyler was unconvinced.

'Did you see what the sunlight did to his skin?' said Jo. 'I mean, it burned him for Christ's sake.' There was a note of desperation in her voice. 'Vic, what are we going to do?'

'Calling the police won't help, especially after that fiasco about Anderson. They'll probably lock us both up.'

'We should get a doctor out here,' she insisted.

'You heard what he said and I believed him. If anyone sticks their head around that door he'll kill them.' They stood facing one another for a moment, then Tyler turned and headed back towards the landrover. 'Come on,' he said.

Jo hesitated, her eye caught by something close by, something which she hadn't noticed when they'd first approached the house.

To the right of the building was a small wooden shed, its door open. The sunlight was glinting on something silvery.

'Vic, come here,' she called and the farmer spun round.

Jo was standing in the doorway of the shed.

'Look at that,' she said.

Inside the shed, piled three or four high in places, were sacks of the Vanderburg multi-purpose feed.

Without a moment's hesitation, Tyler lifted one of the heavy sacks onto his shoulder and, together, they headed back to the landrover. He opened the rear door and threw the sack in alongside his own shotgun then he clambered into the driver's seat, waited until Jo was settled beside him, then turned on the engine. Tyler swung the vehicle around and floored the accelerator. The quicker they left this place the happier he'd be.

They were back in Wakely in less then ten minutes and only when they were safely back in the confines of the town did Tyler ease the pressure on his accelerator. The needle on the speedometer bounced from sixty to thirty and hovered there.

He drove slowly through the tree-lined streets, both he and Jo noticing how quiet things were. There weren't above six people moving about in the blossom-shrouded streets. Garden tools and toys lay discarded in some places, most houses had their curtains drawn and the few people who *were* moving around looked pale and lethargic.

And there was something else, something which

Tyler found even more disturbing than the absence of people, because it was even more inexplicable.

There were no dogs or cats to be seen.

Wakely was becoming a ghost town.

Carlo Fanducci lit up another cigarette, coughing as the acrid fumes burnt his chest, searing his lungs. He spat out of his open window, noticing that the sputum was flecked with blood. What the hell? It was nothing new.

Parked across the road from Dan Hawley's surgery, he had a clear view when Tyler pulled up.

The Italian watched as first the farmer then Jo clambered out, Tyler retrieving the sack of Vanderburg feed from the rear of the vehicle.

Fanducci ran an appreciative eye over Jo and sucked hard on his cigarette. The red T-shirt clung tightly to her body, highlighting the smooth swell of her breasts. Great tits, thought the Italian. He wondered what she was like in bed. A regular little ball-breaker no doubt about it.

And, he was sure now, he'd seen her somewhere before.

He watched as she followed Tyler up the path to Hawley's front door, then he lit up another cigarette, using the butt of the other one to do it. This time he didn't cough.

Fanducci loosened his tie slightly and relaxed back in his seat.

In time it would come to him. Eventually he would remember exactly who that girl was. His memory was one of the things he prided himself on. Names, places, dates. All filed away, waiting to be recalled.

A thin smile spread across his face.

The reporter from the *New York Times*. He'd seen her with that scum-bag Tony Hagen a couple of times. She'd blown the whistle on old man Scalise's rackets and he'd put out a contract on her.

Well, well. What a small world it was turning out to be. Fanducci chuckled to himself and eased the .357 from its holster. He released the cylinder, spun it once, then snapped it back into position. The Italian patted the butt gently.

Twenty-six

Helen Piper sat back on her haunches, laying the trowel before her. She was perspiring despite the fact that she only wore a bikini top and a pair of cut-off denim shorts. The sun had moved full circle in the sky and now, with the advent of afternoon, its rays weren't so powerful. Helen ran a hand through her long black hair and got stiffly to her feet. She'd been out in the garden for most of the day, digging, weeding, planting. Now she decided that it was time to go inside, she was parched. Besides, she'd have to start getting something to eat for herself and the children.

Phil wouldn't be home for another few hours. He'd gone to London on business and she didn't expect him until after seven. He'd been putting in extra hours for the last six months but still Helen was not satisfied. As she passed the pram which stood beneath the porch the sight of their five-month-old daughter, Lorraine, seemed to remind Helen just how badly they needed the money now. Of course everyone had been delighted when she'd announced that she was going to have another child, but she and Phil had already been saddled with a mortgage which they could just about pay and now, with the arrival of the baby, it looked as though they were going to struggle again.

He told her not to worry but she took no notice. It was in her nature. She worried about the bills, she worried about the children. She worried about World War Three. Helen looked in at Lorraine as she passed and smiled down at the sleeping baby. Then she padded inside and put the kettle on.

The house was unusually quiet considering her five-year-old son, Kevin, was upstairs. He'd been up there for hours and she'd not heard a peep out of him. There must be a reason why. Helen decided to find out what he was up to.

As she passed the mirror in the hall she patted her stomach approvingly. She'd worked hard to regain her figure after Lorraine's birth and now, at thirty, she was in as good shape as she'd ever been. Helen moved quietly up the stairs, hoping to surprise her son in the act if he was doing anything he shouldn't be. She tip-toed across the landing and opened the door with the 'Star Wars' poster on it.

The room was in semi-darkness, the curtains drawn.

'Kevin,' she called, unable to see him at first, angry that he'd shut out the light. Then, in the gloom, she saw him crouched by the bed. There were toy soldiers spread across the carpet, the boxes emptied wantonly.

'What are you doing up here?' she asked him, crossing to the window and pulling open the curtains. 'You've been stuck in your room all day. Go out and get some fresh air while I get your tea ready.'

'Oh Mum,' he muttered, his brown hair plastered to his forehead by perspiration. 'I'd rather play in here.'

'Outside, Kevin, please,' she insisted.

'No,' he snapped.

'I told you to go outside, it's not good for you being cooped up in here and with your curtains drawn too.'

'I don't want to go outside. Leave me alone.'

Helen slapped him across the backside.

'Don't talk to me like that, Kevin,' she said. 'Now go on.'

She ushered him out, watching as he shuffled irritably down the stairs. Helen walked into her own bedroom and peered out of the window in time to see the boy emerge in the garden below. He kicked at a stone and, hands dug in the pockets of his jeans, began wandering up and down. She pulled the window closed, leaving just enough room to let some of the late afternoon breeze in.

In the garden, Kevin Piper shielded his eyes from the glare of the sun, glancing alternately up at the window where his mother had been and then at the pram where his baby sister lay. He had a headache and his stomach felt as though he'd eaten too much but he knew that wasn't true. He hadn't been able to eat all day. He hadn't felt like it. His head hurt. He didn't like the sun. Kevin kicked a stone and it banged against the side of the pram. He looked up at the window. No sign of his mother. He picked up a stone and threw it at the pram. The impact rocked it and, from inside, Lorraine began to whimper. He smiled and picked up another stone. A larger one.

This one he hurled with all his strength.

It struck the pram near the hood and Lorraine began to cry.

The shrill sound made his head hurt more.

He threw another stone, this time lobbing it into the pram.

Lorraine screamed and began sobbing loudly.

'Shut up,' grunted Kevin. 'Shut up.'

The crying went on. Louder.

'Shut up,' he shouted, advancing towards the pram.

The window above him opened and Helen looked out. She could hear Lorraine crying, but the porch obscured her view of the pram and also of Kevin.

He gripped the pram by the handle and began to pull on it, using all his weight.

Lorraine was screaming now, her sobs punctuated with racking gasps.

'Lorraine,' Helen called. 'Kevin, what are you doing?' She left the window open and hurried out of the room.

With one final surge of strength, Kevin managed to tip the pram up. It tottered on its back wheels for a second, then pitched forward, catapulting Lorraine out onto the grass. The baby continued screaming, lying helpless on her back before Kevin who was glaring down at her.

He reached for the trowel.

Helen ran down the stairs, tripping at the bottom, nearly losing her footing. She scrambled on, tugging open doors in her haste to reach the garden.

Kevin lifted the trowel in both hands and raised it above the screaming baby.

Helen burst from the back door in time to see him bury the pointed blade in the baby's stomach.

Now it was her turn to scream.

She tried to move towards him but her legs buckled and she could only crawl. Helen saw him bring the weapon down again, this time piercing the little girl's throat. A fountain of blood erupted from the wound, most of it splattering Kevin who bent his head to the jetting flow of crimson, allowing it to flood into his mouth, swallowing hungrily.

Helen Piper passed out.

Twenty-seven

'The one on the right is the broken-down Vanderburg feed, the one on the left is from the bloodstream of the calf.'

Hawley stepped back from the twin microscopes and invited Tyler to look. The farmer pressed his eye to the first of the magnifying instruments and peered at the rapidly moving organisms on the slide beneath. Then he passed to the next one. He looked at Hawley but said nothing. Jo was the next to inspect the findings. It was she who broke the brooding silence.

'They're identical,' she said.

Hawley nodded.

'The same strain of bacteria is present in both the calf's blood and the Vanderburg feed.'

'So the inorganic compound which caused the trouble with the animals *is* the one in the feed? said Tyler.

Hawley nodded.

'But what it is I don't know. It's bacteria, that's true, but what I'm getting at is the fact that the compound itself is made up of proteins. From a breakdown of the Vanderburg feed the other constituents are what you'd expect to find in any animal feed. Maize, barley, wheat, that kind of thing. It's just this protein that shouldn't be there.'

Tyler exhaled deeply.

'What do you mean, it shouldn't be there?' He looked agitated.

'It's been specially introduced into the feed. Manufactured and then added. But it's a synthetic protein. It has no peptide links.'

Tyler held up a hand.

'Look, Dan, can you keep it in a language we can all understand?' he asked.

Hawley apologized, then continued.

'A protein molecule is made up of hundreds of thousands of amino-acid molecules. They're joined together by peptide links. By combining with oxygen, the amino-acid forms bonds which help keep the protein molecule together. The proteins in the Vanderburg feed have not been synthesized from amino-acid. They've been created artificially. That's another reason why the bacteria are still flourishing when they should have been dead ages ago, the proteins have been created from some kind of autotrophic organism. From something inorganic.'

'Man-made, like you said before,' Jo added.

Hawley nodded.

'That's right. This bacteria is virtually indestructible.'

A heavy silence fell over the trio in the room. The vet looked at his two companions, wondering if what he had said had made any sense to them. From the worried looks on their faces he assumed that it had. Tyler peered into the microscopes once more.

'Who could create protein like this?' he asked.

'Someone with very specialized knowledge in this particular field.'

'Like a research scientist?' said Tyler, looking at Jo.

'Anderson,' she said, quietly.

The farmer nodded.

'But why should the protein be consumed by bacteria?' asked Tyler.

'Because with normal protein molecules if you immerse them in water or salt solutions they form colloids. It's like a protective mechanism. These proteins are artificial, they have no protection so, after a while, they simply become engulfed by bacteria which feed off them.'

Tyler wiped a thumb across his eyebrow and swallowed hard.

'There's something else,' said Hawley, crossing to one of the dissection tables where the body of the weaner lay covered by a sheet. He pulled it back, pointing to a small patch of grey coloured skin on the animal's side. 'Spores,' he said. 'The same ones that have been showing up in the bloodstreams and stomachs of the other animals.'

'Have they moved to the outer skin?' asked Tyler.

Hawley nodded.

'On a living animal they'd be invisible.'

'My God,' said Jo. 'What does it mean?'

The vet swallowed hard.

'It means that the idea about a virus spreading through Wakely, amongst its *human* population, is more than likely right,' he announced, wearily.

'But how?' Jo wanted to know. 'You said you didn't know how it was communicated.'

'I didn't before today,' the vet told her.

'So,' demanded Tyler. 'What's the answer?'

'All animals fed on the Vanderburg multi-purpose feed are likely to be carrying this bacteria in them, some more advanced than others. The bacteria, once it has formed spores, then transfers itself to the skin of the animal, sometimes on the hide itself, sometimes in the first layer of muscle.' He paused. 'Anyone who's eaten meat is liable to be infected.'

'Oh God,' muttered Tyler.

'Beef, pork, lamb, mutton, sausages, pies. *Anything* that contains meat is more than certainly contaminated and anyone consuming that meat will be infected.'

'What about poultry and fish?' asked Tyler.

'It hasn't affected them. The feed, as far as I can gather was only designed for use on larger stock.'

'That's something at least,' said Jo.

'At Stuart Nichols's farm we found some dead animals,' Tyler told the vet. 'Could the bacteria have killed them?'

'Some bacteria, once they've finished with the host animal or plant, form spores in order to disperse. To move around. Most are air carried, others water carried.'

'What are you getting at?' asked the farmer.

'We don't know what form the dispersal of these spores takes,' Hawley said. 'The spores from the dead animals you found may already be in the air.'

'Then other people could be infected with this virus?' said Jo. 'People outside Wakely?'

Hawley was silent for long moments.

'Look, at the moment, the only thing I know for sure is that it's confined to animals fed on the Vanderburg compound. They're the ones carrying and transmitting the virus.'

There was another troubled silence.

'Anyone eating meat is at risk,' Hawley reiterated.

Tyler sucked in a weary breath.

'Have you any idea what this disease or virus might be, Dan?' he wanted to know.

'None at all,' the vet said. 'I'm not a doctor.'

The farmer looked at Hawley, noticing the paleness of his skin, the deep black rings around his eyes, the yellowed whites so heavily veined.

Hawley looked at him, aware that he was being stared at. He squinted as the bright lights overhead seemed to sear his eyes.

'Are you feeling all right?' Tyler asked.

'Yes,' he said, defensively. 'Shouldn't I be?'

'Just wondered.'

Hawley tried to swallow but his mouth tasted dry. He said nothing.

'I need to use your phone,' said Tyler.

Hawley motioned him through into reception, keeping his head bowed.

The farmer passed through into the other room and picked up the receiver. He thought for a moment, then dialled. At the other end the phone began to ring.

He let it ring a dozen times, then tried again.

There was still no answer from Wakely's doctor's surgery.

Tyler pressed the cradle down, listening to the persistent buzz for long seconds. There was no point in driving over to the surgery. He felt instinctively that it would prove fruitless. There was obviously no one there.

He dialled Ben Thurston's number.

Nothing.

He tried Reg Gentry's farm.

It was the same story.

Tyler hesitated for a moment, then dialled Thurston's farm once more. God, he hoped nothing had happened to the old boy. As he stood listening to the ringing at the other end, Tyler frowned, thoughts of his own father suddenly coming, unbidden, into his mind. Perhaps, he reasoned, it was because he identified old Ben so closely with his own late father. It would be like losing a parent all over again if Ben was dead.

The phone was still ringing.

'Come on, come on,' muttered Tyler, gripping the receiver more tightly.

He actually had it poised over the cradle when he heard the click which signalled that it had been picked up. He lifted it swiftly to his ear.

'Hello,' he said. 'Ben?'

Tyler heard low, guttural breathing.

'Ben. Is that you?'

A cough.

'It's Vic Tyler.'

'What do you want?'

He recognized the voice. It belonged to Frank Thurston, the eldest of Ben's boys. But the voice had a harsher, deeper quality to it which it didn't usually possess.

'Are you all right?' asked Tyler.

'I'm all right.' The voice was becoming weaker.

There was a long silence.

'Frank, let me talk to Ben will you?'

Another long silence.

'Frank, are you still there?'

'Still here.'

'I want to talk to Ben, is he there?'

There was a bang and Tyler heard footsteps shuffling away from the phone.

'Frank,' he called.

Jo, meantime, had appeared at his elbow.

'Did you reach anyone?' she asked.

Tyler held up a hand for her to be quiet.

More silence. A hiss of static.

'Hello, Vic, what can I do for you?'

Tyler smiled as he recognized Thurston's voice, as bright and cheery as usual.

'Ben, are you feeling OK?' asked Tyler.

'*I* am, but I can't say the same for my boys,' Thurston told him. 'They both look like death warmed up, they've been like it for a few days now. I've tried getting the doctor but there's no bloody answer from the surgery.'

Tyler exhaled deeply.

'What's on your mind, Vic?' Thurston asked.

Tyler looked at Jo. Should he tell Thurston about the virus?

'Nothing Ben, I called Reg Gentry's place but I couldn't reach him. I thought I'd try you. There's nothing wrong.'

'Well then, if you'll excuse me I'll get back outside, I'm doing everything here at the moment.' He chuckled.

Tyler nodded.

Thurston hung up.

'So,' Jo said. 'Not everyone's infected.'

'Not everyone.'

She reached for the phone.

'What are you doing?' he asked.

'Calling my paper, someone's got to know what's happening here,' she announced.

'Don't mention the virus,' Tyler said.

'Why, Vic? The people in Wakely need help.'

'Well, they're not going to get it by having reporters swarming all over them.'

She stepped back and looked deeply at him.

'What's that supposed to mean?' she demanded.

'If you tell your paper what's going on, word will spread. There'll be newsmen from all over the country converging on Wakely.'

'The public have a right to know what's happening. Especially if Vanderburg Chemicals are in back of all this. People's lives might be at risk, we don't know if this virus or disease or whatever it is can kill.'

'Exactly. That's why we don't want more people in the bloody town. They might pick it up, carry it to other places.'

'Goddamit, Vic, this is one hell of a story. Don't try to get in my way. The rest of the country has a right to know.'

'All right,' he said, softly, his voice muted but full of anger. 'Ring your office.' He lifted the receiver and pushed it towards her. 'Do it.'

She took it from him and dialled.

He saw her forehead wrinkle into a frown.

'What's wrong?' he asked.

She flicked the cradle.

'The line's dead.'

She tried again but still there was nothing.

She dialled her own home number.

No sound. Not even a hiss of static.

'The internal lines were all right,' he said.

Jo looked at the receiver for a moment then replaced it.

'Wait,' said Tyler, taking it from her. He dialled 100

and waited for the operator to answer. 'What's your home number?' he asked Jo.

She told him.

Tyler asked the operator to connect him with the number.

There was a moment's silence then a metallic voice told him: 'I'm afraid the number you have requested is no longer in use.'

Jo snatched the receiver from him.

'I want Arkham 62671,' she said.

'The number you have requested is no longer in use.'

Tyler left her with the recalcitrant phone and scuttled back into the surgery. He found Mandy Potter standing beside Hawley. She smiled at the farmer.

Jo re-entered the room a moment later, a worried expression on her face.

'They won't connect me with anywhere outside Wakely,' she said.

Mandy looked surprised.

Tyler glanced down at his watch and saw that it was nearly 7.00 p.m.

'There might be something on the local news,' he said, hopefully.

Mandy led them into the sitting room and turned on the television.

A blue screen greeted them, words spelt out in red letters gleaming like fresh blood against the glowing background:

THERE HAS BEEN A TRANSMITTER FAILURE
NORMAL SERVICE WILL CONTINUE SHORTLY.

Mandy tried the other channels but it was the same on each one. She excused herself and hurried upstairs to try the portable.

'Where's the nearest transmitter?' asked Jo.

'It's in Ducton, about thirty miles from here,' Tyler told her.

Mandy returned a few moments later.

'It's the same message,' she announced.

Tyler switched off the set, gazing at the blank screen for a second.

Through the open door into the surgery he could see Hawley slumped forward across one of the work-tops.

'Is he all right?' the farmer asked.

'He's been a bit under the weather lately,' Mandy explained. 'But he won't go to the doctor.' She shrugged.

'We'd better go,' said Tyler. Both he and Jo left via the surgery. 'Dan,' he called and Hawley turned. 'If you find anything else, anything at all, call me.'

Hawley nodded.

Tyler closed the door behind them as they left. They hurried from the surgery to the waiting landrover and climbed in.

The sky was stained darkly with the colour of the dying sun. Dusk settled over the countryside, the evening clouds gathering in the distance to form a purple shroud which would soon blacken to form the cloak of night.

Twenty-eight

The cassette whirred to a stop and ejected with a loud click.

'Oh sod it,' grunted Gordon Thompson.

Beneath him, her blonde hair plastered across her face, Tina Phillips moaned softly. As he went to pull away she held him close, the touch of their naked bodies causing sensations in her which she did not want to curtail.

'Leave it,' she whispered, running her fingers through his long brown hair.

She leant forward and kissed him, their tongues probing urgently against one another. Tina drew Thompson's bottom lip between her teeth and sucked gently, chuckling as she did. They broke and he rolled to one side, allowing her searching hand to find his erection. She began to move it rhythmically up and down the shaft, bringing her right leg over so that the sensitive area between her legs was rubbing against Thompson's thigh. He felt her wetness on his skin, mingling with the perspiration which was already there.

They had been living together for three months and, to Gordon Thompson, it seemed as if they'd spent all their time in bed. Not that he was complaining. Tina, twenty years old and a year younger than himself, was always eager. Her sexuality knew no bounds. They had never had much time together before, their love-making confined to hurried lunch hours at her home or snatched evenings at friends' dwellings. But now, in the security of their own place, they were taking full advantage.

She leant forward and kissed him again before sliding down and nibbling the flesh of his shoulder, drawing it between her white teeth, nipping him. He groaned, the pain of the small pinch tempered by the building pleasure he was feeling from her hand.

Still stroking his erection, she raised herself onto her knees and turned slightly. Thompson slipped a hand between her legs, his fingers tracing a pattern inside her thigh, probing at her liquescent cleft. He felt her stiffen as he gently stroked the hard bud of her clitoris.

Tina sucked at his chest, leaving a red mark, then

she lapped her way down to his stomach, repeating the procedure.

This time she bit a little too hard and Thompson let out a small yelp of pain but he said nothing, tensing as he felt her hand speeding up on his penis. Allowing him to move his eager fingers inside her, she sat back and looked into his face and, in the darkness of the room, he noticed how her eyes seemed to be ablaze. He had known her passion was intense but he'd never seen her quite so restless as tonight. She kissed him again, fiercely. This time she took his lip between her teeth and sucked harder.

'Jesus,' he gasped, pulling his head away and raising a hand to his mouth.

She had drawn blood.

'Be careful, love,' he said, dabbing a tentative finger at the small gash in his bottom lip.

She didn't speak but merely bent forward again and, this time, Thompson felt her warm breath on his swollen penis head. She manoeuvred herself above him, lowering her slippery sex towards his mouth. His tongue darted forward and he himself felt waves of pleasure run through him as she began to nibble at his stiff organ, finally slipping it into her mouth.

Tina's saliva mingled with the clear liquid which was seeping from the head of his shaft. He thrust forward into her hot mouth.

He felt her stiffen as, for his own part, he lapped at her vagina. She rubbed herself harder against him as she felt her orgasm approaching. Her eyes glowed and Thompson felt her chin nuzzling his pubic hairs as she continued to suck at him, her teeth raking his erection.

For fleeting seconds he realized what was happening.

She bit his penis in half, severing muscle and veins as she clamped her teeth together.

He let out a shriek of agony but it was muffled as she thrust herself at him. Thompson blacked out at once.

Tina sucked hard at the torn root of his manhood, eagerly swallowing the blood which pumped from it, staining the sheets beneath and gushing over his thighs. Her sharp nails tore his scrotum to bloody streamers, shredding the tender flesh.

She lay on top of him, her lips and chin dark with his life fluid.

Finally satiated, she rolled onto her back, ignoring the stench which emanated from Thompson's body.

The breeze which wafted in from the window stirred the strands of her hair. Those that weren't matted with blood.

She closed her eyes, a thin smile on her crimson lips.

PART TWO

'Turn up the lights, I don't want
to go home in the dark . . .'
– O. Henry

'And the day burns through their blood,
like a white candle through a shuttered
hand . . .'
– Roy Campbell

Twenty-nine

The meshed glass partition swung open as Tyler banged on it. The sound of squealing hinges was deafening in the unearthly silence of the police station. Even the two big fans which normally stood over the entry way were silent, the blades immobile.

'There's got to be someone here,' said the farmer, glancing out of the window to where the two Panda cars were parked.

During the short drive to the station that morning, they had seen perhaps two dozen people on the streets. No more.

Tyler reached round and slipped the bolt on the half-door. Jo followed him through. They stood behind the desk, the ticking of the clock above them the only noise in the stillness. The radio stood nearby and Tyler flicked at the 'On' switch. There was a loud crackle and a scream of feedback. He adjusted the volume.

'Ever used one of those things before?' Jo asked him.

Tyler shook his head, fiddling with the frequency regulator in an attempt to pick up a signal of some kind. All he got was a fluctuating buzz and occasional bouts of silence.

'Shit,' he muttered, glaring angrily at the radio. 'We'd better have a look around, the place can't be deserted.'

Jo moved towards a closed door on the left but Tyler stepped in front of her, his hand closing on the knob.

They found themselves in what he took to be the rest

room. There was a large notice board with rotas pinned to it and a couple of photos of cars. On the far wall was a dart board, the arrows jammed into the bull's-eye. The blinds were drawn in the room, plunging it into deep gloom but, in the corner, Tyler saw someone sitting down.

'Who's there?' a voice asked and Tyler recognized it as belonging to Don Mason.

He moved towards the sergeant who tried to rise from his seat. It seemed an effort and he gave up finally, sinking back into the plastic covered chair.

'Don, are you all right?' asked Tyler, drawing closer to the policeman. As he did, he saw that the sergeant's normally lustrous beard was greying, patches of raw skin showing through in places where the bristles had come out in thick hunks. As he raised his hands to his temples, Jo noticed how long his nails had become, the cuticles cracked and riven.

'I feel so bloody tired,' croaked Mason, accepting the hand which Tyler offered.

The farmer shuddered involuntarily as he felt the cold clamminess of the policeman's flesh against his own.

Mason swayed drunkenly for a second, then seemed to regain his footing.

'Where are the other men?' asked Tyler.

'Not here,' Mason told him, heading towards the door. He recoiled slightly as he reached the light and stood in the frame, momentarily frozen. He narrowed his eyes and groaned, one hand pressed to his temple, the other supporting him.

'I don't know what the hell is wrong with me,' he said.

'How long have you felt like this?' Jo asked him.

He shrugged.

'Started to feel bad yesterday afternoon. The wife, she's . . .' he hesitated, as if he'd forgotten what he was going to say next.

Jo and Tyler helped him into the other room where he groaned aloud at the lights and the sun pouring through the unshaded window.

'Is your wife ill too?' Jo wanted to know.

'I couldn't wake her up this morning. So tired.'

Tyler and Jo exchanged anxious glances.

'Look, Don, we've got to contact someone outside Wakely,' explained the farmer.

'Phone them.'

Jo picked up the nearby phone but the line was, as she'd expected, dead. She shook her head and replaced the receiver.

'The lines are down. You'll have to use the radio,' Tyler insisted. 'Get in touch with the Arkham police.'

'Why?'

'Because people here in Wakely could be in danger. We need help.'

'A virus of some kind,' Jo added.

'What the hell are you going on about?' rasped Mason.

'Call the Arkham police,' Tyler said, firmly.

'No good. We're out of range. Arkham's too far from here, besides, they use a different frequency.'

'So find the frequency,' the farmer demanded.

Mason rounded on him.

'They're out of range,' he growled, his yellowed eyes glowing, the veins in them bulging.

'Try,' roared Tyler.

The two men faced each other for a moment, then Mason nodded painfully and reached for the modulator. He turned the dial, the high pitched screams of interference making him wince. Voices drifted, phantom-like, over the air-waves until, finally, Mason grunted and raised the microphone to his mouth.

'This is Wakely Police Station,' he croaked. 'Sergeant Don Mason speaking. Come in Arkham. Over.'

The hum of static was punctuated by sharp crackles, then a distant voice answered:

'This is Arkham. Go ahead. Over.'

Tyler took the microphone from Mason who offered no resistance.

'Arkham Police Station?' said the farmer.

'Affirmative. Please identify yourself.'

'Vic Tyler, I live in Wakely. Listen, send some men over here now I . . .'

'Are you a policeman?'

'No, I told you, I live in Wakely. Will you – '

Again he was cut short.

'You have no right to be using police property, it's an offence.'

'There's no one else here you silly bastard,' snarled the farmer. 'The people in Wakely are in danger, send some men. It's urgent.'

'We've received no reports from Wakely to that effect.'

'That's because the policemen here are gone. For God's sake listen to me . . .'

A hiss of static.

'Did you hear what I said?' Tyler rasped.

'We have received no reports concerning Wakely.'

'Well I'm giving you a fucking report now,' the farmer shouted. 'People are dying. We need help.'

'There have been no formal reports made.'

Tyler gripped the microphone until it threatened to break.

'Let me speak to someone in charge,' he demanded.

'We have received no formal reports. Over and out.'

There was a loud click and then silence.

Tyler hurled the microphone to one side in a paroxysm of rage.

'Bastards,' he fumed. 'Stupid bloody bastards.' He looked down at Mason who was shielding his face from the encroaching sunlight. He pushed past them, heading back into the darkened rest room.

Tyler exhaled deeply.

'There's nothing we can do here,' he said. 'Let's go.'

Tyler was surprised to see one or two members of staff present in 'The King George' hotel. The bar was open and there was even a man sitting on one of the stools sipping at a pint of beer. A rotund chambermaid was hoovering the carpet in reception. She looked up briefly as Jo and the farmer entered.

The American crossed to the desk and rang the bell, wondering if Mark Bates was going to appear. She thought back to the incident the other night when she'd discovered him devouring the raw meat. Was he going to emerge from the staff room with blood dripping from his hands? She hurriedly dismissed the thought.

'I'll have to get your key, miss,' said the chambermaid, appearing beside her. 'There's only a few of us here today.'

'Why is that?' asked the journalist.

'Some of the staff are off sick,' the maid explained. 'My husband, he's not been too good lately.'

'What's wrong with him?' asked Tyler.

'He looks so pale, sir, and during the day all he wants to do is sleep. He's not so bad at night though.' She shrugged.

'But *you* feel OK?' said Jo.

'I'm fine thank you.' The maid looked puzzled and she coloured slightly beneath the combined gaze of Jo and Tyler.

'Is there something wrong?' she asked, handing Jo her key.

The American smiled.

'No.'

The maid crossed to her hoover.

'It seems pointless doing this,' she mused.

'Why,' Tyler wanted to know.

She looked up.

'Well, what with there being hardly any guests here. And I can't see us getting many more in the near future the way things are.' She leant on the cleaner like a navvy on a shovel. 'I'll tell you something else, a lot of people have left the town. Don't ask me why but only two days ago the family who live next door to us moved out. And I've noticed how many people seem to be feeling off colour. You know, ill. I can't understand it.' She paused, shaking her head. 'It's a good job Mr Bates isn't here.'

'Who *is* Bates?' asked Jo.

'The Manager,' explained the maid. 'Why?'

Jo shook her head.

'I was just curious.'

The three of them stood in silence for another moment, then the maid started up her cleaner.

'I suppose I'd better get this done all the same,' she said and bustled off across reception.

Jo and Tyler headed for the lifts, both of which stood empty before them. For some unaccountable reason, the sight of people in the reception and lounge made them feel easier but, as the lift bumped to a halt and the doors slid back, the corridor which stretched away ahead of them seemed curiously forbidding.

They reached Jo's room and went inside.

It was large, containing a double bed, a sideboard and even a desk. The wardrobe had mirrors on its doors and through a white door was the bathroom. A latticed window looked out onto the car park at the back of the building. There were tea-making facilities so Jo filled the kettle from the tap in the bathroom and plugged it into the socket nearby.

Tyler sat down on the edge of the bed.

'If there are people leaving the town, like the maid

said, then that would be one explanation why there aren't so many about.'

'And the ones who haven't left?' said Jo, cryptically.

'We've got to assume they're infected with this virus, whatever it is.'

'You know I've noticed with a lot of them, sunlight or artificial light frightens them. It hurts them. Like that guy Nichols.' She sucked in an anxious breath. 'What kind of virus makes people afraid of the light?'

There was a long silence broken finally by Jo.

'I was thinking about what Hawley said. About the synthetic, man-made proteins in the Vanderburg feed. Geoffrey Anderson *would* have known about it. He would have known the effects it was going to have too. Tests must have been done.'

'What are you getting at, Jo?'

'That night he tried to talk to me, maybe that was what it was about. Anderson must have known what was in the feed. Someone didn't want him shooting his mouth off.'

'He may have known the effect it would have on animals but how could he have known what it would do to human beings?'

'I think he was told to keep quiet. When he wouldn't someone shut him up. Killed him.'

'Come on, Jo, this isn't New York,' said the farmer, wearily.

'Then where is he?' she barked. 'He was scared that night he rang me. He knew someone was on to him.'

'Like who?'

'That's what we've got to find out.'

Tyler exhaled deeply.

'We don't know he's dead. We don't know anything.'

'We know that this town is infected with some kind of virus. We know it's spread by eating contaminated meat. And we know that the victims can't come out in sunlight.'

'That adds up to nothing,' said Tyler. 'Why hasn't everyone in Wakely got this virus? Why haven't you and I caught it?'

'You don't eat meat. I haven't touched any since I arrived in Wakely.'

Tyler stroked his chin thoughtfully.

'If Vanderburg Chemicals are responsible for the virus,' he said, slowly. 'They wouldn't want any publicity. No outside interference.'

'You think they're behind the phone and TV blackouts?' Jo said, incredulously.

'It's a thought, although I doubt if they'd be able to do anything on that scale without help.'

'Help from whom?'

'That's what we've got to find out. We've got to get inside Vanderburg Chemicals.'

Jo looked at him, dumbstruck.

'Are you kidding? That place is like Fort Knox.'

'There has to be a way. We've got no choice.'

'When do we do it?'

'Tonight,' he announced, flatly.

'And in the meantime?'

'I think it would be best if I moved in here with you. I'm not leaving you alone. Not now.'

She kissed him softly on the cheek and he brushed a strand of hair from her forehead.

'What about your farm?' she asked.

'What farm?' he said, sardonically. 'Diseased animals are no good to a farmer. They'll have to be destroyed.' He got to his feet. 'I'll be back in an hour or two,' he said. Then he was gone.

The kettle had begun to boil but Jo didn't notice it. She was gazing out of the window, watching the scudding clouds.

It was just after 1.00 p.m.

Thirty

The oak table sparkled like ice beneath the fluorescent lights. The room smelt of polish and nicotine, the air filled with a bluish haze. It was a large room, twenty feet wide and thirty long, the table being its centre point. The white painted walls bore framed pictures, including an original Turner over the fire place. The painting looked somewhat anachronistic set over an electric fire. Indeed, the entire room seemed to be caught in a kind of chronological limbo. A clash of cultures and times mirrored in what it contained. Antique furniture sat side by side with such modern encumbrances as a computer terminal which, at present, showed a blank screen. The windows, large and airy, were double-glazed, offering added sound proofing.

Five men sat around the table, each with a note pad and pencil before him.

The wall clock ticked noisily in the stillness, the hands having crawled round to 3.00 p.m.

Sir Oliver Thorndike looked at his own watch and coughed exaggeratedly as if to still a babble of conversation, but all eyes were on him anyway.

Thorndike was fifty-three, a tall but heavy set man with thick white hair and sad eyes. He had been knighted in 1978 for his work in the field of genetics. He had worked for Vanderburg Chemicals since 1980. He coughed once more, brushing an imaginary speck of dust from the sleeve of his navy blue suit.

'Gentlemen,' he said. 'If we could begin.'

There were nods of approval.

Thorndike looked at the man closest to him on the right. Charles Muir finished lighting his pipe and sucked contentedly on it.

'The new synthetic compound is almost completed,'

said the older man, his voice a harsh Scots drawl. 'It should be ready for introduction within a week.'

'It will be treated with ultra-violet rays this time,' added Richard Neville.

At forty-five, Neville was the youngest man at the table. He pushed his glasses back on his nose and shuffled in his seat.

'It should have been treated before,' said Muir.

'We had no way of knowing what the effects of the synthetic protein would be,' Neville protested.

'You're a bacteriologist,' the Scot said, challengingly. 'You should have had some idea.'

Thorndike raised a hand.

'Gentlemen, please,' he said. 'We all appreciate that the first batch of the additive was, how shall we say, unproven. The results were merely unfortunate.'

'Why was it not thoroughly checked?' Muir persisted.

'For God's sake,' snapped Martin Glendenning. 'The damage is done now. We made a mistake. That mistake can be rectified this time.'

'Whatever we do now can't be of any help to the people of Wakely,' Muir said, chewing on the stem of his pipe.

'We all knew we were taking a chance,' said Thorndike, sweeping back his white hair. 'We were unfortunate.'

'A masterful understatement,' Muir chided.

'Do we know exactly how the viral infection is affecting the residents of Wakely?' asked Neville, toying with his wedding ring as he spoke.

Thorndike picked up a manilla file and flipped it open.

'First reports indicate that it's manifesting itself as something like pernicious anaemia. We haven't been able to discover the exact effects yet.'

'Does it really matter?' said Glendenning.

'Well, it only matters in as far as knowing its communicability,' Thorndike said. 'It seems confined to the town at the moment so it's reasonably safe to assume that the virus is passed on through ingestion of the affected meat.'

'Is there any possibility of outside interference?' asked Glendenning, plucking at the back of his hand.

'In what form?' Thorndike wanted to know.

'Police. Other authorities.'

Thorndike shook his head.

'If the need arises, we can seal Wakely off,' he said. 'From what I can gather, many of the residents have already left.'

'Infected or virus free?' Muir wanted to know.

Thorndike held up his hands.

'Charles, there's no possible way we could know who was or wasn't infected. Wakely has a population of just under 4,000. From that amount of people it would be impossible to guess how many had the virus.'

'*Try* guessing,' the Scot insisted.

Thorndike looked at the fifth man seated at the table, who was yet to speak, and then at Neville.

'From a population of 4,000,' the younger man began. 'One could expect perhaps a quarter of that number to have contracted the virus in some form.'

'What about those who aren't infected?' asked Glendenning.

'What about them?' Thorndike said.

'What's the likelihood of them contracting the virus?'

'Unless they eat the contaminated meat, they should be safe from the primary infection,' Thorndike told him.

'What about secondary infection?' asked Muir.

Thorndike exhaled deeply.

'As I said before, we have no way of knowing how or even if the virus is communicable except by ingestion.'

'There is the problem of cure,' said Neville. 'Can we find one?'

'It's not our business to find one,' snapped

Glendenning. 'This project is designed to maximize the growth of livestock by the infusion of synthetic proteins. Any adverse effects caused by that work are regrettable but, nonetheless, not our concern.'

'Not our concern,' said Muir, angrily, the pipe bouncing about in his mouth. 'We virtually wipe out an entire town and you say it's not our concern.' He paused. 'I say we should call off the project for the time being.'

A chorus of mutterings greeted his remark.

Thorndike stilled the babble and looked at the Scot.

'That is impractical and unnecessary, Charles, and you know it,' he said.

'Geoffrey Anderson agreed with me,' Muir said.

'To hell with Geoffrey Anderson.'

The voice came from the fifth man who got to his feet and walked to one of the windows which looked out into the grounds of Vanderburg Chemicals. He was tall, nearly six five and his black hair glinted beneath the lights. When he spoke it was with a strong American accent, Mid-West. He was wearing an expensive suit and, when he smiled, which was something of a rarity, a single gold tooth sparkled amidst the expanse of white enamel.

He reached into his pocket and pulled out an engraved silver hip-flask. Unscrewing the cap he took a hefty swig, then turned back to face the men around the table.

'Anderson was a pain in the ass,' said the dark haired man, vehemently. 'This project demands top secrecy at all times, that's why we're working with the co-operation of your Government.' His voice took on a hint of sarcasm. 'To further Anglo-American relations. Now if anybody else wants out that's fine with me but hear this, if one of you bastards breathes a word of what's been said in this room, you'll be wearing your asses for hats.'

John Stark took another swig from his flask, then returned to his seat. As chief financial backer to Vanderburg Chemicals he relished his own importance and was never slow to remind those around him of it too. He had founded the company three years earlier, shortly after the death of his wife, using her maiden name for the concern. She had been killed in a traffic accident, the brakes on her Trans-Am failing as she pulled in front of a Mack truck carrying a tank load of amyl nitrate. There hadn't been much left to bury.

'I don't think any of us want to leave, Mr Stark,' said Thorndike.

'Then what the hell is he bitching about?' snapped the American, pointing at Muir.

'Look, I'll work for you,' said the Scot. 'But that doesn't mean I have to stop caring about the people my work affects. Especially when it's something on this scale.'

'You win some, you lose some,' snapped Stark.

'And in this case we lost an entire town,' said Muir.

'You were the goddam scientists, you should have got it right first time. If anyone's to blame it's you.'

'Well,' said Thorndike, 'I'm sure matters have been put to rights this time.' He smiled at Stark but the gesture was not returned.

'Yeah, well there's something else.'

The men looked, vaguely, at the American.

'I'm talking about that girl and the guy in town, whoever the hell he is. They're too goddam curious.' A rare smile crept across Stark's face. 'Still, curiosity can kill more than cats.' He chuckled.

'What do you propose to do?' asked Glendenning.

'*You* spoke to the girl didn't you?' said Stark.

The older man nodded.

'She did seem rather . . . inquisitive. Especially about Anderson,' the scientist said.

'Too inquisitive.' He turned to Thorndike. 'I want

Wakely sealed off. Cops, telephones, TV, I know that's already been taken care of but, from now on, I don't want anyone leaving. I want this town sewn up tighter than a fish's ass and I mean water-tight. Make that phone call.'

Thorndike reached unhesitatingly for the phone close to him and dialled a London number. It rang for a moment, then the others sat watching as he spoke.

'I'd like to speak to the Minister,' said Thorndike.

The secretary asked for his name, then what he wanted.

'Tell him it's Erebus.'

There was a moment's silence at the other end of the line. A confusion of clicks and crackles as Thorndike was re-connected on another line.

Muir chewed on his pipe.

Stark took another swig from his hip-flask.

The other two men watched Thorndike as he moved the receiver agitatedly from one hand to the other.

Glendenning plucked at the flesh on the back of his hand.

Neville continued twisting his ring.

Thorndike suddenly became animated as he heard a voice at the other end of the phone.

'Yes, sir,' he said. 'This is Erebus.'

He swallowed hard.

'There have been difficulties. We need the town sealed off. No passage for residents or visitors.'

The voice asked what kind of difficulties.

'Project Erebus has precipitated some unforeseen confusion here. We need time to rectify the situation.'

How long, the voice wanted to know.

'Until further notice,' said Thorndike looking across at Stark.

The American nodded.

Thorndike listened for a moment.

'Yes, sir, I understand. No, there is no danger to the project itself.'

There were more hasty enquiries, then Thorndike spoke again.

'Yes, sir. Everything will be taken care of.'

He put the phone down and turned to the waiting American.

'It's done.'

'What, may I ask has been done?' Muir enquired.

'Within forty-eight hours,' Thorndike told him. 'Wakely will be completely sealed off from all outside contact.'

'How?' the Scot wanted to know.

'That's not your worry,' Stark told him.

'What's your solution, *Mr* Stark?' Muir began. 'Complete the annihilation of Wakely that was begun by Project Erebus?'

The American rounded on him.

'Listen to me,' he growled. 'This project is worth millions and we're not the only ones who are going to benefit. Why the hell do you think your Government is behind me too?' There was a long silence. 'Now, there's nothing else to be said. I don't think I have to keep you *gentlemen* from your work any longer.'

The assembled scientists rose and filed from the room. Stark took a swig from his hip-flask, then crossed to a desk in the far corner of the room. He flicked a switch on the console before him and muttered something into the intercom. A moment or two later there was a knock on the door.

'Come in,' he called.

Carlo Fanducci walked in, a cigarette hanging from his mouth. He closed the door behind him.

'The guy and the girl who've been doing the digging in town, who are they?' asked Stark.

Fanducci coughed, fighting to keep down the bitter phlegm.

'The girl's a reporter. She's from the East Side,' he said, his voice raw and gravelly. 'I knew I'd seen her someplace before. She was the one who fingered old man Scalise back in New York. She's been fucking around with this guy, Tyler, for a few days now.'

'Do you know where they are?' Stark asked.

'Tyler runs a farm about a mile outside town. The broad's staying at a hotel in Wakely. But, from what I've seen, he spends most of his time there.'

'What do they know?'

Fanducci shrugged.

'Waste them,' said Stark, flatly. 'And anyone who's with them.'

'When do you want it done?' asked Fanducci.

Stark took another swig from his flask.

'As soon as you can.'

The Italian nodded.

Thirty-one

The attic smelt fusty, the dust of neglect having settled thickly on everything. Particles of it swirled in the beam of Tyler's torch as he clambered up onto the thick rafters. It was a part of the farm house which he used to visit regularly as a youngster, sitting for hours with his father, listening as the older man spoke. Young Tyler would sit cross-legged before the man he held in awe, watching him clean his beloved guns. He had learnt all he knew about guns from his father and now, as he shone the torch around the attic, those memories came flooding back. The beam glinted on some of the trophies which hung on the walls of this most hallowed retreat. Plaques, statuettes, certificates. Everything covered by a film of dust. On the far wall, however, was a canvas sheet. Pinned at either side, it protected the valuable collection beneath.

Tyler reached forward slowly and pulled it down.

There were four shotguns on the rack. Two nickel plated Purdeys, a Franchi automatic and a single barrelled Baikal. Beneath them, in a large cupboard, were countless boxes of ammunition. Tyler still held his own Purdey by his side. It had been given to him on his sixteenth birthday by his father, the stock still bore his faded initials. They had been carved by his father.

Tyler's mother had never been keen on guns, her own brother having been wounded in a hunting accident, but Jack Tyler had taught his son how to use them carefully and skilfully. Many hours of practice and aching shoulders had turned Tyler into a proficient marksman and, at seventeen, he had won the county championships for clay pigeon shooting. Still the youngest person ever to do so.

Now he looked at his own gun and at those of his father.

Already he could feel the tears welling up inside him, not so much for the fact that the memories of his father were so strong but for the purpose to which he intended to put these beloved weapons.

He took down the top gun from the duo of Purdeys and hefted it before him. Then he selected the Franchi. That done, he unlocked the ammunition cupboard and took out as many shells as he could stuff into the pockets of his jacket. He could, he reasoned, come back for more if he needed them. Then, carrying all three weapons, he made his way back down the rickety step ladder which led up to the attic. He paused at the bottom and loaded his own gun and the other two, thumbing five cartridges into the automatic.

When he emerged into the late afternoon sunlight, Tyler felt sick and he had to steady himself against a fence for a moment.

He sucked in huge lungfuls of air, realizing what he had to do but feeling something akin to disgust with himself.

Many of the animals were already gone. Pens and fields were empty. Elsewhere, animals lay dead, some partially decomposed in the heat. But there were still three or four dozen in and around the farm.

Tyler knew they were diseased. He knew they must be destroyed but it made his task no easier. He looked up at the attic window as if expecting to see his father standing there watching him, shaking his head reproachfully as he saw what use his guns were being put to.

Tyler picked up the Franchi and worked the pump action, chambering a round. He crossed to the pig sty and looked in at the oversized weaners, raising the weapon to his shoulder.

He aimed and fired in one movement.

The first animal dropped into the mud as the roar of the shotgun was joined by another. And another. The weaners made no attempt to move as the shot tore into them and, finally, when the hammer slammed down on an empty chamber, the sty was full of carcasses. A bluish haze of smoke wafted gently into the air and the stink of cordite was strong in Tyler's nostrils.

He re-loaded and walked purposefully across to the nearest shed which housed half a dozen cows due for milking.

Tyler gritted his teeth and opened fire, tears now flowing swiftly from his stinging eyes as his ears were filled with the deafening retort of the gun and the loud bellowings of the cattle. And there was another sound.

His own moans of distress.

The smoke cleared slowly and, before it had dispersed, he was firing again. Choking back sobs, trying to keep his aim straight. His shoulder ached from the constant thudding against it of the stock as each fresh impact slammed against him.

He was muttering soundlessly to himself as he fired, passing from one shed to the other. From cattle to pigs, to sheep. The Franchi began to glow red in his hands so he dropped it and, with bloodstained hands, broke the nickel-plated Purdey and checked that it was loaded.

It was.

He gave both barrels to a large bull, watching as the animal went down as if pole-axed.

He felt hot salty tears running freely down his cheeks now because he realized that, in the thundering discharge of those shotgun blasts he was destroying not just diseased animals. He was destroying everything his father had built up. He was slaughtering his own memories. The Purdey roared in his hand.

Each blazing explosion was like an accusatory shout.

Tyler shouted aloud at each discharge, his sorrow gradually giving way to anger as he continued with his grisly task.

The ground was littered with empty shell cases, but there were always plenty more at hand.

'Vanderburg,' he muttered, his jaw set firm.

The rage seemed to grow.

'Bastards,' he growled. He would find out why this had happened. Someone would pay. Tyler was determined that somebody would suffer for what had been done.

The slaughter continued.

It took Tyler over an hour to despatch what livestock he could find on the farm. By the time he'd finished, his arms felt like lead weights. His eyes stung and his nostrils were full of the stench of gun oil and cordite. He dropped to his knees and gulped down the air, trying to ignore the pungent odour of blood which was so strong.

Finally, he got up and trudged wearily back to the house. He collected as much ammunition as he could carry and put it into the landrover with the three shotguns, then he climbed into the vehicle and sat behind the wheel for what seemed like an eternity.

'I'm sorry,' he whispered, wondering whether the words were spoken to the memory of his parents or to appease his own tortured conscience.

He started the engine and swung the vehicle out of the yard. He didn't once look back.

Jo sat on the edge of the bed listening. But for the odd sound of movement from downstairs, the hotel was in silence. The American got to her feet and crossed to her door. She paused for a moment, then opened it, peering to her right and left.

The corridor was empty, the doors to the other rooms were closed.

Jo dropped her own key into the back pocket of her jeans and quietly closed her door behind her. She moved noiselessly towards the first and nearest door and turned the knob. It wouldn't budge. She dropped to one knee and squinted through the keyhole.

The room was well lit inside, the curtains drawn back.

Jo got to her feet and moved down the corridor. It turned at right angles as it approached the lifts, both of which were stationary. The American moved to another door, glancing behind her at the lifts, as if expecting someone to emerge at any second.

She wondered how many of the guests were infected with the mysterious virus, if any. Some of the staff of the hotel certainly were – she knew that only too well after the incident with Bates – and of the other guests she knew nothing.

The second door she tried was also locked.

Jo was about to move away from it when she heard a noise from inside.

She pressed her ear to the white wood and listened.

It came again. A low, guttural rasping. Like asthmatic breathing.

She knelt once more to try and look through the key hole, but all that greeted her prying eye was darkness.

The breathing seemed to grow louder for a moment, then ceased.

The American knocked gently.

The breathing began once more, slow and strained.

Jo paused a moment longer, then moved along to a door which, she noticed, was ajar.

It was dark inside the room and she opened the door inch by inch, allowing the light to dispel the gloom.

It was as quiet as a grave in that room and Jo shuddered involuntarily as she passed across the portal and into the blackness.

The room was like her own except for the fact that it showed no signs of being inhabited. The bed was made, the smell of carpet cleaner strong in the air.

She moved towards the bathroom and pushed open the door, slapping on the light as she did so.

There was hair in the sink. Thick dark hunks of it. Not strands but tufts which had clogged the plug hole. Jo prodded at it with her key, noticing something else too. A thin, almost transparent substance which reminded her of mucous. She turned away, stifling a scream as she looked into the bath.

The white enamel was splashed with blood.

Jo swallowed hard and leant over the bath, dipping one finger tentatively into the crimson liquid.

It was fresh.

She got up and hastily left the room, intent on

returning to her own. The corridor turned at right angles again and Jo realized that she had come almost full circle in her search. Out of curiosity, she tried each door as she went. Finding every one locked.

However, the room next to hers was not locked.

The handle turned smoothly in her grip, the door opening a fraction.

The American hesitated. This was no bedroom. From the smell of freshly laundered sheets she realized that it was the linen cupboard. She wondered whether or not it was worth looking into, then something caught her eye. Something crumpled lying on the floor about two feet inside the room.

She stepped inside.

Had Jo been in the corridor, she may well have seen the lights on the lift flash brightly but, hidden inside the laundry room, she was oblivious to what was going on.

One of the lifts was rising.

Jo took a closer look at the crumpled mass on the floor, prodding it with her key.

It looked like the transparent stuff she'd seen in the sink of the other room. But what the hell was it? She looked around and found a pile of towels nearby. She pulled the top one down and wrapped it around her hand.

The lift bumped to a halt and the doors slid quietly open.

Jo picked up the sticky substance, noticing how tendrils of it hung like rotting streamers. It had a revolting familiarity about it. As she held it before her, it seemed to take on a shape.

Unfolding, the slimy mass fell away like unravelling paper.

Jo saw hair attached to it and she finally realized what she was holding.

It was a large coil of human skin, shed as a snake would shed its old hide.

She dropped it in disgust and got to her feet, backing out of the room, eyes fixed on the lump of skin as if it were a living thing.

The hand closed on her shoulder.

Jo screamed and spun round.

'Sorry,' said Tyler, apologetically.

She could only stand and stare at him, her heart hammering madly against her ribs.

'Didn't you hear the lift coming up?' he asked.

Jo shook her head.

'What's wrong?' Tyler wanted to know.

'Well,' she panted. 'Aside from the fact that I nearly had a goddam heart attack, I've found a couple of things.'

'Like what?'

'Like that.' She pointed to the sloughed skin.

Tyler knelt and glanced at it.

'Skin?' he asked.

She nodded.

'That's not all.'

Jo showed him the blood and hair in the other room, then led him to the locked bedroom where she had heard the breathing.

'There's someone asleep in there,' he said.

'It's four thirty in the afternoon,' she snapped. 'Who sleeps at this time of the day?'

'And what do you propose we do? Kick the door down?' he said. 'There's probably a perfectly logical explanation for . . .'

She cut him short.

'Don't give me that crap,' she rasped.

The door was suddenly pulled open.

Both of them stepped back, surprised to see Mark Bates standing there.

'What are you doing here?' he rasped.

'I heard you breathing,' said Jo. 'I thought maybe you were sick.'

Bates regarded them warily and, in the light, they both saw how the skin had peeled from his face and neck, leaving red and angry patches beneath. He shielded his face from the light, the thick growths of hair on the palms of his hands clearly visible.

'What do you want?' he demanded.

'Nothing,' said Tyler, pulling Jo aside. 'Sorry if we disturbed you.'

Bates glared at them, then slammed the door once more and locked it.

Jo and Tyler were left in the corridor, gazing at the closed door. It was the farmer who made the first movement, urging Jo to join him as he walked back to their own room. Once inside he locked the door behind them.

'Do you think it's safe here?' the American asked him.

Tyler nodded. He crossed to the window and looked out. Jo studied his broad outline as he stood there, unusually silent.

'Vic.' She spoke his name softly. 'What's on your mind?'

He told her what had happened at the farm prior to his return.

'My father built that place up from nothing,' he said. 'Every time I pulled that trigger it was as if I was destroying a piece of his dream.'

Jo crossed to the window and slid her arm around his waist. He pulled her closer.

'You had no choice,' she said.

The words brought him little comfort, but the sadness which had lain so heavy inside him had now turned into a knotted ball of fury. He wanted revenge.

The sun vanished momentarily behind a bank of dark cloud and, in the distance, they could both see the shadow which it cast over the land. Jo shuddered and Tyler held her tighter.

'It'll be dark in a few hours,' he said.

At 7.30 p.m. they returned to the room where they'd found Bates and, surprisingly enough, found the door open.

Tyler checked out the entire room.

Bates was gone.

Thirty-two

Night lay heavy over Wakely. An impenetrable blanket of darkness denied even the welcoming glow of the moon. A few stars glinted against the velvet back-drop but even they were mostly obscured by banks of thick cloud which spread across the gloomy heavens like ink stains on a blotter. There was a storm in the air. The heat of the day had become a cloying humidity and, even as Jo and Tyler sat in the dining room of 'The King George' prodding at the remnants of their dinners, the first low rumblings of thunder could be heard away to the north.

'The fences around Vanderburg Chemicals are electrified,' Jo began. 'If we get past those there's Security guards and patrol dogs. Vic, I'm telling you, it'd take a team of Green Berets to break in there.'

'We'll see,' said Tyler, defiantly.

'So, once we're in, assuming we can *get* in, we're not even sure what we're looking for.'

'Somebody's been doing everything they can to stop us finding out the facts about what's going on in Wakely. The only people who would need to do that are the people at Vanderburg Chemicals.' He paused. 'No phones, no television, not even any police or newsmen. The whole set up is too . . . organized to be a coincidence.'

'You said you thought that Vanderburg couldn't do anything like that without help,' she said.

'I don't. I think someone else is involved. Don't ask me who.'

'Who's powerful enough to seal off an entire town?' Jo said, the question hanging lazily in the air.

Tyler had no answer for her.

A troubled silence descended over them.

Carlo Fanducci brought the car to a halt across the street from the hotel. He lit up another cigarette and inhaled the smoke, gritting his teeth as he felt the pain begin to gnaw at his chest and throat. He coughed, wincing at the effort. Son of a bitch, he thought. It was getting worse. Fucking cancer must have eaten away most of his lung by now. What the hell, there was no good crying about it. He hawked and spat onto the pavement, the bloodied sputum looking black beneath the dull glow of the street lamp.

The lights on the front of the hotel glowed with a rare brilliance and Fanducci noticed how none of the people on the streets went near to the building.

He could see them in the gloom, moving furtively. Like tangible shadows they scuttled about in side streets and doorways, always careful to keep clear of the puddles of yellow light given off by the sodium lamps. Fanducci himself felt at home in the darkness and, as he drew the .357 from its shoulder holster, he did not need to see the heavy cylinder. He knew, from the sound it made as he spun it that every chamber was full. Each one carrying a lethal hollow tipped bullet.

Satisfied, he slid the revolver back into position and reached onto the back seat where he found the Ingram. The machine gun, no bigger than a shoe box, was also loaded, the thirty-two round magazine rammed tight into it. Fanducci pulled back the bolt, priming it.

His little baby. It fired over 1,500 rounds a minute and, from close range, would cut a man in half. He wrapped the leather carrying strap around his wrist and hefted the weapon before him. When he got out of the car, the Ingram dangled at his side.

Fanducci stood for long moments watching the front of the building. Nothing stirred, only the long strands of ivy which clawed at the stone work moved in the shallow breeze.

There was a back entrance which he'd found the other day. Shit, he'd go in that way. Give them a little surprise.

The Italian smiled to himself and set off towards the hotel.

Overhead, the first soundless flash of lightning tore its way across the heavens.

Jo and Tyler walked through the darkened reception towards the lifts and the American jabbed a button. The lights on either side glowed brilliantly for a second, then dimmed. There was a loud rumble of thunder. The lights blazed with their usual power once more.

'Bloody storm,' muttered Tyler.

They were now the only ones in the reception. Off to the left the door to the staff room stood closed. To the right, the bar was empty as well.

The lift purred to a halt and the doors slid open. Outside there was a whiplash crack of lightning followed by a growl of thunder which seemed to shake the building to its foundations. They both stepped into the lift and Jo pressed the button marked '1'. The car began to rise.

Even inside the lift, insulated to a certain degree against the noise from outside, the storm raged with nerve-shredding fury, the celestial explosions continuing at an ever increasing rate as the storm reached its full magnitude.

The lights went out.

The lift was plunged into a blackness so total that Tyler could not see his companion even though she stood just two feet from him. At the same instant, the lift stopped dead.

'Oh Christ,' murmured the farmer.

They stood for interminable seconds, waiting for power to be restored but nothing happened.

'Perhaps the storm's brought down a power line,' said Jo.

'We must be between floors,' Tyler said. 'Perhaps I can get these doors open, then we can see.' He fumbled his way across the small compartment to the sliding doors and worked his fingers into the tiny gap between them, then, with a grunt, he began to pull in both directions. His muscles bulged as he fought to open the doors, the veins throbbing at his temples.

They began to open a fraction.

Jo held up her lighter, the meagre light which it gave off being sufficient to show them that they were, indeed, between floors. But the top of the car showed about two feet above the floor of what would be the first storey.

Tyler suddenly let the doors go as the pressure became too much to bear.

Jo flicked off her lighter and the two of them stood in the gloom. Disembodied voices floated on a sea of darkness.

'Can we climb up through the gap?' asked Jo.

'*You* can,' Tyler said. 'I'll hold the doors open as far as I can, you'll have to try and squeeze through.'

'What about you?'

'There should be an emergency exit in the top of the lift. A maintenance opening or something. If I can get through that, perhaps I can make it to the second floor.'

'No, it's too dangerous. Maybe we should wait until the power comes back on.'

'And if it doesn't?'

The question hung ominously in the air.

'I'll try the doors again,' said Tyler, bracing himself. Jo slipped her shoes off, realizing that she was going to have to clamber over the farmer to reach the small gap. The floor of the compartment felt cold beneath her bare feet and a chill ran through her though she was convinced that not all of it was induced by the cold. She shuddered involuntarily.

Tyler, by now, had managed to force the doors open far enough for her to attempt to slip through. Jo was grateful that she was slim, a few more pounds around the backside and she'd be stuck.

'Ready?' grunted Tyler.

'Ready,' she assured him.

The entire lift was rocked by a powerful impact from above.

Tyler fell back, the doors sliding swiftly shut, nearly trapping his hands.

The car was shaking slightly and they could both hear loud scratching sounds coming from above.

'What the hell is that?' Tyler said, looking up.

Jo was silent, straining her eyes to see.

There was someone on the top of the lift.

The shaking continued for a moment, only to be replaced by what sounded like heavy footsteps

'How could they have got up there?' asked Jo, a note of fear in her voice.

'From the second floor,' Tyler offered. 'They must have climbed down the cable.'

There was a loud scraping sound filling the lift now and, as Jo flicked on her lighter, they both saw that the maintenance hatch was being opened.

Whoever was up there would be through in a minute or two.

The lighter grew hot in Jo's hand and she dropped it, plunging them back into darkness once more. She dropped to her knees, fumbling to find it. Groping like a blind person, her ears ever alert for the sounds from above as the hatch was pulled away.

Tyler felt helpless. Unable to see a hand in front of him, he could only stand there impotently and wait for the intruder to drop from above.

The lights suddenly came back on, the lift simultaneously bucking into action. It rose the required few feet and bumped to a halt on the first floor.

'Get out, quick,' Tyler shouted, pushing her through the half-open doors.

Jo stumbled and fell into the corridor, looking behind her to see Tyler following.

The maintenance hatch was torn free.

Tyler backed off slightly, looking around for something to defend himself with. There was a small fire extinguisher nearby and he snatched it up, hefting it before him like a club. But no one came from the lift and, as the doors slid quietly shut, the farmer lowered his make-shift weapon.

Jo had struggled to her feet and was standing behind him.

'Who was it?' she said, breathlessly.

Tyler merely shook his head.

'You go back to the room, lock yourself in,' he told her. 'Don't open the door for any reason.'

'Where are *you* going?' she demanded.

He dropped the fire extinguisher and headed for the stairs.

'To get us some protection.'

Jo stood for long seconds, listening to his footsteps receding, then she turned and headed up the corridor towards their room, fumbling in her pocket for the key.

She glanced anxiously to her left and right as she walked, watching for the slightest signs of movement from any of the other rooms.

She was in the process of inserting the key in the lock when the lights went out again.

Jo suppressed a scream, relaxing as, a moment later, the power came back on. The thunder rolled ominously around the building and, through the window at the far end of the corridor, she glimpsed jagged barbs of lightning ripping through the thick clouds.

She stepped inside the room and hurriedly locked it.

Across the corridor, the door directly opposite hers opened a fraction.

Carlo Fanducci gripped the Ingram sub-machine gun firmly by its butt and leant against the door. It opened effortlessly and the ex-Mafia man moved silently through the kitchen of the hotel. He strode through the darkness with assurance, his own black shape causing him to melt into it, only his low breathing signalled his presence at all.

He stopped as he heard footsteps in the reception beyond but then he scuttled to the door in time to see Tyler disappear out of the front entrance.

Fanducci smiled. The girl was obviously upstairs alone. Both together or one at a time – it didn't bother him how he had to take them out. He pushed against the door and found himself in reception, behind the desk. The Italian cursed as the light above it flickered again but he flipped open the registration book and ran one nicotine-stained finger down the list of names.

He found Jo's name and checked it against the number of her room.

Behind him, the door to the staff room opened slightly.

Fanducci released the safety catch on the Ingram and steadied the weapon in his hand, eyes fixed on the front entrance. On the glass doors which he knew Tyler must use to re-enter the building.

Away to his left, just out of his field of vision, there was movement. Two shadowy figures, hidden by the gloom, moved closer.

Fanducci ducked down behind the desk, just enough to keep himself hidden but to provide a good view of the main doors. Finger resting on the trigger, he waited.

Tyler unlocked the rear door of the landrover and pulled out the nickel plated Purdey. He broke it and thumbed two cartridges into the hungry chambers. As he looked up the sky seemed to grow darker, clouds gathering like predatory birds above him as the thunder and lightning continued their deafening symphony. The farmer stuffed a box of shells into his jacket pocket then, taking care to lock the vehicle once more, he turned and headed back to the hotel. The rain would not hold off for much longer, Tyler reasoned, although a possible downpour was the last thing on his mind as he trekked back towards the hotel. His mind was in a turmoil.

What *had* happened while they were in the lift? Tyler tried to think of a logical explanation but, lately, things in Wakely had begun to defy rationality.

As he approached the front of the hotel, the farmer glanced behind him.

Across the street, hidden by the deep shadows in a shop doorway, he could see two people. Further down the pavement there were others. Even though he couldn't see their faces he knew they were watching him. Tyler paused for a moment, trying to count the dark shapes, but it was useless. They seemed to move and writhe as one, a large undulating mass which defied close scrutiny.

He walked into the hotel, slowing his pace as he entered the darkened reception. For some reason, it seemed even more forbidding than the storm-blasted street.

Tyler saw the staff room door open and he took a step back.

Fanducci, who was already straightening up, saw the farmer move and thought he'd been spotted. The Italian rose from behind the desk like a malevolent Jack-in-the-box, the Ingram pointed towards Tyler. The farmer barely had time to hurl himself behind one of the oak beams near the door when Fanducci opened up. The hit-man squeezed the trigger and the reception was filled with the staccato rattle of automatic fire. Bullets, sprayed in a wide arc, ploughed through wood, plastic and ricocheted off metal. The sound of breaking glass added to the racket as the shells shattered the doors. Shards of crystal sprayed in all directions and Fanducci kept his finger on the trigger until the hammer struck an empty chamber. He swiftly pulled a fresh magazine from his belt and rammed it in, opening up immediately. Spent cartridge cases rained down like brass confetti as he raked the area where Tyler had been standing.

Tyler hugged the beam, the Purdey gripped in one hand, wondering what was happening. The room smelt of gun oil and cordite and a thick haze of smoke was drifting in the air.

The firing suddenly ceased and Tyler took his chance. He leapt out from behind the beam, throwing the shotgun before him, rolling over until he was sheltered behind a couple of chairs. From his vantage point he could see Fanducci reloading.

He could also see two figures who had emerged from the blackness and were almost upon the Italian.

Despite himself, Tyler shouted a warning.

Fanducci spun round and, for a second, he froze.

Both the figures facing him were dressed in the uniform of the hotel. One of them a maid, the other a chef. The latter of the two carried a kitchen knife.

He struck with lightning speed, slicing open Fanducci's left arm from shoulder to elbow. Blood spurted from the rent and the ex-Mafia man yelped in rage and pain, his finger tightening on the trigger of the Ingram. It spat out its stream of hot lead, the impact blasting both figures against the wall. Bullet holes the size of fists gaped in their chests and stomachs and the wall behind them was splattered crimson.

Immediately, Fanducci turned his attention back to Tyler, the machine gun stuttering loudly.

The farmer ducked low but it was useless.

One of the high powered slugs caught him in the shoulder. It slammed him backward, erupting from his back just above the right scapula. He rolled over, trying to fire the Purdey, pressing the butt to his injured shoulder. He screamed in agony as he fired, the stock slamming into the wound as the recoil shook him. The twin barrels erupted, the discharge missing Fanducci. The power of the explosion blew a hole in the reception desk itself and Tyler fumbled in his pocket for fresh cartridges. He could see his assailant emerging from behind the desk, drawing a revolver.

The first of another two figures in the bar reached up and tore the long pike from the wall, levelling it at Fanducci.

The Italian heard the noise and turned, not sure, for the first time in his life, what to do. He knew Tyler was re-loading but he now found he had two more enemies to deal with.

Tyler saw the figures, a man dressed in a dark suit

who held the pike and a girl in her late thirties, her hair hanging loosely to her shoulders. Patches of her scalp were exposed, raw and angry. Both of them were as white as milk. The man's face was dotted with streaming blisters, his cracked lips drawn back to reveal long teeth now brown in colour.

Fanducci heard the loud metallic snap as Tyler successfully closed the Purdey.

Pike or shotgun?

It all seemed to happen at once.

The diseased man thrust forward with the pike, the vicious point burying itself in Fanducci's side just below the armpit, knocking him over. He went down in a bleeding heap, one hand clapped to the gaping wound which the girl leapt for with a speed that amazed Tyler. She was upon the Italian in seconds, her mouth hungrily seeking the bloody gash. He writhed in agony as she tried to tear his shirt free in an attempt to reach the wound now spilling crimson fluid so freely.

Tyler, his shoulder burning with pain, pulled both triggers, watching as the concentrated shot struck the woman in the back. It lifted her off Fanducci, tearing open her back, snapping her spine as it ripped through her torso to burst forth from her chest, destroying one breast and spattering the pike-carrying man with gobbets of viscera.

The man seemed intent on reaching Fanducci however and he drove the pike forward again, putting all his weight behind it. The wicked point punctured the dying man's stomach, pinning him to the floor like a butterfly to a board. He let out a keening wail of agony which was smothered as blood bubbled up his windpipe and filled his mouth.

Tyler managed to get to his feet, holding the shotgun in one hand, the pain in his shoulder gnawing away at him. He ran for the stairs, by-passing the scene of slaughter before him and ignoring the man who had his face buried in the torn hollow of Fanducci's stomach. The farmer could hear liquid slurping from behind him as the man feasted on the Italian's blood.

He stumbled half way up the stairs, the shotgun falling from his grasp. Tyler turned to retrieve it and saw that the man was now following him. And he was moving with surprising speed.

Tyler snatched up the shotgun and stumbled on, not daring to look round.

As he reached the landing he saw Jo standing in the corridor. She'd heard the noise from downstairs and come to investigate.

'Get back,' screamed Tyler.

The diseased man caught up with him as he stopped to load the shotgun.

Tyler's attacker launched himself at the farmer, crashing into him with the force of a steam train. Both of them slammed into the nearby wall, Tyler already weakened from loss of blood. He rolled onto his back, trying to keep the man's hands away from his throat. He felt long nails gouging his flesh as his attacker fastened both hands around his windpipe in a vice-like grip. Tyler could smell the fetid stench from his opponent, he could feel the strength in those hands, see the fire in the eyes.

The farmer struck out with his good hand, driving two fingers into the man's left eye.

He shrieked but merely tightened his grip.

Jo stood mesmerized for a second, then snatched up the shotgun.

'Do it,' croaked Tyler, his face turning the colour of dark grapes.

The American levelled the shotgun until it was pointing at the man's head. He was straddling Tyler now, using all his power to throttle his victim, but he turned his head and opened his mouth in a defiant roar.

Jo saw blood and pieces of intestine sticking to his

long teeth, more of the red fluid and ragged pieces of flesh hanging from the gaping maw which was his mouth.

'Kill him,' Tyler urged, now a second away from unconsciousness.

Jo gritted her teeth and pulled the trigger.

The roar was deafening, the barrels flaming white for devastating seconds.

From such close range the effect of the blast was incredible. The man's head was literally torn from his shoulders. A sticky mess of crimson and grey porridge was splattered against the far wall and the body, the arteries still jetting blood, remained upright for a second before toppling over.

Tyler was on the point of blacking out. He managed to roll away, gazing up through pain-blurred eyes as Jo dropped the gun and fought to keep down the hot vomit which was clawing its way up her throat.

Further up the corridor, unseen by either of them, Mark Bates moved silently from the room opposite Jo's. He paused, then slipped inside her room, closing the door behind him.

He waited

Tyler propped himself up on one elbow, his free hand reaching for the handkerchief in his trouser pocket. He pressed it to the wound in his shoulder, alarmed at how quickly the linen was soaked with blood. He coughed, finding it difficult to swallow. There were several deep indentations in the flesh of his neck from his attacker's powerful hands and the farmer spat as, once again, he felt his throat stinging from the pressure which had been put upon it.

Jo stood against the other wall, trying to look away from the headless remains of Tyler's assailant. The Purdey lay at her feet, the open chambers smoking.

'Jo,' Tyler rasped.

She was milk white, her breath coming in short gasps.

'Jo.' He said it more forcefully and she seemed to regain her senses somewhat. She looked at him, her green eyes a little glazed.

'Help me,' he said, trying to get up.

She finally tore her gaze from the dead man and aided Tyler as he struggled upright. He took his hand from the wounded shoulder and slipped one arm around Jo for support. His right arm and hand felt numb and he kept flexing his fingers to ensure that he still had control over the appendage. He wondered, for one terrifying moment, whether the bullet had severed some vital nerve, but as he continued flexing his fingers he realized that it hadn't.

Outside, the storm continued to rage across the sky and, as the two of them moved slowly towards their room, the lights in the corridor flickered once more.

'What happened?' Jo asked, finally. Her voice low. 'I heard shooting.'

He nodded.

'There was someone down there with a machine gun,' Tyler said.

'One of the townspeople?'

'No.'

'Is he still down there?'

'He's dead. Two of them killed him.' He paused. 'Tore him apart.'

'Oh God,' she murmured. 'That man who attacked you . . .' The sentence trailed off.

'Diseased. And there was a woman with him. I shot her.'

They reached the door of the room and Jo pushed it open. She frowned, flicking at the light switch.

'Dammit, I thought I left this on,' she said. She tried the switch again but there was still no light.

'The power's on,' said Tyler. 'The corridor lights are working.'

'The bulb must have blown,' she surmised.

Tyler walked across to the bed and sat down, pulling off his jacket carefully, wincing as he did so. The blood had congealed thickly in and around the wound, the material of his shirt and jacket stiff with the red substance.

'You'd better come into the bathroom,' said Jo. 'I'll clean that up for you.' She indicated the wound.

Tyler got up again and crossed to the door, grimacing as he turned the handle.

'Let me,' said Jo.

She twisted the knob.

From inside the bathroom, a clawed hand snaked out and gripped her by the wrist.

She screamed uncontrollably as she felt the hairy palm pressing against her flesh, the long nails tearing into her skin. The door was opening, the attacker emerging.

They both saw that it was Mark Bates.

Jo tried to pull away from him but the strength of his grip was too great. Eyes bulging madly, saliva dripping in reeking ribbons from his swollen lips he advanced from the darkness of the bathroom, pulling Jo towards him.

Her screams drummed in Tyler's ears and he looked around for some way to fight this new horror.

Forgetting the pain in his shoulder, he leapt at Bates and all three of them went down in a heap, Bates releasing his grip on Jo. He seemed more interested in the blood which was now flowing once again from Tyler's bullet-torn shoulder. The farmer may have been injured but he fought with a new-found strength born of desperation. He grabbed Bates by the hair, stepping back in horror as a huge tuft of it came away in his hand to reveal bloodied scalp beneath. But his reactions were fast and he drove his knee up hard into Bates' face. The impact sent the man reeling. He crashed against the open bathroom door, slipping on the floor inside. Tyler was upon him in an instant, driving kicks into his torso, almost shouting in triumph as he heard ribs cracking.

Tyler dragged Bates to his feet and forced him over the bath, bending his back at an impossible angle.

Despite his wound, the farmer was still too heavy for Bates who clawed impotently at his opponent.

Tyler, his face a mask of rage and fear, brought one forearm crashing down on Bates' throat.

There was a sound like splintering wood and the man's spine broke.

Tyler remained lying across the body, pressing down ever harder as if he feared Bates would get up if he released his hold but, finally, he slid off. The corpse dropped to the floor with a forlorn thump.

Jo stood frozen in the doorway, unable to speak.

The farmer hauled himself upright, looking down at the body of his attacker. Bates' eyes were open and staring, the pupils now dilated and glazed. His face, like that of the man further down the corridor, was covered in numerous large blisters, some of which had burst and were weeping watery pus. Others, just forming, appeared like bulges beneath the pale skin.

'Let's get out of here,' said Tyler.

'But where are we going to go?' Jo asked, exasperatedly. 'There could be more of them outside. We can't leave the hotel.' There were tears in her eyes and the farmer could see that she was having trouble holding them back. He pulled her close to him, the burning pain in his shoulder having lessened somewhat.

'Vic, what are we going to do?' she whimpered.

'It's OK,' he said. 'We'll be OK.'

He wasn't sure if he was reassuring Jo or himself.

She looked up at him, wiping the tears away angrily.

'I'm sorry,' she said, 'coming apart on you, like this.'

He said nothing.

Jo laughed sardonically.

'I wasn't this scared when the Mafia were after me.'

Tyler brushed a tear from her cheek.

'We'll move to another room for tonight. Barricade the door if we have to.'

'What about the bodies?' she asked.

'We can't do anything about them until morning.'

He led her across to the room where Bates had been hiding and was relieved to find the key in the lock.

'I've got to get the gun,' he said.

'We ought to check on the guy downstairs. The one who shot you.'

'Right. You stay here. Lock this door and . . .'

She cut him short.

'No way. You're not leaving me alone again. I'm going with you.'

Tyler didn't argue. They walked down the corridor to where Jo had dropped the shotgun. Tyler stooped and retrieved it, breaking it with difficulty, the pain in his shoulder intensifying. The American took it from him and thumbed in two cartridges. Both of them were careful to avoid looking at the body of the headless attacker. They made their way cautiously down the stairs, pausing momentarily as the lights flickered again and a deafening clap of thunder shook the building. Tyler had the Purdey cradled over the crook of his good arm, his finger resting gently on the fore-trigger.

As they emerged into the reception, Jo saw the bodies.

The diseased woman, nearly cut in half by the shotgun blast.

The two staff members, riddled with bullets from the sub-machine gun which lay nearby.

And Fanducci.

He was lying spread-eagled, arms outstretched in the pattern of a crucifixion. His stomach and chest had been ripped open and what remained of his intestines and other internal organs were scattered over the blood-soaked carpet around him. The .357 lay close by, the hammer still pulled back.

'Oh my God,' muttered Jo.

Tyler crossed to the eviscerated corpse and, reining back his revulsion, began fumbling inside the dead man's jacket. The stench which rose from the body was overpowering and Tyler was forced to pause for a second to suck in a reasonably unpolluted breath. Resuming with his task he finally discovered a wallet in the Italian's inside pocket. Tyler wiped the blood from it and flipped the slim leather folder open.

It contained about fifty pounds, mostly in fives, some dollar bills stuffed at the back, a receipt for something and a few other inconsequential pieces of paper.

The I.D. card fell out almost by accident.

Tyler picked it up, looking first at the slim plastic strip.

'Jo,' he said. 'Look at this.'

She appeared at his side, trying to keep her eyes off the riven corpse. Jo read aloud the details on the card.

'Carlo Fanducci, Number 23958. Born 1930.'

And below that was the all too familiar logo with the red and silver initials joined at the curve of the C.

'Vanderburg Chemicals.'

Jo looked at the body then at Tyler.

'Jesus H. Christ,' she murmured.

'Someone at Vanderburg wants us dead,' Tyler observed. 'Why I wonder?'

'Whoever it is thinks we're important enough to go to the trouble of hiring a hit man,' she murmured, looking across at the discarded .357 and the Ingram.

'And we don't know if he's the only one,' the farmer said, nodding towards Fanducci's body. 'When they find out this one's dead they might send others after us.' He slipped the I.D. card into his jacket pocket and turned to pick up the nearby Magnum. The pistol felt heavy in his fist and he passed it to Jo.

'Have you ever used one of these things?' he asked.

'I'll learn,' she told him.

The farmer put one hand to his throbbing shoulder.

'We've wasted enough time,' he said. 'We must get inside Vanderburg Chemicals.'

'Not with your shoulder in that state,' she protested.

'We've got to,' he snapped.

There was a long silence, their eyes locked, neither flinching.

'We've still got five or six hours before daybreak,' said Tyler.

Jo nodded slowly.

'Let's get you patched up first,' she said, wearily.

Outside, there was a whiplash crack of lightning and, in the momentary brilliance, they both glimpsed figures moving in the blackness beyond – writhing and moving like monstrous automatons.

And then there was only darkness again.

Thirty-three

Tyler lay on the bed, watching as Jo cut away his bloodied shirt with a pair of scissors. As she pulled at the gore-stiffened material it stuck to the ragged edges of the wound and pulled some tiny slivers of skin away with it. The farmer winced.

'Sorry,' said Jo, picking up the wet towel which lay beside her. She cleaned the rust-coloured area around the bullet hole, asking Tyler to lean forward while she attended to the exit hole which was slightly larger than her thumb. 'You were lucky,' she told him. 'The bullet couldn't have hit you direct, it must have ricocheted. The deflection took most of the power out of it otherwise it would have taken your arm off.' She wiped away the blood from the exit wound, apologizing once again as she accidentally pulled away a piece of ragged flesh. 'I don't think there's anything broken, it went clean through.'

He worked it around tentatively, making a fist of his right hand as he did so.

'How does it feel?' she asked.

'Sore,' he told her.

They looked into each other's eyes for long moments, then Jo wadded up a clean handkerchief and pressed it to the wound. She did the same at the back, securing the makeshift dressing with lengths of sheet which she had taken from the bed in their room. It lay, torn up, in the corner.

'Tie it tight,' the farmer told her.

When she'd finished he lay back again, one large hand reaching for hers. She looked tired, her mascara had run in places, her hair, normally so lustrous, was matted with blood and her jeans were spattered with dried gore.

She looked down at herself and sighed.

'I feel like shit,' she said. 'I'm going to take a shower.'

He nodded, watching as she walked wearily to the bathroom. Tyler could hear the sputter as the water began to flow from the shower spray. He picked up the .357 which lay beside him and inspected the weapon before finally laying it on the bedside table. The shotgun, together with a dozen or so cartridges, lay beside the bed.

The farmer looked at the I.D. card which bore Fanducci's name and photo and also that red and silver

VC. Their suspicions about Vanderburg Chemicals had obviously been right and also, doubtless, their fears about Geoffrey Anderson. If someone at the chemical plant was willing to kill *them* then Anderson had most probably suffered the ultimate fate. Was the secret of the feed *that* important? Important enough to kill for? Obviously it was, he reasoned. And how many of the townspeople had died or were dying? How many of the people he had known all his life had been transformed into savages by the effects of the contaminated feed? In the past few weeks Tyler had seen his entire world crumble.

He dropped the card and swung himself off the bed, padding across to the door of the bathroom.

Jo had not bothered to pull the shower curtain and the farmer ran appreciative eyes over her tanned body as she stood naked beneath the spurting shower. He watched as she soaped her hands, running them over her breasts and neck, shaking her head to allow the water to run through her hair.

'You're a very beautiful woman,' he said.

Jo turned quickly.

'You scared me,' she said, not attempting to hide herself. 'I didn't know you were standing there.'

'Sorry,' he said, smiling.

She turned off the shower spray and stepped out onto the mat, water dripping from her hair. Tyler noticed how it glistened invitingly on the tightly curled mound beneath her navel. He walked across to her and pulled her close to him, feeling the water on his skin.

Jo shuddered in his arms, her hands fumbling with his trousers which she hurriedly unfastened. Tyler stepped out of them and they stood naked, facing each other, her left hand gently squeezing his penis. It began to stiffen. They kissed and she felt his hands stroking the wet skin of her back, pausing there a second before gliding to her breasts. He kneaded the firm globes, bending his head towards her nipples which had risen to red peaks. She gasped as she felt his tongue licking around them, flicking water away in the process.

She knelt slowly, her hand still on his hard shaft and Tyler ran his hands through the silky slickness of her wet hair. She took one testicle in her mouth and sucked gently before transferring her attention to the other one, then she moved back slightly, fastening her lips around the bulging purple head of his organ.

Her own fluid was flowing now, mingling with the water from the shower and she slid one hand between her own legs as she sucked Tyler's penis, teasing the nub of her clitoris until it too stiffened and grew erect.

Jo stood up slowly, a strand of saliva dripping from the end of Tyler's organ. He felt her hard nipples brush his belly and then his chest as she straightened up and his hand replaced hers in that most delicate area between her legs. She felt only liquid pleasure there, her excitement growing stronger as he pushed two fingers inside her.

Jo pressed her pelvis hard against him, bucking hard on those fingers which probed so deeply. She slipped one leg around his, resting herself on the hard muscle of his thigh, grinding herself against it.

He realized what she was doing and bent his knee slightly, gripping her buttocks in order to add to her movements. The water from the shower dripped onto his thigh but it was her warm moistness which lathered his flesh. Her breathing became more rapid, her movements more frenetic and Tyler held her as tight as he could.

He slid one more finger into her slippery cleft, running the index finger of his other hand over the smooth skin of her back.

She pressed her head against his chest and speeded up her movements, her entire body shaking as the orgasm swept through her. Tyler gripped her tight, still moving his fingers inside her, pressing his thumb to her clitoris, prolonging the moment of pleasure for her until she cried out huskily. She muttered something under her breath and kissed him, now moving slowly against his hard thigh. Finally she pulled free, her face flushed, the upper part of her body glowing pink.

Immediately she began stroking his throbbing penis, tracing the outline of the bulging veins with her long nail. She raised herself onto her toes, allowing him to seek and then find the entrance to her burning sex with the head of his organ. He slid into her and she stepped back, taking the weight against one wall as he moved inside her and, from deep within, she felt that wonderful glow blazing in every fibre of her body.

Their mouths locked, tongues entwining, stirring the warm wetness within.

Tyler gripped her waist and began to thrust urgently. As he reached his climax, Jo felt renewed contractions between her legs and, for the second time, she was enveloped by the most powerful of physical explosions.

They clung to each other for a long moment, then Tyler gently withdrew.

Jo picked up a towel which was lying nearby and began to dry herself.

They both changed into fresh clothes, Tyler slipping on a black shirt, grunting in pain as he pulled it over the makeshift bandage. He clenched his fist, relieved that the numbness and burning sensation had diminished considerably. Then, he checked that the guns were loaded.

Jo glanced at her watch.

'Ready?' he asked.

She nodded.

They had four hours of darkness to hide them. The drive to Vanderburg Chemicals would take them about fifteen minutes.

Thirty-four

The grass was wet beneath his feet and, more than once, Tyler almost slipped over. Hs shot out a hand to steady himself, grasping a nearby tree branch. The wire cutters fell from his belt and he cursed under his breath.

'It's OK,' Jo whispered, stooping before him. 'I've got them.'

She handed the implement back to the farmer who stuck it in his jacket pocket along with the handful of large crocodile clips he'd taken from an electrical store near the centre of Wakely. Jo held a long coil of insulated wire which came from the same source.

They paused, hidden by the enveloping darkness, gazing at the tall wire fence which confronted them. Every fifty yards there were large spotlamps but between these radiant oases the desert of night was impenetrable. Tyler looked to his right and left then, satisfied that nothing was moving, he scuttled towards the fence. Forced to lie on his belly, he could feel the wetness soaking through his clothes. Jo crouched beside him and hastily wound lengths of wire around the ends of the crocodile clips, attaching the mouths to the fence. Then she watched as he slid the wire cutters from his pocket and fastened the sharp jaws on the fence between the crocodile clips.

The wire was thick and it took all of Tyler's considerable strength to cut through it. Fresh pain began to gnaw at his shoulder but he continued with his task, cutting a hole big enough for them to crawl through. If there had been an alarm attached, it had not been activated. Perhaps, Tyler thought, the knowledge that over 60,000 volts coursed through the protective barrier was deterrent enough for most intruders. Not so for Jo and himself.

He finished cutting and wriggled through, turning

on his stomach to help Jo. They both straightened up, Jo brushing the moisture from her clothes as best she could. Tyler stuck the wire cutters back in his belt, his hand brushing against the .357 as he did. The weapon was fully loaded although he doubted his ability to use it if the need arose. Shotguns were one thing, high-powered pistols another.

They both squinted through the gloom, their eyes picking out the massive bulk of the Vanderburg buildings about two hundred yards ahead of them. The ground between them and the buildings was open and Tyler was aware of the spotlights. He ducked low, pulling Jo down with him and, hunched over, they ran as fast as they were able.

They were half-way towards the nearest building when they heard the dog bark.

As if at a given signal, both of them froze.

The barking was close, perhaps fifty or sixty yards to their right. It was coming from the direction of the fence.

Beneath the light from one of the lamps, a Security guard, clad in the familiar Vanderburg dark blue, stood and lit a cigarette. With his other hand he kept a firm hold on the leash of a large black Alsatian. The animal was turned towards Jo and Tyler, its loud barks splitting the stillness.

The guard seemed to pay it no heed. He jerked on the lead and wandered on, casting just a cursory glance in their direction.

The noise the dog was making gradually receded.

'Come on,' Tyler whispered and they continued their sprint, finally coming to a halt against a cold stone wall.

Both stood panting for long seconds, surveying the scene before them.

The gigantic bulk of the main building faced them across a tarmac area about eighty feet wide. There were lights on in one or two of the rooms but most merely reflected the dull glint of the stars above. The main entrance beckoned but Tyler hesitated, sucking in a troubled breath as he saw two Security men walk across the tarmac, one of them holding a Dobermann pinscher by a thick chain. The men were chatting happily, oblivious of the two onlookers.

Jo swallowed hard, frowning when she saw them come to a halt outside the main doors.

'Shit,' she murmured. 'What now?'

Tyler didn't answer, his gaze was fixed on the men and the dog which, he noticed, had pricked up its ears and was looking back and forth. He motioned for Jo to move back further into the shadows.

The dog looked in their direction, froze for a moment, then barked loudly three times.

The farmer slid the sheath knife from its leather scabbard and gripped the handle tightly.

'Have they seen us?' Jo whispered, unable to see the Security men from where she was.

'I don't know,' Tyler answered but he had his suspicions.

The dog continued to bark, straining hard on its chain now. The guard who held it, a tall thin individual, bent and released it and, immediately, the dog bounded towards Tyler and Jo.

'Don't make a sound,' said Tyler, crouching down as the dog drew nearer. He held the knife steady and waited.

The Dobermann came hurtling around the corner of the building, its nose full of scent, but it skidded to a temporary halt in the darkness. The few seconds' respite was all Tyler needed. He threw himself at the animal, raking the knife down its side until it struck bone. He grabbed for its muzzle, trying to avoid the sharp teeth and also to shut the creature up. He succeeded in neither task.

Strong jaws clamped around his forearm for fleeting

moments and, as he struck upwards with the knife a second time, the Dobermann let out a high-pitched wail.

Tyler pushed the lifeless carcass aside, his ears detecting the sound of running feet as the Security men approached.

They, like the dog, came around the corner and paused as they were met by a solid wall of blackness.

The farmer caught the first one across the forehead with the wire cutters, the blow felling him immediately. The second man turned to run but Tyler ran after him, kicking his legs away. The man went down heavily on the tarmac, cracking his head on the wet surface. Yet still he tried to rise and the farmer was forced to drive a boot into the man's face to immobilize him completely. The guard flopped onto his back like a beached fish, blood running from his shattered nose.

'Search them,' said Jo, moving across to the prone bodies, rummaging through their pockets. She found a bunch of keys in the breast pocket of the taller man.

'C-5 report.'

The metallic voice cut through the stillness like a razor blade.

'C-5.'

There was a two-way radio lying nearby.

'Bill, if you're having a piss just say so will you?'

Tyler looked first at Jo and then at the two-way.

'C-5 come in,' the voice demanded. 'Bill, for fuck's sake, what are you playing at?'

Tyler picked up the hand-set.

'C-5' he said, praying that the static on the set would be sufficient to disguise his voice.

'What the bloody hell are you doing down there? Why didn't you answer?' the voice demanded.

'Sorry,' Tyler said, cautiously.

'Is your sector clear?' the voice asked.

'Yes.'

There was a long silence. Jo and Tyler exchanged worried glances.

'Sector is clear,' Tyler repeated, trying to hide the tension in his voice.

There was a harsh chuckle.

'You've been humping that fucking dog again haven't you?' the voice said, merrily.

Tyler gripped the set tightly.

'Sector is clear,' he repeated.

'Yeah, right, I heard you first time. Check back in an hour.' The two-way went dead.

The farmer breathed an audible sigh of relief and wiped his forehead with the back of his hand. Taking another look at the motionless guards, he and Jo crept through the shadows towards the main building.

The massive edifice towered above them, a mass of concrete and glass which looked as impregnable as a fortress. Tyler wondered how they were going to get inside. The entrances, he reasoned, would be alarmed. They couldn't break in without alerting every guard on the site. He glanced behind him. The two unconscious men weren't going to stay out forever. He and Jo didn't have much time.

The farmer reached for the small two-way which he'd slipped into his pocket. He held it before him for a second, his finger poised over the 'ON' button.

'What the hell are you doing, Vic?' Jo gaped, watching as he switched it on.

He waved a hand for her to be quiet.

'C-5,' he said.

Jo shook her head, glancing around anxiously.

The radio crackled.

'C-5' Tyler repeated. 'I have a request.'

'Come in, C-5,' said the metallic voice.

Tyler swallowed hard.

'Intruder sighted,' he said.

'Where?' the voice demanded.

'Main building. Request permission to search.'

'Do you need any help?'

'No,' said the farmer, perhaps a little too quickly.

The radio went silent again.

'Come in,' he said.

Silence.

A bead of perspiration popped onto his forehead.

'Come in,' he said again.

'The alarms are off,' the voice told him. 'Report back immediately if you find anyone.'

He flicked the set off and proceeded towards the main door, followed by Jo. They found that the doors opened easily. Both of them walked into the reception area of Vanderburg Chemicals. The shadows swallowed them up. Jo could feel her heart beating faster as they moved quickly but quietly towards one of the many corridors which grew, spoke-like, from the central hub of the main reception.

'Where do we start?' whispered Tyler, exasperatedly.

'What about the laboratories?' Jo offered.

He nodded.

'If we can find them.'

They walked the length of the corridor, each door which faced them was firmly locked. Tyler suggested searching the first floor. They found the stairs and began ascending, stepping as lightly as possible on the cold stone.

'C-5 report.'

The metallic voice sounded thunderous in the silence of the stair-well.

Tyler grabbed for the hand-set and switched it on.

'C-5, any sign of intruder?'

'No,' said the farmer.

'Check the second floor, if any one *is* inside make sure you stop them before they get to E-1.'

'E-1?' Tyler sounded vague.

Jo shot him an anxious glance, then started up the

stairs to the second floor. He tried to hold her back but she was already disappearing through a set of fire doors at the top of the steps. He followed and found himself in a corridor, at the far end there was a large oak door. Jo was in the process of turning the handle.

'Stop them reaching E-1,' the voice repeated.

'Check,' Tyler snapped.

'I'm going to send more units to help you.'

'No,' the farmer blurted.

There was an ominous silence.

'C-5 identify. Number and code name.'

Jo pushed open the door of the room.

The radio rasped in Tyler's hand again.

'Identify. Number and code name.'

He held the hand-set for long seconds, then hurled it to one side. It smashed against the wall.

'Jo, come on, we've got to get out,' he yelled but she was gazing around the room in amazement.

Computer terminals, filing cabinets and all manner of blue-prints vied for space in the large room which was completely windowless. Thick ring binders were stacked as high as a man in places where they wouldn't fit on the wooden shelves. There were half a dozen large oak desks in the room too. Jo crossed to one of the manilla files laid out on the nearest desk and flipped it open:

BIO-SYNTHETIC MUTATION

She read the top sheet to herself, reaching for another file.

'Jo, for God's sake, this place is going to be swarming with Security men in a minute,' Tyler told her.

'But Vic, it's here,' she said, grabbing up another file headed:

PROTEIN CONSTRUCTION

'Everything we need is here.'

'Come on,' he snarled, gripping her arm, pulling her forcibly from the room.

They ran back down the stairs, the far off sounds of dogs drawing nearer.

'Not the front way,' said Tyler as they reached the reception. He pushed her towards another corridor which ran off to the right. They hurtled along it, the farmer throwing his weight against a flimsy wooden door which barred their way. The impact nearly tore it from the hinges and, as he dashed through, Tyler was thankful that he had hit it with his good shoulder. The wound in his other one was throbbing anyway.

They reached a window and he flung it open. Moist air rushed in and Tyler helped Jo through, then scrambled after her.

The Security men were in the reception by now and two of them let their dogs loose. Confused by the mixture of scents, one ran up the stairs, the other scampered towards the room where the intruders had been.

Outside, Tyler and Jo jumped to the ground, Jo falling on the slick surface but the farmer hauled her upright and they were running again. He prayed that they would make it to the fence.

Lights were beginning to flash on inside the main Vanderburg building now and, from somewhere in the darkness, they heard a siren, its strident wailing filling their ears.

Jo was gasping for breath but she found new strength as she saw the fence drawing closer. Tyler urged her on, glancing around to see dark uniformed men following them. He made sure that she scrambled through the hole in the fence then crawled after her. They got to their feet and rushed into the trees, welcomed by the enveloping darkness. Not until they reached the landrover did they stop running. Tyler wrenched open the door and leapt behind the wheel, starting the engine. Jo slumped into the passenger seat, thrown back as Tyler stepped hard on the accelerator and the vehicle shot forward like some kind of projectile. He spun the wheel, guiding it onto the road back into Wakely, glancing in the rear-view mirror to see if anyone was following.

They weren't.

'Vic, it was there in those files,' Jo gasped, trying to catch her breath. 'I'm sure that was the proof we needed.'

He nodded.

'The Vanderburg scientists *must* have conducted tests. They *knew* the feed was harmful but they went ahead with the project anyway,' she said.

Tyler didn't ease his foot off the pedal, not even when the needle on the speedometer touched sixty.

'Vic, are you listening to me?' she demanded. 'What are we going to do?'

'What we should have done in the first place,' he said. 'Tomorrow morning we'll search the town, see if there's anyone else unaffected by the virus. Then, we'll get out. Leave Wakely.'

Jo nodded.

'Then we'll call every fucking newspaper and TV station we can get hold of and see what they make of Vanderburg's little game.' There was a hard edge to his voice.

Jo sat back in her seat and closed her eyes. She knew she should sleep, she needed to but her mind was too full of ideas, overflowing with thoughts. And fears?

She opened her eyes again and gazed out into the night.

In two hours it would be daylight.

Thirty-five

'Shouldn't we bury them?'

Jo ran a distasteful eye over the pile of corpses which faced her. She had helped Tyler drag them out into the car park of the hotel earlier, now she stood gazing at the untidy heap of bodies. Fanducci's gutted corpse lay face down on top of the others. There were six, counting his.

'We can't take any chances,' said Tyler, reaching for the can of petrol which he'd found amongst many in a shed to the rear of the hotel. There was a cellar beneath, approachable also by a service entrance inside the hotel itself. While he'd been down there he'd discovered a great deal of canned and dried food, hundreds of bottles of wine and a small generator which, he guessed, acted as a source of auxiliary power should anything happen to the mains supply. He began to splash the amber liquid over the corpses.

'We've got to destroy any traces of the bacteria,' he told her, the smell of petrol mingling with that of putrescent flesh. 'If Hawley said it lived on in the dead animals there's every reason to believe it'll live on in the victims.'

Jo shivered, despite the fact that she wore a thick sweatshirt. The watery sun provided little warmth and the early morning dew still lay like a glistening cowl over the ground.

It was 9.17 a.m.

Tyler emptied the last of the petrol over the bodies, then tossed the can onto the make-shift pyre with them. He stepped back, striking a match. For long seconds he hesitated, the sightless eyes of Mark Bates pinning him in a reproachful stare, then the farmer tossed the match onto the pile of corpses.

There was a loud whump as the petrol went up, the

flames eagerly devouring the still forms. Like a collection of obscene effigies on Guy Fawkes night they blazed, the acrid stench of scorched flesh now filling the air, rising with the thick black plume of smoke which billowed from the mound.

Tyler touched his right shoulder, rotating it slightly to remove some of the stiffness. He felt Jo's hand grasp his and he looked at her.

'Are you all right?' he asked.

She nodded, her eyes still fixed on the burning pile of cadavers.

They watched the greedy flames for a moment longer, then turned and headed back to the landrover. They both climbed in, Tyler checking the three shotguns which lay in the back of the vehicle. He had the .357 jammed into his belt.

They looked at one another and there was steel in that gaze. Tyler started the engine.

The streets of Wakely were deserted, the sound of the landrover's engine seeming louder than usual in the stillness. Tyler drove slowly, looking to both sides as well as ahead, not even sure what he was looking for.

'Vic, over there.'

Jo's shout startled him and he stepped hard on the brake. She was pointing at something to the left of them. They both got out of the landrover, Tyler picking up the Franchi as he did so. He left the engine idling and walked slowly across to the shapeless thing which was hunched in the nearby shop doorway.

It was a man. He was squatting, knees drawn up to hide his bowed head, arms dangling limply on either side of him.

Jo looked first at the man and then at Tyler who had not taken his eyes from the motionless figure. He approached within five feet, ensuring that Jo stayed behind him.

The man did not move.

The farmer worked the pump action of the shotgun, chambering a round. He took a step closer and prodded the man with the end of the barrel, one finger hooked around it. Just in case.

The body toppled sideways, face to the sky.

His throat had been cut.

There were three or four ragged tears in the skin, each about the size of a child's fist. Lying close by was a broken bottle, its razor sharp edges stained with dark fluid. And yet, around the body itself, despite the savagery of the cuts, there was little or no blood. Only the front of the man's shirt was stained crimson.

Tyler remarked on it to Jo.

'Maybe the rain washed it away,' she suggested.

Tyler didn't speak. He looked closely at the gaping wounds, noticing a darker, purplish discoloration around them. Like bruising. He stood up.

'Why is there no blood?' he pondered aloud.

Tyler and Jo walked back to the landrover and he drove off, keeping to a steady fifteen as they cruised the deserted streets.

'Maybe all the unaffected people have already left,' Jo suggested.

Tyler shook his head.

'The bloke back there with his throat cut, he wasn't infected. There must be others. Not everyone eats red meat.'

'So where are they?' Jo wanted to know.

'They're probably frightened.'

'I know the feeling,' she muttered.

There were more bodies.

Two of them lay prone in the middle of the road. A man and a small child. The man had been stabbed, his ripped shirt revealing numerous wounds in his chest and stomach.

The child, a boy about five, had been bludgeoned to

death. His head was a shattered ruin. There were pieces of skin and fragments of bone close by, indicating that he'd been killed by having his head slammed repeatedly into the tarmac of the road.

Once again, there was a noticeable lack of blood around the bodies and also, Tyler noticed, the discoloration which tinged the extremities of each wound.

Neither victim was diseased.

Flies swarmed frenziedly over both corpses, entering each orifice eagerly and the farmer watched in disgust as two of them crawled over the child's blackened tongue.

As before he remarked on the lack of blood.

'What are you thinking, Vic?' asked the American.

'I don't know what I'm thinking,' he said. 'If I told you you'd probably laugh.'

'Try me.'

'From what I saw of those infected people last night and what we've found today, I think this disease forces its victims to drink blood.'

He waited for her to say something but she didn't.

'With wounds like these,' he indicated the stabbed man, 'there'd be blood all over the place, the same as that other bloke we found. He'd bleed for ages with a cut throat. There wasn't enough rain last night to wash *that* much blood away.'

'The piglets at the cattle market,' said Jo, 'they attacked the sow. They could have been trying to drink her blood. What we thought was cannibalism was blood-lust.'

There was a long silence.

'Vampires,' Jo murmured, softly.

Tyler didn't hear her. His eyes were fixed on the wounds on the dead man's torso but, more particularly, on the dark areas around the gashes. The flesh looked as if it had been sucked; the wound milked of its crimson fluid by hungry mouths. The very thought disgusted him.

They both stood there looking at the bodies for a moment longer, then Tyler turned and headed back to the landrover.

Jo hesitated, looking first at the corpses and then at the windows of the shops which surrounded them. She wondered what was waiting inside.

The thought made her shudder and she hurried back to the waiting vehicle.

'Let's try Dan Hawley,' said Tyler.

Jo counted half a dozen more bodies on the drive to the vet's surgery. Tyler merely slowed the landrover down as they passed. Neither of them bothered to get out and inspect the corpses.

The farmer finally brought the vehicle to a halt in Hawley's driveway. He clambered down, taking care to bring the shotgun with him, looking up at the drawn curtains of the building as he approached it. Jo was close beside him, her heels clicking noisily on the concrete approach.

Tyler knocked on the door, a little surprised when it swung open at the first impact. He held the shotgun across his chest and stepped into the reception. The curtains downstairs were open, the weak sun lighting their way as they moved cautiously into the surgery itself.

'Dan,' Tyler called, his voice echoing off the white walls.

There was no answer.

Jo paused in the reception and picked up the phone.

It was dead. Not even the hiss of static on the line.

Tyler nudged open the surgery door and found that the blinds were down, the room having been plunged into stifling gloom.

He muttered under his breath as he surveyed the mess before him.

The surgery had been wrecked. Instrument trolleys were turned over, specimen jars smashed, filing cabinets upended. Glass crunched beneath his boots as he walked further into the dusky room. The pungent odour of formaldehyde was strong in the air. Scalpels, probes, saws and all manner of other instruments lay on the floor, combining with ripped and discarded pieces of paper to form a chaotic jigsaw of destruction.

Jo joined him in the room, her eyes widening in shocked surprise. While Tyler moved around the surgery, the American opened the door which led through from the main room into the living quarters beyond.

She found herself in a hallway which, in turn, led through into a spacious living room.

The scene in there was the same. The sofa was upended, a large bookcase had been pulled over, spilling its load on the carpet. Even a fish tank, once a proud possession, had been torn from its base and hurled across the room. There were pieces of broken glass everywhere and, amidst the shattered crystal and tiny stones, lay the stiffened bodies of tropical fish. The room smelt damp. Jo passed through it into a kitchen and from there to the stairs.

She climbed them cautiously, ears alert for the slightest sound of movement. She reached the dim landing and headed for the door closest to her.

She paused in the doorway.

The room had been devastated. As with those downstairs, it looked as if someone had systematically gone through the house and destroyed everything they could lay their hands on. Jo moved cautiously into the room, noticing that several china figures lay smashed at her feet. She bent to inspect one.

Behind her, the door of the wardrobe opened slightly.

Jo held the tiny figure in her hand, shaking her head gently. It seemed as if nothing had escaped the fury.

The hinges on the wardrobe door creaked loudly and Jo spun round.

She saw the knife as it was lifted high above her.

When he heard the scream, Tyler burst from the surgery, not even pausing in the wrecked sitting room. He blundered up the stairs, shotgun held at the ready.

The sight which met him caused him to freeze.

Jo was sitting on the edge of the bed and, beside her, sobbing uncontrollably, was Mandy Potter. She still held the long knife in her shaking hand.

'What happened?' Tyler asked, softly, lowering the gun.

Mandy looked up to see him. She dropped the knife, using both hands to wipe away the tears which were streaming down her cheeks.

'Mandy,' he said. 'The surgery. Did Dan do that? Did he wreck the place?'

Mandy nodded.

'He tried to kill me,' she blubbered, revealing several deep indentations near the top of her arm. They looked like claw marks. Her blouse was ripped and there were flecks of blood on it. Her throat too bore scratches and there was a nasty gash on her left cheek.

'I stabbed him,' she said, her voice a harsh whisper. 'I don't know if I killed him. He ran away. She began to cry once more and Jo slipped a comforting arm around her shoulder. 'He was like an animal. Mad.'

They stood over her for long moments, Tyler watching as she removed her glasses and wiped them on the sheet.

'I'm sorry,' she said, holding up the knife. 'I could have killed you.'

'I'd have done the same thing,' said Jo, smiling.

'We've got to leave here, Mandy,' said Tyler. 'Will you be all right?'

'You're not leaving me alone,' she gasped.

He shook his head.

'I mean all of us, we've got to leave Wakely. Now.'

Mandy nodded.

While they waited downstairs, she cleaned herself up and changed into some fresh clothes. When she joined them in the hall way she looked more assured. Stronger.

'I'm OK,' she said, sniffing slightly.

The three of them walked out, back into the welcoming glow of the sunlight.

'What's happening?' asked Mandy as they climbed into the landrover. 'First the animals, now the people?'

Jo explained briefly what was going on. Mandy sat in silence, not even speaking when she'd finished. She just nodded.

'Are we the only ones left?' she asked, finally.

'That's what we've been trying to find out,' said Tyler. 'So far you're the only uncontaminated person we've found alive. The others have been killed.'

He swung the landrover around a corner, narrowly avoiding the body of a young woman which lay by the kerb.

Mandy looked briefly at it, then closed her eyes.

'Where are we going?' she asked.

'To the nearest big city,' Tyler informed her. 'We've got to let people outside Wakely know what's going on. Someone's got to stop it before it spreads.'

The streets seemed to crowd in on them as they drove, the houses glowering down like watching gargoyles, the sun reflecting off windows which glinted like hundreds of blind eyes.

'There,' shouted Jo, pointing towards a small group of shops nearby.

Tyler slammed on the brakes, the vehicle skidding slightly.

'What is it?' he asked.

'I saw something move in one of those buildings,' said Jo.

Tyler reached for one of the shotguns, his hand closing around the Franchi.

Four buildings confronted them: a small supermarket, a newsagent's, a confectioner's and a butcher's shop.

'Stay here,' Tyler said to Mandy. He and Jo climbed out of the landrover and approached the supermarket. The doors were closed but when Tyler struck at them with the butt of the shotgun they swung open. No alarms went off. Total silence prevailed.

It was relatively light inside the supermarket, the sun cast bright rays through the large windows at the front of the building.

Jo wrinkled her nose. The place smelt of bad food. The fridges were off and some of the frozen produce had begun to rot, as had the fresh vegetables. She passed a pile of apples which were now brown and putrescent. Flies swarmed hungrily over them.

There was a large storeroom at the back of the building but they found it empty. Tyler stood in the middle of the stacked boxes and cans of food and shook his head.

'I know I saw something,' said Jo before he could speak. 'Maybe whoever it was is afraid to come out.'

'Let's try the other buildings,' he said.

The newsagent's was empty. So was the confectioner's.

They moved on to the butcher's.

'There has to be someone here, I know I saw them,' Jo insisted. He nodded and pushed the door.

It was locked.

Without hesitation, the farmer put his weight against the glass and wood partition and drove his shoulder into it. The door flew open, the glass rattling in the frame as it crashed back on its hinges. The blinds were down so Tyler reached for the nearby light switch, waiting until the fluorescents overhead had sputtered into life before walking inside the shop. Both of them moved cautiously, having learnt to fear darkened rooms over the last few days. Now the only sound was the intermittent clicking of Jo's heels on the wooden floor and the steady hum of a fan. It must, Tyler assumed, be on the same circuit as the lights.

The shop itself was large, the two long glass counters forming an 'L' shape. The counters were full of display trays bearing different types of meat. Jo shuddered involuntarily as she looked at the array of beef, lamb and offal, thinking how much damage food like that had done to the residents of Wakely. Once more, there was a smell of decay, a sickly sweet odour which made her wince. Maggots writhed frenziedly on a piece of rotten steak.

Tyler walked behind the counter, touching a couple of discarded knives as he passed a large wooden chopping board. It was stained darkly with blood.

At the back of the shop was the freezer, a large room almost as big as the shop itself, where the carcasses of countless animals hung from meat hooks. There were also several large white fridges at the far end of the room and another work bench where the joints were actually prepared.

There was a man lying on the wooden surface.

His arms were dangling limply from either side of the bench and there was a meat cleaver embedded in his chest. His throat had been sliced open – probably, Tyler thought, with the large knife which lay on the floor beneath him. Apart from a small puddle of frozen blood around the man's head, there was little of the crimson fluid to be found.

'Vic, look,' Jo whispered, pointing to one of the fridges.

Several long slicks of blood had dribbled from the top of one fridge, freezing half-way down.

Tyler crossed to it and hooked two fingers under the lid, the shotgun lowered.

He flipped it open.

The fridge was empty.

Jo shrugged and opened the next one.

The man inside seemed to sit up and grab her as if he possessed some uncanny form of radar. He snatched handfuls of her hair in his clawed hands and pulled her towards him.

Jo shrieked, trying to pull away from the madman's grasp, but she felt him rising.

Tyler dare not use the shotgun for fear of hitting Jo. He could only watch for agonizing seconds as the butcher rose from the fridge and grabbed Jo around the throat. She struck out at him with one hand, her nails raking his dry flesh. Tyler ran at the man and reached for his face, clawing at his eyes. He punched hard and felt brittle bone splinter under the impact but the man merely hurled Jo to one side and turned his full attention to Tyler. It was then that the farmer noticed his adversary held a meat hook.

Jo, thrown by the butcher, had crashed into the nearby bacon slicer which promptly burst into life, its circular blade spinning at over 500 revolutions a minute. She looked up, the droning sound loud in her ears. The diseased man was out of the fridge now, between Tyler and the discarded shotgun. He swung the meat hook in a vicious arc, missing the farmer by inches. Tyler leapt to one side, trying to keep the butcher away from Jo who was still dazed after her fall.

The drone of the moving bacon slicer filled the room, covering the low raspings which the diseased man made as he came at Tyler once more.

The farmer avoided another swipe of the hook, this time managing to grab the meat cleaver. He tore it free of the corpse and brandished it before him. The butcher was grinning, thick streamers of saliva dripping from his mouth as he advanced on the farmer. The hook lashed forward again, this time burying itself in a nearby carcass of meat. Tyler took his chance and brought the cleaver down with bone crushing force.

His aim was good. The vicious blade thudded into the butcher's shoulder, shattering the scapula, scything through an inch or two of muscle. Blood burst from the wound and the injured man backed off.

It was his groping hands that found the shotgun.

Tyler realized that he must act fast. He hurled himself headlong at the madman, knocking him backwards. The gun clattered to the floor and the two of them toppled over. The butcher roared in pain and anger and grabbed Tyler's head between his huge hands, pressing inward. The farmer struck out wildly in an attempt to free himself but the butcher, despite the wound in his arm, was an enormously powerful man and, inch by inch, Tyler felt himself being pushed back.

The man was grinning insanely and, in a moment of panic, the farmer realized that the butcher was forcing his head towards the spinning blade of the bacon slicer.

Jo dragged herself upright moaning aloud as she saw what was about to happen to Tyler.

She looked around desperately for something to attack the butcher with and, she too, found the cleaver. Hefting it in both hands, she went at him.

Tyler gripped the big man's wrists, trying to prise them apart, attempting to relieve the pressure on his skull. It seemed merely a matter of whether his skull was crushed like an egg or his head sliced in two by the swiftly rotating blade. In a few seconds it would all be over. He could actually see the blade out of the corner of his eye.

Screaming in desperation, Jo struck out with the cleaver. It sank into the big man's back just below the nape of the neck. She dragged it free and struck again, this time lower. The swipe laid open his lumbar region and, through a haze of pain, Tyler saw blood begin to dribble from the butcher's mouth. His eyes rolled upward in their sockets and he released his pressure on the farmer's head.

Tyler scrambled clear, grabbing the big man by the hair, forcing his head downwards onto the spinning blade.

There was a sound like sharp nails on a blackboard as the bacon slicer shaved off a sizeable portion of the butcher's skull, exposing the sticky grey matter beneath. The large body bucked violently, blood gushing from the numerous wounds, then he rolled over, the blade of the bacon slicer taking off a chunk of his bottom jaw. He fell to the ground and lay still.

Tyler turned to see Jo standing motionless, the dripping cleaver still held firmly in her hands. She swallowed hard and looked at him, dropping the weapon as she saw the blood spilling out around the corpse at her feet.

He reached out and switched the machine off. Silence descended once more.

'Jo,' he said, softly.

'Yeah, I'm OK,' she told him.

She gazed at the body of the butcher for a moment longer then dropped the cleaver.

Tyler took her in his arms and held her tightly.

After a moment, they walked back out of the shop, leaving the two corpses.

'What happened in there?' asked Mandy.

Tyler told her, keeping details to a minimum.

It was Mandy who heard the far off roar of a car engine. The sound travelled easily in the silence and it didn't take any of them long to realise that it was coming from the centre of town. Without hesitation, Tyler leapt behind the wheel and brought the landrover full circle.

He stepped on the accelerator and drove back into the town centre.

Thirty-six

Tyler brought the landrover skidding to a halt opposite the hotel.

There was a silver-grey Capri outside, its engine idling. The driver's side door opened and a short, tubby man with brown hair and a thick moustache got out to confront Vic who held a shotgun firmly in his grip.

'Do you intend using that?' said the man, his voice as crisp as November frost.

'Who are you?' said Tyler.

'My name is Clayton. Doctor Alec Clayton,' he motioned to the woman who sat in the passenger seat. 'That's my wife, Maria. Might I ask who you are and what you're doing with a shotgun?'

'I'm Vic Tyler, I used to run a farm on the outskirts of Wakely.'

He introduced Jo and Mandy.

'You're not from Wakely,' Tyler said, looking the newcomer up and down.

'No, we've come from Sussex, we've been driving most of the night.'

'What do you want?' asked the farmer.

'I think that's my business, Mr Tyler,' Clayton told him.

'That's true, but we don't get too many strangers around here.'

The doctor's wife got out of the car.

'The town seems deserted,' she said. 'We didn't see a soul on our way through the streets.'

'Where is everyone?' Clayton echoed.

Tyler sighed.

'It's a long story,' he said.

'We've got time,' Clayton told him.

It took Jo and Tyler over an hour to explain what had been happening in Wakely, or at least as much as they knew. Mandy was lying down in the lounge of 'The King George', but the remaining quartet sat in the bar, with the destruction of the previous night still visible, speaking in subdued tones as if in reverence for a town which was no more.

When the whole story had been told Clayton merely sat gazing into the bottom of his wine glass, as if seeking inspiration.

'It's incredible,' he said, softly.

'That's one word for it,' said Tyler. The farmer studied the features of the newcomer. He guessed that Clayton was in his middle forties, his wife about the same age. She was a tall, willowy woman, elegantly dressed in a black two-piece.

'So,' Jo asked. 'Why are you in Wakely?'

'My brother, Edward, and his wife,' said Clayton. 'They live here. We hadn't heard anything from them for a couple of weeks. When I tried to phone two days ago there was a recorded message on the line saying that the number was unavailable.'

Jo looked at Tyler, anxiously.

'I tried two other numbers, friends of Edward, but every time it was the same. A recorded message saying those numbers were no longer in use.' He took a sip from his wine glass. 'I wondered what was wrong. I was worried about Edward anyway. He usually phones or writes regularly. Eventually, we decided to come and see for ourselves.'

'Have you been to his house?' asked Tyler.

Clayton nodded.

'There was no one there but all their belongings were in place. It was as if they'd just walked out. Or vanished.'

'Most people have left the town,' said Tyler. 'Those who haven't are either infected or . . .' He let the sentence trail off.

'Dead,' said Clayton.

There was a long silence. Clayton plucked at his moustache.

'A disease passed on by eating red meat,' he mused, 'it may be some form of food poisoning. You said the strain of bacteria which produced the virus was new, so it stands to reason the symptoms are going to manifest themselves in new ways as well.'

'Food poisoning my ass,' snapped Jo. 'What kind of virus do you know that turns people into vampires?'

Even Tyler looked at her in surprise.

'Vampires?' said Clayton, frowning.

'The contaminated people only come out at night, they have claws, they have large teeth. They drink blood.'

Clayton smiled humourlessly.

'So do haematophiliacs, Miss Ward,' he said.

Jo looked puzzled.

'Have you ever heard of Haigh? John George Haigh?' asked the doctor.

'I've heard the name,' Jo said.

'He was a murderer wasn't he?' added Tyler.

The doctor nodded.

'He was executed in 1949. His defence council tried

to claim he was insane because he confessed to drinking a wine glass full of his victim's blood before he dissolved them in acid. Haigh was haematophiliac. He was aroused by blood. There was a case similar to his in Germany in the 1920s. A man named Peter Kurten killed at least a dozen people and drank their blood. They nicknamed him "The Vampire of Düsseldorf".'

'Could the people in Wakely be suffering from the same disease as Haigh and Kurten?' asked Tyler.

'No. They were not physically ill. An obsession with blood whether it involves drinking it or not, is a psychological problem, not a pathological one,' Clayton explained. He looked at Jo. 'As for your theory about vampires, Miss Ward, they're creatures of folklore. What's happening in Wakely has nothing supernatural about it.'

'Well, whatever the answer is, we've all got to get out of here. Now.'

'I can't leave until I've found my brother,' Clayton protested.

'Doctor,' said Tyler, quietly, 'if your brother is still in Wakely then the chances are he's infected with this virus. I wouldn't advise you to hang around.'

'If my brother *is* infected then he needs help, all the people suffering need help. I can't just turn my back on them,' Clayton said.

'If you're staying you'll need this,' said Tyler, handing him the nickel-plated Purdey.

The doctor regarded the shotgun with horror, drawing back from it as if it were about to strike out at him.

'Take it,' urged Tyler.

'And what am I supposed to do with it?'

'Kill any of them that find you.'

'Tyler, for God's sake, they're human beings. They're ill.'

'They're animals,' snapped the farmer. 'Homicidal maniacs.'

'And your solution is to murder them?' said Clayton, sardonically. 'How many have you already killed?'

'You haven't seen what they're capable of,' growled the farmer.

'What in God's name gives you the right to act as judge, jury and executioner on these people?'

'If you want to find your brother, fine. But if he's infected then he's better off dead and he'll try and kill *you* if he can.'

'Is mindless violence your only answer?' asked the doctor.

Tyler turned to Jo.

'Get Mandy, we're leaving,' he said.

'Tyler,' Clayton shouted. 'We're talking about people, not cattle to be slaughtered. Is that what you'd do with every rabies victim? Shoot them?'

Jo returned a moment later with Mandy who looked on as the two men faced each other.

'You should come with us too,' said Tyler, looking at Maria Clayton.

'My wife's staying with me,' Clayton said, defiantly.

'Suit yourself,' Tyler said and tossed the shotgun onto a nearby chair. Then he turned his back on the doctor and, followed by Jo and Mandy, left the hotel.

They all climbed into the waiting landrover and the farmer started his engine.

The hotel gradually disappeared from view.

Thirty-seven

Tyler looked down at his watch and noticed that it was almost 5.00 p.m. The trees which flanked either side of the road from Wakely to Arkham crowded in like dark battalions, their leaves stirred by the strong breeze which had sprung up. Grey clouds scudded across the late afternoon sky and birds looked like black arrowheads against the dull background.

Dusk was approaching fast and, as if sensing this, Tyler put more pressure on the accelerator, coaxing extra speed from the landrover.

'What do you think will happen to the doctor and his wife?' said Mandy.

Tyler shrugged.

'If they stay inside they should be all right,' he said. 'But, they were warned.'

The road sloped upward sharply, simultaneously curving to the right.

'Jesus Christ,' gasped Tyler, slamming on the brakes.

The road block was about fifty yards from them and he could see uniformed men moving about near to a large truck which was parked on the verge. The men were wearing army uniforms.

As quickly and unobtrusively as possible, the farmer stuck the landrover into reverse and swung it off the road into an outcrop of trees. He let the engine idle and squinted towards the barrier.

'Troops?' said Jo, uncomprehendingly. 'To keep people out?'

Tyler shook his head.

'If they wanted to keep people out they'd have the road block facing the other way,' he said, cryptically.

'You mean it's to keep us *in*?' Jo whispered.

Tyler pointed to a dark-coated man who was talking

to a couple of the soldiers. The man wore the unmistakeable uniform of a Vanderburg Security guard.

'It looks like they're even more thorough than we thought,' said the farmer.

He turned his wheel and drove back the way they'd come, branching off at a junction, taking the road which led to Ducton.

'How the bloody hell did they manage to drag the army into this?' he pondered aloud.

Jo had no answer for him.

Mandy gazed out of the windows in bewilderment, watching as the trees sped past and, beyond them, rolling fields.

Clouds were gathering in greater abundance now.

It took them nearly thirty minutes to reach the Wakely–Ducton road.

The second road block consisted of two large trucks parked bumper to bumper. The troops who manned the obstruction could not have failed to see the approaching landrover but they merely stood, immobile, watching it. Tyler and the two women stared back. They sat there for what seemed like an eternity, then he swung the vehicle around once more, banging the wheel angrily as he drove away.

'We'll have to go across country,' he said and, with that, drove through a gorse hedge which fringed the road. The wheels of the landrover spun on the wet ground for a moment, then gained a grip and the heavy vehicle sped on, bumping over mounds and divots in the earth as it went.

About half a mile ahead of them was a range of low hills, the clouds already gathering ominously above them. Like dusky fingers, they crept over the hills, darkening the sky.

'They can't have covered everywhere,' Tyler said as the landrover reached the top of the hill. He peered through the windscreen and was relieved to see that there were no troops, no trucks. Nothing. A slight smile creased his face. It was clear.

'Next stop Arkham,' he said, triumphantly, and put his foot down. 'We can get back on the road in a while. There's a track about two miles further on, we'll by-pass the block.'

The vehicle moved easily through the mud and grass but after a minute or two Jo gripped his arm.

Ahead of them, clearly visible in the earth, were five or six freshly dug places each about a foot in diameter. Mandy, looking out of the back, noticed more behind them.

'Vic,' said Jo, pointing to the mounds. 'What are they?'

Tyler stepped on the brake and stiffened as if an electric current were being pumped through him. He gripped the wheel until his knuckles turned white.

'We're in a mine-field,' he said, softly.

Thirty-eight

'Sector One report.'

John Stark held the walkie-talkie in one hand and stood poised over the map of Wakely and its surrounding districts which was spread out on the desk before him.

The radio crackled loudly, then a voice came floating into the room.

'Sector One secure,' said the voice.

Stark nodded to himself and drew a large cross on

the black line which represented the Wakely-Arkham road.

'Sector Two report.'

He got a similar answer from the remaining four men he contacted and, at each affirmation, the American drew another cross at the appointed location on the map. The main roads which linked Wakely with the towns around it were blocked, the remainder of the town was ringed by troops.

They had arrived less than three hours ago. Stark didn't know what the troops had been told by their superiors. He didn't really give a shit anyway. The only thing that mattered was that they were there. Wakely was sealed off.

With each unit of troops was a Vanderburg Security man, just to keep an eye on things and, if the need arose, to quell any speculation as to why the troops were where they were. For all they knew, it was some kind of exercise. The only thing which might have puzzled them was the fact that they had been ordered to load up with live ammunition.

Stark wondered how many people *were* still alive in Wakely. He drew a large ring right around the town then dropped his pen. However many there were, they sure as hell weren't going anywhere.

He smiled and took out his hip-flask.

'How long do you propose to keep the troops there?' asked Sir Oliver Thorndike, who was also looking down at the map.

'Until this little mess is cleaned up,' Stark told him.

'And when is that likely to be?'

'What am I, a fortune teller? How the hell do I know?'

'You can't keep troops around the town indefinitely.'

Stark rounded on him.

'Don't tell me what I can or can't do, Thorndike,' rasped the American. 'I wasn't the one who put them there, remember. It was *your* Government. I asked for assistance, they sent troops.'

'It seems rather like using a sledgehammer to swat a fly,' Thorndike said.

'Stop talking in riddles, dammit,' Stark snapped.

'You're after Tyler and the girl. Don't you think using a battalion of troops is being too . . .'

Stark cut him short.

'Look, there could be other people alive in that town. I don't want any of them leaving.'

There was a long silence.

'I'd like to know why the hell Fanducci isn't back yet,' Stark said, finally, unscrewing the cap on his hip-flask. He took a hefty swig.

There was a knock on the office door.

'Come in,' Stark called and looked up as Charles Muir entered.

The Scot had his pipe in his mouth but it wasn't lit. He was carrying a large clip-file.

'The reports on the new additive,' he said, passing the file to Thorndike. 'It should be ready for introduction into the feed in a day or two.'

Thorndike nodded and passed the file on to Stark.

'Any problems?' asked the American.

Muir shrugged.

'It's early days,' he said. 'There didn't seem to be any problems, at first, with the initial batch did there?'

Stark looked at him through eyes narrowed to steely slits.

'You were hired to work here, Muir, not to pass moral judgement on what you're doing.'

'Well,' said the Scot, 'let's see how much damage we can do with the second batch shall we?' His voice was heavy with sarcasm.

Stark slammed the file down.

'I've had it with your complaining,' he snapped. 'If you don't like the work then clear out.'

'Just walk away?' said Muir. 'You'd let me do that, knowing everything I know?' He smiled humourlessly and shook his head. 'I'm not that green *Mr* Stark.'

'Charles, the tests done this time were far more exhaustive,' said Thorndike, trying to put a wedge between the two men.

'I know,' snarled the Scot. 'I've just come from the laboratory. My God, have you seen what it's done to some of the specimens?' His own anger was now rising. 'This . . . "miracle feed" is lethal. How many more towns do you have to wipe out before you realize that, Stark?'

'Why don't you just get the fuck out of here,' Stark rasped. 'You came to work here in the beginning because you were offered a lot of money. What's wrong? Is your conscience starting to get at you? *You* helped wipe out that town, Muir.' Stark pointed an accusatory finger at him. 'You and the rest of you fucking geniuses.' He looked at Thorndike too. 'Well now *I'm* clearing up the mess you made. And I'm doing it my own way.'

A heavy silence filled the room, then the Scot turned and headed for the door.

Thorndike tried to call him back but Muir was already gone.

'He's your friend, right?' said Stark.

Thorndike nodded.

'Then keep him quiet or I swear to Christ he'll wind up like Geoffrey Anderson.'

'Does that apply to any dissenting voice?' asked Thorndike, warily.

Stark looked him in the eye.

'Yes,' he said flatly.

Charles Muir rode alone in the lift. He chewed agitatedly on the stem of his pipe and exhaled deeply.

Conflicting thoughts and emotions raged through him.

Anger. Frustration.

Guilt?

He knew Stark was right about his involvement in the Wakely catastrophe and that made it worse.

Guilt.

Hatred.

Charles Muir had taken all he was going to take from John Stark and Vanderburg Chemicals.

He chewed his pipe and wondered how best to approach the idea he had.

Thirty-nine

Mines.

The word blazed like a beacon in Tyler's mind. No wonder there had been no troops in this area. There had been no need for any. He sat behind the wheel of the landrover staring at the small mounds of earth all around them. They were spread quite well apart and the farmer shuddered as he thought how they had driven so easily and unsuspectingly into the trap. The thing was, how far into the mine-field were they?

'Get out,' he said, pushing open the passenger side door.

Jo hesitated.

'Get out, both of you,' Tyler said more forcefully. 'You'll have to guide me through it.'

Mandy sat immobile in the rear of the vehicle.

'Come on, Mandy. Now.' Tyler felt a bead of perspiration pop onto his forehead.

She shook her head.

'Move,' he bellowed, his voice a mixture of rage and desperation.

The shout seemed to galvanise her into action and, carefully, helped by Jo, she climbed out of the vehicle. The two women stood beside the landrover, looking at the ground around them, moving cautiously towards the back of the vehicle when Tyler instructed them. He pushed open his own door and peered over his shoulder.

Mandy was clinging to Jo's arm and, as they reached the back of the landrover, she slipped.

For interminable seconds, Jo thought she was going to be pulled off balance, only to topple onto one of the waiting booby traps, but she managed to steady herself and, gripping Mandy's hand, she picked her way backward. They both stepped over the mounds carefully.

'All right,' called Jo. 'Come back, slowly.'

Tyler stuck the landrover into reverse and pressed down as lightly as he could on the accelerator. The vehicle began to move.

He could see the first of the mines and tugged on the steering wheel to manoeuvre past it.

'Keep coming,' Jo called, herself backing off, careful to avoid the lethal traps. Mandy was shivering uncontrollably.

Above them, the sky was darkening. Clouds rolling across the heavens like fearful portents.

'There's one to your left,' Jo called, watching as Tyler adjusted the vehicle's path slightly.

He was breathing heavily now, his throat dry.

Mandy screamed as she slipped and fell.

Tyler slammed on his brakes and looked round.

Mandy was lying prone, her head less than a foot from the nearest mine. From where she lay she could see the two prongs which nudged up from beneath the earth. If anything should brush against those. . . .

Jo helped her up.

Tyler cursed under his breath and stuck the vehicle into reverse again, having put it in neutral when he heard the commotion from behind. Now, it edged back tortuously, guided by a combination of Jo's directions and his own careful driving.

'There's another to the left,' Jo called.

To avoid it, Tyler was forced to swing the landrover to his right, up a sharp incline.

His foot slipped from the accelerator and the engine stalled.

The landrover began sliding towards the mine.

'Vic,' screamed Jo.

The farmer grabbed his ignition key and twisted it madly.

The vehicle wouldn't start, it continued sliding inexorably towards the mine.

'Come on,' he shouted, turning it once more.

This time the engine fired and Tyler swung the landrover back, praying that the ground was clear behind him.

Jo leapt to one side, pulling Mandy with her, both of them watching as the rear offside wheel missed a mine by a matter of inches. Tyler brought the vehicle to a halt and sat stiffly behind the wheel. He tried to swallow but couldn't.

Jo too found that her breath was coming in gasps.

Mandy could only stare, wide-eyed as the landrover continued its snail-like progress backwards.

'Another few yards and it's clear,' Jo told him.

At least she hoped it was. The ground behind her was free from any bumps or mounds. Unless, she thought, with a shudder, some other, more insidious form of booby-trap lay hidden beneath the dirt. One invisible until it was too late. It was at that point the thought struck her. The mines had been left conspicuous. As if they were waiting to be found. Silent warnings.

'Keep coming,' she called and Tyler finally reversed to safety.

He allowed his head to sag forward onto the wheel. His palms were sweaty on the plastic which he still gripped as if threatening to break it. Mandy, aided by Jo, clambered back inside the landrover and then the journalist herself got in. They all sat in silence for long moments.

'There's no way out of the town,' said Tyler, quietly. 'We're trapped.'

'What are we going to do?' Jo wanted to know.

'We'll have to go back into Wakely, to the hotel. We've got no choice.'

He spun the wheel, completing a 'U' turn, then he drove back towards the road.

'But it'll be dark soon,' Mandy protested. 'What about the infected people in the town? They'll be on the streets.' She was becoming more and more distraught. 'They'll kill us.'

'We'll make it,' said Tyler, forcefully.

He glanced up at the sky and shuddered. Rain clouds were forming in vast black banks, hastening the onset of evening. He found he was forced to flick his side-lights on as he drove back towards the centre of Wakely. The trees, bustling in the strong wind, seemed even more menacing in the dull light. They bent and snatched at the speeding vehicle as it roared past, skeletal branches tapping on the roof every now and then.

The outskirts of the town loomed nearer and Tyler allowed one hand to drop to his side where the Franchi lay.

Jo gripped his arm momentarily and he could feel her shaking.

A dark shape moved ahead of them, disappearing into the deep shadows.

'I told you they'd be around,' Mandy babbled.

No one answered her.

Tyler swung the landrover around a corner and saw more of the townspeople emerging from shop doorways. They looked at the vehicle as it hurtled past, hunger in their eyes.

'How far to go?' Jo asked.

'About three-quarters of a mile,' he told her. They had been forced to enter Wakely from a different direction. One which, Tyler knew, would add to the journey time.

The man ran out into the street as if appearing from nowhere. He raised both hands towards the speeding landrover, illuminated briefly in the dim light it cast.

The landrover struck him doing about sixty. The impact hurling the body to one side. Tyler flicked on his headlamps, able to see more of the dark shapes now.

They recoiled from the twin beams, skulking back into the shadows, only able to watch as the machine roared past.

The hotel was close now, Tyler could see its lights.

He swung the vehicle around the next corner, almost tipping it over.

Jo screamed.

There was an overturned car blocking the road.

Tyler had no time to stop, he merely twisted the steering wheel and tried to guide the vehicle around the car. The landrover bumped as it mounted the pavement, skidding on the concrete as its rear end spun round. There was a loud crash as it ploughed through the window of a shop. Glass cascaded down from the smashed sheet and Tyler cursed as the impact slammed him against the steering column.

A dozen of the dark shapes converged on the vehicle.

Tyler wrestled with the ignition key as the townspeople drew nearer. Jo snatched up the Franchi, stuck the barrel out of the window and fired. The noise inside the landrover was deafening and Jo shouted aloud as the recoil made her ears ring.

Mandy screamed repeatedly, grabbing the handle of the vehicle's rear doors, anxious to be out of it.

'Mandy, no,' shouted Tyler as the landrover bucked into life again. But it was too late, she had pushed open the rear doors and jumped out onto the pavement, running as fast as she could away from the attacking shapes. In the rear-view mirror, the farmer saw her disappear from view around a corner.

'We can't leave her out there,' said Jo.

Tyler stepped on the accelerator and brought the landrover full circle, speeding away from the frenzied shapes and after Mandy.

When he turned the corner there was no sign of her.

'Shit,' he snarled, scanning the darkened street ahead.

The vehicle was moving slowly now as both he and Jo squinted into the gloom in an effort to catch sight of the terrified girl.

The streets were empty.

He reversed.

'What are you doing?' Jo gasped. 'We've got to find her.'

'We're not risking our lives too,' he snapped.

'Vic, for God's sake.'

The scream came like a knife in soft flesh, ringing through the darkness. A piercing ululation which set their nerves jangling.

Tyler grabbed a shotgun and pushed open his door.

'Keep the lights trained on me,' he said and ran towards the place where the scream had come from. Jo shuffled across into the driver's seat, glancing around her anxiously. She was quivering.

Tyler had pinpointed the sound of the scream, realizing that it came from a house just ahead of him. He kicked open the front door and moved inside, the shotgun held at the ready.

The house smelt fusty from disuse and he wondered how long it had been uninhabited.

In the glow from the landrover's headlamps he saw something glistening on the floor ahead of him.

It was blood.

There was more of it on the stairs.

Tyler moved cautiously upward, working the pump action of the shotgun. He swallowed with difficulty, his throat dry and chalky.

He reached the landing and advanced towards one of the doors which faced him. The farmer braced himself and kicked it open.

Mandy Potter lay on the bed naked. Her clothes lay in bloodied tatters beside her like gory confetti. In her nudity, she looked even more pathetic and Tyler lowered his eyes briefly but it was the nature of her injuries which caused him to look away for a moment. She was still wearing her glasses which, Tyler noticed, had been smashed. Thick lumps of glass had punctured her eyes and blood ran down her cheeks like crimson tears. One breast had been practically ripped off, the other was covered by claw marks – deep, red furrows which made it look as if someone had pulled a rake across her torso. Her mouth was open in a soundless scream, her swollen tongue lolling from one side of it. An inch or so below her left breast there was a large hole. Clogged with black clots of congealed blood it yawned like a monstrous mouth.

On the bed beside her was her heart.

The organ looked grey in colour, parts of it having been gouged open.

Tyler crossed to the body and pulled a blanket over

it, covering both the horrific mutilation and Mandy's nakedness.

Only as he stepped back did Tyler suddenly realize that whoever had done this must still be in the house. He spun round, the shotgun lowered.

Nothing moved.

He made his way back onto the landing, then down the stairs, pausing every now and then to listen for sounds of movement.

There were none.

Above him he heard deep guttural breathing, but he kept on edging down the stairs, the light from the landrover's headlamps beckoning him.

He reached the front door, then turned and ran back to the waiting vehicle.

'Mandy?' Jo said.

He shook his head.

Jo understood.

Tyler stepped on the accelerator and drove as fast as he could in the direction of the hotel.

'I thought you were leaving.'

There was no surprise on Alec Clayton's face as he saw Jo and Tyler enter the hotel. Only Maria showed any signs of bewilderment.

'What happened?' she asked.

They told her about the road blocks. About the troops. About the mine-fields.

About Mandy.

'There's no way out of Wakely,' said Tyler, flatly.

Clayton looked a little shocked.

Tyler crossed to the bar and poured himself a large vodka.

'So what are we going to do?' asked Clayton.

The farmer shrugged.

'I wish I knew.'

Forty

Apart from the red and white collision lights which glowed on the skids and sides of the helicopter, the craft flew in darkness. The steady sweep of its powerful rotor blades cut rapidly through the air until it sounded like a loud sewing machine.

The pilot, a man in his early thirties, was bundled up in a heavy leather flying jacket, his black clothing making him almost invisible in the gloom. The lights from the complex instrument panel before him cast a weak glow across his face, highlighting the parts of his skin which were visible above his scarf. His flesh looked pale in the false light, his cheek bones standing out prominently. It seemed as though the chopper was being flown by a disembodied skull.

In the seat alongside him, John Stark pulled the engraved silver hip-flask from his coat pocket and took a hefty swig. He smacked his lips appreciatively, feeling the brandy burn its way to his stomach. Jesus, it was cold. He wore a thick, fur-lined parka but he was still shivering. He rubbed his hands together, slapping the gloved appendages against his thighs. Beneath him, a blanket of cloud had settled over Wakely, virtually blotting the town from view. There were few lights to be seen. Technicians from Vanderburg Chemicals had shut off the main power supply to the town that very afternoon.

Stark jabbed a finger earthward and nudged the pilot.

'Take her lower,' he shouted, forced to raise his voice to make himself heard above the whoosh of the rotors.

The helicopter dipped violently for a moment, caught for precious seconds in a thermo-draught, but it soon straightened out as the young pilot manipulated the controls and lowered the machine to less than 500 feet.

It skimmed through the air effortlessly, dropping ever lower as Stark demanded a better view of the town.

'I thought you said he was your best man,' said Oliver Thorndike who was sitting behind Stark.

'He was,' snapped the American.

'Then why hasn't he reported back?'

The American didn't answer, he merely took another sip from his flask and peered out into the darkness.

'Could Fanducci have caught the disease?' he asked.

Thorndike cupped a hand to his ear, finding it difficult to hear above the noise of the helicopter. He was cold too, his fingers numb.

'What did you say?' he asked.

Stark repeated his question, raising his voice as he did so.

Thorndike shook his head.

'No. He knew about the meat. Perhaps the girl and her friend were too clever for him.'

'Bullshit,' snapped Stark. 'He's never made a mistake yet.'

The helicopter danced in the air, dipping and swerving until it was just a hundred feet or so above the rooftops.

'We're on the outskirts of Wakely, Mr Stark,' said the pilot. 'Do you want me to land?'

'Are you kidding?' shouted the American. 'Just fly over the place, I want to take a look but only from up here.'

The pilot smiled.

'Just what do you expect to see?' Thorndike asked him.

Stark didn't answer. He reached beneath his seat and pulled out a pair of binoculars, squinting through them at the streets below. He adjusted the focus until everything swam into crystal clarity. In the darkness of the streets he could see moving shapes, dozens of them.

'Take a look,' he said, handing the binoculars to Thorndike. 'There are people down there.'

The scientist leant forward in his seat and looked out.

'They're the infected ones,' he said, studying the black shapes beneath them. 'There's still quite a few left.' He swept the binoculars back and forth as the chopper swung in low over the town. '*They* could have killed Fanducci.'

Once more Stark didn't answer.

He suddenly spotted something about 500 yards ahead and nudged the pilot to get closer.

'Give me the glasses back,' he said to Thorndike who willingly obliged.

As the helicopter drew nearer, Stark trained the twin lenses on the light which he had seen. He found that there were over a dozen large lights glowing in a large building a spot near the centre of Wakely. It took him just a moment or two to realize that it was the hotel.

'Son of a bitch,' he murmured under his breath.

He could actually see some of the diseased townspeople moving about beyond the glare of the hotel lights, skulking in shop doorways and standing in black-shrouded streets nearby looking at the one cursed centre of luminosity in the entire town. The hotel stood out like a beacon amidst the stifling Stygian gloom.

'If the girl and the guy are still in town, I'll lay good money they're in there,' Stark said, pointing towards the hotel. He turned to the pilot. 'Circle it a couple of times.'

The man nodded, taking the chopper up slightly before beginning the first of his sweeps.

Forty-one

The auxiliary power provided by the hotel generator had cut in as soon as the mains supply had gone off and Tyler thought again how fortunate they were to have this reserve. What would have occurred had the hotel been plunged into complete darkness he dared not think. As it was, the street lights were out. Wakely was under a blanket of impenetrable gloom – a premonitory blackness which made all four occupants of the hotel feel somewhat uneasy.

Clayton sat at the bar drinking. Maria paced nervously up and down the lounge. Jo stood close to Tyler, gazing out of the window towards the hordes of people barely visible beyond the range of the hotel's powerful lights.

'What do they want?' said Jo, quietly.

'Us,' Tyler said, flatly.

There was a long pause broken by Tyler himself.

'Fresh blood,' he muttered.

Jo frowned.

'What did you say?'

'I think they need fresh blood. Uncontaminated blood,' he explained. 'Up until now, all the victims we've found had been unaffected by the virus. I think that's why they want us.' He gripped the shotgun tighter. 'I wonder how many are out there?'

No one answered.

'I've been thinking,' Tyler continued. 'Apart from the odd victim of the virus we've found, the majority seem to disappear during the day and yet, at night, they all emerge at roughly the same time.'

'What are you getting at, Vic?' Jo asked.

'I think they're all together. In one communal . . . nest, if you like.'

'It would need to be a big building,' said Jo.

Tyler nodded.

'Are you sure this place is secure, Mr Tyler?' asked Maria, anxiously.

'As long as the lights are on they won't come near us,' Tyler reassured her. He looked down as he felt Jo squeezing his arm. He leant over and kissed her softly on the forehead.

It was Clayton who heard it first.

'Listen,' he said, raising a hand for silence.

'What is it?' asked Tyler.

The doctor cocked an ear towards the imagined sound.

'Listen,' he repeated.

The noise grew louder and they all heard it.

'It's a goddam chopper,' said Jo, peering through the window. She pointed towards the red and white lights which glowed brightly on the craft, appearing suddenly, then soaring out of sight.

'It might be someone from another town, the police perhaps,' said Maria, hopefully.

The sound of the rotor blades receded for a moment, then grew louder as the helicopter swept over the building once more.

'Isn't there some way we can signal to him?' said Clayton. 'He might be looking for somewhere to land.'

The chopper completed another circle and Tyler shook his head almost imperceptibly.

'If he wanted to land he could drop it in the street, the road's wide enough,' said the farmer.

'So why doesn't he?' Maria wondered aloud.

The helicopter passed overhead once more, swinging off to the left and hovering like some gigantic insect preparing to alight on a plant, the thrumming of the rotors sounding like a swarm of bees. In the glare of the hotel lights Jo thought she spotted something. A symbol which she had seen before – a red and silver VC. But in the gloom, could she be sure? She watched the chopper as it hovered, trying to make out the markings on its sides. Was it the Vanderburg logo? She couldn't be sure. The sound of its engine gradually receded.

'Why didn't they land?' said Maria, dejectedly.

No one else spoke.

Clayton returned to the bar and began sipping at his drink once more.

'Why don't you try and get some sleep,' said Tyler to Jo.

'I'm fine,' she said, smiling.

The hands of the wall clock had crawled around to 11.26 p.m.

There was an explosion of glass as the first stone shattered the window.

Tyler jumped back, pulling Jo to one side in an attempt to shield her from the shards of crystal which sprayed inwards. He cursed as he felt a jagged splinter nick his cheek.

Another rock came flying at the glass and smashed through. And, suddenly, they were coming with increasing rapidity.

'What the hell are they doing?' said Clayton, knocking his drink over as he moved towards the window.

'Stay back,' Tyler yelled at him as another stone came hurtling at them.

There was another volley of rocks, then a lull.

Tyler peered out through the broken partition, trying to get a look at the hordes beyond the reach of the hotel lights. He could see them, moving like ghosts, almost invisible in the gloom. He could see enough to realize that a number of them were pointing at the building. Many still held lumps of stone and brick, but it was as if they were awaiting some kind of signal.

The farmer swung the shotgun up to his shoulder and aimed.

'What are you doing?' shouted Clayton, rushing towards him.

Tyler actually had his finger hooked around the trigger when the doctor pulled the barrel down.

The farmer turned on him.

'You stupid bastard, Clayton,' he rasped. 'I should use this on you.'

'I shouldn't imagine you'd find it too difficult,' said the doctor sardonically.

'I've told you before, stay out of my way,' Tyler snarled, turning back towards the window.

'Vic, look,' Jo said, pointing at the townspeople. They had unleashed their salvo of stones but they were aiming higher, many of the projectiles falling on the concrete in front of the main doors. Elsewhere, the occupants of the hotel heard more glass smashing.

'My God, they're trying to smash the lights,' said Tyler and, this time, he raised the Franchi and fired all in one movement. There was a deafening roar as the barrel flamed and he saw one of the diseased horde fall. Swiftly working the pump action of the gun, he fired again.

Maria screamed as another stone came crashing through the glass near to her whilst others were hurled at the lights which covered the front of the building.

Tyler squeezed the trigger a third time, watching as two women dragged the bleeding bodies away into the darkness. He could guess what their motives were and the thought sickened him.

He fired again, killing the first of the women.

'You mad bastard,' roared Clayton, trying to pull the gun away from Tyler. The farmer pushed him hard, knocking him over, then he hurriedly thumbed fresh cartridges into the smoking weapon.

The lights flickered once.

'What's that?' Maria gasped.

Tyler saw the shapes moving back into the shadows,

watching as the hotel illuminations began to perform like strobes, flickering on and off more rapidly now.

'Christ, it must be the generator,' said Tyler, anxiously. 'The fuel must be down.'

The lights glowed brightly for brief seconds then died.

The entire hotel was plunged into darkness.

Forty-two

'Get upstairs now,' Tyler said.

'Where are you going?' Jo wanted to know.

'To see about that bloody generator.' He snatched up the Purdey which was lying close by. 'Clayton, take this,' he said, thrusting the weapon towards the doctor.

Clayton merely shook his head.

Jo took it instead.

'Go quickly,' Tyler shouted, heading for the cellar door which lay to his right through the bar. He heard the sound of their footsteps as they clattered up the stairs. For his own part, he fumbled for his torch, wrenched open the door and hurried, as best he could, down the stone steps into the abyss which was the cellar. He stumbled at the bottom, sprawling on the cold stone, the shotgun falling from his grasp, the torch rolling away from him.

The impact had caused it to go out.

Like a blind man, Tyler groped around.

He heard the sounds of hammering on the outside

cellar door and realized that they were trying to break in.

At last his hand closed over the shotgun but, still in darkness, he continued groping for the torch.

The pounding on the door grew louder.

Outside, the diseased horde ran towards the darkened hotel, some climbing the rope-like ivy which clung to the walls of the building, others pounding at the doors or smashing windows to gain access.

Tyler found the torch and flicked it on, swinging the beam around until it fastened on the outside door. He could see the handle being turned, see the wood bowing inward as more pressure was exerted on it from the outside. He dashed across the cellar and up the other flight of steps, dropping the metal locking bar in place, securing the door. Then, he scurried towards the generator, running the torch beam over the various gauges on it. The needles of all three were lying limply on the red side of the dial indicating that it had indeed run out of fuel. He snatched up a can of petrol and began pouring.

There was enough natural light for Jo and the others to see where they were going once they reached the top of the stairs. Jo ushered them towards the nearest room and they locked the door behind them. The American checked that the shotgun was loaded, praying that Tyler could get the lights back on before she had need to use it.

There was a deafening crash as the window was broken and a large man came hurtling into the room.

He rolled over once, then hauled himself upright. He was followed by two others. A shorter man and a willowy woman. The taller man was carrying a hammer.

Jo aimed for him, but the massive recoil of the shotgun pulled the barrels to one side and the blast hit the shorter man. It lifted him off his feet and slammed him against the far wall where he left a large blot of crimson as he slid down.

The tallest man turned to the three terrified onlookers, the hammer gripped tight in his fist.

Alec Clayton found himself staring into the mad, bulging eyes of his brother.

'Edward,' he said, taking a step towards the man who had once been blood kin but was now little more than a raving maniac.

'Stay away from him,' shouted Jo, trying to aim the gun again.

Maria too was staring dumbfoundedly at Edward and it was towards her that he moved.

The blow from the hammer was both well-aimed and powerful. It caught Maria just below the left temple and stove in most of the side of her face, her cheek bone splintering beneath the impact. She fell sideways and Edward Clayton dropped to his knees, bringing the weapon down again. The head punched a hole in Maria's skull, exposing part of her brain. She was dead by the time he struck again, this time using the claw end of the hammer to tear open the soft flesh of her neck. Great gouts of blood rose from the rent and spattered Edward. The woman with him also moved towards the corpse but Jo squeezed the trigger of the Purdey, shouting aloud as the massive recoil slammed her backwards.

Once more her aim was off. It caused the gun to veer to one side and the blast caught the woman in the arm, almost severing it at the shoulder as it ripped away most of her chest in the pulverizing discharge.

Jo fumbled in her pocket for more cartridges, her eyes fixed on Edward Clayton who, by now, had bent his head to the jetting fountain of blood spurting from Maria's throat. He drank voraciously.

The sight finally seemed to galvanize the doctor into

action and he ran at his diseased brother, knocking him away from Maria.

Edward snarled, his mouth open to reveal dripping teeth.

Jo looked up and saw that more of the killers were attempting to clamber through the smashed window.

She unlocked the bedroom door and tugged at Clayton's arm.

'Come on,' she screamed.

He stood transfixed, gazing at his dead wife and then at his diseased brother, the awful realisation finally sweeping through him.

More of the killers were crashing into the room.

'For God's sake, move,' Jo shouted, almost pulling the doctor over and, as he looked up and found himself pinned in the stare of so many mad eyes, he finally found the strength to move. He and Jo ran from the room, charging headlong down the corridor.

Behind them, three of the townspeople followed.

'Up the stairs,' Jo said, taking them two at a time and nearly falling. She could hear the intruders drawing nearer, their feet pounding as they chased their prey.

Clayton banged into a table as he turned a corner, jarring his hip but he kept going, not daring to look behind him.

They turned into another corner, the killers less than twenty yards behind them.

It was a dead end.

Jo raced towards the door, praying that it would be unlocked.

She twisted the knob frantically but it wouldn't budge.

Clayton kicked at it while Jo held the shotgun ready, waiting for the pursuers to round the corner.

The first to appear was a woman carrying a chisel.

Jo gripped the shotgun tight and pulled the fore-trigger. The weapon bucked violently in her hand, almost knocking her off balance. The blast hit the woman in the thighs and she went down as if pole-axed.

Clayton drove his foot against the door once more and it flew open, crashing back against the wall. He dashed in, followed by Jo, then both of them struggled to pull a chest of drawers across the gap as the people outside tried to force their way in.

Jo was shaking, Clayton was finding it hard to get his breath.

'He killed her,' the doctor gasped. 'Edward killed my wife.'

Jo could hear his voice cracking but she had more important things to think about.

The door was already beginning to open a fraction and there was nothing else in the room to block it with. Another minute or so and the killers would be in and, this time, there was nowhere else to run.

Tyler threw another empty can of petrol to one side and unscrewed the cap of another. He couldn't remember how many gallons he'd poured into the hungry generator yet still the machine seemed to swallow every drop. The sound of the shotgun blasts from above had caused him to quicken his efforts and now, as he tossed yet another container aside, he reached for the switch that would activate the generator.

The needles on the dials rose a fraction, then dropped again.

The hotel remained in darkness.

Jo levelled the shotgun at the door, Clayton picked up a chair leg and prepared to defend himself as the door began to crack from the monumental blows it was receiving. The wood had already split in two places, great long vein-like seams running its full length. The hinges groaned as the furious onslaught seemed to grow in intensity and both Jo and Clayton jumped as a fist burst through the door, clawing at the splintered wood, ripping away the panels. Through the gap they could see the crazed faces, the yellowed eyes gleaming with mad desire as the intruders realized they had almost reached their prey. The chest of drawers, the final obstacle between them, began to topple.

Tyler was sweating as he poured yet another can of petrol into the generator. He hurled it aside and threw the switch. The machine spluttered for a second then hummed into life. He breathed a sigh of relief as the lights came back on, brighter than ever. He switched off the torch, stuck it in his pocket and ran towards the cellar steps.

Jo almost laughed aloud as the lights burst into life. The entire hotel seemed to glow brilliantly and from outside the splintered door both she and Clayton heard screams of pain and rage. As helpless in the brightness as their victims had been in the gloom, the infected group ran for the windows in an effort to escape the searing power of the lights. They stumbled awkwardly, falling over each other in their haste to escape back into the night.

Clayton wrenched the chest of drawers away from the door and ran out into the corridor, watching as one of the intruders writhed contortedly in front of him. Jo too watched mesmerized as the man's skin rose in large welts which burst to emit a thick mucoid fluid. His face began to turn red and the clear pus took on a crimson tinge. He opened his mouth to scream, a furred tongue lolling from his mouth, his swollen lips cracking under the lights until they were shredded by numerous small clefts, each one weeping blood. They saw his eyes bulging in pain as he continued to squirm like an eel on a hot skillet, his fingers opening and closing as he shook violently. Finally, with a last racking spasm, he coughed loudly and a foul-smelling mixture of bile and pus spilled over his lips.

Jo prodded the body with the barrel of the shotgun, looking up as Clayton hurried past in the direction of the room they had first come from.

He paused in the doorway, looking down at the body of his wife.

'Oh God,' he whimpered. 'No, no.'

He knelt beside the body, clasping her hand, tears coursing down his cheeks as he saw the extent of her mutilations.

Her clothes had been torn off, her torso punctured in a dozen different places by various weapons.

'Maria,' he whispered, sobbing uncontrollably but, as he saw another of the killers lying close by, that grief slowly became blind anger. He began kicking at the body, driving great powerful kicks into the neck and head until the bone shattered under the impact.

'No. No,' he sobbed. 'Maria.' He snarled down at the diseased body. 'You filthy bastard. Animal. Murderer.' He continued driving kicks into the body.

By this time Tyler had entered the room. He looked at Jo with relief on seeing that she was uninjured.

'Clayton?' he asked.

'In there,' Jo said, pointing towards the room. 'Maria was killed.'

'Oh Christ,' said Tyler, wearily. He looked down at the body in the corridor and then walked to where Clayton was still raining blows on the dead body of the killer. Almost exhausted now, he was on his knees, digging his thumbs and fingers into the ruined face of his adversary. Punching the still form, his body still lurched violently as the tears stained his cheeks.

Tyler shook his head as he looked down at Maria's body, then he crossed to Clayton and tried to lift him off the pulverized corpse at which he was still clawing.

'They killed her,' he rasped. 'Look what they did to her.'

Tyler nodded.

'If I'd listened to you, this wouldn't have happened,' croaked Clayton.

'It wasn't your fault,' Jo said.

He seemed to quieten down somewhat, his gaze returning to the mutilated body of his wife.

'My brother did this,' he said.

Tyler looked shocked.

'You saw your brother?' he asked.

The doctor nodded.

'He killed my wife.'

There was another heavy silence.

'I should have listened to you, Tyler,' said the older man. 'I should have listened.' He walked out of the room.

Jo put her arm around Tyler's waist and squeezed him tightly.

'Are you all right?' he asked.

She nodded, her eyes drawn to the two bodies lying before them. How easily one of them could have been herself she thought, and the realization made her shudder. Tyler crossed to the window and looked out. There was nothing to be seen out there in the oozing darkness, only the bodies of those he'd killed earlier. The breeze which blew in brought with it the smell of death. It mingled with the stench which already filled the room.

When they walked back out into the corridor, Clayton was nowhere to be seen. Tyler paused for a moment, looking down at the scorched corpse of the killer in the corridor, then he took hold of the ankles, dragged it into the room with the other one and locked the door.

'What about Maria's body?' asked Jo, apparently concerned that it was sharing a room with two other corpses.

'We can't do anything before morning,' Tyler said and, together, they walked downstairs.

They found Clayton in the bar pouring himself a large measure of Scotch which he downed in one, hastily re-filling his glass.

He slammed the bottle down on top of the bar and ran his index finger around the rim.

'I want to bury my wife, Tyler,' he said, quietly. 'I want . . .' The sentence trailed off. He exhaled deeply and took another hefty swig from his glass. 'We'd been married for fifteen years. She was all I cared about, we had no children.' He drained what was left in his glass and poured himself another. 'I'm sorry for that little outburst earlier on,' he smiled, sardonically. 'I've had to tell about twenty patients that they were terminally ill during my time as a doctor. Twenty people in over eighteen years is quite a lot. But it was always from a distance, if you know what I mean. Death never had a tangible face until tonight.' He swallowed more of the fiery liquid. 'Death has my brother's face.' Clayton laughed humourlessly. There was a long silence finally broken by the doctor once more. 'I want to kill him. I want to kill my brother. I will destroy death.' He smiled thinly and raised his glass in salute.

The doctor pulled two more glasses from beneath the bar and filled them with the amber fluid.

'Join me?' he said.

Tyler nodded.

'Why not?' Jo echoed.

They sat on the high stools facing the doctor.

'Whatever you want to do,' said Clayton. 'I'll help you. I owe it to my wife.' He gritted his teeth, the knot of muscles at the side of his jaw pulsing.

'I don't think this is the time to talk about it,' said the farmer.

Clayton shook his head.

'I insist,' he said, his voice taking on a hard edge. 'I want someone to pay for what happened tonight.'

Tyler exhaled deeply.

'We can't get out of here, out of Wakely,' he said. 'As I see it, there's only one thing left for us to do. Something that will bring the whole country down on us.'

Jo frowned.

'What?' she asked.

'Destroy Vanderburg Chemicals,' he said.

Jo was speechless.

'And the infected people in the town?' asked Clayton.

'We've got to destroy them too.'

Jo sipped at her drink.

'You find the townspeople,' she said to Tyler. 'I'll see to Vanderburg.'

'You're not going alone,' he told her.

'She won't be alone,' Clayton interjected. 'I'll go with you, Miss Ward.'

He finished his drink and walked out from behind the bar.

'If you'll excuse me,' he said, quietly. 'I'd like to be alone for a while.'

They watched him as he walked wearily away, turning as he reached the exit.

'Tyler,' he said. 'What about that shotgun?'

The farmer tossed him the nickel-plated Purdey and a box of cartridges, watching as he hefted the weapon before him.

Outside, the dark shapes had returned but, this time, they merely stood motionless, staring at the hotel.

It would be daylight in two hours.

Forty-three

Doctor Alec Clayton placed one solitary flower on the small mound of earth in the hotel garden. Tyler and Jo stood to his right, eyes lowered. The sun had risen bright and shining, casting its warm rays over the sombre proceedings.

It had taken them less than half an hour to bury Maria Clayton. They had dug a makeshift grave using tools from the hardware shop across the street, then they had wrapped the body in a sheet and lowered it gently into the hole. No more than two feet deep, it lay beneath a small willow and, as they stood there, pieces of blossom fell like pink tears to join the flowers atop the grave.

Clayton said a short prayer, his voice cracking half-way through, then he brushed the earth from his hands and walked away.

Tyler felt an uncomfortable familiarity about the ritual, remembering the funeral of his own father not so long ago; the act which had brought him back to his birth-place, now a place of death and disease.

Before they had buried Maria, Tyler had driven alone to Dan Hawley's surgery where he had collected a couple of microscopes, some slides and other paraphernalia which Clayton had asked for. On the journey there and back he had found bodies in the streets, some savaged as Clayton's wife had been, others disfigured almost beyond recognition. And amongst those bodies he had recognized people he knew.

Reg Gentry was one of the men who had farmed around Wakely all his life. Tyler had found him with his eyes torn out and his throat cut.

He had found Ronald Faber, a man he remembered as owning a clothes shop. Faber, normally a fat individual, had wasted away to practically nothing, his skin covered everywhere by hideous growths and sores.

It had seemed to Tyler, as if he were driving through a gigantic graveyard where no one had bothered to bury the dead.

Nevertheless, he had returned with the required instruments and then set about helping Clayton bury his wife. As he had helped lift the body onto the sheet, Tyler had not failed to notice the severity of the mutilations which she had suffered. It seemed as if the ferocity of the attacks was growing worse. And, beside her, had lain the body of one of the diseased killers, the body even more broken and disfigured by the pounding which Clayton himself had given it, venting his frustration and pain on the immobile cadaver. Tyler had looked at it, at the monstrous deformity and obscene appearance and it had reminded him, somehow, of the deformed calf which he had killed. How long ago was it now? A week? Two weeks? Three? It seemed like an eternity. Memories and thoughts flooded through his mind and he was sure the others felt the same way. Each carried their own secret to be stored in the darkest recesses of their minds.

Tyler wondered how much more they would see before it was all over.

The body lay on one of the large stainless steel benches in the kitchen of the hotel. Completely naked, the skin had a yellowish tinge to it, that at least, which wasn't covered by unhealed sores and festering blisters. The stench which rose from the corpse was a pungent mixture of putrefying flesh and blood. Tyler and Clayton had carried it from the room upstairs and stripped it, wearing some rubber gloves which Jo had found in a store cupboard. Now, together with the instruments from his own black bag, Clayton had before him two large butcher's knives, a smaller freezer knife (capable of cutting through bone) and a meat saw. They were not the best implements with which to conduct an autopsy but he had little choice.

The doctor prodded the body with the end of his finger, noticing how tightly the skin was pulled across the bones. In places, it looked as if it were going to break or tear. Small pieces flaked off as he rubbed, exposing grey muscle beneath.

'Very little surface lividity,' he said, reaching for the largest of the butcher's knives. 'The skin looks jaundiced.'

Tyler and Jo watched as he inspected the body, peering closely at the face, probing at one of the gaping blisters with the point of the knife. A small trickle of clear fluid oozed from it and Clayton transferred it onto a microscope slide. 'These lesions look as if they've been caused by a reaction *within* the skin cells,' he said, peering through the microscope. He stroked his chin thoughtfully and returned to the body. Jo gritted her teeth as he pushed the knife into the abdomen of the corpse just below the sternum. With an expert movement, the doctor opened the torso as far as the pelvis.

A cloying stench erupted from the hollow and he waved a hand in front of him for a moment before reaching for a syringe. He located the bladder and ran the syringe deep into the swollen organ, withdrawing about 25ml of fluid which he also deposited on a slide. One drop of it glistened beneath the lights.

'Interesting,' he said, abstractedly. 'The bladder is undamaged yet it's full of blood and, from what I can see, there's no damage to either the liver or kidneys. Filtration of waste has been happening as it would in any normal person.' He pointed to the liver with the end of the knife. 'If the skin coloration was caused by jaundice, or hepatitis, then at least half of the liver cells would be damaged.'

He opened the mouth and inspected the teeth and gums.

'Gum shrinkage,' he said, moving down to the hands with their long fingernails. The doctor also looked at the hair which grew in a thick clump in the palms of both appendages. 'This is very unusual,' he said, pulling at the hairs.

'Have you ever seen anything like it before?' asked Tyler.

Clayton was silent for long moments then he nodded almost imperceptibly.

'Yes, I have,' he said. 'But, it was impossible to make the diagnosis without a full examination of a sufferer.'

'So what is it for God's sake?' asked Tyler.

Clayton looked at Jo.

'It's probably the answer to most of Eastern European myth and folklore,' he said.

'What's that supposed to mean?' Tyler said, agitatedly.

'It was Miss Ward who first mentioned vampires wasn't it?' said the doctor.

Tyler shook his head.

'Oh no, come on Clayton, you're not going to tell me that the people of Wakely have been turned into vampires? What do you think this is, some kind of joke? You'll be telling me next there are werewolves running around here.'

'Vic, let him finish,' said Jo, trying to calm the farmer down.

'This man,' he indicated the body before him, 'in fact, all the infected residents of the town, are suffering from a highly advanced form of a disease known as porphyria.'

'What's that got to do with vampires?' asked Jo.

'You've seen the symptoms yourself,' Clayton said. 'Fear of sunlight, sensitivity to light, growth of nails and teeth, swelling of the lips, yellowing of the skin.

Even the hair on the palms of the hands. The blood-lust, the psychosis. They're all symptoms of porphyria. What, in a less enlightened age, might well have been labelled vampirism.'

'My God,' said Jo, softly.

'Why the need to drink blood?' asked Tyler.

'Porphyria is basically a deficiency of iron in the blood stream,' Clayton told him. 'What is known as a disorder of haem synthesis. The blood cannot absorb iron. At first the symptoms look like anaemia and, much of the time, that's as far as it goes. We still know very little about the diseases.'

'You mean there's more than one strain of it?' Jo enquired.

Clayton nodded.

'There are at least six, each manifesting a different severity of symptoms. The people of Wakely seem to be suffering from an advanced form of *porphyria cutanea tarda*. It can be precipitated by alcohol, oestrogen as is found in some birth control pills, or by any toxic agent. In this case, it would seem to be the bacteria in the Vanderburg feed which was passed on to the humans by way of the diseased animals.'

'I still don't understand the significance of the blood,' said Tyler.

'Blood itself is rich in iron,' Clayton began, 'probably the richest source of iron in nature. As I said, anyone with porphyria would find it impossible to absorb iron but, nevertheless, they would need to replace the lost iron. The quickest way of doing that would be to drink blood. That's why the victims of those infected have been mutilated.' His voice dropped slightly and he lowered his gaze. 'The killers wanted blood.'

'Jesus,' murmured Jo. 'It's not hard to see why or how the vampire myth started.'

'There's another thing which links porphyria to myths,' Clayton told her. 'Vampires, according to folklore, are afraid of garlic. There's an enzyme in garlic which breaks down iron in the blood. It stands to reason that anyone suffering the disease would want to keep well away from garlic. The sufferer also only comes out during the night because once the disease has reached a certain stage the iron-free porphyrins build up under the skin. Any exposure to light or sun causes a chemical reaction leading to these lesions.' He pointed to the disfiguring scars and welts on the face of the corpse.

There was a long silence, broken once more by Clayton.

'At the moment, only one person in every 25,000 suffers from porphyria but that number could increase, with or without the influence of the Vanderburg feed. That has just acted as a catalyst in this case but, as I said before, *any* toxic agent could induce it, even something as simple as alcohol or the birth control pill.'

'How is it cured?' asked Jo.

'It isn't,' Clayton said, flatly. 'So little is known about it that no one knows how to perfect a cure. I only recognize the disease because I've seen it in a much milder form many years ago, but never as virulent as this. The problem with the most common form of the disease, *Erythrohepatic porphyria*, is that people can have it and not even realize they're infected.'

A troubled silence settled over the trio, Tyler looked almost accusingly at the gutted body on the slab before him.

'Is it fatal?' Tyler asked.

Clayton stroked his chin, thoughtfully.

'Normally, no,' he said.

Tyler shook his head.

'In the early stages, the people who were infected must have realized there was something wrong with them, so why didn't they go to the doctor?'

'The disease attacks the central nervous system,' Clayton told him. 'It causes disorders of thought and reason. Eventually, it leads to erosion of brain cells. That's what causes the psychosis.'

'So, theoretically, the people who are already infected may die in a few days anyway?' Jo offered.

'It's impossible to say,' said Clayton. 'Days. Weeks. Months. There's no way of knowing.'

'Which doesn't help us in the meantime,' Tyler added, cryptically.

'Thank God the infected people are inactive during the day,' said Jo.

'Inactive perhaps but, unlike the vampires of myth, they don't go into a coma during the daylight hours. Once awoken, providing they are clear of any kind of light, they're just as dangerous.'

'So, are they vampires or not?' asked Jo.

'They're as close to the concept of the mythical vampire as we'll ever see,' said Clayton. 'Or want to see,' he added as an afterthought.

'Then all those legends were created because people didn't understand about diseases like this?' said Tyler.

'Man has a habit of attaching labels to things,' Clayton said. 'It makes us all feel more secure if we can pigeon-hole people or even beliefs. Ignorance spawned legend in many cases, certainly where porphyria is concerned. If you couple the symptoms of it with the fact that there were also a great many more cases of catatonic coma and premature burial in the middle ages, it's not difficult to see how the legends of vampires, were-wolves and even the living dead came about. If we can't rationalize something, we tend to push it into the area of the sub-normal, the supernatural. We're afraid of what we don't understand. And, what we're afraid of, we tend to destroy.'

There was another long silence.

Tyler looked at his watch and saw that it was almost 12.05 p.m.

'We haven't got much time,' he said. 'Less than seven

hours of daylight and there's a lot of ground to cover. We'd better get moving.'

Forty-four

Sir Oliver Thorndike paced agitatedly back and forth in front of his desk, pausing every few seconds to look at his watch. He brushed first one sleeve then the other, as if the gesture would somehow ensure that the time passed more rapidly. He glanced over at the manilla file on his desk and swallowed hard.

There was a knock on the door.

'Come in,' said Thorndike but Stark was already halfway through the door as he said it.

The American looked at the scientist indifferently.

'OK, what's so goddam important?' he said, seating himself in one of the high-backed leather chairs which faced the older man's desk.

Thorndike walked behind the mahogany cabinet and picked up the file, brandishing it almost accusingly before him.

'This is the report on the latest batch of feed,' he said.

'I read it,' Stark told him, reaching into his pocket for the ever-present hip-flask.

'Then you'll have noticed that it too did not reach the specifications required for an adequate safety level.'

'Cut the crap, Thorndike. If there's something on your mind say it.'

'The protein additive which we are, at this very moment, adding to the new batch of feed, is no safer than the first lot. And look what happened because of that. The Government won't tolerate any more incidents on the scale of the one in Wakely.'

'This Government will tolerate anything once they realize the overall financial gain. Why the hell do you think they agreed to co-operate with this project in the beginning?'

'In a covert capacity, yes, but they won't stand for much more. This incident can't be kept quiet forever.' Thorndike swallowed hard. 'Call a temporary halt to Project Erebus.'

'No,' said the American, flatly. 'The new batch of feed is treated and ready for shipment.'

'How many more people are going to die before your conscience begins to prick you?' Thorndike demanded.

'It seems to me I've heard this shit somewhere before. Have you been talking to Muir?' snarled Stark, vehemently. 'You knew the risks involved when this project was launched, you and all the other men working on it – so don't start lecturing me about conscience, you hypocritical son of a bitch.'

'Deciding to call it Erebus has become somewhat prophetic don't you think?'

'What's that supposed to mean?'

Thorndike threw down the file.

'Erebus. The God of Darkness, ruler of the region beyond Hades. Well, it seems we've created our own little hell just a mile or so away.'

Stark got to his feet.

'Don't try to hand me any of your intellectual crap. You're not indispensable, Thorndike.'

The scientist grinned but there was no humour there.

'It seems to me I've heard *that* somewhere before,' he said. 'First Anderson, then Charles Muir, then myself, is that it?'

'Forget your conscience,' the American said, his voice full of menace. 'There's no room for it anymore.'

He walked out, leaving Thorndike to stare impotently at the discarded file. He sat down, head cradled in his hands.

The file lay there like an accusation.

Forty-five

The map of Wakely which was pinned to the notice-board in the hotel was criss-crossed with red and black pen marks, entire streets had been coloured over. Tyler inked over another part of the map and stepped back in resignation.

'There's nowhere left they could be hiding,' he said.

'Have you searched everywhere?' asked Clayton.

'I think I've been to some places twice, I seem to be going around in circles.'

'What's that?' asked Jo, pointing to an untouched black square towards the north of the town.

'The old cinema,' said Tyler, quietly. He gazed at the map for long moments, thoughts tumbling through his mind.

Clayton looked at him.

'Is it big enough?' he asked.

Tyler nodded.

'How the bloody hell did I miss it?' he muttered to himself.

'You try there then, Vic,' Jo said.

'Are we decided on what to do now?' the doctor added, running over the plans which they had formulated earlier.

'I'll search the rest of the buildings, any that I haven't tried,' said Tyler. 'You and Jo drive out to Vanderburg Chemicals, see what you can find.' He reached into his pocket and pulled out the I.D. card which he'd taken from the body of Carlo Fanducci days earlier. 'Use this to get past the guards,' Tyler said, handing it to the doctor.

'And what if they know who Fanducci is?' asked Clayton.

'Then you'll have to find some other way of getting in.'

'It seems like madness doing it in broad daylight,' said the doctor. 'We'd have a much better chance at night.'

'You know as well as I do that we daren't risk being outside in the dark, not until these . . . creatures have been destroyed.'

Tyler fumbled in his coat pocket, checking that he had enough cartridges for the Franchi. His landrover was already loaded up with a dozen cans of petrol. He felt as secure as he was likely to.

'And we meet back here at eight?' said Jo.

Tyler nodded.

The trio stood in silence for long moments, then Clayton excused himself, walking out of the front door of the hotel. Jo and Tyler gazed into each other's eyes, questions hovering there. Unspoken fears.

He finally reached out and pulled her towards him. She responded fiercely.

'Vic, I'm scared,' she said.

'Join the club,' he mused.

'I don't want to lose you. Not now.'

'You won't,' he reassured her, wishing he could add more conviction to his voice.

'Please be careful,' she said.

'You too,' he told her, smiling. Then they kissed, mouths joined firmly, tongues probing urgently.

When she pulled away, there was a single tear trickling down her cheek which Tyler wiped away with his index finger.

'What happened to the tough lady reporter?' he asked, smiling.

'I think she stayed in New York,' said Jo, angry at herself. When she looked up at him, her eyes were glistening. 'I love you, Vic,' she whispered.

He looked momentarily surprised by the exclamation but then he pulled her close once more.

They remained like that for what seemed like an eternity then, without speaking, they walked outside and around to the rear of the hotel where they found Clayton. The doctor was on his knees, head bowed, beside the small mound of earth which marked the resting place of his dead wife. Tyler could see the man's mouth moving as he spoke silent prayers, muttering inaudible phrases.

Feeling like intruders at the private ritual, Jo and Tyler slipped away to wait for him.

He returned minutes later looking somewhat drawn.

'I'm sorry,' he said, smiling, thinly. 'There was something I had to do.'

Tyler nodded but didn't speak.

The three of them walked out to the car park together, Tyler watching as Clayton unlocked the boot of his Capri, ensuring that there was enough room inside for Jo to lie comfortably. It was an unfortunate necessity. The security men at Vanderburg had seen her. They may not recognise her again but it was a chance no one was willing to take.

Tyler climbed into his landrover and laid the shotgun on the passenger seat. In the rear of the vehicle were several cans of petrol which he'd taken from the hotel cellar.

He watched as Jo slid into the boot of the Capri.

Clayton shut it and walked around to the driver's side door.

He looked at his watch and then up at the sky.

Rain clouds were gathering to the west, a vast grey expanse which stretched across the sky like a shroud, drawing nearer by the minute.

The two men exchanged brief glances then, without speaking, Tyler drove off.

Clayton watched the landrover disappear around a corner, then he too started his engine, guiding the Capri out into the road.

The drive to Vanderburg Chemicals would take less than fifteen minutes.

Forty-six

Tyler glanced anxiously at the sky as he pulled the landrover to a halt. More and more of the blue canopy above him was being obscured by smoky grey cloud which moved in rolling banks towards the town. A light breeze had sprung up and he shivered a little as he stepped out of the vehicle, gripping the Franchi tightly.

The cinema stood before him, a towering red brick building built over forty years earlier. It had been allowed to fall into disrepair, its stonework chipped in places, windows broken here and there. There were still posters up outside, advertising forthcoming attractions and, as Tyler approached the building, he glanced at them. There would be no audience for them this time, he thought. Tyler rattled the glass doors, seeing that they still bore chains and padlocks. If he was going to get in he would have to find a different entrance. He wandered slowly around to one side of the large edifice and tugged on the bar of the twin wooden safety doors.

They wouldn't budge.

He decided to check the rear.

Skirting the building meant passing along a narrow alley way which ran between the cinema and the yard of a furniture store next to it. Tyler had already checked out the store, but it had not struck him to search the cinema until now. He moved slowly down the alley, glancing up at the overcast sky every so often.

Old cans and newspapers lay around his feet as he walked and the breeze whipped one up at him. Tyler pulled it away from him irritably and turned a corner.

The woman's body was lying amidst a pile of rubbish, almost hidden from view. Just her feet and the lower part of her torso were visible.

Tyler crossed to the untidy heap and prodded the corpse with the end of the shotgun, knocking some boxes away in order to get a better look at her. She was lying face down but her head was turned to one side. A woman in her thirties, her hair had come out in thick wads, even her eyebrows were mere tufts. Her eyes, dark rimmed and bloodshot, were open, as was her mouth and Tyler saw that there were several flies crawling eagerly over the corpse, their attention focused on the festering wound just below her right ear. It was already beginning to turn gangrenous, mottled blue and green in places. The knife which had been used to inflict the wound lay a foot or so away, its blade rusty with dried blood. Tyler could see that her throat had been slashed in several other places too.

He exhaled deeply and walked on, past the large incinerator where rubbish from the cinema was burned, finally reaching the other side exit.

It was slightly ajar.

Tyler approached it cautiously, noticing how clammy his hands felt against the wood and metal of the gun. He prodded the door with the end of the barrel and it shrieked alarmingly as it swung open. The farmer paused for long seconds, reaching for his torch, then he moved cautiously inside.

He found himself confronted by a set of stone steps which, he knew, led up to the balcony. As he began to climb them his boots echoed loudly within the cold passageway and Tyler cursed under his breath. It was dark on the staircase but there was enough natural light coming through the frosted glass window ahead to prevent him using the torch. He trod carefully, the shotgun lowered.

The steps finally flattened out into a landing. He needed to turn a corner to climb the other flight, which would take him into the balcony itself. Tyler could hear water dripping from the pipes in the toilets behind him. The steady 'plink, plink' jarred his nerves as he slowly ascended the second flight of steps. The darkness grew more pronounced, closing around him like a glove as he finally reached the doors which were his final obstacle.

He flicked on the torch and leant against the door.

It wouldn't move. Something, Tyler decided, was stopping its passage.

He stepped back a pace then drove a boot into the partition and, this time, it swung open to reveal the gaping black maw within. It was like walking into a coal mine. Even the beam of the torch had difficulty cutting through the all-enveloping darkness. He shone the beam down, bringing it to bear on the object which had been blocking the door.

It was another body, a man this time. His shirt and jacket lay open to reveal a pulped rib-cage and the tattered remnants of intestines. A fetid odour of decay filled the farmer's nostrils and he stepped over the corpse, moving slowly across the balcony, sweeping the torch beam back and forth. The place smelt damp and fusty but there was the ever-present odour of death and decay which he'd come to know only too well in the past week or so.

Something brushed against his ankle.

Tyler almost shouted aloud in surprise, swinging the torch around in an effort to discover what had touched him.

He held the shotgun in one hand, not daring to put the torch down but aware that, if someone did come at him, he would more than likely break his wrist firing the weapon with one hand. He felt a bead of perspiration pop onto his forehead as his eyes scanned the unyielding gloom.

He shone the torch around his feet.

'Oh Christ,' he murmured, softly.

A dismembered hand lay close by, the fingers outstretched. The hand had been torn, not cut, off. Long tendrils of flesh hung from it and Tyler swallowed hard. From the hair on the back of it, the hand looked as if it had belonged to a man.

He heard a slow, rhythmic thudding and it was drawing closer.

The farmer stood bolt upright, the torch moving wildly in his grip as the beam sought out the source of the movement.

The soft thudding grew louder.

It was close now. Very close.

His finger tightened a fraction on the trigger.

Something heavy struck his leg and he almost fired. He swung the torch down immediately, his breath stuck in his throat.

Lying at his feet was the severed head of Ben Thurston. The old man's eyes were open, gazing past Tyler as if looking for his killer. His own movements, he guessed, had dislodged the head.

Tyler gritted his teeth and shone the torch ahead of

him. The rest of Thurston's body lay a few feet away. The head had been severed by a small axe which was still embedded in the back of the corpse. The hand was missing too.

'You bastards,' Tyler shouted and his voice echoed around the cavernous interior, bouncing off the walls until it seemed to rise to a high-pitched scream of anguish.

Only silence greeted his outburst.

He was shaking slightly, as much from rage as from shock. The discovery of Thurston, the man he had loved like his own father, had shaken him more than he'd expected, and what made things worse was the fact that the old man had not been infected. He had been another helpless victim of the diseased killers. Vampires. The word drifted into Tyler's mind. Standing here in this deserted cinema with the severed head of a friend at his feet, surrounded by impenetrable darkness, the word seemed to have a terrifying reality about it.

'Vampires,' he said, quietly.

He stood for long seconds, now sure that the creatures were not hiding in the cinema. But where were they? He'd searched everywhere in town.

The thought struck him like a thunderbolt.

What a fool he'd been. It was so obvious it was ridiculous. He felt, simultaneously, elated and angry. Angry with himself for not having thought of it earlier. He turned and ran for the door.

There was only one place where they could possibly be.

Forty-seven

Clayton wound down his window as the first of the security guards approached, the familiar red and silver Vanderburg logo on his breast pocket.

'Afternoon, sir,' said the guard, running appraising eyes over both Clayton and the car.

The doctor nodded a greeting. He didn't want to speak but even if he'd needed to, he doubted if he could. It was as if someone had clamped a steel vice around his throat and were turning it one notch at a time. He tried to swallow but couldn't.

'There's no unauthorized personnel allowed in,' the guard said. 'If you want to see someone you'll . . .'

Clayton reached into his pocket and produced the I.D. card which had been taken from Fanducci. The guard took it from him, not noticing that the doctor's hands were shaking slightly. He looked at the card and then at Clayton. After a moment he handed the card back, his eyes still fixed on the doctor.

'OK,' said the security man and signalled to his partner. The barrier which blocked the drive was lifted and Clayton drove on. As he guided the vehicle up the long driveway, he peered into his rear-view mirror and saw one of the two guards pointing at the car. Clayton swallowed hard, still watching as the man disappeared inside the yellow porta-cabin. His companion followed closely.

Clayton wiped his sweating palms on his trousers and drove on, finally bringing the car to a halt next to one of the large manufacturing sheds. There was a narrow gap between the shed and the main building and he reversed towards that.

Inside the boot, Jo heard him switch off the engine.

She waited a few moments then slipped the catch, climbing out.

She felt appallingly conspicuous for a moment as she stood behind the car but she rapidly ducked down and sprinted along the narrow passage towards a window in the main building. Clayton watched her in his rear-view mirror, then he scanned the area before him.

A large container lorry had just pulled up in front of the main building. The driver got out.

He looked across, saw Clayton and headed towards the car.

The doctor was frantic as the man drew nearer, glancing at his piece of paper and then at the parked Capri.

Clayton shuffled nervously in his seat. What the hell did this man want?

Jo had disappeared from view behind him. He was alone.

And the man was getting closer.

Clayton heard a loud whistle and looked to his right where another man, dressed in a white overall, was signalling to the driver of the lorry. The man in the overall beckoned the driver to him and Clayton saw them chatting animatedly. The driver returned to his lorry and started it up, guiding the massive juggernaut into its appointed position near the loading bay of the closest manufacturing shed.

The rear end of the lorry now blocked Clayton's exit.

Jo knew the lab coat was too big and she felt conscious of it. She tried tucking the sleeves up but they kept coming down, covering her hands. She pulled it tightly across her and waited for the lift to descend.

She was standing in the main foyer of Vanderburg Chemicals, muzak filling her ears as she waited impatiently, for the metal doors to slide open.

The window by which she had gained entry into the building had led her into a deserted office. She had found the lab coat hanging on a hook on the back of the door. It bore the red and silver VC on the pocket but, from the weight and size of it, Jo was convinced that it belonged to a man. She hoped he didn't come looking for it. However, as she stood watching the numbers light up above her, signalling the approach of the lift, she found that her heart had stopped pounding so hard. Few people had looked at her and, those who had, had cast only cursory glances at her. Hold onto yourself, she thought. Don't get paranoid now.

'Where are you going?'

The voice startled her and she turned to see another young woman standing beside her. The woman, in her late twenties, was carrying several thick files. She too wore the monogrammed lab coat.

'I was looking for the research labs,' said Jo, the lie ready on her tongue. 'I'm new here, I can't find my way around too well yet.'

The other girl smiled.

'I know what you mean, I was like that for the first few *weeks* after I started. This place is like a maze.'

'How long have you worked here?' asked Jo.

'Two years,' said the girl. 'My name's Ruth Wicks by the way.'

'Hi, I'm Janet Grant,' Jo lied.

The lift bumped to a halt and they stepped inside.

'Which floor?' asked Ruth, finger hovering over the buttons.

Jo swallowed hard.

The other girl continued to smile.

The American glanced at the array of buttons.

'Three,' she said, praying she'd said the right thing.

Ruth jabbed the button marked '3' and the doors slid shut.

'You're working with Glendenning then?' she said.

Jo nodded.

'He's away all day, there's no one in the labs,' Ruth said.

'I just thought I'd have a look around, familiarize myself with the place,' the journalist said.

Ruth eyed her, the smile fading slightly.

'I don't think they like people just walking in and out of the labs, not with the work they're doing.'

'Well, like I said, I wanted to get the feel of the place. What kind of work *are* they doing exactly?'

'Didn't they tell you that when you were interviewed?' asked Ruth, the smile now completely gone.

'Not everything,' said Jo, sensing that she was losing her grip here. 'Do *you* know?'

'Yes.'

There was an awkward silence. The lift came to a halt at the second floor and Ruth stepped out.

'Perhaps I'll see you later,' she said.

Jo nodded vigorously, anxious for the girl to leave.

As the doors slid shut, the American breathed an audible sigh of relief. A sound which caught in her throat as, a second later, they opened again.

'By the way,' said Ruth, the smile having returned. 'I'd get them to find you a lab coat that's the right size.'

Jo laughed exaggeratedly, watching as the girl walked away. She jabbed the '3' button again and the lift rose one more floor.

When she stepped out she found that she was in a windowless corridor, fluorescents blazing brightly above her. The passageway ran arrow-straight ahead of her for about twenty yards, then it angled sharply to the right. Jo began walking, her eyes scanning the doors on either side of her, expecting one to open at any moment. There were names on some of them, numbers on others. She sought out the door with Glendenning's name on it. She knew that name from somewhere, she knew him, had spoken to him. Of that she was sure and, as she turned the corner, the realization gradually spread through her. He had been the man she'd spoken to when she'd first visited Vanderburg Chemicals in search of Geoffrey Anderson.

One of the doors she passed was thick, sheet steel and on it was the yellow and black sign which warned of radiation. Jo paused beside the door, looking in front and behind her, listening for the slightest sound of movement. Then, she moved on.

Still the doors showed no signs of Glendenning's name. She tried the handle of one but it was locked.

Jo spun round as she heard a low whimpering sound.

In the stillness of the corridor, with just the steady hum of the fluorescents, the sound seemed louder.

She listened and it came again. It sounded like a dog in pain but a big dog and even then the whining was curiously resonant. She put it down to the acoustics in the corridor.

Jo crossed to the door from behind which the sound was coming. She twisted the knob, surprised to find it unlocked. The blinds in the room were drawn, it was difficult to see. The overcast weather outside offered her very little natural light either. But she was able to see that the room was about twenty feet square. One wall was completely covered by filing cabinets, the centre of it was divided into aisles formed by three workbenches and dozens of cages.

In each of the cages there was a different animal. They were surprisingly quiet as Jo approached them, only the dog continued to whine.

She peered into the first cage where a rhesus monkey lay motionless on the floor, its tail twitching slightly.

It had no eyes.

Where the glistening orbs should have been there were just red-rimmed holes. And yet, when Jo moved, the monkey sat up, following her with those bloodied pits as if tracking her with radar. She shuddered, almost shouting aloud as the bats in the next cage flapped their wings excitedly at her approach. There were two of them, fruit bats or flying foxes she guessed from the size.

Both were completely white, their eyes glinting with a vile pink lustre.

And then she saw the dog.

It was a labrador, at least she thought it was. Its coat had no brilliant sheen to it, rather a dull appearance which made it look dirty. Its muzzle was virtually non-existent, its mouth consisting of a huge gaping maw from which long fangs protruded. One ear was missing and, as Jo looked closely, the dog moved.

There was a long growth sprouting from one of its rear legs and the American was sure she could see claws growing at the end of it. The dog had five legs. It shuffled helplessly in the cage, that cavernous mouth dripping saliva as it watched her with eyes that glowed red.

Jo passed the last of the cages and found two or three files laid out on the nearest work-bench. One of them was open. She scanned the title page:

GENETIC RE-CONSTRUCTION

She looked at the cages behind her, then back at the file. Another lay beside it marked:

PROTEIN SYNTHESIS

Something at the back of her mind clicked. It had been Dan Hawley who had first mentioned proteins. An artificially created protein. The plague carrier. The thing which had transformed the residents of Wakely into the vulpine denizens of legend.

These files were what she sought.

There was another marked simply:

DISTRIBUTION

She picked that one up too, stuffing all three under her arm. As she turned to leave she noticed the steaming mug of coffee on the work-bench nearby. Someone had obviously been working in here and might well return.

Jo swallowed hard and made for the door.

She had taken less than two paces when it opened and Richard Neville stepped inside.

'What are you doing in here?' he snapped. 'This is a restricted area.' He noticed that her lab coat did not fit and, something which Ruth Wicks had not noticed, the absence of an identity tag on her lapel. 'Who are you?' he demanded.

Jo took a step back, her hand brushing against the mug of coffee.

As Neville advanced towards her, she hurled it at him.

The boiling liquid hit the scientist full in the face and he shrieked, clawing madly at his eyes.

Jo side-stepped him and ran for the door.

'Stop,' screamed Neville, his skin blistered by the red hot coffee, his arms flailing about uselessly.

Jo wrenched open the door and ran for the lifts.

The scientist dragged himself upright and staggered blindly across the room towards the alarm on the far wall, crashing into some of the cages as he did so.

There was an explosive cacophony of squawks, shrieks and buckling metal as the cages went flying, some of them bursting open to release their occupants.

A cat with a large tumorous growth on its back scampered free and hid beneath the work-bench. The monkey began to howl, baring long fangs, gripping the bars with the stubby nubs of fingers.

Neville reached the alarm and broke the glass with the heel of his hand. Immediately, the strident wail of a klaxon filled the air, reverberating throughout the entire building.

Alec Clayton heard the siren and he gripped the wheel of the Capri tighter, feeling the plastic slip beneath his sweating palms. The sound could have been started by anyone he reasoned. It may even be a fault in the mechanism, a drill which the employees were obliged to endure every so often. He sought desperately for explanations but his mind could accept nothing but what he knew must be the real reason for the sirens. He wondered if they had caught Jo. Should he start his engine and get away? What if he was wrong? Questions piled up in his tortured mind. Perhaps if he created a diversion of some kind . . . The thought trailed off. He looked anxiously around him. What could he do?

He twisted the key in the ignition and started his engine.

'Security alarm,' said John Stark getting to his feet. He crossed to the window of his office and looked out. Nothing moved. He returned to his desk and flicked one of the switches on the console before him.

'What the hell is going on?' he demanded. 'Who set that alarm off?'

The voice which answered him sounded metallic over the intercom. It belonged to Thorndike.

'There's been a disturbance in one of the laboratories,' he said. 'Neville said that a woman stole some files.'

'A woman?' Stark exclaimed, angrily. 'What does she look like?'

'Neville didn't get a good look at her,' Thorndike said. 'He seemed more concerned about the files. She took the files on the Erebus project.'

The American gritted his teeth and flipped another switch.

'Security, this is a general alert, there is an unauthorized person in the building. No one is to leave. Repeat, no one is to leave.' He flicked the switch off and supped deeply from his flask, grunting angrily. 'Fucking bitch,' he rasped to himself.

Jo gripped the files tightly under her arm as the lift descended. The sound of the siren was loud in her ears, even inside the enclosure. There was a loudspeaker in there too and she heard Stark's angry words. She wondered how she was going to get past the security men downstairs.

Indeed, as the lift doors slid open she stepped out into the cavernous reception area to find blue-uniformed men standing at the exit doors. One was speaking into a two-way radio. Jo hesitated for long seconds, wondering what to do. She dared not try and slip out through the window she had gained entry by, and yet she couldn't stand helplessly staring at the guards. The files suddenly seemed enormous and she felt painfully conspicuous, dressed in her ridiculously ill-fitting lab coat.

She was still trying to decide what to do when one of the security men began walking towards her.

Alec Clayton stuck the Capri into gear and guided it slowly towards the front of the main building. The siren continued to wail and he could see the blue-coated security men blocking the exits.

His shirt was sticking to his back, the perspiration beaded heavily on his face. He gripped the wheel tightly and peered through the double sets of glass doors, his roving eyes finally spotting Jo.

He could see that one of the security men was approaching her. Clayton swallowed hard, realizing what he must do. He put the car into reverse and stepped on the accelerator, pulling back about thirty yards.

Already he could see other security men approaching in his rear view mirror.

He ignored them, gripping the wheel even tighter, ducking as low as he could behind it. Then he pushed his foot down hard on the accelerator, glancing down to see the needle touch forty. There was a scream of burning rubber as the back wheels spun for long seconds, then the Capri shot forward as if fired from a gigantic cannon. It sped towards the glass doors and Clayton opened his mouth in a silent scream as he saw them rushing towards him.

The Capri hurtled into the double doors with the force of a steam train. There was an ear-piercing explosion of glass as the car obliterated the entry way. Huge shards of crystal flew through the air, pieces of wood and metal buckling under the impact. The Capri skidded inside the reception, the rear end swinging round to thud into a security guard. The impact catapulted him several feet and he rolled over in the cascade of glass splinters. The windscreen of the car was cracked but not broken, the front bumper bent badly. Clayton himself sat for long seconds gasping to regain his breath, groaning as he touched his chest. The steering column had slammed into him as he hit the doors but he was sure he hadn't broken any bones.

Jo took advantage of the shattering entrance and lashed out at the security man nearest her, driving her foot hard into his groin. He went down in a heap at her feet. She vaulted him and ran for the car, wrenching open the passenger side door and leaping in.

'Go,' she shouted and Clayton reversed, back over the jagged splinters of crystal, through the pulverized doors.

There was a loud bang and the side window exploded into a thousand pieces as a bullet struck it.

Clayton floored the accelerator, anxious to get away from the two security men who had appeared from another building and were pointing guns in the direction of the Capri. He saw one actually sight the pistol and fire. The bullet ripped off a wing mirror and ricocheted off the bonnet, gouging a deep furrow in the paintwork.

Another security guard emerged from one of the

manufacturing sheds, levelling a .38 at the speeding car.

Clayton spun the wheel, slamming the car into the man before he had a chance to fire. The impact catapulted the guard into the air. His body seemed to hang there for interminable seconds, as if suspended on invisible wires, then it crashed down on the roof of the vehicle before bouncing off.

Clayton drove for the main gate, trying to urge more speed from the Capri.

Both he and Jo saw that the barrier had been dropped. The two guards were both kneeling down, aiming their pistols. A salvo of shots hit the car, one shattering the windscreen. The glass spider-webbed, leaving Clayton momentarily unsighted. The Capri skidded violently and Jo clutched the door handle as the car lurched across the driveway. The doctor punched his fist through the shattered glass, enabling him to see out. He twisted the wheel, ducking low once more as they approached the barrier.

There was another salvo of shots and one of them caught Clayton in the shoulder.

The impact slammed him back in his seat and he yelped in pain as the bullet punched its way through his back leaving an exit hole the size of a fist. His right arm went momentarily numb and the Capri skidded but the doctor gripped the wheel as tightly as he could with his good hand and, seconds later, the car hit the barrier.

What was left of the windscreen was smashed in by the impact and Jo screamed as she was showered with glass. A sliver cut her arm as she shielded her face and she heard the groan of metal as the roof of the vehicle was almost torn free by the collision.

More bullets ploughed into the back of the vehicle as it burst miraculously through the barrier. Behind them,

Jo could see the two security men clambering into a rangerover.

'They're coming after us,' she yelled, watching as the large vehicle roared away in pursuit.

Clayton didn't answer. His face was the colour of rancid butter, blood running freely from the wound in his shoulder. But it was the pain which kept him conscious and, as he too saw the rangerover speeding after them, he seemed able to coax yet more speed from the Capri until the needle on the dashboard nudged eighty.

The Range Rover kept on coming.

Forty-eight

Tyler stood before the main gates of Wakely football ground, the Franchi cradled in his arms.

Above him, the grey clouds were gathering ever more rapidly and, as he pushed open one of the gates, he felt the first light spots of rain begin to fall.

The farmer realized that he would have to move fast. He was no longer safe in weather like this. The floodlights loomed menacingly over him as he walked slowly towards the broken rail which separated the stone embankment steps from the pitch itself. The ground was enclosed by a high wooden fence but, as a child, Tyler could remember sneaking through the gaps to watch the Wakely side play. Now he moved across the steps cautiously, eyes alert for any sign of movement.

There were stands on either side of the pitch and one behind each goal, only the part of the ground which he now patrolled was not under cover. As the rain began to fall more heavily, Tyler hurried to the canopy which overhung the nearest stand.

He pushed open the rusty iron gate and walked through, past the turnstile and the tiny box-like structure which had once been the ticket office. A mouldy yellow sign still proclaimed:

MAIN STAND: ADULTS £1.00 CHILDREN 25p

Tyler looked up at the stand, its roof battered and holed by the ravages of years gone by. However, at the very top, up a flight of covered stairs, was what looked like a press box. It was a room about fifteen feet long and twelve wide, its windows now crusted with dirt and broken in many places.

He had been allowed up there once when he was ten. His father had known most of the ground staff at the club and, as a special treat, young Tyler had been taken up to that special room to see how the floodlights were activated. He could still remember even after all these years.

He stood by the stairs which led up to the first row of stand seats and inhaled. The air smelt of wet grass and decay. He gripped the shotgun tighter and decided to check out the other stands first.

The farmer chose to walk across the pitch itself, coming to the smaller stand directly opposite. It had about 200 seats in it, most of them now rotten, some torn from their brackets and tossed into the aisles. Tyler scanned the delapidated structure hastily then clambered over the rail back onto the pitch.

The goal posts were still standing, the paint peeling and chipped from them like scabrous flesh.

He checked the area behind the right hand goal, it was little more than a covered embankment, then he walked the full length of the pitch and did the same at the other end. Weeds had fought their way up through gaps in the concrete and, here and there, rusted tin cans lay in piles or rolled gently, coaxed by the breeze. A piece of paper, the team sheet from a programme, fluttered mournfully in the air.

Tyler turned and headed back towards the main stand, pausing at the players' tunnel.

Twelve stone steps led down into the maze-like catacombs of changing rooms and showers below. It was as black as pitch down there and the farmer reached for his torch, flicking it on when he was half-way down. An overpoweringly fetid odour rose from the subterranean tunnels but it was not the familiar fusty smell of damp and neglect. It was the pungent, nauseating odour of dead flesh.

Tyler paused as he reached the bottom of the stairs, shining the torch ahead of him. It cut through the blackness, revealing a tunnel. It ran for about twenty yards, then branched off at a sharp angle to both right and left. Tyler advanced cautiously, reigning back his revulsion as the stench grew stronger.

The walls were coated with mildew and he could feel it slimy against his hand as he felt his way along the tunnel.

As he turned to the right he almost tripped over the first of the creatures.

It was a man in his early twenties, huddled up in a foetal position, his mouth open to reveal his long teeth. But for the almost imperceptible rise of his shoulders, Tyler could have mistaken the immobile form for a corpse.

He stepped over the young man, moving as slowly as he could, desperate not to make a sound. As the torch beam cut through the darkness it picked out six, seven. A dozen more sleeping forms. Two dozen.

The tunnel was widening, opening out into another

corridor and, sprawled on the floor were more of them. Many more.

To his left in what had once been the showers he saw three dozen of them huddled close by. To his right, more. The entire place was full of the infected townspeople. Tyler re-traced his steps, careful not to wake any of the sleeping creatures. He tried the other way.

It was the same story. Dozens and dozens of contaminated killers all sleeping in the reeking blackness.

At his feet lay Stuart Nichols. Tyler fought to control himself, a combination of fear and loathing welling up inside him until he felt he would have to scream. The silence was broken only by the occasional rasping ululation, a liquid gurgling. Thick, mucoid snortings.

The farmer tried to control his breathing, to still his hammering heart for fear that they would hear it.

The smell was unbelievable.

All around him they lay, some dead, killed by their own. There were the remnants of corpses lying with those who still breathed and the sight made Tyler feel even sicker. It was like standing in hell itself, in the dank, reeking subterranean gloom surrounded by these monstrosities.

He moved backwards slowly, trying to avoid the numerous sleeping forms, the shotgun hovering in his grip. If he woke them now . . .

Tyler forced himself to think of something else.

He sensed that he was near to the tunnel bend, just a few more yards and he would be back in the players' entrance, able to flee upward from this pit of horror. He could feel the perspiration on his forehead. His throat felt dry and he couldn't swallow.

He would burn them, he decided. There was enough petrol in the landrover, all he had to do was seal the exits from beneath the stand and then set light to the place. Burn every one of them.

Ten yards and he would be able to run.

His torch went out.

Tyler could not restrain himself. A cry of panic escaped him as he shook the useless light, blind in the Stygian darkness.

He turned to run.

A hand caught his ankle and tripped him.

He went sprawling but managed to retain his grip on the shotgun. As he felt the deformed figure clawing at him, he tightened his finger on the trigger.

The blast not only gutted his attacker, it also gave him a second of precious light. In that second, Tyler saw that they were rising. But, there was no slow deliberation to their movements, almost as one they were awake, alert and on their feet. Dozens of them spilled from their hiding places to fill the corridor, hungry eyes fixing him with baleful stares.

Tyler turned and ran, the monstrous horde after him. He hurtled up from beneath the ground, slipping on the wet grass, rolling over in time to see the first of them emerge from the tunnel. The farmer swung the shotgun up and fired, the blast ripping away most of the man's face. The body was catapulted backwards, momentarily blocking the entrance, giving Tyler time to get to his feet.

He was moving without thinking, sheer instinct kept him going and he vaulted the rail, heading for the steps which led up to the main stand.

He could hear the fastest of them clattering up the steps behind him and he turned to see Don Mason approaching him.

Tyler didn't hesitate. He squeezed the trigger, watching as the wad of shot cut through the policeman's chest, splattering those behind with gobbets of lung and fragments of bone. But they kept coming, clambering over Mason's body in their frantic effort to reach Tyler. To reach fresh blood.

He could see the others spilling onto the pitch, looking up at the grey sky as if in gratitude.

If only the sun had been out thought Tyler as he leapt up the next flight of stone steps, the ones which would take him to the little room on top of the stand itself. He took them two at a time, slipping once, looking back to see that there were three of the creatures following him. Led by Stuart Nichols. His face was almost unrecognizable, disfigured by the ravages of the disease but, through all that, his eyes gleamed madly as he sought to catch Tyler.

Tyler reached the door of the room and twisted the handle.

The door was locked.

Nichols was about ten yards from him now and Tyler tugged hard on the recalcitrant handle.

Finally, he realized he had no choice. He spun round and fired. The close range blast eviscerated Nichols, the impact catapulting him backward, blasting him off the steps. He fell screaming.

Tyler realized he had just one cartridge left in the gun. He blew the second attacker's head off, then using the butt of the shotgun as a club, went for his final opponent. The man was in his forties, overweight and a little sluggish. Tyler easily avoided his clumsy gropings and ducked under the first punch, bringing the stock up under the man's chin. The blow staggered him and Tyler struck again, feeling bone splinter as he crushed the man's nose. Blood burst from the ruptured appendage and the farmer pressed his advantage, kicking his opponent hard in the groin.

The man overbalanced and tumbled heavily down the steps. Tyler turned and kicked at the lock of the door, driving desperate blows into it until it finally surrendered to the pressure and flew inwards.

He dashed in, finding himself confronted by a bank of switches and dials. The accumulation of dust made him cough but he scanned the array before him, glancing periodically out of the window down to the pitch below.

Every square inch of grass seemed to be occupied. He could only guess at how many of them there were.

Two hundred? Three hundred? More?

They stood glaring up at the room where he remained. Not one of them attempted to move now. They knew he had to come down eventually. They need do nothing but wait.

Tyler's breath was coming in gasps, as much from frustration as exertion. He looked desperately for some sign on the large control panel which might help him. His fingers traced patterns in the thick dust, brushing it away from the controls.

There was a switch marked:

POWER

He flicked to 'ON' and, somewhere, far below him, there was a rumbling. Like thunder only it sounded as if it were going to erupt from the earth itself. The thrumming grew louder.

Now he saw other switches:

COLUMN ONE
COLUMN TWO

And through to six.

He swallowed hard, the floodlights. The switches had to control the floodlights.

He looked out of the grime-encrusted window once again. The diseased creatures were still standing, looking up at him.

'Just stay there you bastards,' he whispered, fingers poised over the first three switches.

He prayed that the lights would work.

The rumbling from below was now shaking the room.

It was time.

All Tyler heard was a maniacal scream and then

something heavy crashed into him, driving him into the control panel, knocking the breath from him.

He looked up to see Dan Hawley standing over him.

At least what had once been Dan Hawley.

The vet's face was a patchwork of sores and blisters, some of which had burst and were weeping clear pus. Elsewhere, patches of skin had peeled off to reveal raw skin beneath. He had lost most of his hair, his scalp was now infested with suppurating boils. Nails stained darkly with dried blood curved from the ends of his fingers and he snarled at Tyler in a gesture that was more animal than human.

For what seemed like an eternity, they faced each other, then, Hawley launched himself at the farmer. Vic rolled to one side. He lashed out at his attacker as he did so, driving a powerful kick into his stomach.

The vet grunted and rolled over, his bony hand closing over the leg of a broken chair which lay nearby. He brought it down with bone crushing force, missing Tyler by inches, the nail which protruded from the end striking sparks on the control panel.

Tyler grabbed Hawley's arm and twisted it hard against the joint, trying to make him drop the weapon but the vet merely tore at Tyler's face with his long claws, drawing blood.

The farmer backed off, looking for his shotgun.

He snatched it up, hefting it before him like a club. Hawley struck again but Tyler deflected the blow, striking out himself, catching the vet on the temple. The impact sent him reeling and Tyler swung the gun once again, using it like a baseball bat. He drove the stock into Hawley's face, shattering his bottom jaw. But still the vet kept coming, ignoring the blood which oozed from the vicious rent in his flesh. He ducked beneath Tyler's next blow, striking for the farmer's thigh.

Tyler yelped in pain as the nail punctured his flesh.

Blood spurted from the hole and he felt his skin and muscle being torn as Hawley wrenched the spike free.

The farmer had cartridges in his pocket but he knew that he'd never re-load in time and, as he glanced out of the window down onto the pitch, he saw that the others were beginning to move. They could see what was happening in the room on top of the stand and they were becoming restless. Hungry.

Tyler hurled his gun at Hawley but the vet merely ducked and ran at him, bringing the chair leg down in a wide arc.

More by luck than judgement, Tyler managed to grab his assailant's wrist, gripping as hard as he could. Then, using all his strength, he swung Hawley around and hurled him towards the window.

Propelled by Tyler's throw and his own momentum, the vet could not stop himself.

He crashed through the glass with a scream of rage and horror. For what seemed like an eternity, he clutched at empty air, then, with a last caterwaul of despair, he plummeted down, smashing through the rusted roof of the stand and thudding to earth more than fifty feet below. He rolled over once, then lay still in a widening pool of blood.

Tyler threw all six switches.

The floodlights burst into life, bathing the pitch in powerful white light. Thirty bulbs, two hundred watts each, shone from every tower. In all 180 searing points of energy were trained on the vampires of Wakely, pinning them like moths in a candle flame.

Tyler saw them start to fall, hands raised to the offending brightness as their skin blistered and innumerable screams of agony began to rise like a swelling organ note from the contaminated hordes. They writhed helplessly as the light burned them, scorching their flesh as surely as if they'd been put to the torch. Some ran back and forth in an effort to escape their agony but there was no way out. They were trapped by the beams, paralysed into immobility by their pain. Like rabbits before a snake, they remained hypnotised by the blistering lights, unable to look away but dying in consequence. Their eyes were seared in the sockets, their skin stripped away as if by acid and, on all of them, the welts and sores rose like blossoming flowers. The brilliant light blazed down over the field like some purging fire – a white blanket which brought death to all beneath it. Like hundreds of artificial suns, the bulbs poured out their energy.

Tyler watched mesmerised as the last of the infected townspeople died, flopping around like beached fish until, finally, there was no movement at all.

He bowed his head, his breath coming in gasps.

The puncture in his thigh was throbbing madly and he pressed his handkerchief to it as he walked, hobbling from the little room to stand in the rain.

Tyler stood there for a full thirty minutes, eyes scanning the piles of corpses stretched out on the pitch. His whole body ached but he knew that there was one more thing he had to do.

After turning the lights off, Tyler hobbled down from the control room and wandered out to the landrover. From there he drove the vehicle inside the football ground and, working as thoroughly as possible, used up the cans of petrol, sprinkling the golden fluid over as many corpses as possible.

Now he stood watching as the bodies roasted, the acrid stench of burning flesh filling his nostrils, great black plumes of smoke rising above the scene of death.

It was another hour before he left.

Forty-nine

Charles Muir heard the sirens but he paid them no heed, nor did he stop to ask anyone what had happened. He continued walking purposefully towards the oak-panelled door at the end of the windowless corridor. A technician passed him, running, but the Scot didn't spare the man a second glance.

He entered the room and found two other Vanderburg workers there. One, a man in his late thirties, was looking through the maze of filing cabinets. The other, a woman, was seated at one of the computer consoles.

Muir smiled politely at the woman.

'Could you fetch Mr Stark for me,' he asked.

The woman looked puzzled for a moment, then got to her feet and left the room. Muir took her place at the console.

'If you wouldn't mind leaving?' he said to the man.

The technician put down the file he had and followed the woman outside. The Scot heard the sound of their footsteps receding down the corridor. Stark, he guessed, would arrive in five or six minutes.

Perfect timing. He smiled thinly.

The sirens continued to screech but Muir ignored them, turning his attention instead to the keyboard and V.D.U. before him. He pressed a button and the screen went blank, then, after pausing a second, he tapped in the first commands.

Luminous green letters appeared on the screen:

INTERFACE 3095. READY FOR ENQUIRY

Muir hastily relayed his next instruction.

REQUEST PROGRAM

The computer acknowledged.

ALL TERMINALS ERASE

He sat back, looking at what was displayed before him.

DOES NOT COMPUTE

The display unit glowed.

Muir chewed on the stem of his pipe.

ALL TERMINALS SELF-DESTRUCT

NEGATIVE

Muir hit the keyboard harder.

EMERGENCY COMMAND OVERRIDE. ALL TERMINALS SELF-DESTRUCT

FULL POWER

He sat back, watching as the letters on the V.D.U. began first to flash and then to turn red. The room began to fill with a high-pitched whine, drowning out even the siren, but Muir just sat there, the unlit pipe clenched between his teeth.

KEY

He typed:

COMMAND IRREVERSIBLE

Now there was no turning back.

Consoles all over Vanderburg Chemicals began to display the same two words and more than one employee began making for the nearest door.

Muir knew what he had done. He was even quite proud of himself. Once the power began to overload, every electrical circuit in the building would go up. Not just short out but the huge amounts of power running through the circuits would cause fires and, eventually, explosions.

The Scot sat and stared at the screen.

He had known for a while now that it must come to this. The feedstuff programme had to be stopped somehow but, more importantly, John Stark had to be stopped. What he had said to Muir had struck a note deep inside him. As he sat staring at the flashing screen he realized that this was his atonement. It was the only way he could hope to find peace after what he had helped to create. The Vanderburg feed, as he had told Stark, was indeed lethal.

The door opened and John Stark blundered in.

Muir turned slowly in his chair to greet the American.

'What in God's name are you doing?' snarled Stark, peering at the console.

It was beginning to flash wildly:

OVERLOAD

Muir said nothing.

'Stop it, now,' shouted Stark, trying to raise his voice above the sirens and the high-pitched screech which was reaching ever greater intensity.

'There's no way of stopping it, *Mr* Stark,' said the Scot. 'It's all over. Your plans. Everything.'

Stark leapt at Muir and fastened both hands around his throat.

'Turn it off,' he snarled as the first crackles of overloading circuitry began to fill his ears.

Muir tried to force the American's hands away but there was a furious desperation in Stark's grip, something which gave him added strength. The two of them crashed onto the console, Stark slamming the Scot's head repeatedly against the desk top.

'Turn it off,' he roared.

As if a switch had been thrown the entire room suddenly exploded in a searing welter of blistering flame. The walls, as if pushed by gigantic fists, erupted outwards. Huge lumps of stone flew through the air like shrapnel.

Elsewhere on the second floor other terminals exploded, hungry tongues of flame licking through their circuitry. A chorus of deafening blasts rocked the main building as every electrical appliance overloaded. Screams began to punctuate the growing roar of fire. Those fortunate enough to be outside the building ran for their lives as glass from the upper storeys rained down in lethal crystal showers. Long, spear-like shards sped to earth like clear javelins.

A security guard, mesmerised by the sight before

him, was transfixed by a razor sharp length of window which buried itself in his chest.

On the third floor, a blast of seismic proportions sent bodies hurtling through windows as the chemicals in the labs also caught alight. The cries of animals now joined the cacophony of sounds as specimens were burned alive in their cages.

Men and women were picked up, as if by invisible hands, and flung through the air, slamming into walls or crashing through glass. A woman, her hair and clothes ablaze ran screaming down a corridor until another explosion brought the ceiling down on her. Metal began to melt under the intense heat and even the stone steps grew hot as the fires continued to sear everything they touched.

Here and there, people were attempting to fight the fires with extinguishers but it was like trying to put out a forest blaze with a thimbleful of water. Two security men, using extinguishers, tried to make a path for several women through the hungry flames but the fire seemed to rear up at them and they were forced back towards a room near the end of a corridor. It housed several hundred bottles of chemical and, a moment later, an ear-splitting blast simply brushed aside everyone within a hundred yards. Bodies were tossed like bloodied rag dolls, hurtling through the air as if fired from cannons.

In the forecourt below, a lorry exploded, the driver catapulted through the windscreen as the vehicle disappeared beneath a shrieking ball of red and white flame. Lumps of metal went spinning in all directions.

It seemed as if the entire complex which made up Vanderburg Chemicals was ablaze, a roaring beacon which could be seen for miles around.

Powerful explosions continued to rock the place, tearing it apart. Those who could, ran. Those trapped inside were either incinerated or blasted to atoms.

And, above it all, a gigantic mushroom cloud of black smoke rose fully two hundred feet into the air. Like some massive man-made cloud it hung, shroud-like, over the remnants of the complex.

Then, finally, as if the other blasts had been mere portents, there was an explosion which threatened to split the very earth itself: the final, cataclysmic death knell which brought the remnants of Vanderburg Chemicals down like a house of cards. A concussion wave flattened everything within a 500 yard radius and then, almost as an after-thought, there was a vehement detonation which levelled anything left standing. Flames screamed defiantly in the air, shrieking geysers of fire which rose like blazing fingers to point accusingly at the sky.

Even the clouds seemed to be on fire.

Fifty

Jo ducked low in her seat as Clayton swung the car around a tight bend in the road. Behind them, the driver of the rangerover slowed slightly to take the corner but then stepped on the accelerator as the road straightened out once more. His companion was leaning out of the side window trying to aim a gun at the tyre of the speeding Capri.

Jo heard the report but, thankfully, the bullet missed its appointed mark, scraping the side of the vehicle instead.

The doctor gripped the steering wheel as tightly as

he could, blood from the wound in his shoulder seeping down his arm. As she looked at him, Jo could see a shining nub of bone protruding from the ragged wound. The bullet had smashed his scapula.

She peered out of the back window to see that the rangerover was gaining.

'Oh no,' murmured Clayton.

'What is it?' she demanded.

'We're nearly out of petrol,' Clayton told her, indicating the gauge.

He swung the car around another corner and stepped on the brake.

'What the hell are you doing?' Jo asked, in amazement.

'Get out,' he said, watching the rear view mirror.

'Why?'

'Get out,' he bellowed at her. 'Take the files. One of us has got to get away.'

'I can't . . .'

He cut her short, pushing the door open and practically shoving her out. He passed her the files.

'Run,' he told her. 'Go on. There's nothing left for me now. You save yourself. Get to Tyler if you can.'

Before she could protest, he had reached across and slammed the door, spinning the wheel of the Capri, bringing it around in a 'U' turn until it was facing the opposite way.

A second later, the rangerover came hurtling round the corner.

The driver was a little puzzled at first to see the Capri heading back towards them, and that puzzlement turned to horror as he realized what Clayton was doing.

Jo, too, saw what was to happen.

'No,' she shouted but, a second later, her voice was drowned out by a thunderous explosion.

The two vehicles hit each other head on and blew up immediately. There was a blinding ball of fire followed by a billowing orange and black cloud of smoke. Lumps of red hot metal flew into the air and Jo blenched as she saw a severed arm rise on the funnel of flame which erupted from the roaring blast. A wave of pressure rocked her and she shielded her face as the heat rolled over her. The air was filled with the roar of raging flames.

She stood gazing at the pulverized vehicles for as long as she dared, then clutching the three files, she set off across the fields towards town.

It was nearly 6.39 p.m. when Tyler walked into the hotel. He found Jo sitting at the bar, the files before her. As he limped in, she ran to him, throwing her arms around his neck. He responded with equal warmth and relief.

'Thank God you're alive,' she said. Then, stepping back, she asked: 'Is it done?'

He nodded.

'I killed them all,' he told her. 'At least I think I did. There's no way of knowing for sure.' He swallowed hard. 'Jo, I knew so many of them.' He was silent for a moment.

'Clayton's dead,' she told him.

'How?'

Jo explained everything, finally showing him the files.

'But you destroyed Vanderburg Chemicals,' he said, wearily.

She shook her head.

'Not us.'

'I saw the fires,' he said.

'Vic, I don't know *what* happened. But, they're gone.'

Tyler picked up the file marked:

DISTRIBUTION

There was a column on the left hand side of the page which bore the names of cities.

'London. Manchester. Liverpool. Glasgow,' he read.

'Paris. Bonn. Brussels. Vienna.' Tyler swallowed hard. 'New York. Houston. Quebec.' He looked at Jo. 'Jesus, do you realize what this means?'

'They're all places where the new Vanderburg feed is supposed to be distributed, to be sold by their outlets in those cities,' she said. 'Now we have the files we can stop the shipments.'

Tyler shook his head, running his finger across the page.

'The despatch dates on most of these are weeks old,' he said, anxiously.

The smile faded from Jo's face.

'These shipments have already gone,' the farmer said, softly.

'My God,' murmured Jo. 'The virus will spread.' Her voice took on a note of desperation. 'Isn't there any way of stopping it?'

Tyler dropped the file onto the table before him.

'Vic, there has to be a way,' she gasped. 'There must be something.'

He sat down heavily.

'There's nothing,' he said, flatly.

Outside, it began to get dark.

Author's Note

All characters in this novel are figments of my imagination, as are the towns of Wakely and Arkham. There is also no company called Vanderburg Chemicals.

The disease porphyria, on the other hand, *does* exist and the facts given, in *Erebus*, by Dr Alec Clayton are correct. While it is true that one person in every 25,000 suffers from this rare affliction, it is not expected that figures will increase much beyond that particular statistic.

However . . .

Shaun Hutson